ALSO BY JOHN IRVING

Setting Free the Bears

The Water-Method Man

The 158-Pound Marriage

The World According to Garp

The Hotel New Hampshire

The Cider House Rules

A Prayer for Owen Meany

A Son of the Circus

The Imaginary Girlfriend

Trying to Save Piggy Sneed

A Widow for One Year

My Movie Business

The Cider House Rules: A Screenplay

The Fourth Hand

A Sound Like Someone Trying Not to Make a Sound

Until I Find You

Last Night in Twisted River

JOHN IRVING

In One Person

A Novel

Simon & Schuster

New York   London   Toronto   Sydney   New Delhi

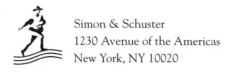
Simon & Schuster
1230 Avenue of the Americas
New York, NY 10020

First Simon & Schuster hardcover edition May 2012

SIMON & SCHUSTER and colophon are registered trademarks
of Simon & Schuster, Inc.

For information about special discounts for bulk purchases,
please contact Simon & Schuster Special Sales at
1-866-506-1949 or business@simonandschuster.com.

The Simon & Schuster Speakers Bureau can bring authors
to your live event. For more information or to book an event,
contact the Simon & Schuster Speakers Bureau at
1-866-248-3049 or visit our website at www.simonspeakers.com.

Designed by Nancy Singer

Manufactured in the United States of America

10   9   8   7   6   5   4   3   2   1

Library of Congress Cataloging-in-Publication Data
Irving, John.
In one person : a novel / John Irving.
p.   cm.
1. Domestic fiction.   2. Psychological fiction.   I. Title.
PS3559.R8I5   2012
813'.54—dc23   2011039707

ISBN 978-1-4516-6412-6
ISBN 978-1-4516-6415-7 (ebook)

*For Sheila Heffernon and David Rowland
and in memory of Tony Richardson*

Thus play I in one person many people,
And none contented.

—WILLIAM SHAKESPEARE, *Richard II*

Chapters

In One Person

AN UNSUCCESSFUL CASTING CALL

I'm going to begin by telling you about Miss Frost. While I say to everyone that I became a writer because I read a certain novel by Charles Dickens at the formative age of fifteen, the truth is I was younger than that when I first met Miss Frost and imagined having sex with her, and this moment of my sexual awakening also marked the fitful birth of my imagination. We are formed by what we desire. In less than a minute of excited, secretive longing, I desired to become a writer and to have sex with Miss Frost—not necessarily in that order.

I met Miss Frost in a library. I like libraries, though I have difficulty pronouncing the word—both the plural and the singular. It seems there are certain words I have considerable trouble pronouncing: nouns, for the most part—people, places, and things that have caused me preternatural excitement, irresolvable conflict, or utter panic. Well, that is the opinion of various voice teachers and speech therapists and psychiatrists who've treated me—alas, without success. In elementary school, I was held back a grade due to "severe speech impairments"—an overstatement. I'm now in my late sixties, almost seventy; I've ceased to be interested in the cause of my mispronunciations. (Not to put too fine a point on it, but fuck the etiology.)

I don't even try to say the *etiology* word, but I can manage to struggle through a comprehensible mispronunciation of *library* or *libraries*—the botched word emerging as an unknown fruit. ("Liberry," or "liberries," I say—the way children do.)

It's all the more ironic that my first library was undistinguished. This was the public library in the small town of First Sister, Vermont—a compact red-brick building on the same street where my grandparents lived. I lived in their house on River Street—until I was fifteen, when my mom remarried. My mother met my stepfather in a play.

The town's amateur theatrical society was called the First Sister Players; for as far back as I can remember, I saw all the plays in our town's little theater. My mom was the prompter—if you forgot your lines, she told you what to say. (It being an *amateur* theater, there were a lot of forgotten lines.) For years, I thought the prompter was one of the actors—someone mysteriously offstage, and not in costume, but a necessary contributor to the dialogue.

My stepfather was a new actor in the First Sister Players when my mother met him. He had come to town to teach at Favorite River Academy—the almost-prestigious private school, which was then all boys. For much of my young life (most certainly, by the time I was ten or eleven), I must have known that eventually, when I was "old enough," I would go to the academy. There was a more modern and better-lit library at the prep school, but the public library in the town of First Sister was my first library, and the librarian there was my first librarian. (Incidentally, I've never had any trouble saying the *librarian* word.)

Needless to say, Miss Frost was a more memorable experience than the library. Inexcusably, it was long after meeting her that I learned her first name. Everyone called her Miss Frost, and she seemed to me to be my mom's age—or a little younger—when I belatedly got my first library card and met her. My aunt, a most imperious person, had told me that Miss Frost "*used to be* very good-looking," but it was impossible for me to imagine that Miss Frost could ever have been better-looking than she was when I met her—notwithstanding that, even as a kid, all I did was imagine things. My aunt claimed that the available men in the town *used to* fall all over themselves when they met Miss Frost. When one of them got up the nerve to introduce himself—to actually tell Miss Frost his name—the then-beautiful librarian would look at him coldly and icily say, "My name is *Miss* Frost. Never been married, never want to be."

With that attitude, Miss Frost was still unmarried when I met her; inconceivably, to me, the available men in the town of First Sister had long stopped introducing themselves to her.

● ● ●

THE CRUCIAL DICKENS NOVEL—THE one that made me want to be
a writer, or so I'm always saying—was *Great Expectations*. I'm sure I was
fifteen, both when I first read it and when I first reread it. I know this was
before I began to attend the academy, because I got the book from the
First Sister town library—twice. I won't forget the day I showed up at the
library to take that book out a second time; I'd never wanted to reread
an entire novel before.

Miss Frost gave me a penetrating look. At the time, I doubt I was as
tall as her shoulders. "Miss Frost *was once* what they call 'statuesque,' "
my aunt had told me, as if even Miss Frost's height and shape existed only
in the past. (She was *forever* statuesque to me.)

Miss Frost was a woman with an erect posture and broad shoulders,
though it was chiefly her small but pretty breasts that got my attention.
In seeming contrast to her mannish size and obvious physical strength,
Miss Frost's breasts had a newly developed appearance—the improbable
but budding look of a young girl's. I couldn't understand how it was possible for an older woman to have achieved this look, but surely her breasts
had seized the imagination of every teenage boy who'd encountered her,
or so I believed when I met her—when was it?—in 1955. Furthermore,
you must understand that Miss Frost never dressed suggestively, at least
not in the imposed silence of the forlorn First Sister Public Library; day
or night, no matter the hour, there was scarcely anyone there.

I had overheard my imperious aunt say (to my mother): "Miss Frost
is past an age where training bras suffice." At thirteen, I'd taken this to
mean that—in my judgmental aunt's opinion—Miss Frost's bras were all
wrong for her breasts, or vice versa. I thought *not*! And the entire time I
was internally agonizing over my and my aunt's different fixations with
Miss Frost's breasts, the daunting librarian went on giving me the afore-
mentioned penetrating look.

I'd met her at thirteen; at this intimidating moment, I was fifteen,
but given the invasiveness of Miss Frost's long, lingering stare, it felt
like a two-year penetrating look to me. Finally she said, in regard to my
wanting to read *Great Expectations* again, "You've already read this one,
William."

"Yes, I loved it," I told her—this in lieu of blurting out, as I almost
did, that I loved *her*. She was austerely formal—the first person to unfailingly address me as *William*. I was always called Bill, or Billy, by my family
and friends.

I wanted to see Miss Frost wearing *only* her bra, which (in my inter-fering aunt's view) offered insufficient restraint. Yet, in lieu of blurting out such an indiscretion as *that,* I said: "I want to reread *Great Expecta-tions.*" (Not a word about my premonition that Miss Frost had made an impression on me that would be no less devastating than the one that Estella makes on poor Pip.)

"So soon?" Miss Frost asked. "You read *Great Expectations* only a month ago!"

"I can't wait to reread it," I said.

"There are a lot of books by Charles Dickens," Miss Frost told me. "You should try a different one, William."

"Oh, I will," I assured her, "but first I want to *reread* this one."

Miss Frost's second reference to me as *William* had given me an in-stant erection—though, at fifteen, I had a small penis and a laughably disappointing hard-on. (Suffice it to say, Miss Frost was in no danger of *noticing* that I had an erection.)

My all-knowing aunt had told my mother I was underdeveloped for my age. Naturally, my aunt had meant "underdeveloped" in other (or in all) ways; to my knowledge, she'd not seen my penis since I'd been an infant—if then. I'm sure I'll have more to say about the *penis* word. For now, it's enough that you know I have extreme difficulty pronouncing "penis," which in my tortured utterance emerges—when I can manage to give voice to it at all—as "penith." This rhymes with "zenith," if you're wondering. (I go to great lengths to avoid the plural.)

In any case, Miss Frost knew nothing of my sexual anguish while I was attempting to check out *Great Expectations* a second time. In fact, Miss Frost gave me the impression that, with so many books in the li-brary, it was an immoral waste of time to *reread* any of them.

"What's so special about *Great Expectations?*" she asked me.

She was the first person I told that I wanted to be a writer "because of" *Great Expectations,* but it was really because of *her.*

"You want to be a *writer!*" Miss Frost exclaimed; she didn't sound happy about it. (Years later, I would wonder if Miss Frost might have expressed indignation at the *sodomizer* word had I suggested that as a profession.)

"Yes, a writer—I think so," I said to her.

"You can't possibly know that you're going to be a *writer!*" Miss Frost said. "It's not a career choice."

She was certainly right about that, but I didn't know it at the time. And I wasn't pleading with her only so she would let me reread *Great Expectations;* my pleas were especially ardent, in part, because the more exasperated Miss Frost became with me, the more I appreciated the sudden intake of her breath—not to mention the resultant rise and fall of her surprisingly girlish breasts.

At fifteen, I was as smitten and undone by her as I'd been two years earlier. No, I must revise that: I was altogether more captivated by her at fifteen than I was at thirteen, when I'd been merely fantasizing about having sex with her *and* becoming a writer—whereas, at fifteen, the imagined sex was more developed (there were more concrete details) and I had already written a few sentences I admired.

Both the sex with Miss Frost and actually being a writer were unlikely, of course—but were they remotely possible? Curiously, I had enough hubris to believe so. As for where such an exaggerated pride or unearned self-confidence came from—well, I could only guess that genes had something to do with it.

I don't mean my mother's; I saw no hubris in her backstage role of the prompter. After all, I spent most of my evenings with my mom in that safe haven for those variously talented (and untalented) members of our town's amateur theatrical society. That little playhouse was not a uniformly prideful or brimming-with-confidence kind of place—hence the prompter.

If my hubris was genetic, it surely came from my biological father. I was told I'd never met him; I knew him only by his reputation, which didn't sound great.

"The code-boy," as my grandfather referred to him—or, less often, "the sergeant." My mom had left college because of the sergeant, my grandmother said. (She preferred "sergeant," which she always said disparagingly, to "code-boy.") Whether William Francis Dean was the contributing cause of my mom leaving college, I didn't really know; she'd gone to secretarial school instead, but not before he'd gotten her pregnant with me. Consequently, my mother would leave secretarial school, too.

My mom told me that she'd married my dad in Atlantic City, New Jersey, in April 1943—a little late for a shotgun wedding, because I'd been born in First Sister, Vermont, back in March of '42. I was already a year old when she married him, and the "wedding" (it was a town-clerk or justice-of-the-peace deal) had been chiefly my grandmother's idea—or so my aunt Muriel said. It was implied to me that William Francis Dean hadn't entered into the marriage all that willingly.

"We were divorced before you were two," my mom had told me. I'd seen the marriage certificate, which was why I remembered the seemingly exotic and far-from-Vermont location of Atlantic City, New Jersey; my father had been in basic training there. No one had shown me the divorce records.

"The sergeant wasn't interested in marriage or children," my grandmother had told me, with no small amount of superiority; even as a child, I could see that my aunt's loftiness had come from my grandmother.

But because of what happened in Atlantic City, New Jersey—no matter at whose insistence—that certificate of marriage legitimized me, albeit belatedly. I was named William Francis Dean, Jr.; I had his name, if not his presence. And I must have had some measure of his code-boy genes—the sergeant's "derring-do," in my mom's estimation.

"What was he like?" I'd asked my mother, maybe a hundred times. She used to be so nice about it.

"Oh, he was *very* handsome—like you're going to be," she would always answer, with a smile. "And he had *oodles* of derring-do." My mom was very affectionate to me, before I began to grow up.

I don't know if all preteen boys, and boys in their early teens, are as inattentive to linear time as I was, but it never occurred to me to examine the sequence of events. My father must have knocked up my mother in late May or early June of 1941—when he was finishing his freshman year at Harvard. Yet there was never any mention of him—not even in a sarcastic comment from Aunt Muriel—as the *Harvard*-boy. He was always called the *code*-boy (or the sergeant), though my mom was clearly proud of his Harvard connection.

"Imagine starting Harvard when you're just fifteen!" I'd heard her say more than once.

But if my derring-do dad had been fifteen at the start of his freshman year at Harvard (in September 1940), he had to be *younger* than my mother, whose birthday was in April. She was already twenty in April of '40; she was just a month short of twenty-two when I was born, in March of '42.

Did they not get married when she learned she was pregnant because my dad was not yet eighteen? He'd turned eighteen in October 1942. As my mom told me, "Obligingly, the draft age was lowered to that level." (I would only later think that the *obligingly* word was not a common one in my mother's vocabulary; maybe that had been the Harvard-boy talking.)

"Your father believed he might better control his military destiny by volunteering for advanced induction, which he did in January 1943," my mom told me. (The "military destiny" didn't sound like her vocabulary, either; the Harvard-boy was written all over it.)

My dad traveled by bus to Fort Devens, Massachusetts—the beginning of his military service—in March 1943. At the time, the air force was part of the army; he was assigned a specialty, that of cryptographic technician. For basic training, the air force had taken over Atlantic City and the surrounding sand dunes. My father and his fellow inductees were bivouacked in the luxury hotels, which the trainees would ruin. According to my grandfather: "No one ever checked IDs in the bars. On weekends, girls—mostly government workers from Washington, D.C.— flocked to town. It was very jolly, I'm sure—the firin' of all sorts of weapons on the sand dunes notwithstandin'."

My mom said that she visited my dad in Atlantic City—"once or twice." (When they were still not married, and I would have been a one-year-old?)

It was together with my grandfather that my mother must have traveled to Atlantic City for that April '43 "wedding"; this would have been shortly before my dad was sent to air force cryptographic school in Pawling, New York—where he was taught the use of codebooks and strip ciphers. From there, in the late summer of '43, my father was sent to Chanute Field in Rantoul, Illinois. "In Illinois, he learned the nuts and bolts of cryptography," my mother said. So they were still in touch, seventeen months after I'd been born. ("Nuts and bolts" was never big in my mom's vocabulary.)

"At Chanute Field, your dad was introduced to the primary military cipher machine—essentially a teletype, with an electronic set of cipher wheels attached to it," my grandfather told me. He might as well have been speaking in Latin; quite possibly, not even my missing father could have made the functions of a cipher machine comprehensible to me.

My grandfather never used "code-boy" or "sergeant" disparagingly, and he enjoyed reciting to me my dad's war story. It must have been as an amateur actor in the First Sister Players that my grandfather had developed the capacity for memorization necessary for him to recall such specific and difficult details; Grandpa was able to reiterate to me *exactly* what had happened to my dad—not that the wartime work of a cryptographer, the coding and decoding of secret messages, was entirely uninteresting.

The U.S. Fifteenth Army Air Force was headquartered in Bari, Italy. The 760th Bomb Squadron, of which my father was a member, was stationed at the Spinazzola Army Air Base—on farmland south of the town.

Following the Allied invasion of Italy, the Fifteenth Army Air Force was engaged in bombing southern Germany, Austria, and the Balkans. From November 1943 till September 1945, more than a thousand B-24 heavy bombers were lost in this combat. But cryptographers didn't fly. My dad would rarely have left the code room at the base in Spinazzola; he spent the remaining two years of the war with his codebooks and the incomprehensible encryption device.

While the bombers attacked the Nazi factory complexes in Austria and the oil fields in Romania, my dad ventured no farther than Bari— mainly for the purpose of selling his cigarettes on the black market. (Sergeant William Francis Dean didn't smoke, my mother had assured me, but he sold enough cigarettes in Bari to buy a car when he got back to Boston—a 1940 Chevrolet coupe.)

My dad's demobilization was relatively swift. He spent the spring of '45 in Naples, which he described as "enchanting and buoyant, and awash in beer." (Described to *whom*? If he'd divorced my mom before I was two—divorced her *how*?—why was he still writing to her when I was already three?)

Maybe he was writing to my grandfather instead; it was Grandpa who told me that my dad had boarded a navy transport ship in Naples. After a short stay in Trinidad, he was flown on a C-47 to a base in Natal, Brazil, where my father said the coffee was "very good." From Brazil, another C-47—this one was described as "aging"—flew him to Miami. A troop train north dispersed the returning soldiers to their points of discharge; hence my dad found himself back in Fort Devens, Massachusetts.

October 1945 was too late for him to return to Harvard in that same academic year; he bought the Chevy with his black-market money and got a temporary job in the toy department of Jordan Marsh, Boston's largest store. He would go back to Harvard in the fall of '46; his field of concentration would be romance studies, which my grandfather explained to me meant the languages and literary traditions of France, Spain, Italy, and Portugal. ("Or at least two or three of 'em," Grandpa said.)

"Your father was a *whiz* at foreign languages," my mom had told me—hence a *whiz* at cryptography, maybe? But why would my mother or my grandpa have cared about my runaway dad's field of concentration at Harvard? Why were these details even known to them? Why had they been informed?

There was a photograph of my father—for years, the only picture I saw of him. In the photograph, he looks very young and very thin. (This was late spring, or early summer, 1945.) He's eating ice cream on that navy transport ship; the photo was taken somewhere between the coast of southern Italy and the Caribbean, before they docked in Trinidad.

I'm guessing that the black panther on my father's flight jacket captured all or most of my childish imagination; that angry-looking panther was the symbol of the 460th Bomb Group. (Cryptography was strictly a ground-crew enterprise—even so, cryptographers were issued flight jackets.)

My all-obscuring fixation was that I had something of the war hero in *me*, though the details of my dad's wartime exploits were not very heroic-sounding—not even to a child. But my grandfather was one of those World War II buffs—you know, the kind who finds every detail intriguing—and he was always telling me, "I see a future hero in you!"

My grandmother had next to nothing positive to say about William Francis Dean, and my mother began and (for the most part) finished her evaluation with "*very* handsome" and "*oodles* of derring-do."

No, that's not entirely true. When I asked her why it hadn't worked out between them, my mom told me that she'd seen my dad kissing some-one. "I saw him kiss someone *else*," was all she said, as perfunctorily as she might have prompted an actor who'd forgotten the *else* word. I could only conclude that she'd observed this kiss after she was pregnant with me—possibly, even after I'd been born—and that she saw enough of the mashed-lips encounter to know that it wasn't an innocent sort of kiss.

"It must have been a Frenchy, a tongue-down-the-throat job," my elder cousin once confided to me—a crude girl, the daughter of that im-perious aunt I keep mentioning. But who was my dad kissing? I wondered if she'd been one of those weekend girls who flocked to Atlantic City, one of those government workers from Washington, D.C. (Why else had my grandfather mentioned them to me?)

At the time, this was all I knew; it was not a lot to know. It was more than enough, however, to make me mistrust myself—even dislike myself—because I had a tendency to attribute all my faults to my biological father. I blamed him for every bad habit, for each mean and secretive thing; essentially, I believed that all my demons were hereditary. Every aspect of myself that I doubted or feared surely had to be one of Sergeant Dean's traits.

Hadn't my mom said I was *going to be* good-looking? Wasn't that a curse, too? As for the derring-do—well, hadn't I presumed (at age thirteen) that I could become a writer? Hadn't I already imagined having sex with Miss Frost?

Believe me, I didn't want to be my runaway dad's offspring, his genetic-package progeny—knocking up young women, and abandoning them, left and right. For that was Sergeant Dean's modus operandi, wasn't it? I didn't want his name, either. I *hated* being William Francis Dean, Jr.—the code-boy's almost-a-bastard son! If there was ever a kid who *wanted* a stepfather, who wished that his mother at least had a serious boyfriend, I was that kid.

Which leads me to where I once considered beginning this first chapter, because I could have begun by telling you about Richard Abbott. My soon-to-be stepfather set the story of my future life in motion; in fact, if my mom hadn't fallen in love with Richard, I might never have met Miss Frost.

BEFORE RICHARD ABBOTT JOINED the First Sister Players, there was what my domineering aunt referred to as a "*dearth* of leading-man material" in our town's amateur theatrical society; there were no truly terrifying villains, and no young males with the romantic capability to make the younger *and* the older ladies in the audience swoon. Richard was not only tall, dark, and handsome—he was the embodiment of the cliché. He was also thin. Richard was so thin that he bore, in my eyes, a remarkable likeness to my code-boy father, who, in the only picture I possessed of him, was permanently thin—and forever eating ice cream, somewhere between the coast of southern Italy and the Caribbean. (Naturally, I would wonder if my mother was aware of the resemblance.)

Before Richard Abbott became an actor with the First Sister Players, the males in our town's little theater were either incoherent mumblers, with downcast eyes and furtive glances, or (the equally predictable) overbearing hams who shouted their lines and made eyes at the easily offended, matronly patrons.

A notable exception in the talent department—for he was a most talented actor, if not in Richard Abbott's league—was my World War II buff grandfather, Harold Marshall, whom everyone (save my grandmother) called Harry. He was the biggest employer in First Sister, Vermont; Harry Marshall had more employees than Favorite River Academy, though the private school was surely the second biggest employer in our small town.

Grandpa Harry was the owner of the First Sister Sawmill and Lumberyard. Harry's business partner—a gloomy Norwegian, whom you will meet momentarily—was the forester. The Norwegian oversaw the logging operations, but Harry managed the sawmill and the lumberyard. Grandpa Harry also signed all the checks, and the green trucks that hauled the logs and the lumber were inscribed, in small yellow capitals, with the name MARSHALL.

Given my grandfather's elevated status in our town, it was perhaps surprising that the First Sister Players always cast him in female roles. My grandpa was a terrific female impersonator; in our town's little playhouse, Harry Marshall had many (some would say *most*) of the leading women's roles. I actually remember my grandfather better as a woman than as a man. He was more vibrant and engaged in his onstage female roles than I ever saw him be in his monotonous real-life role as a mill manager and lumberman.

Alas, it was a source of some family friction that Grandpa Harry's only competition for the most demanding and rewarding female roles was his elder daughter, Muriel—my mother's married sister, my oft-mentioned aunt.

Aunt Muriel was only two years older than my mother; yet she'd done everything before my mom had thought of doing it, and Muriel had done it properly and (in her estimation) to perfection. She'd allegedly "read world literature" at Wellesley and had married my wonderful uncle Bob—her "first and only *beau*," as Aunt Muriel called him. At least I thought Uncle Bob was wonderful; he was always wonderful to *me*. But, as I later learned, Bob drank, and his drinking was a burden and an embarrassment to Aunt Muriel. My grandmother, from whom Muriel had obtained her imperiousness, would often remark that Bob's behavior was "beneath" Muriel—whatever that meant.

For all her snobbishness, my grandmother's language was riddled with proverbial expressions and clichés, and, in spite of her highly prized education, Aunt Muriel seemed to have inherited (or she merely mimicked) the ordinariness of her mother's uninspired speech.

I think that Muriel's love and need for the theater was driven by her desire to find something original for her lofty-sounding voice to say. Muriel was good-looking—a slender brunette, with an opera singer's noteworthy bosom and booming voice—but she had an absolutely vacuous mind. Like my grandmother, Aunt Muriel managed to be both arrogant and judgmental without saying anything that was either verifiable or interesting; in this respect, both my grandmother and my aunt struck me as superior-sounding bores.

In Aunt Muriel's case, her impeccable enunciation made her entirely credible onstage; she was a perfect parrot, but a robotic and humorless one, and she was simply as sympathetic or unsympathetic as the character she played. Muriel's language was elevated, but her own "character" was lacking; she was just a chronic complainer.

In my grandmother's case, she was of an unyielding age and she'd had a conservative upbringing; these constraints led her to believe that the theater was essentially immoral—or, to be more forgiving, amoral—and that women should play no part in it. Victoria Winthrop (the *Winthrop* was my grandmother's maiden name) believed that all the women's roles in any dramatic performance should be played by boys and men; while she confessed to finding my grandfather's many onstage triumphs (as various women) embarrassing, she also believed this was the way drama should be enacted—strictly by male actors.

My grandmother—I called her Nana Victoria—found it tiresome that Muriel was inconsolable (for days) when she lost a plum part to Grandpa Harry. In contrast, Harry was a good sport whenever the sought-after role went to his daughter. "They must have wanted a good-lookin' girl, Muriel—you have me beat in that category, hands down."

I'm not so sure. My grandfather was small-boned and had a pretty face; he was light on his feet, and effortless at girlish laughter *and* at sobbing his heart out. He could be convincing as a scheming woman, or as a wronged one, and he was *more* convincing with the onstage kisses he gave to various miscast men than my aunt Muriel ever managed to be. Muriel cringed at onstage kissing, though Uncle Bob didn't mind. Bob seemed to enjoy seeing his wife *and* his father-in-law bestowing kisses onstage—a good thing, too, since they had the leading female roles in most of the productions.

Now that I'm older, I have more appreciation for Uncle Bob, who "seemed to enjoy" many people and things, and who managed to convey to me an unexpressed but sincere commiseration. I believe that Bob understood where the Winthrop side of the family was coming from; those Winthrop women were long accustomed (or genetically inclined) to looking down their noses at the rest of us. Bob took pity on me, because he knew that Nana Victoria and Aunt Muriel (and even my mother) were watching me warily for telltale signs that I was—as they all feared, as I feared myself—my no-good father's son. I was being judged for the genes of a man I didn't know, and Uncle Bob, perhaps because he drank and was considered "beneath" Muriel, knew what it felt like to be judged by the Winthrop side of the family.

Uncle Bob was the admissions man at Favorite River Academy; that the school's standards for admission were lax did not necessarily make my uncle *personally* accountable for Favorite River's failures. Yet Bob was judged; by the Winthrop side of the family, he was called "overly permissive"—another reason I thought he was wonderful.

Though I remember hearing about Bob's drinking from a variety of sources, I never saw him drunk—well, except for one spectacular occasion. In fact, in the years I was growing up in First Sister, Vermont, I believed that Bob's drinking problem was exaggerated; those Winthrop women were known for their overstatements in the morally outraged category. Righteous indignation was a Winthrop trait.

It was during the summer of '61, when I was traveling with Tom, that it somehow came up that Bob was my uncle. (I know—I haven't told you about Tom. You'll have to be patient with me; it's hard for me to get to Tom.) For Tom and me, this was that allegedly all-important summer between our graduation from prep school and the start of our freshman year in college; Tom's family and mine had granted us a reprieve from our usual summer jobs so that we could travel. We were probably expected to be satisfied with spending no more than a single summer in that doubtful pursuit of "finding" ourselves, but for Tom and me the gift of this summer didn't seem as all-important as that time in your life is supposed to be.

For one thing, we had no money, and the sheer foreignness of European travel frightened us; for another, we'd already "found" ourselves, and there was no making peace with who we were—not publicly. Indeed, there were aspects of ourselves that poor Tom and I found every bit as foreign (and as frightening) as what we managed to see, in our half-assed way, of Europe.

I don't even remember the reason Uncle Bob's name came up, and

Tom already knew I was related to "old Let-'em-in Bob," as Tom called him.

"We're not related by *blood*," I'd started to explain. (Notwithstanding Uncle Bob's blood-alcohol level at any given time, there wasn't a drop of *Winthrop* blood in him.)

"You're not at all alike!" Tom had exclaimed. "Bob is just so *nice*, and so uncomplicated."

Granted, Tom and I had been arguing a lot that summer. We'd taken one of the *Queen* ships (student class) from New York to Southampton; we'd crossed to the continent, landing in Ostend, and the first town in Europe we'd stayed overnight in was the medieval city of Bruges. (Bruges was beautiful, but I was more infatuated with a girl who worked at the pension where we stayed than I was with the belfry atop the old Market Hall.)

"I suppose you were intending to ask her if she had a friend for me," Tom said.

"We just walked all over town—we just talked and talked," I told him. "We barely kissed."

"Oh, is *that* all?" Tom said—so when he later remarked that Uncle Bob was "just so *nice*, and so uncomplicated," I took it that Tom meant I *wasn't* nice.

"I just meant that you're complicated, Bill," Tom told me. "You're not as easygoing as Admissions Man Bob, are you?"

"I can't believe you're pissed off about that girl in Bruges," I told him.

"You should have seen how you stared at her tits—they didn't amount to much. You know, Bill—girls *know* when you're staring at their tits," Tom told me.

But the girl in Bruges was of no importance to me. It was only that her small breasts had reminded me of the rise and fall of Miss Frost's surprisingly girlish breasts, and I'd not gotten over Miss Frost.

OH, THE WINDS OF change; they do not blow gently into the small towns of northern New England. The first casting call that brought Richard Abbott to our town's little theater would even change how the *women's* roles were cast, for it was evident from the start that those parts calling for dashing young men and evil (or plainly bourgeois) husbands and treacherous lovers were all within Richard Abbott's grasp; hence the women chosen to play opposite Richard would have to match up to him.

This posed a problem for Grandpa Harry, who would soon be Richard's father-in-law—Grandpa Harry was too much the older woman to be romantically involved with a handsome young man like Richard in the first place. (There would be no onstage *kissing* for Richard Abbott and Grandpa Harry!)

And, befitting her superior-sounding voice but empty-minded character, this posed a greater problem for my aunt Muriel. Richard Abbott was too much leading-man material for her. His appearance at that very first casting call reduced Muriel to psychosexual babble and dithering; my devastated aunt said later that she could tell my mom and Richard were "*moonstruck* by each other from the start." It was altogether too much for Muriel to imagine being romantically involved with her future brother-in-law—even onstage. (And with my mother *prompting* them, no less!)

At thirteen, I detected little of my aunt Muriel's consternation at encountering (for the first time) what leading-man material was like; nor did I recognize that my mom and Richard Abbott were "*moonstruck* by each other from the start."

Grandpa Harry was charming and entirely welcoming to the graceful young man, who was brand-new to the faculty at Favorite River Academy. "We're always lookin' for new actin' talent," Grandpa said warmly to Richard. "Did you say it was *Shakespeare* you're teachin'?"

"Teaching *and* putting onstage," Richard answered my grandfather. "There are theatrical disadvantages at an all-boys' school, of course—but the best way for young boys *or* girls to understand Shakespeare is for them to put on the plays."

"You mean by 'disadvantages,' I would guess, that the boys have to play the women's roles," Grandpa Harry said slyly. (Richard Abbott, upon first meeting the mill manager Harry Marshall, could not have known about the lumberman's success as an onstage cross-dresser.)

"Most boys haven't the vaguest idea how to be a woman—it's a mortal distraction from the play," Richard said.

"Ah," Grandpa Harry said. "Then how will you manage it?"

"I'm thinking of asking the younger faculty wives to audition for roles," Richard Abbott replied, "and the older faculty daughters, maybe."

"Ah," Grandpa Harry said again. "There might be *townspeople* who are also qualified," my grandfather suggested; he'd always wanted to play

Regan or Goneril, "Lear's loathsome daughters," as Grandpa alliteratively spoke of them. (Not to mention how he longed to play Lady Macbeth!)

"I'm considering open auditions," Richard Abbott said. "But I hope the older women won't be intimidating to the boys at an all-boys' school."

"Ah, well—there's always that," Grandpa Harry said with a know-ing smile. As an older woman, he'd been *intimidating* countless times; Harry Marshall had merely to look at his wife and elder daughter to know how female intimidation worked. But, at thirteen, I was unaware of my grandfather's jockeying for more women's roles; the conversation be-tween Grandpa Harry and the new leading man seemed entirely friendly and natural to me.

What I noticed on that fall Friday night—casting calls were always on Friday nights—was how the dynamic between our theater's dictato-rial director and our variously talented (and untalented) would-be cast was changed by Richard Abbott's knowledge of the theater, as much as by Richard's gifts as an actor. The stern director of the First Sister Play-ers had never been challenged as a *dramaturge* before; our little theater's director, who said he had no interest in "merely acting," was no amateur in the area of dramaturgy, and he was a self-appointed expert on Ibsen, whom he worshipped to excess.

Our heretofore-unchallenged director, Nils Borkman—the afore-mentioned Norwegian who was also Grandpa Harry's business partner and, as such, a forester and logger *and* dramaturge—was the very picture of Scandinavian depression and melancholic forebodings. Logging was Nils Borkman's business—or, at least, his day job—but dramaturgy was his passion.

It further contributed to the Norwegian's ever-blackening pes-simism that the unsophisticated theatergoers in First Sister, Vermont, were unschooled in serious drama. A steady diet of Agatha Christie was expected (even nauseatingly welcome) in our culturally deprived town. Nils Borkman visibly suffered through the ceaseless adaptations of low-brow potboilers like *Murder at the Vicarage*, a Miss Marple mystery; my superior-sounding aunt Muriel had many times played Miss Marple, but the denizens of First Sister preferred Grandpa Harry in that shrewd (but oh-so-feminine) role. Harry seemed more believable at divining other people's secrets—not to mention, at Miss Marple's age, more feminine.

At one rehearsal, Harry had whimsically said—as Miss Marple herself might have—"My word, but who would *want* Colonel Protheroe dead?"

To which my mom, ever the prompter, had remarked, "Daddy, that line isn't even in the script."

"I know, Mary—I was just foolin' around," Grandpa said.

My mother, Mary Marshall—Mary *Dean* (for those unlucky fourteen years before she married Richard Abbott)—always called my grandpa *Daddy*. Harry was unfailingly addressed as *Father* by my lofty-sounding aunt Muriel, in the same black-tie-dinner tone of voice that Nana Victoria unstintingly hailed her husband as *Harold*—never *Harry*.

Nils Borkman directed Agatha Christie's "crowd-pleasers," as he mockingly referred to them, as if he were doomed to be watching *Death on the Nile* or *Peril at End House* on the night of his death—as if his indelible memory of *Ten Little Indians* might be the one he would take to his grave.

Agatha Christie was Borkman's curse, which the Norwegian bore less than stoically—he *hated* her, and he complained about her bitterly—but because he filled the house with Agatha Christie, and similarly shallow entertainments of the time, the morbid Norwegian was permitted to direct "something serious" as the fall play every year.

"Something serious to coincide with that time of year when the *leafs* are dying," Borkman said—the *leafs* word indicating that his command of English was usually clear but imperfect. (That was Nils in a nutshell—usually clear but imperfect.)

On that Friday casting call, when Richard Abbott would change many futures, Nils announced that *this* fall's "something serious" would again be his beloved Ibsen, and Nils had narrowed the choice of *which* Ibsen to a mere three.

"Which three?" the young and talented Richard Abbott asked.

"The *problem* three," Nils answered—he presumed, definitively.

"I take it you mean *Hedda Gabler* and *A Doll's House*," Richard rightly guessed. "And would the third be *The Wild Duck*?"

By Borkman's uncharacteristic speechlessness, we all saw that, indeed, *The* (dreaded) *Wild Duck* was the dour Norwegian's third choice.

"In that case," Richard Abbott ventured, after the telltale silence, "who among us can possibly play the doomed Hedvig—that poor child?" There were no fourteen-year-old girls at the Friday night casting call—no one at all suitable for the innocent, duck-loving (and daddy-loving) Hedvig.

"We've had . . . *difficulties* with the Hedvig part before, Nils," Grandpa Harry ventured. Oh, my—had we ever! There'd been tragicomic fourteen-

year-old girls who were such abysmal actors that when the time came
for them to shoot themselves, the audience had *cheered*! There'd been
fourteen-year-old girls who were so winningly naïve and innocent that
when they shot themselves, the audience was *outraged*!

"And then there's Gregers," Richard Abbott interjected. "That miserable moralizer. I could play Gregers, but only as a meddlesome fool—a
self-righteous and self-pitying clown!"

Nils Borkman often referred to his fellow Norwegians who were suicidal as "fjord-jumpers." Apparently, the abundance of fjords in Norway
provided many opportunities for convenient and unmessy suicides. (Nils
must have noticed, to his further gloom, that there were no fjords in
Vermont—a landlocked state.) Nils now looked at Richard Abbott in
such a scary way—it was as if our depressed director wanted this upstart
newcomer to find the nearest fjord.

"But Gregers is an *idealist*," Borkman began.

"If *The Wild Duck* is a tragedy, then Gregers is a fool and a clown—
and Hjalmar is nothing more than a jealous husband of the pathetic,
before-she-met-me kind," Richard continued. "If, on the other hand, you
play *The Wild Duck* as a comedy, then they're *all* fools and clowns. But
how can the play be a comedy when a child dies because of adult moral-
izing? You need a heartbreaking Hedvig, who must be an utterly innocent and naïve fourteen-year-old; and not only Gregers but Hjalmar and
Gina, and even Mrs. Sørby and Old Ekdal and the villainous Werle, must
be *brilliant* actors! Even then, the play is flawed—not the easiest *amateur*
production of Ibsen that comes to mind."

"*Flawed!*" Nils Borkman cried, as if he (and his wild duck) had been
shot.

"I was Mrs. Sørby in the most recent manifestation," my grandfather
told Richard. "Of course, when I was younger, I got to play Gina—albeit
only once or twice."

"I had thoughts of young Laura Gordon as Hedvig," Nils said. Laura
was the youngest Gordon girl. Jim Gordon was on the faculty at Favorite
River Academy; he and his wife, Ellen, had been actors for the First Sister Players in the past, and two older Gordon daughters had previously
shot themselves as poor Hedvig.

"Excuse me, Nils," my aunt Muriel interposed, "but Laura Gordon
has highly visible breasts."

I saw I was not alone in noticing the fourteen-year-old's astonishing development; Laura was barely a year older than I was, but her breasts were way beyond what an innocent and naïve Hedvig should have.

Nils Borkman sighed; he said (with near-suicidal resignation) to Richard, "And what would the young Mr. Abbott consider an *easier* Ibsen for us mortally mere *amateurs* to perform?" Nils meant "merely mortal," of course.

"Ah . . ." Grandpa Harry began; then he stopped himself. My grandfather was enjoying this. He had the utmost respect and affection for Nils Borkman as a business partner, but—without exception—every keenly devoted and most casual member of the First Sister Players knew Nils to be an absolute tyrant as a director. (And we were almost as sick of Henrik Ibsen, and Borkman's idea of *serious drama,* as we were of Agatha Christie!)

"Well . . ." Richard Abbott began; there was a thoughtful pause. "If it's going to be Ibsen—and we are, after all, only amateurs—it should be either *Hedda Gabler* or *A Doll's House.* No children at all in the former, and the children are of no importance as actors in the latter. Of course, there is the need for a very strong and complicated *woman*—in either play—and for the usual weak or unlikable men, or *both.*"

"Weak or unlikable, or *both?*" Nils Borkman asked, in disbelief.

"Hedda's husband, George, is ineffectual and conventional—an awful combination of weaknesses, but an utterly common condition in men," Richard Abbott continued. "Eilert Løvborg is an insecure weakling, whereas Judge Brack—like his name—is despicable. Doesn't Hedda shoot herself because of her foreseeable future with both her ineffectual husband *and* the despicable Brack?"

"Are Norwegians always shooting themselves, Nils?" my grandfather asked in a mischievous way. Harry knew how to push Borkman's buttons; this time, however, Nils resisted a fjord-jumping story—he ignored his old friend and cross-dressing business partner. (Grandpa Harry had played Hedda many times; he'd been Nora in *A Doll's House,* too—but, at his age, he was no longer suitable for either of these female leads.)

"And what . . . *weaknesses* and other unlikable traits do the male characters in *A Doll's House* present us with—if I may ask the young Mr. Abbott?" Borkman sputtered, wringing his hands.

"Husbands are not Ibsen's favorite people," Richard Abbott began; there was no pausing to think now—he had all the confidence of youth and a brand-new education. "Torvald Helmer, Nora's husband—well, he's not unlike Hedda's husband. He's both boring and conventional—

the marriage is stifling. Krogstad is a wounded man, and a corrupted one; he's not without some redeeming decency, but the *weakness* word also comes to mind in Krogstad's case."

"And Dr. Rank?" Borkman asked.

"Dr. Rank is of no real importance. We need a Nora or a Hedda," Richard Abbott said. "In Hedda's case, a woman who prizes her freedom enough to kill herself in order not to lose it; her suicide is not a weakness but a demonstration of her *sexual strength*."

Unfortunately—or fortunately, depending on your point of view—Richard took this moment to glance at Aunt Muriel. Her good looks and opera singer's swaggering bosom notwithstanding, Muriel was not a tower of *sexual strength*; she fainted.

"Muriel—no histrionics, please!" Grandpa Harry cried, but Muriel (consciously or unconsciously) had foreseen that she did not match up well with the confident young newcomer, the sudden shining star of leading-man material. Muriel had physically taken herself out of the running for Hedda.

"And in the case of *Nora* . . ." Nils said to Richard Abbott, barely pausing to survey my mother's ministrations to her older, domineering (but now fainted) sister.

Muriel suddenly sat up with a dazed expression, her bosom dramatically heaving.

"Breathe in through your nose, Muriel, and out through your mouth," my mother prompted her sister.

"I know, Mary—I *know*!" Muriel said with exasperation.

"But you're doing it the other way—you know, in through your mouth and out through your nose," my mother said.

"Well . . ." Richard Abbott started to say; then he stopped. Even I saw how he looked at my mom.

Richard, who'd lost the toes of his left foot to a lawn-mower accident, which disqualified him from military service, had come to teach at Favorite River Academy directly upon receiving a master's degree in the history of theater and drama. Richard had been born and grew up in western Massachusetts. He had fond memories of family ski vacations in Vermont, when he'd been a child; a job (for which he was overqualified) in First Sister, Vermont, had attracted him for sentimental reasons.

Richard Abbott was only four years older than my code-boy father had been in that photograph—when the sergeant was en route to Trinidad in '45. Richard was twenty-five—my mom was thirty-five. Richard was a whopping ten years younger than my mother. Mom must have liked younger men; she'd certainly liked me better when I was younger.

"And do *you* act, Miss—" Richard began again, but my mom knew he was speaking to her, and she cut him off.

"No, I'm just the prompter," she told him. "I don't act."

"Ah, but, Mary—" Grandpa Harry began.

"I *don't*, Daddy," my mother said. "You and Muriel are the *actresses*," she said, with no uncertain emphasis on the *actresses* word. "I'm always the prompter."

"About Nora?" Nils Borkman asked Richard. "You were something saying—"

"Nora is more about freedom than Hedda," Richard Abbott confidently said. "She not only has the strength to leave her husband; she leaves her children, too! There is such an *untamable* freedom in these women—I say, let your actor who will be Hedda or Nora choose. These women own these plays."

As he spoke, Richard Abbott was surveying our amateur theatrical society for possible Heddas or Noras, but his eyes kept coming back to my mother, who I knew was obdurately (forever) the prompter. Richard would not make a Hedda or a Nora out of my follow-the-script mom.

"Ah, well . . ." Grandpa Harry said; he was reconsidering the part, either Nora or Hedda (his age notwithstanding).

"No, Harry—not you again," Nils said, his old dictatorial self emerging. "Young Mr. Abbott is right. There must be a certain *lawlessness*—both an uncontainable freedom *and* a sexual strength. We need a younger, more sexual *activity* woman than you."

Richard Abbott was regarding my grandfather with growing respect; Richard saw how Grandpa Harry had established himself as a woman to be reckoned with among the First Sister Players—if not as a sexual *activity* woman.

"Won't you consider it, Muriel?" Borkman asked my superior-sounding aunt.

"Yes, will you?" Richard Abbott, who was more than a decade younger than Muriel, asked. "You have an unquestionable sexual *presence*—" he started to say.

Alas, that was as far as young Mr. Abbott got—the *presence* word, modified by *sexual*—before Muriel fainted again.

"I think that's a 'no,' if I had to guess," my mom told the dazzling young newcomer.

I already had a bit of a crush on Richard Abbott, but I hadn't yet met Miss Frost.

IN TWO YEARS' TIME, when I sat as a fifteen-year-old freshman in my first morning meeting at Favorite River Academy, I would hear the school physician, Dr. Harlow, invite us boys to treat the most common afflictions of our tender age aggressively. (I am certain that he used the word *afflictions*; I'm not making this up.) As for what these "most common" afflictions were, Dr. Harlow explained that he meant acne and "an unwelcome sexual attraction to other boys or men." For our pimples, Dr. Harlow assured us there was a variety of remedies. In regard to those early indications of homosexual yearnings—well, either Dr. Harlow or the school psychiatrist, Dr. Grau, would be happy to talk to us.

"There is a cure for these afflictions," Dr. Harlow told us boys; there was a doctor's customary authority in his voice, which was at once scientific and cajoling—even the cajoling part was delivered in a confident, man-to-man way. And the gist of Dr. Harlow's morning-meeting speech was perfectly clear, even to the greenest freshmen—namely, we had only to present ourselves and ask to be treated. (What was also painfully apparent was that we had only ourselves to blame if we didn't ask to be cured.)

I would wonder, later, if it might have made a difference—that is, if I'd been exposed to Dr. Harlow's (or Dr. Grau's) buffoonery at the time I first met Richard Abbott, instead of two years after meeting him. Given what I know now, I sincerely doubt that my crush on Richard Abbott was *curable*, though the likes of Dr. Harlow and Dr. Grau—the available authorities in the medical sciences of that time—emphatically believed that my crush on Richard was in the category of a treatable affliction.

Two years after that life-changing casting call, it would be too late for a cure; on the road ahead, a world of crushes would open before me. That Friday night casting call was my introduction to Richard Abbott; to everyone present—not least to Aunt Muriel, who fainted twice—it was obvious that Richard had taken charge of us all.

"It seems that we need a Nora, or a Hedda, if we're going to do Ibsen at all," Richard said to Nils.

"But the *leafs*! They are already color-changing; they will keep falling," Borkman said. "It is the dying time of the year!"

He was not the easiest man to understand, except that Borkman's beloved Ibsen and fjord-jumping were somehow connected to the *serious drama*, which was always our fall play—and to, no less, the so-called dying time of the year, when the *leafs* were unstoppably falling.

Looking back, of course, it seems such an innocent time—both the dying time of the year and that relatively uncomplicated time in my life.

Chapter 2

CRUSHES ON THE WRONG PEOPLE

How long was it, after that unsuccessful casting call, before my mom and young Richard Abbott were dating? "Knowing Mary, I'll bet they were *doing it* immediately," I'd overheard Aunt Muriel say.

Only once had my mother ventured away from home; she'd gone off to college (no one ever said where), and she had dropped out. She'd managed only to get pregnant; she didn't even finish secretarial school! Moreover, to add to her moral and educational failure, for fourteen years, my mother and her almost-a-bastard son had borne the Dean name—for the sake of conventional legitimacy, I suppose.

Mary Marshall Dean did not dare to leave home again; the world had wounded her too gravely. She lived with my scornful, cliché-encumbered grandmother, who was as critical of her black-sheep daughter as my superior-sounding aunt Muriel was. Only Grandpa Harry had kind and encouraging words for his "baby girl," as he called her. From the way he said this, I got the impression that he thought my mom had suffered some lasting damage. Grandpa Harry was ever my champion, too—he lifted my spirits when I was down, as he repeatedly tried to bolster my mother's ever-failing self-confidence.

In addition to her duties as prompter for the First Sister Players, my mom worked as a secretary in the sawmill and lumberyard; as the owner and mill manager, Grandpa Harry chose to overlook the fact that my mother had failed to finish secretarial school—her typing sufficed for him.

There must have been remarks made about my mother—I mean,

among the sawmill men. The things they said were not about her typing, and I'll bet they'd heard them first from their wives or girlfriends; the sawmill men would have noticed that my mom was pretty, but I'm sure the women in their lives were the origin of the remarks made about Mary Marshall Dean around the lumberyard—or, more dangerously, in the logging camps.

I say "more dangerously" because Nils Borkman supervised the logging camps; men were always getting injured there, but were they sometimes "injured" because of their remarks about my mom? One guy or another was always getting hurt at the lumberyard, too—occasionally, I'll bet it was a guy who was repeating what he'd heard his wife or girlfriend say about my mother. (Her so-called husband hadn't been in any hurry to marry her; he'd never lived with her, married or not, and *that boy* had no father—those were the remarks made about my mom, I imagine.)

Grandpa Harry wasn't a fighting man; I'm guessing that Nils Borkman stuck up for his beloved business partner, and for my mother.

"He can't work for six weeks—not with a busted collarbone, Nils," I'd heard Grandpa Harry say. "Every time you 'straighten out' someone, as you put it, we're stuck payin' the workers' compensation!"

"We can afford the workers' compensation, Harry—he'll watch what he says the time next, won't he?" Nils would say.

"The 'next time,' Nils," Grandpa Harry would gently correct his old friend.

In my eyes, my mom was not only a couple of years younger than her mean sister, Muriel; my mother was by far the prettier of the two Marshall girls. It didn't matter that my mom lacked Muriel's operatic bosom and booming voice. Mary Marshall Dean was altogether better-proportioned. She was almost Asian-looking to me—not only because she was petite, but because of her almond-shaped face and how strikingly wide open (and far apart) her eyes were, not to mention the acute smallness of her mouth.

"A jewel," Richard Abbott had dubbed her, when they were first dating. It became what Richard called her—not "Mary," just "Jewel." The name stuck.

And how long was it, after they were dating, before Richard Abbott discovered that I didn't have my own library card? (Not long; it was still early in the fall, because the leaves had just begun to change color.)

My mom had revealed to Richard that I wasn't much of a reader, and this led to Richard's discovery that my mother and grandmother were bringing books home from our town library for me to read—or *not* to read, which was usually the case.

The other books that were brought into my life were hand-me-downs from my meddlesome aunt Muriel; these were mostly romance novels, the ones my crude elder cousin had read and rejected. Occasionally, Cousin Geraldine had expressed her contempt for these romances (or for the main characters) in the margins of the books.

Gerry—only Aunt Muriel and my grandmother ever called her *Geraldine*—was three years older than I was. In that same fall when Richard Abbott was dating my mom, I was thirteen and Gerry sixteen. Since Gerry was a girl, she wasn't allowed to attend Favorite River Academy. She was vehemently angry about the "all-boys' factor" at the private school, because she was bused every school day to Ezra Falls—the nearest public high school to First Sister.

Some of Gerry's hatred of boys found its way into the marginalia she contributed to the hand-me-down romance novels; some of her disdain for boy-crazy girls was also vented in the margins of those pages. Whenever I was given a hand-me-down romance novel courtesy of Aunt Muriel, I read Gerry's comments in the margins immediately. The novels themselves were stultifyingly boring. But to the tiresome description of the heroine's first kiss, Gerry wrote in the margin: "Kiss *me*! I'll make your gums bleed! I'll make you *piss* yourself!"

The heroine was a self-congratulatory prig, who would never let her boyfriend touch her breasts—Gerry responded in the margin with: "I would rub your tits *raw*! Just try to stop me!"

As for the books my mother and grandmother brought home from the First Sister Public Library, they were (at best) adventure novels: seafaring stories, usually with pirates, or Zane Grey Westerns; worst of all were the highly unlikely science-fiction novels, or the equally implausible futuristic tales.

Couldn't my mom and Nana Victoria see for themselves that I was both mystified and frightened by life on Earth? I had no need of stimulation from distant galaxies and unknown planets. And the present gripped me with sufficient incomprehension, not to mention the daily terror of being misunderstood; even to contemplate the future was nightmarishly unwelcome.

"But why doesn't Bill choose what books he likes for himself?" Richard Abbott asked my mother. "Bill, you're thirteen, right? What are you interested in?"

Except for Grandpa Harry and my ever-friendly uncle Bob (the ac-cused drinker), no one had asked me this question before. All I liked to read were the plays that were in rehearsal at the First Sister Players; I imagined that I could learn these scripts as word-for-word as my mother always learned them. One day, if my mom were sick, or in an automobile accident—there were car crashes galore in Vermont—I imagined I might be able to replace her as the prompter.

"Billy!" my mother said, laughing in that seemingly innocent way she had. "Tell Richard what you're interested in."

"I'm interested in *me*," I said. "What books are there about someone like me?" I asked Richard Abbott.

"Oh, you would be surprised, Bill," Richard told me. "The subject of childhood giving way to early adolescence—well, there are many mar-velous novels that have explored this pivotal coming-of-age territory! Come on—let's go have a look."

"At this hour? Have a look *where?*" my grandmother said with alarm. This was after an early school-night supper—it was not quite dark out-side, but it soon would be. We were still sitting at the dining-room table.

"Surely Richard can take Bill to our town's little library, Vicky," Grandpa Harry said. Nana looked as if she'd been slapped; she was so very much a *Victoria* (if only in her own mind) that no one but my grandpa ever called her "Vicky," and when he did, she reacted with resentment every time. "I'm bettin' that Miss Frost keeps the library open till nine most nights," Harry added.

"*Miss* Frost!" my grandmother declared, with evident distaste.

"Now, now—tolerance, Vicky, tolerance," my grandfather said.

"Come on," Richard Abbott said again to me. "Let's go get you your own library card—that's a start. The books will come later; if I had to guess, the books will soon *flow*."

"*Flow!*" my mom cried happily, but with no small measure of dis-belief. "You don't know Billy, Richard—he's just not much of a reader."

"We'll see, Jewel," Richard said to her, but he winked at me. I had a growingly incurable crush on him; if my mother was already falling in love with Richard Abbott, she wasn't alone.

I remember that captivating night—even such a commonplace thing as walking on the River Street sidewalk with the enthralling Richard Abbott seemed romantic. It was muggy, like a summer night, with a far-off thunderstorm brewing. All the neighborhood children and dogs were at play in the River Street backyards, and the bell in the clock tower of Favorite River Academy tolled the hour. (It was only seven on a September school night, and my childhood, as Richard had said, was giving way to early adolescence.)

"Exactly what about you are you interested in, Bill?" Richard Abbott asked me.

"I wonder why I have sudden, unexplainable . . . *crushes*," I said to him.

"Oh, *crushes*—you'll soon have many more of them," Richard said encouragingly. "Crushes are common, and to be expected—to be *enjoyed!*" he added.

"Sometimes, the crushes are on the wrong people," I tried to tell him.

"But there are no 'wrong' people to have crushes on, Bill," Richard assured me. "You cannot will yourself to have, or not to have, a crush on someone."

"Oh," I said. At thirteen, this must have meant to me that a crush was more dire than I'd first thought.

It's so funny to think that, only six years later, when I took that summer-long trip with Tom—that trip to Europe, which got off to a bit of a bad start in Bruges—the very idea of falling in love seemed no longer likely; it even seemed impossible. That summer, I was only nineteen, but I was already convinced that I would never fall in love again.

I'm not entirely sure what expectations poor Tom had for that summer, but I was still so inexperienced that I imagined I'd seen the last of a crush that was dire enough to hurt me. In fact, I was so woefully naïve—so was Tom—that I further imagined I had the rest of my life to recover from whatever slight damage I had done to myself in the throes of my love for Miss Frost. I'd not been in enough relationships to realize the lasting effect that Miss Frost would have on me; the damage wasn't "slight."

As for Tom, I simply thought I had to be more circumspect in the looks I gave to the younger chambermaids, or to those other small-breasted girls and young women Tom and I encountered in our travels.

I was aware that Tom was insecure; I knew how sensitive he was about being "marginalized," as he called it—he was always feeling overlooked or taken for granted, or flat-out ignored. I thought I was being careful not to let my eyes linger on anyone else for too long.

But one night—we were in Rome—Tom said to me, "I wish you would just *stare* at the prostitutes. They like to be looked at, Bill, and it's frankly excruciating how I know you're thinking about them—especially that very tall one with the faint trace of a mustache—but you won't even *look!*"

Another night—I don't remember where we were, but we'd gone to bed and I thought Tom was asleep—he said in the dark, "It's as if you've been shot in the heart, Bill, but you're unaware of the hole or the loss of blood. I doubt you even heard the shot!"

But I'm getting ahead of myself; alas, it's what a writer who knows the end of the story tends to do. I'd better be getting back to Richard Abbott, and that charming man's quest to get me my first library card—not to mention Richard's valiant efforts to assure me, a thirteen-year-old, that there were no "wrong" people to have crushes on.

THERE WAS ALMOST NO one in the library that September evening; as I would later learn, there rarely was. (Most remarkably, there were never any children in that library; it would take me years to realize why.) Two elderly women were reading on an uncomfortable-looking couch; an old man had surrounded himself with stacks of books at one end of a long table, but he seemed less determined to read all the books than he was driven to barricade himself from the two old ladies.

There were also two despondent-looking girls of high school age; they and Cousin Gerry were fellow sufferers at the public high school in Ezra Falls. The high school girls were probably doing what Gerry had described to me as their "forever minimal" homework.

The dust, long accumulated in the countless book bindings, made me sneeze. "Not allergic to *books*, I hope," someone said—these were Miss Frost's first words to me, and when I turned around and saw her, I couldn't speak.

"This boy would like a library card," Richard Abbott said.

"And just who would '*this boy*' be?" Miss Frost asked him, not looking at me.

"This is Billy Dean—I'm sure you know Mary Marshall Dean," Richard explained. "Well, Bill is Mary's boy—"

"Oh, my—yes!" Miss Frost exclaimed. "So this is *that boy*!"

The thing about a small town like First Sister, Vermont, was that everyone knew the circumstances of my mother having me—with one of those husbands *in-name-only*. I had the feeling that everybody knew the history of my code-boy dad. William Francis Dean was the disappearing kind of husband and father, and all that remained of the sergeant in First Sister, Vermont, was his name—with a *junior* tacked on at the end of it. Miss Frost may not have officially met me until this September night in 1955, but she surely knew all about me.

"And you, I presume, are *not* Mr. Dean—you're not this boy's *father*, are you?" Miss Frost asked Richard.

"Oh, no—" Richard started to say.

"I thought not," said Miss Frost. "You are then . . ." She waited; she had no intention of finishing that halted sentence.

"Richard Abbott," Richard announced.

"The new *teacher*!" Miss Frost declared. "Hired with the fervent hope that *someone* at Favorite River Academy should be able to teach those boys Shakespeare."

"Yes," Richard said, surprised that the public librarian would know the details of the private school's mission in hiring him—not only to teach English but to get the boys to read and understand Shakespeare. I was marginally more surprised than Richard; while I'd heard him tell my grandfather about his interest in Shakespeare, this was the first I'd heard of his Shakespearean *mission*. It seemed that Richard Abbott had been hired to beat the boys silly with Shakespeare!

"Well, good luck," Miss Frost told him. "I'll believe it when I see it," she added, smiling at me. "And are you going to put on any of Shakespeare's plays?" she asked Richard.

"I believe that's the only way to make the boys read and understand Shakespeare," Richard told her. "They've got to see the plays performed—better yet, they've got to perform them."

"All those boys, playing girls and women," Miss Frost speculated, shaking her head. "Talk about 'willing suspension of disbelief,' and all the other stuff that Coleridge said," Miss Frost remarked, still smiling at me. (I normally disliked it when someone ruffled my hair, but when Miss Frost did it, I just beamed back at her.) "That *was* Coleridge, wasn't it?" she asked Richard.

"Yes, it was," he said. He was quite taken with her, I could tell, and if he hadn't so recently fallen in love with my mother—well, who knows? Miss Frost was a knockout, in my unseasoned opinion. Not the hand that ruffled my hair, but her other hand now rested on the table next to Richard Abbott's hands; yet, when Miss Frost saw me looking at their hands, she took her hand off the table. I felt her fingers lightly touch my shoulder.

"And what might you be interested in reading, William?" she asked. "It *is* William, isn't it?"

"Yes," I answered her, thrilled. "William" sounded so grown up. I was embarrassed to have developed a crush on my mother's boyfriend; it seemed much more permissible to be developing an even bigger crush on the statuesque Miss Frost.

Her hands, I had noticed, were both broader in the palms and longer in the fingers than Richard Abbott's hands, and—standing as they were, beside each other—I saw that Miss Frost's upper arms were more substantial than Richard's, and her shoulders were broader; she was taller than Richard, too.

There was one similarity. Richard was so very youthful-looking—he seemed to be almost as young as a Favorite River Academy student; he might have needed to shave only once or twice a week. And Miss Frost, despite the broad shoulders and her strong-looking upper arms, and (I only now noticed) the conspicuous breadth of her chest, had these small breasts. Miss Frost had young, barely emerging breasts—or so they seemed to me, though, at thirteen, I was a relatively recent noticer of breasts.

My cousin Gerry had bigger ones. Even fourteen-year-old Laura Gordon, who was too bosomy to play Hedvig in *The Wild Duck,* had more "highly visible breasts" (as my breast-conscious aunt Muriel had observed) than the otherwise imposing Miss Frost.

I was too smitten to utter a word—I couldn't answer her—but Miss Frost (very patiently) asked me her question again. "William? You're interested in reading, I presume, but could you tell me if you like fiction or nonfiction—and what subject in particular you prefer?" Miss Frost asked. "I've seen *this boy* at our little theater!" she said suddenly to Richard. "I've spotted you backstage, William—you seem very *observant.*"

"Yes, I am," I scarcely managed to say. Indeed, I'd been so *observant* of Miss Frost that I could have masturbated on the spot, but instead I summoned the strength to say: "Do you know any novels about young people who have . . . dangerous crushes?"

Miss Frost stared at me unflinchingly. "Dangerous crushes," she repeated. "Explain what's dangerous about a crush."

"A crush on the wrong person," I told her.

"I said, in effect, there's no such thing," Richard Abbott interjected. "There are no 'wrong' people; we're free to have crushes on anyone we want."

"There are no 'wrong' people to have crushes on—are you *kidding?*"
Miss Frost asked Richard. "On the contrary, William, there is some notable literature on the subject of crushes on the wrong people," she said
to me.

"Well, that's what Bill is into," Richard told Miss Frost. "Crushes on
the wrong people."

"That's quite a category," Miss Frost said; she was all the while smiling beautifully at me. "I'm going to start you out slowly—trust me on this
one, William. You can't rush into crushes on the wrong people."

"Just what do you have in mind?" Richard Abbott asked her. "Are we
talking *Romeo and Juliet* here?"

"The problems between the Montagues and the Capulets were not
Romeo's and Juliet's problems," Miss Frost said. "Romeo and Juliet were
the *right* people for each other; it was their families that were fucked up."

"I see," Richard said—the "fucked up" remark shocked him and me.
(It seemed so unlike a librarian.)

"Two sisters come to mind," Miss Frost said, quickly moving on. Both
Richard Abbott and I misunderstood her. We were thinking that she
meant to say something clever about my mother and Aunt Muriel.

I'd once imagined that the town of First Sister had been named
for Muriel; she exuded sufficient self-importance to have had a whole
town (albeit a small one) named for her. But Grandpa Harry had set me
straight about the origins of our town's name.

Favorite River was a tributary of the Connecticut River; when the first
woodsmen were logging the Connecticut River Valley, they renamed some
of the rivers from which they ran logs into and down the Connecticut—
from both the New Hampshire and Vermont sides of the big river. (Maybe
they hadn't liked all the Indian names.) Those early river drivers named
Favorite River—what they called a straight shot into the Connecticut,
with few bends that could cause log jams. As for naming our town First
Sister, that was because of the millpond, which was created by the dam
on the Favorite River. With our sawmill and the lumberyard, we became
a "first sister" to those other, bigger mill towns on the Connecticut River.

I found Grandpa Harry's explanation of First Sister's origins to be
less exciting than my earliest assumption that our small town had been
named for my mother's older, bullying sister.

But both Richard Abbott and I were thinking about those two Marshall girls, when Miss Frost made her remark—"Two sisters come to

mind." Miss Frost must have noticed that I appeared puzzled, and Richard had lost his leading-man aura; he seemed confused, even unsure of himself. Miss Frost then said, "I mean the Brontë sisters, obviously."

"Obviously!" Richard cried; he looked relieved.

"Emily Brontë wrote *Wuthering Heights*," Miss Frost explained to me, "and Charlotte Brontë wrote *Jane Eyre*."

"Never trust a man with a lunatic wife in an attic," Richard told me. "And anyone named Heathcliff should make you suspicious."

"Those are some *crushes*," Miss Frost said meaningfully.

"But aren't they *women's* crushes?" Richard asked the librarian. "Bill might have a young *man's* crush, or crushes, more in mind."

"Crushes are crushes," Miss Frost said, without hesitation. "It's the *writing* that matters; you're not suggesting that *Wuthering Heights* and *Jane Eyre* are novels 'for women only,' are you?"

"Certainly not! Of course it's the *writing* that matters!" Richard Abbott exclaimed. "I just meant that a more *masculine* adventure—"

"More *masculine*!" Miss Frost repeated. "Well, I suppose there's Fielding," she added.

"Oh, yes!" Richard cried. "Do you mean *Tom Jones*?"

"I do," Miss Frost replied, with a sigh. "If one can count sexual escapades as one result of *crushes*—"

"Why not?" Richard Abbott quickly said.

"You're *how* old?" Miss Frost asked me. Once again, her long fingers touched my shoulder. I recalled how Aunt Muriel had fainted (twice), and briefly feared I would soon lose consciousness.

"I'm thirteen," I told her.

"Three novels are enough of a beginning at thirteen," she said to Richard. "It wouldn't be wise to overload him with crushes at too young an age. Let's just see where these three novels lead him, shall we?" Once more Miss Frost smiled at me. "Begin with the Fielding," she advised me. "It's arguably the most primitive. You'll find that the Brontë sisters are more emotional—more psychological. They're more grown-up novelists."

"Miss Frost?" Richard Abbott said. "Have you ever been *onstage*— have you ever *acted*?"

"Only in my mind," she answered him, almost flirtatiously. "When I was younger—all the time."

Richard gave me a conspiratorial look; I knew perfectly well what the talented young newcomer to the First Sister Players was thinking.

A tower of *sexual strength* stood before us; to Richard and me, Miss Frost was a woman with an *untamable* freedom—a certain *lawlessness* definitely accompanied her.

To a younger man, Richard Abbott, and to me—I was a thirteen-year-old daydreamer who suddenly desired to write the story of my crushes on the wrong people *and* to have sex with a librarian in her thirties—Miss Frost was an unquestionable sexual *presence*.

"There's a part for you, Miss Frost," Richard Abbott ventured, while we followed her through the stacks, where she was gathering my first three *literary* novels.

"Actually, one of two possible parts," I pointed out.

"Yes, you have to choose," Richard quickly added. "It's either Hedda in *Hedda Gabler*, or Nora in *A Doll's House*. Do you know Ibsen? These are often called *problem* plays—"

"That's some choice," Miss Frost said, smiling at me. "Either I get to shoot myself in the temple, or I get to be the kind of woman who abandons her three young children."

"I think it's a *positive* decision, in both cases," Richard Abbott tried to reassure her.

"Oh, how very *positive*!" Miss Frost said, laughing—with a wave of her long-fingered hand. (When she laughed, there was something hoarse and low in her voice, which almost immediately jumped to a higher, clearer register.)

"Nils Borkman is the director," I warned Miss Frost; I was feeling protective of her already, and we'd only just met.

"My dear boy," Miss Frost said to me, "as if there's a soul in First Sister who doesn't know that a neuroses-ridden Norwegian—no neophyte to 'serious drama'—is our little theater's director."

She said suddenly to Richard: "I would be interested to know—if *A Doll's House* is the Ibsen that we choose, and I am to be the much-misunderstood Nora—how *you* will be cast, Mr. Richard Abbott." Before Richard could answer her, Miss Frost went on: "My guess is that you would be Torvald Helmer, Nora's dull and uncomprehending husband—he whose life Nora saves, but he can't save hers."

"I would guess that is how I will be cast," Richard ventured cautiously. "Of course I'm not the director."

"You must tell me, Richard Abbott, if you intend to *flirt* with me—I don't mean in our onstage roles," Miss Frost said.

"No—not at all!" Richard cried. "I'm seriously flirting with Bill's mom."

"Very well, then—that's the right answer," she told him—once more ruffling my hair, but she kept talking to Richard. "And if it's *Hedda Gabler* that we do, and I'm Hedda—well, the decision regarding *your* role is a more complicated one, isn't it?"

"Yes, I suppose it is," Richard said thoughtfully. "I hope, in the case of *Hedda Gabler*, I am not the dull, uncomprehending husband—I would *hate* to be George," Richard said.

"Who *wouldn't* hate to be George?" Miss Frost asked him.

"There's the writer Hedda destroys," Richard speculated. "I don't put it past Nils to cast me as Eilert Løvborg."

"You would be wrong for the part!" Miss Frost declared.

"That leaves Judge Brack," Richard Abbott surmised.

"That might be fun," Miss Frost told him. "I shoot myself to escape your clutches."

"I could well imagine being destroyed by that," Richard Abbott said, most graciously. They were acting, even now—I could tell—and they were not amateurs. My mother wouldn't need to be doing much prompting in their cases; I didn't imagine that Richard Abbott or Miss Frost would ever forget a line or misspeak a single word.

"I shall think about it and get back to you," Miss Frost told Richard. There was a tall, narrow, dimly lit mirror in the foyer of the library, where a long row of coat hooks revealed a solitary raincoat—probably Miss Frost's. She glanced at her hair in the mirror. "I've been considering longer hair," she said, as if to her double.

"I imagine Hedda with somewhat longer hair," Richard said.

"*Do* you?" Miss Frost asked, but she was smiling at me again. "Just look at you, William," she said suddenly. "Talk about 'coming of age'— just look at *this boy*!" I must have blushed, or looked away—clutching those three coming-of-age novels to my heart.

MISS FROST CHOSE WELL. I would read *Tom Jones, Wuthering Heights,* and *Jane Eyre*—in that order—thus becoming, to my mom's surprise, a reader. And what those novels taught me was that adventure was not confined to seafaring, with or without pirates. One could find considerable excitement by not escaping to science fiction or futuristic fantasies; it wasn't necessary to read a Western or a romance novel in order to transport oneself. In reading, as in writing, all one needed—that is, in

order to have an utterly absorbing journey—was a believable but formidable relationship. What else, after all, did crushes—especially crushes
on the wrong people—lead to?

"Well, Bill, let's get you home so you can start reading," Richard Abbott
said that warm September evening, and—turning to Miss Frost, in the foyer
of the library—he said (in a voice not his own) the last thing Judge Brack
says to Hedda in act 4, " 'We shall get on capitally together, we two!' "

There would be two months of rehearsals for *Hedda Gabler* that
fall, so I would become most familiar with that line—not to mention
the last lines Hedda says, in response. She has already exited the stage,
but—speaking offstage, *loud and clear*, as the stage directions say—Miss
Frost (as Hedda) responds, " 'Yes, don't you flatter yourself we will, Judge
Brack? Now that you are the one cock in the basket—' " *A shot is heard
within*, the stage directions then say.

Do I sincerely love that play, or did I adore it because Richard Abbott
and Miss Frost brought it to life for me? Grandpa Harry was outstanding
in a small role—that of George's aunt Juliana, Miss Tesman—and my
aunt Muriel was the needy comrade of Eilert Løvborg, Mrs. Elvsted.

"Well, *that* was some performance," Richard Abbott said to me, as
we strolled along the River Street sidewalk on that warm September
evening. It was dark now, and a distant thunder was in the air, but the
neighborhood backyards were quiet; children and dogs had been brought
indoors, and Richard was walking me home.

"*What* performance?" I asked him.

"I mean Miss Frost!" Richard exclaimed. "I mean *her* performance!
The books you should read, all that stuff about *crushes*, and her elaborate
dance about whether she would play Nora or Hedda—"

"You mean she was always *acting*?" I asked him. (Once again, I felt
protective of her, without knowing why.)

"I take it that you liked her," Richard said.

"I *loved* her!" I blurted out.

"Understandable," he said, nodding his head.

"Didn't *you* like her?" I asked him.

"Oh, yes, I did—I *do* like her—and I think she'll be a perfect Hedda,"
Richard said.

"If she'll do it," I cautioned him.

"Oh, she'll do it—of course she's going to *do* it!" Richard declared.
"She was just toying with me."

"Toying," I repeated, not sure if he was criticizing Miss Frost. I was not at all certain that Richard had liked her *sufficiently*.

"Listen to me, Bill," Richard said. "Let the librarian be your new best friend. If you like what she's given you to read, trust her. The library, the theater, a passion for novels and plays—well, Bill, this could be the door to your future. At your age, I lived in a library! Now novels and plays are my life."

This was all so overwhelming. It was staggering to imagine that there were novels about crushes—even, perhaps especially, crushes on the wrong people. Furthermore, our town's amateur theatrical society would be performing Ibsen's *Hedda Gabler* with a brand-new leading man, and with a tower of *sexual strength* (and *untamable* freedom) in the leading female role. And not only did my wounded mother have a *"beau,"* as Aunt Muriel and Nana Victoria referred to Richard Abbott, but my uncomfortable crush on Richard had been supplanted. I was now in love with a librarian who was old enough to be my mother. My seemingly unnatural attraction to Richard Abbott notwithstanding, I felt a new and unknown lust for Miss Frost—not to mention that I suddenly had all this serious reading to do.

No wonder that, when Richard and I came in the house from our excursion to the library, my grandmother felt my forehead—I must have looked flushed, as if I had a fever. "Too much excitement for a school night, Billy," Nana Victoria said.

"Nonsense," Grandpa Harry said. "Show me the books you have, Bill."

"Miss Frost chose them for me," I told him, handing him the novels.

"*Miss* Frost!" my grandmother again declared, her contempt rising.

"Vicky, Vicky," Grandpa Harry cautioned her, like little back-to-back slaps.

"Mommy, please don't," my mother said.

"They're great novels," my grandfather announced. "In fact, they're classics. I daresay Miss Frost knows what novels a young boy should read."

"I *daresay*!" Nana repeated haughtily.

There then followed some difficult-to-understand nastiness from my grandmother, concerning Miss Frost's actual age. "I don't mean her *professed* age!" Nana Victoria cried. I offered that I thought Miss Frost was my mom's age, or a little younger, but Grandpa Harry and my mother looked at each other. Next came what I was familiar with, from the theater—a pause.

"No, Miss Frost is closer to Muriel's age," my grandpa said.

"That *woman* is older than Muriel!" my grandmother snapped.

"Actually, they're about the same age," my mother very quietly said.

At the time, all this meant to me was that Miss Frost was younger-looking than Muriel. In truth, I gave the matter little thought. Nana Victoria evidently didn't like Miss Frost, and Muriel had issues with Miss Frost's breasts or her bras—or both.

It would be later—I don't remember when, exactly, but it was several months later, after I was regularly in the habit of getting novels from Miss Frost in our town's public library—when I overheard my mean aunt Muriel talking about Miss Frost (to my mother) in that same tone of voice my grandmother had used. "And I suppose that *she* has not progressed from the ridiculous training bra?" (To which my mom merely shook her head.)

I would ask Richard Abbott about it, albeit indirectly. "What are *training* bras, Richard?" I asked him, seemingly out of the blue.

"Something you're reading about, Bill?" Richard asked.

"No, I just wondered," I told him.

"Well, Bill, training bras aren't something I know a great deal about," Richard began, "but I believe they are designed to be a young girl's first bra."

"Why *training*?" I asked.

"Well, Bill," Richard continued, "I guess the *training* part of the bra works like this. A girl whose breasts are newly forming wears a training bra so that her breasts begin to get the idea of what a bra is all about."

"Oh," I said. I was completely baffled; I couldn't imagine why Miss Frost's breasts needed to be *trained* at all, and the concept that breasts have *ideas* was also new and troubling to me. Yet my infatuation with Miss Frost had certainly shown me that my penis had ideas that seemed entirely separate from my own thoughts. And if penises could have ideas, it was not such a stretch (for a thirteen-year-old) to imagine that breasts could also think for themselves.

In the literature Miss Frost was presenting me with, at an ever increasing rate, I'd not yet encountered a novel from a penis's point of view, or one where the *ideas* that a woman's breasts have are somehow disturbing to the woman herself—or to her family and friends. Yet such novels seemed possible, if only in the way that my ever having sex with Miss Frost also seemed (albeit remotely) *possible*.

WAS IT PRESCIENT OF Miss Frost to make me wait for Dickens—to work up to him, as it were? And the first Dickens she allowed me was not what I've called the "crucial" one; she made me wait for *Great Expectations*, too. I began, as many a Dickens reader has, with *Oliver Twist*, that young and Gothic novel—the hangman's noose at Newgate casts its macabre shadow over several of the novel's most memorable characters. One thing Dickens and Hardy have in common is the fatalistic belief that, particularly in the case of the young and innocent, the character with a good heart and unbudging integrity is at the greatest risk in a menacing world. (Miss Frost had the good sense to make me wait for Hardy, too. Thomas Hardy is not thirteen-year-old material.)

In the case of Oliver, I readily identified with the resilient orphan's progress. The criminal, rat-infested alleys of Dickens's London were excitingly far, far away from First Sister, Vermont, and I was more forgiving than Miss Frost, who criticized the early novel's "creaky plot mechanism," as she called it.

"Dickens's inexperience as a novelist *shows*," Miss Frost pointed out to me.

At thirteen, going on fourteen, I wasn't critical of inexperience. To me, Fagin was a lovable monster. Bill Sikes was purely terrifying—even his dog, Bull's-eye, was evil. I was seduced, actually kissed, by the Artful Dodger in my dreams—no more winning or fluid a pickpocket ever existed. I cried when Sikes murdered the good-hearted Nancy, but I also cried when Sikes's loyal Bull's-eye leaps from the parapet for the dead man's shoulders. (Bull's-eye misses his mark; the dog falls to the street below, dashing out his brains.)

"Melodramatic, don't you think?" Miss Frost asked me. "And Oliver cries too much; he is more of a cipher for Dickens's abundant passion for damaged children than he is ever a fully fleshed-out character." She told me that Dickens would write better of these themes, and of such children, in his more mature novels—most notably in *David Copperfield*, the next Dickens she gave me, and *Great Expectations*, for which I was made to wait.

When Mr. Brownlow takes Oliver to those "dreadful walls of Newgate,

which have hidden so much misery and such unspeakable anguish"—
where Fagin is waiting to be hanged—I cried for poor Fagin, too.

"It's a good sign when a boy cries reading a novel," Miss Frost assured me.

"A good sign?" I asked her.

"It means you have more of a heart than most boys have," was all she
would say about my crying.

When I was reading with what Miss Frost described as the "reckless
desperation of a burglar ravishing a mansion," she one day said to me,
"Slow down, William. Savor, don't gorge. And when you love a book,
commit one glorious sentence of it—perhaps your favorite sentence—to
memory. That way you won't forget the language of the story that moved
you to tears." (If Miss Frost thought Oliver cried too much, I wondered
what she really thought of me.) In the case of *Oliver Twist*, alas, I forget
which sentence I chose to memorize.

After *David Copperfield*, Miss Frost gave me my first taste of Thomas
Hardy. Was I then fourteen, going on fifteen? (Yes, I think so; Richard
Abbott happened to be teaching the same Hardy novel to the boys at
Favorite River Academy, but they were prep-school seniors and I was still
in the lowly eighth grade, I'm sure.)

I remember looking, with some uncertainty, at the title—*Tess of the
d'Urbervilles*—and asking Miss Frost, with apparent disappointment, "It's
about a girl?"

"Yes, William—a most unlucky girl," Miss Frost quickly said. "But—
more important, for your benefit as a young man—it's also about the men
she meets. May you never be one of the men Tess meets, William."

"Oh," I said. I would know soon enough what she meant about the
men Tess meets; indeed, I would never want to be one of them.

Of Angel Clare, Miss Frost said simply: "What a wet noodle he is."
And when I looked uncomprehending, she added: "Overcooked spa-
ghetti, William—think *limp*, think *weak*."

"Oh."

I RACED HOME FROM school to read; I raced when I read, unable to
heed Miss Frost's command to slow down. I raced to the First Sister Public Library after every school-night supper. I modeled myself on what
Richard Abbott had told me of his childhood—I lived in the library,
especially on the weekends. Miss Frost was always making me move to

a chair or a couch or a table where there was better light. "Don't ruin your eyes, William. You'll need your eyes for the rest of your life, if you're going to be a reader."

Suddenly I was fifteen. It was *Great Expectations* time—also, it was the first time I wanted to reread a novel—and Miss Frost and I had that awkward conversation about my desire to become a writer. (It was not my only desire, as you know, but Miss Frost and I didn't discuss that other desire—not then.)

It was suddenly time for me to attend Favorite River Academy, too. Fittingly—since she would be so instrumental in my overall education—it was Miss Frost who pointed out to me what a "favor" my mother and Richard Abbott had done for me. Because they got married in the summer of 1957—more to the point, because Richard Abbott legally adopted me—my name was changed from William Francis Dean, Jr., to William Marshall Abbott. I would begin my prep-school years with a brand-new name—one I liked!

Richard had a faculty apartment in one of the dormitories of the boarding school, which he and my mom shared in their new life together, and I had my own bedroom there. It was not a long walk, on River Street, to my grandparents' house, where I'd grown up, and I was a frequent visitor there. As little as I liked my grandmother, I was very fond of Grandpa Harry; of course I would continue to see my grandfather onstage, as a woman, but once I became a student at Favorite River, I would no longer be a backstage regular at the rehearsals of the First Sister Players.

I had much more homework at the academy than I'd ever seen in middle or elementary school, and Richard Abbott was in charge of the Drama Club (as it was called) at the prep school. Richard's Shakespearean ambitions would draw me more to the Drama Club, and away from all but the finished performances at the First Sister Players. The Drama Club's stage, the academy's theater, was both bigger and more sophisticated than our town's quaint little playhouse. (The *quaint* word was a new one for me. I became a bit of a snob in my years at Favorite River, or so Miss Frost would one day inform me.)

And if my inappropriate crush on Richard Abbott had been "supplanted" (as I've said) by my lust and ardent longing for Miss Frost, so had two gifted amateurs (Grandpa Harry and Aunt Muriel) been replaced by two vastly more talented actors. Richard Abbott and Miss Frost were soon superstars on the stage of the First Sister Players. Not only was Miss

Frost cast as the neurotic Hedda to Richard's hideously controlling Judge Brack; in the fall of '56, she played Nora in *A Doll's House*. Richard, as he'd guessed, was cast as her dull, uncomprehending husband, Torvald Helmer. An uncharacteristically subdued Aunt Muriel did not speak to her own father for almost a month, because Grandpa Harry (not Muriel) was cast as Mrs. Linde. And Richard Abbott and Miss Frost managed to persuade Nils Borkman to play the unfortunate Krogstad, which the grim Norwegian brought off with a creepy combination of doom and righteousness.

More important than what this mixed bag of amateurs made of Ibsen, a new faculty family had arrived at Favorite River Academy at the start of the academic year of 1956 and '57—a couple named Hadley. They had an only child—a gawky-looking daughter, Elaine. Mr. Hadley was a new history teacher. Mrs. Hadley, who played the piano, gave voice and singing lessons; she directed the school's several choruses and conducted the academy choir. The Hadleys became friends with Richard and my mom, and so Elaine and I often found ourselves thrust together. I was a year older, which—at the time—made me feel a lot older than Elaine, who lagged far behind in the breast-development department. (Nor would Elaine *ever* have any breasts, I imagined, for I'd also noticed that Mrs. Hadley was virtually flat-chested—even when she sang.)

Elaine was extremely nearsighted; in those days, there was no remedy for this, save those super-thick lenses that magnified your eyes and made them appear as if they were exploding out of your head. But her mother had taught her to sing, and Elaine also had a vibrant, well-enunciated speaking voice. When she spoke, it was almost as if she were singing— you could hear every word.

"Elaine really knows how to *project*," was how Mrs. Hadley put it. Her name was Martha; she was not pretty, but she was very nice, and she was the first person to notice with some accuracy that there were certain words I couldn't pronounce properly. She told my mother that there were vocal exercises I could try, or that singing might be of some benefit to me, but that fall of '56 I was still in middle school, and I was consumed by reading. I wanted nothing to do with "vocal exercises" or singing.

All these significant changes in my life came together and moved forward with an unexpected momentum: In the fall of '57, I was a student at Favorite River Academy; I was still rereading *Great Expectations,* and (as you know) I'd let it slip to Miss Frost that I wanted to be a writer. I was fifteen, and Elaine Hadley was a nearsighted, flat-chested, clarion-voiced fourteen-year-old.

One night that September, there came a knocking on the door of Richard's faculty apartment, but it was study hours in the dormitory—no boy came to our apartment door then, unless he was sick. I opened the door, expecting to see a sick student standing anxiously in the dorm hall, but there was Nils Borkman, the distraught director; he looked as if he'd seen a ghost, possibly some previous fjord-jumper he had known.

"I've seen her! I've heard her speak! She would be a perfect Hedvig!" Nils Borkman cried.

Poor Elaine Hadley! It was her bad luck to be half blind—and breast-less and shrill. (In *The Wild Duck*, a big deal is made of what is wrong with Hedvig's eyes.) Elaine, that sexless but crystal-clear child, would be cast as the wretched Hedvig, and once more Borkman would unleash *The* (dreaded) *Wild Duck* on the aghast citizens of First Sister. Fresh from his surprising success as Krogstad in *A Doll's House*, Nils would cast himself as Gregers.

"That miserable moralizer," Richard Abbott had called Gregers.

Determined, as he was, to personify the *idealist* in Gregers, Nils Bork-man would play the clownish aspect of the character to unwitting perfec-tion.

No one, least of all the suicidal Norwegian, could explain to the fourteen-year-old Elaine Hadley whether Hedvig means to shoot the wild duck and *accidentally* shoots herself, or if—as Dr. Relling says—Hedvig *intends* to kill herself. Nevertheless, Elaine was a ter-rific Hedvig—or at least a loud and clear Hedvig.

It was sadly funny, when the doctor says of the bullet that has gone through Hedvig's heart, "The ball has entered her breast." (Poor Elaine had no breasts.)

Startling the audience, the fourteen-year-old Hedvig cries out, "The wild duck!"

This is just before Hedvig exits the stage. The stage directions say: *She steals over and takes the pistol*—well, not quite. Elaine Hadley actually brandished the weapon and stomped offstage.

What bothered Elaine most about the play was that no one says a word about what will become of the wild duck. "The poor thing!" Elaine lamented. "It's *wounded*! It tries to *drown* itself, but the horrid dog brings it up from the bottom of the sea. And the duck is confined in a garret!

What kind of life can a wild duck have in a *garret*? And after Hedvig *offs* herself, who's to say that the crazy old military man—or even Hjalmar, who's such a *wimp*, who feels so sorry for himself—won't just *shoot* it? It's simply *awful* how that duck is treated!"

I know now, of course, it was not sympathy for the *duck* that Henrik Ibsen so arduously sought, or that Nils Borkman attempted to elicit from the unsophisticated audience in First Sister, Vermont, but Elaine Hadley would be marked for life by her too-young, altogether too-innocent immersion in what a mindless melodrama Borkman made of *The Wild Duck*.

To this day, I've not seen a professional production of the play; to see it done right, or at least as right as it could be done, might be unbearable. But Elaine Hadley would become my good friend, and I will not be disloyal to Elaine by disputing her interpretation of the play. Gina (Miss Frost) was by far the most sympathetic human being onstage, but it was the wild duck itself—we never see the stupid bird!—that garnered the lion's share of Elaine's sympathy. The unanswered or unanswerable question—"What happens to the duck?"—is what resonates with me. This has even become one of the ways Elaine and I greet each other. All children learn to speak in codes.

GRANDPA HARRY DIDN'T WANT a part in *The Wild Duck*; he would have feigned laryngitis to get free from that play. Also, Grandpa Harry had grown tired of being directed by his long-standing business partner, Nils Borkman.

Richard Abbott was having his way with the staid all-boys' academy; not only was he teaching Shakespeare to those boringly single-sex boys at Favorite River—Richard was putting Shakespeare onstage, and the female roles would be played by girls and women. (Or by an expert female impersonator, such as Harry Marshall, who could at least teach those prep-school boys how to act like girls and women.) Richard Abbott hadn't only married my abandoned mother and given me a crush on him; he had found a kindred soul in Grandpa Harry, who (especially as a woman) much preferred having Richard as his director than the melancholic Norwegian.

There was a moment, in those first two years Richard Abbott was performing for the First Sister Players—and he was teaching and directing Shakespeare at Favorite River Academy—when Grandpa Harry would yield to a familiar temptation. In the seemingly endless list of

Agatha Christie plays that were waiting to be performed, there was more than one Hercule Poirot mystery; the fat Belgian was an acknowledged master at getting murderers to betray themselves. Both Aunt Muriel and Grandpa Harry had played Miss Marple countless times, but there was what Muriel would have called a *"dearth"* of cast-worthy fat Belgians in First Sister, Vermont.

Richard Abbott didn't do fat, and he refused to perform Agatha Christie at all. We simply had no Hercule Poirot, and Borkman was fjord-jumping morose about it. "An idea fairly leaps to mind, Nils," Grandpa Harry told the troubled Norwegian one day. "Why must it be *Hercule* Poirot. Would you consider instead a *Hermione?*"

Thus was *Black Coffee* performed by the First Sister Players, with Grandpa Harry in the role of a sleek and agile (almost balletic) Belgian woman, Hermione Poirot. A formula for a new explosive is stolen from a safe; a character named Sir Claud is poisoned, and so on. It was no more memorable than Agatha Christie ever is, but Harry Marshall brought the house down as Hermione.

"Agatha Christie is rolling in her grave, Father," was all my disapproving aunt Muriel could say.

"I daresay she is, Harold!" my grandmother joined in.

"Agatha Christie isn't dead yet, Vicky," Grandpa Harry told Nana Victoria, winking at me. "Agatha Christie is very much alive, Muriel."

Oh, how I loved him—especially as a *her*!

Yet in those same two years when Richard Abbott was new in our town, he could not persuade Miss Frost to make a guest appearance in a single one of the Shakespeare plays that he directed for the Drama Club at Favorite River Academy. "I don't think so, Richard," Miss Frost told him. "I'm not at all sure it would be good for those boys to have me put myself 'out there,' so to speak—by which I mean, they are all boys, they are all young, and they are all *impressionable*."

"But Shakespeare can be fun, Miss Frost," Richard argued with her. "We can do a play that is strictly *fun*."

"I don't think so, Richard," she repeated, and that appeared to be the end of the discussion. Miss Frost didn't do Shakespeare, or she wouldn't—not for those oh-so-*impressionable* boys. I didn't know what to make of her refusal; seeing her onstage was thrilling to me, not that I needed an added incentive to love and desire her.

But once I started being a student, a mere freshman, at Favorite

River, there were all these older boys around; they weren't especially friendly to me, and some of them were distractions. I developed a distant infatuation with a striking-looking boy on the wrestling team; it wasn't only that he had a beautiful body. (I say "distant," because initially I did my best to keep my distance from him—to keep as far away from him as I could get.) Talk about a crush on the wrong person! And it was *not* my imagination that every other word out of many of the older boys' mouths was "homo" or "fag" or "queer"; these purposely hurtful words seemed to me to be the worst things you could say about another boy at the prep school.

Were these "distractions," my crushes on the wrong people, part of the genetic package I had inherited from my code-boy father? Curiously, I doubted it; I thought these particular crushes were all my fault, for hadn't the sergeant been a notorious womanizer? Hadn't my combative cousin Gerry labeled him with the *womanizer* word? Gerry may have heard it, or she got that impression, from my uncle Bob or my aunt Muriel. (Didn't *womanizer* sound like a word Muriel might have used?)

I suppose I should have talked to Richard Abbott about it, but I didn't; I didn't dare mention it to Miss Frost, either. I kept these new, unhappy crushes entirely to myself, the way—so often—children do.

I began to stay away from the First Sister Public Library. I must have felt that Miss Frost was smart enough to sense that I was being unfaithful to her—if only in my imagination. In fact, my first two years as a Favorite River student were spent almost entirely in my imagination, and the new library in my life was the more modern and better-lit one at the academy. I did all my homework there, and what amounted to my earliest attempts at writing.

Was I the only boy at the all-boys' school who found that the wrestling matches gave me a homoerotic charge? I doubt it, but boys like me kept their heads down.

I went from having these unmentionable crushes on this or that boy to masturbating with the dubious aid of one of my mother's mail-order clothing catalogs. The advertisements for bras and girdles got my attention. The models for the girdles were mostly older women. For me, it was an early exercise in creative writing—at least I managed some clever cutting and pasting. I took the faces of these older women and moved them to the young-girl models for the training bras; thus did Miss Frost come to life for me, albeit (like most other things) only in my imagination.

Girls my own age didn't usually interest me. While she was flat-chested and not pretty, as I've said, I took a preternatural interest in Mrs. Hadley—I suppose because she was around a lot, and she took a sincere interest in me (or in my mounting number of speech impediments, anyway). "What words are the hardest for you to pronounce, Billy?" she asked me once, when she and Mr. Hadley (and the trombone-voiced Elaine) were having dinner with my mother and Richard and me.

"He has trouble with the *library* word." Elaine spoke up—loudly and clearly, as always. (I had absolutely zero sexual interest in Elaine, but she was growing on me in other ways. She never teased me about my mispronunciations; she seemed as genuinely interested in helping me to say a word the right way as her mother was.)

"I was asking *Billy*, Elaine," Mrs. Hadley said.

"I think Elaine knows, better than I do, which words give me the most trouble," I said.

"Billy makes a mess of the last two syllables in *ominousness* every time," Elaine went on.

"I say *penith*," I ventured.

"I see," Martha Hadley said.

"Don't ask him to say the plural," Elaine told her mother.

If Favorite River Academy had admitted girls in those days, Elaine Hadley and I would probably have become best friends sooner than we did, but I didn't get to go to school with Elaine. I managed to see as much of her as I did only because the Hadleys so frequently socialized with my mom and Richard—they were becoming such good friends.

Thus, occasionally, it was the homely and flat-chested Mrs. Hadley I imagined in those training bras—I thought of Martha Hadley's small breasts when I perused the young-girl models in my mom's mail-order catalogs.

In the academy library, where I was becoming a writer—or, more accurately, dreaming of becoming one—I especially liked the room with the vast collection of Favorite River yearbooks. Other students seemed to take no interest in that reading room; the occasional faculty member could be found there, either reading or grading papers and blue books.

Favorite River Academy was old; it had been founded in the nineteenth century. I liked looking at the old yearbooks. (Perhaps *all* the past held secrets; I knew my past did.) If I kept at it, I imagined, I might eventually catch up to the yearbook of my own graduating class—but not before the spring of my senior year. In the fall of my junior year, I was still looking through yearbooks from 1914 and 1915. World War I was going on; those Favorite River boys must have been frightened. I looked closely at the faces of the graduating seniors, and at their college choices and career ambitions; many of the seniors were "undecided" about both. Almost all the seniors had nicknames, even back then.

I looked very closely at the wrestling-team photographs, and somewhat less closely at the Drama Club photos; in the latter case, there were many boys in makeup and dressed as girls. It seemed that there'd always been a wrestling team and a Drama Club at Favorite River. (You must remember that this particular 1914–1915 yearbook searching was in the fall of 1959; the much-admired traditions in single-sex boarding schools were vigorously upheld through the fifties, and into the sixties.)

I suppose I liked that reading room with all the yearbooks, and with the occasional faculty member, because there were never any other students there—no bullies, in other words, and no distracting crushes. How lucky was I to have had my own room in my mom and Richard's faculty apartment? All the boarders at the academy had roommates. I cannot imagine what abuse, or what more subtle form of cruelty, I might have suffered from a roommate. And what would I have done with my mother's mail-order clothing catalogs? (The very thought of not being able to masturbate was abusive enough—I mean, just *imagining* it!)

At seventeen, which I was in the fall of 1959, I had no reason to go back to the First Sister Public Library—that is, no reason I would have dared to express. I'd found a haven to get my homework done; the yearbook room in the academy library was a place to write, or just to imagine. But I must have missed Miss Frost. She was not onstage enough to satisfy me, and now that I skipped the rehearsals at the First Sister Players, I saw her only when she was in an actual performance; these were "too few and far between," as my cliché-spouting grandmother might have said.

I could have talked to Grandpa Harry about it; he would have understood. I could have told him about missing Miss Frost, about my crush on her *and* on those older boys—even about my earliest, inappropriate crush on my stepfather, Richard Abbott. But I didn't talk to Grandpa Harry about any of it—not then.

Was Harry Marshall an actual transvestite? Was Grandpa Harry more than the occasional cross-dresser? Today, would we call my grandpa a closeted gay man who only *acted* as a woman under the most permissible circumstances of his time? I honestly don't know. If my generation was repressed, and we certainly were, I can only imagine that my grandfather's generation—whether or not Grandpa Harry truly was a homosexual—flew well under the existing radar.

Thus it seemed to me, at the time, that there was no remedy for missing Miss Frost—except making up a reason to see her. (If I was going to be a writer, after all, I should be able to make up a believable reason for my frequenting the First Sister Public Library again.) And so I settled upon a story—namely, that the only place I could work on my writing was the public library, where my academy friends wouldn't keep interrupting me. Maybe Miss Frost wouldn't know that I didn't have many friends, and what few friends I had at Favorite River kept their heads down and were as timid as I was; they wouldn't have dared to interrupt anyone.

Since I'd told Miss Frost that I wanted to become a writer, she might accept that the First Sister town library was where I wanted to try my hand at it. In the evening, I knew, there were mostly elderly people there, and few of them; there might also be scant representation of those sullen high school girls, condemned to further their education in Ezra Falls. There was no one who would interrupt me in our town's forlorn library. (No children, especially.)

I was afraid that Miss Frost wouldn't recognize me. I had started to shave, and I thought I was somehow altered—I was so much more grown up, in my estimation. I knew that Miss Frost knew my name had changed, and that she must have seen me—albeit only occasionally, in the last two years, either backstage or in the audience at the First Sister Players' little theater. She certainly knew I was the prompter's son—I was *that boy.*

On the night I presented myself at the public library—not to take out a book, or even read one, but to actually work on my own writing— Miss Frost stared at me for the longest time. I assumed she was having trouble remembering me, and my heart was breaking, but she remembered far more than I'd imagined.

"Don't tell me—it's William Abbott," Miss Frost suddenly said. "I suppose you want to read *Great Expectations* a record-breaking *third* time."

I confessed to her that I hadn't come to the library to read. I told Miss Frost that I was trying to get away from my friends—so that I could *write.*

"You've come here, to the library, to *write,*" she repeated. I remembered that Miss Frost had a habit of repeating what you said. Nana Victoria said that Miss Frost must have enjoyed the repetition, because by repeating what you said to her, she could keep the conversation going a little longer. (Aunt Muriel had claimed that no one liked to talk to Miss Frost.)

"Yes, I do," I told Miss Frost. "I want to write."

"But why *here*? Why this place?" Miss Frost demanded.

I couldn't think of what to say. A word (and then another word) just popped into my head, and Miss Frost made me so nervous that I spontaneously said the first word, which was quickly followed by the second. "Nostalgia," I said. "Maybe I'm *nostalgic*."

"Nostalgia!" Miss Frost cried. "You're *nostalgic*!" she repeated. "Just how old are you, William?" she asked.

"Seventeen," I told her.

"Seventeen!" Miss Frost cried, as if she'd been stabbed. "Well, William Dean—forgive me, I mean William *Abbott*—if you're *nostalgic* at seventeen, maybe you *are* going to be a writer!"

She was the first one who said so—for a while, she was the only one who knew what I wanted to be—and I believed her. At the time, Miss Frost struck me as the most genuine person I knew.

Chapter 3

MASQUERADE

The wrestler with the most beautiful body was named Kittredge. He had a hairless chest with absurdly well-defined pectoral muscles; those muscles were of an exaggerated, comic-book clarity. A thin line of dark-brown, almost-black hair ran from his navel to his pubes, and he had one of those cute penises—I have such a dread of that plural! His penis was inclined to curl against his right thigh, or it appeared to be preternaturally pointed to the right. There was no one I could ask concerning what the rightward inclination of Kittredge's penis signified. In the showers, at the gym, I lowered my eyes; for the most part, I wouldn't look at him above his strong, hairy legs.

Kittredge had a heavy beard, but he had perfect skin and was generally clean-shaven. I found him at his most devastatingly handsome with two or three days' stubble, when he looked older than the other students, and even some of the Favorite River faculty—including Richard Abbott and Mr. Hadley. Kittredge played soccer in the fall, and lacrosse in the spring, but wrestling was the foremost showcase for his beautiful body, and the wrestling seemed well suited to his innate cruelty.

While I rarely saw him bully anyone—that is, physically—he was aggressive and intimidating, and his sarcasm was of a cutting-edge kind. In that all-boys', boarding-school world, Kittredge was honored as an athlete, but I remember him best for how effectively abusive he was. Kittredge was brilliant at inflicting verbal pain, and he had the body to back up what he said; no one stood up to him. If you despised him, you kept quiet about it. I both despised and adored him. Alas, the despising-him part did little to lessen my crush on him; my attraction to him was a burden I bore through my junior year, when Kittredge was a senior—when I believed I had only one year of agony remaining. I foresaw a day, just around the corner, when my longing for him would cease to torment me.

It would be a blow, and an additional burden, to discover that Kittredge had failed to pass the foreign-language requirement; he would stay at the school for a fifth year. We would be seniors together. By then, Kittredge not only looked older than the other Favorite River students—he truly was older.

If only at the beginning of those seemingly endless years of our incarceration together, I misheard the nuance in the pronunciation of Kittredge's first name—"Jock," I thought everyone called him. It fit. Surely, I thought, Jock was a nickname—anyone who was as cool as Kittredge had one. But his first name, his *actual* name, was Jacques.

"*Zhak*," we called Kittredge. In my infatuation with him, I must have imagined that my fellow students found him as beautiful as I did—that we'd instinctively *Frenchified* the *jock* word because of Kittredge's good looks!

He was born and grew up in New York City, where his father had something to do with international banking—or maybe it was international law. Kittredge's mother was French. She was a Jacqueline—in French, the feminine of *Jacques*. "My mom, who I don't believe really *is* my mom, is very vain," Kittredge said, repeatedly—as if *he* weren't vain. I wondered if it was a measure of Jacqueline Kittredge's vanity that she had named her son—he was an only child—after herself.

I saw her only once—at a wrestling match. I admired her clothes. She certainly was beautiful, though I thought her boy was better-looking. Mrs. Kittredge had a masculine kind of attractiveness; she looked chiseled—she even had her son's prominent jaw. How could Kittredge have believed she wasn't his mom? They looked so much alike.

"She looks like Kittredge with breasts," Elaine Hadley said to me—with her typical, clarion-voiced authority. "How could she *not* be his mother?" Elaine asked me. "Unless she's his much-older sister. Come on, Billy—if they were the same age, she could be his *twin*!"

At the wrestling match, Elaine and I had stared at Kittredge's mother; she seemed unfazed by it. With her striking bones, her jutting breasts, her perfectly fitted and most flattering clothes, Mrs. Kittredge was surely used to being stared at.

"I wonder if she waxes her face," I said to Elaine.

"Why would she have to?" Elaine asked me.

"I can imagine her with a mustache," I said.

"Yeah, but with no hair on her chest, like him," Elaine replied. I suppose that Kittredge's mom was riveting to us because we could see Kittredge in her, but Mrs. Kittredge was also riveting in her own disturbing way. She was the first older woman who made me feel I was too young and inexperienced to understand her. I remember thinking that it must have been intimidating to have her as a mother—even for Kittredge.

I knew that Elaine had a crush on Kittredge because she'd told me. (Embarrassingly, we'd both memorized Kittredge's chest.) That fall of '59, when I was seventeen, I hadn't been honest with Elaine about *my* crushes; I'd not yet been brave enough to tell her that both Miss Frost and Jacques Kittredge turned me on. And how could I have told Elaine about my confounding lust for her mom? Occasionally, I was still masturbating to the homely and flat-chested Martha Hadley—that tall, big-boned woman with a wide, thin-lipped mouth, whose long face I imagined on those young girls who were the training-bra models in my mom's mail-order catalogs.

It might have comforted Elaine to know that I shared her misery over Kittredge, who at the outset was as scathing or indifferent (or both) to her as he was to me, though he had been treating us slightly better lately—since Richard Abbott had cast the three of us in *The Tempest*. It was wise of Richard to have cast himself as Prospero, because there was no mere boy among the Favorite River students who could have properly played the "true" Duke of Milan, as Shakespeare calls him, and Miranda's loving father. His twelve years of island life have honed Prospero's magical powers, and there are few prep-school boys who can make such powers evident onstage.

Okay—maybe Kittredge could have done it. He was well cast as a ravishingly sexy Ferdinand; Kittredge was convincing in his love for Miranda, though this caused Elaine Hadley, who was cast as Miranda, no end of suffering.

"I would not wish / Any companion in the world but you," Miranda tells Ferdinand.

And Ferdinand says to Miranda: "I, / Beyond all limit of what else i' the world, / Do love, prize, honor you."

How hard it must have been for Elaine to hear that—in one rehearsal after another—only to be ignored (or belittled) by Kittredge whenever she encountered him offstage. That he was treating us "slightly better" since the start of rehearsals for *The Tempest* didn't mean that Kittredge couldn't still be awful.

Richard had cast me as Ariel; in the dramatis personae for the play, Shakespeare calls Ariel "an airy Spirit."

No, I don't believe that Richard was being particularly prescient in regard to my emerging and confusing sexual orientation. He told the cast that Ariel's gender was "polymorphous—more a matter of habiliment than anything organic."

From the first *Enter Ariel* moment (act 1, scene 2), Ariel says to Prospero: "To thy strong bidding task / Ariel and all his quality." Richard had called the cast's attention—especially my attention—to the male pronoun. (In the same scene, the stage direction for Ariel reads: *he demonstrates*.)

It was unfortunate for me that Prospero commands Ariel: "Go make thyself like a nymph o' th' sea, be subject / To no sight but thine and mine—invisible / To every eyeball else."

Alas, I would not be invisible to the audience. The *Enter Ariel as a water nymph* always got a big laugh—even before I was in costume with makeup. That stage direction was what led Kittredge to start calling me "Nymph."

I remember exactly how Richard had put it: "Keeping the character of Ariel in the male gender is simpler than tricking out one more choirboy in women's garb." (But women's garb—well, at least the *wig*—was how I would be tricked out!)

Nor was it lost on Kittredge when Richard said, "It's possible that Shakespeare saw a continuum from Caliban through Prospero to Ariel—a kind of spiritual evolution. Caliban is all earth and water, brute force and guile. Prospero is human control and insight—he's the ultimate alchemist. And Ariel," Richard said, smiling at me—no smile was ever lost on Kittredge—"Ariel is a spirit of air and fire, freed from mortal concerns. Perhaps Shakespeare felt that presenting Ariel as explicitly female might detract from this notion of a continuum. I believe that Ariel's gender is *mutable*."

"Director's choice, in other words?" Kittredge asked Richard.

Our director and teacher regarded Kittredge cautiously before answering him. "The sex of angels is also mutable," Richard said. "Yes, Kittredge—director's choice."

"But what will the so-called water nymph *look* like?" Kittredge asked. "Like a *girl*, right?"

"Probably," Richard said, more cautiously.

I was trying to imagine how I would be costumed and made up as an invisible water nymph; I could never have foreseen the algae-green wig I wore, nor the crimson wrestling tights. (Crimson and silver-gray—"death-gray," Grandpa Harry had called it—were the Favorite River Academy colors.)

"So Billy's gender is . . . *mutable*," Kittredge said, smiling.

"Not Billy's—*Ariel's*," Richard said.

But Kittredge had made his point; the cast of *The Tempest* would not forget the *mutable* word. "Nymph," Kittredge's nickname for me, would stick. I had two years to go at Favorite River Academy; a Nymph I would be.

"It doesn't matter what costume and makeup do to you, Nymph," Kittredge said to me privately. "You'll never be as hot as your mother."

I was aware that my mom was pretty, and—at seventeen—I was increasingly conscious of how the other students at an all-boys' academy like Favorite River regarded her. But no other boy had told me that my mom was "hot"; as I often found myself with Kittredge, I was at a loss for words. I'm sure that the *hot* word was not yet in use—not the way Kittredge had used it. But Kittredge definitely meant "hot" in that way.

When Kittredge spoke of his own mother, which he rarely did, he usually raised the issue of there being a possible mix-up. "Maybe my real mom died in childbirth," Kittredge said. "My father found some unwed mother in the same hospital—an unfortunate woman (her child was still-born, but the woman never knew), a woman who *looked like* my mother. There was a switch. My dad would be capable of such a deception. I'm not saying the woman knows she's my stepmother. She may even believe my dad is my stepfather! At the time, she might have been taking a lot of drugs—she must have been depressed, maybe suicidal. I have no doubt that she *believes* she's my mom—she just doesn't always *act* like a mother. She's done some contradictory things—contradictory to motherhood. All I'm saying is that my dad has never been answerable for his behavior with women—with *any* woman. My dad just makes deals. This woman may look like me, but she's not my mom—she's not *anyone's* mother."

"Kittredge is in denial—big time," Elaine had told me. "That woman looks like his mother *and* his father!"

When I told Elaine Hadley what Kittredge had said about my mom, Elaine suggested that I tell Kittredge our opinion of his mother—based on our shameless staring at her, at one of his wrestling matches. "Tell him his mom looks like him, with *tits*," Elaine said.

"*You* tell him," I told her; we both knew I wouldn't. Elaine wouldn't talk to Kittredge about his mom, either.

Initially, Elaine was almost as afraid of Kittredge as I was—nor would she ever have used the *tits* word in his company. She was very conscious of having inherited her mom's flat chest. Elaine was nowhere near as homely as her mother; Elaine was thin and gawky, and she had no boobs, but she had a pretty face—and, unlike her mom, Elaine would never be big-boned. Elaine was delicate-looking, which made her trombone of a voice all the more surprising. Yet, at first, she was so intimidated in Kittredge's presence that she often croaked or mumbled; at times, she was incoherent. Elaine was so afraid of sounding too loud around him. "Kittredge fogs up my glasses," was the way she put it.

Their first meeting onstage—as Ferdinand and Miranda—was dazzlingly clear; one never saw two souls so unmistakably drawn to each other. Upon seeing Miranda, Ferdinand calls her a "wonder"; he asks, "If you be maid or no?"

"'No wonder sir, / But certainly a maid,'" Elaine (as Miranda) replies in a vibrant, gonglike voice. But offstage, Kittredge had managed to make Elaine self-conscious about her booming voice. After all, she was only sixteen; Kittredge was eighteen, going on thirty.

Elaine and I were walking back to the dorm after rehearsal one night—the Hadleys had a faculty apartment in the same dorm where I lived with Richard Abbott and my mom—when Kittredge magically materialized beside us. (Kittredge was always doing that.) "You two are quite a couple," he told us.

"We're not a *couple!*" Elaine blurted out, much louder than she'd meant to. Kittredge pretended to stagger, as if from an unseen blow; he held his ears.

"I must warn you, Nymph—you're in danger of losing your hearing," Kittredge said to me. "When this little lady has her first orgasm, you better be wearing earplugs. And I wouldn't do it in the dormitory, if I were you," Kittredge warned me. "The whole dorm would hear her." He then drifted away from us, down a different, darker path; Kittredge lived in the jock dorm, the one nearest the gym.

It was too dark to see if Elaine Hadley had blushed. I touched her face lightly, just enough to ascertain if she was crying; she wasn't, but her cheek was hot and she brushed my hand away. "No one's giving me an orgasm anytime soon!" Elaine cried after Kittredge.

We were in a quadrangle of dormitories; in the distance, there were lights in the surrounding dorm windows, and a chorus of voices whooped and cheered—as if a hundred unseen boys had heard her. But Elaine was very agitated when she cried out; I doubted that Kittredge (or anyone but me) had understood her. I was wrong, though what Elaine had cried with police-siren shrillness sounded like, "No nun's liver goes into spasm for a raccoon!" (Or nonsense of a similar, incomprehensible kind.)

But Kittredge had grasped Elaine's meaning; his sweetly sarcastic voice reached us from somewhere in the dark quadrangle. Cruelly, it was as the sexy Ferdinand that Kittredge called out of the darkness to my friend Elaine, who was (at that moment) not feeling much like Miranda.

"O, if a virgin, / And your affection not gone forth, I'll make you / The Queen of Naples," Ferdinand swears to Miranda—and so Kittredge amorously called. The quad of dorms was eerily quiet; when those Favorite River boys heard Kittredge speak, they were silenced by their own awe and stupefaction. "Good night, Nymph!" I heard Kittredge call. "Good night, Naples!"

Thus Elaine Hadley and I had our nicknames. When Kittredge named you, it may have been a dubious honor, but the designation was both lasting and traumatic.

"Shit," Elaine said. "It could be worse—Kittredge could be calling me *Maid* or *Virgin*."

"Elaine?" I said. "You're my one true friend."

" 'Abhorrèd slave,' " she said to me.

This was uttered as sharply as a bark; there was a doglike echo in the quadrangle of dorms. We both knew it is what Miranda says to Caliban— "a savage and deformed slave," Shakespeare calls him, but Caliban is an unfinished monster.

Prospero berates Caliban: "thou didst seek to violate / The honor of my child."

Caliban doesn't deny it. Caliban hates Prospero *and* his daughter ("toads, beetles, bats, light on you!"), though the monster once lusted after Miranda and wishes he "had peopled" the island with little Calibans. Caliban is evidently male, but it's uncertain how human he is.

When Trinculo, the jester, first notices Caliban, Trinculo says, "What have we here? A man or a fish? Dead or alive?"

I knew that Elaine Hadley had been kidding—speaking to me as Miranda speaks to Caliban, Elaine was just fooling around—but as we drew near to our dormitory, the lights from the windows illuminated her tear-streaked face. In only a minute or two, Kittredge's mockery of Ferdinand and Miranda's romance had taken effect; Elaine was crying. "You're my *only* friend!" she blubbered to me.

I felt sorry for her, and put my arm around her shoulders; this provoked more whoops and cheers from those unseen boys who'd whooped and cheered before. Did I know that this night was the beginning of my masquerade? Was I conscious of giving those Favorite River boys the impression that Elaine Hadley was my girlfriend? Was I acting, even then? Consciously or not, I was making Elaine Hadley my disguise. For a while, I would fool Richard Abbott and Grandpa Harry—not to mention Mr. Hadley and his homely wife, Martha, and (if not for long, and to a lesser extent) my mother.

Yes, I was aware that my mom was changing. She'd been so nice to me when I was little. I used to wonder, when I was a teenager, what had become of the small boy she'd once loved.

I even began an early novel with this tortured and overlong sentence: "According to my mother, I was a fiction writer before I'd written any fiction, by which she meant not only that I invented things, or made things up, but that I preferred this kind of fantasizing or pure imagining to what other people generally liked—she meant reality, of course."

My mom's assessment of "pure imagining" was not flattering. Fiction was frivolous to her; no, it was worse than frivolous.

One Christmas—I believe it was the first Christmas I'd come home to Vermont, for a visit, in several years—I was scribbling away in a notebook, and my mother asked me, "What are you writing *now*, Billy?"

"A novel," I told her.

"Well, that should make *you* happy," she suddenly said to Grandpa Harry, who'd begun to lose his hearing—sawmill damage, I suppose.

"Me? Why should it make *me* happy that Bill is writing another novel? Not that I didn't love the last one, Bill, because I sure-as-shit *did* love it!" Grandpa Harry quickly assured me.

"Of course you loved it," my mother told him. "Novels are just another kind of cross-dressing, aren't they?"

"Ah, well . . ." Grandpa Harry had started to say, but then stopped. As Harry got older, he stopped himself from saying what he was going to say—more and more.

I know the feeling. When I was a teenager, when I began to sense that my mom wasn't as *nice* to me as she'd been before, I got in the habit of stopping myself from saying what I wanted to say. Not anymore.

MANY YEARS LATER, LONG after I'd left Favorite River Academy, at the height of my interest in she-males—I mean dating them, not being one—I was having dinner with Donna one night, and I told her about Grandpa Harry's onstage life as a female impersonator.

"Was it only onstage?" Donna asked.

"As far as I know," I answered her, but you couldn't lie to her. One of a couple of uncomfortable things about Donna was that she always knew when you were holding out on her.

Nana Victoria had been dead for more than a year when I first heard from Richard that no one could persuade Grandpa Harry to part with my late grandmother's clothes. (At the sawmill, of course, Harry Marshall was sure-as-shit still dressing like a lumberman.)

Eventually, I would come clean to Donna about Grandpa Harry spending his evenings in his late wife's attire—if only in the privacy of his River Street home. I would leave out the part about Harry's cross-dressing adventures after he was moved to that assisted-living facility he and Nils Borkman had (years before) generously built for the elderly in First Sister. The other residents had complained about Harry repeatedly surprising them in drag. (As Grandpa Harry would one day tell me, "I think you've noticed that rigidly conventional or ignorant people have no sense of humor about cross-dressers.")

Fortunately, when Richard Abbott told me what had happened at the assisted-living facility, Grandpa Harry's River Street home had not yet been sold; it was still on the market. Richard and I quickly moved Harry back into the familiar surroundings of the house he'd lived in with Nana Victoria for so many years. Nana Victoria's clothes were moved back into the River Street house with him, and the nurse Richard and I hired, for Grandpa Harry's round-the-clock care, made no objection to Harry's apparently permanent transformation as a woman. The nurse fondly remembered Harry Marshall's many female impersonations onstage.

"Did the cross-dressing bug ever bite you, Billy?" Donna asked me one night.

"Not really," I'd answered her.

My attraction to transsexuals was pretty specific. (I'm sorry, but we didn't use to say "transgender"—not till the eighties.) Transvestites never did it for me, and the transsexuals had to be what they call "passable"— one of few adjectives I still have trouble with, in the pronunciation department. Furthermore, their breasts had to be natural—hormones were okay, but no surgical implants—and, not surprisingly, I preferred small breasts.

How feminine she was mattered a lot to Donna. She was tall but thin—even her upper arms were slender—and she was flawlessly smooth-skinned. (I've known many women who were hairier.) She was always having her hair done; she was very stylish.

Donna was self-conscious about her hands, though they were not as noticeably big and strong-looking as Miss Frost's. Donna didn't like to hold hands with me, because my hands were smaller.

She came from Chicago, and she tried living in New York—after we broke up, I heard she'd moved to Toronto—but Donna believed that Europe was the place for someone like her. I used to take her with me on publishing trips, when my novels were translated into various European languages. Donna said that Europe was more accepting of transsexuals— Europe was more sexually accepting *and* sophisticated, generally—but Donna was insecure about learning another language.

She'd dropped out of college, because her college years coincided with what she called her "sexual-identity crisis," and she had little confidence in herself intellectually. This was crazy, because she read all the time—she was very smart—but there are those years when we're supposed to feed and grow our minds, and Donna felt that she'd lost those years to her difficult decision to live as a woman.

Especially when we were in Germany, where I could speak the language, Donna was at her happiest—that is, when we were together on those German-language translation trips, not only in Germany but also in Austria and German-speaking Switzerland. Donna loved Zurich; I know it struck her, as Zurich does everyone, as a very well-to-do city. She loved Vienna, too—from my student days in Vienna, I still knew my way around (a little). Most of all, Donna was delighted with Hamburg—to her, I think, Hamburg was the most elegant-seeming German city.

In Hamburg, my German publishers always put me up at the Vier Jahreszeiten; it was such an elegant hotel, I think it gave Donna most of her delight with Hamburg. But then there was that awful evening, after which Donna could never be happy in Hamburg—or, perhaps, with me—again.

It began innocently enough. A journalist who'd interviewed me invited us to a nightclub on the Reeperbahn; I didn't know the Reeperbahn, or what kind of club it was, but this journalist (and his wife, or girlfriend) invited Donna and me to go out with them and see a show. Klaus (with a *K*) and Claudia (with a *C*) were their names; we took a taxi together to the club.

I should have known what kind of place it was when I saw those skinny boys at the bar on our way in. A *Transvestiten-Cabaret*—a transvestite show. (I'm guessing the skinny boys at the bar were the performers' boyfriends, because it wasn't a pickup place, and, the boys at the bar excepted, there wasn't a visible gay presence.)

It was a show for sex tourists—guys in drag, entertaining straight couples. The all-male groups were young men there for the laughs; the all-women groups were there to see the penises. The performers were comedians; they were very aware of themselves as men. They were not half as passable as my dear Donna; they were the old-fashioned transvestites who weren't really trying to pass as female. They were meticulously made up, and elaborately costumed; they were very good-looking, but they were good-looking men dressed as women. In their dresses and wigs, they were very feminine-looking men, but they weren't fooling anybody— they weren't even trying to.

Klaus and Claudia clearly had no idea that Donna was one of them (though she was much more convincing, and infinitely more committed).

"I didn't know," I told Donna. "I really didn't. I'm sorry."

Donna couldn't speak. It had not occurred to her—this was the seventies—that one of the more sophisticated and accepting things about Europe, when it came to difficult decisions regarding sexual identity, was that the Europeans were so used to sexual differences that they had already begun to make fun of them.

That the performers were making fun of themselves must have been terribly painful for Donna, who'd had to work so hard to take herself seriously as a woman.

There was one skit with a very tall tranny driving a make-believe car, while her date—a frightened-looking, smaller man—is attempting to go down on her. What frightens the small man is how big the tranny's cock is, and how his inexpert attentions to this monster cock are interfering with the tranny's driving.

Of course Donna couldn't understand the German; the tranny was talking nonstop, offering breathless criticism of what a bad blow job she was getting. Well, I had to laugh, and I don't think Donna ever forgave me.

Klaus and Claudia clearly thought I had a typical American girl-friend; they thought Donna was not enjoying the show because she was a sexually uptight prude. There was no way to explain anything to them—not there.

When we left, Donna was so distraught that she jumped when one of the waitresses spoke to her. The waitress was a tall transvestite; she could have passed for one of the performers. She said to Donna (in German), "You are looking really fine." It was a compliment, but I knew that the tranny knew Donna was a transsexual. (Almost no one could tell, not at that time. Donna didn't advertise it; her entire effort went into being a woman, not getting away as one.)

"What did she say?" Donna kept asking me, as we left the club. In the seventies, the Reeperbahn wasn't the tourist trap that it is today; there were the sex tourists, of course, but the street itself was seedier then—the way Times Square used to be seedier, too, and not so overrun with gawkers.

"She was complimenting you—she thought you looked 'really fine.' She meant you were beautiful," I told Donna.

"She meant 'for a man,' right—isn't that what she *meant?*" Donna asked me. She was crying. Klaus and Claudia still didn't get it. "I'm not some two-bit cross-dresser!" Donna cried.

"We're sorry if this was a bad idea," Klaus said rather stiffly. "It's meant to be *funny*—it's not intended to be *offensive.*" I just kept shaking my head; there was no way to save the night, I knew.

"Look, pal—I've got a bigger dick than the tranny driving that non-existent car!" Donna said to Klaus. "You want to *see* it?" Donna asked Claudia.

"Don't," I said to her—I knew Donna was no prude. Far from it!

"Tell them," she told me.

Naturally, I had already written a couple of novels about sexual differ-ences—about challenging and, at times, confusing sexual identities. Klaus had read my novels; he'd *interviewed* me, for Christ's sake—he and his wife (or girlfriend) should have known that my girlfriend wasn't a prude.

"Donna definitely has a bigger dick than the tranny driving the make-believe car," I said to Klaus and Claudia. "Please don't ask her to show it to you—not here."

"Not *here?*" Donna screamed.

I truly don't know why I said that; the stream of traffic, both cars and pedestrians, along the Reeperbahn must have made me anxious about Donna whipping out her penis *there*. I certainly didn't mean—as I told Donna repeatedly, back at our hotel—that Donna would (or should) show them her penis at another time, or in another place! It just came out that way.

"I'm not an *amateur* cross-dresser," Donna was sobbing. "I'm not, I'm *not*—"

"Of course you're not," I was telling her, when I saw Klaus and Claudia slipping away. Donna had put her hands on my shoulders; she was shaking me, and I suppose that Klaus and Claudia got a good look at Donna's big hands. (She *did* have a bigger dick than the tranny gagging the guy who was giving her a bad blow job in that make-believe car.)

That night, back at the Vier Jahreszeiten, Donna was still crying when she washed her face before going to bed. We left the light on in the walk-in closet, with the closet door ajar; it served as a night-light, a way to find the bathroom in the dark. I lay awake looking at Donna, who was asleep. In the half-light, and with no makeup on, Donna's face bore a hint of something masculine. Maybe it was because she wasn't trying to be a woman when she slept; perhaps it was something in the contours of her jaw and cheekbones—something chiseled.

That night, looking at Donna asleep, I was reminded of Mrs. Kittredge; there'd been something masculine in her attractiveness, too—something of Kittredge himself about her, something all-male. But if a woman is aggressive, she can *look* male—even in her sleep.

I fell asleep, and when I woke up, the door to the walk-in closet was closed—I knew we'd left it ajar. Donna was not in bed beside me; in the light that was coming from the walk-in closet, from under the door, I could see the shadows of her moving feet.

She was naked, looking at herself in the full-length mirror in the walk-in closet. I knew this routine.

"Your breasts are perfect," I told her.

"Most men like them bigger," Donna said. "You're not like most men I know, Billy. You even like *actual* women, for Christ's sake."

"Don't hurt your beautiful breasts—please don't do anything to them," I told her.

"What's it matter that I have a big dick? You're strictly a top, Billy— that won't ever change, right?" she asked me.

"I *love* your big dick," I said.

Donna shrugged; her small breasts were the target. "You know the difference between an *amateur* cross-dresser and someone like me?" Donna asked.

I knew the answer—it was always her answer. "Yes, I know—you're committed to changing your body."

"I'm not an amateur," Donna repeated.

"I know—just don't change your breasts. They're perfect," I told her, and went back to bed.

"You know what's the matter with you, Billy?" Donna asked me. I was already in bed, with my back turned to the light coming from under the door of the walk-in closet. I knew her answer to this question, too, but I didn't say anything. "You're not like anyone else, Billy—that's what's the matter with you," Donna said.

As for cross-dressing, Donna could never interest me in trying on her clothes. She would talk, from time to time, about the seemingly remote possibility of surgery—not just the breast implants, which were tempting to many transsexuals, but the bigger deal, the sex-change surgery. Technically speaking, Donna—and every other transsexual who ever attracted me—was what they call a "pre-op." (I know only a few post-op transsexuals. The ones I know are very courageous. It's daunting to be around them; they know themselves so well. Imagine knowing yourself *that* well! Imagine being that sure about who you are.)

Donna would say, "I suppose you were never curious—I mean, to be like me."

"That's right," I told her, truthfully.

"I suppose, all your life, you've wanted to keep your penis—you probably really *like* it," she said.

"I like yours, too," I told her—also truthfully.

"I know you do," she said, sighing. "I just don't always like it so much myself. But I always like *yours*," Donna quickly added.

Poor Tom would have found Donna too "complicated," I think, but I thought she was very brave.

I found it intimidating that Donna was so certain about who she was, but that was also one of the things I loved about her—that and the cute, rightward inclination of her penis, which reminded me of you-know-who.

As it would turn out, my only exposure to Kittredge's penis was what I managed to glimpse of him—always furtively—in the showers at the Favorite River gym.

I had much more exposure to Donna's penis. I saw as much of her as I wanted, though—in the beginning—I had such an insatiable hunger for her (and for other transsexuals, albeit only the ones who were like her) that I couldn't imagine ever seeing or having *enough* of Donna. In the end, I didn't move on because I was tired of her, or because she ever doubted or had second thoughts about who she was. In the end, it was *me* she doubted. It was *Donna* who moved on, and her distrust of me made me doubt myself.

When I stopped seeing Donna (more accurately, when she stopped seeing me), I became more cautious with transsexuals—not because I no longer desired them, and I still find them extraordinarily brave, but because transsexuals (Donna, especially) forced me to acknowledge the most confusing aspects of my bisexuality every fucking day! Donna was exhausting.

"I usually like straight guys," she would constantly remind me. "I also like other transsexuals—not just the ones like me, you know."

"I know, Donna," I would assure her.

"And I can deal with straight guys who also like women—after all, I'm trying to live my life, all the time, as a woman. I'm just a woman with a penis!" she would say, her voice rising.

"I know, I know," I would tell her.

"But you also like other guys—*just* guys—*and* you like women, Billy."

"Yes, I do—*some* women," I would admit to her. "And cute guys—not *all* cute guys," I would remind her.

"Yeah, well—fuck what *all* means, Billy," Donna would say. "What gets to me is that I don't know what you like about me, and what it is about me that you *don't* like."

"There's nothing about you I *don't* like, Donna. I like *all* of you," I promised her.

"Yeah, well—if you're going to leave me for a woman, like a straight guy one day would, I get it. Or if you're going to go back to guys, like a gay guy one day would—well, I get that, too," Donna said. "But the thing about you, Billy—and I don't get this *at all*—is that I don't know who or what you're going to leave me for."

"I don't know, either," I would tell her, truthfully.

"Yeah, well—that's why I'm leaving you, Billy," Donna said.

"I'm going to miss you like crazy," I told her. (This was also true.)

"I'm already getting over you, Billy," was all she said. But until that night in Hamburg, I believed that Donna and I had a chance together.

I USED TO BELIEVE my mom and I had a chance together, too. I mean more than the "chance" of staying friends; I mean that I used to think nothing could ever drive us apart. My mother once worried about my most minor injuries—she imagined my life was in danger at the first cough or sneeze. There was something childlike about her fears for me; my nightmares gave her nightmares, my mom once said.

My mother told me that, as a child, I had "fever dreams"; if so, they persisted into my teenage years. Whatever they were, they seemed more real than dreams. If there was any reality to the most recurrent of these dreams, it eluded me for the longest time. But one night, when I'd been sick—I was actually recuperating from scarlet fever—it seemed that Richard Abbott was telling me a war story, yet Richard's only war story was the lawn-mower accident that had disqualified him from military service. This wasn't Richard Abbott's story; it was my *father's* war story, or one of them, and Richard couldn't possibly have told it to me.

The story (or the dream) began in Hampton, Virginia—Hampton Roads, Port of Embarkation, was where my code-boy father boarded a transport ship for Italy. The transports were Liberty ships. The ground cadre of the 760th Bomb Squadron left Virginia on a dark and threatening January day; within the sheltered harbor, the soldiers had their first meal at sea—pork chops, I was told (or dreamed). When my dad's convoy hit the open seas, the Liberty ships encountered an Atlantic winter storm. The enlisted personnel occupied the fore and aft holds; each man had his helmet hung by his bunk—the helmets would soon become vomit basins for seasick soldiers. But the sergeant didn't get seasick. My mom had told me that he'd grown up on Cape Cod; as a boy, he'd been a sailor—he was immune to seasickness.

Consequently, my code-boy dad did his duty—he emptied the sea-sick soldiers' helmets. Amidships, at deck level—a laborious climb from the bunks, below the deck—was a huge head. (Even in the dream, I had to interrupt the story and ask what a "head" was; the person I thought was Richard, but it couldn't have been Richard, told me that the head was a huge latrine—the toilets stretched across the entire ship.)

During one of many helmet-emptying ordeals, my father stopped to sit down on one of the toilets. There was no point in trying to pee while standing up; the ship was pitching and rolling—you had to sit down. My dad sat on the toilet with both his hands gripping the seat. Seawater sloshed around his ankles, soaking his shoes and pants. At the farthest end of the long row of toilets, another soldier sat holding the seat, but this soldier's grip was precarious. My dad saw that the other soldier was also immune to seasickness; he was actually reading, holding on to the toilet seat with only one hand. When the ship suddenly pitched more steeply, the bookworm lost his grip. He came skipping over the toilet seats—his ass made a slapping sound—until he collided with my father at the opposite end of the row of toilets.

"Sorry—I just had to keep reading!" he said. Then the ship rolled in the other direction, and the soldier sallied forth, skipping over the seats again. When he'd slid all the way to the last toilet, he either lost control of the book or he let it go, gripping the toilet seat with both hands. The book floated away in the seawater.

"What were you reading?" the code-boy called.

"*Madame Bovary*!" the soldier shouted in the storm.

"I can tell you what happens," the sergeant said.

"Please don't!" the bookworm answered. "I want to read it for my-self!"

In the dream, or in the story someone (who was *not* Richard Abbott) was telling me, my father never saw this soldier for the rest of the voyage. "Past a barely visible Gibraltar," I remember the dream (or someone) say-ing, "the convoy slipped into the Mediterranean."

One night, off the coast of Sicily, the soldiers belowdecks were awak-ened by crashing noises and the sounds of cannon fire; the convoy was under aerial attack by the *Luftwaffe*. Subsequently, my dad heard that an adjacent Liberty ship had been hit and sunk with all hands. As for the soldier who'd been reading *Madame Bovary* in the storm, he failed to introduce himself to my dad before the convoy made landfall at Taranto.

The code-boy's war story would continue and conclude without my disappearing dad ever encountering the toilet-traveling man.

"Years later," said the dream (or the storyteller), my father was "finishing up" at Harvard. He was riding on the Boston subway, the MTA; he'd got on at the Charles Street station, and was on his way back to Harvard Square.

A man who got on at Kendall Square began to stare at him. The sergeant was "discomfited" by the strange man's interest in him; "it felt like an *unnatural* interest—a foreboding of something violent, or at least unpleasant." (It was the language of the story that made this recurrent dream seem more real to me than other dreams. It was a dream with a first-person narrator—a dream with a *voice*.)

The man on the subway started changing seats; he kept moving closer to my dad. When they were almost in physical contact with each other, and the subway was slowing down for the next stop, the stranger turned to my father and said, "Hi. I'm Bovary. Remember me?" Then the subway stopped at Central Square, where the bookworm got off, and the sergeant was once more on his way to Harvard Square.

I WAS TOLD THAT the fever part of scarlet fever abates within a week—usually within three to five days. I'm pretty sure that I was over the fever part when I asked Richard Abbott if he'd ever told me this story—perhaps at the onset of the rash, or during the sore-throat part, which began a couple of days before the rash. My tongue had been the color of a strawberry, but when I first spoke to Richard about this most vivid and recurrent dream, my tongue was a beefy dark red—more of a raspberry color—and the rash was starting to go away.

"I don't know this story, Bill," Richard told me. "This is the first time I've heard it."

"Oh."

"It sounds like a Grandpa Harry story to me," Richard said.

But when I asked my grandfather if he'd told me the *Madame Bovary* story, Grandpa Harry started his "Ah, well" routine, hemming and hawing his way in circles around the question. No, he "*definitely* didn't" tell me the story, my grandfather said. Yes, Harry had *heard* the story—"a secondhand version, if I recall correctly"—but he conveniently couldn't remember who'd told him. "It was Uncle Bob, maybe—perhaps it was Bob who told you, Bill." Then my grandfather felt my forehead, and mumbled words to the effect that my fever seemed to be gone. When he peered into my mouth, he announced: "That's still a pretty ugly-lookin' tongue, though I would say the rash is disappearin' a bit."

"It was too real to be a dream—at least, to begin with," I told Grandpa Harry.

"Ah, well—if you're good at *imaginin'* things, which I believe you *are* pretty good at, Bill, I would say that some dreams can seem very real," my grandfather hemmed and hawed.

"I'll ask Uncle Bob," I said.

Bob was always putting squash balls in my pockets, or in my shoes—or under my pillow. It was a game; when I found the balls, I gave them back. "Oh, I've been *looking* for that squash ball all over, Billy!" Bob would say. "I'm so glad you found it."

"What's *Madame Bovary* about?" I asked Uncle Bob. He'd come to see how I was recuperating from the scarlet fever, and I'd given him the squash ball I had found in the glass for my toothbrush—in the bathroom I shared with Grandpa Harry.

Nana Victoria "would rather die" than share a bathroom with him, Harry had told me, but I liked sharing a bathroom with my grandfather.

"Truth be told, I haven't actually read *Madame Bovary*, Billy," Uncle Bob told me; he peered into the hallway, outside my bedroom, checking to be sure that my mom (or my grandmother, or Aunt Muriel) wasn't within listening distance. Even though the coast was clear, Bob lowered his voice: "I believe it's about adultery, Billy—an unfaithful wife." I must have looked baffled, utterly uncomprehending, because Uncle Bob quickly said, "You should ask Richard what *Madame Bovary* is about—literature, you know, is Richard's department."

"It's a novel?" I asked.

"I don't think it's a true story," Uncle Bob answered. "But Richard would know."

"Or I could ask Miss Frost," I suggested.

"Uh-huh, you could—just don't say it was my idea," Uncle Bob said.

"I know a story," I started to say. "Maybe you told me."

"You mean the one about the guy reading *Madame Bovary* on a hundred toilets at the same time?" Bob cried. "I absolutely love that story!"

"Me, too," I said. "It's very funny!"

"Hilarious!" Uncle Bob declared. "No, I never told you that story, Billy—at least I don't *remember* telling you that story," he said quickly.

"Oh."

"Maybe your *mom* told you?" Uncle Bob asked. I must have given him an incredulous look, because Bob suddenly said, "Probably not."

"It's a dream I keep having, but someone must have told me first," I said.

"Dinner-party conversation, perhaps—one of those stories children overhear, when the adults think they've gone to bed or they can't possibly be listening," Uncle Bob said. While this was more credible than my mother being the source of the toilet-seat story, neither Bob nor I looked very convinced. "Not all mysteries are meant to be solved, Billy," he said to me, with more conviction.

It was shortly after he'd left when I discovered another squash ball, or the same squash ball, under my covers.

I knew perfectly well that my mother hadn't told me the *Madame Bovary*, multiple-toilet-seats story, but of course I asked her. "I never thought that story was the least bit funny," she said. "I wouldn't have had anything to do with telling you that story, Billy."

"Oh."

"Maybe Daddy told you—I asked him *not* to!" my mother said.

"No, Grandpa *definitely* didn't tell me," I said.

"I'll bet Uncle Bob did," my mom said.

"Uncle Bob says he doesn't *remember* telling me," I replied.

"Bob drinks—he doesn't remember everything," my mother told me. "And you've had a fever recently," she reminded me. "You know the dreams a fever can give you, Billy."

"I thought it was a funny story, anyway—how the man's ass made a slapping sound as he was skipping over the toilet seats!" I said.

"It's not the least bit funny to *me*, Billy."

"Oh."

It was after I'd completely recovered from the scarlet fever that I asked Richard Abbott his opinion of *Madame Bovary*. "I think you would appreciate it more when you're older, Bill," Richard told me.

"How much older?" I asked him. (I would have been fourteen—I'm guessing. I'd not yet read and reread *Great Expectations*, but Miss Frost had already started me on my life as a reader—I know that.)

"I could ask Miss Frost how old she thinks I should be," I suggested.

"I would wait a while before you ask her, Bill," Richard said.

"How long a while?" I asked him.

Richard Abbott, who I thought knew everything, answered: "I don't know, exactly."

I DON'T KNOW EXACTLY when my mom became the prompter for Richard Abbott's theatrical productions in the Drama Club at Favorite River Academy, but I was very much aware of her being the prompter for *The Tempest*. There were the occasional scheduling conflicts, because my mother was still prompting for the First Sister Players, but prompters could miss rehearsals now and then, and the performances—the actual shows put on by our town's amateur theatrical society and Favorite River's Drama Club—never overlapped.

In rehearsals, Kittredge would pretend to botch a line just to have my mom prompt him. "O most dear maid," Ferdinand misspoke to Miranda in one of our rehearsals, when we were newly off-script.

"No, Jacques," my mother said. "That would be 'O most dear *mistress*,' not *maid*."

But Kittredge was acting—he was only pretending to flub the line, so that he could engage my mother in conversation. "I'm so sorry, Mrs. Abbott—it won't happen again," he said to her; then he blew the very next dialogue assigned him.

"No, precious creature," Ferdinand is supposed to say to Miranda, but Kittredge said, "No, precious mistress."

"Not this time, Jacques," my mom told him. "It's 'No, precious *creature*'—not *mistress*."

"I think I'm trying too hard to please you—I want you to like me, but I'm afraid you don't, Mrs. Abbott," Kittredge said to my mother. He was flirting with her, and she blushed. I was embarrassed by how often I thought of my mom as easily seduced; it was almost as if I believed she was somewhat retarded, or so sexually naïve that anyone who flattered her could win her over.

"I *do* like you, Jacques—I certainly don't *not* like you!" my mom blurted out, while Elaine (as Miranda) stood there seething; Elaine knew that Kittredge had used the *hot* word for my mom.

"I get so nervous around you," Kittredge told my mother, though he didn't look nervous; he seemed increasingly confident.

"What a lot of bullshit!" Elaine Hadley croaked. Kittredge cringed at the sound of her voice, and my mother flinched as if she'd been slapped.

"Elaine, mind your language," my mom said.

"Can we just get on with the *play?*" Elaine asked.

"Oh, Naples—you're so impatient," Kittredge said with a most disarming smile, first to Elaine and then to my mother. "Elaine can't wait to get to the hand-holding part," Kittredge told my mom.

Indeed, the scene they were rehearsing—act 3, scene 1—ends with Ferdinand and Miranda holding hands. It was Elaine's turn to blush, but Kittredge, who was in complete control of the moment, had fixed his most earnest gaze on my mother. "I have a question, Mrs. Abbott," he began, as if Elaine and Miranda didn't exist—as if they'd never existed. "When Ferdinand says, 'Full many a lady / I have eyed with best regard, and many a time / The harmony of their tongues hath into bondage / Brought my too diligent ear'—you know, *that* line—I wonder if that means I have been with a lot of women, and if I shouldn't somehow imply that I am, you know, *sexually experienced.*"

My mom blushed more deeply than before.

"Oh, *God!*" Elaine Hadley cried.

And I—where was I? I was Ariel—"an airy Spirit." I was waiting for Ferdinand and Miranda to *exeunt—separately,* like the stage direction said. I was standing by, with Caliban, Stephano ("a drunken butler," Shakespeare calls him), and Trinculo; we were all in the next scene, in which I was invisible. With my mother blushing at Kittredge's clever manipulations, I felt invisible—or I wanted to be.

"I'm just the prompter," my mother said hastily to Kittredge. "That's a question for the director—you should ask Mr. Abbott," she said. My mom's agitation was obvious, and I suddenly saw her as she must have looked years ago, when she was either pregnant with me or already my mother—when she'd seen my *womanizing* father kissing someone else. I remembered how she'd said the *else* word when she told me about it, in the same perfunctory way she had corrected Kittredge's purposeful flubs. (Once we were in performances of *The Tempest,* Kittredge wouldn't muff a line—not a single word. I realize that I haven't acknowledged this, but Kittredge was very good onstage.)

It was painful for me to see how easily undone my mom was—by the slightest sexual suggestion, from a *teenager!* I hated myself, because I saw that I was ashamed of my own mother, and I knew that whatever shame I felt for her had been formed by Muriel's constant condescension and her chiding gossip. Naturally, I hated Kittredge for how effortlessly he had rattled my damaged mom—for how smoothly he was able to rattle Elaine and me, too—and then my mother called for help. "Richard!" she called. "Jacques has a question about his *character*!"

"Oh, *God*," Elaine said again—this time, under her breath; she was barely audible, but Kittredge had heard her.

"Patience, dear Naples," Kittredge said to her, taking her hand. He grasped her hand exactly as Ferdinand takes Miranda's hand—before they part at the end of act 3, scene 1—but Elaine yanked her hand away from him.

"What is it about your character, Ferdinand?" Richard Abbott asked Kittredge.

"This is more bullshit," Elaine said.

"Your *language*, Elaine!" my mother said.

"Some fresh air would be good for Miranda," Richard said to Elaine. "Just a couple of deep breaths, and perhaps a needed expulsion of whatever words spontaneously come to mind. Take a break, Elaine—you should take a break, too, Bill," Richard told me. "We want our Miranda and our Ariel *in character*." (I guess Richard could see that I was agitated, too.)

There was a loading dock off the carpentry shop, to the rear of the backstage area, and Elaine and I stepped out on the dock in the cool night air. I tried to take her hand; at first she pulled her hand away from me, though not as violently as she'd jerked it away from Kittredge. Then, with the door to the loading dock still open, Elaine gave me back her hand; she rested her head against my shoulder. "They're a cute couple, aren't they?" we heard Kittredge say to someone, or to them all, before the door closed.

"Motherfucker!" Elaine Hadley yelled. "Penis-breath!" she shouted; then she gulped the cold air, until her breathing had returned to almost normal, and we went back inside the theater, where Elaine's glasses instantly fogged up.

"Ferdinand is *not* saying to Miranda that he is sexually experienced," Richard was telling Kittredge. "Ferdinand is saying how *attentive* he has been to women, and how often women have made an impression on him. All he means is that no one has *impressed* him as forcefully as Miranda."

"It's a speech about *impressions*, Kittredge," Elaine managed to say. "It's not a speech about sex."

Enter Ariel, invisible—that was the stage direction to my upcoming scene (act 3, scene 2). But I was already *truly* invisible; I had somehow succeeded in giving them all the impression that Elaine Hadley was my love interest. For Elaine's part, she seemed to be going along with it—maybe for self-protective reasons of her own. But Kittredge was smiling at us—in that sneering, superior way he had. I do not think the *impressions* word ever meant very much to Kittredge. I believe that everything was always about sex—about *actual* sex—to him. And if the present company was convinced that Elaine and I were interested in each other in a sexual way, possibly Kittredge alone remained unconvinced—at least this was the *impression* that his sneer gave Elaine and me.

Maybe this was why Elaine suddenly turned from him and kissed me. She barely brushed her lips against mine, but there was actual (if fleeting) contact; I suppose I even appeared to kiss her back, albeit briefly. That was all. It wasn't much of a kiss; it didn't even fog up her glasses.

I doubt that Elaine had an iota of sexual interest in me, and I believe she knew from the beginning that I was only pretending to be interested in her in that way. We were the most amateur actors—her innocent Miranda and my largely invisible Ariel—but we were acting, and there was an unspoken complicity in our deception.

After all, we both had something to hide.

Chapter 4

ELAINE'S BRA

To this day, I don't know what to make of the wretched Caliban—the monster whose attempted rape of Miranda earns Prospero's unforgiving condemnation. Prospero seems to take minimal responsibility for Caliban—"this thing of darkness I / Acknowledge mine."

For someone as self-centered as Kittredge, of course, *The Tempest* was all about Ferdinand; it's a love story, in which Ferdinand woos and wins Miranda. But Richard Abbott called the play a "tragicomedy," and for those two (almost three) months in the fall of '59 when Elaine Hadley and I were in rehearsals for the play, we felt that our close-enough-to-touch proximity to Kittredge was our tragicomedy—notwithstanding that *The Tempest* has a happy ending for Miranda and Ariel.

My mother, who always maintained she was just the prompter, had the curiously mathematical habit of timing each actor; she used a cheap stove timer, and (in the margins of her copy of the play) she noted the approximate percent of the characters' actual time onstage. The value of my mom's calculations seemed questionable to me, though both Elaine and I enjoyed the fact that Ferdinand was onstage for only 17 percent of the play.

"What about Miranda?" Elaine made a point of asking my mom, within Kittredge's keenly competitive hearing.

"Twenty-seven percent," my mother replied.

"What about me?" I asked my mom.

"Ariel is onstage thirty-one percent of the time," she told me.

Kittredge scoffed at this degrading news. "And Prospero, our peerless director—he of the much-*ballyhooed* magical powers?" Kittredge inquired sarcastically.

"Much-*ballyhooed!*" Elaine Hadley thunderously echoed.

"Prospero is onstage approximately fifty-two percent of the time," my mother told Kittredge.

"Approximately," Kittredge repeated, sneering.

Richard had told us that *The Tempest* was Shakespeare's "farewell play," that the bard was knowingly saying good-bye to the theater, but I didn't understand the necessity for act 5—especially the tacked-on epi-logue, spoken by Prospero.

Perhaps it was a small measure of my becoming a writer (though never for the stage) that I believed *The Tempest* should have ended with Prospero's speech to Ferdinand and Miranda—the "Our revels now are ended" speech in act 4, scene 1. And surely Prospero should have ended that speech (and the play) with the wonderful "We are such stuff / As dreams are made on, and our little life / Is rounded with a sleep." Why does Prospero need to say more? (Maybe he *does* feel responsible for Cali-ban.)

But when I expressed these thoughts to Richard, he said, "Well, Bill—if you're rewriting Shakespeare at seventeen, I expect great things of you!" Richard wasn't given to satire at my expense, and I was hurt by it; Kittredge was quick to pick up on someone else's pain.

"Hey, *Rewriter!*" Kittredge called to me, across the quadrangle of dorms. Alas, that nickname didn't stick; Kittredge never said it again, preferring Nymph. I would have preferred Rewriter; at least it was true to the kind of writer I would one day become.

But I've strayed from the Caliban character; I have digressed, which is also the kind of writer I would become. Caliban is onstage 25 percent of the time. (My mother's approximations never took into account the lines spoken, only the onstage time of the characters.) This was my very first experience with *The Tempest*, but as many times as I've seen the play performed, I always find Caliban a deeply disturbing character; as a writer, I would call him an "unresolved" character. By how harshly Pros-pero treats him, we know how unforgivingly Prospero thinks of Caliban, but I wonder what Shakespeare wanted us to feel about the monster. Sympathy, maybe—some guilt, perhaps.

That fall of '59, I wasn't at all sure what Richard Abbott made of

Caliban; that Richard had cast Grandpa Harry as the monster sent a mixed message. Harry had never been onstage as a male *anything;* that Caliban was less than human was further "unresolved" by Grandpa Harry's steadfastly *female* impersonation. Caliban may indeed have lusted after Miranda—we know the monster has tried to *rape* her!—but Harry Marshall, even when he was cast as a villain, was almost never unsympathetic onstage, nor was he ever entirely *male.*

Perhaps Richard had acknowledged that Caliban was a confusing monster, and Richard knew that Grandpa Harry would find a way to add to the confusion. "Your grandfather is weird," was how Kittredge unambiguously put it to me. ("Queen Lear," Kittredge called him.)

Even I believe that Harry out-weirded himself in Caliban's case; Grandpa Harry gave a sexually ambiguous performance—he played Caliban as an androgynous hag.

The wig (Grandpa Harry was bald) would have worked for either sex. The costume was something an eccentric urban bag lady might have worn—floppy sweatpants with an oversize sweatshirt, both as workout-gray as the wig. To complete the gender-unknown image, Harry had whorishly painted the toenails of his bare feet. There was a mannishly chunky rhinestone earring attached to the lobe of one ear—more appealing to a pirate, or a professional wrestler, than a hooker—and a fake-pearl necklace (the cheapest costume jewelry) over the sweatshirt.

"What is Caliban, exactly?" Kittredge would ask Richard Abbott.

"Earth and water, Kittredge—brute force and guile," Richard had repeated.

"But what *sex* is the guile supposed to be?" Kittredge asked. "Is Caliban a *lesbian* monster? Is it a she or a he who tried to rape Miranda?"

"Sex, sex, sex!" Elaine Hadley screamed. "All you think about is sex!"

"Don't forget those earplugs, Nymph," Kittredge said, smiling at me.

Elaine and I couldn't look at him without seeing his mother, with her legs so perfectly crossed on those uncomfortable bleacher seats at Kittredge's wrestling match; Mrs. Kittredge had seemed to watch her son's systematic mauling of his overmatched opponent as if it were a pornographic film, but with the detached confidence of an experienced woman who knew she could do it better. "Your mother is a man with breasts," I wanted to say to Kittredge, but of course I didn't dare.

I could only guess how Kittredge might have responded. "Do you mean my *stepmother?*" he would have asked, before breaking my arms and legs.

I spoke to my mom and Richard in the privacy of our dormitory apartment. "What is it about Grandpa Harry?" I asked them. "I know that Ariel's gender is polymorphous—more a matter of *habiliment* than anything organic, as you say," I said to Richard. "Okay, so my trappings, my equipment—the wig, the tights—suggest that Ariel's gender is mutable. But isn't Caliban a *male* monster? Isn't Grandpa Harry playing Caliban like some kind of . . ." I paused. I refused to call my grandfather *Queen Lear*, because that was Kittredge's nickname for him. "Like some kind of *dyke?*" was how I put it. The *dyke* word was in vogue at Favorite River—among those students (like Kittredge) who never tired of *homo*, *fag*, and *queer*, which they used viciously.

"Daddy isn't a *dyke!*" my mother snapped. Snapping had once seemed so unlike her; now, increasingly, when she snapped, she snapped at *me*.

"Well, Bill . . ." Richard Abbott started to say; then he stopped. "Don't get upset, Jewel," he said to my mom, whose agitation had distracted Richard. "What I really think, Bill," Richard began again, "is that gender mattered a whole lot less to Shakespeare than it seems to matter to us."

A lame response, I thought, but I didn't say so. Was I growing disappointed in Richard, or was I just growing up?

"I guess that wasn't an answer to your question, was it?" Elaine Hadley asked me later, when I confessed to her that the sexual identity of Grandpa Harry as Caliban was confusing to me.

IT WAS FUNNY HOW, when Elaine and I were alone, we didn't usually hold hands, or anything like that, but when we were out in public, we spontaneously reached for each other's hands, and we would maintain contact for only as long as we had an audience. (It was another kind of code between us, like the way we would ask each other, "What happens to the duck?")

Yet, on our initial visit together to the First Sister Public Library, Elaine and I didn't hold hands. It was my impression that Miss Frost wouldn't be fooled into thinking that Elaine and I were romantically involved—not for a minute. Elaine and I were just seeking a possible place where we could run our lines for *The Tempest*. Our dormitory apartments were claustrophobic and very public—unless we ran our lines in her bedroom or mine, with the door closed. We'd been too successful in masquerading as boyfriend and girlfriend. My mom and Richard, or the

Hadleys, would have had a cow if we'd closed our bedroom doors when we were together.

As for the yearbook room in the academy library, there was the occasional faculty member at work there, and it wasn't a room with a door you could close; our voices would have been heard elsewhere in the building. (Elaine and I feared we could be heard *throughout* the much smaller First Sister Public Library!)

"We wondered if there might be a more *private* room here," I explained to Miss Frost.

"More *private*," the librarian repeated.

"Where we wouldn't be heard," Elaine said, in her sonic-boom voice. "We want to run our lines for *The Tempest*, but we don't want to *bother* anyone!" Elaine hastily added—lest Miss Frost think we were seeking some soundproof asylum for Elaine's aforementioned first orgasm.

Miss Frost looked at me. "You want to run lines in a library," she said, as if this were a well-fitted piece to the puzzle of my earlier wanting to *write* in a library. But Miss Frost didn't betray my intentions—namely, becoming a writer. (I had not yet been candid with my good friend Elaine on the writing subject; my desire to be a writer and my *other* desires were still kept secret from Elaine.)

"We can try to run our lines *quietly*," Elaine said, in an abnormally soft voice—for her.

"No, no, dear—you must feel free to run lines as they should be said, onstage," Miss Frost told Elaine, patting my friend's hand with her much bigger hand. "I think I know a place where you could *scream* and no one would hear you." As it turned out, the concept that there was a contained space in the First Sister Public Library where one could scream unheard was not as much of a miracle as the room itself.

Miss Frost led Elaine and me down the basement stairs to what, at first glance, appeared to be the furnace room of the old library. It was a red-brick building of the Georgian period, and the building's first furnace had been coal; the blackened remains of the coal chute were still hanging from a transom window. But the hulking coal burner had been toppled on its side and dragged to an unused corner of the basement; its replacement was a more modern oil furnace. Quite a new-looking propane hot-water heater stood near the oil-burning furnace, and a separate room (with a door) had been assembled in the vicinity of the transom window. A rectangular notch, near the basement ceiling, had been cut in one wall of the room—where the remnants of the coal chute dangled from the lone window. At one time, the coal chute had run from the transom window into the room—formerly, the coal bin. It was now a furnished bedroom and bathroom.

There was an old-fashioned brass bed with a headboard of brass rails, as sturdy-looking as prison bars, to which a reading lamp had been affixed. There was a small sink and mirror in one corner of the room, and in another corner, unconcealed, stood a solitary sentinel—not an actual guard but a toilet with a wooden seat. There was a night table by the bed, where I saw an orderly stack of books and a squat, scented candle. (It smelled like cinnamon in the room; I guessed that the candle concealed the smell of oil fumes from the nearby furnace.)

There was also an open wardrobe closet, where Elaine and I could see some shelves and hangers—with what appeared to be a most minimal assortment of Miss Frost's clothes. What was unquestionably the centerpiece of the small room—"my converted coal bin," Miss Frost called it—was a bathtub of Victorian opulence, with very visible plumbing. (The floor of the room was unfinished plywood, and the wiring was very visible, too.)

"When there's a snowstorm, and I don't feel like driving or walking home," Miss Frost said—as if this explained everything that was at once cozy but rudimentary about the basement room. (Neither Elaine nor I knew where Miss Frost lived, but we gathered it must have been within walking distance of the town library.)

Elaine stared at the bathtub; it had lion paws for feet, and lion heads for faucets. I was, I confess, fixated on the brass bed with the prison-bars headboard.

"Unfortunately, there's nowhere to sit but the bed," Miss Frost said, "unless you want to run lines in the tub." She seemed not in the least concerned that Elaine and I might ever *do* anything on the bed, or take a bath together.

Miss Frost was about to leave us alone, to actually close the door on us—in her makeshift bedroom, her expedient home-away-from-home—when Elaine Hadley exclaimed, "The room is *perfect*! Thank you for helping us, Miss Frost."

"You're very welcome, Elaine," Miss Frost said. "I assure you that you and William can scream your heads off in here, and no one will hear you." But before closing the door, Miss Frost looked at me and smiled.

"If you need any help running lines—if there's a question of emphasis, or a pronunciation problem—well, you know where to find me." I didn't know that Miss Frost had noticed my pronunciation problems; I'd actually spoken very little in her company.

I was too embarrassed to speak, but Elaine didn't hesitate. "Now that you mention it, Miss Frost, Billy has encountered only one difficulty in Ariel's vocabulary, and we're working on it," Elaine said.

"What difficulty is that, William?" Miss Frost asked me, with her most penetrating look. (Thank God there were no *penises* in Ariel's vocabulary!)

When Caliban calls Prospero a tyrant, Ariel (invisible) says, "Thou liest." Since Ariel is invisible, Caliban thinks *Trinculo* has called him a liar. In the same scene, Ariel says "Thou liest" to Stephano, who thinks Trinculo has called *him* a liar—Stephano hits Trinculo.

"I have to say 'Thou liest' twice," I told Miss Frost, being careful to say the *liest* word correctly—with two syllables.

"Sometimes he says 'least'—one syllable, rhymes with *yeast*," Elaine told Miss Frost.

"Oh, my," the librarian said, briefly closing her eyes at the horror of it. "Look at me, William," Miss Frost said. I did as she told me; for once, I didn't need to sneak a look at her. "Say 'finest' to me, William," she said.

This was not hard to do. Miss Frost was the *finest* of my all-over-the-place infatuations. "Finest," I said to her, still looking right at her.

"Well, William—just remember that *liest* rhymes with *finest*," Miss Frost said.

"Go on, say it," Elaine told me.

"Thou liest," I said, as the invisible Ariel is supposed to say. I made a perfect two-syllable match for the *finest* word.

"May all your difficulties be so easy to fix, William," Miss Frost said. "I love running lines," she told Elaine, as she closed the door.

I was impressed that Miss Frost even knew what "running lines" meant. When Richard had asked her if she'd ever *acted*, Miss Frost had quickly answered him: "Only in my mind. When I was younger—all the time." Yet she'd certainly made a name for herself as a standout in the First Sister Players.

"Miss Frost *is* an Ibsen woman!" Nils had said to Richard, but she'd not had many roles—not beyond those of the severely tested women in *Hedda Gabler*, *A Doll's House*, and *The Wild* (fucking) *Duck*.

It suffices to say: For someone who'd heretofore acted only in her mind, but who seemed a natural at portraying Ibsen's women, Miss Frost was clearly familiar with all that "running lines" entailed—and she couldn't have been more supportive of Elaine Hadley and me.

It was awkward, at first—how Elaine and I arranged ourselves on Miss Frost's bed. It was only a queen-size mattress, but the brass bed frame was rather high; when Elaine and I sat (somewhat primly) side by side, our feet didn't reach the floor. But when we stretched out on our stomachs, we had to contort ourselves to look at each other; it was only when we propped the pillows up against the headboard (those brass rails like prison bars) that we could lie on our sides, facing each other, and run our lines—our copies of the play held between us, for reference.

"We're like an old married couple," Elaine said; I was already thinking the same thing.

Our first evening in Miss Frost's snowstorm room, Elaine fell asleep. I knew she had to get up earlier than I did; due to the bus ride to Ezra Falls, she was always tired. When Miss Frost knocked on the door, Elaine was startled; she threw her arms around my neck, and she was still holding tight when Miss Frost came inside the small room. Notwithstanding these amorous-looking circumstances, I don't believe that Miss Frost assumed we'd been making out. Elaine and I certainly didn't look as if we'd been necking, and Miss Frost merely said, "It's almost time for me to close the library. Even Shakespeare has to go home and get some sleep."

As everyone who's ever been part of a theatrical production knows, after all the stressful rehearsals, and the interminable memorization—I mean when your lines are truly *run*—even Shakespeare comes to an end. We put on four shows of *The Tempest*. I managed to make *liest* rhyme with *finest* in every performance, though on opening night I almost said "finest breasts," when I thought I saw Kittredge's wonderfully dressed mother in the audience—only to learn from Kittredge, during the intermission, that I was mistaken. The woman wasn't his mom.

"The woman you think is my mom is in Paris," Kittredge dismissively said.

"Oh."

"You must have seen some other middle-aged woman who spends too much money on her clothes," Kittredge said.

"Your mother is very beautiful," I told him. I genuinely meant this, in the nicest possible way.

"Your mom is *hotter*," Kittredge told me matter-of-factly. There was no hint of sarcasm, nor anything the slightest suggestive, in his remark; he spoke in the same empirical way in which he'd said his mother (or the woman who wasn't his mother) was in Paris. Soon, the *hot* word, the way Kittredge meant it, would be the rage at Favorite River.

Later, Elaine would say to me, "What are you doing, Billy—trying to be his *friend?*"

Elaine was an excellent Miranda, though opening night was not her best performance; she'd needed prompting. It was probably my fault.

"Good wombs have borne bad sons," Miranda says to her father—in reference to Antonio, Prospero's brother.

I'd talked to Elaine about the good-wombs idea, possibly too much. I'd told Elaine my own ideas about my biological father—how whatever seemed bad in me I had ascribed to the code-boy, to the sergeant's genes (not my mom's). At the time, I still counted my mother among the good wombs in the world. She may have been embarrassingly *seducible*—the very word I used to describe my mom to Elaine—but Mary Marshall Dean *or* Abbott was essentially innocent of any wrongdoing. Maybe my mother was gullible, occasionally *backward*—I said this to Elaine, in lieu of the *retarded* word—but never "bad."

Admittedly, it was funny how I couldn't pronounce the *wombs* word—not even the singular. Both Elaine and I had laughed about how hard I came down on the letter *b*.

"It's a *silent b*, Billy!" Elaine had cried. "You don't *say* the *b!*"

It was comical, even to me. What need did I have of the *womb* (or *wombs*) word?

But I'm sure this was why Elaine had *moms* on her mind on opening night—"Good *moms* have borne bad sons," Elaine (as Miranda) almost said. Elaine must have heard the *moms* word coming; she stopped herself short after "Good—" There was then what every actor fears: an incriminating silence.

"Wombs," my mother whispered; she had a prompter's perfect whisper—it was almost inaudible.

"*Wombs!*" Elaine Hadley had shouted. Richard (as Prospero) had jumped. "Good *wombs* have borne bad sons!" Miranda, back in character, too emphatically said. It didn't happen again.

Naturally, Kittredge would say something to Elaine about it—after our opening-night performance.

"You need to work on the *wombs* word, Naples," he told her. "It's probably a word that causes you some nervous excitement. You should try saying to yourself, 'Every woman has a womb—even *I* have a womb. Wombs are no big deal.' We can work on saying this together—if it helps. You know, I say 'womb,' you say 'wombs are no big deal,' or I say 'wombs,' and you say '*I've* got one!'—that kind of thing."

"Thanks, Kittredge," Elaine said. "How very thoughtful." She was biting her lower lip, which I knew she did only when she was pining for him and hating herself for it. (I was accustomed to the feeling.)

Then suddenly, after months of such histrionic closeness, our contact with Kittredge was over; Elaine and I were despondent. Richard tried to talk to us about the postpartum depression that occasionally descends on actors following a play. "We didn't give birth to *The Tempest*," Elaine said impatiently. "*Shakespeare* did!"

Speaking strictly for myself, I missed running lines on Miss Frost's brass bed, too, but when I confessed this to Elaine, she said, "Why? It's not like we ever fooled around, or anything."

I was increasingly fond of Elaine, if not in that way, but you have to be careful what you say to your friends when you're trying too hard to make them feel better.

"Well, it wasn't because I didn't *want* to fool around with you," I told her.

We were in Elaine's bedroom—with the door open—on a Saturday night at the start of winter term. This would have been the New Year, 1960, though our ages hadn't changed; I was still seventeen, and Elaine was sixteen. It was movie night at Favorite River Academy, and from Elaine's bedroom window, we could see the flickering light of the movie projector in the new onion-shaped gym, which was attached to the old gym—where, on winter weekends, Elaine and I often watched Kittredge wrestle. Not this weekend; the wrestlers were away, competing some-where to the south of us—at Mount Hermon, maybe, or at Loomis.

When the team buses returned, Elaine and I would see them from her fifth-floor bedroom window. Even in the January cold, with all the windows closed, the sound of shouting boys reverberated in the quad-rangle of dormitories. The wrestlers, and the other athletes, would carry their gear from the buses to the new gym, where the lockers and the showers were. If the movie was still playing, some of the jocks would stay in the gym to see the end.

But they were showing a Western on this Saturday night; only morons watched the end of a Western without seeing the beginning of the movie—the endings were all the same. (There would be a shoot-out, a predictable comeuppance.) Elaine and I had been betting on whether or not Kittredge would stay in the gym to see the end of the Western—that is, if the wrestling-team bus returned before the movie was over.

"Kittredge isn't stupid," Elaine had said. "He won't hang around the gym to watch the final fifteen minutes of a horse opera." (Elaine had a low opinion of Westerns, which she called "horse operas" only when she was being kind; she more often called them "male propaganda.")

"Kittredge is a jock—he'll hang around the gym with the other jocks," I had said. "It doesn't matter what the movie is."

The jocks who did not hang around the gym after their road trips didn't have far to go. The jock dorm, which was called Tilley, was a five-story brick rectangle next to the gym. For whatever mindless reason, the jocks always whooped it up in the quad of dorms when they walked or ran to Tilley from the gym.

Mr. Hadley and his homely wife, Martha, were out; they'd gone off with Richard and my mom—as they often did together, especially when there was a foreign film playing in Ezra Falls. The marquee at the movie house in Ezra Falls capitalized it when a film had SUBTITLES. This wasn't just a warning to those local Vermonters who were disinclined (or unable) to read subtitles; this amounted to a caveat of a different kind—namely, that a foreign film was likely to have more sexual content than many Vermonters were used to.

When my mom and Richard and the Hadleys went to Ezra Falls to see those films with subtitles, Elaine and I weren't usually invited. Therefore, while our parents were out watching sex movies, Elaine and I were alone—either in her bedroom or in mine, always with the door open.

Elaine did not attend movie night in the Favorite River gym—not even when they weren't showing a Western. The atmosphere in the academy gym on movie nights was too all-boys for Elaine's liking. Faculty daughters of a certain age did not feel comfortable in that young-male environment. There was intentional farting, and far worse signs of loutish behavior. Elaine hypothesized that if they showed the foreign sex films in the academy gym on movie nights, some of the boys would beat off on the basketball court.

Generally, when we were left alone, Elaine and I preferred her bed-

room to mine. The Hadleys' fifth-floor dormitory apartment had more
of an overview of the quad; Richard and my mom's apartment, and my
bedroom, were on the third floor of the dorm. Our dormitory was called
Bancroft, and there was a bust of old Bancroft, a long-dead professor
emeritus at Favorite River, in the ground-floor common room—the *butt*
room, it was called. Bancroft (or at least his bust) was bald, and he had
bushy eyebrows.

I was in the process of acquainting myself with Favorite River
Academy's past. I had encountered photographs of the actual Professor
Bancroft. He'd been a young faculty member once, and I'd seen his photos—when he had a full head of hair—in those long-ago yearbooks in
the academy library. (You shouldn't guess about someone's past; if you
don't see any evidence of it, a person's past remains unknown to you.)

When Elaine went with me to the yearbook room, she demonstrated
little interest in the older yearbooks that fascinated me. I had barely
inched my way through the First World War, but Elaine Hadley had
begun with the contemporary yearbooks; she liked looking at the photographs of boys who were still at the school, or who'd only recently graduated. At the rate we were going, Elaine and I estimated that we might
arrive at the *same* yearbook in the early years of World War II—or just
before that war, maybe.

"Well, *he's* good-looking," Elaine would say, when she fancied this or
that boy in the yearbook photos.

"Show me," I would say—ever her loyal friend, but not yet giving
myself away to her. (We had somewhat similar taste in young men.)

It's a wonder I dared to suggest that I'd *wanted* to fool around with
Elaine. While this was a well-meaning lie, I may also have been trying to
throw her off the track; I might have been worried that Elaine somehow
sensed I was given to those homosexual yearnings Dr. Harlow and Dr.
Grau sought to treat "aggressively."

At first, Elaine didn't believe me. "You just said *what?*" she asked me.
We had been flopping around on her bed—certainly *not* in a sexual way.
We were bored, listening to a rock-'n'-roll station on Elaine's radio while
keeping an eye out her fifth-floor window. The return of the team buses
meant little to us, though this nonevent would mean that Kittredge was
once again at large in the quad.

There was a reading lamp with a dark-blue shade on Elaine's windowsill; the lamp shade was made of glass, as thick as a Coke bottle.

Kittredge knew that the dark-blue light in the fifth-floor window of Bancroft was coming from Elaine's bedroom. Ever since we'd been in *The Tempest* together, Kittredge would occasionally serenade that blue light in Elaine's bedroom, which he could see from anywhere in the quadrangle of dormitories—even from Tilley, the jock dorm. I had not spotted Professor Tilley in my search of the faculty photographs in the yearbook room. If Tilley was a professor emeritus at Favorite River, he must have taught at the school in more modern times than those school days of yore—the ones old Bancroft had once whinnied in.

I didn't realize how much Kittredge's infrequent serenades meant to Elaine; they were, of course, mocking in tone—"Shakespearean patois," as Elaine described it. Yet I knew that Elaine often fell asleep with that dark-blue lamp on—and that when Kittredge *didn't* serenade her, she was unhappy about it.

It was into this rock-'n'-roll-radio atmosphere of idle waiting, in the loneliness of Elaine Hadley's dark-blue bedroom, where I introduced the idea of my *wanting* to fool around with her. It wasn't that this was such a bad idea; it just wasn't true. It's not surprising that Elaine's initial response was one of disbelief.

"You just said *what?*" my friend Elaine asked.

"I don't want to do or say anything that would endanger our friendship," I told her.

"You want to fool around with *me?*" Elaine asked.

"Yes, I do—a little," I said.

"No . . . *penetration,* is that what you mean?" she asked.

"No . . . *yes,* that's what I mean," I said. Elaine knew that I had a little trouble with the *penetration* word; it was one of those nouns that could cause a pronunciation problem for me, but I would soon get over it.

"Say it, Billy," Elaine said.

"No . . . going all the way," I told her.

"But what kind of fooling around, exactly?" she asked.

I lay facedown on her bed and covered my head with one of her pillows. This must have been unacceptable to her, because she straddled my hips and sat on my lower back. I could feel her breathing on the back of my neck; she nuzzled my ear. "Kissing?" she whispered. "Touching?"

"Yes," I said, in a muffled voice.

Elaine pulled the pillow off my head. "Touching *what?*" she asked.

"I don't know," I said.

"Not *everything*," Elaine said.

"No! Certainly not," I said.

"You can touch my breasts," she said. "I don't have any breasts, any-way."

"Yes, you do," I told her. She had *something* there, and I admit that I wanted to touch her breasts. (I confess to wanting to touch all kinds of breasts, especially small ones.)

Elaine lay next to me on the bed, and I turned on my side to look at her. "Do I give you a hard-on?" she asked me.

"Yes," I lied.

"Oh, my God—it's always so hot in this room!" she suddenly cried, sitting up. The colder the weather was outside, the hotter it was in those old dormitories—and the higher the floor you were on, the hotter it got. At bedtime, or after lights-out, the students were always opening their windows, albeit only a crack, to let a little cold air in, but the ancient radiators would keep cranking up the heat.

Elaine was wearing a boy's dress shirt—white, with a button-down collar, though she never buttoned the collar, and she always left the top two buttons unbuttoned. Now she untucked the shirt from her jeans; she pinched the shirt between her thumb and index finger, and, holding it away from her stick-thin body, she blew on her chest to cool herself off.

"Do you have a hard-on *now?*" she asked me; she'd opened the win-dow a crack before lying down on the bed beside me.

"No—I must be too nervous," I told her.

"Don't be nervous. We're just kissing and touching, right?" Elaine asked me.

"Right," I said.

I could feel a razor-sharp draft of cold air from the cracked-open win-dow when Elaine kissed me, a chaste little peck on the lips, which must have been as disappointing to her as it was to me—because she said, "Tongues are okay. French kissing is allowed."

The next kiss was much more interesting—tongues change every-thing. There is a gathering momentum to French kissing; Elaine and I were unfamiliar with what to do about it. Perhaps to distract myself, I thought of my mother overseeing my wayward father kissing some-one *else*. There's a *waywardness* to French kissing, I remember thinking. Elaine must have needed to distract herself, too. She broke free from our kiss and breathlessly said, "Not the Everly Brothers *again!*" I'd been un-aware of what was playing on the rock-'n'-roll station, but Elaine rolled away from me; reaching for her night table, she turned the radio off.

"I want to be able to hear us breathing," Elaine said, rolling into my arms again.

Yes, I thought—breathing is very different when you're French kiss-ing someone. I lifted her untucked shirt and tentatively touched her bare stomach; she slid my hand up to her breast—well, to her *bra,* anyway—which was soft and small and fit easily in the palm of my hand.

"Is this a . . . *training* bra?" I asked her.

"It's a *padded* bra," Elaine said. "I don't know about the training part."

"It feels nice," I told her. I wasn't lying; the *training* word had trig-gered something, though I wasn't sure exactly what I held in the palm of my hand. (I mean, how much of what I felt was her breast—or was it mostly the bra?)

Elaine, as if heralding what our future relationship would become, must have read my mind, for she said—as always, loud and clear—"There's more padding than breast, if you want to know the truth, Billy. Here, I'll show you," she said; she sat up and unbuttoned the white shirt, slipping it off her shoulders.

It was a pretty bra, more pearl-gray than white, and when she reached behind her back to unfasten it, her bra seemed to expand. I had only a glimpse of her small, pointy breasts before she put her shirt back on; her nipples were bigger than any boy's, and those darker-colored rings around the nipples—the areolae, another unpronounceable plural!—were al-most as big as her breasts. But while Elaine was buttoning her shirt, it was her bra—now on the bed, between us—that captured my attention. I picked it up; the soft, breast-shaped pads were sewn into the silky fabric. To my surprise, I instantly wanted to try it on—I wanted to know what it felt like to *wear* a bra. But I was no more honest about this feeling than I'd been about those other desires I had withheld from my friend Elaine.

It was only the slightest deviation from the norm that signaled to me a fallen boundary in our emerging relationship: As always, Elaine had left the top two buttons of her boy's dress shirt unbuttoned, but this time she'd also left the bottommost button unbuttoned. My hand slipped more easily under her untucked shirt; it was the real thing (what little there was of it) that fit so perfectly in my palm.

"I don't know about you, Billy," Elaine said, as we lay face-to-face on one of her pillows, "but I had always imagined a boy touching my breasts for the first time as *messier* than it actually is."

"*Messier*," I repeated. I must have been stalling.

I was remembering Dr. Harlow's annual morning-meeting talk to us boys, concerning our *treatable afflictions*; I was recalling that "an unwelcome sexual attraction to other boys and men" fell into this dubiously curable category.

I must have repressed the annual morning-meeting presentation of Dr. Grau—"Herr Doktor" Grau, as we boys called Favorite River's school psychiatrist. Dr. Grau gave us the same lunatic spiel every year—how we were all of an age of arrested development, "frozen," the Herr Doktor said, "like bugs in amber." (By our frightened expressions, we boys could tell that not all of us had seen bugs in amber—or even knew what they were.) "You are in the *polymorphous-perverse* phase," Dr. Grau assured us. "It is only natural, at this phase, that you exhibit infantile sexual tendencies, in which the genitals are not yet identified as the sole or principal sexual organs." (But how could we fail to recognize such an obvious thing about our genitals? we boys thought with alarm.) "At this phase," Herr Doktor Grau continued, "coitus is not necessarily the recognizable goal of erotic activity." (Then why did we think about coitus nonstop? we boys wondered with dread.) "You are experiencing pregenital libidinal fixations," old Grau told us, as if this were somehow reassuring. (He also taught German at the academy, in the same unintelligible fashion.) "You must come talk to me about these *fixations*," the old Austrian always concluded. (No boy I knew at Favorite River admitted to having such fixations; no one I knew ever talked to Dr. Grau about *anything*!)

Richard Abbott told me and the cast of *The Tempest* that Ariel's gender was "polymorphous—more a matter of habiliment than anything organic." This later led Richard to conclude that the gender of the character I played was "*mutable*," and I was further confused regarding my (and Ariel's) sexual orientation.

Yet, when I asked Richard if he meant anything at all resembling the "*polymorphous-perverse* phase" of the "bugs in amber" bullshit Dr. Grau had gone on (and on) about in morning meeting, Richard adamantly denied there was any connection.

"No one listens to old Grau, Bill," Richard had told me. "Don't you listen to him, either."

Wise advice—but while it was possible not to heed what Dr. Grau said, we boys were forced to *hear* him. And, lying next to Elaine, with my hand on her bare breast, and our tongues once more entangled in a way that made us imagine what the next most erotic thing to do with each other was, I became aware of my growing erection.

With our mouths still pressed together, Elaine managed to ask: "Are you getting a hard-on *yet*?" Yes, I was, and I'd noted Elaine's impatience in her overloud utterance of the *yet* word, but my confusion was such that I was unsure what had initiated my erection.

Yes, the French kissing was exciting, and (to this day) the touch of a woman's bare breasts is not something I am indifferent to; yet I believe my hard-on began when I imagined wearing Elaine's padded bra. At that moment, wasn't I exhibiting the "infantile sexual tendencies" Dr. Grau had warned us boys about?

But all I said to Elaine, in the midst of our darting tongues, was a strangled-sounding "Yes!"

This time, when Elaine broke free from me, she bit my lower lip in the hurried-up process. "You actually have a boner," Elaine said to me, seriously.

"Yes, I actually do," I admitted. I felt my lower lip, to be sure I wasn't bleeding. (I was looking all around for her bra.)

"Oh, God—I don't want to see it!" Elaine cried. This was sexually confusing to me, too. I hadn't suggested *showing* my hard-on to her! I didn't want her to see it. In fact, I would have been embarrassed for her to see it; I thought it would probably disappoint her, or make her laugh (or throw up).

"Maybe I could just *touch* it," Elaine considered, more thoughtfully. "I don't mean your bare boner!" she quickly added. "Maybe I could just *feel* it—I mean, through your clothes."

"Sure—why not?" I said, as casually as I could, though I would wonder (for years) if anyone else ever went through a sexual initiation of such a highly negotiated kind.

The boys at Favorite River Academy were not permitted to wear jeans; dungarees, as we called them then, were not allowed in class or in the dining hall, where we were obliged to wear coats and ties. Most boys wore khakis, or—in the winter months—flannel trousers or corduroys. I was wearing a baggy pair of corduroys on this January Saturday night. It was a comfortable pair of pants to have a boner in, but I was also wearing

Jockey briefs, and they were increasingly uncomfortable. Maybe it was the only men's underwear you could buy in Vermont in 1960—white Jockey briefs. (I don't know; at the time, my mom still bought all my clothes.)

I'd seen Kittredge's underwear, at the gym—blue cotton boxers, the color of a blue dress shirt. Maybe his French mother had bought them in Paris, or in New York. "That woman *has* to be his mother," Elaine had said. "She could *be* Kittredge, if she didn't have those breasts—that woman would know where to buy boxers like that." And Kittredge's blue boxers were *pressed;* this wasn't an affectation of Kittredge's, because the school laundry pressed everything—not just your trousers and dress shirts, but even your underwear and your stupid socks. (This was talked about with a derision almost equal to that assigned to the advice of Dr. Harlow and Dr. Grau.)

Notwithstanding this social history, my first erection inspired by Elaine Hadley (or by her bra) was stiffening in a tight-fitting pair of Jockey briefs, which were threatening to cut off circulation to my "inspired" hard-on. Elaine—with an aggressiveness I was unprepared for—suddenly put her hand on those very genitals that Dr. Grau had told us we'd "not yet identified" as our own goddamn sexual organs! There was no question in my mind concerning what and where my "sole or principal sexual organs" were, and when Elaine grabbed hold of them, I flinched.

"Oh . . . my . . . God!" Elaine cried, momentarily deafening the nearer of my ears. "I can't imagine what having one of those is like!"

This was sexually confusing, too. Did Elaine mean that she couldn't imagine what having a penis *inside* her was like, or did Elaine mean that she couldn't imagine being a boy and having her own penis? I didn't ask. I was relieved that she'd released my balls from her not inconsiderable grasp, but Elaine held fast to my penis, and I continued to fondle her breasts. Had we resumed the French kissing where we'd left off, there's no telling what the aforementioned "gathering momentum" might have led to, but in fact we'd just begun to kiss again—tentatively, at first, with only the tips of our tongues making contact. I watched Elaine close her eyes, and I closed mine.

Thus I discovered that it was possible to be holding Elaine Hadley's breast while I imagined I was fondling an equally permissive Miss Frost. (Miss Frost's breasts would only be slightly bigger than Elaine's, I had long imagined.) With my eyes closed, I could even conceive that the fierce grip of Elaine's small hand on my penis was in truth Miss Frost's far bigger hand—in which case, Miss Frost must have been restraining herself. And, as the French kissing quickened—both Elaine and I were soon breathless—I fantasized that it was Miss Frost's long tongue thrusting against mine, and that we were entwined on the brass bed in her basement hideaway in the First Sister Public Library.

When the diesel fumes from the first of the returning team buses reached the cracked-open window of Elaine's fifth-floor room, I managed to think I was smelling the oil-burning furnace next to Miss Frost's former coal bin of a bedroom. When I opened my eyes, I half expected to be face-to-face with Miss Frost, but there instead was my friend Elaine Hadley, with her eyes tightly closed.

All the time I'd been imagining Miss Frost, it had not occurred to me that Elaine might have been imagining, too. Not surprisingly, the name on her lips, which she somehow managed to say in my mouth, was "Kittredge!" (Elaine had correctly identified the diesel fumes from the returning team bus; she was wondering if it was the wrestling-team bus, because she'd been imagining Kittredge while I was imagining Miss Frost.)

Elaine's eyes were wide open now. I must have looked as guilty as she did. There was a pulse in my penis; if I could feel it throbbing, I knew that Elaine could feel it, too.

"Your heart's beating, Billy," she said.

"That's not my heart," I told her.

"Yes, it is—your heart is beating in your penis," Elaine said. "Do all boys' hearts beat there?"

"I can't speak for other boys," I answered. But she'd let go of my penis, and had rolled away from me.

There was more than one parked bus at the gym with its diesel engine running; the flickering light from the movie projector was still blinking from the basketball court, and the meaningless shouts and whoops of the returning jocks echoed in the dormitory quadrangle—the wrestlers were among them, maybe, or maybe not.

Elaine now lay on the bed with her forehead almost touching the windowsill, where the draft of cold air from the cracked-open window was the coldest. "When I was kissing you, and holding your penis, and you were touching my breasts, I was thinking of Kittredge—that bastard," Elaine told me.

"I know—it's okay," I said to her. I knew what a good and truthful friend she was, but—even so—I couldn't tell her that I'd been thinking of Miss Frost.

"No, it's *not* okay," Elaine said; she was crying.

Elaine was lying on her side at the foot of her bed, facing the window, and I stretched out behind her with my chest flush to her back; I could kiss the back of her neck that way, and (with one hand) I could manage to touch her breasts under her untucked shirt. The heartbeat in my penis was still pounding away. Through her jeans, through my corduroy pants, I doubted that Elaine could detect the pulse in my penis, though I had pressed myself against her and she'd thrust her small bum into me.

Elaine had a boy's nonexistent bottom, and no hips to speak of; she was wearing a pair of boy's dungarees (to go with her boy's shirt), and I suddenly thought, as I kissed her neck and her damp hair, that Elaine actually smelled like a boy, too. After all, she'd been sweating; she wore no perfume, no makeup of any kind, not even lipstick, and here I was rubbing myself against her boyish bum.

"You still have a hard-on, don't you?" she asked me.

"Yes," I said. I was embarrassed that I couldn't stop rubbing against her, but Elaine was moving her hips; she was rubbing against me, too.

"It's okay—what you're doing," Elaine told me.

"No, it's *not* okay," I said, but I lacked the conviction I'd heard in Elaine's voice—when, only a moment ago, she'd said the same thing to me. (What I meant, of course, was that I was thinking of Kittredge, too.)

Miss Frost was a big woman; she was broad-shouldered, and her hips were wide. Miss Frost did *not* have a young boy's bum; by no stretch of my imagination was I thinking of Miss Frost while I rubbed myself against Elaine Hadley, who was quietly crying.

"No, really, it's okay—I like it, too," Elaine was saying softly, when we both heard Kittredge calling from the quad.

"My sweet Naples—is that your blue light burning?" Kittredge called. I felt Elaine's body stiffen. There were other boys' voices in the quadrangle—in the area of Tilley, the jock dorm—but only Kittredge's voice stood out distinctly.

"I told you he wouldn't watch the end of a Western—that bastard," Elaine whispered to me.

"Oh, Naples—is your blue light a beacon for *me?*" Kittredge called. "Are you still a maid, Naples, or a maid no more?" he called out. (I would realize, one day, that Kittredge was mock-Shakespearean—a kind of *faux* Shakespeare—to his core.)

Elaine was sobbing when she reached to turn off her lamp with the dark-blue shade. When she thrust herself back into me, her sobs were louder; she was grunting as she rubbed against me. Her sobs and grunts were strangely commingled, not unlike the yelps a dog makes when it's dreaming.

"Don't let him get to you, Elaine—he's such an asshole," I whispered in her ear.

"*Shhh!*" she hushed me. "No actual talking," she said breathlessly, between her half-strangled cries.

"Is that *you*, Naples?" Kittredge called to her. "Lights out so soon? To bed alone, alas!"

My dress shirt had come untucked from my corduroys; it must have been the incessant rubbing. The shirt was blue—the same color as Kittredge's boxers, I was thinking. Elaine began to moan. "Keep doing it! Do it *harder!*" she moaned. "Yes! Like *that*—God, don't stop!" she cried loudly.

I could see her breath in that cold razor of air from the open window; I was grinding against her for what seemed the longest time, before I realized what I was saying. "Like that?" I kept asking her. "Like *that?*" (No actual talking, as Elaine had requested, but our voices were being broadcast to the quadrangle of dorms—all the way to Tilley and the gym, where the returning team buses were still unloading.)

The flickering light from the movie projector had stopped; the windows of the basketball court were in darkness. The Western was over; the gun smoke from the shoot-out had drifted away—like the Favorite River boys, drifting back to their dormitories, but not Kittredge.

"Cut it out, Naples!" Kittredge called. "Are you there, too, Nymph?" he called to me.

Elaine had begun a prolonged, orgasmic scream. She would say later: "More like childbirth than orgasm, or so I imagine—I'm never having any children. Have you seen the size of babies' *heads?*" she asked me.

Her caterwauling may have sounded like an orgasm to Kittredge. Elaine and I were still straightening out the bedcovers when we heard the knock on the door from the dormitory hall.

"God, where's my bra?" Elaine asked; she couldn't find it in the bedcovers, but she wouldn't have had time to put it on, anyway. (She had to answer the door.)

"It's *him*," I warned her.

"Of course it is," she said. She went into the living room of the apartment; she looked at herself in the long mirror, in the foyer, before opening the door.

I found her bra on the bed; it had been lost in the crazy patterns of the rumpled quilt, but I quickly stuffed it into my Jockey briefs. My erection had completely subsided; there was more room for Elaine's little bra in my briefs than there had been for my hard-on.

"I wanted to be sure you were all right," I heard Kittredge saying to Elaine. "I was afraid there was a fire, or something."

"There was a fire, all right, but I'm fine," Elaine told him.

I came out of Elaine's bedroom. She'd not invited Kittredge into the apartment; he stood in the doorway to the dorm. Some of the Bancroft boys scurried by in the hall, peering into the foyer.

"So you're here, too, Nymph," Kittredge said to me.

I saw that he had a fresh mat burn on one cheek, but the mat burn made him no less cocksure than before.

"I suppose you won your match," I said to him.

"That's right, Nymph," he said, but he kept looking at Elaine. Because her shirt was white, you could see her nipples through the fabric, and the darker rings around her nipples—those unpronounceable areolae—looked like wine stains on her fair skin.

"This doesn't look good, Naples. Where's your bra?" Kittredge asked her.

Elaine smiled at me. "Did you find it?" she asked me.

"I didn't really look all that hard for it," I lied.

"You should think about your reputation, Naples," Kittredge told her. This was a new tack for him; it caught both Elaine and me off-guard.

"There's nothing wrong with my reputation," Elaine said defensively.

"You should think about her reputation, too, Nymph," Kittredge told me. "A girl can't get her reputation back—if you know what I mean."

"I didn't know you were such a *prude*," Elaine said to him, but I could tell that the *reputation* word—or everything Kittredge had insinuated about it—truly upset her.

"I'm not a prude, Naples," he said, smiling at her. It was a smile you give a girl when you're alone with her; I could see that she'd allowed him to get to her.

"I was just *faking* it, Kittredge!" she yelled at him. "I was just *acting*—we both were!" she shouted.

"It didn't sound like acting—not entirely," he said to her. "You have to be careful who you pretend to be, Nymph," Kittredge said to me, but he kept looking at Elaine as if he were alone with her.

"Well, if you'll excuse me, Kittredge, I should find my bra and put it on before my parents come home—you should go, too, Billy," Elaine said to me, but she never took her eyes off Kittredge. Neither of them looked at me.

It was not yet eleven o'clock when Kittredge and I stepped into the fifth-floor hall of the dorm; the Bancroft boys who were loitering in the hall, or gawking at Kittredge from the open doorways of their rooms, were clearly shocked to see him. "Did you win again?" some kid asked him. Kittredge just nodded.

"I heard the wrestling team lost," another boy said.

"I'm not the team," Kittredge told him. "I can only win my weight-class."

We went down the stairwell to the third floor, where I said good night to him. Dorm check-in—even for seniors, on a Saturday night—was at eleven.

"I suppose Richard and your mom are out with the Hadleys," Kittredge said, matter-of-factly.

"Yes, there's a foreign film in Ezra Falls," I told him.

"Humping in French, Italian, or Swedish," Kittredge said. I laughed, but he wasn't trying to be funny. "You know, Nymph—you're not in France, Italy, or Sweden. You've got to be more careful with that girl you're humping, or not humping."

At the moment, I wondered if Kittredge might be genuinely concerned for Elaine's "reputation," as he'd referred to it, but you could never tell with Kittredge; you often didn't see where he was going with what he said.

"I would never do anything to hurt Elaine," I told him.

"Listen, Nymph," he said. "You can hurt people by having sex with them and by *not* having sex with them."

"I guess that's true," I said cautiously.

"Does your mom sleep naked, or does she wear something?" Kittredge asked me, as if he hadn't suddenly changed the subject.

"She wears something," I told him.

"Well, that's mothers for you," he said. "Most mothers, anyway," he added.

"It's almost eleven," I warned him. "You don't want to be late for check-in."

"Does Elaine sleep naked?" Kittredge asked me.

Of course, what I should have told him was that my desire never to do anything to hurt Elaine prevented me from telling the likes of Kittredge whether she slept naked or not, but in truth I didn't know if Elaine slept naked. I thought it would be perfectly mysterious to say to Kittredge, which I did, "When Elaine's with me, she's not asleep."

To which Kittredge simply said: "You're a mystery, aren't you, Nymph? I just don't know about you, but I'll figure you out one day—I really will."

"You're going to be late for check-in," I told him.

"I'm going to the infirmary—I'm going to get this mat burn checked out," he said, pointing to his cheek. It wasn't much of a mat burn, in my opinion, but Kittredge said, "I like the weekend nurse at the infirmary— the mat burn's just an excuse to see her. Saturday night is a good night to stay in the infirmary," he told me.

On that provocative note, he left me—that was Kittredge. If he was still figuring me out, I hadn't yet figured *him* out. Was there really a "weekend nurse" at the Favorite River infirmary? Did Kittredge have an older-woman thing going? Or was he acting, as Elaine and I had been? Was he just faking it?

I HADN'T BEEN BACK in our dormitory apartment for very long, not more than a couple of minutes, before my mom and Richard came home from the movie. I'd barely had time to take Elaine's padded bra from my Jockey briefs. (I'd no sooner put the bra under my pillow when Elaine phoned me.)

"You have my bra, don't you?" she asked me.

"What happens to the duck?" I asked her, but she wasn't in the mood for it.

"Do you have my bra, Billy?"

"Yes," I said. "It was a spur-of-the-moment thing."

"That's okay," she said. "I want you to have it." I didn't tell her that Kittredge had asked me if she slept naked.

Then Richard and my mom came home, and I asked them about the foreign film. "It was *disgusting!*" my mother said.

"I didn't know you were such a *prude*," I said to her.

"Take it easy, Bill," Richard said.

"I'm not a prude!" my mom told me. She seemed unreasonably upset.

I had been kidding. It was just something I'd heard Elaine say to Kittredge.

"I didn't know what the movie was about, Jewel," Richard said to her. "I'm sorry."

"Look at you!" my mom said to me. "You look more wrinkled than an unmade bed. I think you should have that conversation with Billy, Richard."

My mom went into their bedroom and closed the door. "*What* conversation?" I asked Richard.

"It's about being careful with Elaine, Bill," Richard said. "She's younger than you are—it's about being sure you're *protecting* her," Richard told me.

"Are you talking to me about *rubbers?*" I asked him. "Because you can only get them in Ezra Falls, and that asshole pharmacist won't give condoms to kids."

"Don't say 'asshole,' Bill," Richard said, "at least not around your mom. You want *rubbers?* I'll get you rubbers."

"There's no danger with Elaine," I told him.

"Did I see Kittredge leaving Bancroft as we were coming home?" Richard asked.

"I don't know," I said. "Did you?"

"You're at a . . . *pivotal* age, Bill," Richard told me. "We just want you to be careful with Elaine."

"I *am* careful with her," I told him.

"You'd better keep Kittredge away from her," Richard said.

"Just how do I do that?" I asked him.

"Well, Bill . . ." Richard had started to say, when my mother came out of their bedroom. I remember thinking that Kittredge would have been disappointed by what she was wearing—flannel pajamas, not at all sexy.

"You're still talking about *sex*, aren't you?" my mom asked Richard and me. She was angry. "I know that's what you were talking about. Well, it's not funny."

"We weren't laughing, Jewel," Richard tried to tell her, but she wouldn't let him continue.

"You keep your pecker in your pants, Billy!" my mom told me. "You go slowly with Elaine, and you tell her to watch out for Jacques Kittredge—she better watch out for him! That Kittredge is a boy who doesn't just want to *seduce* women—he wants women to *submit* to him!" my mother said.

"Jewel, Jewel—let it rest," Richard Abbott was saying.

"You don't know everything, Richard," my mother told him.

"No, I don't," Richard admitted.

"I know boys like Kittredge," my mom said; she said it to me, not to Richard—even so, she blushed.

It occurred to me that, when my mother was angry at me, it was because she saw something of my *womanizing* father in me—perhaps, increasingly, I looked like him. (As if I could help *that*!)

I thought of Elaine's bra, which was waiting for me under my pillow—"more a matter of habiliment than anything organic," as Richard had said about Ariel's gender. (If that small padded bra didn't fit the *habiliment* word, what did?)

"What was the foreign film about?" I asked Richard.

"It's not an appropriate subject for *you*," my mother told me. "Don't you tell him about it, Richard," my mother said.

"Sorry, Bill," Richard said sheepishly.

"Nothing Shakespeare would have shied away from, I'll bet," I said to Richard, but I kept looking at my mom. She wouldn't look at me; she went back inside her bedroom and closed the door.

If I was less than forthcoming to my one true friend, Elaine Hadley, I needed only to think of my mother; if I couldn't tell Richard about my crush on Kittredge, or admit to Miss Frost that I loved her, I had no doubt concerning where my lack of candor came from. (From my mother, unquestionably, but possibly from my *womanizing* father, too. Maybe from both of them, it only now occurred to me.)

"Good night, Richard—I love you," I said to my stepfather. He quickly kissed me on my forehead.

"Good night, Bill—I love you, too," Richard said. He gave me a please-forgive-me kind of smile. I really did love him, but I was fighting against my disappointment in him at the same time.

Also, I was mortally tired; it is exhausting to be seventeen and not know who you are, and Elaine's bra was summoning me to my bed.

Chapter 5

LEAVING ESMERALDA

Perhaps you need to have your world change, your entire world, to under-stand why anyone would write an epilogue—not to mention why there is an act 5 to *The Tempest*, and why the epilogue to that play (spoken by Prospero) is absolutely fitting. When I made that juvenile criticism of *The Tempest*, my world hadn't changed.

"Now my charms are all o'erthrown," Prospero begins the epilogue—not unlike the way Kittredge might have started a conversation, offhand and innocent-seeming.

That winter of 1960, when Elaine and I were continuing our mas-querade, which even extended to our holding hands while we watched Kittredge wrestle, was marked by Martha Hadley's first official efforts to address the probable cause (or causes) of my pronunciation problems. I use the *official* word because I made appointments to see Mrs. Hadley, and I met with her in her office—it was in the academy music building.

At seventeen, I'd not yet seen a psychiatrist; had I ever been tempted to talk to Herr Doktor Grau, I'm certain that my beloved stepfather, Richard Abbott, would have persuaded me not to. Besides, that same winter when I was faithfully keeping my appointments with Mrs. Hadley, old Grau died. Favorite River Academy would eventually replace him with a younger (if no less modern) school psychiatrist, but not before the fall term of the next academic year.

Moreover, while I was seeing Martha Hadley, I had no need of a psy-chiatrist; in the ferreting out of those myriad words I couldn't pronounce, and in her far-reaching speculations regarding the reason (or reasons) for my mispronunciations, Mrs. Hadley, an expert voice and singing teacher, became my first psychiatrist.

My closer contact with her gave me a better understanding of my attraction to her—her homeliness notwithstanding. Martha Hadley had a masculine kind of homeliness; she was thin-lipped but she had a big mouth, and big teeth. Her jaw was as prominent as Kittredge's, but her neck was long and contrastingly feminine; she had broad shoulders and big hands, like Miss Frost. Mrs. Hadley's hair was longer than Miss Frost's, and she wore it in a severe ponytail. Her flat chest never failed to remind me of Elaine's overlarge nipples, and those darker-skinned rings around them—the areolae, which I imagined were a mother-daughter thing. But, unlike Elaine, Mrs. Hadley was very strong-looking. I was realizing how much I liked that look.

When the *areola* and *areolae* words were added to my long list of troublesome pronunciations, Martha Hadley asked me: "Does the difficulty lie in what they are?"

"Maybe," I answered her. "Fortunately, they're not words that come up every day."

"Whereas *library* or *libraries*, not to mention *penis*—" Mrs. Hadley started to say.

"It's more of a problem with the plural," I reminded her.

"I suppose you don't have much use for penises—I mean the plural, Billy," Martha Hadley said.

"Not every day," I told her. I meant that the occasion to say the *penises* word rarely came up—not that I didn't think about penises every day, because I did. And so—maybe because I hadn't told Elaine or Richard Abbott or Grandpa Harry, and probably because I didn't dare tell Miss Frost—I told Mrs. Hadley everything. (Well, *almost* everything.)

I began with my crush on Kittredge. "You *and* Elaine!" Martha Hadley said. (Elaine had even been forthcoming to her *mother* about it!)

I told Mrs. Hadley that, before I ever saw Kittredge, I'd had a homoerotic attraction to other wrestlers, and that—in my perusal of the old yearbooks in the Favorite River Academy library—I had a special fondness for the wrestling-team photographs, in comparison to a merely passing interest in the photos of the school Drama Club. ("I see," Mrs. Hadley said.)

I even told her about my slightly fading crush on Richard Abbott;

it had been at its strongest before he became my stepfather. ("My good-ness—*that* must have been awkward!" Martha Hadley exclaimed.)

But when it came to confessing my love for Miss Frost, I stopped; my eyes welled with tears. "What is it, Billy? You can tell me," Mrs. Hadley said. She took my hands in her bigger, stronger hands. Her long neck, her throat, was possibly the only pretty thing about her; without much evidence, I could merely speculate that Martha Hadley's small breasts were like Elaine's.

In Mrs. Hadley's office, there was just a piano with a bench, an old couch (where we always sat), and a desk with a straight-backed chair. The third-floor view out her office window was uninspiring—the twisted trunks of two old maple trees, some snow on the more horizontal limbs of the trees, the sky streaked with gray-white clouds. The photo of Mr. Hadley (on Mrs. Hadley's desk) was also uninspiring.

Mr. Hadley—I've long forgotten his first name, if I ever knew it—seemed unsuited to boarding-school life. Mr. Hadley—shaggy, spottily bearded—would one day become a more active figure on the Favorite River campus, where he lent his history-teaching expertise to discussions (which later led to protests) of the Vietnam War. More memorable, by far, than Mr. Hadley was the day of my confession in Martha Hadley's office, when I concentrated all my attention on Mrs. Hadley's throat. "Whatever you tell me, Billy, will not leave this office—I swear," she said.

Somewhere in the music building, a student was practicing the piano—not with the greatest competence, I thought, or perhaps there were two students playing two different pianos. "I look at my mother's mail-order catalogs," I confessed to Mrs. Hadley. "I imagine *you* among the training-bra models," I told her. "I masturbate," I admitted—one of the few verbs that gave me a little trouble, though not this time.

"Oh, Billy, this isn't criminal activity!" Martha Hadley said happily. "I'm only surprised that you would think of *me*—I'm not in the least good-looking—and it's a mild surprise that *training bra* is so easy for you to pronounce. I'm not finding a discernible pattern here," she said, wav-ing the growing list of those words that challenged me.

"I don't know what it is about you," I confessed to her.

"What about girls your own age?" Mrs. Hadley asked me. I shook my head. "Not Elaine?" she asked. I hesitated, but Martha Hadley put her strong hands on my shoulders; she faced me on the couch. "It's all right, Billy—Elaine doesn't believe that you're interested in her in that way. And this is strictly between us, remember?" My eyes filled with tears again; Mrs. Hadley pulled my head to her hard chest. "Billy, Billy— you've done nothing *wrong*!" she cried.

Whoever knocked on the door to her office surely had heard the *wrong* word. "Come in!" Mrs. Hadley called, in such a strident way that I realized where Elaine's stop-you-in-your-tracks voice came from.

It was Atkins—an acknowledged loser, but I'd not known he was a music student. Maybe Atkins had a voice issue; perhaps there were words he couldn't pronounce. "I can come back," Atkins said to Martha Had- ley, but he wouldn't stop staring at me, or he couldn't look at her—one or the other. Any idiot would have known I'd been crying.

"Come back in half an hour," Mrs. Hadley told Atkins.

"Okay, but I don't have a watch," he said, still staring at me.

"Take mine," she told him. It was when she took her watch off and handed it to him that I saw what it was that attracted me to her. Martha Hadley not only had a masculine appearance—she was dominant, like a man, in everything she did. I could only imagine, sexually, that she was dominant, too—that she would impose what she wanted on anyone, and that it would be difficult to resist what she wanted you to do. But why would that appeal to me? (Naturally, I wouldn't make these thoughts part of my selective confession to Mrs. Hadley.)

Atkins was mutely staring at the watch. It made me wonder if he was such a loser and an idiot that he couldn't tell time.

"In half an hour," Martha Hadley reminded him.

"The numbers are Roman numerals," Atkins said despondently.

"Just keep your eye on the minute hand. Count to thirty minutes. Come back then," Mrs. Hadley said to him. Atkins walked off, still star- ing at the watch; he left the office door open. Mrs. Hadley got up from the couch and closed the door. "Billy, Billy," she said, turning to me. "It's all right to feel what you're feeling—it's okay."

"I thought of talking to Richard about it," I told her.

"That's a good idea. You can talk to Richard about anything—I'm sure of that," Martha Hadley said.

"But not my mother," I said.

"Your mother, Mary. My dear friend Mary . . ." Mrs. Hadley began; then she stopped. "No, not your mother—don't tell her yet," she said.

"Why?" I asked. I thought I knew why, but I wanted to hear Mrs.

Hadley say it. "Because she's a little *damaged?*" I asked. "Or because she seems angry at me—I'm not sure why."

"I don't know about the *damaged* part," Martha Hadley said. "Your mother *does* seem angry at you—I'm not sure why, either. I was mainly thinking that she becomes rather easily *unhinged*—in some areas, given certain subjects."

"What areas?" I asked. "What subjects?"

"Certain sexual matters upset her," Mrs. Hadley said. "Billy, I know there are things she's kept from you."

"Oh."

"Secrecy isn't my favorite thing about New England!" Mrs. Hadley suddenly cried; she looked at her wrist, where her watch had been, and then laughed at herself. "I wonder how Atkins is managing the Roman numerals," she said, and we both laughed. "You can tell Elaine, too, you know," Martha Hadley said. "You can tell Elaine anything, Billy. Besides, I think she already knows."

I thought so, too, but I didn't say it. I was thinking about my mother becoming rather easily *unhinged*. I was regretting that I hadn't consulted Dr. Grau before he died—if only because I could have familiarized myself with his doctrine of how *curable* homosexuality was. (It might have made me less angry in the coming years, when I would be exposed to more of that punitive, dumber-than-dog-shit doctrine.)

"It's really helped me to talk to you," I told Mrs. Hadley; she moved away from her office door to let me pass. I was afraid she was going to grasp my hands or my shoulders, or even pull my head to her hard chest again, and that I would be unable to stop myself from hugging her—or kissing her, though I would have had to stand on my toes to do that. But Martha Hadley didn't touch me; she just stood aside.

"There's nothing wrong with your voice, Billy—there's nothing physically the matter with your tongue, or with the roof of your mouth," she said. I'd forgotten that she had looked in my mouth at our very first appointment.

She'd asked me to touch the roof of my mouth with my tongue, and she'd held the tip of my tongue with a gauze pad, and—with another gauze pad—she'd poked around on the floor of my mouth, apparently feeling for something that wasn't there. (I'd been embarrassed that her playing around in my mouth had given me an erection—more evidence of what old Grau had called "infantile sexual tendencies.")

"Not to defame the dead," Mrs. Hadley said, as I was leaving, "but I hope you're aware, Billy, that the late Dr. Grau and our sole surviving faculty member in the medical sciences—I mean Dr. Harlow—are both imbeciles."

"That's what Richard says," I told her.

"Listen to Richard," Mrs. Hadley said. "He's a sweet man."

It would be years later, when I had this thought: In a small, less-than-first-rate boarding school, there were various indications of the adult world—some truly sensitive and good-hearted grown-ups who were trying to make the adult world more comprehensible and more bearable for young people, while there were also those dinosaurs of an inflexible rectitude (the Dr. Graus and the Dr. Harlows) and the tirelessly intractable *homophobes* men of their ilk and generation have spawned.

"How did Dr. Grau really die?" I asked Mrs. Hadley.

The story they'd told us boys—Dr. Harlow had told us, in morning meeting—was that Grau had slipped and fallen in the quadrangle one winter night. The paths were icy; the old Austrian must have hit his head. Dr. Harlow did not say that Herr Doktor Grau actually froze to death—I believe that "hypothermia" was the term Dr. Harlow used.

The boys who were on the kitchen crew found the body in the morning. One of them said that Grau's face was as white as the snow, and another boy told us that the old Austrian's eyes were open, but a third boy said the dead man's eyes were closed; there was agreement among the kitchen boys that Dr. Grau's Tyrolean hat (with a greasy-looking pheasant feather) was discovered at some distance from the body.

"Grau was drunk," Martha Hadley told me. "There'd been a faculty dinner party in one of the dorms. Grau probably *did* slip and fall—he *may* have hit his head, but he was definitely drunk. He was passed out in the snow all night! He froze."

Dr. Grau, like no small number of the faculty at Favorite River, had applied for a job at the academy because of the nearby skiing, but old Grau hadn't skied for years. Dr. Grau was terribly fat; he said he could still ski very well, but he admitted that, when he fell down, he couldn't get up—not without taking his skis off first. (I used to imagine Grau fallen on the slope, flailing to release his bindings, shouting "infantile sexual tendencies" in English and German.)

I'd chosen German for my language requirement at Favorite River, but only because I'd been assured that there were three other German teachers at the academy; I never had to be taught by Herr Doktor Grau. The other German teachers were also Austrians—two of them skiers. My favorite, Fräulein Bauer, was the only nonskier.

As I was leaving Mrs. Hadley's office, I suddenly remembered what Fräulein Bauer had told me; I made many grammatical mistakes in German, and the word-order business gave me fits, but my pronunciation was perfect. There was no German word I couldn't pronounce. Yet when I told Martha Hadley this news, she seemed barely interested—if at all. "It's psychological, Billy. You can say anything, in the sense that you're able to say it. But you either won't say a word, because it triggers something, or—"

I interrupted her. "It triggers something *sexual,* you mean," I said.

"Maybe," said Mrs. Hadley; she shrugged. She seemed barely interested in the *sexual* part of my pronunciation problems, as if sexual speculation (of any kind) was in a category as uninteresting to her as my excellent pronunciation in German. I had an Austrian accent, naturally.

"I think you're as angry at your mother as she is at you," Martha Hadley told me. "At times, Billy, I think you're too angry to speak."

"Oh."

I heard someone coming up the stairs. It was Atkins, still staring at Mrs. Hadley's watch; I was surprised he didn't trip on the stairs. "It hasn't been thirty minutes yet," Atkins reported.

"I'm leaving—you can go in," I told him, but Atkins had paused on the stairs, one step away from the third floor. I passed him as I headed down the stairs.

The stairwell was wide; I must have been close to the ground floor when I heard Mrs. Hadley say, "Please come in."

"But it hasn't been thirty minutes. It's not . . ." Atkins didn't (or couldn't) finish his thought.

"It's not *what?*" I heard Martha Hadley ask him. I remember pausing on the stairs. "I know you can say it," she said gently to him. "You're wearing a tie—you can say *tie,* can't you?"

"It's not . . . *tie,*" Atkins managed.

"Now say *mmm*—like when you eat something good," Mrs. Hadley told him.

"I can't!" Atkins blurted out.

"Please come in," Mrs. Hadley said again.

"It's not *tie—mmm!*" Atkins struggled to say.

"That's good—that's *better*, anyway. Please come in now," Martha Hadley told him, and I continued down the stairs and out of the music building, where I'd also heard snippets of songs, choral voices, and a second-floor segment of stringed instruments, and (on the ground floor) another in-progress piano practice. But my thoughts were entirely on what a loser and an idiot Atkins was—he couldn't pronounce the *time* word! What a fool!

I was halfway across the quad, where Grau had died, when I thought that the hatred of homosexuals was perfectly in tune with my thinking. I couldn't pronounce *penises*, yet here I was feeling utterly superior to a boy who couldn't manage to say *time*.

I remember thinking that, for the rest of my life, I would need to find more people like Martha Hadley, and surround myself with them, but that there would always be other people who would hate and revile me—or even try to cause me physical harm. This thought was as bracing as the winter air that killed Dr. Grau. It was a lot to absorb from one appointment with a sympathetic voice-and-singing teacher—this in addition to my disturbing awareness of Mrs. Hadley as a dominant personality, and that something to do with her dominance appealed to me sexually. Or was there something about her dominance that *didn't* appeal to me? (It only then occurred to me that maybe I wanted to *be* like Mrs. Hadley—that is, sexually—not be *with* her.)

Maybe Martha Hadley was a hippie ahead of her time; the *hippie* word was not in use in 1960. At that time, I'd heard next to no mention of the *gay* word; it was a little-used word in the Favorite River Academy community. Maybe "gay" was too friendly a word for Favorite River—at least it was too neutral a word for all those homo-hating boys. I did know what "gay" meant, of course—it just wasn't said much, in my limited circles—but, as sexually inexperienced as I was, I'd given scant consideration to what was meant by "dominant" and "submissive" in the seemingly unattainable world of gay sex.

NOT THAT MANY YEARS later, when I was living with Larry—of the men and women I've tried to live with, I lasted with Larry the longest—he liked to make fun of me by telling everyone how "shocked" I was at the way he picked me up in that gay coffeehouse, which was such a mysterious place, in Vienna.

This was my junior year abroad. Two years of college German—not to mention my studying the language at Favorite River Academy—had prepared me for a year in a German-speaking country. These same two college years of living in New York City had both prepared me and *not* prepared me for how underground a gay coffeehouse in Vienna would be in that academic year of 1963–64. At that time, the gay bars in New York were being shut down; the New York World's Fair was in '64, and it was the mayor's intention to clean up the city for the tourists. One New York bar, Julius', remained open the whole time—there may have been others—but even at Julius', the men at the bar weren't permitted to touch one another.

I'm not saying Vienna was more underground than New York at that time; the situation was similar. But in that place where Larry picked me up, there was some touching among the men—permitted or not. I just remember it was Larry who shocked me, not Vienna.

"Are you a top or a bottom, beautiful Bill?" Larry had asked me. (I was shocked, but not by the question.)

"A top," I answered, without hesitation.

"Really!" Larry said, either genuinely surprised or feigning surprise; with Larry, this was often hard to tell. "You look like a bottom to me," he said, and after a pause—such a long pause that I'd thought he was going to ask someone else to go home with him—he added, "Come on, Bill, let's leave now."

I was shocked, all right, but only because I was a college student, and Larry was my professor. This was the Institut für Europäische Studien in Vienna—*das Institut*, the students called it. We were Americans, from all over, but our faculty was a mixed bag: some Americans (Larry was by far the best-known among them), one wonderful and eccentric Englishman, and various Austrians from the faculty at the University of Vienna.

In those days, the Institute for European Studies was on that end of the Wollzeile nearest the Doktor-Karl-Lueger-Platz and the Stubenring. The students complained about how far *das Institut* was from the university; many of our students (the ones with better German) took additional courses at the University of Vienna. Not me; I wasn't interested in more courses. I'd gone to college in New York because I wanted to be in New York; I was studying abroad in Vienna to be in Vienna. I didn't care how near to or far from the university I was.

My German was good enough to get me hired at an excellent restaurant on the Weihburggasse—near the opposite end of the Kärntnerstrasse from the opera. It was called Zufall ("Coincidence"), and I got the job both because I had worked as a waiter in New York and because, shortly after I arrived in Vienna, I learned that the only English-speaking waiter at Zufall had been fired.

I'd heard the story in that mysterious gay coffeehouse on the Doro-theergasse—one of those side streets off the Graben. The Kaffee Käfig, it was called—the "Coffee Cage." During the day, it appeared to be mostly a student hangout; there were girls there, too—in fact, it was daytime when a girl told me that the waiter at Zufall had been fired. But after dark, the older men showed up at the Kaffee Käfig, and there weren't any girls around. That was how it was the night I ran into Larry, and he popped the top-or-bottom question.

That first fall term at the Institute, I was not one of Larry's students. He was teaching the plays of Sophocles. Larry was a poet, and I wanted to be a novelist—I thought I was done with theater, and I didn't write poems. But I knew that Larry was a respected writer, and I'd asked him if he would consider offering a writing course—in either the winter or the spring term, in '64.

"Oh, God—not a *creative* writing class!" Larry said. "I know—don't tell me. One day, creative writing will be taught *everywhere!*"

"I just wanted to be able to show my writing to another writer," I told him. "I'm not a poet," I admitted. "I'm a fiction writer. I understand if you're not interested." I was walking away—I was trying to look hurt—when he stopped me.

"Wait, wait—what is your name, young *fiction* writer?" Larry asked. "I do *read* fiction," he told me.

I told him my name—I said "Bill," because Miss Frost owned the *William* name. (I would publish my novels under the name William Abbott, but I let no one else call me William.)

"Well, Bill—let me think about it," Larry said. I knew then that he was gay, and everything else he was thinking, but I wouldn't become his student until January 1964, when he offered a creative writing course at the Institute in the winter term.

Larry was the already-distinguished poet—*Lawrence* Upton, to his colleagues and students, but his gay friends (and a coterie of lady admir-ers) called him Larry. By then, I'd been with a few older men—I'd not lived with them, but they'd been my lovers—and I knew who I was when it came to the top-or-bottom business.

It was not the crudeness of Larry's top-or-bottom question that shocked me; even his first-time students knew that Lawrence Upton was a famous snob who could also be notoriously crass. It was simply that my teacher, who was such a renowned literary figure, had hit on me—*that* shocked me. But that was never how Larry told the story, and there was no contradicting him.

According to Larry, he *hadn't* asked me if I was a top or a bottom. "In the sixties, dear Bill, we did not say 'top' and 'bottom'—we said 'pitcher' and 'catcher,' though of course you *Vermonters* might have been prescient," Larry said, "or so far ahead of the rest of us that you were already asking, 'Plus or minus?' while we less-progressive types were still stuck with the pitcher-or-catcher question, which soon *would become* the top-or-bottom question. Just not in the sixties, dear Bill. In Vienna, when I picked you up, I *know* I asked you if you were a pitcher or a catcher."

Then, turning from me to our friends—*his* friends, for the most part; both in Vienna and later, back in New York, most of Larry's friends were older than I was—Larry would say, "Bill is a *fiction* writer, but he writes in the first-person voice in a style that is tell-all confessional; in fact, his fiction sounds as much like a memoir as he can make it sound."

Then, turning back to me—just me, as if we were alone—Larry would say, "Yet you insist on anachronisms, dear Bill—in the sixties, the *top* and *bottom* words are anachronisms."

That was Larry; that was how he talked—he was always right. I learned not to argue about the smaller stuff. I would say, "Yes, Professor," because if I'd said he was mistaken, that he had absolutely used the *top* and *bottom* words, Larry would have made another crack about my being from Vermont, or he would have shot the breeze about my saying I was a pitcher when, all along, I'd looked like a catcher to him. (Didn't everyone think I looked like a catcher? Larry would usually ask his friends.)

The poet Lawrence Upton was of that generation of older gay men who basically believed that most gay men were bottoms, no matter what they said—or that those of us who *said* we were tops would eventually be bottoms. Since Larry and I met in Vienna, our enduring disagreement concerning exactly what was said on our first "date" was further clouded by what many Europeans felt in the sixties, and still feel today—namely, that we Americans make entirely too much of the top-or-bottom business. The Europeans have always believed we were too rigid about these distinctions, as if everyone gay is either one or the other—as some young, cocksure types tell me nowadays.

Larry—who was a bottom, if I ever knew one—could be both petu-
lant and coy about how misunderstood he was. "I'm more versatile than
you are!" he once said to me, in tears. "You may say you also like women,
or you pretend that you do, but I'm not the truly inflexible one in this
relationship!"

By the late seventies, in New York, when we were still seeing each
other but no longer living together—Larry called the seventies the "Bliss-
ful Age of Promiscuity"—you could only be absolutely sure of someone's
sexual role in those overobvious leather bars, where a hankie in the back
left pocket meant you were a top, and a hankie in the back right pocket
signified that you were a bottom. A blue hankie was for fucking, a red
one was for fist-fucking—well, what does it matter anymore? There was
also that utterly annoying signal concerning where you clipped your
keys—to the belt loop to the right or left of the belt buckle on your
jeans. In New York, I paid no attention to where I clipped my keys; I was
always getting hit on by some signal-conscious top, and I was a top! (It
could be irritating.)

Even in the late seventies, almost a decade after gay liberation, the
older gays—I mean not only older than me but also older than Larry—
would complain about the top-or-bottom advertising. ("Why do you guys
want to take all the mystery away? Isn't the mystery an exciting part of
sex?")

I liked to look like a gay boy—or enough like one to make other
gay boys, and men, look twice at me. But I wanted the girls and women
to wonder about me—to make them look twice at me, too. I wanted to
retain something provocatively masculine in my appearance. ("Are you
trying to look *toppish* tonight?" Larry once asked me. Yes, maybe I was.)

I remembered, when we were rehearsing *The Tempest*, how Richard
had said that Ariel's gender was "mutable"; he'd said the sex of angels
was mutable, too.

"Director's choice?" Kittredge had asked Richard, about Ariel's mu-
tability.

I suppose I was trying to look sexually *mutable*, to capture something
of Ariel's unresolved sexuality. I knew I was small but good-looking. I
could also be invisible when I wanted to be—like Ariel, I could be "an
airy Spirit." There is no one way to *look* bisexual, but that was the look
I sought.

Larry liked to make fun of me for having what he called a "Utopian notion of androgyny"; for his generation, I think that so-called liberated gays were no longer supposed to be "sissies." I know that Larry thought I looked (and dressed) like a sissy—that was probably why I looked like a bottom to him, not a top.

But I saw myself as an almost regular guy; by "regular," I mean only that I was never into leather or the bullshit hankie code. In New York— as in most cities, through the seventies—there was a lot of street cruising. Then, and now, I liked the androgynous look—nor were *androgynous* and *androgyny* ever words that gave me pronunciation problems.

"You're a pretty boy, Bill," Larry often said to me, "but don't think you can stay ultra-thin forever. Don't imagine that you can dress like a razor blade, or even in drag, and have any real effect on the macho codes you're rebelling against. You won't change what real men are like, nor will you ever be one!"

"Yes, Professor," was all I usually said.

In the fabulous seventies, when I picked up a guy, or I let myself be picked up, there was always that moment when my hand got hold of his butt; if he liked to be fucked, he would start moaning and writhing around—just to let me know I'd hit the magic spot. But if he turned out to be a top, we would settle for a super-fast 69 and call it a night; sometimes, this would turn into a super-*rough* 69. (The "macho codes," as Larry called them, might prevail. My "Utopian notion of androgyny" might not.)

It was Larry's formidable jealousy that eventually drove me away from him; even when you're as young as I was, there's a limit to enduring admiration being a substitute for love. When Larry thought I'd been with someone else, he would try to touch my asshole—to feel if I was wet, or at least lubricated. "I'm a top, remember?" I used to tell him. "You should be sniffing my cock instead." But Larry's jealousy was insanely illogical; even knowing me as well as he did, he actually believed I was capable of being a bottom with someone else.

When I met Larry in Vienna, he was making himself a student of opera there—the opera was why he'd come. The opera was partly why I'd chosen Vienna, too. After all, Miss Frost had made me a devoted reader of nineteenth-century novels. The operas I loved *were* nineteenth-century novels!

Lawrence Upton was a well-established poet, but he'd always wanted to write a libretto. ("After all, Bill, I know how to *rhyme*.") Larry had this wish to write a gay opera. He was very strict with himself as a poet; maybe he imagined he could be more relaxed as a librettist. He may have wanted to write a gay opera, but Lawrence Upton never wrote an openly gay poem—that used to piss me off, more than a little.

In Larry's opera, some cynical queen—someone a lot like Larry—is the narrator. The narrator sings a lament—it's deliberately foolish, and I forget how it rhymes. "Too many Indians, not enough chiefs," the narrator laments. "Too many chickens, not enough roosters." It was very relaxed, all right.

There is a chorus of bottoms—*numerous* bottoms, naturally—and a comically much-smaller chorus of tops. If Larry had continued his opera, it's possible he would have added a medium-size chorus of bears, but the bear movement didn't begin until the mid-eighties—those big hairy guys, consciously sloppy, rebelling against the chiseled, neat-and-trim men, with their shaved balls and gym bodies. (Those bears were so refreshing, at first.)

Needless to say, Larry's libretto was never made as an opera; his career as a librettist was abandoned in-progress. Larry would be remembered only as a poet, though I remember his gay-opera idea—and those many nights at the Staatsoper, the vast Vienna State Opera, when I was still so young.

It was a valuable lesson for the young would-be writer that I was: to see a great man, an accomplished poet, fail. You must be careful when you stray from an acquired discipline—when I first hooked up with Larry, I was still learning that writing is such a discipline. Opera may be a flamboyant form of storytelling, but a librettist also follows some rules; good writing isn't "relaxed."

To Larry's credit, he was the first to acknowledge his failure as a librettist. That was a valuable lesson, too. "When you compromise your standards, Bill, don't blame the form. Opera is not at fault. I'm not the victim of this failure, Bill—I'm the perpetrator."

You can learn a lot from your lovers, but—for the most part—you get to keep your friends longer, and you learn more from them. (At least I have.) I would even say that my friend Elaine's mother, Martha Hadley, had a greater influence on me than Lawrence Upton truly had.

In fact, at Favorite River Academy, where I was a junior in the winter of 1960—and, Vermont boy that I was, given my naïveté—I had never heard the *top* or *bottom* words used in that way Larry (or any number of my gay friends and lovers) would later use them, but I knew I was a top before I'd ever had sex with anyone.

That day I made my partial confession to Martha Hadley, when Mrs. Hadley's obvious dominance made such a strong but bewildering impression on me, I absolutely knew that I ceaselessly desired fucking other boys and men, but always with my penis in their bottoms; I never desired the penis of another boy or man penetrating me. (In my mouth, yes—in my asshole, no.)

Even as I desired Kittredge, I knew this much about myself: I wanted to fuck him, and to take his penis in my mouth, but I didn't want him to fuck me. Knowing Kittredge, how utterly crazy I was, because if Kittredge were ever to entertain the possibility of a gay relationship, it was painfully clear to me what he would be. If Kittredge was gay, he sure looked like a top to me.

IT'S REVEALING HOW I have skipped ahead to my junior year abroad in Vienna, choosing to begin that interlude in my future life by telling you about Larry. You might think I should have begun that Vienna interlude by telling you about my first actual girlfriend, Esmeralda Soler, because I met Esmeralda shortly after I arrived in Vienna (in September of 1963), and I'd been living with Esmeralda for several months before I became Larry's writing student—and, not long after that, Larry's lover.

But I believe I know why I have waited to tell you about Esmeralda. It's all too common for gay men of my generation to say how much easier it is today to "come out" as a teenager. What I want to tell you is: At that age, it's never easy.

In my case, I had felt ashamed of my sexual longings for other boys and men; I'd fought against those feelings. Perhaps you think I've overemphasized my attraction to Miss Frost and Mrs. Hadley in a desperate effort to be "normal"; maybe you have the idea that I was never really attracted to women. But I *was*—I *am* attracted to women. It was just that—at Favorite River Academy, especially, no doubt because it was an all-boys' school—I had to suppress my attraction to other boys and men.

After that summer in Europe with Tom, when I'd graduated from Favorite River, and later, when I was on my own—in college, in New York—I was finally able to acknowledge the homosexual side of myself. (Yes, I *will* say more about Tom; it's just that Tom is so difficult.) And after Tom, I had *many* relationships with men. When I was nineteen and twenty—I turned twenty-one in March of '63, shortly before I learned I'd been accepted to the Institute for European Studies in Vienna—I had already "come out." When I went to Vienna, I'd been living in New York City as a young gay guy for two years.

It *wasn't* that I was no longer attracted to women; I *was* attracted to them. But to give in to my attractions to women struck me as a kind of going back to being the repressed gay boy I'd been. Not to mention the fact that, at the time, my gay friends and lovers *all* believed that anyone calling himself a bisexual man was really just a gay guy with one foot in the closet. (I suppose—when I was nineteen and twenty, and had only recently turned twenty-one—there was a part of me that believed this, too.)

Yet I knew I was bisexual—as surely as I'd known I was attracted to Kittredge, and exactly how I was attracted to him. But in my late teens and early twenties, I was holding back on my attractions to women—as I'd once repressed my desires for other boys and men. Even at such a young age, I must have sensed that bisexual men were not trusted; perhaps we never will be, but we certainly weren't trusted then.

I was never ashamed of being attracted to women, but once I'd had gay lovers—and, in New York, I had an ever-increasing number of gay friends—I quickly learned that being attracted to women made me distrusted and suspected, or even feared, by other gay guys. So I held back, or I was quiet about it; I just *looked* at a lot of women. (That summer of '61 in Europe—when I was traveling with Tom—poor Tom had caught me looking.)

WE WERE A SMALL group: I mean the American students who'd been accepted to the Institut für Europäische Studien in Vienna for the academic year of 1963–64. We boarded one of the cruise ships in New York Harbor and made the trans-Atlantic crossing—as Tom and I had done, two summers before. I quickly concluded that there were no gay boys among the Institute's students that year, or none who'd come out—or no one who interested me, in that way.

We traveled by bus across Western Europe to Vienna—vastly more educational sightseeing, in a hasty two weeks, than Tom and I had managed in an entire summer. I had no history with my fellow junior-year-abroad students. I made some friends—straight boys and girls, or so they seemed to me. I thought about a few of the girls, but even before we arrived in Vienna, I decided it was an awfully small group; it really wouldn't have been smart to sleep with one of the Institute girls. Besides, I had already initiated the fiction that I was "trying to be" faithful to a girlfriend back in the States. I'd established to my fellow Institut students that I was a straight guy, apparently inclined to keep to myself.

When I landed that job as the only English-speaking waiter at Zufall on the Weihburggasse, my aloofness from the Institute for European Studies was complete—it was too expensive a restaurant for my fellow students to ever eat there. Except for attending my classes on the Doktor-Karl-Lueger-Platz, I could continue to act out the adventure of being a young writer in a foreign country—namely, that most necessary exercise of finding the time to be alone.

It was an accident that I ever met Esmeralda. I'd noticed her at the opera; this was both because of her size (tall, broad-shouldered girls and women attracted me) and because she took notes. She stood at the rear of the Staatsoper, scribbling furiously. The first night I saw Esmeralda, I mistook her for a critic; though she was only three years older than I was (Esmeralda was twenty-four in the fall of '63), she looked older than that.

When I continued to see her—she was always standing in the rear—I realized that if she were a critic, she would at least have had a seat. But she stood in the back, like me and the other students. In those days, if you were a student, you were welcome to stand in the back; for students, standing room at the opera was free.

The Staatsoper dominated the intersection of the Kärntnerstrasse and the Opernring. The opera house was less than a ten-minute walk from Zufall. When there was a show at the Staatsoper, Zufall had two dinner seatings. We served an early supper before the opera, and we served a later, more extravagant dinner afterward. When I worked both seatings, which was the case most nights, I got to the opera after the first act had begun, and I left before the final act was finished.

One night, during an intermission, Esmeralda spoke to me. I must have looked like an American, which deeply disappointed me, because she spoke to me in English.

"What is it with you?" Esmeralda asked me. "You're always late and you always leave early!" (She was clearly American; as it turned out, she was from Ohio.)

"I have a job—I'm a waiter," I told her. "What is it with *you*? How come you're always taking notes? Are you trying to be a writer? *I'm* trying to be one," I admitted.

"I'm just an understudy—I'm trying to be a *soprano*," Esmeralda said. "You're trying to be a writer," she repeated slowly. (I was immediately drawn to her.)

One night, when I wasn't working the late shift at Zufall, I stayed at the opera till the final curtain, and I proposed that I walk Esmeralda home.

"But I don't want to go 'home'—I don't like where I live. I don't spend much time there," Esmeralda said.

"Oh."

I didn't like where I lived in Vienna, either—I also didn't spend much time there. But I worked at that restaurant on the Weihburggasse most nights; I wasn't, as yet, very knowledgeable about where to go in Vienna at night.

I brought Esmeralda to that gay coffeehouse on the Dorotheergasse; it was near the Staatsoper, and I'd been there only in the daytime, when there were mostly students hanging out—girls included. I hadn't learned that the nighttime clientele at the Kaffee Käfig was all-male, all-gay.

It took Esmeralda and me little time to recognize my mistake. "It's not like this during the day," I told her, as we were leaving. (Thank God Larry wasn't there that night, because I'd already approached him about teaching a writing course at the Institute; Larry had not yet told me his decision.)

Esmeralda was laughing about me taking her to the Kaffee Käfig— "for our first date!" she exclaimed, as we walked up the Graben to the Kohlmarkt. There was a coffeehouse on the Kohlmarkt; I'd not been there, but it looked expensive.

"There's a place I know in my neighborhood," Esmeralda said. "We could go there, and *then* you could walk me home."

To our mutual surprise, we lived in the same neighborhood—across the Ringstrasse, away from the first district, in the vicinity of the Karls-kirche. At the corner of the Argentinierstrasse and the Schwindgasse, there was a café-bar—like so many in Vienna. It was a coffeehouse and a bar; it was my neighborhood place, too, I was telling Esmeralda as we sat down. (I often wrote there.)

Thus we began to describe our less-than-happy living situations. It turned out that we both lived on the Schwindgasse, in the same building. Esmeralda had more of an actual apartment than I did. She had a bed-room, her own bathroom, and a tiny kitchen, but she shared a front hall with her landlady; almost every night, when Esmeralda came "home," she had to pass her landlady's living room, where the old and disapproving woman was ensconced on her couch with her small, disagreeable dog. (They were always watching television.)

The drone from the TV could be constantly heard from Esmeralda's bedroom, where she listened to operas (usually, in German) on an old phonograph. She'd been instructed to play her music softly, though "softly" wasn't suitable for opera. The opera was sufficiently loud to mask the sound from the landlady's television, and Esmeralda listened and listened to the German, singing to herself—also softly. She needed to improve her German accent, she'd told me.

Because I needed to improve my German grammar and word order—not to mention my vocabulary—I instantly foresaw how Esmeralda and I could help each other. My accent was the only aspect of my German that was better than Esmeralda's.

The waitstaff at Zufall had tried to prepare me: When the fall was over—when the winter came, and the tourists were gone—there would be nights when there'd be no English-speaking customers in the restaurant. I had better improve my German before the winter months, they had warned me. The Austrians weren't kind to foreigners. In Vienna, *Ausländer* ("foreigner") was never said nicely; there was something truly xenophobic about the Viennese.

At that café-bar on the Argentinierstrasse, I began to describe my living situation to Esmeralda—in German. We'd already decided that we should speak German to each other.

Esmeralda had a Spanish name—*esmeralda* means "emerald" in Spanish—but she didn't speak Spanish. Her mother was Italian, and Esmeralda spoke (and sang) Italian, but if she wanted to be an opera singer, she had to improve her German accent. She said it was a joke at the Staatsoper that she was a soprano understudy—a soprano "in-waiting," Esmeralda called herself. If they ever let her onstage in Vienna, it would happen only if the regular soprano—the "starting" soprano, Esmeralda called her—*died*. (Or if the opera was in Italian.)

Even as she told me this in grammatically perfect German, I could hear strong shades of Cleveland in her accent. A music teacher in a Cleveland elementary school had discovered that Esmeralda could sing; she'd gone to Oberlin on a scholarship. Esmeralda's junior year abroad had been in Milan; she'd had a student internship at La Scala, and had fallen in love with Italian opera.

But Esmeralda said that German felt like chips of wood in her mouth. Her father had run out on her and her mother; he'd gone to Argentina, where he met another woman. Esmeralda had concluded that the woman her father hooked up with in Argentina must have had Nazi ancestors.

"What else could explain why I can't handle the accent?" Esmeralda asked me. "I've studied the shit out of German!"

I still think about the bonds that drew Esmeralda and me together: We each had absconding fathers, we lived in the same building on the Schwindgasse, and we were talking about all this in a café-bar on the Argentinierstrasse—in our flawed German. *Unglaublich!* ("Unbelievable!")

The Institute students were housed all over Vienna. It was common to have your own bedroom but to share a bathroom; a remarkable number of our students had widows for landladies, and no kitchen privileges. I had a widow for a landlady and my own bedroom, and I shared a bathroom with the widow's divorced daughter and the divorcée's five-year-old son, Siegfried. The kitchen was in constant, chaotic use, but I was permitted to make coffee for myself there, and I kept some beer in the fridge.

My widowed landlady wept regularly; day and night, she shuffled around in an unraveling terry-cloth bathrobe. The divorcée was a big-breasted, take-charge sort of woman; it wasn't her fault that she reminded me of my bossy aunt Muriel. The five-year-old, Siegfried, had a sly, demonic way of staring at me; he ate a soft-boiled egg for breakfast every morning—including the eggshell.

The first time I saw Siegfried do this, I went immediately to my bedroom and consulted my English-German dictionary. (I didn't know the German for "eggshell.") When I told Siegfried's mother that her five-year-old had eaten the shell, she shrugged and said it was probably better for him than the egg. In the mornings, when I made my coffee and watched little Siegfried eat his soft-boiled egg, shell and all, the divorcée was usually dressed in a slovenly manner, in a loose-fitting pair of men's pajamas—conceivably belonging to her ex-husband. There were always too many unbuttoned buttons, and Siegfried's mother had a deplorable habit of scratching herself.

What was funny about the bathroom we shared was that the door had a peephole, which is common on hotel-room doors, but not on bathroom doors. I speculated that the peephole had been installed in the bathroom door so that someone leaving the bathroom—perhaps half-naked, or wrapped in a towel—could see if the coast was clear in the hall (if someone was *out there*, in other words). But why? Who would want or need to walk around naked in the hall, even if the coast was clear?

This mystery was aggravated by the curious fact that the peephole cylinder on the bathroom door could be reversed. I discovered that the cylinder was *often* reversed; the reversal became commonplace—you could peek into the bathroom from the hall, and plainly see who was there and what he or she was doing!

Try explaining *that* to someone in German, and you'll see how good or bad your German is, but all of this I somehow managed to tell Esmeralda—in German—on our first date.

"Holy cow!" Esmeralda said at one point, in English. Her skin had a milky-coffee color, and there was the faintest, softest trace of a mustache on her upper lip. She had jet-black hair, and her dark-brown eyes were almost black. Her hands were bigger than mine—she was a little taller than I was, too—but her breasts (to my relief) were "normal," which to me meant "noticeably smaller" than the rest of her.

Okay—I'll say it. If I had hesitated to have my first actual girlfriend experience, a part of the reason was that I'd discovered I *liked* anal intercourse. (I liked it a *lot!*) No doubt there was a part of me that feared what *vaginal* intercourse might be like.

That summer in Europe with Tom—when poor Tom became so insecure and felt so threatened, when all I really did was just look at girls and women—I remember saying, with no small amount of exasperation, "For Christ's sake, Tom—haven't you noticed how much I *like* anal sex? What do you think I imagine making love to a *vagina* would be like? Maybe like having sex with a *ballroom!*"

Naturally, it had been the *vagina* word that sent poor Tom to the bathroom—where I could hear him gagging. But although I'd only been kidding, it was the *ballroom* word that had stuck with me. I couldn't get it out of my mind. What if having vaginal sex *was* like making love to a ballroom? Yet I continued to be attracted to larger-than-average women.

Our less-than-ideal living situations were not the only obstacles that stood between Esmeralda and me. We had cautiously visited each other, in our respective rooms.

"I can deal with the reverse-peephole-bathroom-door thing," Esmeralda had told me, "but that kid gives me the creeps." She called Siegfried "the eggshell-eater"; as my relationship with Esmeralda developed, though, it would turn out that it wasn't Siegfried, per se, who creeped out Esmeralda.

Far more disturbing to Esmeralda than that reverse-peephole-bathroom-door thing was the bigger thing she had about kids. She was terrified of having one; like many young women at that time, Esmeralda was preternaturally afraid of getting pregnant—for good reasons.

If Esmeralda got pregnant, that would be the end to her career hopes of becoming an opera singer. "I'm not ready to be a housewife soprano," was how she put it to me. We both knew there were countries in Europe where it was possible to get an abortion. (Not Austria, a Catholic country.) But, for the most part, abortion was unavailable—or unsafe and illegal. We knew that, too. Besides, Esmeralda's Italian mother was *very* Catholic; Esmeralda would have had misgivings about getting an abortion, even if the procedure had been available and safe *and* legal.

"There isn't a condom made that can keep me from getting knocked up," Esmeralda told me. "I am fertile times ten."

"How do you know that?" I'd asked her.

"I *feel* fertile, all the time—I just *know* it," she said.

"Oh."

We were sitting chastely on her bed; the pregnancy terror stuck me as an insurmountable obstacle. The decision, in regard to which bedroom we might try to *do it* in, had been made for us; if we were going to live together, we would share Esmeralda's small apartment. My weeping widow had complained to the Institute; I'd been accused of reversing the peephole thing on the bathroom door! *Das Institut* accepted my claim that I was innocent of this deviant behavior, but I had to move out.

"I'll bet it was the eggshell-eater," Esmeralda had said. I didn't argue with her, but little Siegfried would have had to stand on a stool or a chair just to reach the stupid peephole. My bet was on the divorcée with the unbuttoned buttons.

Esmeralda's landlady was happy to have the extra rent money; she'd probably never imagined that Esmeralda's apartment, which had such a tiny kitchen, could be shared by two people, but Esmeralda and I never cooked—we always ate out.

Esmeralda said that her landlady's disposition had improved since I'd moved in; if the old woman frowned upon Esmeralda having a live-in boyfriend, the extra rent money seemed to soften her disfavor. Even the disagreeable dog had accepted me.

That same night when Esmeralda and I sat, not touching, on her bed, the old lady had invited us into her living room; she'd wanted us to see that she and her dog were watching an *American* movie on the television. Both Esmeralda and I were still in culture shock; it's not easy to recover from hearing Gary Cooper speak German. "How could they have dubbed *High Noon?*" I kept saying.

The drone from the TV wafted over us in Esmeralda's bedroom. Tex Ritter was singing "Do Not Forsake Me."

"At least they didn't *dub* Tex Ritter," Esmeralda was saying, when I— very tentatively—touched her perfect breasts. "Here's the thing, Billy," she said, letting me touch her. (I could tell she'd said this before; in the past, I would learn, this speech had been a boyfriend-stopper. Not this time.)

I'd not noticed the condom until she handed it to me—it was still in its shiny foil wrapper. "You have to wear this, Billy—even if the damn thing breaks, it's cleaner."

"Okay," I said, taking the condom.

"But the thing is—this is the hard part, Billy—you can only do *anal*. That's the only intercourse I allow—anal," she repeated, this time in a shameful whisper. "I know it's a compromise for you, but that's just how it is. It's anal or nothing," Esmeralda told me.

"Oh."

"I understand if that's not for you, Billy," she said.

I shouldn't say too much, I was thinking. What she proposed was hardly a "compromise" for me—I *loved* anal intercourse! As for "anal or nothing" being a boyfriend-stopper—on the contrary, I was relieved. The dreaded *ballroom* experience was once more postponed! I knew I had to be careful—not to appear too enthusiastic.

It wasn't completely a lie, when I said, "I'm a little nervous—it's my first time." (Okay, so I didn't add "with a woman"—okay, okay!)

Esmeralda turned on her phonograph. She put on that famous '61 recording of Donizetti's *Lucia di Lammermoor*—with Joan Sutherland as the crazed soprano. (I then understood that this was not a night when Esmeralda was focusing on improving her German accent.) Donizetti was certainly more romantic background music than Tex Ritter.

Thus I excitedly embarked on my first girlfriend experience—the compromise, which was no compromise for me, being that the sex was "anal or nothing." The *or-nothing* part wasn't strictly true; we would have lots of oral sex. I wasn't afraid of oral sex, and Esmeralda *loved* it—it made her sing, she said.

Thus I was introduced to a vagina, with one restriction; only the ballroom (or not-a-ballroom) part was withheld—and for that part I was content, even happy, to wait. For someone who had long viewed that part with trepidation, I was introduced to a vagina in ways I found most intriguing and appealing. I truly loved having sex with Esmeralda, and I loved *her,* too.

There were those après-sex moments when, in a half-sleep or forgetting that I was with a woman, I would reach out and touch her vagina—only to suddenly pull back my hand, as if surprised. (I had been reaching for Esmeralda's penis.)

"Poor Billy," Esmeralda would say, misunderstanding my fleeting touch; she was thinking that I wanted to be *inside* her vagina, that I was feeling a pang for all that was denied me.

"I'm not 'poor Billy'—I'm *happy* Billy, I'm *fully satisfied* Billy," I always told her.

"You're a very good sport," Esmeralda would say. She had no idea how happy I was, and when I reached out and touched her vagina—in my sleep, sometimes, or otherwise unconsciously—Esmeralda had no clue what I was reaching for, which was what she didn't have and what I must have been missing.

DER OBERKELLNER ("THE HEADWAITER") at Zufall was a stern-looking young man who seemed older than he was. He'd lost an eye and wore an eye patch; he was not yet thirty, but either the eye patch or how he'd lost the eye gave him the gravity of a much older man. His name was Karl, and he never talked about losing the eye—the other waiters had told me the story: At the end of World War II, when Karl was ten, he'd seen some Russian soldiers raping his mother and had tried to intervene. One of the Russians had hit the boy with his rifle, and the blow cost Karl his sight in one eye.

Late that fall of my junior year abroad—it was nearing the end of November—Esmeralda was given her first chance to be the lead soprano on the tripartite stage of the Staatsoper. As she'd predicted, it was an Italian opera—Verdi's *Macbeth*—and Esmeralda, who'd been patiently waiting her turn (actually, she'd been thinking that her turn would never come), had been the soprano understudy for Lady Macbeth for most of that fall (in fact, for as long as we'd been living together).

"*Vieni, t'affretta!*" I'd heard Esmeralda sing in her sleep—when Lady

Macbeth reads the letter from her husband, telling her about his first meeting with the witches.

I asked Karl for permission to leave the restaurant's first seating early, and to get to the après-opera seating late; my girlfriend was going to be Lady Macbeth on Friday night.

"You have a girlfriend—the understudy really is your girlfriend, correct?" Karl asked me.

"Yes, that's correct, Karl," I told him.

"I'm glad to hear it, Bill—there's been talk to the contrary," Karl said, his one eye transfixing me.

"Esmeralda is my girlfriend, and she's singing the part of Lady Macbeth this Friday," I told the headwaiter.

"That's a one-and-only chance, Bill—don't let her blow it," Karl said.

"I just don't want to miss the beginning—and I want to stay till the end, Karl," I said.

"Of course, of course. I know it's a Friday, but we're not that busy. The warm weather is gone. Like the leaves, the tourists are dropping off. This might be the last weekend we really *need* an English-speaking waiter, but we can manage without you, Bill," Karl told me. He had a way of making me feel bad, even when he was on my side. Karl made me think of Lady Macbeth calling on the ministers of hell.

"*Or tutti sorgete.*" I'd heard Esmeralda sing that in her sleep, too; it was chilling, and of no help to my German.

"*Fatal mia donna!*" Lady Macbeth says to her weakling husband; she takes the dagger Macbeth has used to kill Duncan and smears the sleeping guards with blood. I couldn't wait to see Esmeralda pussy-whipping Macbeth! And all this happens in act 1. No wonder I didn't want to arrive late—I didn't want to miss a minute of the witches.

"I'm very proud of you, Bill. I mean, for having a girlfriend—not just that big soprano of a girlfriend, but *any* girlfriend. That should silence the talk," Karl told me.

"Who's talking, Karl?" I asked him.

"Some of the other waiters, one of the sous-chefs—you know how people talk, Bill."

"Oh."

In truth, if anyone in the kitchen at Zufall needed proof that I *wasn't* gay, it was probably Karl; if there'd been talk that I *was* gay, I'm sure Karl was the one doing the talking.

I'd kept an eye on Esmeralda when she was sleeping. If Lady Macbeth made a nightly appearance as a sleepwalker, in act 4—lamenting that there was still blood on her hands—Esmeralda never sleepwalked. She was sound asleep, and lying down, when she sang (almost every night) *"Una macchia."*

The lead soprano, who was taking Friday night off, had a singer's polyp in the area of her vocal cords; while this was not uncommon for opera singers, much attention had been paid to Gerda Mühle's tiny polyp. (Should the polyp be surgically removed or not?)

Esmeralda worshipped Gerda Mühle; her voice was resonant, yet never forced, through an impressive range. Gerda Mühle could be vibrant but effortless from a low G to dizzying flights above high C. Her soprano voice was large and heavy enough for Wagner, yet Mühle could also manage the requisite agility for the swift runs and complicated trills of the early-nineteenth-century Italian style. But Esmeralda had told me that Gerda Mühle was a pain in the ass about her polyp.

"It's taken over her life—it's taking over *all* our lives," Esmeralda said. She'd gone from worshipping Gerda Mühle, the soprano, to hating Gerda Mühle, the woman—the "Polyp," Esmeralda now called her.

On Friday night, the Polyp was resting her vocal cords. Esmeralda was excited to be getting what she called her "first start" at the Staatsoper. But Esmeralda was dismissive of Gerda Mühle's polyp. Back in Cleveland, Esmeralda had endured a sinus surgery—a risky one for a would-be singer. As a teenager, Esmeralda's nasal passages were chronically clogged; she sometimes wondered if that sinus surgery was responsible for the persistent American accent in her German. Esmeralda had zero sympathy for Gerda Mühle making such a big deal out of her singer's polyp.

I'd learned to ignore the jokes among the kitchen crew and the waitstaff about what it was like to have a soprano for a girlfriend. Everyone teased me about this except Karl—he didn't kid around.

"It must be *loud*, at times," the chef at Zufall had said, to general laughter in the kitchen.

I didn't tell them, of course, that Esmeralda had orgasms only when I went down on her. By her own account, Esmeralda's orgasms were "pretty spectacular," but I was shielded from the sound. Esmeralda's thighs were clamped against my ears; I truly heard nothing.

"God, I think I just hit a high E-flat—and I really *held* it!" Esmeralda said, after one of her more prolonged orgasms, but my ears were warm and sweaty, and my head had been held so tightly between her thighs that I hadn't heard anything.

I don't remember what the weather was like in Vienna on this particular November Friday. I just remember that when Esmeralda left our little apartment on the Schwindgasse, she was wearing her JFK campaign button. It was her good-luck charm, she'd told me. She was very proud of volunteering for Kennedy's election campaign in Ohio in 1960; Esmeralda had been hugely pissed off when Ohio, by a narrow margin, went Republican. (Ohio had voted for Nixon.)

I wasn't as political as Esmeralda. In 1963, I believed I was too intent on becoming a writer to have a political life; I'd said something terribly lofty-sounding to Esmeralda about that. I told her that I wasn't hedging my bets about becoming a writer—I said that political involvement was a way that young people left the door open to failing in their artistic endeavors, or some such bullshit.

"Do you mean, Billy, that *because* I'm more politically involved than you, I don't *care* about making it as a soprano as much as you care about being a writer?" Esmeralda asked me.

"Of course I don't mean *that!*" I answered.

What I should have told her, but I didn't dare, was that I was bisexual. It wasn't my *writing* that kept me from being politically involved; it was that, in 1963, my dual sexuality was all the politics I could handle. Believe me: When you're twenty-one, there's a lot of politics involved in being sexually *mutable*.

That said, on this November Friday, I would soon regret I'd ever given Esmeralda the idea that I thought she was hedging her bets about becoming a soprano—or leaving the door open to failing as an opera singer—*because* she was such a political person.

FOR THE FIRST SEATING at Zufall, there were more Americans among the clientele than either Karl or I had expected. There were no other foreign tourists—no English-speaking ones, anyway—but there were several American couples past retirement age, and a table of ten obstetricians and gynecologists (all of them Americans) who told me they were in Vienna for an OB-GYN conference.

I got a generous tip from the doctors, because I told them they'd picked a good opera for obstetricians and gynecologists. I explained that part in *Macbeth* (act 3) when the witches conjure up a bloody child—the child famously tells Macbeth that "none of woman born" can harm him. (Of course, Macbeth is screwed. Macduff, who kills Macbeth, announces that he had a caesarean birth.)

"It's possibly the only opera with a c-section theme," I told the OB-GYN table of ten.

Karl was telling everyone that my girlfriend was the soprano singing the Lady Macbeth part tonight, so I was pretty popular with the early-seating crowd, and Karl made good on his promise to let me leave the restaurant in plenty of time for the start of act 1. But something was wrong.

I had the weird impression that the audience wouldn't settle down—especially the uncouth Americans. One couple seemed on the verge of a divorce; she was sobbing, and nothing her husband had to say could soothe her. I'm guessing that many of you know which Friday night this was—it was November 22, 1963. It was 12:30 P.M., Central Standard Time, when President Kennedy was shot in Dallas. I was seven hours ahead of Texas time in Vienna, and *Macbeth*—to my surprise—didn't start on time. Esmeralda had told me that the Staatsoper always started on time, but not this night.

I couldn't have known, but things were as unsettled backstage as they appeared to me in the audience. The American couple I'd identified as headed for a divorce had already left; both of them were inconsolable. Now there were other Americans who seemed in distress. I suddenly noticed the empty seats. Poor Esmeralda! It was her debut, but it wasn't a full house. (It would have been 1 P.M. in Dallas when JFK died—8 P.M. in Vienna.)

When the curtain simply would not open on that barren heath in Scotland, I began to worry about Esmeralda. Was she suffering from stage fright? Had she lost her voice? Had Gerda Mühle changed her mind about taking a night off? (The program had an insert page, announcing that Esmeralda Soler was Lady Macbeth on Friday, November 22, 1963. I'd already decided that I would have this page framed; I was going to give it to Esmeralda for Christmas that year.) More irritating Americans were talking in the audience—more were leaving, too, some in tears. I decided that Americans were culturally deprived, socially inept imbeciles, or they were all philistines!

Finally the curtain went up, and there were the witches. When Macbeth and Banquo appeared—the latter, I knew, would soon be a ghost—I thought that this Macbeth was far too old and fat to be Esmeralda's husband (even in an opera).

You can imagine my surprise, in the very next scene in act 1, when it was *not* my Esmeralda singing *"Vieni, t'affretta!"* Nor was it Esmeralda calling on the ministers of hell to assist her (*"Or tutti sorgete"*). There onstage was Gerda Mühle and her polyp. I could only imagine how shocked the English-speaking clientele at our early seating at Zufall must have been—those ten obstetricians and gynecologists included. They must have been thinking: How is it possible that this matronly-looking load of a soprano is the *girlfriend* of our young, good-looking waiter?

When Lady Macbeth smeared the sleeping guards with the bloody dagger, I imagined that Esmeralda had been murdered backstage—or that something no less dire had happened to her.

It seemed that half the audience was crying by the end of act 2. Was it the news of Banquo's assassination that moved them to tears, or was it Banquo's ghost at the dinner table? About the time Macbeth saw Banquo's ghost that second time, near the end of act 2, I might have been the only person at the Vienna State Opera who *didn't* know that President Kennedy had been assassinated. It wasn't until the intermission that I would learn what had happened.

After the intermission, I stayed to see the witches again—and that terrifying bloody child who tells Macbeth that "none of woman born" can harm him. I stayed until the middle of act 4, because I wanted to see the sleepwalking scene—Gerda Mühle, and her polyp, singing *"Una macchia"* (about the blood that still taints Lady Macbeth's hands). Maybe I'd imagined that Esmeralda would emerge from backstage and join me and the other students faithfully standing at the rear of the Staatsoper, but—by act 4—there were so many vacated seats that most of my fellow students had found places to sit down.

I did not know that there was a soundless TV set backstage, and that Esmeralda was glued to it; she would tell me later that you didn't need the sound to understand what had happened to JFK.

I did not wait till the end of act 4, the final act. I didn't need to see "Birnam Wood remove to Dunsinane," as Shakespeare puts it, or hear Macduff tell Macbeth about the caesarean birth. I ran along the crowded Kärntnerstrasse to Weihburggasse, passing people with tears streaming down their faces—most of them *not* Americans.

In the kitchen at Zufall, the crew and the waitstaff were all watching television; we had a small black-and-white TV set. I saw the same sound-less accounts of the shooting in Dallas that Esmeralda must have seen.

"You're early, not late," Karl observed. "Did your girlfriend blow it?"

"It wasn't her—it was Gerda Mühle," I told him.

"*Blöde Kuh!*" Karl cried. "Stupid cow!" (The Viennese operagoers who were fed up with Gerda Mühle had called her a stupid cow long before Esmeralda started calling her the Polyp.)

"Esmeralda must have been too upset to perform—she must have lost it backstage," I said to Karl. "She was a Kennedy fan."

"So she *did* blow it," Karl said. "I don't envy you living with the outcome."

There was already a scattering of English-speaking customers, Karl warned me—not operagoers, evidently.

"More obstetricians and gynecologists," Karl observed disdainfully. (He thought there were too many babies in the world. "Overpopulation is the number-one problem," Karl kept saying.) "And there's a table of queers," Karl told me. "They just got here, but they're already drunk. Definitely fruits. Isn't that what you call them?"

"That's one of the things we call them," I told our one-eyed head-waiter.

It wasn't hard to spot the OB-GYN table; there were twelve of them—eight men, four women, all doctors. Since President Kennedy had just been killed, I didn't think it would be a good idea for me to break the ice by telling them that they'd all missed the c-section scene in *Macbeth*.

As for the table of queers—or "fruits," as Karl had called them—there were four men, all drunk. One of them was the well-known American poet who was teaching at the Institute, Lawrence Upton.

"I didn't know you worked here, young fiction writer," Larry said. "It's Bill, isn't it?"

"That's right," I told him.

"Jesus, Bill—you look *awful*. Is it Kennedy, or has something else happened?" Larry asked me.

"I saw *Macbeth* tonight—" I started to say.

"Oh, I heard it was the soprano understudy's night—I skipped it," Larry interrupted me.

"Yes, it was—it was *supposed to be* the understudy's night," I told him.

"But she's American—she must have been too upset about Kennedy. She didn't go on—it was Gerda Mühle, as usual."

"Gerda's great," Larry said. "It must have been wonderful."

"Not for me," I told him. "The soprano understudy is my girlfriend—I was hoping to see her as Lady Macbeth. I've been listening to her sing in her sleep," I told the table of drunken queers. "Her name is Esmeralda Soler," I told the fruits. "One day, maybe, you'll all know who she is."

"You have a girlfriend," Larry said—with the same, sly disbelief he would later express when I claimed to be a top.

"Esmeralda Soler," I repeated. "She must have been too upset to sing."

"Poor girl," Larry said. "I don't suppose there is a *plethora* of opportunities for understudies."

"I suppose not," I said.

"I'm still thinking about your writing-course idea," Larry told me. "I haven't ruled it out, Bill."

Karl had said he didn't envy me "living with the outcome" of Esmeralda not singing the part of Lady Macbeth, but—looking at Lawrence Upton and his queer friends—I suddenly foresaw another, not-so-pretty outcome of my living with Esmeralda.

There weren't many English-speaking operagoers who came to Zufall after that Friday-night performance of Verdi's *Macbeth*. I'm guessing that JFK's assassination kind of kicked the late-night-dinner urge out of most of my fellow Americans who were in Vienna that November. The OB-GYN table was morose; they left early. Only Larry and the fruits stayed late.

Karl urged me to go home. "Go find your girlfriend—she can't be doing too good," the one-eyed headwaiter told me. But I knew that either Esmeralda was with her opera people or she'd already gone back to our little apartment on the Schwindgasse. Esmeralda knew where I worked; if she wanted to see me, she knew where to find me.

"The fruits are never leaving—they've decided to die here," Karl kept saying. "You seem to know the handsome one—the *talker*," Karl added.

I explained who Lawrence Upton was, and that he taught at the Institute, but he was not my teacher.

"Go home to your girlfriend, Bill," Karl kept saying.

But I shuddered to think of watching the already-repetitious reports of JFK's assassination on that television in the living room of Esmeralda's landlady's apartment; visions of the disagreeable dog kept me at Zufall, where I could keep an eye on the small black-and-white TV in the restaurant's kitchen.

"It's the death of American culture," Larry was saying to the three other fruits. "Not that there *is* a culture for books in the United States, but Kennedy offered us some hope of having a culture for writers. Witness Frost—that inaugural poem. It wasn't bad; Kennedy at least had taste. How long will it be before we have another president who even has taste?"

I know, I know—this is not the most appealing way to present Larry. But what was wonderful about the man was that he spoke the truth, without taking into account the context of other people's "feelings" at that moment.

Someone overhearing Larry might have been awash in sentiments for our slain president—or feeling shipwrecked on a foreign shore, battered by surging waves of patriotism. Larry didn't care; if he believed it was true, he said it. This boldness didn't make Larry unappealing to me.

But it was somewhere in the middle of Larry's speech when Esmeralda got to the restaurant. She could never eat before she sang, she'd told me, so I knew she hadn't eaten, and she'd already had some white wine—not a good idea, on an empty stomach. Esmeralda first sat at the bar, crying; Karl had quickly ushered her into the kitchen, where she sat on a stool in front of the small TV. Karl gave her a glass of white wine before he told me she was in the kitchen; I'd not seen Esmeralda at the bar, because I was opening yet another bottle of red wine for Larry's table.

"It's your girlfriend, Bill—you should take her home," Karl told me. "She's in the kitchen." Larry's German wasn't bad; he'd understood what Karl had said.

"Is it your soprano understudy, Bill?" Larry asked me. "Let her sit with us—we'll cheer her up!" he told me. (I rather doubted it; I was pretty sure that a death-of-American-culture conversation wouldn't have cheered up Esmeralda.)

But that was how it happened—how Larry got a look at Esmeralda, as we were making our exit from the restaurant.

"Leave the fruits with me," Karl said. "I'll split the tip with you. Take the girl home, Bill."

"I think I'll throw up if I keep watching television," Esmeralda told me in the kitchen. She looked a little wobbly on the stool. I knew she would probably throw up, anyway—because of the white wine. We would have an awkward-looking walk, all the way across the Ringstrasse to the Schwindgasse, but I hoped the walk would be good for her.

"An unusually *pretty* Lady Macbeth," I heard Larry say, as I was steering Esmeralda out of the restaurant. "I'm still thinking about that writing course, young fiction writer!" Larry called to me, as Esmeralda and I were leaving.

"I think I'm going to throw up, eventually," Esmeralda was saying.

It was late when we got back to the Schwindgasse; Esmeralda had thrown up when we were crossing the Karlsplatz, but she said she was feeling better when we got to the apartment. The landlady and her disagreeable dog had gone to bed; the living room was dark, the television was off—or they were all as dead as JFK, the TV included.

"Not Verdi," Esmeralda said, when she saw me standing undecided at the phonograph.

I put on Joan Sutherland in what everyone said was her "signature role"; I knew how much Esmeralda loved *Lucia di Lammermoor*, which I put on softly.

"It's your big night, Billy—mine, too. I've never had vaginal sex, either. It doesn't matter if I get pregnant. When an understudy *clutches*, that's it—it's over," Esmeralda said; she'd brushed her teeth and washed her face, but she was still a little drunk, I think.

"Don't be crazy," I told her. "It *does* matter if you get pregnant. You'll have lots more opportunities, Esmeralda."

"Look—do you want to try it in my vagina, or don't you?" Esmeralda asked me. "I want to try it in my vagina, Billy—I'm *asking* you, for Christ's sake! I want to know what it's like in my vagina!"

"Oh."

Of course I used a condom; I would have put on two of the things, if she'd told me. (She was definitely still a little drunk—no question.)

That's how it happened. On the night our president died, I had vaginal sex for the first time—I really, *really* liked it. I think it was during Lucia's mad scene when Esmeralda had her very loud orgasm; to be honest with you, I'll never know if it was Joan Sutherland hitting that high E-flat, or if it was Esmeralda. My ears weren't protected by her thighs this time; I still managed to hear the landlady's dog bark, but my ears were ringing.

"Holy *shit*!" I heard Esmeralda say. "That was *amazing*!"

I was amazed (and relieved) myself; I'd not only really, *really* liked it—I had *loved* it! Was it as good as (or better than) *anal* sex? Well, it was *different*. To be diplomatic, I always say—when asked—that I love anal and vaginal sex "equally." My earlier worries about vaginas had been unfounded.

But, alas, I was a little slow in responding to Esmeralda's "Holy *shit*!" and her "That was *amazing*!" I was thinking how much I'd loved it, but I didn't say it.

"Billy?" Esmeralda asked. "How was it for you? Did you like it?"

You know, it's not only writers who have this problem, but writers really, *really* have this problem; for us, a so-called train of thought, though unspoken, is unstoppable.

I said: "Definitely not a ballroom." On top of what a day poor Esmeralda had had, that was what I told her.

"Not a *what*?" she said.

"Oh, it's just a *Vermont* expression!" I quickly said. "It's meaningless, really. I'm not even sure what 'not a ballroom' means—it doesn't translate very well."

"Why would you say something *negative*?" Esmeralda asked me. " 'Not an' *anything* is negative—'not a ballroom' sounds like a big disappointment, Billy."

"No, no—I'm *not* disappointed. I *loved* your vagina!" I cried. The disagreeable dog barked again; Lucia was repeating herself—she had gone back to the beginning, when she was still the trusting but easily unhinged young bride.

"I'm 'not a ballroom'—like I'm just a *gym*, or a *kitchen*, or something," Esmeralda was saying. Then her tears came—tears for Kennedy, for her one chance to be a *starting* soprano, for her unappreciated vagina—lots of tears.

You can't take back something like "Definitely not a ballroom"; it's simply not what you should ever say after your first vaginal sex. Of course, I also couldn't take back what I'd said to Esmeralda about her politics—about her lack of commitment to becoming a soprano.

We would live together through that Christmas and the first of the New Year, but the damage—the *distrust*—had begun. One night, I must have said something in my sleep. In the morning, Esmeralda asked me: "That rather good-looking older man in Zufall—you know, that terrible night. What did he mean about the writing course? Why did he call you 'young fiction writer,' Billy? Does he know you? Do you know him?"

Ah, well—there was no easy answer to that. Then, another night— that January of '64, after I got off work—I crossed the Kärntnerstrasse and turned down Dorotheergasse to the Kaffee Käfig. I knew perfectly well what the clientele was like late at night; it was all-male, all-gay.

"Well, if it isn't the fiction writer," Larry might have said, or maybe he just asked, "It's Bill, isn't it?" (This would have been the night he told me that he'd decided to teach that writing course I had asked him about, but before my first couple of classes with him as my teacher.)

That night in the Kaffee Käfig—not all that long before he hit on me—Larry might have asked, "No soprano understudy tonight? Where is that pretty, pretty girl? Not your *average* Lady Macbeth, Bill—is she?"

"No, she's not *average*," I might have mumbled. We just talked; nothing happened that night.

In fact, later that same night, I was in bed with Esmeralda when she asked me something significant. "Your German accent—it's so perfectly *Austrian*, it just kills me. Your German isn't that great, but you speak it so authentically. Where does your German *come from*, Billy—I can't believe I've never asked you!"

We had just made love. Okay, it hadn't been that spectacular—the landlady's dog didn't bark, and my ears weren't echoing—but we'd had vaginal sex, and we both loved it. "No more anal for us, Billy—I'm over it," Esmeralda had said.

Naturally, I knew that I *wasn't* over anal sex. I also understood that I not only loved Esmeralda's vagina; I'd already accepted the enslaving idea that I would never get "over" vaginas, either. Of course, it wasn't only Esmeralda's vagina that had enslaved me. It wasn't her fault that she didn't have a penis.

I blame the "Where does your German *come from*" question. That started me thinking about where our *desires* "come from"; that is a dark, winding road. And that was the night I knew I would be leaving Esmeralda.

Chapter 6

THE PICTURES I KEPT OF ELAINE

I was in German III my junior year at Favorite River Academy. That winter after old Grau died, Fräulein Bauer's section of German III acquired some of Dr. Grau's students—Kittredge among them. They were an ill-prepared group; Herr Doktor Grau was a confusing teacher. It was a graduation requirement at Favorite River that you had to take three years of the same language; if Kittredge was taking German III as a senior, this meant that he had flunked German in a previous year, or that he'd started out studying another foreign language and, for some unknown reason, had switched to German.

"Isn't your mom French?" I asked him. (I assumed he'd spoken French at home.)

"I got tired of doing what my alleged mother wanted," Kittredge said. "Hasn't that happened to you yet, Nymph?"

Because Kittredge was so witheringly smart, I was surprised he was such a weak German student; I was less surprised to discover he was lazy. He was one of those people things came easily to, but he did little to demonstrate that he deserved to be gifted. Foreign languages demand a willingness to memorize and a tolerance for repetition; that Kittredge could learn his lines for a play showed he had the capacity for this kind of self-polishing—onstage, he was a poised performer. But he lacked the necessary discipline for studying a foreign language—German, especially. The articles—"The frigging *der, die, das, den, dem* shit!" as Kittredge angrily stated—were beyond his patience.

That year, when Kittredge *should have* graduated, I didn't help his final grade by agreeing to assist him with his homework; that Kittredge virtually copied my translations of our daily assignments would be of no help to him in the in-class exams, which he had to write by himself. I most certainly didn't want Kittredge to fail German III; I foresaw the repercussions of him repeating his senior year, when I would also be a senior. But it was hard to say no to him when he asked for help.

"It's hard to say no to him, period," Elaine would later say. I blame myself that I didn't know they were involved.

That winter term, there were auditions for what Richard Abbott called "the spring Shakespeare"—to distinguish it from the Shakespeare play he had directed in the fall term. At Favorite River, Richard sometimes made us boys do Shakespeare in the winter term, too.

I hate to say this, but I believe that Kittredge's participation in the Drama Club was responsible for a surge in the popularity of our school plays—notwithstanding all the Shakespeare. There was more than usual interest when Richard read aloud the cast list for *Twelfth Night* at morning meeting; the list was later posted in the academy dining hall, where students actually stood in line for their opportunity to stare at the dramatis personae.

Orsino, Duke of Illyria, was our teacher and director, Richard Abbott. Richard, as the Duke, begins *Twelfth Night* with those familiar and rhapsodic lines " 'If music be the food of love, play on,' " not ever needing any prompting from my mother on that subject.

Orsino first professes his love for Olivia, a countess played by my complaining aunt Muriel. Olivia rejects the Duke, who (wasting no time) quickly falls in love with Viola, thus making Orsino an overproclaiming figure—"maybe more in love with love than with either lady," as Richard Abbott put it.

I always thought that, because Olivia turns down Orsino as her lover, Muriel must have felt comfortable in accepting the role of the countess. Richard was still a little too much leading-man material for Muriel; she never entirely relaxed in her handsome brother-in-law's company.

Elaine was cast as Viola, later disguised as Cesario. Elaine's immediate response was that Richard had anticipated Viola's necessary cross-dressing of herself as Cesario—"Viola *has* to be flat-chested, because for much of the play she's a guy," was how Elaine put it to me.

I actually found it a little creepy that Orsino and Viola end up in love—given that Richard was noticeably older than Elaine—but Elaine didn't seem to care. "I think girls got married younger back then," was all she said about it. (With half a brain, I might have realized that Elaine already had a real-life lover who was older than she was!)

I was cast as Sebastian—Viola's twin brother. "That's perfect for you two," Kittredge said condescendingly to Elaine and me. "You've already got a brother-sister thing going, as anyone can see." (At the time, I didn't pick up on that; Elaine must have told Kittredge that she and I weren't interested in each other in that way.)

I'll admit I was distracted; that Muriel, as Olivia, is first smitten with Elaine (disguised as Cesario) and later falls for *me*, Sebastian—well, that was a test of the previously mentioned disbelief business. For my part, I found it impossible to imagine falling in love with Muriel—hence I stared fixedly at my aunt's operatic bosom. Not once did *this* Sebastian look in *that* Olivia's eyes—not even when Sebastian exclaims, "If it be thus to dream, still let me sleep!"

Or when Olivia, whose bossiness was right up Muriel's alley, demands to know, "Would thou'dst be rul'd by me!"

I, as Sebastian, staring straight ahead at my aunt Muriel's breasts, which were laughably at eye level to me, answer her in a lovestruck fashion: " 'Madam, I will.' "

"Well, you best remember, Bill," Grandpa Harry said to me, "*Twelfth Night* is sure-as-shit a comedy."

When I grew just a little taller, and a little older, Muriel would object to my staring at her breasts. But that later play wasn't a comedy, and it only now occurs to me that when we were cast as Olivia and Sebastian in *Twelfth Night*, Muriel probably couldn't see that I was staring at her breasts, because her breasts were in the way! (Given my height at the time, Muriel's breasts blocked her line of vision.)

Aunt Muriel's husband, my dear uncle Bob, well understood the comic factor in *Twelfth Night*. That Bob's drinking was such a burden for Muriel to bear seemed a subject of mockery when Richard cast Uncle Bob as Sir Toby Belch, Olivia's kinsman and—in his most memorable moments in the play—a misbehaving drunk. But Bob was as much loved by the Favorite River students as he was by me—after all, he was the school's overly permissive admissions man. Bob thought it was no big deal that the students liked him. ("Of course they like me, Billy. They met me when I interviewed them, and I let them in!")

Bob also coached the racquet sports, tennis and squash—ergo the squash balls. The squash courts were on the basement level of the gym, underground and dank. When one of the squash courts stank of beer, the boys said that Coach Bob must have been playing there—sweating out the poisons of the night before.

Both Aunt Muriel and Nana Victoria complained to Grandpa Harry that casting Bob as Sir Toby Belch "encouraged" Bob's drinking. Richard Abbott would be blamed for "making light" of the deplorable pain caused to poor Muriel whenever Bob drank. But while Muriel and my grandmother would bitch to Grandpa Harry about Richard, they would never have breathed a word of discontent to Richard himself.

After all, Richard Abbott had come along "in the nick of time" (to use Nana Victoria's cliché) to save my *damaged* mother; they spoke of this rescue as if no one else might have managed the job. My mother was seen as no longer Nana Victoria's or Aunt Muriel's responsibility, because Richard had shown up and taken her off their hands.

At least this was very much the impression that my aunt and my grandmother gave to me—Richard could do no wrong, or what wrongdoing Nana Victoria and Aunt Muriel *thought* that Richard had done would be spelled out for Grandpa Harry, as if *he* could ever be expected to speak to Richard about it. My cousin Gerry and I overheard it all, because when Richard and my mother weren't around, my disapproving grandmother and my meddlesome aunt talked ceaselessly about them. I got the feeling they would still be calling them "the newlyweds," however facetiously, after my mom and Richard had been married for twenty years! As I grew older, I was realizing that *all* of them—not only Nana Victoria and Aunt Muriel, but also Grandpa Harry and Richard Abbott—treated my mother like a temperamental child. (They pussyfooted around her, the way they would have done with a child who was in danger of doing some unwitting damage to herself.)

Grandpa Harry would never criticize Richard Abbott; Harry might have agreed that Richard was my mom's savior, but I think Grandpa Harry was smart enough to know that Richard had chiefly saved my mother from Nana Victoria and Aunt Muriel—more than from the next man who might have come along and swept my *easily seducible* mom off her feet.

However, in the case of this ill-fated production of *Twelfth Night*, even Grandpa Harry had his doubts about the casting. Harry was cast as Maria, Olivia's waiting-gentlewoman. Both Grandpa Harry and I had thought of Maria as much younger, though Harry's chief difficulty with the role was that he was supposed to be married off to Sir Toby Belch.

"I can't believe that I'm going to be betrothed to my much-younger son-in-law," Grandpa Harry said sadly, when I was having dinner with him and Nana Victoria one winter Sunday night.

"Well, you best remember, Grandpa, *Twelfth Night* is sure-as-shit a comedy," I reminded him.

"A good thing it's only onstage, I guess," Harry had said.

"You and your *only-onstage* routine," Nana Victoria snapped at him. "I sometimes think you live to be weird, Harold."

"Tolerance, have tolerance, Vicky," Grandpa Harry intoned, winking at me.

Maybe that was why I decided to tell him what I had told Mrs. Hadley—about my slightly faded crush on Richard, my deepening attraction to Kittredge, even my masturbation to the unlikely contrivance of Martha Hadley as a training-bra model, but not (still not) my unmentioned love for Miss Frost.

"You're the sweetest boy, Bill—by which I mean, of course, you have feelin's for other people, and you take the greatest care not to hurt *their* feelin's. This is admirable, most admirable," Grandpa Harry said to me, "but you must be careful not to have *your* feelin's hurt. Some people are safer to be attracted to than others."

"Not other boys, you mean?" I asked him.

"I mean not *some* other boys. Yes. It takes a *special* boy—to safely speak your heart to. Some boys would hurt you," Grandpa Harry said.

"Kittredge, probably," I suggested.

"That would be my guess. Yes," Harry said. He sighed. "Maybe not here, Bill—not in this school, not at this time. Maybe these attractions to other boys, or men, will have to wait."

"Wait till when, and where?" I asked him.

"Ah, well . . ." Grandpa Harry started to say, but he stopped. "I think that Miss Frost has been very good at findin' books for you to read," Grandpa Harry started again. "I'll bet you that she could recommend somethin' for you to read—I mean on the subject of bein' attracted to other boys, or men, and regardin' when and where it may be possible to act on such attractions. Mind you, I haven't read that book, Bill, but I bet there are such stories; I know such books exist, and maybe Miss Frost would know about them."

I almost told him on the spot that Miss Frost was one of my confusing attractions, though something held me back from saying this; perhaps that she was the most powerful of all my attractions was what stopped me. "But how do I *begin* to tell Miss Frost," I said to Grandpa Harry. "I don't know how to *start*—I mean before I get to the business of there being books on the subject, or not."

"I believe you can tell Miss Frost what you told me, Bill," Grandpa Harry said. "I have a feelin' she would be *sympathetic*." He kissed me on the forehead and gave me a hug—there was both affection and concern for me in my grandfather's expression. I saw him suddenly as I had so often seen him—onstage, where he was almost always a woman. It was the way he'd used the *sympathetic* word that had triggered a long-ago memory; it may have been something I completely imagined, but, if I had to bet, it was a memory.

How old I was, I couldn't say—ten or eleven, at most. This was long before Richard Abbott appeared; I was Billy Dean, and my single mom was suitorless. But Mary Marshall Dean was already the long-established prompter for the First Sister Players, and, whatever my age, and notwithstanding my innocence, I'd been a long-accepted presence backstage. I had the run of the place—provided I kept out of the actors' way, and I stayed quiet. ("You're not backstage to talk, Billy," I remember my mom saying to me. "You're here to watch and listen.")

I believe it was one of the English poets—was it Auden?—who said that before you could write anything, you had to notice something. (Admittedly, it was Lawrence Upton who told me this; I'm just guessing it was Auden, because Larry was a fan of Auden's.)

It doesn't really matter who said it—it's so obviously true. Before you can write anything, you have to notice something. That part of my childhood—when I was backstage in the little theater of our town's amateur theatrical society—was the *noticing* phase of my becoming a writer. One of the things I noticed, if not the very first thing, was that not everyone thought it was wonderful or funny that my grandfather took so many women's roles in the productions of the First Sister Players.

I loved being backstage, just watching and listening. I liked the transitions, too—for example, that moment when all the actors were off-script, and my mother was called upon to start prompting. There then came a magical interlude, even among amateurs, when the actors seemed completely in character; regardless of how many rehearsals I'd attended,

I remember that quickly passing illusion when the play suddenly seemed real. Yet there was always something you saw or heard in the dress rehearsal that struck you as entirely new. Last, on opening night, there was the excitement of seeing and hearing the play for the first time with an audience.

I remember that, even as a child, I was as nervous on opening night as the actors. I had a pretty good (albeit partial) view of the actors from my hiding place backstage. I had a better view of the audience—though I saw only those faces in the first two or three rows of seats. (Depending on where my mother had positioned herself as the prompter, this was either a stage-right or stage-left view of the people in those first few rows of seats.)

I saw those faces in the audience only slightly more head-on than in profile, though the people in the audience were looking at the actors onstage; they were never looking at me. To tell you the truth, it was a kind of eavesdropping—I felt as if I were spying on the audience, or just this small segment of it. The houselights were dark, but the faces in the first couple of rows of seats were illuminated by whatever light there was onstage; naturally, in the course of the play, the light on the people in the audience varied, though I could almost always see their faces and make out their expressions.

The feeling that I was "spying" on these most exposed theatergoers of First Sister, Vermont, came from the fact that when you're in the audience in a theater, and your attention is captured by the actors onstage, you never imagine that someone is watching *you*. But I was observing them; in their expressions, I saw everything they thought and felt. Come opening night, I knew the play by heart; after all, I'd been to most of the rehearsals. By then, I was much more interested in the audience's reaction than I was in what the actors onstage were doing.

In every opening-night performance—no matter which woman, or what kind of woman, Grandpa Harry was playing—I was fascinated to observe the audience's reactions to Harry Marshall as a female.

There was the delightful Mr. Poggio, our neighborhood grocer. He was as bald as Grandpa Harry, but woefully shortsighted—he was always a first-row customer, and even in the first row, Mr. Poggio was a squinter. The moment Grandpa Harry came onstage, Mr. Poggio was convulsed with suppressed laughter; tears rolled down his cheeks, and I had to look away from his openmouthed, gap-toothed smile or I would have burst out laughing.

Mrs. Poggio was curiously less appreciative of Grandpa Harry's female impersonations; she frowned when she first saw him and bit her lower lip. She also did not seem to enjoy how happy her husband was with Grandpa Harry as a woman.

And there was Mr. Ripton—Ralph Ripton, the sawyer. He operated the main blade at Grandpa Harry's sawmill and lumberyard; it was a highly skilled (and dangerous) position in the mill, to be the main-blade operator. Ralph Ripton was missing the thumb and first two joints of his index finger on his left hand. I'd heard the story of the accident many times; both Grandpa Harry and his partner, Nils Borkman, liked to tell the blood-spattered tale.

I'd always believed that Grandpa Harry and Mr. Ripton were *friends*—they were more than fellow workers, surely. Yet Ralph didn't like Grandpa Harry as a woman; Mr. Ripton had an angry, condemning expression whenever he saw Grandpa Harry onstage in a female role. Mr. Ripton's wife—she was completely expressionless—sat beside her over-critical husband as if she'd been brain-damaged by the very idea of Harry Marshall performing as a woman.

Ralph Ripton skillfully managed to pack his pipe with fresh tobacco; at the same time, he never took his hard eyes from the stage. I guessed, at first, that Mr. Ripton was loading up his pipe for a smoke at the intermission—he always used the stump of his severed left index finger to tamp the tobacco tightly into the bowl of his pipe—but I later noticed that the Riptons never returned after the intermission. They came to the theater for the devout purpose of hating what they saw and leaving early.

Grandpa Harry had told me that Ralph Ripton had to sit in the first or second row in order to hear; the main blade in the sawmill made such a high-pitched whine that the saw had deafened him. But I could see for myself that there was more wrong with the sawyer than his deafness.

There were other faces in the collective audiences—many regular customers in those front-row seats—and while I didn't know most of their names or their professions, I had no difficulty (even as a child) recognizing their obdurate dislike of Grandpa Harry as a woman. To be fair: When Harry Marshall *kissed* as a woman—I mean when he kissed another man onstage—most of the audience laughed or cheered or applauded. But I had a knack for finding the unfriendly faces—there were always a few. I saw people cringe, or angrily look away; I saw their eyes narrow with disgust at Grandpa Harry *kissing* as a woman.

Harry Marshall played all kinds of women—he was a crazy lady who repeatedly bit her own hands, he was a sobbing bride who was ditched at the altar, he was a serial killer (a hairstylist) who poisoned her boyfriends, he was a policewoman with a limp. My grandfather loved the theater, and I loved watching him perform, but perhaps there were folks in First Sister, Vermont, who had rather limited imaginations; they knew Harry Marshall was a lumberman—they couldn't accept him as a woman.

Indeed, I saw more than obvious displeasure and condemnation in the faces of our townsfolk—I saw more than derision, worse than meanness. I saw *hatred* in a few of those faces.

One such face I wouldn't know by name until I saw him in my first morning meeting as a Favorite River Academy student. This was Dr. Harlow, our school's physician—he who, when he spoke to us boys, was usually so hearty and cajoling. On Dr. Harlow's face was the conviction that Harry Marshall's love of performing as a woman was an *affliction*; in Dr. Harlow's expression was the hardened belief that Grandpa Harry's cross-dressing was *treatable*. Thus I feared and hated Dr. Harlow before I knew who he was.

And, even as a backstage child, I used to think: *Come on! Don't you get it? This is make-believe!* Yet those hard-eyed faces in the audience weren't buying it. Those faces said: "You can't make-believe *this*; you can't make-believe *that*."

As a child, I was frightened by what I saw in those faces in the audience from my unseen, backstage position. I never forgot some of their expressions. When I was seventeen, and I told my grandfather about my crushes on boys and men, and my contradictory attraction to a made-up version of Martha Hadley as a training-bra model, I was still frightened by what I'd seen in those faces in the audience at the First Sister Players.

I told Grandpa Harry about watching some of our fellow townspeople, who were caught in the act of watching him. "They didn't care that it was make-believe," I told him. "They just knew they didn't like it. They *hated* you—Ralph Ripton and his wife, even Mrs. Poggio, no question about Dr. Harlow. They *hated* you pretending to be a woman."

"You know what I say, Bill?" Grandpa Harry asked me. "I say, you can make-believe what you want." There were tears in my eyes then, because I was afraid for myself—not unlike the way, as a child, I had been afraid backstage for Grandpa Harry.

"I stole Elaine Hadley's bra, because I wanted to wear it!" I blurted out.

"Ah, well—that's a good fella's failin', Bill. I wouldn't worry about that," Grandpa Harry said.

It was strange what a relief it was—to see that I couldn't shock him. Harry Marshall was only worried about my safety, as I'd once been afraid for his.

"Did Richard tell you?" Grandpa Harry suddenly asked me. "Some morons have banned *Twelfth Night*—I mean, over the years, total imbeciles have actually banned Shakespeare's *Twelfth Night*, many times!"

"Why?" I asked him. "That's *crazy*! It's a *comedy*, it's a *romantic* comedy! What could possibly be the reason for *banning* it?" I cried.

"Ah, well—I can only guess why," Grandpa Harry said. "Sebastian's twin sister, Viola—she looks a lot like her brother; that's the story, isn't it? That's why people mistake Sebastian for Viola—after Viola has disguised herself as a man, and she's goin' around callin' herself Cesario. Don't you see, Bill? Viola is a cross-dresser! *That's* what got Shakespeare in trouble! From everythin' you told me, I think you've noticed that rigidly conventional or ignorant people have no sense of humor about cross-dressers."

"Yes, I've noticed," I said.

But it was what I had failed to notice that would haunt me. All those years when I was backstage, when I had the prompter's perspective of those front-row faces in the audience, I had neglected to look at the prompter herself. I had not once noticed my mother's expression, when she saw and heard her father onstage as a woman.

That winter Sunday night, when I walked back to Bancroft, after my little talk with Grandpa Harry, I vowed I would watch my mom's face when Harry was performing as Maria in *Twelfth Night*.

I knew there would be opportunities—when Sebastian was not onstage but Maria was—when I could spy on my mother backstage and observe her expression. I was frightened of what I might see in her pretty face; I doubted she would be smiling.

I had a bad feeling about *Twelfth Night* from the start. Kittredge had talked a bunch of his wrestling teammates into auditioning. Richard had given four of them what he'd called "some smaller parts."

But Malvolio *isn't* a small part; the wrestling team's heavyweight, a sullen complainer, was cast in the role of Olivia's steward—an arrogant pretender who is tricked into thinking that Olivia desires him. I must say that Madden, the heavyweight who thought of himself as a perpetual

victim, was well cast; Kittredge had told Elaine and me that Madden suffered from "going-last syndrome."

In those days, all dual meets in wrestling began with the lightest
weight-class; heavyweights wrestled last. If the meet was close, it came
down to who won the heavyweight match—Madden usually lost. He had
the look of someone wronged. How perfect that Malvolio, who is jailed
as a lunatic, protests his fate—" 'I say there was never man thus abused,' "
Madden, as Malvolio, whines.

"If you want to be in character, Madden," I heard Kittredge say to
his unfortunate teammate, "just think to yourself how *unfair* it is to be a
heavyweight."

"But it *is* unfair to be a heavyweight!" Madden protested.

"You're going to be a great Malvolio. I know you are," Kittredge told
him—as ever, condescendingly.

Another wrestler—one of the lightweights who struggled to make
weight at every weigh-in—was cast as Sir Toby's companion, Sir Andrew
Aguecheek. The boy, whose name was Delacorte, was ghostly thin. He
was often so dehydrated from losing weight that he had cotton-mouth.
He rinsed his mouth out with water from a paper cup—he spat the water
out into another cup. "Don't mix your cups up, Delacorte," Kittredge
told him. ("Two Cups," I'd once heard Kittredge call him.)

We would not have been surprised to see Delacorte faint from hunger; one rarely saw him in the dining hall. He was constantly running his
fingers through his hair to be sure it wasn't falling out. "Loss of hair is a
sign of starvation," Delacorte told us gravely.

"Loss of common sense is another sign," Elaine said to him, but this
didn't register with Delacorte.

"Why doesn't Delacorte move up a weight-class?" I'd asked Kittredge.

"Because he would get the shit kicked out of him," Kittredge had said.

"Oh."

Two other wrestlers were cast as sea captains. One of the captains
isn't very important—he's the captain of the wrecked ship, the one who
befriends Viola. I can't remember the name of the wrestler who played
him. The second sea captain is Sebastian's friend Antonio. I'd earlier
feared that Richard might cast Kittredge as Antonio, who is a brave and
swashbuckling type. There is something so genuinely affectionate in
Sebastian's friendship with Antonio, I was anxious how that affection
would play out—I mean, in the case of Kittredge being Antonio.

But Richard either sensed my anxiety or knew that Kittredge would have been wasted as Antonio. In all likelihood, Richard, from the start, had a better part in mind for Kittredge.

The wrestler Richard chose for Antonio was a good-looking guy named Wheelock; whatever was swashbuckling about Antonio, Wheelock could convey.

"Wheelock can convey little else," Kittredge told me about his teammate. I was surprised that Kittredge seemed to feel superior to his wrestling teammates; I'd heretofore thought it was only the likes of Elaine and me he felt superior to. I saw that I'd underestimated Kittredge: He felt superior to everyone.

Richard cast Kittredge as the Clown, Feste—a very clever clown, and a somewhat cruel one. Like others of Shakespeare's fools, Feste is smart and superior. (It's no secret that Shakespeare's fools are often wiser than the ladies and gentlemen they share the stage with; the Clown in *Twelfth Night* is one of those smart fools.) In fact, in most productions I've seen of *Twelfth Night,* Feste steals the show—Kittredge certainly did. That late winter of 1960, Kittredge stole more than the show.

I SHOULD HAVE KNOWN as I crossed the quadrangle that night, following my conversation with Grandpa Harry, that the blue light in Elaine's fifth-floor bedroom window was—as Kittredge had called it—a "beacon." Kittredge had been right: That lamp with the blue shade was shining for him.

I'd once imagined that the blue light in Elaine's bedroom window was the last light old Grau saw—if only dimly, as he lay freezing. (A far-fetched idea, perhaps. Dr. Grau had hit his head; he'd passed out in the snow. Old Grau probably saw no lights at all, not even dimly.)

But what had Kittredge seen in that blue light—what about that *beacon* had encouraged him? "*I* encouraged him, Billy," Elaine would tell me later, but she didn't tell me at the time; I had no idea she was fucking him.

And all the while, my good stepfather, Richard Abbott, was bringing *me* condoms—"Just to be safe, Bill," Richard would say, as he bestowed another dozen rubbers on me. I had no use for them, but I kept them proudly; occasionally, I masturbated in one.

Of course, I should have given a dozen (or more) condoms to Elaine. I would have somehow summoned the courage to give them all to Kittredge, if I'd known!

Elaine didn't tell me when she knew she was pregnant. It was the spring term, and *Twelfth Night* was only a few weeks away from production; we'd been off-script for a while, and our rehearsals were improving. Uncle Bob (as Sir Toby Belch) was making us howl every time he said, " 'Dost thou think because thou art virtuous, there shall be no more cakes and ale?' "

And Kittredge had a strong singing voice—he was quite a good singer. That song the Clown, Feste, sings to Sir Toby and Sir Andrew Aguecheek—the "O mistress mine, where are you roaming?" song—well, it's a sweet but melancholic kind of song. It's the one that ends, "Youth's a stuff will not endure." It was hard to hear Kittredge sing that song as beautifully as he did, though the slight mockery in his voice—in Feste's character, or in Kittredge's—was unmistakable. (When I knew about Elaine being pregnant, I would remember a line from one of the middle stanzas of that song: "Journeys end in lovers meeting.")

There's no question that Elaine and Kittredge did their "meeting" in her fifth-floor bedroom. The Hadleys were still in the habit of going to the movies in Ezra Falls with Richard and my mom. I remember there were a few foreign films with subtitles that did *not* qualify as sex films. There was a Jacques Tati film showing in Vermont that year—*Mon Oncle*, was it, or maybe the earlier one, *Mr. Hulot's Holiday?*—and I went to Ezra Falls with my mom and Richard, and with Mr. and Mrs. Hadley.

Elaine didn't want to come; she stayed home. "It's not a sex film, Elaine," my mother had assured her. "It's French, but it's a comedy—it's very *light*."

"I don't feel like *light*—I don't feel like a *comedy*," Elaine had said. She was already throwing up at *Twelfth Night* rehearsals, but no one had figured out that she had morning sickness.

Maybe that's when Elaine told Kittredge that he'd knocked her up—when her family and mine were watching a Jacques Tati film, with subtitles, in Ezra Falls.

When Elaine knew she was pregnant, she eventually told her mother; either Martha Hadley or Mr. Hadley must have told Richard and my mom. I was in bed—naturally, I was wearing Elaine's bra—when my mother burst into my bedroom. "Don't, Jewel—try to take it easy," I heard Richard saying, but my mom had already snapped on my light.

I sat up in bed, holding Elaine's bra as if I were hiding my nonexistent breasts.

"Just look at you!" my mother cried. "Elaine is *pregnant!*"

"It wasn't me," I told her; she slapped me.

"Of course it wasn't you—I *know* it wasn't you, Billy!" my mom said. "But why *wasn't* it you—why *wasn't* it?" she cried. She went out of my room, sobbing, and Richard came in.

"It must have been Kittredge," I said to Richard.

"Well, Bill—of course it's Kittredge," Richard said. He sat on the side of my bed, trying his hardest not to notice the bra. "You'll have to forgive your mom—she's upset," he said.

I didn't reply. I was thinking about what Mrs. Hadley had said to me—that bit about "certain sexual matters" upsetting my mother. ("Billy, I know there are things she's kept from you," Martha Hadley had told me.)

"I think Elaine will have to go away for a while," Richard Abbott was saying.

"Away *where?*" I asked him, but Richard either didn't know or didn't want to tell me; he just shook his head.

"I'm really sorry, Bill—I'm sorry about everything," Richard said. I had just recently turned eighteen.

It was then I realized that I didn't have a crush on Richard anymore—not even a slight one. I knew I loved Richard Abbott—I still *do* love him—but that night I'd found something I disliked about him. In a way, he was weak—he let my mother push him around. Whatever my mom had kept from me, I knew then that Richard was keeping it from me, too.

IT HAPPENS TO MANY teenagers—that moment when you feel full of resentment or distrust for those adults you once loved unquestioningly. It happens to some teenagers when they're younger than I was, but I was a brand-new eighteen when I simply tuned out my mother and Richard. I trusted Grandpa Harry more, and I still loved Uncle Bob. But Richard Abbott and my mom had drifted into that discredited area occupied by Aunt Muriel and Nana Victoria—in their case, an area of carping, undermining commentary to be ignored or avoided. In the case of Richard and my mother, it was their secrecy I shunned.

As for the Hadleys, they sent Elaine "away" in stages. I can only guess what passed between Mrs. Kittredge and the Hadleys—the deals adults make aren't often explained to kids—but Mr. and Mrs. Hadley agreed to let Kittredge's mother take Elaine to Europe. I have no doubt that Elaine wanted the abortion. Martha Hadley and Mr. Hadley must have agreed it was best. It was definitely what Mrs. Kittredge had wanted. I'm guessing that, being French, she knew where to go in Europe; being Kittredge's mom, she may have had some previous experience with an unwanted pregnancy.

At the time, I imagined that a boy like Kittredge had gotten girls pregnant before—he easily could have. But I was also thinking that Mrs. Kittredge might have needed to get herself out of a jam—I mean, when she was younger. It's hard to explain what gave me that idea. I had overheard a conversation at a *Twelfth Night* rehearsal; I'd wandered into the middle of something Kittredge and his teammate Delacorte were saying—Delacorte, the rinser and spitter. It sounded as if they'd been arguing; it seemed to me that Delacorte was frightened of Kittredge, but so was everyone.

"No, I didn't mean that—I just said she was the most beautiful mother of the mothers I've met. Your mom is the best-looking—that's all I said," Delacorte was anxiously saying; then he rinsed and spat.

"If she's anyone's mother, you mean," Kittredge said. "She doesn't have a very *motherly* look, does she? She looks like someone who's asking for trouble—*that's* what she looks like."

"I didn't say what your mom looks *like*," Delacorte insisted. "I just said she was the most beautiful. She's the best-looking mom of *all* the moms!"

"Maybe she doesn't look like a mom because she *isn't* one," Kittredge said. Delacorte looked too frightened to speak; he just kept rinsing and spitting, clutching the two paper cups.

My idea that Mrs. Kittredge might have needed to get herself out of a jam came from *Kittredge;* he was the one who said, "She looks like someone who's asking for trouble."

Quite possibly, Mrs. Kittredge had more in mind than helping Elaine out of a jam; the deal she made with the Hadleys probably kept Kittredge in school. "Moral turpitude" was among the stated grounds for dismissal at Favorite River Academy. For a senior at the school to impregnate a faculty child—remember, Elaine was not yet eighteen; she was under the age of legal maturity—certainly struck me as base or depraved or vile behavior, but Kittredge stayed.

"You're *traveling* with Kittredge's mother—just the two of you?" I'd asked Elaine.

"Of course it's just the two of us, Billy—who *else* needs to come along?" Elaine responded.

"*Where* in Europe?" I asked.

Elaine shrugged; she was still throwing up, though less frequently. "What does it matter where it is, Billy? It's somewhere Jacqueline knows."

"You're calling her Jacqueline?"

"She asked me to call her Jacqueline—not Mrs. Kittredge."

"Oh."

Richard had cast Laura Gordon as Viola; Laura was now a senior in the high school in Ezra Falls. According to my cousin Gerry, Laura "put out"—not that I saw, but Gerry seemed well informed about such matters. (Gerry was a university student now, at last liberated from Ezra Falls.)

If Laura Gordon's breasts had been too developed for her to be cast as Hedvig in *The Wild Duck*, they should have disqualified her for Viola, who somehow has to disguise herself as a man. (Laura would need to be wrapped flat with Ace bandages, and, even so, there was no flattening her.) But Richard knew that Laura could learn her lines on short notice; that she looked nothing like my twin notwithstanding, she wouldn't be a bad Viola. The show went on, though Elaine would miss our performances; she would linger in Europe—recuperating, I could only guess.

The Clown's song concludes *Twelfth Night*. Feste is alone onstage. "'For the rain it raineth every day,'" Kittredge sang four times.

"The poor kid," Kittredge had said to me, about Elaine. "Such bad luck—her first time, and everything." As had happened to me before, I was speechless.

I didn't notice that Kittredge's German homework was any worse, or any better. I didn't even notice my mother's expression when she saw her father onstage as a woman. I was so upset about Elaine that I forgot about my plan to observe the prompter.

When I say that the Hadleys sent Elaine away "in stages," I mean that the trip to Europe—not to mention the obvious reason for that trip—was just the beginning.

The Hadleys had decided that their dormitory apartment in an all-boys' school was the wrong place for Elaine to finish her high school years. They would send her away to an all-girls' boarding school, but not until the fall. That spring of 1960 was a write-off for Elaine, and she would have to repeat her sophomore year.

It was said publicly that Elaine had had "a nervous breakdown," but everyone in a town as small as First Sister, Vermont, knew what had happened when a girl of high school age withdrew from school. Everyone at Favorite River Academy knew what had happened to Elaine, too. Even Atkins understood. I came out of Mrs. Hadley's office in the music building, not long after Elaine had disembarked for Europe with Mrs. Kittredge. Martha Hadley had been undone by the ease with which I'd pronounced the *abortion* word; she'd dismissed me from our appointment twenty minutes early, and I encountered Atkins on the stairwell between the first and second floors. I could see it crossing his mind—that it was not yet time for his appointment with Mrs. Hadley, but his struggle with the *time* word clearly prevented him from saying it. Instead he said, "What kind of breakdown was it? What does Elaine have to be *nervous* about?"

"I think you know," I said to him. Atkins had an anxious, feral-looking face, but with dazzling blue eyes and a girl's smooth complexion. He was a junior, like me, but he looked younger—he wasn't yet shaving.

"She's pregnant, isn't she? It was Kittredge, wasn't it? That's what everybody's saying, and he isn't denying it," Atkins said. "Elaine was really nice—she always said something nice to me, anyway," he added.

"Elaine really *is* nice," I told him.

"But what's she doing with Kittredge's *mother*? Have you *seen* Kittredge's mom? She's not like a mom. She's like one of those old movie stars who is secretly a witch or a dragon!" Atkins declared.

"I don't know what you mean," I told him.

"A woman who used to be that beautiful can never accept how—" Atkins stopped.

"How time passes?" I guessed.

"Yes!" he cried. "Women like Mrs. Kittredge *hate* young girls. Kittredge told me," Atkins added. "His dad left his mom for a younger woman—she wasn't more beautiful, just younger."

"Oh."

"I can't imagine traveling with Kittredge's mother!" Atkins exclaimed. "Will Elaine have her own room?" he asked me.

"I don't know," I told him. I hadn't thought about Elaine sharing a room with Mrs. Kittredge; it gave me the shivers just to think about it. What if she *wasn't* Kittredge's mother, or *anyone's* mother? But Mrs. Kittredge *had* to be Kittredge's mom; there was no way those two were unrelated.

Atkins had inched his way past me, up the stairs. I took a step or two down the stairs; I thought we were through talking. Suddenly Atkins said, "Not everyone here understands people like us, but Elaine did—Mrs. Hadley does, too."

"Yes," was all I said, continuing down the stairs. I tried not to consider too carefully what he'd meant by *people like us*, but I was sure that Atkins wasn't exclusively referring to our pronunciation problems. Had Atkins made a pass at me? I wondered, as I crossed the quad. Was that the first pass that a boy *like me* ever made at me?

The sky was lighter now—it didn't get dark so soon in the afternoon—but it would already be past nightfall in Europe, I knew. Elaine would be going to bed soon, in a room of her own or not. It was warmer now, too—not that there was ever much of a spring in Vermont—but I shivered as I crossed the quadrangle, on my way to my *Twelfth Night* rehearsal. I should have been thinking of my lines, of what Sebastian says, but I could only think of that song the Clown sings before the final curtain—Feste's song, the one Kittredge sang. ("For the rain it raineth every day.")

Just then, it began to rain, and I thought about how Elaine's life had been changed forever, while I was still just acting.

I HAVE KEPT THE photographs Elaine sent me; they were never very good photos, just black-and-white or color snapshots. Because of how many of my desktops these pictures have sat on—often in sunlight, and for so many years—the photographs are badly faded, but of course I have no trouble recalling the circumstances.

I just wish that Elaine had sent me some pictures of her trip to Europe with Mrs. Kittredge, but who would have taken those photographs? I can't imagine Elaine snapping photos of Kittredge's fashion-model mother—doing what? Brushing her teeth, reading in bed, getting dressed or undressed? And what might Elaine have been doing to inspire the artist-as-photographer in Mrs. Kittredge? Vomiting into a toilet from a kneeling position? Waiting, nauseated, in the lobby of this or that hotel, because her room—or the room she would share with Kittredge's mom—wasn't ready?

I doubt there were many photo opportunities that captured Mrs. Kittredge's imagination. Not the visit to the doctor's office—or was it a clinic?—and certainly not the messy but matter-of-fact procedure itself.

(Elaine was in her first trimester. I'm sure the procedure was a standard dilation and curettage—you know, the usual scraping.)

Elaine would later tell me that, after the abortion, when she was still taking the painkillers—when Mrs. Kittredge would regularly check the amount of blood on the pad, to be sure the bleeding was "normal"— Kittredge's mom felt her forehead, to ascertain that Elaine didn't have a fever, and that was when Mrs. Kittredge told Elaine those outrageous stories.

I used to think the painkillers might have been a factor in what Elaine remembered, or believed she heard, in those stories. "The painkillers weren't that strong, and I didn't take them for more than a day or two," Elaine always said. "I wasn't in a whole lot of pain, Billy."

"But weren't you drinking wine? You told me that Mrs. Kittredge gave you all the red wine you wanted," I would remind Elaine. "I'm sure that you weren't supposed to mix the painkillers with alcohol."

"I never had more than a glass or two of red wine, Billy," Elaine always told me. "I heard every word that Jacqueline said. Either those stories are true, or Jacqueline was lying to me—and why would anyone's mother lie about that kind of thing?"

Admittedly, I don't know why "anyone's mother" would make up stories about her only child—at least, not that kind—but I don't hold Kittredge or his mom in the highest moral esteem. Whatever I believed, or didn't, about the stories Mrs. Kittredge told Elaine, Elaine seemed to believe every word.

According to Mrs. Kittredge, her only child was a sickly little boy; he had no confidence in himself and was picked on by the other children, especially by the boys. While this was truly difficult to imagine, it was even harder to believe that Kittredge was once intimidated by girls; he apparently was so shy that he stuttered when he tried to talk to girls, and the girls either teased him or ignored him.

In the seventh grade, Kittredge would fake being sick so that he could stay home from school—these were "very competitive schools," in Paris and New York, Mrs. Kittredge had explained to Elaine—and at the start of eighth grade, he'd stopped talking to both the boys and the girls in his class.

"So I seduced him—it's not as if I had lots of other options," Mrs. Kittredge told Elaine. "The poor boy—he had to gain a little confidence *somewhere*!"

"I guess he gained quite a *lot* of confidence," Elaine ventured to say to Kittredge's mom, who'd simply shrugged.

Mrs. Kittredge had an insouciant shrug; one can only wonder if she was born with it, or if—after her husband had left her for a younger but indisputably less attractive woman—she'd developed an instinctive indifference to any kind of rejection.

Mrs. Kittredge matter-of-factly told Elaine that she'd slept with her son "as much as he'd wanted to," but only until Kittredge demonstrated a lack of fervor or a wandering sexual attention span. "He can't help it that he loses interest every twenty-four hours," Kittredge's mom told Elaine. "He didn't gain all that confidence by being bored—believe me."

Did Mrs. Kittredge imagine she was giving Elaine what amounted to an excuse for her son's behavior? All the time she was talking, Mrs. Kittredge went on checking to see if the blood on Elaine's pad was "normal," or feeling Elaine's forehead to be sure she didn't have a fever.

There are no pictures of their time together in Europe—only what I have managed (over the years) to coax out of Elaine, and what I've inevitably imagined of my dear friend aborting Kittredge's child, and her subsequent recuperation in the company of Kittredge's mother. If Mrs. Kittredge had seduced her own son, so that he might gain a little confidence, did this explain why Kittredge felt so strongly that his mom was somewhat less (or maybe more) than *motherly*?

"For how long did Kittredge have sex with his mom?" I asked Elaine.

"That eighth-grade year, when he would have been thirteen and fourteen," Elaine answered, "and maybe three or four times after he'd started at Favorite River—he would have been fifteen when it stopped."

"Why did it stop?" I asked Elaine—not that I completely believed it had happened!

Perhaps the insouciance of Elaine's shrug was something she'd picked up from Mrs. Kittredge.

"Knowing Kittredge, I suppose he got tired of it," Elaine had said. She was packing her bags for what would be her sophomore year at Northfield—fall term, 1960—and we were in her bedroom in Bancroft. It would have been late August; it was hot in that room. The lamp with the dark-blue shade had been replaced with a colorless job, like the desk lamp in an anonymous office, and Elaine had cut her hair short—almost like a boy's.

Although the phases of her going away would be marked by an increasingly conscious masculinity in her appearance, Elaine said she would never be in a lesbian relationship; yet she told me she'd experimented with being a lesbian. Had she "experimented" with Mrs. Kittredge? If Elaine had ever been attracted to women, I imagined how Mrs. Kittredge might have ended that, but Elaine was vague about it. I think of my dear friend as someone doomed to be attracted to the wrong men, but Elaine was vague about that, too. "They're just not the sort of men who last," was how she put it.

As for the photographs: The pictures Elaine sent me of her three years at Northfield are the ones I have kept. They may be black-and-white or color, and utterly amateur snapshots, but they are not as artless as they first appear.

I'll begin with the photo of Elaine standing on the porch of a three-story wooden house; she doesn't look like she belongs there—perhaps she was only visiting. Together with the name of the building, and the date of its construction—*Moore Cottage, 1899*—there is also this hope expressed, in Elaine's careful longhand, on the back of the photograph: *I wish this were my dorm.* (Apparently, it wasn't—nor would it be.)

On the ground floor of Moore Cottage, there were wooden clapboards, painted white, but there were white-painted wooden shingles on the second and third floors—as if to suggest not only the passage of time but a lingering indecision. Possibly this uncertainty had to do with Moore Cottage's use. Over the years, it would be used as a dormitory for girls—later, as a guesthouse for visiting parents. From the spread-out look of the building, there were probably a dozen or more bedrooms—far fewer bathrooms, I'll bet—and a large kitchen with an adjoining common room.

More bathrooms might have made the visiting parents happier, whereas the students (when they lived there) were long accustomed to making do with less. The porch, where Elaine stood—she seemed uncharacteristically unsure of herself—had a contradictory appearance. What use do students have for porches? In a good school, which Northfield was, students are too busy for porches, which are better suited for people with more time for leisure—such as guests.

In the picture of herself on the porch at Moore Cottage—it was among the very first of the photographs Elaine sent me from Northfield—maybe she felt like a guest. Curiously, there is someone in the window of one of the ground-floor rooms overlooking the porch: a woman of indeterminate age, to judge her by her clothes and the length of her hair—her face lost in the shadows, or obscured by an unclear reflection in the window.

Also among the earliest photos Elaine sent me from her new school, which was, in fact, a very *old* school, was that picture of the birthplace of Dwight L. Moody. *Our founder's birthplace, alleged to be haunted,* Elaine had written on the back of this photo, though that can't be the ghost of D.L. himself in a small upstairs window of the birthplace. It is a woman's face in profile—neither young nor old, but definitely pretty—her expression unknown. Elaine, smiling, is in the foreground of the photograph; she appears to be pointing in the direction of that upstairs window. (Maybe the girl was a friend of hers, or so I first imagined.)

Then there's the picture labeled *The Auditorium, 1894—on a slight hill.* I guess Elaine meant "slight" by Vermont standards. (I remember it as the first of the photos where the mystery woman seemed to be consciously posed; after seeing this picture, I began to look for her.) The Auditorium was a red-brick building with arched windows and doorways, and with two castle-size towers. A shadow cast by one of the towers fell across the lawn where Elaine was standing, near the trunk of an imposing tree. Sticking out, from behind the tree—in sunlight, *not* in the tower's shadow—was a woman's shapely leg. Her foot, which was pointed toward Elaine, was in a dark and sensible shoe; her kneesock was properly pulled up to her bare knee, above which her long gray skirt had been hiked to mid-thigh.

"Who's the other girl, or woman?" I'd asked Elaine.

"I don't know who you mean," Elaine replied. "*What* girl or woman?"

"In the pictures. There's always someone else there, in the photographs," I said. "Come on—you can tell me. Who is it—a friend of yours, maybe, or a teacher?"

In the photo of East Hall, the woman's face is very small—and partially hidden by a scarf—in an upper-story window. East Hall was, evidently, a dormitory, though Elaine didn't say; the fire escape gave it away.

In the picture of Stone Hall, there is a clock tower of that copper-green color, and very tall windows; it must have had warm light inside, on those few ungray days in the school-year months in western Massachusetts. Elaine is somewhat awkwardly positioned at the far side of the photograph; she is facing the camera, but she is standing almost perfectly back-to-back with someone. You can count two or three extra fingers on Elaine's left hand; holding her right hip is a third hand.

There's the one of the school chapel, I guess you would call it—a massive-looking cathedral with one of those big wooden doors inlaid with cast iron. A woman's bare arm is holding the heavy-looking door open for Elaine, who seems not to notice the arm—a bracelet on the wrist, rings on both the pinkie and the index finger—or maybe Elaine didn't care whether or not the woman was there. One can read the Latin engraved on the chapel: ANNO DOMINI MDCCCCVIII. Elaine had translated this on the back of the photo: *In the year of the Lord 1908.* (She'd added, *Where I want to get married, if I'm ever desperate enough to get married—if so, please just shoot me.*)

I believe I love best the picture of Margaret Olivia Hall, Northfield's music building, because I knew how much Elaine loved to sing—singing was one thing her big voice was born to do. ("I love to sing until I cry, and then sing some more," she once wrote to me.)

The names of composers were engraved between the upper-story windows of the music hall; I have memorized the names. Palestrina, Bach, Handel, Beethoven, Wagner, Gluck, Mozart, Rossini. In the window above the *u* in *Gluck*, which had been carved like a *v*, was a headless woman—just her torso—wearing only a bra. Unlike Elaine, who is leaning against the building, the headless woman in the window has very noticeable breasts—big ones.

"Who is she?" I asked Elaine, again and again.

If you didn't know it already, the music building with the names of those composers was an accurate indication of how sophisticated a school Northfield was; it put a place like Favorite River Academy to shame. It was a quantum leap heavenward from what Elaine had been used to at the public high school in Ezra Falls.

Most of the prep schools in New England were single-sex schools at that time. Many all-boys' schools provided faculty daughters with a tuition stipend; the girls could attend an all-girls' boarding school, and not be adrift in whatever public high school served the community. (To be fair: The public schools in Vermont were not all as bad as the one in Ezra Falls.)

As a result of the Hadleys' sending Elaine to Northfield—at first, at their expense—Favorite River did the right thing: It provided what amounted to vouchers for its faculty daughters. I would never hear the end of it from my crude cousin Gerry—namely, that this change in policy had happened too late to rescue her from the public high school in Ezra

Falls. As I've said, Gerry was a college girl that same spring when Elaine traveled to Europe with Mrs. Kittredge. "I guess I would have been wise to get myself knocked up a few years ago—provided the lucky guy had a French mother," was how Gerry put it. (I could easily imagine Muriel saying this when Muriel had been a teenager—although, after staring nonstop at my aunt's breasts in *Twelfth Night,* it was terrifying to think of Aunt Muriel as a teenager.)

I could describe other photographs that Elaine sent me from Northfield—I've kept them all—but the pattern would simply repeat itself. There was always a partial, imperfect image of another woman in the pictures of Elaine and those impressive buildings on the Northfield campus.

"Who is she? I know you know who I mean—she's always there, Elaine," I said repeatedly. "Don't be coy about it."

"I'm not being coy, Billy—you should talk about being *coy,* if that's the word you're using for being evasive, or not talking about things directly. If you know what I mean," Elaine would say.

"Okay, okay—so I have to *guess* who she is, is that it? So you're paying me back for being less than candid with you—am I getting warm?" I asked my dear friend.

ELAINE AND I WOULD try living together, though this would be many years later, after we'd both had sufficient disappointments in our lives. It wouldn't work out—not for very long—but we were too good friends not to have tried it. We were also old enough, when we embarked on this adventure, to know that friends were more important than lovers—not least for the fact that friendships generally lasted longer than relationships. (It's best not to generalize, but this was certainly the case for Elaine and me.)

We had a seedy eighth-floor apartment on Post Street in San Francisco—in that area of Post Street between Taylor and Mason, near Union Square. Elaine and I had our own rooms, to write. Our bedroom was large and accommodating—it overlooked some rooftops on Geary Street, and the vertical sign for the Hotel Adagio. At night, the neon for the HOTEL word was dark—burned out, I guess—so that only the ADAGIO was lit. In my insomnia, I would get out of bed and go to the window and stare at the bloodred ADAGIO sign.

One night, when I came back to bed, I inadvertently woke up Elaine, and I asked her about the *adagio* word. I knew it was Italian; not only had I heard Esmeralda say it, but I'd seen the word in her notes. In my forays into the world of opera and other music—both with Esmeralda and with Larry, in Vienna—I knew that the word had some use in music. I knew that Elaine would know what it meant; like her mother, Elaine was very musical. (Northfield had been a good fit for her—it was a great school for music.)

"What's it mean?" I asked Elaine, as we lay awake in that seedy Post Street apartment.

"*Adagio* means slowly, softly, gently," Elaine answered.

"Oh."

That would be about the best you could say for our efforts at love-making, which we tried, too—with no more success than the living-together part, but we tried. "*Adagio*," we would say, when we tried to make love, or afterward, when we were trying to fall asleep. We say it still; we said it when we left San Francisco, and we say it when we close letters or emails to each other now. It's what love means to us, I guess—only *adagio*. (Slowly, softly, gently.) It works for friends, anyway.

"So who was she, really—the lady in all those pictures?" I would ask Elaine, in that accommodating bedroom overlooking the neon-damaged Hotel Adagio.

"You know, Billy—she's still looking after me. She'll always be hovering somewhere nearby, taking my temperature by hand, checking the blood on my pad to see if the bleeding is still 'normal.' It was always 'normal,' by the way, but she's still checking—she wanted me to know that I would never leave her care, or her thoughts," Elaine said.

I lay there thinking about it—the only light out the window being the dull glow of lights from Union Square and that damaged neon sign, the vertical ADAGIO in bloodred, the HOTEL unlit.

"You actually mean that Mrs. Kittredge is *still*—"

"Billy!" Elaine interrupted me. "I was never as intimate with anyone as I was with that awful woman. I will never be as close to anyone again."

"What about Kittredge?" I asked her, though I should have known better—after all those years.

"Fuck Kittredge!" Elaine cried. "It's his mother who *marked* me! It's *her* I'll never forget!"

"*How* intimate? Marked you *how*?" I asked her, but she'd begun to cry, and I thought that I should just hold her—slowly, softly, gently—and say nothing. I'd already asked her about the abortion; it wasn't that. She'd had another abortion, after the one in Europe.

"They're not so bad, when you consider the alternative," was all Elaine ever said about her abortions. However Mrs. Kittredge had *marked* her, it wasn't about that. And if Elaine had "experimented" with being a lesbian—I mean with Mrs. Kittredge—Elaine would go to her grave being vague about *that*.

The pictures I kept of Elaine were what I could imagine about Kittredge's mother, or how "close" Elaine ever was to her. The shadows and body parts of the woman (or women) in those photographs are more vivid to me than my one memory of Mrs. Kittredge at a wrestling match, the first and only time I actually saw her. I know "that awful woman" best by her effect on my friend Elaine—the way I know myself best by my persistent crushes on the wrong people, the way I was formed by how long I kept the secret of myself from the people I loved.

Chapter 7

My Terrifying Angels

If an unwanted pregnancy was the "abyss" that an intrepid girl could fall into—the *abyss* word was my mother's, though I'll bet she'd heard it first from fucking Muriel—surely the abyss for a boy like me was to succumb to homosexual activity. In such love lay madness; in acting out my most dire imaginings, I would certainly descend to the bottomless pit of the universe of desire. Or so I believed in the fall of my senior year at Favorite River Academy, when I once more ventured to the First Sister Public Library—this time, I thought, to save myself. I was eighteen, but my sexual misgivings were innumerable; my self-hatred was huge.

If you were, like me, at an all-boys' boarding school in the fall of 1960, you felt utterly alone—you trusted no one, least of all another boy your age—and you loathed yourself. I'd always been lonely, but self-hatred is worse than loneliness.

With Elaine starting her new life at Northfield, I was spending more and more time in the yearbook room of the academy library. When my mom or Richard asked me where I was going, I always answered: "I'm going to the library." I didn't tell them *which* library. And without Elaine to slow me down—she could never resist showing me those hot-looking boys from the more contemporary of the yearbooks—I was blazing my way through the graduating classes of the decreasingly distant past. I'd left World War I behind; I was way ahead of my imagined schedule. At the rate I was going through those yearbooks, I would catch up with the present well before the spring of '61 and my own graduation from Favorite River.

In fact, I was a mere thirty years behind myself; on the same September evening I decided to leave the academy library and pay a visit to Miss Frost, I'd begun to peruse the yearbook for the Class of '31. An absolutely heart-stopping boy in the wrestling-team photo had caused me to abruptly close the yearbook. I thought: I simply can't keep thinking about Kittredge, and boys like him; I must not give in to those feelings, or I am doomed.

Just what exactly was holding my doom at bay? My contrived image of Martha Hadley as a training-bra model in a mail-order catalog wasn't working anymore. It was increasingly difficult to masturbate to even the most imaginative transposing of Mrs. Hadley's homely face on the least bosomy of those small-breasted young girls. All that held Kittredge (and boys like him) at bay was my ardent fantasizing about Miss Frost.

The Favorite River Academy yearbook was called *The Owl*. ("Anyone who knows why is probably dead," Richard Abbott had replied, when I'd asked him why.) I pushed the '31 *Owl* aside. I gathered up my notebooks, and my German homework—cramming everything but *The Owl* into my book bag.

I was taking German IV, though it wasn't required. I was still helping Kittredge with German III, which he'd flunked but was perforce repeating. It was somewhat easier to help him, since we were no longer taking German III together. Essentially, all I did was save Kittredge a little time. The hard stuff in German III was the introduction to Goethe and Rilke; there was more of them in German IV. When Kittredge got stuck on a phrase, I saved him time by giving him a quick and rudimentary translation. That some of the *same* Goethe and Rilke was as confounding to Kittredge the second time truly incensed him, but frankly the notes and hurried comments that now passed between us were easier for me than our previous conversations. I was trying to be in Kittredge's presence as little as I possibly could.

To that end, I dropped out of the fall Shakespeare play—to Richard's oft-expressed disappointment. Richard had cast Kittredge as Edgar in *King Lear*. Furthermore, there was an unforeseen flaw in Richard's having cast me as Lear's Fool. When I was telling Mrs. Hadley that I wanted no part in the play, because Kittredge had "a hero's part"—not to mention that Edgar is later disguised as Poor Tom, so that Kittredge had essentially been given "a dual role"—Martha Hadley wanted to know how closely I'd looked over my lines. Given that my number of *unpronounceables* was growing, did I foresee that the Fool presented me with any vocabulary issues? Was Mrs. Hadley hinting that my pronunciation problems could excuse me from the play?

"What are you getting at?" I asked her. "You think I can't handle 'cutpurses' or 'courtesan,' or are you worried that 'codpiece' will throw me for a loop—just because of the *whatchamacallit* the codpiece covers, or because I have trouble with the word for the *whatchamacallit* itself?"

"Don't be defensive, Billy," Martha Hadley said.

"Or was it the 'arrant whore' combination that you thought might trip me up?" I asked her. "Or maybe 'coxcomb'—either the singular or the plural, or both!"

"Calm down, Billy," Mrs. Hadley said. "We're both upset about Kittredge."

"Kittredge had the last lines in *Twelfth Night*!" I cried. "Now Richard gives him the last lines again! We have to hear *Kittredge* say, 'The weight of this sad time we must obey: / Speak what we feel, not what we ought to say.' "

" 'The oldest hath borne most,' " Kittredge-as-Edgar continues.

In the story of *King Lear*—given what happens to Lear, not to mention the blinding of Gloucester (Richard had cast himself as Gloucester)—this is certainly true. But when Edgar ends the play by declaring that "we that are young / Shall never see so much nor live so long"—well, I don't know if that is *universally* true.

Do I dispute the concluding wisdom of this great play because I can't distinguish Edgar from Kittredge? Can *anyone* (even Shakespeare) know how future generations will or will not *suffer*?

"Richard is doing what's best for the play, Billy," Martha Hadley told me. "Richard isn't rewarding Kittredge for seducing Elaine." Yet it somehow seemed that way to me. Why give Kittredge as good a part as Edgar, who is later disguised as Poor Tom? After what had happened in *Twelfth Night*, why did Richard have to give Kittredge a role in *King Lear* at all? I wanted out of the play—being, or not being, Lear's Fool wasn't the issue.

"Just tell Richard you don't want to be around Kittredge, Billy," Mrs. Hadley said to me. "Richard will understand."

I couldn't tell Martha Hadley that I also didn't want to be around Richard. And what point was there, in this production of *King Lear*, to observe my mother's expression when she watched her father onstage as a woman? Grandpa Harry was cast as Goneril, Lear's eldest daughter;

Goneril is such a horrid daughter, why wouldn't my mom look at *anyone* playing Goneril with the utmost disapproval? (Aunt Muriel was Regan, Lear's other awful daughter; I assumed that my mother would glower at her sister, Muriel, too.)

It wasn't only because of Kittredge that I wanted nothing to do with this *King Lear*. I had no heart to see Uncle Bob fall short in the leading-man department, for the good-hearted Bob—*Squash Ball* Bob, Kittredge called him—was cast as King Lear. That Bob lacked a tragic dimension seemed obvious, if not to Richard Abbott; perhaps Richard pitied Bob, *and* found him tragic, because Bob was (tragically) married to Muriel.

It was Bob's body that was all wrong—or was it his head? Bob's body was big, and athletically robust; compared to his body, Bob's head seemed too small, and improbably round—a squash ball lost between two hulking shoulders. Uncle Bob was both too good-natured and too strong-looking to be Lear.

It is relatively early in the play (act 1, scene 4) when Bob-as-Lear bellows, " 'Who is it that can tell me who I am?' "

Who could forget how Lear's Fool answers the king? But I did; I forgot that I even had a line. " 'Who is it that can tell me who I am,' *Bill?*" Richard Abbott asked me.

"It's your line, Nymph," Kittredge whispered to me. "I had anticipated that you might have a little trouble with it." Everyone waited while I found the Fool's line. At first, I wasn't even aware of the pronunciation problem; my difficulty in saying this word was so recent that I hadn't noticed it, nor had Martha Hadley. But Kittredge, clearly, had detected the potential unpronounceable. "Let's hear you say it, Nymph," Kittredge said. "Let's hear you *try* it, anyway."

"Who is it that can tell me who I am?" Lear asks.

The Fool answers: "Lear's shadow."

Since when had the *shadow* word given me any grief in the pronunciation department? Since Elaine had come back from that trip to Europe with Mrs. Kittredge, when Elaine seemed as insubstantial as a shadow— at least in comparison to her former self. Since Elaine had come back from Europe, and there seemed to be an unfamiliar shadow dogging her every step—a shadow that bore a ghostly but ultrasophisticated resemblance to Mrs. Kittredge herself. Since Elaine had gone away again, to Northfield, and I was left with a shadow following me around—perhaps the disquieting, unavenged shadow of my absent best friend.

" 'Lear's . . . *shed*,' " I said.

"His *shed*!" Kittredge exclaimed.

"Try it again, Bill," Richard said.

"I can't say it," I replied.

"Maybe we need a new Fool," Kittredge suggested.

"That would be my decision, Kittredge," Richard told him.

"Or mine," I said.

"Ah, well—" Grandpa Harry started to say, but Uncle Bob interrupted him.

"It seems to me, Richard, that Billy could say 'Lear's *reflection*,' or even 'Lear's *ghost*'—if, in your judgment, this fits with what the Fool means or is implying," Uncle Bob suggested.

"Then it wouldn't be Shakespeare," Kittredge said.

"The line is 'Lear's *shadow*,' Billy," my mother, the prompter, said. "Either you can say it or you can't."

"Please, Jewel—" Richard started to say, but I interrupted him.

"Lear should have a proper Fool—one who can say everything," I told Richard Abbott. I knew, as I was leaving, that I was walking out of my final rehearsal as a Favorite River Academy student—my last Shakespeare play, perhaps. (As it would turn out, *King Lear* was my last Shakespeare play *as an actor*.)

The faculty daughter whom Richard cast as Cordelia was and remains so completely unknown to me that I can't recall her name. "An unformed girl, but with a crackerjack memory," Grandpa Harry had said about her.

"Neither a present nor a future beauty," was all my aunt Muriel said of the doomed Cordelia, implying that, in *King Lear*, no one would ever have married *this* Cordelia—not even if she'd lived.

Lear's Fool would be played by Delacorte. Since Delacorte was a wrestler, he'd probably learned that the part was available because Kittredge had told him. Kittredge would later inform me that, because the fall Shakespeare play was rehearsed and performed before the start of the wrestling season, Delacorte wasn't as ill affected as he usually was by the complications of cutting weight. Yet the lightweight who, according to Kittredge, would have had the shit kicked out of him in a heavier weight-class, still suffered from cotton-mouth, even when he wasn't dehydrated—or perhaps Delacorte dreamed of cutting weight, even in the off-season. Therefore, Delacorte *constantly* rinsed his mouth out with water from a paper cup; he *eternally* spat out the water into another paper cup. If Delacorte were alive today, I'm sure he would still be running his fingers through his hair. But Delacorte is dead, along with so many others. Awaiting me, in the future, was seeing Delacorte die.

Delacorte, as Lear's Fool, would wisely say: " 'Have more than thou showest, / Speak less than thou knowest, / Lend less than thou owest.' " Good advice, but it won't save Lear's Fool, and it didn't save Delacorte.

Kittredge acted strangely in Delacorte's company; he could behave affectionately and impatiently with Delacorte in the same moment. It was as if Delacorte had been a childhood friend, but one who'd disappointed Kittredge—one who'd not "turned out" as Kittredge had hoped or expected.

Kittredge was preternaturally fond of Delacorte's rinsing-and-spitting routine; Kittredge had even suggested to Richard that there might be onstage benefits to Lear's Fool repeatedly rinsing and spitting.

"Then it wouldn't be Shakespeare," Grandpa Harry said.

"I'm not *prompting* the rinsing and spitting, Richard," my mom said.

"Delacorte, you will kindly do your rinsing and spitting backstage," Richard told the compulsive lightweight.

"It was just an idea," Kittredge had said with a dismissive shrug. "I guess it will suffice that we at least have a Fool who can say the *shadow* word."

To me, Kittredge would be more philosophical. "Look at it this way, Nymph—there's no such thing as a working actor with a restricted vocabulary. But it's a positive discovery, to be made aware of your limitations at such a young age," Kittredge assured me. "How fortuitous, really—now you know you can never be an actor."

"You mean, it's not a career choice," I said, as Miss Frost had once declared to me—when I'd first told her that I wanted to be a writer.

"I should say not, Nymph—not if you want to give yourself a fighting chance."

"Oh."

"And you might be wise, Nymph, to clarify another choice—I mean, before you get to the career part," Kittredge said. I said nothing; I just waited. I knew Kittredge well enough to know when he was setting me up. "There's the matter of your sexual proclivities," Kittredge continued.

"My sexual proclivities are crystal-clear," I told him—a little surprised at myself, because I was acting and there wasn't a hint of a pronunciation problem.

"I don't know, Nymph," Kittredge said, with that deliberate or involuntary flutter in the broad muscles of his wrestler's neck. "In the area of sexual proclivities, you look like a work-in-progress to me."

"OH, IT'S YOU!" MISS Frost said cheerfully, when she saw me; she sounded surprised. "I thought it was your friend. He was here—he just left. I thought it was him, coming back."

"Who?" I asked her. (I had Kittredge on my mind, of course—not exactly a friend.)

"Tom," Miss Frost said. "Tom was just here. I'm never sure why he comes. He's always asking about a book he says he can't find at the academy library, but I know perfectly well the school has it. Anyway, I never have what he's looking for. Maybe he comes here looking for you."

"Tom *who?*" I asked her. I didn't think I knew a Tom.

"Atkins—isn't that his name?" Miss Frost asked. "I know him as Tom."

"I know him as Atkins," I said.

"Oh, William, I wonder how long the last-name culture of that awful school will persist!" Miss Frost said.

"Shouldn't we be whispering?" I whispered.

After all, we were in a library. I was puzzled by how loudly Miss Frost spoke, but I was also excited to hear her say that Favorite River Academy was an "awful school"; I secretly thought so, but out of loyalty to Richard Abbott and Uncle Bob, faculty brat that I was, I would never have *said* so.

"There's no one else here, William," Miss Frost whispered to me. "We can speak as loudly as we want."

"Oh."

"You've come to *write*, I suppose," Miss Frost loudly said.

"No, I need your advice about what I should read," I told her.

"Is the subject still crushes on the wrong people, William?"

"*Very* wrong," I whispered.

She leaned over, to be closer to me; she was still so much taller than I was, she made me feel that I hadn't grown. "We can whisper about this, if you want to," she whispered.

"Do you know Jacques Kittredge?" I asked her.

"Everyone knows Kittredge," Miss Frost said neutrally; I couldn't tell what she thought about him.

"I have a crush on Kittredge, but I'm trying not to," I told her. "Is there a novel about that?"

Miss Frost put both her hands on my shoulders. I knew she could feel me shaking. "Oh, William—there are worse things, you know," she said. "Yes, I have the very novel you should read," she whispered.

"I know why Atkins comes here," I blurted out. "He's not looking for me—he probably has a crush on *you!*"

"Why would he?" Miss Frost asked me.

"Why *wouldn't* he? Why wouldn't *any* boy have a crush on you?" I asked her.

"Well, no one's had a crush on me for a while," she said. "But it's very flattering—it's so sweet of you to say so, William."

"I have a crush on you, too," I told her. "I always have, and it's stronger than the crush I have on Kittredge."

"My dear boy, you *are* so very wrong!" Miss Frost declared. "Didn't I tell you there were worse things than having a crush on Jacques Kittredge? Listen to me, William: Having a crush on Kittredge is *safer!*"

"How can Kittredge be safer than *you?*" I cried. I could feel that I was starting to shake again; this time, when she put her big hands on my shoulders, Miss Frost hugged me to her broad chest. I began to sob, uncontrollably.

I hated myself for crying, but I couldn't stop. Dr. Harlow had told us, in yet another lamentable morning meeting, that excessive crying in boys was a homosexual tendency we should guard ourselves against. (Naturally, the moron never told us *how* we should guard ourselves against something we couldn't control!) And I'd overheard my mother say to Muriel: "Honestly, I don't know what to do when Billy cries like a *girl!*"

So there I was, in the First Sister Public Library, crying like a girl in Miss Frost's strong arms—having just told her that I had a stronger crush on her than the one I had on Jacques Kittredge. I must have seemed to her like such a sissy!

"My dear boy, you don't really know me," Miss Frost was saying. "You don't know who I am—you don't know the first thing about me, do you? William? You *don't,* do you?"

"I don't *what?*" I blubbered. "I don't know your first name," I admitted; I was still sobbing. I was hugging her back, but not as hard as she hugged me. I could feel how strong she was, and—once again—the smallness of her breasts seemed to stand in surprising contrast to her strength. I could also feel how soft her breasts were; her small, soft breasts struck me as such a contradiction to her broad shoulders, her muscular arms.

"I didn't mean my *name*, William—my first name isn't important," Miss Frost said. "I mean you don't know *me*."

"But what *is* your first name?" I asked her.

There was a theatricality in the way Miss Frost sighed—a staged exaggeration in the way she released me from her hug, almost pushing me away from her.

"I have a lot at stake in being *Miss* Frost, William," she said. "I did not acquire the *Miss* word accidentally."

I knew something about not liking the name you were given, for I hadn't liked being William Francis Dean, Jr. "You don't *like* your first name?" I asked her.

"We could begin with that," she answered, amused. "Would you ever name a girl Alberta?"

"Like the province in Canada?" I asked. I could not imagine Miss Frost as an Alberta!

"It's a better name for a province," Miss Frost said. "Everyone used to call me Al."

"Al," I repeated.

"You see why I like the *Miss*," she said, laughing.

"I love everything about you," I told her.

"Slow down, William," Miss Frost said. "You can't rush into crushes on the wrong people."

Of course, I didn't understand why she thought of herself as "wrong" for me—and how could she possibly imagine that my crush on Kittredge was *safer*? I believed that Miss Frost must have meant merely to warn me about the difference in our ages; maybe an eighteen-year-old boy with a woman in her forties was a taboo to her. I was thinking that I was *legally* an adult, albeit barely, and if it were true that Miss Frost was about my aunt Muriel's age, I was guessing that she would have been forty-two or forty-three.

"Girls my own age don't interest me," I said to Miss Frost. "I seem to be attracted to older women."

"My dear boy," she said again. "It doesn't matter how old I am—it's *what* I am. William, you don't know what I *am*, do you?"

As if that existential-sounding question wasn't confusing enough, Atkins chose this moment to enter the dimly lit foyer of the library, where he appeared to be startled. (He told me later he'd been frightened by the reflection of himself he had seen in the mirror, which hung silently in the foyer like a nonspeaking security guard.)

"Oh, it's *you*, Tom," Miss Frost said, unsurprised.

"Do you see? What did I tell you?" I asked Miss Frost, while Atkins went on fearfully regarding himself in the mirror.

"You're so very *wrong*," Miss Frost told me, smiling.

"Kittredge is looking for you, Bill," Atkins said. "I went to the yearbook room, but someone said you'd just left."

"The yearbook room," Miss Frost repeated; she sounded surprised. I looked at her; there was an unfamiliar anxiety in her expression.

"Bill is conducting a study of Favorite River yearbooks from past to present," Atkins said to Miss Frost. "Elaine told me," Atkins explained to me.

"For Christ's sake, Atkins—it sounds like you're conducting a study of *me*," I told him.

"It's Kittredge who wants to talk to you," Atkins said sullenly.

"Since when are you Kittredge's messenger boy?" I asked him.

"I've had enough *abuse* for one night!" Atkins cried dramatically, throwing up his slender hands. "It's one thing to have Kittredge insulting me—he insults everyone. But having *you* insult me, Bill—well, that's just too much!"

In an effort to leave the First Sister Public Library in a flamboyant pique, Atkins once again encountered that menacing mirror in the foyer, where he paused to deliver a parting shot. "I'm not your *shadow*, Bill—Kittredge is," Atkins said.

He was gone before he could hear me say, "Fuck Kittredge."

"Watch your language, William," Miss Frost said, putting her long fingers to my lips. "After all, we're in a fucking *library*."

The *fucking* word was not one that came to mind when I thought of her—in the same way that Miss Frost seemed an implausible Alberta—but when I looked at her, she was smiling. She was just teasing me; her long fingers now brushed my cheek.

"A curious reference to the *shadow* word, William," she said. "Would it be the unpronounceable word that caused your unplanned exit from *King Lear*?"

"It would," I told her. "I guess you heard. In a town this small, I think everyone hears everything!"

"Maybe not quite everyone—possibly not quite everything, William," Miss Frost said. "It appears to me, for example, that *you* haven't heard everything—about me, I mean."

I knew that Nana Victoria didn't like Miss Frost, but I didn't know why. I knew that Aunt Muriel had issues with Miss Frost's choice in bras, but how could I have brought up the training-bra subject when I had just expressed my love for everything about Miss Frost?

"My grandmother," I started to say, "and my aunt Muriel—"

But Miss Frost lightly touched my lips with her long fingers again. "*Shhh*, William," she whispered. "I don't need to hear what those ladies think of me. I'm much more interested in hearing about that project of yours in the old yearbook room."

"Oh, it's not really a project," I told her. "I just look at the wrestling-team photos, mostly—and at the pictures of the plays that the Drama Club performed."

"*Do* you?" Miss Frost somewhat absently asked. Why was it I got the feeling that she was acting—in a kind of on-again, off-again way? What was it she'd said, when Richard Abbott had asked her if she'd ever been *onstage*—if she'd ever *acted?*

"Only in my mind," she'd answered him, almost flirtatiously. "When I was younger—all the time."

"And what year are you up to in those old yearbooks, William—which graduating class?" Miss Frost then asked.

"Nineteen thirty-one," I answered. Her fingers had strayed from my lips; she was touching the collar of my shirt, almost as if there were something about a boy's button-down dress shirt that had affected her—a sentimental attachment, maybe.

"You're so close," Miss Frost said.

"Close to *what?*" I asked her.

"Just close," she said. "We haven't much time."

"Is it time to close the library?" I asked her, but Miss Frost only smiled; then, as if giving the matter more thought, she glanced at her watch.

"Well, what harm is there in closing a little early tonight?" she said suddenly.

"Sure—why not?" I said. "There's no one here but us. I don't think Atkins is coming back."

"Poor Tom," Miss Frost said. "He doesn't have a crush on *me*, William— Tom Atkins has a crush on *you!*"

The second she said so, I knew it was true. "Poor Tom," which would become how I thought of Atkins, probably sensed I had a crush on Miss Frost; he must have been jealous of her.

"Poor Tom is just spying on me, *and* you," Miss Frost told me. "And what does Kittredge want to talk to you about?" she suddenly asked me.

"Oh, that's nothing—that's just a German thing. I help Kittredge with his German," I explained.

"Tom Atkins would be a safer choice for you than Jacques Kittredge, William," Miss Frost said. I knew this was true, too, though I didn't find Atkins attractive—except in the way that someone who adores you can become a *little* attractive to you, over time. (But that almost never works out, does it?)

Yet, when I began to tell Miss Frost that I wasn't really attracted to Atkins—that not *all* boys were attractive to me, just a very few boys, actually—well, this time she put her lips to mine. She simply kissed me. It was a fairly firm kiss, moderately aggressive; there was only one assertive thrust, a single dart of her warm tongue. Believe me: I'll soon be seventy; I've had a long lifetime of kisses, and this one was more confident than any man's handshake.

"I know, I know," she murmured against my lips. "We have so little time—let's not talk about poor Tom."

"Oh."

I followed her into the foyer, where I was still thinking that her concern with "time" had only to do with the closing time of the library, but Miss Frost said: "I presume that check-in time for seniors is still ten o'clock, William—except on a Saturday night, when I'm guessing it's still eleven. Nothing ever changes at that awful school, does it?"

I was impressed that Miss Frost even knew about check-in time at Favorite River Academy—not to mention that she was exactly right about it.

I watched her lock the door to the library and turn off the outdoor light; she left the dim light in the foyer on, while she went about the main library, killing the other lights. I had completely forgotten that I'd asked her advice—on the subject of a book about my having a crush on Kittredge, and "trying not to"—when Miss Frost handed me a slender novel. It was only about forty-five pages longer than *King Lear,* which happened to be the story I'd read most recently.

It was a novel by James Baldwin called *Giovanni's Room*—the title

of which I could barely read, because Miss Frost had extinguished all the lights in the main library. There was only the light from the dimly lit foyer—scarcely sufficient for Miss Frost and me to see our way to the basement stairs.

On the dark stairs, lit only by what scant light followed us from the foyer of the library—and a dull glowing ahead of us, which beckoned us to Miss Frost's cubicle, partitioned off from the furnace room—I suddenly remembered that there was another novel I wanted the confident librarian's advice about.

The name *Al* was on my lips, but I could not bring myself to say it. I said, instead: "Miss Frost, what can you tell me about *Madame Bovary*? Do you think I would like it?"

"When you're older, William, I think you'll *love* it."

"That's kind of what Richard said, and Uncle Bob," I told her.

"Your uncle Bob has read *Madame Bovary*—you can't mean *Muriel's* Bob!" Miss Frost exclaimed.

"Bob hasn't read it—he was just telling me what it was about," I explained.

"Someone who hasn't read a novel doesn't really know what it's *about*, William."

"Oh."

"You should wait, William," Miss Frost said. "The time to read *Madame Bovary* is when your romantic hopes and desires have crashed, and you believe that your future relationships will have disappointing—even devastating—consequences."

"I'll wait to read it until then," I told her.

Her bedroom and bathroom—formerly, the coal bin—was lit only by a reading lamp, affixed to the headboard of rails on the old-fashioned brass bed. Miss Frost lit the cinnamon-scented candle on the night table, turning off the lamp. In the candlelight, she told me to undress. "That means everything, William—please don't keep on your socks."

I did as she told me, with my back turned to her, while she said she would appreciate "some privacy"; she briefly used the toilet with the wooden seat—I believe I heard her pee, and flush—and then, from the sound of running water, I think she had a quick wash-up and brushed her teeth in the small sink.

I lay naked on her brass bed; in the flickering candlelight, I read that *Giovanni's Room* was published in 1956. From the attached library card,

I saw that only one patron of the First Sister Public Library had checked out the novel—in four years—and I wondered if Mr. Baldwin's solitary reader had in fact been Miss Frost. I did not finish the first two paragraphs before Miss Frost said, "Please don't read that now, William. It's very sad, and it will surely upset you."

"Upset me *how?*" I asked her. I could hear her hanging her clothes in the wardrobe closet; it was distracting to imagine her naked, but I kept reading.

"There's no such thing as trying not to have a crush on Kittredge, William—'trying not to' doesn't work," Miss Frost said.

That was when the penultimate sentence of the second paragraph stopped me; I just closed the book and shut my eyes.

"I told you to stop reading, didn't I?" Miss Frost said.

The sentence began: "There will be a girl sitting opposite me who will wonder why I have not been flirting with her"—I stopped there wondering if I would dare to continue.

"It's not a novel your mother should see," Miss Frost was saying, "and if you're not prepared to talk about your crush on Kittredge with Richard—well, I wouldn't let Richard know what you're reading, either." I could feel her lie down on the bed, behind me; her bare skin touched my back, but she'd not taken off all her clothes. She gently took hold of my penis in her big hand.

"There's a fish called a shad," Miss Frost said.

"A shad?" I asked; my penis was stiffening.

"Yes—that's what it's called," Miss Frost told me. "It migrates upstream to spawn. Shad roe is a delicacy. You know what roe is, don't you?" she asked me.

"The eggs, right?"

"The unborn eggs, yes—they take them out of the female fish, and some people love to eat them," Miss Frost explained.

"Oh."

"Say 'shad roe' for me, William."

"Shad roe," I said.

"Try saying it without the *r*," she told me.

"Shadow," I said, without thinking; my penis and her hand had most of my attention.

"Like Lear's shadow?" she asked me.

"Lear's shadow," I said. "I didn't want a part in the play, anyway," I told her.

"Well, at least you didn't say Lear's shad roe," Miss Frost said.

"Lear's shadow," I repeated.

"And what's *this* that I've got in my hand?" she asked me.

"My *penith*," I answered.

"I wouldn't change that *penith* for all the world, William," Miss Frost said. "I believe you should say that word any fucking way you want to."

What happened next would usher in the unattainable; what Miss Frost did to me would prove inimitable. She pulled me suddenly to her—I was flat on my back—and she kissed me on my mouth. She was wearing a bra—not a padded one, like Elaine's, but a see-through bra with only slightly bigger cups than I'd expected. The material was sheer, and much silkier than the soft cotton of Elaine's bra, and—to compare it to the more utilitarian undergarments in my mother's mail-order catalogs— Miss Frost's bra was not in the training-bra category; it was altogether sexier and more sophisticated. Miss Frost also wore a half-slip, of the slinky kind women wear under a skirt—this one was a beige color—and when she straddled my hips and sat on me, she appeared to hike up the half-slip, well above mid-thigh. Her weight, and how firmly she held me, pressed me into the bed.

I held one of her small, soft breasts in one hand; with my other hand, I tried to touch her, under her half-slip, but Miss Frost said, "No, William. Please don't touch me there." She took my straying hand and clasped it to her other breast.

It was my penis that she guided under her half-slip. I had never penetrated anyone, and when I felt this most amazing friction, of course this felt like penetration to me. There was a slippery sensation—there was absolutely no pain, yet my penis had never been so tightly gripped— and when I ejaculated, I cried out against her small, soft breasts. I was surprised that my face was pressed against her breasts and her silky bra, because I didn't remember the moment when Miss Frost had stopped kissing me. (She'd said, "No, William. Please don't touch me there." Obviously, she couldn't have been kissing me *and* speaking to me at the same time.)

There was so much I wanted to say to her, and ask her, but Miss Frost was not in a mood for conversation. Perhaps she was feeling the curious constraints of "so little time" again, or so I managed to convince myself.

She drew a bath for me; I was hoping that she would take off the rest of her clothes and get into the big tub with me, but she did not. She knelt beside that bathtub with the lion paws for feet, and the lion heads for faucets, and she gently bathed me—she was especially gentle with my penis. (She even spoke of it affectionately, using the *penith* word in a way that made us both laugh.)

But Miss Frost kept looking at her watch. "Late for check-in means a restriction, William. A restriction might entail an earlier check-in time. No visits to the First Sister Public Library after closing time—we wouldn't like that, would we?"

When I had a look at her watch, I saw it was not even nine-thirty. I was just a few minutes' walk from Bancroft Hall, which I pointed out to Miss Frost.

"Well, you might run into Kittredge and have a German discussion— you never know, William," was all she said.

I had noticed a wet, silky feeling, and when I touched my penis— before stepping into the bath—my fingers had a vaguely perfumy smell. Maybe Miss Frost had used a lubricant of some kind, I imagined—something I would be reminded of years later, when I first smelled those liquid soaps that are made from almond or avocado oil. But, whatever it was, the bath had washed it away.

"No detours to that old yearbook room—not tonight, William," Miss Frost was saying; she helped me get dressed, as if I were a child going off to my first day of school. She even put a dab of toothpaste on her finger, and stuck it in my mouth. "Go rinse your mouth in the sink," she told me. "I assume you can find your way out—I'll lock up again, when I go." She kissed me then—a long, lingering kiss that caused me to put both my hands on her hips.

Miss Frost quickly intercepted my hands, taking them from her slinky, knee-length half-slip and clasping them to her breasts, where (I had the distinct impression) she believed my hands belonged. Or perhaps she believed that my hands *didn't* belong below her waist—that I should not, or must not, touch her "there."

As I made my way up the dark basement stairs, toward the faint light that was glowing from the foyer of the library, I was remembering an idiot admonition in a long-ago morning meeting—the always-numbing warning from Dr. Harlow, on the occasion of a weekend dance we were having with a visiting all-girls' school. "Don't touch your dates below their waists," our peerless school physician said, "and you *and* your dates will be happier!"

But this *couldn't* be true, I was thinking, when Miss Frost called to me—I was still on the stairs. "Go straight home, William—and come see me soon!"

We have so little time! I almost called back to her—one of those premonitory thoughts I would remember later, and forever, though at the time I imagined I was thinking of saying it just to see what *she* would say. Miss Frost was the one who seemed to think we had so little time, for whatever reason.

Outside, I had a passing thought about poor Atkins—poor *Tom*. I was sorry that I'd been mean to him, though it made me laugh at myself to recall I had ever imagined he might have a crush on Miss Frost. It was funny to think of them being together—Atkins with his pronunciation problem, his complete incapability of saying the *time* word, and Miss Frost saying it every other minute!

I had passed the mirror in the dimly lit foyer, scarcely looking at myself, but—in the star-bright September night—I considered that I had looked much more grown up to myself (than before my encounter with Miss Frost, I mean). Yet, as I made my way along River Street to the Favorite River campus, I reflected that I could not tell from my expression in the mirror that I'd just had sex for the first time.

And that thought had an unnerving, disturbing companion—namely, I suddenly imagined that maybe I *hadn't* had sex. (Not *actual* sex—no actual *penetration*, I mean.) Then I thought: How can I be thinking such a thing on what is the most pleasurable night of my young life?

I as yet had no idea that it was possible not to have actual sex (*or* actual penetration) and still have unsurpassable sexual pleasure—a pleasure that, to this day, has been unmatched.

But what did I know? I was only eighteen; that night, with James Baldwin's *Giovanni's Room* in my book bag, my crushes on the wrong people were just beginning.

THE COMMON ROOM IN Bancroft Hall was, like the common rooms in other dorms, called the butt room; the seniors who were smokers were allowed to spend their study hours there. Many nonsmokers who were seniors thought it was a privilege too important to be missed; even they chose to spend their study hours there.

No one warned us of the dangers of secondhand smoke in those fear-less years—least of all our imbecilic school physician. I don't recall a sin-gle morning meeting that addressed the *affliction* of smoking! Dr. Harlow had devoted his time and talents to the treatment of excessive crying in boys—in the doctor's stalwart belief that there was a cure for homosexual tendencies in the young men we were becoming.

I was fifteen minutes early for check-in; when I walked into the fa-miliar blue-gray haze of smoke in the Bancroft butt room, Kittredge ac-costed me. I don't know what wrestling hold it was. I would later try to describe it to Delacorte—who I heard didn't do a bad job as Lear's Fool, by the way. Between rinsing and spitting, Delacorte said: "It sounds like an arm-bar. Kittredge arm-bars the shit out of everyone."

Whatever the name of the wrestling hold is, it didn't hurt. I just knew I couldn't get away from him, and I didn't try. It was frankly over-whelming to be held so tightly by Kittredge, when I had just been held by Miss Frost.

"Hi, Nymph," Kittredge said. "Where have you been?"

"The library," I answered.

"I heard you left the library a while ago," Kittredge said.

"I went to the *other* library," I told him. "There's a public library, the town library."

"I suppose one library isn't enough for a busy boy like you, Nymph. Herr Steiner is hitting us with a quiz tomorrow—I'm guessing more Rilke than Goethe, but what do *you* think?"

I'd had Herr Steiner in German II—he was one of the Austrian ski-ers. He wasn't a bad teacher, or a bad guy, but he was pretty predict-able. Kittredge was right that there would be more Rilke than Goethe on the quiz; Steiner liked Rilke, but who didn't? Herr Steiner also liked big words, and so did Goethe. Kittredge got in trouble in German because he was always guessing. You can't guess in a foreign language, especially not in a language as precise as German. Either you know it or you don't.

"You've got to know the big words in Goethe, Kittredge. The quiz won't be all Rilke," I told him.

"The phrases Steiner likes in Rilke are all the *long* ones," Kittredge complained. "They're hard to remember."

"There are some short phrases in Rilke, too. Everyone likes them—not just Steiner," I warned him. " '*Musik: Atem der Statuen.*' "

"Shit!" Kittredge cried. "I know that—what *is* that?"

" 'Music: breathing of statues,' " I translated for him, but I was thinking about the arm-bar, if that was the wrestling hold; I was hoping he would hold me forever. "And there's this one: '*Du, fast noch Kind*'—do you know that one?"

"All the childhood shit!" Kittredge cried. "Did fucking Rilke never get over his childhood, or something?"

" 'You, almost still a child'—I guarantee that'll be on the quiz, Kittredge."

"And '*reine Übersteigung*'! The 'pure transcendence' bullshit!" Kittredge cried, holding me tighter. "That one will be there!"

"With Rilke, you can count on the childhood thing—it'll be there," I warned him.

" '*Lange Nachmittage der Kindheit,*' " Kittredge sang in my ear. " 'Long afternoons of childhood.' Aren't you impressed that I know that one, Nymph?"

"If it's the *long* phrases you're worried about, don't forget this one: '*Weder Kindheit noch Zukunft werden weniger*—neither childhood nor future grows any smaller.' Remember that one?" I asked him.

"Fuck!" Kittredge cried. "I thought that was Goethe!"

"It's about childhood, right? It's Rilke," I told him. *Dass ich dich fassen möcht*—If only I could clasp you! I was thinking. (*That* was Goethe.) But all I said was " '*Schöpfungskraft.*' "

"Double-fuck!" Kittredge said. "I know *that's* Goethe."

"It doesn't mean 'double-fuck,' though," I told him. I don't know what he did with the arm-bar, but it started hurting. "It means 'creative power,' or something like that," I said, and the pain stopped; I had almost liked it. "I'll bet you don't know '*Stossgebet*'—you missed it last year," I reminded him. The pain was back in the arm-bar; it felt pretty good.

"You're feeling dauntless tonight, aren't you, Nymph? The two libraries must have boosted your confidence," Kittredge told me.

"How's Delacorte doing with 'Lear's shadow'—and all the rest of it?" I asked him.

He let up on the arm-bar; he seemed to hold me almost soothingly. "What's a fucking '*Stossgebet*,' Nymph?" he asked me.

"An 'ejaculatory prayer,' " I told him.

"Triple-fuck," he said, with uncharacteristic resignation. "Fucking Goethe."

"You had trouble with *'überschlechter'* last year, too—if Steiner gets sneaky and throws an adjective in. I'm just trying to help you," I told him.

Kittredge released me from the arm-bar. "I think I know this one—it means 'really bad,' right?" he asked me. (You must understand that the entire time we were not exactly wrestling—and not exactly *conversing*, either—the denizens of the Bancroft butt room were enthralled. Kittredge was ever the eye magnet, in any crowd, and here I was—at least appearing to hold my own with him.)

"Don't get fooled by *'Demut,'* will you?" I asked him. "It's a short word, but it's still Goethe."

"I know that one, Nymph," Kittredge said, smiling. "It's 'humility,' isn't it?"

"Yes," I said; I was surprised he knew the word, even in English. "Just remember: If it sounds like a homily or a proverb, it's probably Goethe," I told him.

" 'Old age is a polite gentleman'—you mean that sort of bullshit." To my further surprise, Kittredge even knew the German, which he then recited: " '*Das Alter ist ein höflich' Mann.*' "

"There's one that sounds like Rilke, but it's Goethe," I warned him.

"It's the one about the fucking kiss," Kittredge said. "Say it in German, Nymph," he commanded me.

" '*Der Kuss, der letzte, grausam süss,*' " I said to him, thinking of Miss Frost's frank kisses. I couldn't help but think of kissing Kittredge, too; I was starting to shake again.

" 'The kiss, the last one, cruelly sweet,' " Kittredge translated.

"That's right, or you could say 'the last kiss of all,' if you wanted to," I told him. " '*Die Leidenschaft bringt Leiden!*' " I then said to him, taking every word to heart.

"Fucking Goethe!" Kittredge cried. I could tell he didn't know it—there was no *guessing* it, either.

" 'Passion brings pain,' " I translated for him.

"Oh, yeah," he said. "Lots of pain."

"You guys," one of the smokers said. "It's almost check-in time."

"Quadruple-fuck," Kittredge said. I knew he could sprint across the quadrangle of dorms to Tilley, or—if he was late—Kittredge could be counted on to make up a brilliant excuse.

" '*Ein jeder Engel ist schrecklich,*' " I said to Kittredge, as he was leaving the butt room.

"Rilke, right?" he asked me.

"It's Rilke, all right. It's a famous one," I told him. " 'Every angel is terrifying.' "

That stopped Kittredge in the doorway to the butt room. He looked at me before he ran on; it was a look that frightened me, because I thought I saw both complete understanding and total contempt in his handsome face. It was as if Kittredge suddenly knew everything about me—not only who I was, and what I was hiding, but everything that awaited me in my future. (My menacing *Zukunft,* as Rilke would have called it.)

"You're a special boy, aren't you, Nymph?" Kittredge quickly asked me. But he ran on, not expecting an answer; he just called to me as he ran. "I'll bet every fucking one of *your* angels is going to be terrifying!"

I know it isn't what Rilke meant by "every angel," but I was thinking of Kittredge and Miss Frost, and maybe poor Tom Atkins—and who knew who *else* there would be in my future?—as *my* terrifying angels.

And what was it Miss Frost had said, when she advised me to wait before reading *Madame Bovary?* What if my terrifying angels, beginning with Miss Frost and Jacques Kittredge (my "future relationships," was what Miss Frost had said), *all* had "disappointing—even devastating—consequences," as she'd also put it?

"What's wrong, Bill?" Richard Abbott asked, when I came into our dormitory apartment. (My mother had already gone to bed; at least their bedroom door was closed, as it often was.) "You look as if you've seen a ghost!" Richard said.

"Not a ghost," I told him. "Just my future, maybe," I said. I chose to leave him with the mystery of my remark; I went straight to my bedroom, and closed the door.

There was Elaine's padded bra, where it nearly always was—under my pillow. I lay looking at it for a long time, seeing little of my future—or my terrifying angels—in it.

Chapter 8

BIG AL

"It is Kittredge's cruelty that I chiefly dislike," I wrote to Elaine that fall.

"He came by it genetically," she wrote me back. Of course I couldn't dispute Elaine's superior knowledge of Mrs. Kittredge. Elaine and "that awful woman" had been intimate enough for Elaine to become assertive on the matter of those mother-to-son genes that were passed. "Kittredge can deny she's his mom till the cows come home, Billy, but I'm telling you she's one of those moms who breast-fed the fucker till he was shaving!"

"Okay," I wrote to Elaine, "but what makes you so sure cruelty is genetic?"

"What about kissing?" Elaine wrote me back. "Those two kiss the same way, Billy. Kissing is definitely genetic."

Elaine's genetic dissertation on Kittredge was in the same letter where she announced her intention to be a writer; even in the area of that most sacred ambition, Elaine had been more candid with me than I'd managed to be with her. Here I was embarking on my long-desired adventure with Miss Frost, yet I still hadn't told Elaine about *that*!

I'd not told anyone about that, naturally. I had also resisted reading more of *Giovanni's Room*, until I realized that I wanted to see Miss Frost again—as soon as I could—and I believed that I shouldn't show up at the First Sister Public Library without being prepared to discuss the writing of James Baldwin with Miss Frost. Thus I plunged ahead in the novel—not very far ahead, in fact, before I was stopped cold by another sentence. This one was just after the beginning of the second chapter, and it rendered me incapable of reading further for an entire day.

"I understand now that the contempt I felt for him involved my self-contempt," I read. I immediately thought of Kittredge—how my dislike of him was completely entangled with my dislike of myself for being attracted to him. I thought that James Baldwin's writing was a little too true for me to handle, but I forced myself to try again the very next night.

There is that description, still in the second chapter, of "the usual, knife-blade lean, tight-trousered boys," from which I inwardly recoiled; I would soon model myself on those boys, and seek their company, and the thought of an abundance of "knife-blade boys" in my future frightened me.

Then, in spite of my fear, I was suddenly halfway into the novel, and I couldn't stop reading. Even that part where the narrator's hatred for his male lover is as powerful as his love for him, and is "nourished by the same roots"; or the part where Giovanni is described as somehow always desirable, while at the same time his breath makes the narrator "want to vomit"—I truly detested those passages, but only because of how much I loathed and feared those feelings in myself.

Yes, having these disturbing attractions to other boys and men also made me afraid of what Baldwin calls "the dreadful whiplash of public morality," but I was much more frightened by the passage that describes the narrator's reaction to having sex with a woman—"I was fantastically intimidated by her breasts, and when I entered her I began to feel that I would never get out alive."

Why hadn't that happened to *me*? I wondered. Was it only because Miss Frost had small breasts? If she'd had big ones, would I have felt "intimidated"—instead of so amazingly aroused? And, once again, there came the unbidden thought: Had I really "entered" her? If I had not, and I did enter her the next time, would I subsequently feel disgusted—instead of so completely satisfied?

You must understand that, until I read *Giovanni's Room*, I'd never read a novel that had shocked me, and I'd already (at eighteen) read a lot of novels—many of them excellent. James Baldwin wrote excellent stuff, *and* he shocked me—most of all when Giovanni cries to his lover, "You want to leave Giovanni because he makes you stink. You want to despise Giovanni because he is not afraid of the stink of love." That phrase, "the stink of love," shocked me, and it made me feel so awfully naïve. What had I thought making love to a boy or a man *might* smell like? Did Baldwin actually mean the smell of *shit*, because wouldn't that be the smell on your cock if you fucked a man or a boy?

I was terribly agitated to read this; I wanted to talk to someone about it, and I almost went and woke up Richard to talk to him.

But I remembered what Miss Frost had said. I wasn't prepared to talk to Richard Abbott about my crush on Kittredge. I just stayed in bed; I was wearing Elaine's bra, as usual, and I read on and on in *Giovanni's Room*—on into the night.

I remembered the perfumy smell on my fingers, after I'd touched my penis and before I stepped into the bath Miss Frost had drawn for me; that almond- or avocado-oil scent wasn't at all like the smell of shit. But, of course, Miss Frost was a *woman*, and if I *had* penetrated her, surely I had not penetrated her *there*!

Mrs. Hadley was suitably impressed that I had conquered the *shadow* word, but because I couldn't (or wouldn't) tell Martha Hadley about Miss Frost, I had some difficulty describing how I'd mastered one of my unpronounceables.

"Whatever made you think of saying 'shad roe' without the *r*, Billy?"

"Ah, well . . ." I started to say, and then stopped—in the manner of Grandpa Harry.

It was a mystery to Mrs. Hadley, and to me, how "the shad-roe technique" (as Martha Hadley called it) could be applied to my other pronunciation problems.

Naturally, upon leaving Mrs. Hadley's office—once again, on the stairs in the music building—I ran into Atkins.

"Oh, it's *you*, Tom," I said, as casually as I could.

"So now it's 'Tom,' is it?" Atkins asked me.

"I'm just sick of the last-name culture of this awful school—aren't you?" I asked him.

"Now that you mention it," Atkins said bitterly; I could tell that poor Tom's feathers were still ruffled from our run-in at the First Sister Public Library.

"Look, I'm sorry about the other night," I told him. "I didn't mean to add to whatever misery Kittredge had caused you by calling you his 'messenger boy.' I apologize."

Atkins had a way of often seeming on the verge of tears. If Dr. Harlow had ever wanted to summon before us a quaking example of what our school physician meant by "excessive crying in boys," I imagined that he needed only to snap his fingers and ask Tom Atkins to burst into tears at morning meeting.

"It seemed that I probably *interrupted* you and Miss Frost," Atkins said searchingly.

"Miss Frost and I talk a lot about writing," I told him. "She tells me what books I should read. I tell her what I'm interested in, and she gives me a novel."

"What novel did she give you the other night?" Tom asked. "What *are* you interested in, Bill?"

"Crushes on the wrong people," I told Atkins. It was astonishing how quickly my first sexual relationship, with anyone, had emboldened me. I felt encouraged—even compelled—to say things I'd heretofore been reluctant to say, not only to a timid soul like Tom Atkins but even to such a powerful nemesis and forbidden love as Jacques Kittredge.

Granted, it was a lot easier to be brave with Kittredge in German. I didn't feel sufficiently "emboldened" to tell Kittredge my true feelings and actual thoughts; I wouldn't have dared to say "crushes on the wrong people" to Kittredge, not even in German. (Not unless I pretended it was something Goethe or Rilke had written.)

I saw that Atkins was struggling to say something—maybe about what time it was, or something with the *time* word in it. But I was wrong; it was "crushes" that poor Tom couldn't say.

Atkins suddenly blurted: "*Thrushes* on the wrong people—that's a subject that interests me, too!"

"I said 'crushes,' Tom."

"I can't say that word," Atkins admitted. "But I am *very* interested in that subject. Perhaps, when you're finished reading whatever novel Miss Frost gave you on that subject, you could give it to me. I like to read novels, you know."

"It's a novel by James Baldwin," I told Atkins.

"It's about being in love with a *black* person?" Atkins asked.

"No. What gave you that idea, Tom?"

"James Baldwin is black, isn't he, Bill? Or am I thinking of another Baldwin?"

James Baldwin was black, of course, but I didn't know that. I'd not read any of his other books; I had never heard of him. And *Giovanni's*

Room was a library book—as such, it didn't have a dust jacket. I'd not seen an author photo of James Baldwin.

"It's a novel about a man who's in love with another man," I told Tom quietly.

"Yes," Atkins whispered. "That's what I thought it would be about, when you first mentioned the 'wrong people.'"

"I'll let you read it when I'm finished," I said. I had finished *Giovanni's Room*, of course, but I wanted to read it again, and talk to Miss Frost about it, before I let Atkins read it, though I was certain there was nothing about the narrator being black—and poor Giovanni, I knew, was Italian.

In fact, I even remembered that line near the end of the novel when the narrator is looking at himself in a mirror—"my body is dull and white and dry." But I simply wanted to reread *Giovanni's Room* right away; it had had that profound an effect on me. It was the first novel I'd wanted to reread since *Great Expectations*.

Now, when I'm nearly seventy, there are few novels I can reread and *still* love—I mean among those novels I first read and loved when I was a teenager—but I recently reread *Great Expectations* and *Giovanni's Room*, and I admired those novels no less than I ever had.

Oh, all right, there are passages in Dickens that go on too long, but so what? And who the trannies were in Paris, in Mr. Baldwin's time there—well, they were probably not very passable transvestites. The narrator of *Giovanni's Room* doesn't like them. "I always found it difficult to believe that they ever went to bed with anybody, for a man who wanted a woman would certainly have rather had a real one and a man who wanted a man would certainly not want one of *them*," Baldwin wrote.

Okay, I'm guessing that Mr. Baldwin never met one of the *very* passable transsexuals one can meet today. He didn't know a Donna, one of those she-males with breasts and not a trace of facial hair—one of those totally *convincing* females. You would swear that there wasn't an iota of anything masculine in the kind of transsexual I'm talking about, except for that fully functioning *penith* between her legs!

I'm also guessing that Mr. Baldwin never wanted a lover with breasts *and* a cock. But, believe me, I don't fault James Baldwin for failing to be attracted to the trannies of his time—*"les folles,"* he called them.

All I say is: Let us leave *les folles* alone; let's just leave them be. Don't judge them. You are not superior to them—don't put them down.

In rereading *Giovanni's Room* just recently, I not only found the novel to be as perfect as I'd remembered it; I also discovered something I had missed, or I'd read without noticing, when I was eighteen. I mean the part where Baldwin writes that "people can't, unhappily, invent their mooring posts, their lovers and their friends, anymore than they can invent their parents."

Yes, that's true. Naturally, when I was eighteen, I was still *inventing myself* nonstop; I don't only mean sexually. And I was unaware that I needed "mooring posts"—not to mention how many I would need, or who my mooring posts would be.

Poor Tom Atkins needed a mooring post, in the worst way. That much was evident to me, as Atkins and I conversed, or we tried to, on the subject of crushes (or *thrushes!*) on the wrong people. For a moment it seemed we would never progress from where we stood on the stairs of the music building, and that what passed for our conversation had permanently lagged.

"Have you had any breakthroughs with your pronunciation problems, Bill?" Atkins awkwardly asked me.

"Just one, actually," I told him. "I seem to have conquered the *shadow* word."

"Good for you," Atkins said sincerely. "I've not conquered any of mine—not in a while, anyway."

"I'm sorry, Tom," I told him. "It must be tough having trouble with one of those words that comes up all the time. Like the *time* word," I said.

"Yes, that's a tough one," Atkins admitted. "What's one of your worst ones?"

"The word for your *whatchamacallit*," I told him. "You know—dong, schlong, dick, dork, willy, dipstick, dipping wick, quim-stuffer," I said.

"You can't say *penis?*" Atkins whispered.

"It comes out *penith*," I told him.

"Well, at least it's comprehensible, Bill," Atkins said encouragingly.

"Do you have one that's worse than the *time* word?" I asked him.

"The female equivalent of your penis," Atkins answered. "I can't come close to saying it—it just kills me to try it."

"You mean 'vagina,' Tom?"

Atkins nodded vigorously; I thought poor Tom had that verge-of-tears aspect, in the way he wouldn't stop nodding his head, but Mrs. Hadley saved him from crying—albeit only momentarily.

"Tom Atkins!" Martha Hadley called down the stairwell. "I can hear your voice, but you are *late* for your appointment! I am *waiting* for you!"

Atkins started to run up the stairs, without thinking. He gave me a friendly but vaguely embarrassed look, over his shoulder; I distinctly heard him call to Mrs. Hadley as he continued up the stairs. "I'm sorry! I'm coming!" Atkins shouted. "I just lost track of the time!" Both Martha Hadley and I had clearly heard him.

"That sounds like a breakthrough to me, Tom!" I hollered up the stairs.

"What did you just say, Tom Atkins? Say it again!" I heard Mrs. Hadley call down to him.

"Time! Time! Time!" I heard Atkins crying, before his tears engulfed him.

"Oh, don't *cry*, you silly boy!" Martha Hadley was saying. "Tom, Tom—please stop crying. You should be *happy*!" But I heard Atkins blubbering on and on; once the tears started, he couldn't stop them. (I knew the feeling.)

"Listen to me, Tom!" I called up the stairwell. "You're on a roll, man. Now's the time to try 'vagina.' I know you can do it! If you can conquer 'time,' trust me—'vagina' is easy! Let me hear you say the *vagina* word, Tom! Vagina! Vagina! Vagina!"

"Watch your language, Billy," Mrs. Hadley called down the stairwell. I would have kept up the encouragements to poor Tom, but I didn't want Martha Hadley—or another faculty person in the music building—to give me a restriction.

I had a date—a fucking date!—with Miss Frost, so I didn't repeat the *vagina* word. I just went on my way down the stairs; all the way out of the music building, I could hear Tom Atkins crying.

IT'S EASY TO SEE, with hindsight, how I gave myself away. I wasn't in the habit of showering and shaving before I went out in the evening to the library. While I was in the habit of not saying to Richard or my mom which library I was going to, I suppose I should have been smart enough to take *Giovanni's Room* with me. (I left the novel under my pillow, with Elaine's bra, but that was because I wasn't intending to return the book to the library. I wanted to lend it to Tom Atkins, but only after I'd asked Miss Frost if she thought that was a good idea.)

"You look *nice*, Billy," my mother commented, as I was leaving our dormitory apartment. She almost never complimented me on my appearance; while she'd more than once said I was "*going to be* good-looking," she hadn't said that in a couple of years. I'm guessing that I was already *too* good-looking, in my mom's opinion, because the way she said the *nice* word wasn't very nice.

"Going to the library, Bill?" Richard asked me.

"That's right," I said. It was stupid of me not to take my German homework with me. Because of Kittredge, I was almost never without my Goethe and my Rilke. But that night my book bag was practically empty. I had one of my writing notebooks with me—that was all.

"You look too *nice* for the library, Billy," my mom said.

"I suppose I can't go around looking like Lear's *shadow*, can I?" I asked the two of them. I was just showing off, but, in retrospect, it was inadvisable to give my mother and Richard Abbott a taste of my new-found confidence.

It was only a little later that same evening—I'm sure I was still in the yearbook room of the academy library—when Kittredge showed up at Bancroft Hall, looking for me. My mother answered the door to our apartment, but when she saw who it was, I'm certain she wouldn't have invited Kittredge in. "Richard!" she no doubt called. "Jacques Kittredge is here!"

"I was hoping for a word with the German scholar," Kittredge said charmingly.

"Richard!" my mom would have called again.

"I'm coming, Jewel!" Richard would have answered. It was a small apartment; while my mother wanted nothing to do with talking to Kittredge, I'm sure she overheard every word of Kittredge's conversation with Richard.

"If it's the German scholar you're looking for, Jacques, I'm afraid he's gone to the library," Richard told Kittredge.

"*Which* library?" Kittredge asked. "He's a two-library student, that German scholar. The other night, he was hanging out in the town library—you know, the *public* one."

"What's Billy doing in the *public* library, Richard?" my mom might have asked. (She would have thought this, anyway; she would have asked Richard later, if not while Kittredge was still there.)

"I guess Miss Frost is continuing to advise him about what to read," Richard Abbott may have answered—either then or later.

"I gotta be going," Kittredge probably said. "Just tell the German scholar that I did pretty well on the quiz—my best grade ever. Tell him he was dead-on about the 'passion brings pain' part. Tell him he even guessed right about the 'terrifying angel'—I nailed that part," Kittredge told Richard.

"I'll tell him," Richard would have said to Kittredge. "You got the 'passion brings pain' part—you nailed the 'terrifying angel,' too. I'll be sure to tell him."

By then, my mother would already have found the library book in my bedroom. She knew that I kept Elaine's bra under my pillow; I'll bet that's the first place she looked.

Richard Abbott was a well-informed guy; he may have already heard what *Giovanni's Room* was about. Of course, my German homework—the ever-present Goethe and Rilke—would have been visible in my bedroom, too. Whatever was preoccupying me, in *which* library, it didn't appear to be my German homework. And folded in the pages of Mr. Baldwin's superb novel would have been my handwritten notes—quotations from *Giovanni's Room* included, of course. Naturally, "stink of love" would have been among my jottings, and that sentence I thought of whenever I thought of Kittredge: "With everything in me screaming *No!* yet the sum of me sighed *Yes.*"

Kittredge would have been long gone from Bancroft by the time Richard and my mom drew their conclusions and called the others. Maybe not Mrs. Hadley—that is, not at first—but certainly my meddlesome aunt Muriel and my much-abused uncle Bob, and of course Nana Victoria and First Sister's most famous female impersonator, Grandpa Harry. They must have all drawn their conclusions, and even come up with a rudimentary plan, while I was still in the process of leaving the old yearbook room; by the time their plan of attack took its final form, I'm sure I was already en route to the First Sister Public Library, where I arrived shortly before closing time.

I HAD A LOT on my mind about Miss Frost—especially after seeing the 1935 *Owl*. I did my best not to linger over that heartthrob of a boy on the '31 wrestling team; there wasn't anyone who arrested my attention in the Favorite River Academy yearbook of 1932, not even among the wrestlers. In the Drama Club photos from '33 and '34, there were some boys-as-girls who looked convincingly feminine—at least onstage—but I didn't pay very close attention to those photographs, and I completely missed *Miss* Frost in the wrestling-team pictures of the '33 and '34 teams, when she was in the back row.

It was the '35 *Owl* that was the shocker—what would have been Miss Frost's senior year at Favorite River Academy. In that year, Miss Frost—even as a boy—was unmistakable. She was seated front-row center, because "A. Frost" was noted as the wrestling captain in '35; just the initial "A." was used in the captions under the team photo. Even sitting down, her long torso made her a head taller than any of the other boys in the front row, and I spotted her broad shoulders and big hands as easily as I doubtless would have if she'd been dressed and made up as a girl.

Her long, pretty face had not changed, though her thick hair was cut unfamiliarly short. I quickly flipped to the head shots of the graduating seniors. To my surprise, *Albert* Frost was from the town of First Sister, Vermont—a day student, not a boarder—and while the eighteen-year-old Albert's choice of college or university was cited as "undecided," the young man's chosen career was revealing. Albert had designated "fiction"—most fitting for a future librarian and a handsome boy on his way to becoming a passable (albeit small-breasted) woman.

I guessed that Aunt Muriel must have remembered Albert Frost, the handsome wrestling-team captain—Class of '35—and that it was *as a boy* that Muriel meant Miss Frost "*used to be* very good-looking." (Albert certainly was.)

I was not surprised to see Albert Frost's nickname at Favorite River Academy. It was "Big Al."

Miss Frost hadn't been kidding when she'd told me that "everyone used to" call her Al—including, very probably, my aunt Muriel.

I *was* surprised that I recognized another face among the head shots of the graduating seniors in the Class of 1935. Robert Fremont—my uncle Bob—had graduated in Miss Frost's class. Bob, whose nickname was "Racquet Man," must have known Miss Frost when she was Big Al. (It was one of life's little coincidences that, in the '35 *Owl*, Robert Fremont was on the page opposite Albert Frost.)

I realized, on that short walk from the yearbook room to the First Sister Public Library, that everyone in my family, which for a few years now included Richard Abbott, had to have known that Miss Frost had been born—and, in all likelihood, still was—a *man*. Naturally, no one had told *me* that Miss Frost was a man; after all, a lack of candor was endemic in my family.

It occurred to me, as I stood looking at my frightened face in that mirror in the dimly lit foyer of the town library, where Tom Atkins had so recently startled himself, that almost anyone of a certain age in First Sister, Vermont, would have known that Miss Frost was a man; this surely included everyone over the age of forty who had seen Miss Frost onstage as an Ibsen woman in those amateur productions of the First Sister Players.

I had subsequently found Miss Frost in the wrestling-team photos in the '33 and '34 yearbooks, where A. Frost was not quite so big and broad-shouldered; in fact, she'd stood so unsure of herself in the back row of those team photos that I had overlooked her.

I'd overlooked her, too, in the Drama Club photographs. A. Frost was always cast as a woman; she'd been onstage in a variety of female roles, but wearing such absurd wigs, and with breasts so unsuitably big, that I had failed to recognize her. What a lark that must have been for the boys—to see their wrestling-team captain, Big Al, flouncing around onstage, pretending to be a *girl*! Yet, when Richard had asked Miss Frost if she'd ever been *onstage*—if she'd ever *acted*—she'd answered, "Only in my mind."

What a lot of lies! I was thinking, as I saw myself shaking in the mirror.

"Is someone here?" I heard Miss Frost call. "Is that *you*, William?" she called, loudly enough that I knew we were alone in the library.

"Yes, it's me, Big Al," I answered.

"Oh, dear," I heard Miss Frost say, with an exaggerated sigh. "I told you we didn't have much time."

"There's quite a lot you *didn't* tell me!" I called to her.

I saw that, in anticipation of my arrival, Miss Frost had already killed the lights in the main library. The light that glowed upward, from the bottom of the basement stairs—the basement door was open—bathed Miss Frost in a soft, flattering light. She sat at the checkout desk with her big hands folded in her lap. (I say the light was "flattering" because it made her look younger; of course that also might have been the influence of my seeing her in those old yearbooks.)

"Come kiss me, William," Miss Frost said. "There's no reason for you *not* to kiss me, is there?"

"You're a *man*, aren't you?" I asked her.

"Goodness me, what makes a man?" she asked. "Isn't Kittredge a man? You want to kiss *him*. Don't you still want to kiss me, William?"

I *did* want to kiss her; I wanted to do *everything* with her, but I was angry and upset, and I knew by the way I was shaking that I was very close to crying, which I didn't want to do.

"You're a *transsexual!*" I told her.

"My dear boy," Miss Frost said sharply. "My dear boy, please don't put a *label* on me—don't make me a *category* before you get to know me!"

When she stood up from her desk, she seemed to tower over me; when she opened her arms to me, I didn't hesitate—I ran to her strong embrace, and kissed her. Miss Frost kissed me back, very hard. I couldn't cry, because she took my breath away.

"My, my—what a busy boy you've been, William," she said, leading me to the basement stairs. "You've read *Giovanni's Room*, haven't you?"

"Twice!" I managed to say.

"*Twice,* already! *And* you've found the time to read those old yearbooks, haven't you, William? I knew it wouldn't take you long to get from 1931 to 1935. Was it that wrestling-team photo in '35—was that the one that caught your eye, William?"

"Yes!" I scarcely managed to tell her. Miss Frost was lighting the cinnamon-scented candle in her bedroom; then she turned off the reading lamp that was fastened to the headboard of her brass bed, where the covers were already turned down.

"I couldn't very well have kept you from seeing those old yearbooks—could I, William?" she went on saying. "I'm not welcome in the academy library. And if you hadn't seen that picture of me in my wrestling days, surely somebody would have told you about me—eventually. I'm frankly astonished that someone *didn't* tell you," Miss Frost said.

"My family doesn't tell me much," I told her. I was undressing as quickly as I could, and Miss Frost had already unbuttoned her blouse and taken off her skirt. This time, when she used the toilet, she didn't mention the matter of her privacy.

"Yes, I know about that family of yours!" she said, laughing. She hiked up her half-slip, and—first lifting the wooden toilet seat—she peed standing up, rather loudly, but with her back to me. I didn't see her penis, but there was no doubt, from the forceful way she was pissing, that she had one.

I lay naked on the brass bed and watched her washing her hands and face, and brushing her teeth, in that little sink. I saw her wink at me in the mirror. "I guess you must have been a pretty good wrestler," I said to her, "if they made you captain of the team."

"I didn't ask to be captain," she told me. "I just kept beating every-body—I beat everyone, so they made me captain. It wasn't the kind of thing you could refuse."

"Oh."

"Besides, the wrestling kept them all from questioning me," Miss Frost said. She was hanging up her skirt and blouse in the wardrobe closet; this time, she took her bra off, too. "They don't question you—I mean *sexually*—if you're a wrestler. It kind of keeps them off the track—if you know what I mean, William."

"I know what you mean," I told her. I thought that her breasts were wonderful—so small, and with such perfect nipples, but her breasts were bigger than poor Elaine's. Miss Frost had a fourteen-year-old's breasts, and they looked small on her only because she was so big and strong.

"I love your breasts," I said to her.

"Thank you, William. They won't get any bigger, but it's a wonder what hormones can induce. I guess I don't really *need* to have bigger ones," Miss Frost said, smiling at me.

"I think they're the perfect size," I told her.

"I assure you, I didn't have them when I *wrestled*—that wouldn't have worked out very well," Miss Frost said. "I kept wrestling—thus, I kept the questions at bay, all through college," she told me. "No breasts—no liv-ing as a woman, William—until *after* I was out of college."

"Where'd you go to college?" I asked her.

"Someplace in Pennsylvania," she told me. "It's no place you've ever heard of."

"Were you as good a wrestler as Kittredge?" I asked her. She lay down beside me on the bed, but this time when she took my penis in her big hand, I was facing her.

"Kittredge isn't that good," Miss Frost said. "He just hasn't had any competition. New England isn't exactly a hotbed for wrestling. It's noth-ing like Pennsylvania."

"Oh."

I touched her half-slip, in the area where I thought her penis was; she let me touch her. I didn't try to reach under the half-slip. I just touched her penis through the slinky material of her half-slip; this one was a pearl-gray color, almost the same color as Elaine's bra. When I thought of Elaine's bra, I remembered *Giovanni's Room*, which was under the same pillow.

The James Baldwin novel was so unbearably sad that I suddenly didn't want to talk about it with Miss Frost; instead, I asked her, "Wasn't it difficult being a wrestler, when you wanted to be a girl and you were attracted to other boys?"

"It wasn't that difficult when I was winning. I like to be on top," she told me. "When you're winning in wrestling, you're on top. It was more difficult in Pennsylvania, because I wasn't winning all the time there. I was on the bottom more than I liked," she said, "but I was older then—I could handle losing. I *hated* being pinned, but I was pinned only twice—by the same fucking guy. Wrestling was my *cover*, William. Back then, boys like us needed a cover. Wasn't Elaine a cover, William? She looked like your cover to me," Miss Frost said. "Nowadays, don't boys like us still need a little cover?"

"Yes, we do," I whispered.

"Oh, now we're whispering again!" Miss Frost whispered. "Whispering is a kind of cover, too, I guess."

"You must have studied something in that college in Pennsylvania—not just wrestling," I said to her. "The yearbook said your choice of career was 'fiction'—kind of a funny career path, isn't it?" I asked her. (I believe I was just babbling, as a way to distract myself from Miss Frost's penis.)

"In college, I studied library science," Miss Frost was saying, while we went on holding each other's penises. Hers wasn't as hard as mine—not yet, anyway. I thought that, even not hard, her penis was bigger than mine, but if you're not experienced, you can't really estimate the size of someone's penis—not if you can't see it. "I thought that a library would be a fairly safe and forgiving place for a man who was on his way to becoming a woman," Miss Frost continued. "I even knew *which* library I wanted to work in—the very same academy library where those old yearbooks are, William. I thought: What other library would appreciate me as much as my old school library? I'd been a good student at Favorite River, and I'd been a *very* good wrestler—not so good by Pennsylvania standards, maybe, but I'd been very good in New England. Of course, when I came back to First Sister *as a woman*, Favorite River Academy wanted nothing to do with someone like me—not around all those *impressionable* boys! Everyone is naïve about something, William, and I was naïve about that. I knew my old school had liked me when I was Big Al; I was naïve enough to be unprepared for them *not* liking me as *Miss* Frost. It was only because your grandpa Harry was on the board of the town library—this funny old public library, where I was *way* overqualified to be the librarian—that they gave me the job here."

"But why did you want to stay here in First Sister—*or* be at Favorite River Academy, which you say yourself is an *awful* school?" I asked her.

I was only eighteen, but I already never wanted to come back to Favorite River Academy or the Podunk town of First Sister, Vermont. I couldn't wait to get away, to be somewhere—to be *anywhere*—where I could have sex with whomever I wanted to, without being stared at and judged by all these overly familiar people who presumed they *knew* me!

"I have an ailing parent, William," Miss Frost explained. "My father died the year I started at Favorite River Academy; if he hadn't passed away, my becoming a woman probably would have killed him. But my mother hasn't been healthy for quite some time; I barely got through college because of my mother's health problems. She's one of those people who's been sick so long that if she ever got well, she wouldn't know she was cured. She's sick in her *mind*, William; she doesn't even *notice* that I'm a woman, or maybe she doesn't remember that her little boy was *ever* a man. I'm sure she doesn't remember that she used to have a little boy."

"Oh."

"Your grandpa Harry used to employ my dad. Harry knew I was the one who took care of my mom. That's the only reason I had to come back to First Sister—whether Favorite River Academy would have me or not, William."

"I'm sorry," I said.

"Oh, it's not so bad," Miss Frost replied, in that *acting* way. "Small towns may revile you, but they have to keep you—they can't turn you away. And I got to meet *you*, William. Who knows? Perhaps I'll be remembered as the crazy cross-dressing librarian who got you *started* as a writer. You have started, haven't you?" she asked me.

But the story of her life, so far, seemed extraordinarily unhappy to me. While I went on touching her penis through that pearl-gray half-slip, I thought about *Giovanni's Room*, which was all wrapped up in Elaine's bra, under my pillow, and I said, "I *loved* the James Baldwin novel. I didn't bring it back to the library because I wanted to lend it to Tom Atkins. He and I have talked about it—I think he would love *Giovanni's Room*, too. Is it all right with you if I lend it to him?"

"Is *Giovanni's Room* in your book bag, William?" Miss Frost asked me suddenly. "Where is the actual book right now?"

"It's at home," I told her. I was suddenly afraid to say it was under my pillow—not to mention that the novel was in contact with Elaine Hadley's padded pearl-gray bra.

"You mustn't leave that novel at home," Miss Frost told me. "Of course you can lend it to Tom. But tell Tom not to let his roommate see it."

"I don't know who Atkins has for a roommate," I told her.

"It doesn't matter who Tom's roommate *is*—just don't let the roommate see that novel. I told you not to let your mother—or Richard Abbott—see it. If I were you, I wouldn't even let your grandpa Harry know you have it."

"Grandpa knows I have a crush on Kittredge," I said to Miss Frost. "Nobody but you knows I have a crush on *you*," I told her.

"I hope you're right about that, William," she whispered. She bent over me and put my penis in her mouth—in less time than it took me to write this sentence. Yet, when I reached under her half-slip for *her* penis, she stopped me. "No—we're not doing that," she said.

"I want to do everything," I told her.

"Of course you do, William, but you'll have to do everything with someone else. It is not appropriate for a young man your age to do *everything* with someone my age," Miss Frost told me. "I will not be responsible for your first time at trying *everything*."

With that, she put my penis back in her mouth; for the time being, she would not explain herself further. When she was still sucking me, I said: "I don't think we had *actual* sex the last time—I mean the penetration part. We did something else, didn't we?"

"Talking is not very easily accomplished during a blow job, William," Miss Frost said, sighing in such a way—while she lay down next to me, face-to-face—that I got the feeling this was probably curtains for the blow job, and it was. "You seemed to enjoy the 'something else' we did last time, William," she said.

"Oh, yes, I *did*!" I cried. "I was just wondering about the penetration part."

"You can wonder about it all you want, William, but there will be *no* 'penetration part' with me. Don't you see?" she asked me suddenly. "I am trying to *protect* you from 'actual sex.' At least a *little*," Miss Frost added, smiling.

"But I don't want to be *protected*!" I cried.

"I will not have 'actual sex' with an eighteen-year-old on my conscience, William. As for who you will become, I've probably been of too much influence already!" Miss Frost declared. She was certainly right about that, though she must have imagined she was being more theatrical than prophetic—and I didn't yet know just how much of an "influence" (on the rest of my *life*!) Miss Frost would be.

This time, she showed me the lotion she used—she let me smell it on her fingers. It had an almond fragrance. She didn't straddle me, or sit on me; we lay sideways with our penises touching. I still didn't see her penis, but Miss Frost rubbed her penis and mine together. When she rolled over, she took my penis between her thighs and pushed her buttocks against my stomach. Her half-slip was hiked up to her waist; I held one of her bare breasts in one hand, and her penis in the other. Miss Frost slid my penis between her thighs until I ejaculated into the palm of her hand.

We seemed to lie in each other's arms for the longest time afterward, but I realize that we couldn't have been alone like that for nearly as long as I imagined; we truly *didn't* have much time together. I think it was because I loved listening to her talk, and the sound of her voice, that I imagined the time as passing more slowly than it actually did.

She drew me a bath, like the first time, but she still wouldn't completely undress, and when I suggested that she climb into the big bathtub with me, she laughed and said: "I'm still trying to *protect* you, William. I wouldn't want to risk *drowning* you!"

I was happy enough that her breasts were bare, and that she'd let me hold her penis, which I still hadn't seen. She'd gotten harder and bigger in my hand, but I had the feeling that even her penis was holding back— a little. I can't explain this, but I felt certain that Miss Frost was simply not *allowing* her penis to get any harder or bigger; perhaps this was, in her mind, another way in which she was *protecting* me.

"Does it have a *name*—having sex the way we did it?" I asked.

"It *does*, William. Can you say the word *intercrural*?" she asked me.

"Intercrural," I replied, without hesitating. "What does it mean?"

"I'm sure you're familiar with the prefix *inter*, in this sense meaning 'between,' William," Miss Frost answered. "As for *crural*, it means 'of or pertaining to the leg'—between the thighs, in other words."

"I see," I said.

"It was favored by homosexual men in ancient Greece, or so I've read," Miss Frost explained. "Not a part of my library-science studies, but I did get to spend a lot of free time in a library!"

"What did the ancient Greeks like about it?" I asked her.

"I read this long ago—I may have forgotten all the reasons," Miss Frost said. "The from-behind part, maybe."

"But we don't live in ancient Greece," I reminded Miss Frost.

"Trust me, William: It's possible to have sex intercrurally without *exactly* imitating the Greeks," Miss Frost explained. "One doesn't always have to do it from behind. Between the thighs will work sideways, or in other positions—even in the missionary position."

"The *what?*" I asked her.

"We'll try it next time, William," she whispered. It might have been in the midst of her quiet whisper when I thought I heard the first creak on the basement stairs. Either Miss Frost heard it, too, or it was merely a coincidence that she took that moment to glance at her watch.

"You told Richard and me that you'd been *onstage*—that you had *acted*—only in your mind. But I saw you in those Drama Club photos. You'd been onstage—you *had* acted before," I said to her.

"Poetic license, William," Miss Frost replied, with one of her theatrical sighs. "Besides, that wasn't *acting*. That was merely dressing up—that was *over*acting! Those boys were clowns—they were just fooling around! There was no Richard Abbott at Favorite River Academy in those days. There was no one in charge of the Drama Club who knew half as much as *Nils* knows, and Nils Borkman is a dramaturgical *pedant!*"

There was a second creak on the basement stairs, which both Miss Frost and I heard; there was no mistaking it this time. I was mainly surprised that Miss Frost seemed so unsurprised. "In our haste, William, did we forget to lock the library door?" she whispered to me. "Oh, dear—I think we did."

We had so little time—as Miss Frost knew, from the beginning.

Upon the third creak on those basement stairs, on that most memorable night in the clearly unlocked First Sister Public Library, Miss Frost—who'd been kneeling beside her big bathtub while she thoughtfully attended to my penis and we talked about all sorts of interesting things—stood up and said in a clarion voice, which would have impressed my friend Elaine and her voice-teacher mother, Mrs. Hadley: "Is that you, Harry? I've been thinking that those cowards would send *you*. It *is* you, isn't it?"

"Ah, well—yes, it's me," I heard Grandpa Harry say sheepishly, from the basement stairs. I sat up straight in the bathtub. Miss Frost stood very erect, with her shoulders back and her small but pointy breasts aimed at her open bedroom door. Miss Frost's nipples were rather long, and her unpronounceable areolae were the intimidating size of silver dollars.

When my grandfather stepped tentatively into Miss Frost's basement room, he was not the confident character I'd so often seen onstage; he was not a woman with a commanding presence, but just a man—bald and small. Grandpa Harry had clearly not volunteered to be the one to come and rescue me.

"I'm disappointed that Richard didn't have the balls to come," Miss Frost said to my embarrassed grandfather.

"Richard asked to be the one, but Mary wouldn't let him," my grandfather said.

"Richard is pussy-whipped, like all of you men married to those Winthrop women," Miss Frost told him. My grandfather couldn't look at her, with her bare breasts showing, but she would not turn away from him—nor did she seek her clothes. She wore just the pearl-gray half-slip in front of him, as if it were a formal gown and she had overdressed for the occasion.

"I don't imagine Muriel was willing to let Bob come," Miss Frost continued. Grandpa Harry just shook his head.

"That Bobby is a sweetheart, but he was always a pussy—even before he was pussy-whipped," Miss Frost went on. I'd never heard Uncle Bob called "Bobby," but I now knew that Robert Fremont had been Albert Frost's classmate at Favorite River Academy, and when you're in a boarding school in those formative years, you call one another names you never hear or use again. (No one calls me Nymph anymore, for example.)

I was attempting to get out of the bathtub without showing all of myself to my grandpa, when Miss Frost handed me a towel. Even with the towel, it was awkward getting out of the tub, and drying myself, and trying to put on my clothes.

"Let me tell you something about your aunt Muriel, William," Miss Frost said, standing as a barrier between my grandfather and me. "Muriel actually had a crush on *me*—before she started hanging out with her 'first and only *beau*,' your uncle Bob. Imagine if I had taken Muriel up—I mean on her *offering* herself to me!" Miss Frost cried, in her best Ibsenwoman fashion.

"Al, please don't be crude," Grandpa Harry said. "Muriel is my daughter, after all."

"Muriel is a bossy bitch, Harry. It might have made her *nicer* if she'd ever gotten to know me," Miss Frost said. "There's no pussy-whipping *me*, William," she said, looking at how I was managing to get myself dressed—badly.

"No, there isn't, Al—I daresay!" Grandpa Harry exclaimed. "There's no pussy-whippin' you!"

"Your grandpa is a good guy, William," Miss Frost told me. "He *built* this room for me. When I first moved back to town, my mother thought I was still a man. I needed a place to change before I went to work as a woman—and before I went home every night, to my mother, as a man. You might say it's a blessing—at least it's easier for me—that my poor mom doesn't appear to notice what gender I am, or should be, anymore."

"I wish you had let me finish this place properly, Al," Grandpa Harry was saying. "Jeez—there should have been a wall around that toilet, anyway!" he observed.

"It's too small a room to have more walls," Miss Frost said. This time, when she stood at the toilet and flipped up the wooden seat, Miss Frost didn't turn her back on me, or on Grandpa Harry. Her penis was not even a little hard, but she had a pretty big one—like the rest of her, except for her breasts.

"Come on, Al—you're a decent fella. I've always stood up for you," Grandpa Harry said. "But this isn't right—you and Bill, I mean."

"She was *protecting* me!" I blurted out. "We never had sex. No penetration," I added.

"Jeez, Bill—I don't want to hear about you *doin'* it!" Grandpa Harry cried; he cupped his hands over his ears.

"But we *didn't* do it!" I told him.

"That night when Richard first brought you here, William—when you got your library card, and Richard offered me those roles in the Ibsen plays—do you remember?" Miss Frost asked me.

"Yes, of course I *remember*!" I whispered.

"Richard thought he was offering the part of Nora, and the part of Hedda, to a woman. It was when he took you home, and he must have talked to your mom—who talked to Muriel, I'm sure—well, that was when they all told him about me. But Richard still wanted to cast me! Those Winthrop women had to accept me, at least *onstage*—as they've had to accept you, Harry, when you were just *acting*. Isn't that the way it happened?" she asked my grandfather.

"Ah, well—*onstage* is one thing, isn't it, Al?" Grandpa Harry asked Miss Frost.

"You're pussy-whipped, too, Harry," Miss Frost told him. "Aren't you sick of it?"

"Come on, Bill," my grandfather said to me. "We should be goin'."

"I always respected you, Harry," Miss Frost told him.

"I always respected *you*, Al!" my grandfather declared.

"I know you did—that's why the craven fuckers sent you," Miss Frost said to him. "Come here, William," she suddenly commanded me. I went to her, and she pulled my head to her bare breasts and held me there; I knew she could feel me shaking. "If you want to cry, do it in your room—but don't let them hear you," she told me. "If you want to cry, close your door and pull your pillow over your head. Cry with your good friend Elaine, if you want to, William—just don't cry in front of *them*. Promise me!"

"I promise you!" I told her.

"So long, Harry—I *did* protect him, you know," Miss Frost said.

"I believe you did, Big Al. I've always protected *you*, you know!" Grandpa Harry exclaimed.

"I know you have, Harry," she told him. "It might not be possible for you to protect me *now*. Don't kill yourself trying," she added.

"I'll do the best I can, Al."

"I know you will, Harry. Good-bye, William—or, 'till we meet again,' as they say," Miss Frost said.

I was shaking more, but I didn't cry; Grandpa Harry took my hand, and we went up those dark basement stairs together.

"I'm guessin' that must have been some book Miss Frost gave you, Bill—on that subject we were discussin'," Grandpa Harry said, as we walked along River Street in the direction of Bancroft Hall.

"Yes, it is an awfully good novel," I told him.

"I'm thinkin' I might like to read it myself—if Al will let me," Grandpa Harry said.

"I promised to lend it to a friend," I told him. "Then *I* could give it to you."

"I'm thinkin' I better get it from Miss Frost, Bill—I wouldn't want you to get in trouble for givin' it to me! I believe you're in enough trouble, for the time bein'," Grandpa Harry whispered.

"I see," I said, still holding his hand. But I *didn't* see; I was merely scratching the surface of all of them. I was just getting started with the *seeing* part.

When we got to Bancroft, the idolatrous boys in the butt room seemed disappointed to see us. I suppose they now expected the occasional sighting of the idolized Kittredge in my company, and here I was with my grandfather—bald and small, and dressed in the working clothes of a lumberman. Grandpa Harry was clearly not a faculty type, and he'd not attended Favorite River Academy; he'd gone to the high school in Ezra Falls, and had not gone to college. The butt-room boys paid no attention to my grandfather and me; I'm sure Grandpa Harry didn't care. How would those boys have recognized Harry, anyway? Those who'd ever seen him before had seen Harry Marshall onstage, when he'd been a woman.

"You don't have to come up to the third floor with me," I told my grandpa.

"If I *don't* come up with you, Bill, you'll be doin' the explainin'," Grandpa Harry said. "You've had quite a night already—why don't you leave the explainin' to me?"

"I love you—" I began, but Harry wouldn't let me continue.

"Of course you do, and I love you, too," he told me. "You trust me to say all the right things, don't you, Bill?"

"Of course I do," I told him. I *did* trust him, and I was tired; I just wanted to go to bed. I needed to hold Elaine's bra to my face, and cry in such a way that none of them would hear me.

But when Grandpa Harry and I entered that third-floor apartment, the assembled family gathering—which *had* included Mrs. Hadley, I only later learned—had dispersed. My mother was in her bedroom, with the door meaningfully closed; maybe there would be no further *prompting* from my mom tonight. Only Richard Abbott was there to greet us, and he looked about as comfortable as a dog with fleas.

I went straight to my bedroom, without saying a word to Richard—that pussy-whipped coward!—and there was *Giovanni's Room* on top of my pillow, not under it. They'd had no right to poke around my bedroom, pawing over my stuff, I was thinking; then I looked under my pillow. Elaine Hadley's pearl-gray bra was gone.

I went back into the living room of our small apartment, where I could tell that Grandpa Harry had not yet started "doin' the explainin'," as he'd put it to me.

"Where's Elaine's bra, Richard?" I asked my stepfather. "Did my mom take it?"

"Actually, Bill, your mother was not herself," Richard told me. "She *destroyed* that bra, Bill, I'm sorry to say—she cut it up in small pieces."

"Jeez—" Grandpa Harry began, but I interrupted him.

"No, Richard," I said. "That was Mom *being* herself, wasn't it? That wasn't Mom being 'not herself.' That's who Mom *is*."

"Ah, well—Bill," Grandpa Harry chimed in. "There are more discreet places to put your women's clothes than under your pillow—speakin' from experience."

"I'm disgusted with both of you," I said to Richard Abbott, not looking at Grandpa Harry; I didn't mean him, and my grandfather knew it.

"I'm pretty disgusted with *all* of us, Bill," Grandpa Harry said. "Now why don't you be goin' to bed, and let me do the explainin'.'"

Before I could leave them, I heard my mother crying in her bedroom; she was crying loudly enough for us all to hear her. That was the point of her crying loudly, of course—so that we would all hear her, and Richard would go into her bedroom to attend to her, which Richard did. My mom wasn't done *prompting*.

"I know my Mary," Grandpa Harry whispered to me. "She wants to be in on the explainin' part."

"I know her, too," I told my grandfather, but I had much more to learn about my mother—more than I knew.

I kissed Grandpa Harry on top of his bald head, only then realizing that I'd grown taller than my diminutive grandfather. I went into my bedroom and closed the door. I could hear my mom; she was still sobbing. That was when I resolved that I truly would never cry loudly enough for them to hear me, as I'd promised Miss Frost.

There was a bible of knowledge and compassion on the subject of gay love on my pillow, but I was too tired and too angry to consult James Baldwin any further.

I would have been better informed if I'd reread the passage near the end of that slender novel—I mean the one about "the heart growing cold with the death of love." As Baldwin writes: "It is a remarkable process. It is far more terrible than anything I have ever read about it, more terrible than anything I will ever be able to say."

If I'd reread that passage on this terrible night, I might have realized Miss Frost had been saying good-bye to me, and what she'd meant by the curious "till we meet again" business was that we would *never* meet again as lovers.

Perhaps it's a good thing I didn't reread the passage then, or know all this then. I had enough on my mind when I went to bed that night—hearing, through my walls, my mother manipulatively crying.

I could vaguely hear Grandpa Harry's preternaturally high voice, too, though not what he was saying. I knew only that he had begun "doin' the explainin'," a process that I also knew had just been seriously jump-started inside me.

From here on, I thought—at the age of eighteen, as I lay in bed, seething—*I'm* the one who'll be "doin' the explainin'!"

Chapter 9

DOUBLE WHAMMY

I don't want to overuse the *away* word, and I've already told you how Elaine Hadley was sent away "in stages." As in any small town or village, where the public coexists with a private school, there were town-gown matters of disagreement between the townsfolk of First Sister, Vermont, and the faculty and administrators of Favorite River Academy—yet *not* in the case of Miss Frost, who was fired by the board of trustees of the First Sister Public Library.

Grandpa Harry was no longer a member of that board; had Harry even been the board *chair*, it is unlikely that he could have persuaded his fellow citizens to keep Miss Frost. In the transsexual librarian's case, the higher-ups at Favorite River Academy were in agreement with the town: The very pillars of the private school, and their counterparts in the public community, believed they had demonstrated the most commendable tolerance toward Miss Frost. It was Miss Frost who had "gone too far"; it was Miss Frost who'd "overstepped her bounds."

Moral outrage and righteous indignation aren't unique to small towns and backward schools, and Miss Frost was not without her champions. Though it caused him to suffer my mother's "silent treatment" for several weeks, Richard Abbott took up Miss Frost's cause. Richard argued that, when faced with an earnest young man's determined infatuation, Miss Frost had actually shielded the young man from the full array of sexual possibilities.

Grandpa Harry, though it caused him the unbridled scorn of Nana Victoria, also spoke up for Miss Frost. She'd shown admirable restraint and sensitivity, Harry had said—not to mention the fact that Miss Frost was a source of inspiration to the *readers* of First Sister.

Even Uncle Bob, risking more vigorous derision from my most indignant aunt Muriel, said that Big Al deserved a break. Martha Hadley, who continued to counsel me in the aftermath of my forcibly aborted relationship with Miss Frost, said that the transsexual librarian had been a boost to my chronically weak self-confidence. Miss Frost had even managed to help me overcome a pronunciation problem, which Mrs. Hadley claimed was caused by my psychological and sexual insecurity.

If anyone had ever listened to Tom Atkins, poor Tom might have had a good word to say for Miss Frost, but Atkins—as Miss Frost had understood—was jealous of the alluring librarian, and when she was persecuted, Tom Atkins was true to his timid nature and remained silent.

Tom did say to me, when he'd finished reading *Giovanni's Room*, that the James Baldwin novel had both moved and disturbed him, though I later learned that Atkins had developed a few more pronunciation problems as a result of his stimulating reading. (Not surprisingly, the *stink* word was chief among the culprits.)

Perhaps it was counterproductive that the most outspoken of Miss Frost's defenders was a known eccentric who was foreign-born. The grim forester, that lunatic logger, the Norwegian dramaturge with a suicidal streak—none other than Nils Borkman—presented himself at a First Sister town meeting by declaring he was Miss Frost's "biggest fan." (It may have undermined Borkman's defense of Miss Frost that Nils had been known to beat up various sawmill men and loggers who'd made unkind comments about Grandpa Harry's onstage appearances as a woman—especially those offenders who'd objected to Harry *kissing* as a woman.)

In Borkman's opinion, not only was Miss Frost an Ibsen woman—to Nils, this meant that Miss Frost was both the best and most complicated kind of woman imaginable—but the obsessed Norwegian went so far as to say that Miss Frost was *more* of a woman than any woman Nils had met in the state of Vermont. Quite possibly, the only woman who was not offended by Borkman's outrageous assertion had been Mrs. Borkman, because Nils had met his wife in Norway; she was not from the Green Mountain State.

Borkman's wife was little seen, and she'd been more rarely heard. Almost no one in First Sister could remember what Mrs. Borkman looked like, nor could anyone recall if she—like her husband, Nils—spoke with a Norwegian accent.

Yet the damage done by Nils was instantaneous. Hearts were hardened against Miss Frost; she encountered a more entrenched resistance because Nils Borkman had boasted that she was *more* of a woman than any woman he'd met in Vermont.

"Not good, Nils—not good, not good," Harry Marshall had muttered to his old friend at that First Sister town meeting, but the damage had been done.

A GOOD-HEARTED BULLY IS still a bully, but Nils Borkman was resented for other reasons. A former biathlete, Nils had introduced southern Vermont to his love of the biathlon—the curious sporting event that entails cross-country skiing and shooting. This was at a time before cross-country skiing had gained the popularity in the northeastern United States that the sport enjoys now. In Vermont, there already existed a few informed and determined zealots who were cross-country skiers in those days, but no one I knew skied with a loaded rifle on his (or her) back.

Nils had introduced his business partner, Harry Marshall, to hunting deer on cross-country skis. A kind of deer-hunting biathlon ensued; Nils and Harry silently skied down (and shot) a lot of deer. There was nothing illegal about it, although the local game warden—an unimaginative soul—had complained.

What the game warden *should* have complained about simply filled him with a complacent sullenness. His name was Chuck Beebe, and he ran a deer-checking station—a so-called biology station, where he compiled deer ages and measurements.

The first Saturday of deer season, the checking station was overrun with women, many of whom, if the weather was nice, were wearing open-toed shoes. The women displayed other signs that they had *not* been deer-hunting, but there they were—lipstick and halter tops, and all—presenting Chuck Beebe with a stiffened deer, caked with congealed blood. The women had hunting licenses, and they'd been issued deer tags, but they had *not*, Chuck knew, shot these deer. Their husbands or fathers or brothers, or their boyfriends, had shot these deer on opening day, and those men were now out shooting more deer. (One deer tag, per licensed hunter, entitled you to shoot one deer.)

"Where'd you shoot this here buck?" Chuck would ask one woman after another.

The women would say something like, "On the mountain." Or: "In the woods." Or: "In a field."

Grandpa Harry made Muriel and Mary do this—that is, claim that they had killed Harry's first two deer of the season. (Nana Victoria refused.) Uncle Bob had made my cousin Gerry do it—until Gerry was old enough to say she wouldn't. I had done it for Nils Borkman, on occasion—as had the elusive Mrs. Borkman.

Chuck Beebe had long accepted this perpetual fiction, but that Nils Borkman and Harry Marshall hunted deer on *skis*—well, that just struck the game warden as *unfair*.

Deer-hunting regulations were pretty primitive in Vermont—they still are. Shooting deer from a motorized vehicle is not permitted; almost anything else goes. There is a bow season, a rifle season, a black-powder season. "Why not a *knife* season?" Nils Borkman had asked, in an earlier, now-famous town meeting. "Why not a *slingshot* season? There are too many deers, right? We should kill more of them, yes?"

Nowadays, there are also too few hunters; their numbers decline each year. Over the years, deer-hunting regulations have attempted to address the deer-population problem, but the overpopulation has endured; nevertheless, there are townspeople in First Sister, Vermont, who remember Nils Borkman as a raving asshole for proposing a *knife* season and a *slingshot* season for "deers"—even though Nils was just kidding, of course.

I remember when you could shoot only buck, then buck and doe, then buck and just *one* doe—that is, *if* you had a special permit, and the buck couldn't be a spike-horn.

"How about we shoot out-of-staters, no limit?" Nils Borkman had once asked. (Limitless shooting of out-of-staters might have been a pretty popular proposal in Vermont, but Borkman was just kidding about the out-of-staters, too.)

"Nils has a *European* sense of humor," Grandpa Harry had said, in defense of his old friend.

"*European!*" Nana Victoria had exclaimed with scorn—no, with more than scorn. My grandmother spoke of Borkman being *European* in a similar manner to how she might have expressed her disgust at Nils having dog shit on his shoes. But the way Nana Victoria said the *Euro-*

pean word was mild in comparison to how derisively she spat out the *she* word, the spittle foaming on her lips, whenever she spoke of *Miss* Frost.

You might say that, as a result of her not having actual sex with me, Miss Frost was banished from First Sister, Vermont; she would, like Elaine, be sent away "in stages," and the first stage of Miss Frost's removal from First Sister began with her being fired from the library.

After she'd lost her job, Miss Frost could not long afford to maintain her ailing mother in what had been their family home; the house would be sold, but this took a little time, and Miss Frost made the necessary arrangements to move her mom to that assisted-living facility Harry Marshall and Nils Borkman had built for the town.

It seems likely that Grandpa Harry and Nils probably gave Miss Frost a special deal, but it would not have been a deal of the magnitude of the one that Favorite River Academy made with Mrs. Kittredge—the deal that permitted Kittredge to stay in school and graduate, even though he had knocked up a faculty daughter who was underage. No one would offer Miss Frost a deal of that kind.

WHEN I HAPPENED UPON Aunt Muriel, she greeted me in her usual insincere fashion: "Oh, hi, Billy—how's everything? I hope all the *normal* pursuits of a young man your age are as gratifying to you as they *should* be!"

To which I would unfailingly respond, as follows: "There was no penetration—no what most people call sex, in other words. The way I look at it, Aunt Muriel, I'm still a virgin."

This must have sent Muriel running to my mother to complain about my reprehensible behavior.

As for my mom, she was subjecting both Richard and me to the "silent treatment"—not realizing, in my case, that I *liked* it when she didn't speak to me. In fact, I vastly preferred her not speaking to me to her constant and conventional disapproval; furthermore, that my mother now had nothing to say to me didn't prevent me from speaking to her first.

"Oh, hi, Mom—how's it going? I should tell you that, contrary to feeling *violated*, I feel that Miss Frost was protecting me—she truly *prevented* me from penetrating her, and I hope it goes without saying that she didn't penetrate me!"

I usually didn't get to say more than that before my mother would run into her bedroom and close the door. "Richard!" she would call, forgetting that she was giving Richard the "silent treatment" because he'd taken up Miss Frost's lost cause.

"No what most people call sex, Mom—that's what I'm telling you," I would continue saying to her, on the other side of her closed bedroom door. "What Miss Frost truly did to me amounted to nothing more than a fancy kind of *masturbation*. There's a special name for it and everything, but I'll spare you the *details*!"

"Stop it, Billy—stop it, stop it, stop it!" my mom would cry. (I guess she forgot that she was giving me the "silent treatment," too.)

"Take it easy, Bill," Richard Abbott would caution me. "I think your mom is feeling pretty fragile these days."

"Pretty fragile these days," I repeated, looking straight at him—until Richard looked away.

"Trust me on this one, William," Miss Frost had said to me, when we were holding each other's penises. "Once you start repeating what people say to you, it's a hard habit to break."

But I didn't want to break that habit; it had been *her* habit, and I decided to embrace it.

"I'm not judging you, Billy," Mrs. Hadley said. "I can see for myself, without you belaboring the details, that your experience with Miss Frost has affected you in certain positive ways."

"Belaboring the details," I repeated. "Positive ways."

"However, Billy, I feel it is my duty to inform you that in a sexual situation of this awkward kind, there is an expectation, in the minds of many adults." Here Martha Hadley paused; so did I. I was considering repeating that bit about "in a sexual situation of this awkward kind," but Mrs. Hadley suddenly continued her arduous train of thought. "What many adults hope to hear you express, Billy, is something you have not, as yet, expressed."

"There is an expectation that I will express *what?*" I asked her.

"Remorse," Martha Hadley said.

"Remorse," I repeated, looking straight at her, until Mrs. Hadley looked away.

"The repetition thing is annoying, Billy," Martha Hadley said.

"Yes, isn't it?" I asked her.

"I'm sorry that they're making you see Dr. Harlow," she told me.

"Do you think Dr. Harlow is hoping to hear me express *remorse?*" I asked Mrs. Hadley.

"That would be my guess, Billy," she said.

"Thank you for telling me," I told her.

Atkins was on the music-building stairs again. "It's so very tragic," he started. "Last night, when I was thinking about it, I threw up."

"You were thinking about *what?*" I asked him.

"*Giovanni's Room!*" he cried; we'd already discussed the novel, but I gathered that poor Tom wasn't done. "That part about the smell of love—"

"The *stink* of love," I corrected him.

"The *reek* of it," Atkins said, gagging.

"It's *stink*, Tom."

"The *stench*," Atkins said, vomiting on the stairs.

"Jesus, Tom—"

"And that awful woman with the cavernous cunt!" Atkins cried.

"The *what?*" I asked him.

"The terrible girlfriend—you know who I mean, Bill."

"I guess that was the point of it, Tom—how someone he once desired now turns him off," I said.

"They smell like fish, you know," Atkins told me.

"Do you mean women?" I asked him.

He gagged again, then recovered himself. "I mean their *things*," Atkins said.

"Their *vaginas*, Tom?"

"Don't say that word!" poor Tom cried, retching.

"I have to go, Tom," I told him. "I have to prepare myself for a little chat with Dr. Harlow."

"Talk to Kittredge, Bill. They're always making Kittredge have a talk with Dr. Harlow. Kittredge knows how to handle Dr. Harlow," Atkins told me. I didn't doubt it; I just didn't want to talk to Kittredge about anything.

But, of course, Kittredge had heard about Miss Frost. Nothing of a sexual nature escaped him. If you were a boy at Favorite River and you received a restriction, Kittredge not only knew your crime; he knew who had caught you, and the terms of confinement your restriction entailed.

Not only was the public library off limits to me; I was told not to see Miss Frost—not that I knew where to find her. The whereabouts of the family home she'd shared with her mental-case mother were unknown to me. Besides, that house was for sale; for all I knew, Miss Frost (and her mom) had already moved out.

I did my homework, and what writing I could manage, in the year-book room of the academy library. It was always a little before check-in when I passed, as quickly as I could, through the Bancroft Hall butt room, where both the smoking and the nonsmoking boys seemed uncharacteristically disturbed to see me. I suppose that my sexual reputation troubled them; whatever convenient pigeonhole they'd put me in might not be the right fit for me now.

If those boys had heretofore thought of me as a miserable faggot, what were they to make of my apparent friendship with Kittredge? And now there was this story about the transsexual town librarian. Okay, so she was some guy in drag; she wasn't a *real* woman, but she *presented* as a woman. Maybe more to the point, I had acquired an undeniable mystique—if only to the Bancroft butt-room boys. Don't forget: Miss Frost was an *older* woman, and that goes a long way with boys—even if the older woman has a penis!

Don't forget this, too: Rumors aren't interested in the unsensational story; rumors don't care what's true. The truth was, I hadn't had what most people call sex—there'd been no penetration! But those butt-room boys didn't know that, nor would they have believed it. In the minds of my fellow students at Favorite River Academy, Miss Frost and I had done *everything*.

I'd climbed the stairs to the second floor of Bancroft when Kittredge suddenly swept me into his arms; at a dead run, Kittredge carried me up the third flight of stairs and into the hall of the dormitory. Worshipful boys gaped at us from the open doorways to their rooms; I could feel their sad envy, a familiar and pathetic longing.

"Holy shit, Nymph—you are the *nooky* master!" Kittredge whispered in my ear. "You are the *poontang* man! Way to go, Nymph! I am *so* impressed with you—you are my new hero! *Listen up!*" Kittredge called to the gawking boys in the third-floor hall, and in their doorways. "While you jerk-offs are beating your meat, and only dreaming about getting laid, this guy is really *doing it*. You there," Kittredge suddenly said to a round-faced underclassman who stood terror-frozen in the hall; his name was Trowbridge, he was wearing pajamas, and he held his toothbrush (with a gob of toothpaste already on it) as if he hoped the toothbrush were a magic wand.

"I'm Trowbridge," the starstruck boy said.

"Where are you going, Trowbridge?" Kittredge asked him.

"I'm going to brush my teeth," Trowbridge said in a trembling voice.

"And after that, Trowbridge?" Kittredge asked the boy. "No doubt you'll soon be pulling your pud, imagining your face pressed between a couple of enormous knockers." But by his aghast expression, I thought it unlikely that Trowbridge had yet dared to jerk off in the dormitory; he surely had a roommate—Trowbridge was probably afraid to beat off in Bancroft. "Whereas *this* young man, Trowbridge," Kittredge continued, still holding me in his strong arms, "*this* young man has not only challenged the public image of gender roles. *This* nooky master, *this* poontang man," Kittredge cried, jouncing me up and down, "this *stud* has actually porked a *transsexual*! Do you have any idea, Trowbridge, what transsexual snatch even *is*?"

"No," Trowbridge said in a small voice.

Even holding me in his arms, Kittredge managed his signature shrug; it was his mother's insouciant shrug, the one Elaine had learned. "My dear Nymph," Kittredge whispered, as he continued to carry me down the hall. "I am *so* impressed with you!" he said again. "An actual transsexual—in *Vermont*, of all places! I've seen some, of course, but in Paris—and in New York. The transvestites in Paris tend to hang out with one another; they're quite a colorful crowd, but you get the feeling that they do everything together. I regret I've never tried one," Kittredge whispered, "but I have the impression that if you pick up one, the others will come along. *That* must be different!"

"Do you mean *les folles*?" I asked him.

I couldn't stop thinking about *les folles*—"screaming like parrots the details of their latest love affairs," as Baldwin describes them. But either Kittredge hadn't heard me, or my French accent was so off the mark that he ignored me.

"Naturally, the transsexuals are another story in New York," Kittredge continued. "They strike me as loners—a lot of them are hookers, maybe. There's one who hangs out on Seventh Avenue—I'm pretty sure she's a hooker. She is really *tall*! I hear there's a club they all go to—I don't know where. Nowhere you want to go by yourself, I'll bet. I think if I were going to try it, I would try it in Paris. But *you*, Nymph—you've already *done* it! How *was* it?" he asked me—seemingly with the utmost sincerity, but I knew enough to be careful. With Kittredge, you were never sure where the conversation was headed.

"It was absolutely wonderful," I told him. "I don't imagine I'll ever have a sexual experience exactly like it again."

"Really," Kittredge said flatly. We'd stopped in front of the door to the faculty apartment I shared with my mom and Richard Abbott, but Kittredge didn't look the least tired from carrying me, and he gave me no indication that he ever intended to put me down. "I suppose she had a penis," Kittredge said then, "and you saw it, touched it, and did all those things one does with a penis—right, Nymph?"

Something in his voice had changed, and I was afraid of it. "To be honest with you, I was so caught up in the moment that I kind of lose track of the details," I told him.

"*Do* you?" Kittredge softly asked, but he didn't seem to care. It was as if the details of *any* sexual adventure were already known to him, and he was bored by them. For a moment, Kittredge looked surprised that he was holding me—or perhaps repulsed. He suddenly put me down. "You know, Nymph, they're going to make you talk to Harlow—you know that, don't you?" he asked.

"Yes," I said. "I was wondering what I should say to him."

"I'm glad you asked me," Kittredge said. "Here's how to handle Harlow," Kittredge began. There was something oddly soothing and (at the same time) indifferent in his voice; in the way Kittredge coached me, I felt that our roles had been reversed. I'd been the Goethe and Rilke expert, tutoring him through the tricky parts. Now here was Kittredge, tutoring me.

At Favorite River Academy, when you were caught committing an act of carnal folly, you were interrogated by Dr. Harlow; Kittredge, who (I presumed) had a wealth of experience with carnal acts, was an expert at dealing with Dr. Harlow.

I listened intently to Kittredge's advice; I hung (as they say) on his every word. It was painful to hear, at times, because Kittredge insisted on spelling out for me the details of his sexual misadventure with Elaine. "Forgive the specific example, Nymph, but just so you know how Harlow operates," Kittredge would say, before launching into his short-term hearing loss—the result of how *loud* Elaine Hadley's orgasms were.

"What Harlow wants to hear from you is how *sorry* you are, Nymph. He's expecting you to *repent.* What you give him, instead, is nonstop titillation. Harlow will try to make you feel *guilty,*" Kittredge told me. "Don't buy into that shit, Nymph—just pretend you're reciting a pornographic novel."

"I see," I said. "No remorse, right?"

"No remorse, Nymph—that's exactly right. Mind you," Kittredge said, in that eerily changed voice—the one I was afraid of. "Mind you, Nymph—I think what you've done is *disgusting*. But I applaud you for having the courage to do it, and you absolutely have a *right* to do it!"

Then, as suddenly as he'd swept me into his arms on the dormitory stairs, he was gone—he was disappearing down the third-floor hall, with those admiring boys in the doorways all watching him run. It had been classic Kittredge. You could be careful, but you could never be careful enough with him; only Kittredge knew where the conversation would end. I often had the feeling with him that he knew the end of our conversation before he started.

It was then that the door to our faculty apartment opened; both Richard Abbott and my mother were standing there, as if they'd been standing on the other side of the door for quite a while.

"We heard voices, Bill," Richard said.

"I heard Kittredge's voice—I would know his voice anywhere," my mother said.

I looked all around me in the suddenly deserted hall.

"Then you must be hearing things," I told my mom.

"I heard Kittredge's voice, too, Bill—he sounded rather *passionate*," Richard said.

"You should both get your ears checked—have your hearing tested or something," I told them. I walked past them into the living room of our apartment.

"I know you're seeing Dr. Harlow tomorrow, Bill," Richard said. "Perhaps we should talk about that."

"I know everything I'm going to say to Dr. Harlow, Richard—in fact, the details are pretty fresh," I told him.

"You should be careful what you say to Dr. Harlow, Billy!" my mother exclaimed.

"What do I have to be careful about?" I asked her. "I don't have anything to hide—not anymore."

"Just take it easy, Bill—" Richard started to say, but I wouldn't let him finish.

"They didn't kick out Kittredge for having sex, did they?" I asked Richard. "Are you afraid they're going to kick me out for *not* having sex?" I asked my mother.

"Don't be silly—" my mom started to say.

"Then what *are* you afraid of?" I asked her. "One day I'm going to have all the sex I want—the way I want it. Are you afraid of *that?*"

She didn't answer me, but I could see that she *was* afraid of my having all the sex I wanted, the way I wanted it. This time, Richard didn't jump into the conversation; he didn't try to help her out. As I went to my bedroom and closed the door, I was thinking that Richard Abbott probably knew something I *didn't* know.

I lay down on my bed and tried to imagine everything that I might not know. It must have been something my mother had kept from me, I thought, and maybe Richard had disapproved of her not telling me. That would explain why Richard hadn't rushed in to help my mom out of whatever mess she'd made for herself. (Richard hadn't even managed to say his usual "Take it easy, Bill" bullshit!)

Later, as I was trying to fall asleep, I was thinking that, if I ever had children, I would tell them everything. But the *everything* word only led me to remember the details of my sexual experience with Miss Frost. Those details, which I would impart—in as titillating (even in as *pornographic*) a fashion as I could manage—to Dr. Harlow in the morning, led me next to imagine the sex that I *hadn't* had with Miss Frost. Naturally, with all there was to imagine, I was awake rather late into the night.

KITTREDGE HAD PREPARED ME so well for my meeting with Dr. Harlow that the meeting itself was anticlimactic. I simply told the truth; I left no detail out. I even included the part about my not knowing, at first, if I'd had what most people call sex with Miss Frost—if there'd been any penetration. The *penetration* word seized Dr. Harlow's attention to such a degree that he stopped writing on his pad of lined paper; he flat out asked me.

"Well, *was* there any penetration?" the doctor said impatiently.

"In due time," I told him. "You can't rush that part of the story."

"I want to know *exactly* what happened, Bill!" Dr. Harlow exclaimed.

"Oh, you *will!*" I cried excitedly. "The not-knowing is part of the story."

"I don't *care* about the not-knowing part!" Dr. Harlow declared, pointing his pencil at me. But I was not about to be rushed. The longer I talked, the more the bald-headed owl-fucker had to listen.

At Favorite River Academy, we called the faculty and staff we intensely disliked "bald-headed owl-fuckers." The origin of this is obscure. If the Favorite River yearbook was called *The Owl*, I'm guessing that this hinted at an owl's presumed wisdom—as expressed in the questionable claim "wise as an owl," or the equally unprovable "wise old owl." (Our stupid sports teams were called the Bald Eagles, which was additionally confusing—eagles were not owls.)

"The 'bald-headed' reference may indicate the physical appearance of a circumcised penis," Mr. Hadley had said once—when all the Hadleys were having dinner with Richard and my mom and me.

"What on earth makes you think so?" Mrs. Hadley asked her husband. I remember that Elaine and I were riveted by this conversation—my mother's obvious discomfort with the *penis* word being part of our enthrallment.

"You see, Martha, the 'owl-fucker' part is indicative of the homo-hating culture of an all-boys' school," Mr. Hadley continued, in his history-teacher way. "The boys call those of us they most detest 'bald-headed owl-fuckers' because they are presuming that the very *worst* of us are homosexual men who diddle—or dream of diddling—young boys."

Elaine and I howled; we thought this was so *funny*. We'd never imagined that the expression "bald-headed owl-fucker" actually meant *anything*!

But my mother suddenly spoke up. "It's just one of those vulgar things the boys say, because they're *always* saying vulgar things—it's how they *think*," my mom said, bitterly.

"But it originally *meant* something, Mary," Mr. Hadley had insisted. "It surely originated for a *reason*," the history teacher had intoned.

In my deliberate and detailed recounting to Dr. Harlow of my sexual experience with Miss Frost, I very much enjoyed remembering Mr. Hadley's historical speculations concerning what a bald-headed owl-fucker actually was. Dr. Harlow clearly was one, and—as I prolonged my discovery that Miss Frost and I had had an *intercrural* sexual experience—I admit that I borrowed a few of James Baldwin's well-chosen words. "There was *no* penetration," I told Dr. Harlow, in due time, "therefore no 'stink of love,' but I so *wanted* there to be!"

"Stink of love!" Dr. Harlow repeated; I could see he was writing this down, and that he suddenly didn't look well.

"I may never have a better orgasm," I told Dr. Harlow, "but I still want to do *everything*—all those things Miss Frost was protecting me from, I mean. She made me want to do all those things—in fact, I can't wait to do them!"

"Those *homosexual* things, Bill?" Dr. Harlow asked me. Through his thinning, lusterless hair, I could see him sweating.

"Yes, of *course* 'homosexual things'—but also other things, to both men *and* women!" I said eagerly.

"*Both*, Bill?" Dr. Harlow asked.

"Why not?" I said to the bald-headed owl-fucker. "I was attracted to Miss Frost when I believed she was a woman. When I realized she was a man, I was no *less* attracted to her."

"And are there other people, of *both* sexes—at this school, and in this town—who *also* attract you, Bill?" Dr. Harlow asked.

"Sure. Why not?" I said again. Dr. Harlow had stopped writing; perhaps the task of the opus ahead of him seemed unending.

"Students, Bill?" the bald-headed owl-fucker asked.

"Sure," I said. I closed my eyes for dramatic effect, but this had more of an effect on me than I'd anticipated. I suddenly saw myself in Kittredge's powerful embrace; he had me in the arm-bar, but of course there was more to it than that.

"Faculty wives?" Dr. Harlow suggested, less than spontaneously.

I needed only to think of Mrs. Hadley's homely face, superimposed again and again on those training-bra models in my mother's mail-order catalogs.

"Why not?" I asked, a third time. "*One* faculty wife, anyway," I added.

"Just *one?*" Dr. Harlow asked, but I could tell that the bald-headed owl-fucker wanted to ask me *which* one.

At that instant, it occurred to me how Kittredge would have answered Dr. Harlow's insinuating question. First of all, I looked bored—as if I had much more to say, but just couldn't be bothered.

My acting career was almost over. (I didn't know this at the time, when I was the center of attention in Dr. Harlow's office, but I had only one, extremely minor, role remaining.) Yet I was able to summon my best imitation of Kittredge's shrug and Grandpa Harry's evasions.

"Ah, well . . ." I started to say; then I stopped talking. Instead of speaking, I mastered that insouciant shrug—the one Kittredge had inherited from his mother, the one Elaine had learned from Mrs. Kittredge.

"I see, Bill," Dr. Harlow said.

"I doubt that you do," I told him. I saw the old homo-hater stiffen.

"You doubt that I do!" the doctor cried indignantly. Dr. Harlow was furiously writing down what I'd told him.

"Trust me on this one, Dr. Harlow," I said, remembering every word that Miss Frost had spoken to me. "Once you start repeating what people say to you, it's a hard habit to break."

. That was my meeting with Dr. Harlow, who sent a curt note to my mother and Richard Abbott, describing me as "a poor prospect for rehabilitation"; Dr. Harlow didn't elaborate on his evaluation, except to say that, in his professional estimation, my sexual problems were "more a matter of attitude than action."

All I said to my mother was that, in *my* professional estimation, the talk with Dr. Harlow had been a great success.

Poor, well-meaning Richard Abbott attempted to have a friendly tête-à-tête with me about the meeting. "What do you think Dr. Harlow meant by your *attitude*, Bill?" dear Richard asked me.

"Ah, well . . ." I said to Richard, pausing only long enough to meaningfully shrug. "I suppose a visible lack of remorse lies at the heart of it."

"A visible lack of remorse," Richard repeated.

"Trust me on this one, Richard," I began, confident that I had Miss Frost's domineering intonation exactly right. "Once you start repeating what people say to you, it's a hard habit to break."

I SAW MISS FROST only two more times; on both occasions, I was completely unprepared—I'd not been expecting to see her.

The sequence of events that led to my graduation from Favorite River Academy, and my departure from First Sister, Vermont, unfolded fairly quickly.

King Lear was performed by the Drama Club before our Thanksgiving vacation. For a period of time, not longer than a week or two, Richard Abbott joined my mother in giving me the "silent treatment"; I'd clearly hurt Richard's feelings by not seeing the fall Shakespeare play. I'm sure I would have enjoyed Grandpa Harry's performance in the Goneril role—more than I would have liked seeing Kittredge in the dual roles of Edgar and Poor Tom.

The *other* "poor Tom"—namely, Atkins—told me that Kittredge had pulled off both parts with a noble-seeming indifference, and that Grandpa Harry had luxuriously indulged in the sheer awfulness of Lear's eldest daughter.

"How was Delacorte?" I asked Atkins.

"Delacorte gives me the creeps," Atkins answered.

"I meant, how was he as Lear's Fool, Tom."

"Delacorte wasn't bad, Bill," Atkins admitted. "I just don't know why he always looks like he needs to *spit!*"

"Because Delacorte *does* need to spit, Tom," I told Atkins.

It was after Thanksgiving—hence the winter-sports teams had commenced their first practices—when I ran into Delacorte, who was on his way to wrestling practice. He had an oozing mat burn on one cheek and a deeply split lower lip; he was carrying the oft-seen paper cup. (I noted that Delacorte had just *one* cup, which I hoped was not a multipurpose cup—that is, for both rinsing *and* spitting.)

"How come you didn't see the play?" Delacorte asked me. "Kittredge said you didn't see it."

"I'm sorry I missed it," I told him. "I've had a lot of other stuff going on."

"Yeah, I know," Delacorte said. "Kittredge told me about it." Delacorte took a sip of water from the paper cup; he rinsed his mouth, then spit the water into a dirty snowbank alongside the footpath.

"I heard you were a very good Lear's Fool," I told him.

"Really?" Delacorte asked; he sounded surprised. "Who told you that?"

"Everybody said so," I lied.

"I tried to do all my scenes with the awareness that I was dying," Delacorte said seriously. "I see each scene that Lear's Fool is in as a kind of death-in-progress," he added.

"That's very interesting. I'm sorry I missed it," I told him again.

"Oh, that's all right—you probably would have done it better," Delacorte told me; he took another sip of water, then spit the water in the snow. Before he hurried on his way to wrestling practice, Delacorte suddenly asked me: "Was she *pretty?* I mean the transsexual librarian."

"Yes, *very* pretty," I answered.

"I have a hard time imagining it," Delacorte admitted worriedly; then he ran on.

Years later, when I knew that Delacorte was dying, I often thought of him playing Lear's Fool as a death-in-progress. I really *am* sorry I missed it. Oh, Delacorte, how I misjudged you—you were more of a death-in-progress than I ever imagined!

It was Tom Atkins who told me, that December of 1960, how Kittredge was telling everyone I was "a sexual hero."

"Kittredge said that to you, Tom?" I asked.

"He says it to everyone," Atkins told me.

"Who knows what Kittredge really thinks?" I said to Atkins. (I was still suffering from the way Kittredge had delivered the *disgusting* word when I'd least expected it.)

That December, the wrestling team had no home matches—their earliest matches were away, at other schools—but Atkins had expressed his interest in seeing the home wrestling matches with me. I'd earlier resolved to see no more wrestling matches—in part because Elaine wasn't around to see the matches with me, but also because I was bullshitting myself about trying to boycott Kittredge. Yet Atkins was interested in watching the wrestling, and his interest had rekindled mine.

Then, that Christmas of 1960, Elaine came home; the Favorite River dormitories had emptied for the Christmas break, and Elaine and I had the deserted campus largely to ourselves. I told Elaine absolutely everything about Miss Frost; my session with Dr. Harlow had provided me with sufficient storytelling practice, and I was eager to make up for those years when I'd been less than candid with my dear friend Elaine. She was a good listener, and not once did she try to make me feel guilty for not telling her about my various sexual infatuations sooner.

We were able to speak frankly about Kittredge, too, and I even told Elaine that I "had once had" a crush on her mother. (That Mrs. Hadley no longer attracted me in that way made it easier for me to tell Elaine about it.)

Elaine was such a good friend to me that she actually volunteered to be the go-between—that is, should I want to try to arrange a meeting with Miss Frost. I thought about such a meeting all the time, of course, but Miss Frost had so clearly indicated to me her unwavering intentions to say good-bye—her "till we meet again" had such a *businesslike* sound to it. I couldn't imagine that Miss Frost had meant anything clandestine or suggestive about how we might manage to "meet again."

I appreciated Elaine's willingness to be the go-between, but I didn't for a moment delude myself by imagining that Miss Frost would ever make herself available to me again. "You have to understand," I said to Elaine. "I think Miss Frost is pretty serious about *protecting* me."

"As first experiences go, Billy, I think you've had a pretty good one," Elaine told me.

"Except for the interference of my whole fucking *family*!" I cried.

"That's just weird," Elaine said. "It can't be Miss Frost they're all so afraid of. Surely they didn't believe that Miss Frost would ever hurt you."

"What do you mean?" I asked her.

"There's something about *you* they're afraid of, Billy," Elaine told me.

"That I'm a homosexual, or that I'm bisexual—is that what you mean?" I asked her. "Because I think they've already figured that out, or at least they *suspect* it."

"They're afraid of something you don't know yet, Billy," Elaine told me.

"I'm sick of everybody trying to *protect* me!" I shouted.

"That may indeed be Miss Frost's motive, Billy," Elaine said. "I'm not so sure about what's motivating your whole fucking *family*, as you say."

MY CRUDE COUSIN GERRY came home from college that same Christmas break. In Gerry's case, I use the *crude* word affectionately. Please don't dismiss Gerry as a stridently angry lesbian who hated her parents and all heterosexuals; she had always loathed boys, but I'd foolishly imagined that she might like me a little bit, because I knew she would have heard about my scandalous relationship with Miss Frost. Yet, at least for a few more years, Gerry wouldn't like gay or bisexual boys any better than she liked straight ones.

Nowadays, I hear my friends say that our society tends to be more accepting of gay and bi women than we are of gay and bi men. In our family's case, there was little apparent reaction to Gerry being a lesbian, at least compared to almost everyone having a cow about my relationship with Miss Frost—not to mention my mom's horror at how I was "turning out," sexually. Yes, I know, it's true that many people treat lesbians and bi women *differently* than they treat gay and bi men, but Gerry wasn't *accepted* by our family as much as she was simply *ignored* by them.

Uncle Bob loved Gerry, but Bob was a coward; he loved his daughter, in part, because she was more courageous than he was. I think Gerry deliberately misbehaved, and not only to build a barrier around herself; I think she was aggressive and "crude" because this forced our family to *notice* her.

I had always liked Gerry, but I kept my fondness for her a secret. I wish I'd *told* her that I liked her—I mean, sooner than I did.

We would become better friends when we were older; nowadays, we're quite close. I'm truly fond of Gerry—okay, in an odd way—but Gerry was not very likable when she was a young woman. All I'm saying is that Gerry *purposely* made herself unlikable. Elaine detested her, and would never like her—not even a little.

That Christmas, Elaine and I were up to our usual but separate pursuits in the yearbook room of the academy library. The library was open over the Christmas break—except for Christmas Day. Many of the faculty liked to work there, and Christmastime was when a lot of prospective students and their parents visited Favorite River Academy. My summer job, for the past three years, had been as a tour guide; I showed prospective students and their parents my awful school. I got a part-time job as a tour guide over the Christmas break, too; the boys among the faculty brats frequently did this. Uncle Bob, the admissions man, was our overly permissive boss.

Elaine and I were in the yearbook room when my cousin Gerry found us. "I hear you're queer," Gerry said to me, ignoring Elaine.

"I guess so," I said, "but I'm attracted to some women, too."

"I don't want to know," Gerry told me. "No one's sticking anything up my ass, or anywhere else."

"You never know till you try it," Elaine said. "You might like it, Gerry."

"I see you're not pregnant," Gerry said to her, "unless you're already pregnant again, Elaine, and you're not yet showing."

"You got a girlfriend?" Elaine asked her.

"She could beat the shit out of you, Elaine," Gerry said. "You, too—probably," Gerry told me.

I could be forgiving of Gerry, knowing that Muriel was her mother; that couldn't have been easy, especially for a lesbian. I was less inclined to forgive Gerry for how harsh she was with her father, because I had always liked Uncle Bob. But Elaine felt no forgiveness for Gerry at all. There must have been some history between them; maybe Gerry had hit on her, or when Elaine had been pregnant with Kittredge's child, it's entirely possible that Gerry had said or written something cruel to her.

"My dad's looking for you, Billy," Gerry said. "There's a family he wants you to show the school to. The kid looks like a bed-wetter to me, but maybe he's a homo, and you can suck each other off in one of the empty dorm rooms."

"Jesus, you're crass!" Elaine said to Gerry. "I was naïve enough to imagine that college would have civilized you—at least to some small degree. But I think whatever tasteless culture you acquired from your Ezra Falls high school experience is the only culture you're capable of acquiring."

"I guess the culture *you* acquired didn't teach you to keep your thighs together, Elaine," Gerry told her. "Why not ask my dad to give you the master key to Tilley, when you're showing the bed-wetter and his parents around?" Gerry asked me. "That way, you and Elaine can sneak a look at Kittredge's room. Maybe you two jerk-offs can masturbate each other on Kittredge's bed," Gerry told us. "What I mean, Billy, is that you have to have a master key to show someone a dorm room, don't you? Why not get the key to Tilley?" With that, Gerry left Elaine and me in the year-book room. Like her mother, Muriel, Gerry could be an insensitive bitch, but—unlike her mother—Gerry wasn't conventional. (Maybe I admired how angry Gerry was.)

"I guess your whole fucking family—as you say, Billy—talks *about* you," Elaine said. "They just don't talk *to* you."

"I guess so," I said, but I was thinking that Aunt Muriel and my mother were probably the chief culprits—that is, when it came to talking *about* me but not *to* me.

"Do you want to see Kittredge's room in Tilley?" Elaine asked me.

"If *you* do," I told her. Of course I wanted to see Kittredge's room—and Elaine did, too.

I HAD LOST A little of my enthusiasm for perusing the old yearbooks, following my discovery that Miss Frost had been the Favorite River wrestling-team captain in 1935. Since then, I hadn't made much progress—nor had Elaine.

Elaine was still stuck in the contemporary yearbooks; specifically, she was held in thrall by what she called "the Kittredge years." She devoted herself to finding photos of the younger, more innocent-seeming Kittredge. Now that Kittredge was in his fifth and final year at Favorite River, Elaine sought out those photographs of him in his freshman and sophomore years. Yes, he'd looked younger then; the innocent-seeming part, however, was hard to see.

If one could believe Mrs. Kittredge's story—if Kittredge's own mother had really had sex with him when she said she did—Kittredge had not been innocent for very long, and he'd definitely not been innocent by the time he attended Favorite River. Even as a freshman—on the very day Kittredge had shown up in First Sister, Vermont—Kittredge hadn't been innocent. (It was almost impossible for me to imagine that he'd *ever* been innocent.) Yet Elaine kept looking through those earliest photographs for some evidence of Kittredge's innocence.

I don't remember the boy Gerry had called the bed-wetter. He was (in all likelihood) a prepubescent boy, probably on his way to becoming straight or gay—but not on his way to becoming *bi*, or so I imagine. I don't recall the alleged bed-wetter's parents, either. My exchange with Uncle Bob, about the master key to Tilley, is more memorable.

"Sure, show 'em Tilley—why not?" my easygoing uncle said to me. "Just don't show 'em Kittredge's room—it's not typical."

"Not typical," I repeated.

"See for yourself, Billy—just show 'em another room," Uncle Bob told me.

I don't recall whose room I showed to the bed-wetter and his parents; it was the standard double, with two of everything—two beds, two desks, two chests of drawers.

"Everyone has a roommate?" the bed-wetter's mom asked; it was usually the mothers who asked the roommate question.

"Yes, everyone—no exceptions," I said; those were the rules.

"What's 'not typical' about Kittredge's room?" Elaine asked, after the visiting family was through their tour.

"We'll soon see," I said. "Uncle Bob didn't tell me."

"Jesus, no one in your family tells you *anything*, Billy!" Elaine exclaimed.

I'd been thinking the same thing. In the yearbook room, I was up only to the Class of '40. I had twenty years to go before I got to my own graduating class, and I'd just discovered that the yearbook for 1940 was missing. I'd skipped from the '39 *Owl* to '41 and '42, before I realized that '40 was gone.

When I asked the academy librarian about it, I said: "Nobody can check out a yearbook. *The Owl* for 1940 must have been stolen."

The academy librarian was one of Favorite River's fussy old bachelors; everyone thought that such older, unmarried males on the Favorite River faculty were what we called at that time "nonpracticing homosexuals." Who knew if they were or weren't "practicing," or if they were or were not homosexuals? All we'd observed was that they lived alone, and there was a particular fastidiousness about the way they dressed, and the way they ate and spoke—hence we imagined that they were unnaturally effeminate.

"*Students* may not check out a yearbook, Billy—the *faculty* can," the academy librarian said primly; his name was Mr. Lockley.

"The *faculty* can," I repeated.

"Yes, of course they can," Mr. Lockley told me; he was looking through some filing cards. "Mr. Fremont has checked out the 1940 *Owl*, Billy."

"Oh."

Mr. Fremont—Robert Fremont, Class of '35, Miss Frost's classmate—was my uncle Bob, of course. But when I asked Bob if he was finished with the '40 *Owl*, because I was waiting to have a look at it, good old easygoing Bob wasn't so easygoing about it.

"I'm pretty sure I returned that yearbook to the library, Billy," my uncle said; he was a good guy, basically, but a bad liar. Uncle Bob was a fairly forthright fella, but I knew he was hanging on to the '40 *Owl*, for some unknown reason.

"Mr. Lockley thinks you still have it, Uncle Bob," I told him.

"Well, I'll look all around for it, Billy, but I swear I took it back to the library," Bob said.

"What did you need it for?" I asked him.

"A member of that class is newly deceased," Uncle Bob replied. "I wanted to say some nice things about him, when I wrote to his family."

"Oh."

Poor Uncle Bob would never be a writer, I knew; he couldn't make up a story to save his ass.

"What was his name?" I asked.

"*Whose* name, Billy?" Bob said in a half-strangled voice.

"The *deceased*, Uncle Bob."

"Gosh, Billy—I can't for the life of me remember the fella's name!"

"Oh."

"More fucking secrets," Elaine said, when I told her the story. "Ask Gerry to find the yearbook and give it to you. Gerry hates her parents—she'll do it for you."

"I think Gerry hates me, too," I told Elaine.

"Gerry hates her parents *more*," Elaine said.

We'd located the door to Kittredge's room in Tilley, and I let us in with the master key Uncle Bob had given me. At first, the only "not typical" thing about the dorm room was how neat it was, but neither Elaine nor I was surprised to see that Kittredge was tidy.

The one bookshelf had very few books on it; there was a lot of room for more books. The one desk had very little on it; the one chair had no clothes draped over it. There were just a couple of framed photographs on top of the lone chest of drawers, and the wardrobe closet, which typically had no door—not even a curtain—revealed Kittredge's familiar (and expensive-looking) clothes. Not even the solitary single bed had any stray clothes on it, and the bed was perfectly made—the sheets and blanket uncreased, the pillowcase unwrinkled.

"Jesus," Elaine suddenly said. "How did the bastard swing a *single?*"

It was a single room; Kittredge had no roommate—that's what was "not typical" about it. Elaine and I speculated that the single room might have been part of the deal Mrs. Kittredge made with the academy when she'd told them—and Mr. and Mrs. Hadley—that she would take Elaine to Europe and get the unfortunate girl a safe abortion. It was also possible that Kittredge had been an overpowering and abusive roommate; perhaps no one had *wanted* to be Kittredge's roommate, but this struck both Elaine and me as unlikely. At Favorite River Academy, it would have been prestigious to be Kittredge's roommate; even if he abused you, you wouldn't want to give up the honor. The single room, in combination with Kittredge's evidently compulsive neatness, smacked of privilege. Kittredge exuded privilege, as if he'd managed (even in utero) to create his own sense of entitlement.

What was most upsetting to Elaine about Kittredge's room was that there was absolutely no evidence in it that he'd ever known her; maybe she'd expected to see a photograph of herself. (She admitted to me that she'd given him several.) I didn't ask her if she'd given Kittredge one of her bras, but that was because I was hoping to ask her if she would give me another one.

There were some school-newspaper photographs, and yearbook photos, of Kittredge wrestling. There were no pictures of girlfriends (or ex-girlfriends). There were no photographs of Kittredge as a child; if he'd ever had a dog, there were no pictures of the dog. There were no photos of anyone who could have been his father. The only picture of Mrs. Kittredge had been taken the one time she'd come to Favorite River to see her son wrestle. The photo must have been taken after the match; Elaine and I had been at that match—it was the only time I saw Mrs. Kittredge. Elaine and I didn't remember seeing anyone take a picture of Kittredge and his mom at the match, but someone had.

What Elaine and I noticed, simultaneously, was that an unseen hand—it must have been Kittredge's—had cut off Mrs. Kittredge's face and glued it to Kittredge's body. There was Kittredge's mother in Kittredge's wrestling tights and singlet. And there was Kittredge's handsome face glued to his mother's beautiful and exquisitely tailored body. It was a funny photograph, but Elaine and I didn't laugh about it.

The truth is, Kittredge's face *worked* on a woman's body, with a woman's clothes, and Mrs. Kittredge's face went very well with Kittredge's wrestler's body (in tights and a singlet).

"I suppose it's *possible*," I said to Elaine, "that Mrs. Kittredge could have switched the faces in the photograph." (I didn't really think so, but I said it.)

"No," Elaine flatly said. "Only Kittredge could have done it. That woman has no imagination and no sense of humor."

"If you say so," I told my dear friend. (As I've already told you, I wouldn't question Elaine's authority on the subject of Mrs. Kittredge. How could I?)

"You'd better go to work on Gerry and find that 1940 yearbook, Billy," Elaine told me.

I did this at our family dinner on Christmas Day—when Aunt Muriel and Uncle Bob and Gerry joined my mom and me, and Richard Abbott, at Grandpa Harry's house on River Street. Nana Victoria always made a big to-do about the essential and necessary "old-fashionedness" of Christmas dinner.

It was also a tradition in our family that the Borkmans joined us for Christmas dinner. In my memory, Christmas was one of the few days of the year I saw Mrs. Borkman. At Nana Victoria's insistence, we all called her "Mrs." Borkman; I never knew her first name. When I say "all," I don't mean only the children. Surprisingly, that is how Aunt Muriel and my mother addressed Mrs. Borkman—and Uncle Bob and Richard Abbott, when they spoke to the presumed "Ibsen woman" Nils had married. (She had not left Nils, nor had she shot herself in the temple, but we assumed that Nils Borkman would never have married a woman who *wasn't* an Ibsen woman, and we therefore wouldn't have been surprised to learn that Mrs. Borkman had done something dire.)

The Borkmans did not have children, which indicated to my aunt Muriel and Nana Victoria that there was something amiss (or indeed dire) in their relationship.

"Motherfucking Christ," Gerry said to me on that Christmas Day,

1960. "Isn't it perfectly possible that Nils and his wife are too depressed to have kids? The prospect of having kids depresses the shit out of me, and I'm neither suicidal nor Norwegian!"

On that warmhearted note, I decided to introduce Gerry to the mysterious subject of the missing 1940 *Owl*, which—according to Mr. Lockley's records—Uncle Bob had checked out of the academy library and had not returned.

"I don't know what your dad is doing with that yearbook," I told Gerry, "but I want it."

"What's in it?" Gerry asked me.

"Some members of our illustrious family don't want me to see what's in it," I said to Gerry.

"Don't sweat it. I'll find the fucking yearbook—I'm dying to see what's in it myself," Gerry told me.

"It's probably something of a delicate nature," I said to her.

"Ha!" Gerry cried. "Nothing I get my hands on is 'of a delicate nature' for very long!"

When I repeated what she'd said to Elaine, my dear friend remarked: "The very idea of having sex with Gerry is nauseating to me."

To me, too, I almost told Elaine. But that's not what I said. I thought my sexual forecast was cloudy; I wasn't at all sure about my sexual future. "Sexual desire is pretty specific," I said to Elaine, "and it's usually pretty decisive, isn't it?"

"I guess so," Elaine answered. "What do you mean?"

"I mean that, in the past, my sexual desire has been very specific— my attraction to someone very decisive," I said to Elaine. "But all that seems to be changing. Your breasts, for example—I love them *specifically*, because they're yours, not just because they're small. Those dark parts," I tried to tell her.

"The areolae," Elaine said.

"Yes, I *love* those parts. And kissing you—I love kissing you," I told her.

"Jesus—*now* you tell me, Billy!" Elaine said.

"I only know it now—I'm *changing*, Elaine, but I'm not at all sure *how*," I told her. "By the way, I wonder if you would give me one of your bras—my mother cut up the old one."

"She *did?*" Elaine cried.

"Maybe there's one you've outgrown, or you're just tired of it," I said to her.

"My stupid breasts grew only a little, even when I was pregnant," she told me. "Now I think I've stopped growing. You can have as many of my bras as you want, Billy," Elaine said.

One night, after Christmas, we were in my bedroom—with the door open, of course. Our parents were seeing a movie together in Ezra Falls; we'd been invited to join them, but we hadn't wanted to go. Elaine had just started kissing me, and I was fondling her breasts—I'd managed to get one of her breasts out of her bra—when there was a pounding on the apartment door.

"Open the fucking door, Billy!" my cousin Gerry was shouting. "I know your parents and the Hadleys are at a movie—my asshole parents went with them!"

"Jesus—it's that awful girl!" Elaine whispered. "She's got the yearbook, I'll bet you."

It hadn't taken Gerry long to find the '40 *Owl*. Uncle Bob may have been the one to check it out of the academy library, but Gerry found the yearbook under her mother's side of the bed. It had doubtless been my aunt Muriel's idea to keep the yearbook of that graduating class away from me, or maybe Muriel and my mom had cooked up the idea together. Uncle Bob was just doing what those Winthrop women had told him to do; according to Miss Frost, Uncle Bob had been a pussy *before* he was pussy-whipped.

"I don't know what the big deal is," Gerry said, handing me the yearbook. "So it's your runaway father's graduating class—so fucking *what!*"

"My dad went to Favorite River?" I asked Gerry. I'd known that William Francis Dean was a Harvard-boy at fifteen, but no one had told me he'd gone to Favorite River before that. "He must have met my mother here, in First Sister!" I said.

"So fucking *what!*" Gerry said. "What's it matter where they met?"

But my mom was older than my dad; this meant that William Francis Dean had been even younger than I thought when they first met. If he'd graduated from Favorite River in 1940—and he'd been only fifteen when he started his freshman year at Harvard in the fall of that same year—he might have been only twelve or thirteen when they met. He could have been a prepubescent boy.

"So fucking *what!*" Gerry kept saying. She'd obviously not looked over the yearbook in close detail, nor had she seen those earlier yearbooks ('37, '38, '39), where there might have been photographs of William Francis Dean when he was only twelve, thirteen, and fourteen. How had I overlooked him? If he'd been a four-year senior in '40, he could have started at Favorite River in the fall of 1936—when William Francis Dean would have been only *eleven*!

What if my mom had known him then, when he'd been an eleven-year-old? Their "romance," such as it was, might have been vastly different from the one I'd imagined.

"Did you see anything of the alleged *womanizer* in him?" I asked Gerry, as Elaine and I quickly searched through the head shots of the graduating seniors in the Class of 1940.

"Who said he was a *womanizer?*" Gerry asked me.

"I thought *you* did," I said, "or maybe it was something you heard your mother say about him."

"I don't remember the *womanizer* word," Gerry told me. "All I heard about him was that he was kind of a *pansy*."

"A *pansy*," I repeated.

"Jesus—the repetition, Billy. It's got to stop," Elaine said.

"He wasn't a *pansy*!" I said indignantly. "He was a *womanizer*—my mom caught him kissing someone *else*!"

"Yeah—some other *boy*, maybe," my cousin Gerry said. "That's what I heard, anyway, and he sure looks like a *poofter* to me."

"Like a *poofter*!" I cried.

"My dad said your dad was as flaming a fag as he ever saw," Gerry said.

"As flaming a fag," I repeated.

"Dear God, Billy—please stop it!" Elaine said.

There he was: William Francis Dean, as pretty a boy as I'd ever seen; he could have passed for a girl, with a whole lot less effort than Miss Frost had put into *her* transformation. It was easy to see why I might have missed him in those earlier yearbooks. William Francis Dean looked like me; his features were so familiar to me that I must have skipped over him without really seeing him. His choice of college or university: "Harvard." His career path: "performer."

"Performer," I repeated. (This was before Elaine and I had seen any other photographs; we'd seen only the requisite head shot.)

William Francis Dean's nickname was "Franny."

"Franny," I repeated.

"Look, Billy—I thought you knew," Gerry was saying. "My dad always said it was a double whammy."

"*What* was?" I asked her.

"It was a double whammy that you would be queer," Gerry told me. "You had Grandpa Harry's homo genes on the maternal side of your family, and on the paternal side—well, shit, just *look* at him!" Gerry said, pointing to the picture of the pretty boy in the Class of '40. "On the paternal side of your frigging gene pool, you had flaming Franny Dean! That's a double fucking whammy," Gerry said. "No wonder Grandpa Harry adored the guy."

"Flaming Franny," I repeated.

I was reading William Francis Dean's abbreviated bio in the '40 *Owl. Drama Club (4)*. I had little doubt that Franny would have had strictly women's roles—I couldn't wait to see those photos. *Wrestling team, manager (4)*. Naturally, he'd not been a wrestler—just the manager, the guy who made sure the wrestlers had water and oranges, and a bucket to spit in, and all the handing out and picking up of towels that a wrestling-team manager has to do.

"Genetically speaking, Billy, you were up against a stacked deck," Gerry was saying. "My dad's not the sharpest saw in the mill, but you were dealt the double-whammy card, for sure."

"Jesus, Gerry—that's enough for now," Elaine said. "Would you just leave us, please?"

"Anyone would know you've been making out, Elaine," Gerry told her. "Your tits are so small—one of them's fallen out of your bra, and you don't even know."

"I love Elaine's breasts," I said to my cousin. "Fuck you, Gerry, for not telling me what I never knew."

"I thought you *did* know, asshole!" Gerry shouted at me. "Shit, Billy—how could you *not* know? It's so fucking *obvious*! How could you be as queer as you are and *not* know?"

"That's not fair, Gerry!" Elaine was shouting, but Gerry was gone. She left the door to the dormitory hall wide open when she went. That was okay with Elaine and me; we left the apartment shortly after Gerry. We wanted to get to the academy library while it was still open; we wanted to see all the photos we could find of William Francis Dean in those earlier yearbooks, where I had missed him.

Now I knew where to look: Franny Dean would be the prettiest girl in the Drama Club pictures, in the '37, '38, and '39 *Owl*; he would be the most effeminate-looking boy in the wrestling-team photos, where he would *not* be bare-chested and wearing wrestling tights. (He would be wearing a jacket and a tie, the standard dress code in those years for the wrestling-team manager.)

Before Elaine and I went to the old yearbook room in the academy library, we took the '40 *Owl* up to the fifth floor of Bancroft Hall, where we hid it in Elaine's bedroom. Her parents didn't search through her things, Elaine had told me. She had caught them at it, shortly after she'd returned from her trip to Europe with Mrs. Kittredge. Elaine suspected them of trying to discover if she was having sex with anyone else.

After that, Elaine put condoms everywhere in her room. Naturally, Mrs. Kittredge had given her the condoms. Perhaps Mr. and Mrs. Hadley took the condoms as a sign that Elaine was being sexually active with an *army* of boys; more likely, I knew, Mrs. Hadley was smarter than that. Martha Hadley probably knew what the plethora of condoms meant: Stay the fuck out of my room! (After that one time, Mr. and Mrs. Hadley did.)

The '40 *Owl* was safe in Elaine Hadley's bedroom, if not in mine. Elaine and I could look at all the photos of flaming Franny Dean in that yearbook, but we both wanted to see the pictures of the *younger* William Francis Dean first. We would have the rest of our Christmas vacation to learn everything we could about the Favorite River Class of 1940.

OVER THAT SAME CHRISTMAS dinner of 1960, when I'd asked Gerry to get me the '40 *Owl*, Nils Borkman had managed a moment—when we were briefly alone—to confide in me.

"Your librarian friend—they are *roadrailing* her, Bill!" Borkman whispered harshly to me.

"*Railroading* her—yes," I said.

"They are stereo sex-types!" Borkman exclaimed.

"Sexual stereotypes?" I asked.

"*Yes*—that's what I said!" the Norwegian dramaturge declared. "It's a pity—I had the perfect parts for you two," the director whispered. "But of course I cannot put Miss Frost onstage—the Puritan sex-types would *stone* her, or something!"

"The perfect parts in *what?*" I asked.

"He is the *American* Ibsen!" Nils Borkman cried. "He is the *new* Ibsen, from your backward American South!"

"*Who* is?" I asked.

"Tennessee Williams—the most important playwright since Ibsen," Borkman reverentially intoned.

"What play is it?" I asked.

"*Summer and Smoke*," Nils answered, trembling. "The repressed female character has another woman smoldering inside her."

"I see," I said. "That would be the Miss Frost character?"

"Miss Frost would have been a *perfect* Alma!" Nils cried.

"But now—" I started to say; Borkman wouldn't let me finish.

"Now I have no choice—it's Mrs. Fremont as Alma, or nobody," Nils muttered darkly. I knew "Mrs. Fremont" as Aunt Muriel.

"I think Muriel can do *repressed*," I told Nils encouragingly.

"But Muriel doesn't *smolder*, Bill," Nils whispered.

"No, she doesn't," I agreed. "What was my part going to be?" I asked him.

"It's still yours, if you want it," Nils told me. "It's a small role—it won't interfere with your work-home."

"My homework," I corrected him.

"*Yes*—that's what I said!" the Norwegian dramaturge declared again. "You play a traveling salesman, a young one. You make a pass at the Alma character in the last scene of the play."

"I make a pass at my aunt Muriel, you mean," I said to the ardent director.

"But not onstage—don't worry!" Borkman cried. "The hanky-panky is all imagined; the repetitious sexual activity happens later, offstage."

I was pretty sure that Nils Borkman didn't mean the sexual activity was "repetitious"—not even offstage.

"*Surreptitious* sexual activity?" I asked the director.

"Yes, but there's no hanky-panky with your auntie onstage!" Borkman assured me, excitedly. "It just would have been so *symbolic* if Alma could have been Miss Frost."

"So *suggestive*, you mean?" I asked him.

"Suggestive *and* symbolic!" Borkman exclaimed. "But with Muriel, we stick to the suggestive—if you know what I mean."

"Maybe I could read the play first—I don't even know my character's name," I said to Nils.

"I have a copy for you," Borkman whispered. The paperback was badly beaten up—the pages had come unglued from the binding, as if the excitable director had read the little book to death. "Your name is Archie Kramer, Bill," Borkman informed me. "The young salesman is supposed to wear a derby hat, but in your case we can *piss-dense* with the derby!"

"*Dispense* with the derby," I repeated. "As a salesman, what do I sell?"

"Shoes," Nils told me. "In the end, you're taking Alma on a date to a casino—you have the last line in the play, Bill!"

"Which is?" I asked the director.

" 'Taxi!' " Borkman shouted.

Suddenly, we were no longer alone. The Christmas-dinner crowd was startled by Nils Borkman shouting for a taxi. My mother and Richard Abbott were staring at the paperback copy of Tennessee Williams's *Summer and Smoke*, which I held in my hands; no doubt they feared it was a sequel to *Giovanni's Room*.

"You want a *taxi*, Nils?" Grandpa Harry asked his old friend. "Didn't you come in your own car?"

"It's all right, Harry—Bill and I were just shop-talking," Nils explained to his colleague.

"That would be 'talkin' shop,' Nils," Grandpa Harry said.

"What part does Grandpa Harry have?" I asked the Norwegian dramaturge.

"You haven't offered me a part in anything, Nils," Grandpa Harry said.

"Well, I was *about* to!" Borkman cried. "Your grandfather would be a brilliant Mrs. Winemiller—Alma's mother," the wily director said to me.

"If you do it, I'll do it," I said to Grandpa Harry. It would be the spring production for the First Sister Players, the premiere of a serious drama in the spring—my last onstage performance before my departure from First Sister and that summer in Europe with Tom Atkins. It would not be for Richard Abbott and the Drama Club, but I would sing my swan song for Nils Borkman and the First Sister Players—the last time my mother would have the occasion to *prompt* me.

I liked the idea of it already—even before I read the play. I'd only glanced at the title page, where Tennessee Williams had included an epigraph from Rilke. The Rilke was good enough for me. "Who, if I were to cry out, would hear me among the angelic orders?" It seemed that, everywhere I looked, I just kept happening upon Rilke's terrifying angels. I wondered if Kittredge knew the German.

"Okay, Bill—if you do it, I'll do it," Grandpa Harry said; we shook on it.

Later, I found a discreet way to ask Nils if he'd already signed up Aunt Muriel and Richard Abbott in the Alma and John roles. "Don't worry, Bill," Borkman told me. "I have Muriel and Richard in my pocket-back!"

"In your back pocket—yes," I said to the crafty deerstalker on skis.

That Christmastime night when Elaine and I ran across the deserted Favorite River campus to the academy library—on our eager way to the old yearbook room—we saw the cross-country ski tracks crisscrossing the campus. (There was good deer-hunting on the academy cross-country course, and the outer athletic fields, when the Favorite River students had gone home for Christmas vacation.)

It being Christmas break, I did not necessarily expect to see Mr. Lockley at the check-out desk of the academy library, but there he was—as if it were a working night, or perhaps the alleged "nonpracticing homosexual" (as Mr. Lockley was called, behind his back) had nothing else to do.

"No luck with Uncle Bob finding the '40 *Owl,* huh?" I asked him.

"Mr. Fremont believes he returned it, but he did *not*—that is, not to my knowledge," Mr. Lockley stiffly replied.

"I'll just keep bugging him about it," I said.

"You do that, Billy," Mr. Lockley said sternly. "Mr. Fremont does not often frequent the library."

"I'll bet he doesn't," I said, smiling.

Mr. Lockley did not smile—certainly not at Elaine, anyway. He was one of those older men who lived alone; he would not take kindly to the coming two decades—by which time most (if not all) of the all-boys' boarding schools in New England would finally become coeducational.

In my estimation, coeducation would have a humanizing effect on those boarding schools; Elaine and I could testify that boys treat other boys better when there are girls around, and the girls are not as mean to one another in the presence of boys.

I know, I know—there are those diehards who maintain that single-sex education was more rigorous, or less distracting, and that coeducation came with a cost—a loss of "purity," I've heard the Mr. Lockleys of the boarding-school world argue. (Less concentration on "academics," they usually mean.)

That Christmastime night, all Mr. Lockley could manage to direct to Elaine was a minimally cordial bow—as if he were saying the unutterable, "Good evening, knocked-up faculty daughter. How are you managing now, you smelly little slut?"

But Elaine and I went about our business, paying no attention to Mr. Lockley. We were alone in the yearbook room—and more alone than usual in the otherwise abandoned academy library. Those old *Owls* from

'37, '38, and '39 beckoned us, and we soon found much to marvel about in their revealing pages.

WILLIAM FRANCIS DEAN WAS a smiling little boy in the 1937 *Owl*, when he would have been twelve. He seemed a charmingly elfin manager of the 1936–37 wrestling team, and the only other evidence Elaine and I could find of him was as the prettiest little girl in the Drama Club photos of that long-ago academic year—a scant five years before I would be born.

If Franny Dean had met the older Mary Marshall in '37, there was no record of it in the *Owl* of that year—nor was there any record of their meeting in the '38 and '39 *Owls*, wherein the wrestling-team manager grew only a little in stature but seemingly a lot in self-assurance.

Onstage, for the Drama Club, in those '38 and '39 yearbooks, Elaine and I could tell that the future Harvard-boy, who'd chosen "performer" as his career path, had developed into a most fetching femme fatale—he was a nymphlike presence.

"He was good-looking, wasn't he?" I asked Elaine.

"He looks like you, Billy—he's handsome but different," Elaine said.

"He already must have been dating my mother," I said, when we'd finished with the '39 *Owl* and were hurrying back to Bancroft Hall. (My dad was fifteen when my mom was nineteen!)

"If 'dating' is the right word, Billy," Elaine said.

"What do you mean?" I asked.

"You have to talk to your grandpa, Billy—if you can get him alone," Elaine told me.

"I could try talking to Uncle Bob first, if I can get Bob alone. Bob isn't as smart as Grandpa Harry," I said.

"I've got it!" Elaine suddenly said. "You talk to the admissions man first, but you tell him you've *already* talked to Grandpa Harry—and that Harry has told you everything he knows."

"Bob's not that dumb," I told Elaine.

"Yes, he is," Elaine said.

We had about an hour alone in Elaine's fifth-floor bedroom before Mr. and Mrs. Hadley came home from the movie in Ezra Falls. It being the Christmas holiday, we figured that the Hadleys and my mother and Richard—together with Aunt Muriel and Uncle Bob—would have stopped for a drink somewhere after the movie, and they had.

We'd had more than enough time to peruse the '40 *Owl* and look at all the photos of flaming Franny Dean—the prettiest boy in the class. William Francis Dean was a cross-dressing knockout in the photos from the Drama Club of that year, and there—at last, at the Senior Dance—was the missing picture Elaine and I had so fervently sought. There was little Franny holding my mom, Mary Marshall, in a slow-dancing embrace. Watching them, with evident disapproval, was big-sister Muriel. Oh, those Winthrop girls, "those Winthrop women," as Miss Frost had labeled my mother and my aunt Muriel—giving them Nana Victoria's maiden name of Winthrop. (When it came to who had the balls in the Marshall family, the Winthrop genes were definitely the ball-carriers.)

I wouldn't wait long to trap Uncle Bob. The very next day, a prospective student and his parents were visiting Favorite River Academy; Uncle Bob gave me a call and asked if I felt like being a tour guide.

When I'd finished the tour, I found Uncle Bob alone in the Admissions Office; it being Christmas break, the secretaries weren't necessarily working.

"What's up, Billy?" Uncle Bob asked me.

"I guess you forgot that you actually *did* take the '40 *Owl* back to the library," I began.

"I *did?*" Uncle Bob asked. I could see he was wondering how he would ever explain this to Muriel.

"It didn't show up in the yearbook room by itself," I said. "Besides, Grandpa Harry has told me all about 'flaming Franny' Dean, and what a pretty boy he was. What I don't get is how it all began with my mom—I mean why and when. I mean, how did it start in the first place?"

"Franny wasn't a bad guy, Billy," Uncle Bob quickly said. "He was just a little light in his loafers, if you know what I mean."

I'd heard the expression—from Kittredge, of course—but all I said was, "Why did my mom ever fall for him in the first place? How did it *start?*"

"He was an awfully young boy when he met your mother—she was four years older, which is a big difference at that age, Billy," Uncle Bob said. "Your mom saw him in a play—as a girl, of course. Afterward, he complimented her clothes."

"Her clothes," I repeated.

"It seems he liked girls' clothes—he liked trying them on, Billy," Uncle Bob said.

"Oh."

"Your grandmother found them in your mom's bedroom—one day, after your mother had come home from the high school in Ezra Falls. Your mom and Franny Dean were trying on your mom's clothes. It was just a childish game, but your aunt Muriel told me Franny had tried on *her* clothes, too. The next thing we knew, Mary had a crush on him, but by then Franny must have known he liked boys better. He was genuinely fond of your mom, Billy, but he mainly liked her clothes."

"She still managed to get *pregnant*," I pointed out. "You don't get a girl pregnant by fucking her clothes!"

"Think about it, Billy—there was all this dressing and undressing going on," Uncle Bob said. "They must have been in their underwear a lot—you know."

"I have trouble imagining it," I told him.

"Your grandpa thought the world of Franny Dean, Billy—I think Harry believed it could work," Uncle Bob said. "Don't forget, your mother was always a little *immature*—"

"A little simpleminded, do you mean?" I interrupted him.

"When Franny was a young boy, I think your mom sort of *managed* him—you know, Billy, she could kind of boss him around a little."

"But then Franny grew up," I said.

"There was also the guy—the one Franny met in the war, and they reconnected later," Uncle Bob began.

"It *was* you who told me that story—wasn't it, Uncle Bob?" I asked. "You know, the toilet-seat skipper, the man on the ship—he lost control of *Madame Bovary*; he went sliding over the toilet seats. Later, they met on the MTA. The guy got on at the Kendall Square station—he got off at Central Square—and he said to my dad, 'Hi. I'm Bovary. Remember me?' I mean *that* guy. You told me that story—didn't you, Uncle Bob?"

"No, I didn't, Billy," Uncle Bob said. "Your dad himself told you that story, and that guy *didn't* get off at the Central Square station—that guy stayed on the train, Billy. Your father and that guy were a *couple*. They may *still* be a couple, for all I know," Uncle Bob told me. "I thought your grandfather told you *everything*," he added suspiciously.

"It looks like there's more to ask Grandpa Harry about," I told Uncle Bob.

The admissions man was staring sadly at the floor of his office. "Did you have a good tour, Billy?" he asked me, a little absently. "Did that boy strike you as a promising candidate?"

Of course I had no memory of the prospective student or his parents.

"Thanks for everything, Uncle Bob," I said to him; I really did like him, and I felt sorry for him. "I think you're a good fella!" I called to him, as I ran out of the Admissions Office.

I knew where Grandpa Harry was; it was a workday, so he wouldn't be at home, under Nana Victoria's thumb. Harry Marshall didn't get a schoolteacher's Christmas break. I knew that Grandpa Harry was at the sawmill and the lumberyard, where I soon found him.

I told him I'd seen my father in the Favorite River Academy year-books; I said that Uncle Bob had confessed everything he knew about flaming Franny Dean, the effeminate cross-dressing boy who'd once tried on my mother's clothes—even, I'd heard, my aunt *Muriel's* clothes!

But what was this I'd heard about my dad actually visiting *me*—when I was sick with scarlet fever, wasn't it? And how was it possible that my father had actually told me that story of the soldier he met in the head of the Liberty ship during an Atlantic winter storm? The transport ship had just hit the open seas—the convoy was on its way to Italy from Hampton Roads, Virginia, Port of Embarkation—when my dad made the acquaintance of a toilet-seat skipper who was reading *Madame Bovary*.

"Who the hell was that fella?" I asked Grandpa Harry.

"That would be the someone *else* your mom saw Franny kissin', Bill," Grandpa Harry told me. "You had scarlet fever, Bill. Your dad heard you were sick, and he wanted to see you. I suspect, knowin' Franny, he wanted to get a look at Richard Abbott, too," Grandpa Harry said. "Franny just wanted to know you were in good hands, I guess. Franny wasn't a bad guy, Bill—he just wasn't really a *guy*!"

"And nobody told me," I said.

"Ah, well—I don't think any of us is proud of *that*, Bill!" Grandpa Harry exclaimed. "That's just how such things work out, I think. Your mom was hurt. Poor Mary just never understood the dressin'-up part— she thought it was somethin' Franny would outgrow, I guess."

"And what about the *Madame Bovary* guy?" I asked my grandfather.

"Ah, well—there's people you meet, Bill," Grandpa Harry said. "Some of 'em are merely encounters, nothin' more, but occasionally there's a love-of-your-life meetin', and that's different—you know?"

I had only two times left when I would see Miss Frost. I *didn't* know about the long-lasting effects of a "love-of-your-life meetin' "—not yet.

Chapter 10

ONE MOVE

The next-to-last time I saw Miss Frost was at a wrestling match—a dual meet at Favorite River Academy in January 1961. It was the first home meet of the season; Tom Atkins and I went together. The wrestling room—at one time, it was the only gym on the Favorite River campus— was an ancient brick building attached to the more modern, bigger gym by an enclosed but unheated cement catwalk.

The old gym was encircled by a wooden running track, which hung over the wrestling room; the track sloped downward at the four corners. The student spectators sat on the wooden track with their arms resting on the center bar of the iron railing. On this particular Saturday, Tom Atkins and I were among them, peering down at the wrestlers below.

The mat, the scorers' table, and the two team benches took up most of the gym floor. At one end of the wrestling room was a slanted rectangle of bleachers, with not more than a dozen rows of seats. The students considered the bleachers to be appropriate seating for the "older types." Faculty spectators sat there, and visiting parents. There were some townspeople who regularly attended the wrestling matches, and they sat in the bleachers. The day Elaine and I had seen Mrs. Kittredge watch her son wrestle, Mrs. Kittredge had sat in the bleachers—while Elaine and I had closely observed her from the sloped wooden running track above her.

I was remembering my one and only sighting of Mrs. Kittredge, when Tom Atkins and I noticed Miss Frost. She was sitting in the first row of the bleacher seats, as close to the wrestling mat as she could get. (Mrs. Kittredge had sat in the back row of the bleachers, as if to signify her immortal-seeming aloofness from the grunting and grimacing of human combat.)

"Look who's here, Bill—in the first row. Do you see her?" Atkins asked me.

"I *know*, Tom—I see her," I said. I instantly wondered if Miss Frost often, or always, attended the wrestling matches. If she'd been a frequent spectator at the home meets, how had Elaine and I missed seeing her? Miss Frost was not only tall and broad-shouldered; as a woman, it wasn't just her size that was imposing. If she'd frequently had a front-row seat at the wrestling matches, how could anyone have missed seeing her?

Miss Frost seemed very much at home where she was—at the edge of the wrestling mat, watching the wrestlers warm up. I doubted that she'd spotted Tom Atkins and me, because she didn't glance up at the surrounding running track—even during the warm-ups. And once the competition started, didn't everyone watch the wrestlers on the mat?

Because Delacorte was a lightweight, he wrestled in one of the first matches. If Delacorte had played Lear's Fool as a death-in-progress, that was certainly the way he wrestled; it was agonizing to watch him. Delacorte managed to make a wrestling match resemble a death-in-progress. The weight-cutting took a toll on him. He was so sucked down—he was all loose skin and super-prominent bones. Delacorte looked as if he were starving to death.

He was noticeably taller than most of his opponents; he often outscored them in the first period, and he was usually leading at the end of the second period, when he began to tire. The third period was Delacorte's time to pay for the weight-cutting.

Delacorte finished every wrestling match desperately trying to protect an ever-diminishing lead. He stalled, he fled the mat; his opponent's hands appeared to grow heavy on him. Delacorte's head hung down, and his tongue lolled out a corner of his open mouth. According to Kittredge, Delacorte ran out of gas every third period; a wrestling match was always a couple of minutes too long for him.

"Hang on, Delacorte!" one of the student spectators inevitably cried; soon all of us would echo this plea.

"Hang on! Hang on! Hang on!"

At this point in Delacorte's matches, Elaine and I had learned to look at Favorite River's wrestling coach—a tough-looking old geezer with cauliflower ears and a crooked nose. Almost everyone called Coach Hoyt by his first name, which was Herm.

When Delacorte was dying in the third period, Herm Hoyt predictably took a towel from a stack at the end of the wrestling-team bench nearest the scorers' table. Coach Hoyt unfailingly sat next to the towels, as near as he could get to the scorers' table.

As Delacorte tried to "hang on" a little longer, Herm unfolded the towel; he was bowlegged, in that way a lot of old wrestlers are, and when he stood up from the team bench, he (for just a moment) looked like he wanted to strangle the dying Delacorte with the towel, which Herm instead put over his own head. Coach Hoyt wore the towel as if it were a hood; he peered out from under the towel at Delacorte's final, expiring moments—at the clock on the scorers' table, at the ref (who, in the waning seconds of the third period, usually first warned Delacorte, and then penalized him, for stalling).

While Delacorte died, which I found unbearable to watch, I looked instead at Herm Hoyt, who seemed to be dying of both anger and empathy under the towel. Naturally, I advised Tom Atkins to keep his eyes on the old coach instead of enduring Delacorte's agonies, because Herm Hoyt knew before anyone else (including Delacorte) whether Delacorte would hang on and win or finish dying and lose.

This Saturday, following his near-death experience, Delacorte actually hung on and won. He came off the mat and collapsed into Herm Hoyt's arms. The old coach did as he always did with Delacorte—win or lose. Herm covered Delacorte's head with the towel, and Delacorte staggered to the team bench, where he sat sobbing and gasping for breath under the all-concealing mantle.

"For once, Delacorte isn't rinsing or spitting," Atkins sarcastically observed, but I was watching Miss Frost, who suddenly looked at me and smiled.

It was an unselfconscious smile—accompanied by a spontaneous little wave, just the wiggling of her fingers on one hand. I instantly knew: Miss Frost had known all along that I was there, and she'd expected that I would be.

I was so completely undone by her smile, and the wave, that I feared I would faint and slip under the railing; I foresaw myself falling from the wooden track to the wrestling room below. In all likelihood, it wouldn't have been a life-threatening fall; the running track was not at a great height above the gym floor. It just would have been humiliating to fall in a heap on the wrestling mat, or to land on one or more of the wrestlers.

"I don't feel well, Tom," I said to Atkins. "I'm a little dizzy."

"I've got you, Bill," Atkins said, putting his arm around me. "Just don't look down for a minute."

I kept looking at the far end of the gym, where the bleachers were, but Miss Frost had returned her attention to the wrestling; another match had started, while Delacorte was still wracked by sobs and gasps— his head was bobbing up and down under the consoling towel.

Coach Herm Hoyt had sat back down on the team bench next to the stack of clean towels. I saw Kittredge, who was beginning to loosen up; he was standing behind the bench, just bouncing on the balls of his feet and turning his head from side to side. Kittredge was stretching his neck, but he never stopped looking at Miss Frost.

"I'm okay, Tom," I said, but the weight of his arm rested on the back of my neck for a few seconds more; I counted to five to myself before Atkins took his arm from around my shoulders.

"We should think about going to Europe together," I told Atkins, but I still watched Kittredge, who was skipping rope. Kittredge couldn't take his eyes off Miss Frost; he continued to stare at her, skipping rhythmically, the speed of the jump rope never changing.

"Look who's *captivated* by her now, Bill," Atkins said petulantly.

"I *know*, Tom—I see him," I said. (Was it my worst fear, or was it secretly thrilling—to imagine Kittredge and Miss Frost together?)

"We would go to Europe this summer—is that what you mean, Bill?" Atkins asked me.

"Why not?" I replied, as casually as I could—I was still watching Kittredge.

"If your parents approve, and mine do—we could ask them, couldn't we?" Atkins said.

"It's in our hands, Tom—we have to make them understand it's a priority," I told him.

"She's looking at you, Bill!" Atkins said breathlessly.

When I glanced (as casually as I could) at Miss Frost, she was smiling at me again. She put her index and middle fingers to her lips and kissed them. Before I could blow her a kiss, she was once more watching the wrestling.

"Boy, did *that* get Kittredge's attention!" Tom Atkins said excitedly. I kept looking at Miss Frost, but only for a moment; I didn't need Atkins to tell me in order to know that Kittredge was looking at me.

"Bill, Kittredge is—" Atkins began.

"I *know*, Tom," I told him. I let my gaze linger on Miss Frost a little longer, before I glanced—as if accidentally—at Kittredge. He'd stopped jumping rope and was staring at me. I just smiled at him, as unmeaningfully as I'd ever managed to smile at him, and Kittredge began to skip rope again; he had picked up the pace, either consciously or unconsciously, but he was once again staring at Miss Frost. I couldn't help wonder if Kittredge was reconsidering the *disgusting* word. Perhaps the *everything* that Kittredge imagined I'd done with Miss Frost didn't disgust him anymore, or was this wishful thinking?

The atmosphere in the wrestling room changed abruptly when Kittredge's match began. Both team benches viewed the mauling with a clinical appreciation. Kittredge usually beat up his opponents before he pinned them. It was confusing for a nonwrestler like myself to differentiate among the displays of Kittredge's technical expertise, his athleticism, and the brute force of his physical superiority; Kittredge thoroughly dominated an opponent before pinning him. There was always a moment in the third and final period when Kittredge glanced at the clock on the scorers' table; at that moment, the home crowd began chanting, "Pin! Pin! Pin!" By then, the torturing had gone on for so long that I imagined Kittredge's opponent was *hoping* to be pinned; moments later, when the referee signaled the fall, the pin seemed both overdue and merciful. I'd never seen Kittredge lose; I hadn't once seen him challenged.

I don't remember the remaining matches that Saturday afternoon, or which team won the dual meet. The rest of the competition is clouded in my memory by Kittredge's nearly constant staring at Miss Frost, which continued long after his match—Kittredge interrupting his fixed gaze only with cursory (and occasional) glances at me.

I, of course, continued to look back and forth between Kittredge and Miss Frost; it was the first time I could see both of them in the same place, and I admit I was deeply disturbed about that imagined split second when Miss Frost would look at Kittredge. She didn't—not once. She continued to watch the wrestling and, albeit briefly, to smile at me—while the entire time Tom Atkins kept asking, "Do you want to leave, Bill? If this is uncomfortable for you, we should just leave—I would go with you, you know."

"I'm *fine*, Tom—I want to stay," I kept telling him.

"*Europe*—well, I never imagined I would see *Europe*!" Atkins at one point exclaimed. "I wonder *where* in Europe, and how we would travel. By train, I suppose—by bus, maybe. I wish I knew what we would need for clothes—"

"It will be summer, Tom—we'll need summer clothes," I told him.

"Yes, but how formal, or not—that's what I mean, Bill. And how much *money* would we need? I truly have no idea!" Atkins said in a panicky voice.

"We'll ask someone," I said. "Lots of people have been to Europe."

"Don't ask Kittredge, Bill," Atkins continued, in his panic-stricken mode. "I'm sure we couldn't afford any of the places Kittredge goes, or the hotels he stays in. Besides, we don't want Kittredge to know we're going to Europe together—do we?"

"Stop blithering, Tom," I told him. I saw that Delacorte had emerged from under the towel; he appeared to be breathing normally, paper cup in hand. Kittredge said something to him, and Delacorte instantly started to stare at Miss Frost.

"Delacorte gives me the—" Atkins began.

"I *know*, Tom!" I told him.

I realized that the wrestling-team manager was a servile, furtive-looking boy in glasses; I'd not noticed him before. He handed Kittredge an orange, cut in quarters; Kittredge took the orange without looking at the manager or saying anything to him. (The manager's name was Merry-weather; with a last name like that, as you might imagine, no one ever called him by his first name.)

Merryweather handed Delacorte a clean paper cup; Delacorte gave Merryweather the old, spat-in cup, which Merryweather dropped in the spit bucket. Kittredge was eating the orange while he and Delacorte stared at Miss Frost. I watched Merryweather, who was gathering up the used and discarded towels; I was trying to imagine my father, Franny Dean, doing the things a wrestling-team manager does.

"I must say, Bill—you're rather remote for someone who's just asked me to spend a summer in Europe with him," Atkins said tearfully.

"Rather remote," I repeated. I was beginning to regret that I'd asked Tom Atkins to go to Europe with me for a whole summer; his neediness was already irritating me. But suddenly the wrestling was over; the student spectators were filing down the corrugated-iron stairs, which led from the running track to the gym floor. Parents and faculty—and the other adult spectators, from the bleacher seats—were milling around on the wrestling mat, where the wrestlers were talking to their families and friends.

"You're not going to *speak* to her, are you, Bill? I thought you weren't *allowed*," Atkins was fretting.

I must have wanted to see what might happen, if I accidentally bumped into Miss Frost—if I just said, "Hi," or something. (Elaine and I used to mill around on the wrestling mat after we'd watched Kittredge wrestle—probably hoping, and fearing, that we would bump into Kittredge "accidentally.")

It was not hard to spot Miss Frost in the crowd; she was so tall and erect, and Tom Atkins was whispering beside me with the nervous constancy of a bird dog. "There she is, Bill—over there. Do you see her?"

"I see her, Tom."

"I don't see Kittredge," Atkins said worriedly.

I knew that Kittredge's timing was not to be doubted; when I had made my way to where Miss Frost was standing (not coincidentally, in the intimidating center of that starting circle on the wrestling mat), I found myself stopping in front of her at the very instant Kittredge materialized beside me. Miss Frost probably realized that I couldn't speak; Atkins, who'd been blathering compulsively, was now struck speechless by the awkward gravity of the moment.

Smiling at Miss Frost, Kittredge—who was never at a loss for words—said to me: "Aren't you going to introduce me to your friend, Nymph?"

Miss Frost continued smiling at me; she did not look at Kittredge when she spoke to him.

"I know you onstage, Master Kittredge—on *this* stage, too," Miss Frost said, pointing a long finger at the wrestling mat. (Her nail polish was a new color to me—magenta, maybe, more purplish than red.) "But Tom Atkins will have to introduce us. William and I," she said, not once looking away from me as she spoke, "are not permitted to speak to each other, or otherwise *engage*."

"I'm sorry, I didn't—" Kittredge started to say, but he was interrupted.

"Miss Frost, this is Jacques Kittredge—Jacques, this is Miss Frost!" Atkins blurted out. "Miss Frost is a great . . . *reader*!" Atkins told Kittredge; poor Tom then considered what options remained for him. Miss Frost had only tentatively extended her hand in Kittredge's direction;

because she kept looking at me, Kittredge was perhaps unsure if she was offering her hand to him or to me. "Kittredge is our best wrestler," Tom Atkins forged ahead, as if Miss Frost had no idea who Kittredge was. "This will be his third undefeated season—that is, if he remains undefeated," Atkins bumbled on. "It will be a school record—three undefeated seasons! Won't it?" Atkins asked Kittredge uncertainly.

"Actually," Kittredge said, smiling at Miss Frost, "I can only *tie* the school record, if I remain undefeated. Some stud did it in the thirties," Kittredge said. "Of course, there was no New England tournament back then. I don't suppose they wrestled as many matches as we do today, and who knows how tough their competition was—"

Miss Frost stopped him. "It wasn't bad," she said, with a disarming shrug; by how perfectly she'd captured Kittredge's shrug, I suddenly realized for how long (and how closely) Miss Frost had been observing him.

"Who's the stud—whose record is it?" Tom Atkins asked Kittredge. Of course I knew by the way Kittredge answered that he had no idea whose record he was trying to tie.

"Some guy named Al Frost," Kittredge said dismissively. I feared the worst from Tom Atkins: nonstop crying, explosive vomiting, insane and incomprehensible repetition of the *vagina* word. But Atkins was mute and twitching.

"How's it goin', Al?" Coach Hoyt asked Miss Frost; his battered head came up to her collarbones. Miss Frost affectionately put her magenta-painted hand on the back of the old coach's neck, pulling his face to her small but very noticeable breasts.

(Delacorte would explain to me later that wrestlers called this a collar-tie.) "How are you, Herm?" Miss Frost said fondly to her former coach.

"Oh, I'm hangin' in there, Al," Herm Hoyt said. An errant towel protruded from one of the side pockets of his rumpled sports jacket; his tie was askew, and the top button of his shirt was unbuttoned. (With his wrestler's neck, Herm Hoyt could never button that top button.)

"We were talking about Al Frost, and the school record," Kittredge explained to his coach, but Kittredge continued to smile at Miss Frost. "All Coach Hoyt will ever say about Frost is that he was 'pretty good'— of course, that's what Herm says about a guy who's *very* good *or* pretty good," Kittredge was explaining to Miss Frost. Then he said to her: "I don't suppose *you* ever saw Frost wrestle?"

I don't think that Herm Hoyt's sudden and obvious discomfort gave it away; I honestly believe that Kittredge realized who Al Frost was in the split second that followed his asking Miss Frost if she'd ever seen Frost wrestle. It was the same split second when I saw Kittredge look at Miss Frost's hands; it wasn't the nail polish he was noticing.

"Al—Al Frost," Miss Frost said. This time, she unambiguously extended her hand to Kittredge; only then did she look at him. I knew that look: It was the *penetrating* way she'd once looked at me—when I was fifteen and I wanted to reread *Great Expectations*. Both Tom Atkins and I noticed how small Kittredge's hand looked in Miss Frost's grip. "Of course we weren't—we *aren't*, I should say—in the same weight-class," Miss Frost said to Kittredge.

"Big Al was my one-seventy-seven-pounder," Herm Hoyt was telling Kittredge. "You were a little light to wrestle heavyweight, Al, but I started you at heavyweight a couple of times—you kept askin' me to let you wrestle the big guys."

"I was pretty good—*just* pretty good," Miss Frost told Kittredge. "At least they didn't think I was *very* good—not when I got to Pennsylvania."

Both Atkins and I saw that Kittredge couldn't speak. The handshaking part was over, but either Kittredge couldn't let go of Miss Frost's hand or she didn't *let* him let go.

Miss Frost had lost a lot of muscle mass since her wrestling days; yet, with the hormones she'd been taking, I'm sure her hips were bigger than when she used to weigh in at 177 pounds. In her forties, I'm guessing Miss Frost weighed 185 or 190 pounds, but she was six feet two—in heels, she'd told me, she was about six-four—and she carried the weight well. She didn't look like a 190-pounder.

Jacques Kittredge was a 147-pounder. I'm estimating that Kittredge's "natural" weight—when it wasn't wrestling season—was around 160 pounds. He was five-eleven (and a bit); Kittredge had once told Elaine that he'd just missed being a six-footer.

Coach Hoyt must have seen how unnerved Kittredge was—this was so uncharacteristic—not to mention the prolonged hand-holding between Kittredge and Miss Frost, which was making Atkins breathe irregularly.

Herm Hoyt began to ramble; his impromptu dissertation on wrestling history filled the void (our suddenly halted conversation) with an odd combination of nervousness and nostalgia.

"In your day, Al, I was just thinkin', you wore nothin' but tights—everyone was bare-chested, don'tcha remember?" the old coach asked his former 177-pounder.

"I most certainly do, Herm," Miss Frost replied. She released Kittredge's hand; with her long fingers, Miss Frost straightened her cardigan, which was open over her fitted blouse—the *bare-chested* word having drawn Kittredge's attention to her girlish breasts.

Tom Atkins was wheezing; I'd not been told that Atkins suffered from asthma, in addition to his pronunciation problems. Perhaps poor Tom was merely hyperventilating, in lieu of bursting into tears.

"We started wearin' the singlets *and* the tights in '58—if you remember, Jacques," Herm Hoyt said, but Kittredge had not recovered the ability to speak; he managed only a disheartened nod.

"The singlets *and* the tights are redundant," Miss Frost said; she was examining her nail polish disapprovingly, as if someone else had chosen the color. "It should either be *just* a singlet, and *no* tights, or you wear *only* tights and you're bare-chested," Miss Frost said. "Personally," she added, in a staged aside to the silent Kittredge, "I *prefer* to be bare-chested."

"One day, it will be just a singlet—no tights, I'll bet ya," the old coach predicted. "No bare chests allowed."

"Pity," Miss Frost said, with a theatrical sigh.

Atkins emitted a choking sound; he'd spotted the scowling Dr. Harlow, maybe a half-second before I saw the bald-headed owl-fucker. I had my doubts that Dr. Harlow was a wrestling fan—at least Elaine and I had never noticed him when we'd watched Kittredge wrestle before. (But why would we have paid any attention to Dr. Harlow then?)

"This is strictly forbidden, Bill—there's to be no contact between you two," Dr. Harlow said; he didn't look at Miss Frost. The "you two" was as close as Dr. Harlow could come to saying her name.

"Miss Frost and I haven't said a word to each other," I told the bald-headed owl-fucker.

"There's to be no *contact*, Bill," Dr. Harlow sputtered; he still wouldn't look at Miss Frost.

"*What* contact?" Miss Frost said sharply; her big hand gripped the doctor's shoulder, causing Dr. Harlow to spring away from her. "The only *contact* I've had is with young Kittredge here," Miss Frost told Dr. Harlow; she now put both her hands on Kittredge's shoulders. "Look at me," she commanded him; when Kittredge looked up at her, he seemed as suddenly impressionable as a submissive little boy. (If Elaine had been there, she at last would have seen the innocence she'd sought, unsuccessfully, in Kittredge's younger photographs.) "I wish you luck—I hope you tie that record," Miss Frost told him.

"Thank you," Kittredge managed to mumble.

"See you around, Herm," Miss Frost said to her old coach.

"Take care of yourself, Al," Herm Hoyt told her.

"I'll see you, Nymph," Kittredge said to me, but he didn't look at me—or at Miss Frost. Kittredge quickly jogged off the mat, catching up to one of his teammates.

"We were talkin' about *wrestlin'*, Doc," Herm Hoyt said to Dr. Harlow.

"*What* record?" Dr. Harlow asked the old coach.

"My record," Miss Frost told the doctor. She was leaving when Tom Atkins made a gagging sound; Atkins couldn't contain himself, and now that Kittredge was gone, poor Tom was no longer afraid to say it.

"Miss Frost!" Atkins blurted out. "Bill and I are going to Europe together this summer!"

Miss Frost smiled warmly at me, before turning her attention to Tom Atkins. "I think that's a *wonderful* idea, Tom," she told him. "I'm sure you'll have a great time." Miss Frost was walking away when she stopped and looked back at us, but it was clear, when Miss Frost spoke to us, that she was looking straight at Dr. Harlow. "I hope you two get to do *everything* together," Miss Frost said.

Then they were gone—both Miss Frost and Dr. Harlow. (The latter didn't look at me as he was leaving.) Tom Atkins and I were left alone with Herm Hoyt.

"Ya know, fellas—I gotta be goin'," the old coach told us. "There's a team meetin'—"

"Coach Hoyt," I said, stopping him. "I'm curious to know who would win—if there were ever a match between Kittredge and Miss Frost. I mean, if they were the same age and in the same weight-class. You know what I mean—if everything were equal."

Herm Hoyt looked around; maybe he was checking to be sure that none of his wrestlers was near enough to overhear him. Only Delacorte had lingered in the wrestling room, but he was standing far off by the exit door, as if he were waiting for someone. Delacorte was too far away to hear us.

"Listen, fellas," the old coach growled, "don't quote me on this, but

Big Al would *kill* Kittredge. At any age, no matter what weight-class—Al could kick the shit out of Kittredge."

I won't pretend that it wasn't gratifying to hear this, but I would rather have heard it privately; it wasn't something I wanted to share with Tom Atkins.

"Can you *imagine*, Bill—" Atkins began, when Coach Hoyt had left us for the locker room.

I interrupted Atkins. "Yes, of course I can *imagine*, Tom," I told him.

We were at the exit to the old gym when Delacorte stopped us. It was *me* he'd been waiting for.

"I saw her—she's truly beautiful!" Delacorte told me. "She spoke to me as she was leaving—she said I was a 'wonderful' Lear's Fool." Here Delacorte paused to rinse and spit; he was holding two paper cups and no longer resembled a death-in-progress. "She also told me I should move up a weight-class, but she put it in a funny way. 'You might lose more matches if you move up a weight, but you won't suffer so much.' She *used to be* Al Frost, you know," Delacorte confided to me. "She used to *wrestle!*"

"We *know*, Delacorte!" Tom Atkins said irritably.

"I wasn't talking to *you*, Atkins," Delacorte said, rinsing and spitting. "Then Dr. Harlow interrupted us," Delacorte told me. "He said something to your friend—some bullshit about it being 'inappropriate' for her even to be here! But she just kept talking to me, as if the bald-headed owl-fucker weren't there. She said, 'Oh, what is it Kent says to Lear—act one, scene one, when Lear has got things the wrong way around, concerning Cordelia? Oh, what *is* the line? I just saw it! You were just *in* it!' But I didn't know what line she meant—I was Lear's Fool, I wasn't Kent—and Dr. Harlow was just standing there. Suddenly, she cries out: 'I've got it—Kent says, "*Kill thy physician*"—that's the line I was looking for!' And the bald-headed owl-fucker says to her, 'Very funny—I suppose you think that's very funny.' But she turns on him, she gets right in Dr. Harlow's face, and she says, 'Funny? I think you're a *funny* little man—that's what I think, Dr. Harlow.' And the bald-headed owl-fucker scurried off. Dr. Harlow just ran away! Your friend is marvelous!" Delacorte told me.

Someone shoved him. Delacorte dropped both paper cups—in a doomed effort to regain his balance, to try to stop himself from falling. Delacorte fell in the mess from his rinsing and spitting cups. It was Kittredge who'd shoved him. Kittredge had a towel wrapped around his waist—his hair was wet from the shower. "There's a team meeting after showers, and you haven't even showered. I could get laid twice in the time it takes to wait for you, Delacorte," Kittredge told him.

Delacorte got to his feet and ran down the enclosed cement catwalk to the new gym, where the showers were.

Tom Atkins was attempting to make himself invisible; he was afraid that Kittredge would shove him next.

"How did you not know she was a man, Nymph?" Kittredge suddenly asked me. "Did you overlook her Adam's apple, did you not notice how *big* she is? Except her tits. Jesus! How could you not know she was a man?"

"Maybe I *did* know," I said to him. (It just came out, as the truth only occasionally will.)

"Jesus, Nymph," Kittredge said. He was starting to shiver; there was a draft of cold air from the unheated catwalk that led to the bigger, newer gym, and Kittredge was wearing just a towel. It was unusual to see Kittredge appear vulnerable, but he was half naked and shivering from the cold. Tom Atkins was not a brave boy, but even Atkins must have sensed Kittredge's vulnerability—even Atkins could summon a *moment* of fearlessness.

"How did *you* not know she was a *wrestler?*" Atkins asked him. Kittredge took a step toward him, and Atkins—again fearful—stumbled backward, almost falling. "Did you see her shoulders, her *neck,* her *hands?*" Atkins cried to Kittredge.

"I gotta go," was all Kittredge said. He said it to me—he didn't answer Atkins. Even Tom Atkins could tell that Kittredge's confidence was shaken.

Atkins and I watched Kittredge run along the catwalk; he clutched the towel around his waist as he ran. It was a small towel—as tight around his hips as a short skirt. The towel made Kittredge run like a girl.

"You don't think Kittredge could lose a match this season—do you, Bill?" Atkins asked me.

Like Kittredge, I didn't answer Atkins. How could Kittredge lose a wrestling match in New England? I would have loved to ask Miss Frost that question, among other questions.

THAT MOMENT WHEN YOU are tired of being treated like a child— tired of adolescence, too—that suddenly opening but quickly closing passage, when you irreversibly want to grow up, is a dangerous time. In a future novel (an early one), I would write: "Ambition robs you of your childhood. The moment you want to become an adult—in *any* way—something in your childhood dies." (I might have been thinking of that simultaneous desire to become a writer and to have sex with Miss Frost, not necessarily in that order.)

In a later novel, I would approach this idea a little differently—a little more carefully, maybe. "In increments both measurable and not, our childhood is stolen from us—not always in one momentous event but often in a series of small robberies, which add up to the same loss." I suppose I could have written "betrayals" instead of "robberies"; in my own family's case, I might have used the *deceptions* word—citing lies of both omission and commission. But I'll stand by what I wrote; it suffices.

In another novel—very near the beginning of the book, in fact—I wrote: "Your memory is a monster; *you* forget—*it* doesn't. It simply files things away; it keeps things for you, or hides things from you. Your memory summons things to your recall with a will of its own. You imagine you have a memory, but your memory has you!" (I'll stand by that, too.)

It would have been late February or early March of '61 when the Favorite River Academy community learned that Kittredge had lost; in fact, he'd lost twice. The New England Interscholastic Wrestling Championships were in East Providence, Rhode Island, that year. Kittredge was beaten badly in the semifinals. "It wasn't even close," Delacorte told me in an almost-incomprehensible sentence. (I could detect the vowels but not the consonants, because Delacorte was speaking with six stitches in his tongue.)

Kittredge had lost again in the consolation round to determine third place—this time, to a kid he'd beaten before.

"That first loss kind of took it out of him—after that, Kittredge didn't seem to care if he finished third or fourth," was all Delacorte could manage to say. I saw blood in his spitting cup; he'd bitten through his tongue—hence the six stitches.

"Kittredge finished *fourth*," I told Tom Atkins.

For a two-time defending champion, this must have hurt. The New England Interscholastic Wrestling Championships had begun in '49, fourteen years after Al Frost finished his third undefeated season, but in the Favorite River school newspaper, nothing was said about Al Frost's record—or Kittredge's failure to tie it. In thirteen years, there'd been eighteen two-time New England champions—Kittredge among them. If he'd managed to win a third championship, that would have been a first. "A first and a last," Coach Hoyt was quoted as saying, in our school newspaper. As it would turn out, '61 was the final year there were all-inclusive New England schoolboy wrestling championships; starting in '62, the public high schools and the private schools would have separate tournaments.

I asked Herm Hoyt about it one early spring day, when our paths crossed in the quad. "Somethin' will be lost—havin' one tournament for everyone is tougher," the old coach told me.

I asked Coach Hoyt about Kittredge, too—if there was anything that could explain those two losses. "Kittredge didn't give a shit about that consolation match," Herm said. "If he couldn't win it all, he didn't give a good fuck about the difference between third and fourth place."

"What about the first loss?" I asked Coach Hoyt.

"I kept tellin' Kittredge, there's always someone who's better," the old coach said. "The only way you beat the better guy is by bein' *tougher*. The other guy was better, and Kittredge *wasn't* tougher."

That seemed to be all there was to it. Atkins and I found Kittredge's defeat anticlimactic. When I mentioned it to Richard Abbott, he said, "It's Shakespearean, Bill; lots of the important stuff in Shakespeare happens offstage—you just hear about it."

"It's Shakespearean," I repeated.

"It's *still* anticlimactic," Atkins said, when I told him what Richard had to say.

As for Kittredge, he seemed only a little subdued; he didn't strike me as much affected by those losses. Besides, it was that time in our senior year when we were hearing about what colleges or universities we'd been admitted to. The wrestling season was over.

Favorite River was not in the top tier of New England preparatory schools; understandably, the academy kids didn't apply to the top tier of colleges or universities. Most of us went to small liberal-arts colleges, but Tom Atkins saw himself as a state-university type; he'd seen what *small* was like, and what he wanted was *bigger*—"a place you could get lost in," Atkins wistfully said to me.

I cared less about the getting-lost factor than Tom Atkins did. I cared about the English Department—whether or not I could continue to read those writers Miss Frost had introduced me to. I cared about being in or near New York City.

"Where'd you go to college?" I had asked Miss Frost.

"Someplace in Pennsylvania," she'd told me. "It's no place you've ever heard of." (I liked the "no place you've ever heard of" part, but it was the New York City factor that mattered most to me.)

I applied to every college and university I could think of in the New York City area—ones you've heard of, ones you've never heard of. I made a point of speaking to someone in the German Department, too. In every case, I was assured that they would help me find a way to study abroad in a German-speaking country.

I already had the feeling that a summer in Europe with Tom Atkins would only serve to stimulate my desire to be far, far away from First Sister, Vermont. It seemed to me to be what a would-be writer should do— that is, live in a foreign country, where they spoke a foreign language, while (at the same time) I would be making my earliest serious attempts to write in my own language, as if I were the first and only person to ever do it.

Tom Atkins ended up at the University of Massachusetts, in Amherst; it was a big school, and Atkins would manage to get lost there— maybe more lost than he'd meant, or had wanted.

No doubt, my application to the University of New Hampshire provoked some suspicion at home. There'd been a rumor that Miss Frost was moving to New Hampshire. This had prompted Aunt Muriel to remark that she wished Miss Frost were moving farther away from Vermont than *that*—to which I responded by saying I hoped to move farther away from Vermont than *that*, too. (This must have mystified Muriel, who knew I'd applied to the University of New Hampshire.)

But that spring, there was no confirmation that Miss Frost's rumored move to New Hampshire was true—nor did anyone say *where* in New Hampshire she might be moving to. Truly, my reasons for applying to the University of New Hampshire had nothing to do with Miss Frost's future whereabouts. (I'd only applied there to worry my family—I had no intention of going there.)

It was frankly more of a mystery—chiefly, to Tom Atkins and me—that Kittredge was going to Yale. Granted, Atkins and I had the kind of SAT scores that made Yale—or any of the Ivy League schools— unattainable. My grades had been better than Kittredge's, however, and how could Yale have overlooked the fact that Kittredge had been forced to repeat his senior year? (Tom Atkins had erratic grades, but he had graduated on schedule.) Atkins and I knew that Kittredge had great SAT scores, but Yale must have been motivated to take him for other reasons; Atkins and I knew that, too.

Atkins mentioned Kittredge's wrestling, but I think I know what Miss Frost would have said about that: It wasn't the wrestling that got Kittredge into Yale. (As it turned out, he wouldn't wrestle in college, anyway.) His SAT scores probably helped, but Kittredge's father, from whom he was estranged, had gone to Yale.

"Trust me," I told Tom. "Kittredge didn't get into Yale for his *German*—that's all I can tell you."

"Why does it matter to you, Billy—where Kittredge is going to college?" Mrs. Hadley asked me. (I was having a pronunciation problem with the *Yale* word, which was why the subject came up.)

"I'm not envious," I told her. "I assure you, I don't want to go there—I can't even *say* it!"

As it turned out, it meant nothing—where Kittredge went to college, or where I went—but, at the time, it was infuriating that Kittredge was accepted to Yale.

"Forget about *fairness*," I said to Martha Hadley, "but doesn't *merit* matter?" It was an eighteen-year-old question to ask, though I had turned nineteen (in March 1961); in due time, of course, I would get over where Kittredge went to college. Even in that spring of '61, Tom Atkins and I were more interested in planning our summer in Europe than we were obsessed by the obvious injustice of Kittredge getting into Yale.

I admit: It was easier to forget about Kittredge, now that I rarely saw him. Either he didn't need my help with his German or he'd stopped asking for it. Since Yale had admitted him, Kittredge wasn't worried about what grade he got in German—all he had to do was graduate.

"May I remind you?" Tom Atkins asked me sniffily. "*Graduating* was all Kittredge had to do last year, too."

But in '61, Kittredge did graduate—so did we all. Frankly, graduation seemed anticlimactic, too. Nothing happened, but what were we expecting? Apparently, Mrs. Kittredge hadn't been expecting anything; she didn't attend. Elaine also stayed away, but that was understandable.

Why hadn't Mrs. Kittredge come to see her only child graduate? ("Not very *motherly*, is she?" was all Kittredge had to say about it.) Kittredge seemed unsurprised; he was notably unimpressed with graduating. His aura was one of already having moved beyond the rest of us.

"It's as if he's started at Yale—it's like he's not here anymore," Atkins observed.

I met Tom's parents at graduation. His father took a despairing look at me and refused to shake my hand; he didn't *call* me a fag, but I could feel him thinking it.

"My father is very . . . unsophisticated," Atkins told me.

"He should meet my mom," was all I said. "We're going to Europe together, Tom—that's all that matters."

"That's all that matters," Atkins repeated. I didn't envy him his days at home before we left; it was evident that his dad would give him endless shit about me while poor Tom was home. Atkins lived in New Jersey. Having seen only the New Jersey people who came to Vermont to ski, I didn't envy Atkins that, either.

Delacorte introduced me to his mom. "This is the guy who was *going to be* Lear's Fool," Delacorte began.

When the pretty little woman in the sleeveless dress and the straw hat also declined to shake my hand, I realized that my being the original Lear's Fool was probably connected to the story of my having had sex with the transsexual town librarian.

"I'm so sorry for your *troubles*," Mrs. Delacorte told me. I only then remembered that I didn't know where Delacorte was going to college. Now that he's dead, I'm sorry I never asked him. It may have mattered to Delacorte—where he went to college—maybe as much as where I went *didn't* matter to me.

THE REHEARSALS FOR THE Tennessee Williams play weren't time-consuming—not for my small part. I was only in the last scene, which is all about Alma, the repressed woman Nils Borkman believed Miss Frost would be perfect for. Alma was played by Aunt Muriel, as *repressed* a woman as I've ever known, but I managed to invigorate my role as "the young man" by imagining Miss Frost in the Alma part.

It seemed suitable to the young man's infatuation with Alma that I stare at my aunt Muriel's breasts, though they were gigantic (in my opinion, *gross*) in comparison to Miss Frost's.

"*Must* you stare at my breasts, Billy?" Muriel asked me, in one memorable rehearsal.

"I'm supposed to be infatuated with you," I replied.

"With *all* of me, I would imagine," Aunt Muriel rejoined.

"I think it's *appropriate* for the young man to stare at Alma's bosoms," our director, Nils Borkman, intoned. "After all, he's a shoe salesman—he's not very *refinery*."

"It's not healthy for my *nephew* to look at me like that!" Aunt Muriel said indignantly.

"Surely, Mrs. Fremont's bosoms have attracted the stares of *many* young mens!" Nils said, in an ill-conceived effort to flatter Muriel. (I've momentarily forgotten why my aunt didn't complain when I stared at her breasts in *Twelfth Night*. Oh, yes—I was a little shorter then, and Muriel's breasts had blocked me from her view.)

My mother sighed. Grandpa Harry, who was cast as Alma's mother—he was wearing a huge pair of falsies, accordingly—suggested that it was "only natural" for *any* young man to stare at the breasts of a woman who was "well endowed."

"You're calling me, your own daughter, 'well endowed'—I can't believe it!" Muriel cried.

My mom sighed again. "*Everyone* stares at your breasts, Muriel," my mother said. "There was a time when you *wanted* everyone to stare at them."

"You don't want to go down that road with me—there was a time when *you* wanted something, Mary," Muriel warned her.

"Girls, girls," said Grandpa Harry.

"Oh, shut up—you old cross-dresser!" my mother said to Grandpa Harry.

"Maybe I could just stare at *one* of the breasts," I suggested.

"Not that *you* care about *either* of them, Billy!" my mom shouted.

I was getting a lot of shouts and sighs from my mother that spring; when I'd announced my plans to go to Europe with Tom Atkins for the summer, I got both the sigh and the shout. (First the sigh, of course, which was swiftly followed by: "Tom Atkins—that *fairy*!")

"Ladies, ladies," Nils Borkman was saying. "This is a *forward* young man, Mr. Archie Kramer—he asks Alma, 'What's there to do in this town after dark?' That's pretty *forward*, isn't it?"

"Ah, yes," Grandpa Harry jumped in, "and there's a stage direction about Alma—'*she gathers confidence before the awkwardness of his youth*'—and there's another one, when Alma '*leans back and looks at him under half-closed lids, perhaps a little suggestively.'* I think Alma is kind of *en-couragin'* this young fella to look at her breasts!"

"There can be only one director, Daddy," my mother told Grandpa Harry.

"I don't do 'suggestively'—I don't *encourage* anyone to look at my breasts," Muriel said to Nils Borkman.

"You're so full of shit, Muriel," my mom said.

There's a fountain in that final scene—so that Alma can give one of her sleeping pills to the young man, who washes the pill down by drinking from the fountain. There were originally benches in the scene, too, but Nils didn't like the benches. (Muriel had been too agitated to sit still, given that I was staring at her breasts.)

I foresaw a problem with losing the benches. When the young man hears that there's a casino, which offers "all kinds of after-dark entertainment" (as Alma puts it), he says to Alma, "Then what in hell are we sitting here for?" But there were no benches; Alma and the young man couldn't be *sitting.*

When I pointed this out to Nils, I said: "Shouldn't I say, 'Then what in hell are we *doing here?'* Because Alma and I *aren't* sitting—there's nothing to sit on."

"You're not writing this play, Billy—it's already written," my mother (ever the prompter) told me.

"So we bring the benches back," Nils said tiredly. "You'll have to sit *still,* Muriel. You've just absorbed a sleeping pill, remember?"

"Absorbed!" Muriel exclaimed. "I should have *absorbed* a whole bottle of sleeping pills! I can't possibly sit still with Billy staring at my breasts!"

"Billy isn't *interested* in breasts, Muriel!" my mother shouted. (This was not true, as I know you know—I simply wasn't interested in *Muriel's* breasts.)

"I'm just *acting*—remember?" I said to Aunt Muriel and my mom.

In the end, I leave the stage; I go off shouting for a taxi. Only Alma remains—*"she turns slowly about toward the audience with her hand still raised in a gesture of wonder and finality as . . . the curtain falls."*

I hadn't a clue as to how Muriel might bring that off—*"a gesture of wonder"* seemed utterly beyond her capabilities. As for the *"finality"* aspect, I had little doubt that my aunt Muriel could deliver finality.

"Let's one more time try it," Nils Borkman implored us. (When our director was tired, his word order eluded him.)

"Let's try it one more time," Grandpa Harry said helpfully, although Mrs. Winemiller isn't in that final scene. (It is dusk in the park in *Summer and Smoke*; only Alma and the young traveling salesman are onstage.)

"Behave yourself, Billy," my mom said to me.

"For the last time," I told her, smiling as sweetly as I could—at both Muriel and my mother.

" 'The water—is—cool,' " Muriel began.

" 'Did you say something?' " I asked her breasts—as the stage direction says, *eagerly*.

THE FIRST SISTER PLAYERS opened *Summer and Smoke* in our small community theater about a week after my Favorite River graduation. The academy students never saw the productions of our local amateur theatrical society; it didn't matter that the boarders, Kittredge and Atkins among them, had left town.

I spent the whole play backstage, until the twelfth and final scene. I was past caring about observing my mother's disapproval of Grandpa Harry as a woman; I'd seen all I needed to know about that. In the stage directions, Mrs. Winemiller is described as *a spoiled and selfish girl who evaded the responsibilities of later life by slipping into a state of perverse childishness. She is known as Mr. Winemiller's "Cross."*

It was evident to my mom and me that Grandpa Harry was drawing on Nana Victoria—and what a *"Cross"* she was for him to bear—in his testy portrayal of Mrs. Winemiller. (This was evident to Nana Victoria, too; my disapproving grandmother sat in the front row of the audience looking as if she'd been poleaxed, while Harry brought the house down with his antics.)

My mother had to prompt the shit out of the two child actors who virtually ruined the prologue. But in scene 1—specifically, the third time Mrs. Winemiller shrieked, "Where is the ice cream man?"—the audience was roaring, and Mrs. Winemiller brought the curtain down at the end of scene 5 by taunting her pussy-whipped husband. " 'Insufferable cross yourself, you old—windbag . . .' " Grandpa Harry cackled, as the curtain fell.

It was as good a production as Nils Borkman had ever directed for the First Sister Players. I have to admit that Aunt Muriel was excellent as Alma; it was hard for me to imagine that Miss Frost could have matched Muriel in the *repressed* area of my aunt's agitated performance.

Beyond prompting the child actors in the prologue, my mom had nothing to do; no one muffed a line. It is fortunate that my mother had no further need to prompt anyone, because it was fairly early in the play when we both spotted Miss Frost in the front row of the audience. (That Nana Victoria found herself sitting in the same row as Miss Frost perhaps contributed to my grandmother's concussed appearance; in addition to suffering her husband's scathing portrayal of a shrewish wife and mother, Nana Victoria had to sit not more than two seats away from the trans-sexual wrestler!)

Upon seeing Miss Frost, my mom might have inadvertently prompted her mother to crap in a cat's litter box. Of course, Miss Frost had chosen her front-row seat wisely. She knew where the prompter had positioned herself backstage; she knew I always hung out with the prompter. If we could see her, my mother and I knew, Miss Frost could see us. In fact, for entire scenes of *Summer and Smoke,* Miss Frost paid no attention to the actors onstage; Miss Frost just kept smiling at me, while my mother increasingly took on the brained-by-a-two-by-four expressionlessness of Nana Victoria.

Whenever Muriel-as-Alma was onstage, Miss Frost removed a compact from her purse. While Alma repressed herself, Miss Frost admired her lipstick in the compact's small mirror, or she applied some powder to her nose and forehead.

At the closing curtain, when I'd run offstage, shouting for a taxi—leaving Muriel to find the gesture that implies (without words) both *"wonder and finality"*—I encountered my mother. She knew where I exited the stage, and she had left her prompter's chair to intercept me.

"You will not speak to that *creature*, Billy," my mom said.

I had anticipated such a showdown; I'd rehearsed so many things that I wanted to say to my mother, but I had *not* expected her to give me such a perfect opportunity to attack her. Richard Abbott, who'd played John, must have been in the men's room; he wasn't backstage to help her. Muriel was still onstage, for a few more seconds—to be followed by resounding and all-concealing applause.

"I *will* speak to her, Mom," I began, but Grandpa Harry wouldn't let me continue. Mrs. Winemiller's wig was askew, and her enormous falsies were crowded too closely together, but Mrs. Winemiller wasn't asking for ice cream now. She was nobody's cross to bear—not in *this* scene—and Grandpa Harry needed no prompting.

"Just *stop* it, Mary," Grandpa Harry told my mother. "Just forget about Franny. For once in your life, stop feelin' so sorry for yourself. A good man finally married you, for Christ's sake! What have you got to be so *angry* about?"

"I am speaking to my *son*, Daddy," my mom started to say, but her heart wasn't in it.

"Then *treat* him like your son," my grandfather said. "Respect Bill for who he is, Mary. What are you gonna do—change his genes, or somethin'?"

"That *creature*," my mother said again, meaning Miss Frost, but just then Muriel exited the stage. There was thunderous applause; Muriel's massive chest was heaving. Who knew whether the *wonder* or the *finality* had taken it out of her? "That *creature* is here—in the audience!" my mom cried to Muriel.

"I *know*, Mary. Do you think I didn't see him?" Muriel said.

"See *her*," I corrected my aunt Muriel.

"*Her!*" Muriel said scornfully.

"Don't you call her a *creature*," I said to my mother.

"She was doin' her best to look after Bill, Mary," Grandpa Harry (as Mrs. Winemiller) said. "She really *was* lookin' after him."

"Ladies, ladies . . ." Nils Borkman was saying. He was trying to ready Muriel and Grandpa Harry to go back onstage for their bows. Nils was a tyrant, but I appreciated how he allowed me to miss the all-cast curtain call; Nils knew I had a more important role to play backstage.

"Please don't speak to that . . . *woman*, Billy," my mom was pleading. Richard was with us, preparing to take his bows, and my mother threw herself into his arms. "Did you see who's here? She came *here*! Billy wants to *speak* to her! I can't bear it!"

"Let Bill speak to her, Jewel," Richard said, before running onstage.

The audience was treating the cast to more rousing applause when Miss Frost appeared backstage, just seconds after Richard had left.

"Kittredge lost," I said to Miss Frost. For months I had imagined speaking to her; now this was all I could say to her.

"Twice," Miss Frost said. "Herm told me."

"I thought you'd gone to New Hampshire," my mom said to her. "You shouldn't be here."

"I *never* should have been here, Mary—I shouldn't have been *born* here," Miss Frost told her.

Richard and the rest of the cast had come offstage. "We should go,

Jewel—we should leave these two alone for a minute," Richard Abbott was saying to my mother. Miss Frost and I would never be "alone" together again—that much was obvious.

To everyone's surprise, it was Muriel Miss Frost spoke to. "Good job," Miss Frost told my haughty aunt. "Is Bob here? I need a word with the Racquet Man."

"I'm right here, Al," Uncle Bob said uncomfortably.

"You have the keys to everything, Bob," Miss Frost told him. "There's something I would like to show William, before I leave First Sister," Miss Frost said; there was no theatricality in her delivery. "I need to show him something in the wrestling room," Miss Frost said. "I could have asked Herm to let us in, but I didn't want to get Herm in any trouble."

"In the *wrestling* room!" Muriel exclaimed.

"You and Billy, in the wrestling room," Uncle Bob said slowly to Miss Frost, as if he had trouble picturing it.

"You can stay with us, Bob," Miss Frost said, but she was looking at my mom. "You and Muriel can come, too, Mary—if you think William and I need more than one chaperone."

I thought my whole fucking family might die on the spot—merely to hear the *chaperone* word—but Grandpa Harry once more distinguished himself. "Just give me the keys, Bob—*I'll* be the chaperone."

"*You?*" Nana Victoria cried. (No one had noticed her arrival backstage.) "Just *look* at you, Harold! You're a sexual *clown*! You're in no condition to be anyone's chaperone!"

"Ah, well . . ." Grandpa Harry started to say, but he couldn't continue. He was scratching under one of his falsies; he was fanning his bald head with his wig. It was hot backstage.

This was exactly how it unfolded—the last time I would see Miss Frost. Bob went to the Admissions Office to get his keys to the gym; he would have to come with us, my uncle explained, because only he and Herm Hoyt knew where the lights were in the new gym. (You had to enter the new gym, and cross to the old gym on the cement catwalk; there was no getting into the wrestling room any other way.)

"There was no new gym in my day, William," Miss Frost was saying, as we traipsed across the dark Favorite River campus with Uncle Bob and Grandpa Harry—*not* with Mrs. Winemiller, alas, because Harry was once more wearing his lumberman's regalia. Nils Borkman had decided to come along, too.

"I'm interested in seeing *gives-what* with the wrestling!" the eager Norwegian said.

"In seein' *what gives* with the wrestlin'," Grandpa Harry repeated.

"You're going out in the world, William," Miss Frost said matter-of-factly. "There are homo-hating assholes everywhere."

"Homo-assholes?" Nils asked her.

"Homo-hating assholes," Grandpa Harry corrected his old friend.

"I've never let anyone into the gym at night," Uncle Bob was telling us, apropos of nothing. Someone was running to catch up to us in the darkness. It was Richard Abbott.

"Increasin' popular interest in seein' what gives with the wrestlin', Bill," Grandpa Harry said to me.

"I wasn't planning on a coaching clinic, William—please try to pay attention. We don't have much time," Miss Frost added—just as Uncle Bob found the light switch, and I could see that Miss Frost was smiling at me. It was our story—not to have much *time* together.

Having Uncle Bob, Grandpa Harry, Richard Abbott, and Nils Borkman for an audience didn't necessarily make what Miss Frost had to show me a spectator sport. The lighting in the old gym was spotty, and no one had cleaned the wrestling mats since the end of the '61 season; there was dust and grit on the mats, and some dirty towels on the gym floor in the area of the team benches. Bob, Harry, Richard, and Nils sat on the home-team bench; it was where Miss Frost had told them to sit, and the men did as they were directed. (In their own ways, and for their own reasons, these four men were genuine fans of Miss Frost.)

"Take your shoes off, William," Miss Frost began; I could see that she'd taken off hers. Miss Frost had painted her toenails a turquoise color—or maybe it was an aqua color, a kind of greenish blue.

It being a warm June night, Miss Frost was wearing a white tank top and Capri pants; the latter, in a blue-green color that matched her toenail polish, were a little tight for wrestling. I was wearing some baggy Bermuda shorts and a T-shirt.

"Hi," Elaine suddenly said. I hadn't noticed her in the theater. She'd followed us to the old gym—at a discreet distance behind us, no doubt—and now sat watching us from the wooden running track above the wrestling room.

"More wrestling," was all I said to Elaine, but I was happy my dear friend was there.

"You will one day be bullied, William," Miss Frost said. She clamped what Delacorte had called a collar-tie on the back of my neck. "You're going to get pushed around, sooner or later."

"I suppose so," I said.

"The bigger and more aggressive he is, the more you want to crowd him—the closer you want to get to him," Miss Frost told me. I could smell her; I could feel her breath on the side of my face. "You want to make him lean on you—you want him cheek-to-cheek, like this. Then you jam one of his arms into his throat. Like *this*," she said; the inside of my own elbow was constricting my breathing. "You want to make him push back—you want to make him lift that arm," Miss Frost said.

When I pushed back against her—when I lifted my arm, to take my elbow away from my throat—Miss Frost slipped under my armpit. In a split second, she was at once behind me and to one side of me. Her hand, on the back of my neck, pulled my head down; with all her weight, she drove me shoulder-first into the warm, soft mat. I felt a tweak in my neck. I landed at an awkward angle; how I fell put a lot of strain on that shoulder, and in the area of my collarbone.

"Imagine the mat is a cement sidewalk, or just a plain old wood floor," she said. "That wouldn't feel so good, would it?"

"No," I answered her. I was seeing stars; I'd never seen them before.

"Again," Miss Frost said. "Let me do it to you a few more times, William—then you do it to me."

"Okay," I said. We did it again and again.

"It's called a duck-under," Miss Frost explained. "You can do it to anyone—he just has to be pushing you. You can do it to anyone who's being *aggressive*."

"I get it," I told her.

"No, William—you're *beginning* to get it," Miss Frost told me.

We were in the wrestling room for over an hour, just drilling the duck-under. "It's easier to do to someone who's taller than you are," Miss Frost explained. "The bigger he is, and the more he's leaning on you, the harder his head hits the mat—or the pavement, or the floor, or the ground. You get it?"

"I'm *beginning* to," I told her.

I will remember the contact of our bodies, as I learned the duck-under; as with most things, there is a rhythm to it when you start to do it correctly. We were sweating, and Miss Frost was saying, "When you hit it ten more times, without a glitch, you can go home, William."

"I don't *want* to go home—I want to keep doing *this*," I whispered to her.

"I wouldn't have missed making your acquaintance, William—not for all the world!" Miss Frost whispered back.

"I love you!" I told her.

"Not now, William," she said. "If you can't stick the guy's elbow in his throat, stick it in his mouth," she told me.

"In his mouth," I repeated.

"Don't kill each other!" Grandpa Harry was shouting.

"What's goin' on here?" I heard Coach Hoyt ask. Herm had noticed all the lights; the old gym and that wrestling room were sacred to him.

"Al's showing Billy a duck-under, Herm," Uncle Bob told the old coach.

"Well, I showed it to Al," Herm said. "I guess Al oughta know how it goes." Coach Hoyt sat down on the home-team bench—as close as he could get to the scorers' table.

"I'll never forget you!" I was whispering to Miss Frost.

"I guess we're done, William—if you can't concentrate on the duck-under," Miss Frost said.

"Okay, I'll concentrate—ten more duck-unders!" I told her; she just smiled at me, and she ruffled my sweat-soaked hair. I don't believe she'd ruffled my hair since I was thirteen or fifteen—not for a long time, anyway.

"No, we're done now, William—Herm is here. Coach Hoyt can take over the duck-unders," Miss Frost said. I suddenly saw that she looked tired—I'd never seen her look tired before.

"Give me a hug, but don't kiss me, William—let's just play by the rules and make everyone happy," Miss Frost told me.

I hugged her as hard as I could, but she didn't hug me back—not nearly as hard as she could have.

"Safe travels, Al," Uncle Bob said.

"Thanks, Bob," Miss Frost said.

"I gotta get home, before Muriel sends out the police and the firemen to find me," Uncle Bob said.

"I can lock up the place, Bob," Coach Hoyt told my uncle. "Billy and I will just hit a few more duck-unders."

"A few more," I repeated.

"Till I see how you're gettin' it," Coach Hoyt said. "How 'bout *all* of you goin' home?" the old coach asked. "You, too, Richard—you, too, Harry," Herm was saying; the coach probably didn't recognize Nils Borkman, and if Coach Hoyt recognized Elaine Hadley, he would have known her only as the unfortunate faculty daughter who'd been knocked up by Kittredge.

"I'll see you later, Richard—I love you, Elaine!" I called, as they were leaving.

"I love *you*, Billy!" I heard Elaine say.

"I'll see you at home—I'll leave some lights on, Bill," I heard Richard say.

"Take care of yourself, Al," Grandpa Harry said to Miss Frost.

"I'm going to miss you, Harry," Miss Frost told him.

"I'm gonna miss you, too!" I heard Grandpa Harry say.

I understood that I shouldn't watch Miss Frost leave, and I didn't. Occasionally, you know when you won't see someone again.

"The thing about a duck-under, Billy, is to make the guy kinda do it to himself—that's the key," Coach Hoyt was saying. When we locked up with the growingly familiar collar-ties, I had the feeling that grabbing hold of Herm Hoyt was like grabbing hold of a tree trunk—he had such a thick neck that you couldn't get much of a grip on him.

"The place to stick the guy's elbow is anywhere it makes him uncomfortable, Billy," Herm was saying. "In his throat, in his mouth—stick it up his nose, if you can find a way to fit it up there. You're only stickin' his elbow in his face to get him to react. What you want him to do is *over*-react, Billy—that's all you're doin'."

The old coach did about twenty duck-unders on me; they were very fluid, but my neck was killing me.

"Okay—your turn. Let's see you do it," Herm Hoyt told me.

"Twenty times?" I asked him. (He could see that I was crying.)

"We'll start countin' the times as soon as you stop cryin', Billy. I'm guessin' you'll be cryin' for the first forty times, or so—then we'll start countin'," Coach Hoyt said.

We were there in the old gym for at least another two hours—maybe three. I had stopped counting the duck-unders, but I was beginning to get the feeling that I could do a duck-under in my sleep, or drunk, which was a funny thing for me to think because I'd not yet been drunk. (There was a first time for everything, and I had a lot of first times ahead of me.)

At some point, I made the mistake of saying to the old coach: "I think I could do a duck-under *blindfolded*."

"Is that so, Billy?" Herm asked me. "Stay right here—don't leave the mat." He went off somewhere; I could hear him on the catwalk, but I couldn't see him. Then the lights went out, and the wrestling room was in total darkness.

"Don't worry—just stay where you are!" the coach called to me. "I can find you, Billy."

It wasn't long before I felt his presence; his strong hand clamped me in a collar-tie and we were locked up in the surrounding blackness.

"If you can feel me, you don't need to see me," Herm said. "If you've got hold of my neck, you kinda know where my arms and legs are gonna be, don'tcha?"

"Yes, sir," I answered.

"You better do your duck-under on me before I do mine on you, Billy," Herm told me. But I wasn't quick enough. Coach Hoyt hit his duck-under first; it was a real head-banger. "I guess it's your turn, Billy— just don't make me wait all night," the old coach said.

"Do you know where she's going?" I asked him later. It was pitch-dark in the old gym, and we were lying on the mat—both of us were resting.

"Al told me not to tell you, Billy," Herm said.

"I understand," I told him.

"I always knew Al wanted to be a girl." The old coach's voice came out of the darkness. "I just didn't know he had the balls to go through with it, Billy."

"Oh, he has the balls, all right," I said.

"She—*she* has the balls, Billy!" Herm Hoyt said, laughing crazily.

There were some windows surrounding the wooden track above us; an early-dawn light gave them a dull glow.

"Listen up, Billy," the old coach said. "You've got one move. It's a pretty good duck-under, but it's just one move. You can take a guy down with it—maybe hurt him a little. But a tough guy is gonna get up and keep comin' after you. One move won't make you a wrestler, Billy."

"I see," I said.

"When you hit your duck-under, you get the hell out of there— wherever you are, Billy. Do you get what I'm sayin'?" Coach Hoyt asked me.

"It's just one move—I hit it and run. Is that what you're telling me?" I asked him.

"You hit it and run—you know how to run, don'tcha?" the old coach said.

"What will happen to her?" I asked him suddenly.

"I can't tell you that, Billy," Herm said, sighing.

"She's got more than one move, doesn't she?" I asked him.

"Yeah, but Al's not gettin' any younger," Coach Hoyt told me. "You best get home, Billy—there's enough light to see by."

I thanked him; I made my way across the absolutely empty Favorite River campus. I wanted to see Elaine, and hug her and kiss her, but I didn't think that would be our future. I had a summer ahead of me to explore the much-ballyhooed sexual *everything* with Tom Atkins, but I liked boys *and* girls; I knew Atkins couldn't provide me with everything.

Was I enough of a romantic to believe Miss Frost knew this about me? Did I believe she was the first person to understand that no one person could *ever* give me everything?

Yes, probably. After all, I was only nineteen—a bisexual boy with a pretty good duck-under. It was just one move, and I was no wrestler, but you can learn a lot from good teachers.

Chapter 11

ESPAÑA

"You should wait, William," Miss Frost had said. "The time to read *Ma-dame Bovary* is when your romantic hopes and desires have crashed, and you believe that your future relationships will have disappointing—even devastating—consequences."

"I'll wait to read it until then," I'd told her.

Is it any wonder that this was the novel I took with me to Europe in the summer of 1961, when I was traveling with Tom?

I'd just begun reading *Madame Bovary* when Atkins asked me, "Who is she, Bill?" In his tone of voice, and by the pitiful-looking way poor Tom was biting his lower lip, I perceived that he was jealous of Emma Bovary. I hadn't yet met the woman! (I was still reading about the oafish Charles.)

I even shared with Atkins that passage about Charles's father encouraging the boy to "take great swigs of rum and to shout insults at religious processions." (A promising upbringing, I'd oh-so-wrongly concluded.) But when I read poor Tom that defining observation of Charles—"the audacity of his desire protested against the servility of his conduct"—I could see how hurtful this was. It would not be the last time I underestimated Atkins's inferiority complex. After that first time, I couldn't read *Madame Bovary* to myself; I was permitted to read that novel only if I read every word of it aloud to Tom Atkins.

Granted: Not every new reader of *Madame Bovary* takes away from that novel a distrust (bordering on hatred) of monogamy, but my contempt of monogamy was born in the summer of '61. To be fair to Flaubert, it was poor Tom's craven need for monogamy that I loathed.

What an awful way to read that wonderful novel—out loud to Tom Atkins, who feared infidelity even as the first sexual adventure of his young life was just getting started! The aversion Atkins felt for Emma's adultery was akin to his gag reflex at the *vagina* word; yet well before Emma's descent into infidelity, poor Tom was revolted by her—the description of "her satin slippers, with their soles yellowed from the beeswax on the dance-floor" disgusted him.

"Who cares about that sickening woman's *feet?*" Atkins cried.

Of course it was Emma's *heart* that Flaubert was exposing—"contact with the rich had left it smeared with something that would never fade away."

"Like the beeswax on her slippers—don't you see?" I asked poor Tom.

"Emma is nauseating," Atkins replied. What I soon found nauseating was Tom's conviction that having sex with me was the only remedy for how he'd "suffered" while listening to *Madame Bovary*.

"Then let me read it to myself!" I begged him. But, in that case, I would have been guilty of neglecting him—worse, I would have been choosing Emma's company over his!

And so I read aloud to Atkins—"she was filled with lust, with rage, with hatred"—while he writhed; it was as if I were torturing him.

When I read aloud that part where Emma is so enjoying the very idea of having her first lover—"as if a second puberty had come upon her"—I believed that Atkins was going to throw up in our bed. (I thought Flaubert would have appreciated the irony that poor Tom and I were in France at the time, and there was no toilet in our room at the pension—only a bidet.)

While Atkins went on vomiting in the bidet, I considered how the infidelity that poor Tom truly feared—namely, mine—was thrilling to me. With the accidental assistance of *Madame Bovary*, I see now why I added monogamy to the list of distasteful things I associated with the exclusively heterosexual life, but—more accurately—it was Tom Atkins who was to blame. Here we were, in Europe—experiencing the sexual *everything* that Miss Frost had so protectively withheld from me—and Atkins was already agonizing over the eventuality of my leaving him (perhaps, but not necessarily, for someone else).

While Atkins was barfing in that bidet in France, I kept reading aloud to him about Emma Bovary. "She summoned the heroines from the books she had read, and the lyric host of these unchaste women began their chorus in her memory, sister-voices, enticing her." (Don't you just love that?)

Okay, it was cruel—how I raised my voice with that bit about the "unchaste women"—but Atkins was noisily retching, and I wanted to be heard over the running water in the bidet.

Tom and I were in Italy when Emma poisoned herself and died. (This was around the time I was compelled to keep looking at that prostitute with the faintest trace of a mustache on her upper lip, and poor Tom had noticed me looking at her.)

"'Soon she was vomiting blood,'" I read aloud. By then, I thought I understood those things that Atkins disapproved of—even as they attracted me—but I'd not foreseen the vehemence with which Tom Atkins could disapprove. Atkins cheered when the end was near, and Emma Bovary was vomiting blood.

"Let me see if I understand you correctly, Tom," I said, pausing just before that moment when Emma starts screaming. "Your cheers indicate to me that Emma is getting what she *deserves*—is that what you're saying?"

"Well, Bill—of course she *deserves* it. Look what she's done! Look how she's behaved!" Atkins cried.

"She has married the dullest man in France, but because she fucks around, she deserves to die in agony—is that your point, Tom?" I asked him. "Emma Bovary is bored, Tom. Should she just *stay* bored—and by so doing earn the right to die peacefully, in her sleep?"

"*You're* bored, aren't you, Bill? You're bored with *me*, aren't you?" Atkins asked pitifully.

"Not everything is about *us*, Tom," I told him.

I would regret this conversation. Years later, when Tom Atkins was dying—at that time when there were so many righteous souls who believed poor Tom, and others like him, *deserved* to die—I regretted that I had embarrassed Atkins, or that I'd ever made him feel ashamed.

Tom Atkins was a good person; he was just an insecure guy and a cloying lover. He was one of those boys who'd always felt unloved, and he loaded up our summer relationship with unrealistic expectations. Atkins was manipulative and possessive, but only because he wanted me to be the love of his life. I think poor Tom was afraid he would *always* be unloved; he imagined he could force the search for the love of his life into a single summer of one-stop shopping.

As for my ideas about finding the love of my life, I was quite the opposite to Tom Atkins; that summer of '61, I was in no hurry to stop shopping—I'd just started!

Not that many pages further on in *Madame Bovary*, I would read aloud Emma's actual death scene, her final convulsion—upon hearing the blind man's tapping stick and his raucous singing. Emma dies imagining "the beggar's hideous face, stationed in the eternal darkness like a monster."

Atkins was shaking with guilt and terror. "I wouldn't wish that on *anyone*, Bill!" poor Tom cried. "I didn't mean it—I didn't mean she deserved *that*, Bill!"

I remember holding him while he cried. *Madame Bovary* is not a horror story, but the novel had that effect on Tom Atkins. He was very fair-skinned, with freckles on his chest and back, and when he got upset and cried, his face flushed pink—as if someone had slapped him—and his freckles looked inflamed.

When I read on in *Madame Bovary*—that part where Charles finds Rodolphe's letter to Emma (Charles is so stupid, he tells himself that his unfaithful wife and Rodolphe must have loved each other "platonically")—Atkins was wincing, as if in pain. "'Charles was not one of those men who like to get to the bottom of things,'" I continued, while poor Tom moaned.

"Oh, Bill—no, no, no! Please tell me I'm *not* one of those men like Charles. I *do* like to get to the bottom of things!" Atkins cried. "Oh, Bill—I honestly do, I do, I *do*!" He once more dissolved in tears—as he would again, when he was dying, when poor Tom indeed got to the bottom of things. (It was not the bottom that any of us saw coming.)

"*Is* there eternal darkness, Bill?" Atkins would one day ask me. "Is there a monster's face, waiting there?"

"No, no, Tom," I would try to assure him. "It's either *just* darkness—*no* monster, no *anything*—or it's very bright, truly the most amazing light, and there are lots of wonderful things to see."

"No monsters, either way—right, Bill?" poor Tom would ask me.

"That's right, Tom—no monsters, either way."

We were still in Italy, that summer of '61, when I got to the end of *Madame Bovary*; by then, Atkins was such a self-pitying wreck that I'd snuck into the WC and read the ending to myself. When it was time for the reading-aloud part, I skipped that paragraph about the autopsy on

Charles—that horrifying bit when they open him up and find *nothing*. I didn't want to deal with poor Tom's distress at the *nothing* word. ("How could there have been *nothing*, Bill?" I imagined Atkins asking.)

Maybe it was the fault of the paragraph I omitted from my reading, but Tom Atkins wasn't content with the ending of *Madame Bovary*.

"It's just not very *satisfying*," Atkins complained.

"How about a blow job, Tom?" I asked him. "I'll show you *satisfying*."

"I was being serious, Bill," Atkins told me peevishly.

"So was I, Tom—so was I," I said.

After that summer, it wasn't a surprise to either of us that we went our separate ways. It was easier, for a while, to maintain a limited but cordial correspondence than to see each other. I wouldn't hear from Atkins for a couple of our college years; I guessed that he might have tried having a girlfriend, but someone told me Tom was lost on drugs, and that there'd been an ugly and very public exposure of a homosexual kind. (In Amherst, Massachusetts!) This was early enough in the sixties that the *homosexual* word had a forbiddingly clinical sound to it; at that time, of course, homosexuals had no "rights"—we weren't even a "group." I was still living in New York in '68, and even in New York there wasn't what I would have called a gay "community," not a *true* community. (Just all the cruising.)

I suppose the frequency with which gay men encountered one another in doctors' offices might have constituted a different kind of community; I'm kidding, but it was my impression that we had more than our fair share of gonorrhea. In fact, a gay doctor (who was treating me for the clap) told me that bisexual men should wear condoms.

I don't remember if the clap doctor said *why*, or if I asked him; I probably took his unfriendly advice as further evidence of prejudice against bisexuals, or maybe this doctor reminded me of a gay Dr. Harlow. (In '68, I knew a lot of gay guys; *their* doctors weren't telling *them* to wear condoms.)

The only reason I remember this incident at all is that I was about to publish my first novel, and I had just met a woman I was interested in, in that way; at the same time, of course, I was constantly meeting gay guys. And it wasn't only because of this clap doctor (with the apparent prejudice against bisexuals) that I started wearing a condom; I credit Esmeralda for making condoms appealing to me, and I missed Esmeralda—I definitely did.

In any case, the next time I heard from Tom Atkins, I had become a condom-wearer and poor Tom had a wife and children. As if that weren't shocking enough, our correspondence had degenerated to Christmas cards! Thus I learned, from a Christmas photo, that Tom Atkins had a family—an older boy, a younger girl. (Needless to say, I hadn't been invited to the wedding.)

In the winter of 1969, I became a published novelist. The woman I'd met in New York around the time I was persuaded to wear a condom had lured me to Los Angeles; her name was Alice, and she was a screenwriter. It was somehow reassuring that Alice had told me she wasn't interested in "adapting" my first novel.

"I'm not going down that road," Alice said. "Our relationship means more to me than a job."

I'd told Larry what Alice had said, thinking this might reassure him about her. (Larry had met Alice only once; he hadn't liked her.)

"Maybe you should consider, Bill, what Alice means," Larry said. "What if she already pitched your novel to all the studios, and no one was interested?"

Well, my old pal Larry was the first to tell me that no one would ever make a film from my first novel; he also told me I would hate living in L.A., although I think what Larry meant (or hoped) was that I would hate living with Alice. "She's not your soprano understudy, Bill," Larry said.

But I *liked* living with Alice—Alice was the first woman I'd lived with who knew I was bisexual. She said it didn't matter. (*Alice* was bisexual.)

Alice was also the first woman I'd talked to about having a child together—but, like me, she was no fan of monogamy. We'd gone to Los Angeles with a bohemian belief in the enduring superiority of friendship; Alice and I were friends, and we both believed that the concept of "the couple" was a dinosaur idea. We'd given each other permission to have other lovers, though there were limitations—namely, it was okay with Alice if I saw men, just not other women, and I told her it was okay with me if she saw women, just not other men.

"Uh-oh," Elaine had said. "I don't think those kinds of arrangements work."

At the time, I wouldn't have considered Elaine to be an authority on "arrangements"; I also knew that, even in '69, Elaine had expressed an on-again, off-again interest in *our* living together. But Elaine was stead-fast in her resolution never to have any children; she hadn't changed her mind about the size of babies' heads.

Alice and I additionally believed, most naïvely, in the enduring su-periority of writers. Naturally, we didn't see each other as rivals; she was a screenwriter, I was a novelist. What could possibly go wrong? ("Uh-oh," as Elaine would say.)

I'd forgotten that my first conversation with Alice had been about the draft. When I got summoned for a physical—I can't remember exactly when this was, or many other details, because I had a terrible hangover that day—I checked the box that said something along the lines of "homo-sexual tendencies," which I vaguely recall whispering to myself in an Aus-trian accent, as if Herr Doktor Grau were still alive and speaking to me.

The army psychiatrist was a tight-assed lieutenant; I remember *him*. He kept his office door open while he interrogated me—so that the recruits who were waiting their turn could overhear us—but I'd lived through earlier and vastly smarter intimidation tactics. (Think of Kit-tredge.)

"And *then* what?" Alice had asked, when I was telling her the story. She was a great person to tell a story to; Alice always gave me the impres-sion that she couldn't wait to hear what happened next. But Alice was impatient with the vagueness of my draft story.

"You don't like girls?" the lieutenant had asked me.

"Yes, I do—I *do* like girls," I told him.

"Then what are your 'homosexual tendencies,' exactly?" the army psychiatrist asked.

"I like guys, too," I told him.

"You do?" he asked. "Do you like guys *better* than you like girls?" the psychiatrist continued loudly.

"Oh, it's just so hard to *choose*," I said, a little breathlessly. "I really, really like them *both*!"

"Uh-huh," the lieutenant said. "And do you see this tendency *con-tinuing*?"

"Well, I certainly *hope* so!" I said—as enthusiastically as I could man-age. (Alice loved this story; at least she said she did. She thought it would make a funny scene in a movie.)

"The *funny* word should have warned you, Bill," Larry would tell me much later, when I was back in New York. "Or the *movie* word, maybe."

What might have warned me about Alice was that she took notes when we were talking. "Who takes *notes* on conversations?" Larry had asked me; not waiting for an answer, he'd also asked, "And which of you *likes* it that she doesn't shave her armpits?"

About two weeks after I'd checked the box for "homosexual tendencies," or whatever the stupid form said, I received my classification notice—or maybe it was my *re*classification notice. I think it was a 4-F; I was found "not qualified"; there was something about the "established physical, mental, or moral standards."

"But exactly what did the notification say—what was your actual classification?" Alice had asked me. "You can't just *think* it was a Four-F."

"I don't remember—I don't care," I told her.

"But that's just so *vague*!" Alice said.

Of course the *vague* word should have warned me, too.

There'd been a follow-up letter, perhaps from the Selective Service, but maybe not, telling me to see a shrink—not just any shrink, but a particular one.

I'd sent the letter to Grandpa Harry; he and Nils knew a lawyer, for their logging and lumber business. The lawyer said that I couldn't be forced to see a shrink; I didn't, and I never heard from the draft again. The problem was that I'd written about this—albeit in passing—in my first novel. I didn't realize it was my *novel* Alice was interested in; I thought she was interested in every little thing about *me*.

"Most places we leave in childhood grow less, not more, fancy," I wrote in that novel. (Alice had told me how much she loved that line.) The first-person narrator is an out-of-the-closet gay man who's in love with the protagonist, who refuses to check the "homosexual tendencies" box; the protagonist, who is an in-the-closet gay man, will die in Vietnam. You might say it is a story about how *not* coming out can kill you.

One day, I could tell that Alice was really agitated. She seemed to be working on so many projects at the same time—I never knew which screenplay she was writing, at any given moment. I just assumed that one of these scripts-in-progress was causing her agitation, but she confessed to me that one of the studio execs she knew had been "bugging" her about me and my first novel.

He was a guy she regularly made a point of putting down. "Mr. Sharpie," she sometimes called him—or "Mr. Pastel," more recently. I had the impression of an immaculate dresser, but a guy who wore golfing clothes—light-colored clothes, anyway. (You know: lime-green pants, pink polo shirts—*pastel* colors.)

Alice told me that Mr. Pastel had asked her if I would try to "interfere" with a film based on my novel—*if* there ever were a movie made. Mr. Sharpie must have known she lived with me; he'd asked her if I would be "compliant" to changes in my story.

"Just the usual novel-to-screenplay sort of changes, I guess," Alice said vaguely. "The guy just has a lot of *questions*."

"Like what?" I asked her.

"Where does the service-to-my-country part come into the story?" the studio exec in the light-colored clothing had asked Alice. I was a little confused by the question; I thought I'd written an anti-Vietnam novel.

But in the exec's opinion, the reason the closeted gay protagonist doesn't check the "homosexual tendencies" box is that he feels an obligation to serve his country—*not* that he's so afraid to come out, he would rather risk dying in an unjust war!

In this studio exec's opinion, "our voice-over character" (he meant my first-person narrator) admits to homosexual tendencies because he's a coward; the exec even said, "We should get the idea that he's faking it." The *faking-it* idea was Mr. Sharpie's substitute for *my* idea, in the novel—namely, that my first-person narrator is being brave to come out!

"Who *is* this guy?" I asked Alice. No one had made me an offer for the film rights to my novel; I still owned those rights. "It sounds like someone is writing a script," I said.

Alice's back was to me. "There's no script," she mumbled. "This guy just has a lot of questions about what you're like to *deal* with," Alice said.

"I don't know the guy," I told her. "What's *he* like to 'deal with,' Alice?"

"I was trying to spare you meeting this guy, Bill," was all Alice said. We were living in Santa Monica; she was always the driver, so she was sparing me the driving, too. I just stayed in the apartment and wrote. I could walk to Ocean Avenue and see the homeless people—I could run on the beach.

What was it Herm Hoyt had said to me about the duck-under? "You hit it and run—you know how to run, don'tcha?" the old coach had said.

I started to run in Santa Monica, in '69. I would soon be twenty-seven; I was already writing my second novel. It had been eight years since Miss Frost and Herm Hoyt had showed me how to hit a duck-under; I was probably a little rusty. The running suddenly seemed like a good idea.

Alice drove me to the meeting. There were four or five studio execs gathered around an egg-shaped table in a glassy building in Beverly Hills, with near-blinding sunlight pouring through the windows, but only Mr. Sharpie spoke.

"This is William Abbott, the novelist," Mr. Sharpie said, introducing me; it was probably my extreme self-consciousness, but I thought the *novelist* word made all the execs uneasy. To my surprise, Mr. Sharpie was a slob. The *Sharpie* word wasn't a compliment to how the guy dressed; it referred to the brand of waterproof pen he twirled in his hand. I hate those permanent markers. You can't really *write* with them—they bleed through the page; they make a mess. They're only good for making short remarks in the wide margins of screenplays—you know, manageable words like "This is shit!" or "Fuck this!"

As for where the "Mr. Pastel" nickname came from—well, I couldn't see it. The guy was an unshaven slob dressed all in black. He was one of those execs who was trying to look like an artist of some indeterminate kind; he wore a sweat-stained black jogging suit over a black T-shirt, with black running shoes. Mr. Pastel looked very fit; since I'd just started running, I could see at a glance he ran harder than I did. Golf wasn't his game—it would have been insufficient exercise for him.

"Perhaps Mr. Abbott will tell us his thoughts," Mr. Sharpie said, twirling his waterproof pen.

"I'll tell you when I might take seriously the idea of service to my country," I began. "When local, state, and federal legislation, which currently criminalizes homosexual acts between consenting adults, is repealed; when the country's archaic anti-sodomy laws are overturned; when psychiatrists stop diagnosing me and my friends as clinically abnormal, medically incompetent freaks in need of 'rehabilitation'; when the media stops representing us as sissy, pansy, fairy, child-molesting *perverts*! I would actually like to have children one day," I said, pausing to look at Alice, but she had lowered her head and sat at the table with one hand on her forehead, shielding her eyes. She was wearing jeans and a man's blue-denim work shirt with the sleeves rolled up—her customary uniform. In the sunlight, her hairy arms sparkled.

"In short," I continued, "I might take seriously the idea of service to my country when my country begins to demonstrate that it gives a shit about me!" (I had rehearsed this speech while running on the beach—from the Santa Monica Pier to where Chautauqua Boulevard ends at the Pacific Coast Highway, and back again—but I'd not realized that the hairy mother of my future children and the studio exec who thought my first-person narrator should be *faking* his homosexual tendencies were in cahoots.)

"You know what I love?" this same studio exec said then. "I love that voice-over about childhood. How's it go, Alice?" the craven shit asked her. That's when I knew they were fucking each other; it was the way he'd asked the question. And if the "voice-over" existed, *someone* was already writing the script.

Alice knew she'd been caught. With her hand on her forehead—still shielding her eyes—she recited, with resignation, " 'Most places we leave in childhood grow less, not more, fancy.' "

"Yeah—that's it!" the exec cried. "I love that so much, I think it should begin and end our movie. It bears repeating, doesn't it?" he asked me, but he wasn't waiting for an answer. "It's the tone of voice we want—*isn't* it, Alice?" he asked.

"You know how much I love that line, Bill," Alice said, still shielding her eyes. Maybe Mr. Pastel's *underwear* was light-colored, I thought—or perhaps his *sheets*.

I couldn't just get up and leave. I didn't know how to get back to Santa Monica from Beverly Hills; Alice was the driver in our little would-be family.

"Look at it this way, dear Bill," Larry said, when I came back to New York in the fall of '69. "If you'd had children with that conniving ape, your kids would have been born with hairy armpits. Women who want babies will say and do *anything*!"

But I think I'd wanted children, with someone—okay, maybe with *anyone*—as sincerely as Alice had. Over time, I would give up the idea of having children, but it's harder to stop *wanting* to have children.

"Do you think I would have been a good mother, William?" Miss Frost had asked me once.

"*You?* I think you would be a *fantastic* mother!" I said to her.

"I said 'would have been,' William—not 'would be.' I'm not ever going to be a mother *now*," Miss Frost told me.

"I think you would have been a terrific mom," I told her.

At the time, I didn't understand why Miss Frost had made such a big deal of the "would have been" or "would be" business, but I get it now. She'd given up the idea of ever having children, but she couldn't stop the *wanting* part.

WHAT REALLY PISSED ME off about Alice and the fucking movie business is that I was living in Los Angeles when the police raided the Stonewall Inn, a gay bar in Greenwich Village—in June of '69. I missed the Stonewall riots! Yes, I know it was street hustlers and drag queens who first fought back, but the resultant protest rally in Sheridan Square—the night after the raid—was the start of something. I wasn't happy that I was stuck in Santa Monica, still running on the beach and relying on Larry to tell me what had happened back in New York. Larry had certainly not been to the Stonewall with me—not *ever*—and I doubt he was among the patrons on that June night when some gays resisted the now-famous raid. But to hear Larry talk, you would think he was the first gay man to cruise Greenwich Avenue and Christopher Street, and that he was among the regulars at the Stonewall—even that he'd been carted off to jail with the kicking, punching drag queens, when (as I later learned) Larry had been with his patrons-of-poetry people in the Hamptons, or with that young poetaster of a Wall Street guy Larry was fucking on Fire Island. (His name was Russell.)

And it wasn't until I came back to New York that my dearest friend, Elaine, admitted to me that Alice had hit on her the one time Elaine had visited us in Santa Monica.

"Why didn't you *tell* me?" I asked Elaine.

"Billy, Billy," Elaine began, as her mother used to preface her admonitions to me, "did you not know that your most insecure lovers will *always* try to discredit your friends?"

Of course I *did* know that, or I should have. I'd already learned it from Larry—not to mention Tom Atkins.

And it was right around that time when I heard again from poor Tom. A dog (a Labrador retriever) had been added to the photograph on the Atkins family Christmas card of 1969; at the time, Tom's children struck me as too young to be going to school, but the breakup with Alice had caused me to pay less attention to children. Enclosed with the Christmas card was what I first mistook for one of those third-person Christmas letters; I almost didn't read it, but then I did.

It was Tom Atkins trying hard to write a book review of my first novel—a most generous (albeit awkward) review, as it turned out. As I would later learn, all of poor Tom's reviews of my novels would conclude with the same outrageous sentence. "It's better than *Madame Bovary*, Bill—I know you don't believe me, but it really is!" Coming from Atkins, of course I knew that *anything* would be better than *Madame Bovary*.

LAWRENCE UPTON'S SIXTIETH BIRTHDAY party was on a bitter-cold Saturday night in New York, in February of 1978. I was no longer Larry's lover—not even his occasional fuck buddy—but we were close friends. My third novel was about to be published—around the time of my birthday, in March of that same year—and Larry had read the galleys. He'd pronounced it my best book; that Larry's praise had been unqualified spooked me somewhat, because Larry wasn't known for withholding his reservations.

I'd met him in Vienna, when he'd been forty-five; I'd had fifteen years of listening to Lawrence Upton's edgy endorsements, which had included his often barbed appreciation of me and my writing.

Now, even at the sumptuous bash for his sixtieth—at the Chelsea brownstone of his young Wall Street admirer, Russell—Larry had singled me out for a toast. I was going to be thirty-six in another month; I was unprepared to have Larry toast me, and my soon-to-be-published novel—especially among his mostly older, oh-so-superior friends.

"I want to thank *most* of you for making me feel younger than I am—beginning with you, dear Bill," Larry had begun. (Okay—perhaps Larry was being a *little* barbed, to Russell.)

I knew it wouldn't be a late night, not with all the old farts in that crowd, but I'd not expected such a warmhearted event. I wasn't living with anyone at the time; I had a few fuck buddies in the city—they were men my age, for the most part—and I was very fond of a young novelist who was teaching in the writing program at Columbia. Rachel was just a few years younger than I was, in her early thirties. She'd published two novels and was working on a book of short stories; at her invitation, I'd visited one of her writing classes, because the students were reading one of my novels. We'd been sleeping with each other for a couple of months, but there'd been no talk of living together. Rachel had an apartment on the Upper West Side, and I was in a comfortable-enough apartment on Third Avenue and East Sixty-fourth. Keeping Central Park between us seemed an acceptable idea. Rachel had just escaped from a long, claustrophobic relationship with someone she described as a "serial-marriage zealot," and I had my fuck buddies.

I'd brought Elaine to Larry's birthday party. Larry and Elaine really liked each other; frankly, until my third novel, which Larry praised so generously, I'd had the feeling that Larry liked Elaine's writing better than mine. This was okay with me; I felt the same way, though Elaine was a doggedly slow writer. She'd published only one novel and one small collection of stories, but she was always busy writing.

I mention how cold it was in New York that night, because I remember that was why Elaine decided she would come uptown and spend the night in my apartment on East Sixty-fourth Street; Elaine was living downtown, where she was renting the loft of a painter friend on Spring Street, and that fuck-head painter's place was freezing. Also, how cold it was in Manhattan serves as a convenient foreshadow to how much colder it must have been in Vermont on that same February night.

I was in the bathroom, getting ready for bed, when the phone rang; it hadn't been a late party for Larry, as I've said, but it was late for me to be getting a phone call, even on a Saturday night.

"Answer it, will you?" I called to Elaine.

"What if it's Rachel?" Elaine called to me.

"Rachel knows you—she knows we're not *doing it*, Elaine!" I called from the bathroom.

"Well, it will be weird if it's Rachel—believe me," Elaine said, answering the phone. "Hello—this is Billy's old friend, Elaine," I heard her say. "We're *not* having sex; it's just a cold night to be alone downtown," Elaine added.

I finished brushing my teeth; when I came out of the bathroom, Elaine wasn't talking. Either the caller had hung up, or whoever it was was giving an earful to Elaine—maybe it *was* Rachel and I *shouldn't* have let Elaine answer the phone, I was thinking.

Then I saw Elaine on my bed; she'd found a clean T-shirt of mine to wear for pajamas, and she was already under the covers with the phone pressed to her ear and tears streaking her face. "Yes, I'll tell him, Mom," Elaine was saying.

I couldn't imagine under what circumstances Mrs. Hadley might have been prompted to call me; I thought it unlikely that Martha Hadley would have had my phone number. Perhaps because it was a milestone night for Larry, I was inclined to imagine other potential milestones.

Who had died? My mind raced through the likeliest suspects. Not Nana Victoria; she was already dead. She'd "slipped away" when she was still in her seventies, I'd heard Grandpa Harry say—as if he were envious. Maybe he was—Harry was eighty-four. Grandpa Harry was fond of spending his evenings in his River Street home—more often than not, in his late wife's attire.

Harry had not yet "slipped away" into the dementia that would (one day soon) cause Richard Abbott and me to move the old lumberman into the assisted-living facility that Nils Borkman and Harry had built for the town. I know I've already told you this story—how the other residents of the Facility (as the elderly of First Sister ominously called the place) complained about Grandpa Harry "surprising" them in drag. I would think at the time: After a few episodes when Harry was in drag, how could anyone have been *surprised*? But Richard Abbott and I immediately moved Grandpa Harry back to the privacy of his River Street home, where we hired a round-the-clock nurse to look after him. (All this—and more, of course—awaited me, in my not-too-distant future.)

Oh, *no*! I thought—as Elaine hung up the phone. Don't let it be Grandpa Harry!

I wrongly imagined that Elaine knew my thoughts. "It's your mom, Billy. Your mom and Muriel were killed in a car crash—nothing's happened to Miss Frost," Elaine quickly said.

"Nothing's happened to Miss Frost," I repeated, but I was thinking: How could I not once have contacted her, in all these years? I hadn't even tried! Why did I never seek her out? She would be sixty-one. I was suddenly astonished that I hadn't seen Miss Frost, or heard one word about her, in seventeen years. I hadn't even asked Herm Hoyt if he'd heard from her.

On this bitter-cold night in New York, in February of 1978, when I was almost thirty-six, I had already decided that my bisexuality meant I would be categorized as more unreliable than usual by straight women, while at the same time (and for the same reasons) I would never be entirely trusted by gay men.

What would Miss Frost have thought of me? I wondered; I didn't mean my *writing*. What would she have thought of my relationships with men and women? Had I ever "protected" anyone? For whom had I truly been worthwhile? How could I be almost forty and not love anyone as sincerely as I loved Elaine? How could I not have lived up to those expectations Miss Frost must have had for me? She'd protected me, but for what reason? Had she simply delayed my becoming promiscuous? That was never a word used positively, for if gay men were more openly pro-miscuous—even more deliberately so than straight guys—bisexuals were often accused of being more promiscuous than *anybody*!

If Miss Frost were to meet me now, who would she think I most resembled? (I don't mean in my choice of partners; I mean in the sheer number, not to mention the shallowness, of my relationships.)

"Kittredge," I answered myself, aloud. What tangents I would take—not to think about my mother! My mom was dead, but I couldn't or wouldn't let myself think about her.

"Oh, Billy, Billy—come here, come here. Don't go down that road, Billy," Elaine said, holding out her arms to me.

THE CAR, WHICH MY aunt Muriel had been driving, was hit head-on by a drunk driver who had strayed into Muriel's lane on Vermont's Route 30. My mother and Muriel were returning home from one of their Satur-day shopping trips to Boston; on that Saturday night, they were probably talking up a storm—just yakking away, nattering about nothing or ev-erything—when the carload of partying skiers came down the road from Stratton Mountain and turned east-southeast on Route 30. My mom and Muriel were headed west-northwest on Route 30; somewhere between Bondville and Rawsonville, the two cars collided. There was plenty of snow for the skiers, but Route 30 was bone-dry and crusted with road salt; it was twelve degrees below zero, too cold to snow.

The Vermont State Police reported that my mother and Muriel were killed instantly; Aunt Muriel had only recently turned sixty, and my mom would have been fifty-eight in April of that year. Richard Abbott was just forty-eight. "Kinda young to be a widower," as Grandpa Harry would say. Uncle Bob was on the young side to be a widower, too. Bob was Miss Frost's age—he was sixty-one.

Elaine and I rented a car and drove to Vermont together. We argued the whole way about what I "saw" in Rachel, the thirty-something fic-tion writer who was teaching at Columbia.

"You're flattered when younger writers like your writing—or you're oblivious to how they come on to you, maybe," Elaine began. "All the time you've spent around Larry has at least taught you to be wary of *older* writers who suck up to you."

"I guess I'm oblivious to it—namely, that Rachel is sucking up to me. But Larry *never* sucked up to me," I said. (Elaine was driving; she was an aggressive driver, and when she drove, it made her more aggressive in other ways.)

"Rachel is sucking up to you, and you don't see it," Elaine said. I didn't say anything, and Elaine added: "If you ask me, I think my tits are bigger."

"Bigger than—"

"Rachel's!"

"Oh."

Elaine was never sexually jealous of anyone I was sleeping with, but she didn't like it when I was hanging out with a *writer* who was younger than she was—man or woman.

"Rachel writes in the present tense—'I go, she says, he goes, I think.' That *shit*," Elaine declared.

"Yes, well—"

"And the 'thinking, wishing, hoping, wondering'—*that* shit!" Elaine cried.

"Yes, I know—" I started to say.

"I hope she doesn't verbalize her orgasms: 'Billy—I'm coming!' That shit," Elaine said.

"Well, no—not that I remember," I replied.

"I think she's one of those young-women writers who baby her students," Elaine said.

Elaine had taught more than I had; I never argued with her about teaching, or Mrs. Kittredge. Grandpa Harry was generous to me; he gave me a little money for Christmas every year. I'd had part-time college-teaching jobs, the occasional writer-in-residence stint—the latter never longer than a single semester. I didn't dislike teaching, but it hadn't invaded my writing time—as I knew it *did* invade the writing time of many writer friends, Elaine among them.

"Just so you know, Elaine—I find there's more to like about Rachel than her small breasts," I said.

"I would sincerely hope so, Billy," Elaine said.

"Are you seeing anyone?" I asked my old friend.

"You know that guy Rachel almost married?" Elaine asked me.

"Not personally," I told her.

"He hit on me," Elaine said.

"Oh."

"He told me that, one time, Rachel shit in the bed—that's what he told me, Billy," Elaine said.

"Nothing like that has happened, yet," I told Elaine. "But I'll be on the lookout for anything suspicious."

After that, we drove for a while in silence. When we left New York State and crossed into Vermont, a little west of Bennington, there were more dead things in the road; the bigger dead things had been dragged to the side of the road, but we could still see them. I remember a couple of deer, in the *bigger* category, and the usual raccoons and porcupines. There's a lot of roadkill in northern New England.

"Would you like me to drive?" I asked Elaine.

"Sure—yes, I would," Elaine answered quietly. She found a place to pull off the road, and I took over the driving. We turned north again, just before Bennington; there was more snow in the woods, and more dead things in the road and along the roadside.

We were a long way from New York City when Elaine said, "That guy didn't hit on me, Billy—I made up the story about Rachel shitting in bed, too."

"That's okay," I said. "We're writers. We make things up."

"I *did* run into someone you went to school with—this is a true story," Elaine told me.

"Who? In school with *where?*" I asked her.

"At the Institute, in Vienna—she was one of those Institute girls," Elaine said. "When she met you, you told her you were trying to be faithful to a girlfriend back in the States."

"I did tell some girls that," I admitted.

"I told this Institute girl that *I* was the girlfriend you were trying to be faithful to, when you were in Vienna," Elaine said.

We both had a laugh about that, but Elaine then asked me—more seriously—"Do you know what that Institute girl said, Billy?"

"No. What?" I asked.

"She said, 'Poor *you!*' That's what she said—this is a true story, Billy," Elaine told me.

I didn't doubt it. *Das Institut* was awfully small; every student there knew when I was fucking a soprano understudy—and, later, when I was fucking a famous American poet.

"If you'd been my girlfriend, I would have been faithful to *you,*

Elaine—or I would have sincerely tried," I told her. I let her cry for a while in the passenger seat.

"If you'd been my boyfriend, I would have sincerely tried, too, Billy," Elaine finally said.

We drove northeast, then headed west from Ezra Falls—the Favorite River running beside us, to the north side of the road. Even in February, as cold as it was, that river was never entirely frozen over. Of course I'd thought about having children with Elaine, but there was no point in bringing that up; Elaine wasn't kidding about the size of babies' heads— in her view, they were *enormous*.

When we drove down River Street, past the building that had once been the First Sister Public Library—it was now the town's historical society—Elaine said, "I ran lines with you on that brass bed, for *The Tempest*, about a century ago."

"Almost twenty years ago, yes," I said. I wasn't thinking about *The Tempest*, or running lines with Elaine on that brass bed. I had other memories of that bed, but as I drove past what used to be the public library, it occurred to me—a mere seventeen years after the much-maligned librarian had left town—that Miss Frost might have *protected* (or not) other young men in her basement bedroom.

But what other young men would Miss Frost have met in the library? I suddenly remembered that I'd never seen *any* children there. As for teenagers, there were only those occasional *girls*—the high school students condemned to Ezra Falls. I'd never seen any teenage *boys* in the First Sister Public Library—except for the night Tom Atkins came, looking for me.

Except for *me*, our town's young boys would not have been encouraged to visit that library. Surely, no responsible parents in First Sister would have wanted their young male children to be in the company of the transsexual wrestler who was in charge of the place!

I suddenly realized why I'd been so late in getting a library card; no one in my family would *ever* have introduced me to Miss Frost. It was only because Richard Abbott proposed taking me to the First Sister Public Library, and no one in my family could ever say no to Richard— nor was anyone in my family quick enough to overrule Richard's good-hearted and impromptu proposition. I'd managed to meet Miss Frost only because Richard recognized the absurdity of a small-town thirteen-year-old boy not having a library card.

"Almost twenty years ago feels like a century to me, Billy," Elaine was saying.

Not to *me*, I was trying to say, but the words wouldn't come. It feels like *yesterday* to me! I wanted to shout, but I couldn't speak.

Elaine, who saw I was crying, put her hand on my thigh. "Sorry I brought up that brass bed, Billy," Elaine said. (Elaine, who knew me so well, knew I wasn't crying for my mother.)

GIVEN THE SECRETS MY family watched over—those silent vigils we kept, in lieu of anything remotely resembling honest disclosure—it is a wonder I didn't also suffer a religious upbringing, but those Winthrop women were not religious. Grandpa Harry and I had been spared that falsehood. As for Uncle Bob and Richard Abbott, I know there were times when living with my aunt Muriel and my mother must have resembled a religious observance—the kind of demanding devotion that fasting requires, or perhaps a nocturnal trial (such as staying up all night, when going to sleep would be both customary and more natural).

"What is it that's so appealin' about a *wake?*" Grandpa Harry asked Elaine and me. We went first to his house on River Street; I'd half expected Harry to greet us *as a woman*, or at least dressed in Nana Victoria's clothes, but he was looking like a lumberman—jeans, a flannel shirt, unshaven. "I mean, why would anyone *livin'* find it suitable to watch over the bodies of the dead—that is, before you get to the *buryin'* part? Where are the dead bodies gonna go? Why do dead bodies need *watchin'?*" Grandpa Harry asked.

It was Vermont; it was February. Nobody was burying Muriel or my mother until April, after the ground had thawed. I could only guess that the funeral home had asked Grandpa Harry if he'd wanted to have a proper wake; that had probably started the tirade.

"Jeez—we'll be *watchin'* the bodies till *spring!*" Harry had shouted.

There was no religious service planned. Grandpa Harry had a big house; friends and family members would show up for cocktails and a catered buffet. The *memorial* word was allowed, but not a "memorial service"; Elaine and I didn't hear the *service* word mentioned. Harry seemed distracted and forgetful. Elaine and I both thought he didn't behave like a man who'd just lost his only children, his two daughters; instead, Harry struck us as an eighty-four-year-old who had misplaced his reading glasses—Grandpa Harry was eerily disconnected from the moment. We left him to ready himself for the "party"; Elaine and I were not mistaken—Harry had used the *party* word.

"Uh-oh," Elaine had said, as we were leaving the River Street house.

It was the first time I had been "home" when school was in session—that is, to Richard Abbott's faculty apartment in Bancroft Hall—since I'd been a Favorite River student. But how young the students looked was more unnerving to Elaine.

"I don't see anyone I could even *imagine* having sex with," Elaine said.

At least Bancroft was still a boys' dorm; it was disconcerting enough to see all the girls on the campus. In a process that was familiar to most of the single-sex boarding schools in New England, Favorite River had become a coed institution in 1973. Uncle Bob was no longer working in Admissions. The Racquet Man had a new career in Alumni Affairs. I could easily see Uncle Bob as a glad-hander, a natural at soliciting goodwill (and money) from a sentimental Favorite River alum. Bob also had a gift for inserting his queries into the class notes in the academy's alumni magazine, *The River Bulletin*. It had become Bob's passion to track down those elusive Favorite River graduates who'd failed to keep in touch with their old school. (Uncle Bob called his queries "Cries for Help from the Where-Have-You-Gone? Dept.")

Cousin Gerry had forewarned me that Bob's drinking had been "unleashed" by all his traveling for Alumni Affairs, but I counted Gerry as the last surviving Winthrop woman—albeit a watered-down, lesbian version of that steadfastly disapproving gene. (You will recall that I'd always imagined Uncle Bob's reputation for drinking was exaggerated.)

On another subject: Upon our return to Bancroft Hall, Elaine and I discovered that Richard Abbott couldn't speak, and that Mr. and Mrs. Hadley weren't talking to each other. The lack of communication between Martha Hadley and her husband was not unknown to me; Elaine had long predicted that her parents were headed for a divorce. ("It won't be acrimonious, Billy—they're already indifferent to each other," Elaine had told me.) And Richard Abbott had confided to me—that is, before my mother died, when Richard could still speak—that he and my mom had stopped socializing with the Hadleys.

Elaine and I had speculated on the mysterious "stopped socializing" part. Naturally, this dovetailed with Elaine's twenty-year theory that her mother was in love with Richard Abbott. Since I'd had crushes on Mrs. Hadley *and* Richard, what could I possibly contribute to this conversation?

I'd always believed that Richard Abbott was a vastly better man than my mother deserved, and that Martha Hadley was entirely too good for Mr. Hadley. Not only could I never remember that man's first name, if he ever had one; something about Mr. Hadley's fleeting brush with fame—the fame was due to his emergence as a political historian, and a voice of protest, during the Vietnam War—had served to dislocate him. If he'd once appeared aloof from his family—not only remote-seeming to his wife, Mrs. Hadley, but even distant from his only child, Elaine—Mr. Hadley's identification with a cause (his anti-Vietnam crusades with the Favorite River students) completely severed him from Elaine and Martha Hadley, and further led him to have little (if anything) to do with adults.

It happens in boarding schools: There's occasionally a male faculty member who is unhappy with his life as a grown-up. He tries to become one of the students. In Mr. Hadley's case—according to Elaine—his unfortunate regression to become one of the students when he himself was already in his fifties coincided with Favorite River Academy's decision to admit *girls*. This was just two years before the end of the Vietnam War.

"Uh-oh," as I'd heard Elaine say, so many times, but this time she'd added something. "When the war is over, what crusade will my father be leading? How's he going to engage all those *girls?*"

Elaine and I didn't see my uncle Bob until the "party." I had just read the Racquet Man's query in the most recent issue of *The River Bulletin;* attached to the class notes for the Class of '61, which was my class, there was this plaintive entry in the "Cries for Help from the Where-Have-You-Gone? Dept."

"What's up with you, Jacques Kittredge?" Uncle Bob had written. Following his undergraduate degree from Yale ('65), Kittredge had completed a three-year residence at the Yale School of Drama; he'd earned an MFA in '67. Thereafter, we'd heard nothing.

"An MFA in fucking *what?*" Elaine had asked more than ten years ago—when *The River Bulletin* had last heard a word from (or about) Kittredge. Elaine meant that it could have been a degree in acting, design, sound design, directing, playwriting, stage management, technical design and production, theater management—even dramaturgy and dramatic criticism. "I'll bet he's a fucking *critic,*" Elaine said. I told her I didn't care what Kittredge was; I said I didn't want to know.

"Yes, you *do* want to know. You can't bullshit me, Billy," Elaine had said.

Now here was the Racquet Man, slumped on a couch—actually *sunken into* a couch in Grandpa Harry's living room, as if it would take a wrestling team to get Bob back on his feet.

"I'm sorry about Aunt Muriel," I told him. Uncle Bob reached up from the couch to give me a hug, spilling his beer.

"Shit, Billy," Bob said, "it's the people you would least expect who are disappearing."

"Disappearing," I repeated warily.

"Take your classmate, Billy. Who would have picked Kittredge as a likely disappearance?" Uncle Bob asked.

"You don't think he's dead, do you?" I asked the Racquet Man.

"An unwillingness to communicate is more likely," Uncle Bob said. His speech was so slowed down that the *communicate* word sounded as if it had seven or eight syllables; I realized that Bob was quietly but spectacularly drunk, although the gathering in memory of my aunt Muriel and my mother was just getting started.

There were some empty beer bottles at Bob's feet; when he dropped the now-empty bottle he'd been drinking (and spilling), he deftly kicked all but one of the bottles under the couch—somehow, without even looking at the bottles.

I'd once wondered if Kittredge had gone to Vietnam; he'd had that hero-looking aspect about him. I knew two other Favorite River wrestlers had died in the war. (Remember Wheelock? I barely remember him— an adequately "swashbuckling" Antonio, Sebastian's friend, in *Twelfth Night*. And how about Madden, the self-pitying heavyweight who played Malvolio in that same production? Madden always saw himself as a "perpetual victim"; that's all I remember about him.)

But, drunk as he was, Uncle Bob must have read my mind, because he suddenly said, "Knowing Kittredge, I'll bet he ducked Vietnam— somehow."

"I'll bet he did," was all I said to Bob.

"No offense, Billy," the Racquet Man added, accepting another beer from one of the passing caterers—a woman about my mom's age, or Muriel's, with dyed-red hair. She looked vaguely familiar; maybe she worked with Uncle Bob in Alumni Affairs, or she might have worked with him (years ago) in the Admissions Office.

"My dad was sloshed before he got here," Gerry told Elaine and me, when we were standing together in the line for the buffet. I knew Gerry's girlfriend; she was an occasional stand-up comic at a club I went to in the Village. She had a deadpan delivery and always wore a man's black suit, or a tuxedo, with a loose-fitting white dress shirt.

"No bra," Elaine had observed, "but the shirt's too big for her, and it's not see-through material. The point is, she doesn't want you to know she has breasts—or what they look like."

"Oh."

"I'm sorry about your mom, Billy," Gerry said. "I know she was completely dysfunctional, but she *was* your mother."

"I'm sorry about yours," I told Gerry. The stand-up comic made a horsey snorting sound.

"Not as deadpan as usual," Elaine would say later.

"Someone's gotta get the car keys from my fucking father," Gerry said.

I was keeping an eye on Grandpa Harry. I was afraid he would sneak away from the party, only to reappear as a surprise reincarnation of Nana Victoria. Nils Borkman was keeping an eye on his old partner, too. (If *Mrs.* Borkman was there, I either didn't see her or didn't recognize her.)

"I'm back-watching your grandfather, Bill," Nils told me. "If the funny stuff gets out of hand, I am emergency-calling you!"

"What funny stuff?" I asked him.

But just then, Grandpa Harry suddenly spoke up. "They're always late, those girls. I don't know where they are, but they'll show up. Everyone just go ahead and eat. There's plenty of food. Those girls can find somethin' to eat when they get here."

That quieted the crowd down. "I already told him that his girls aren't coming to the party, Bill. I mean, he knows they're dead—he's just forgetfulness *exemplified*," Nils told me.

"Forgetfulness *personified*," I said to the old Norwegian; he was two years older than Grandpa Harry, but Nils seemed a little more reliable in the *remembering* department, and in some other departments.

I asked Martha Hadley if Richard had spoken yet. Not since the news of the accident, Mrs. Hadley informed me. Richard had hugged me a lot, and I'd hugged him back, but there'd been no words.

Mr. Hadley appeared lost in thought—as he often did. I couldn't remember the last time he'd talked about anything but the war in Vietnam.

Mr. Hadley had made himself a droll obituarist of every Favorite River boy who'd bitten the dust in Vietnam. I saw that he was waiting for me at the end of the buffet table.

"Get ready," Elaine warned me, in a whisper. "Here comes another death you didn't know about."

There was no prologue—there never was, with Mr. Hadley. He was a history teacher; he just announced things. "Do you remember Merry-weather?" Mr. Hadley asked me.

Not Merryweather! I thought. Yes, I remembered him; he was still an underclassman when I graduated. He'd been the wrestling-team manager—he handed out oranges, cut in quarters; he picked up the bloody and discarded towels.

"Not Merryweather—not in *Vietnam*!" I automatically said.

"Yes, I'm afraid so, Billy," Mr. Hadley said gravely. "And Trow-bridge—did you know Trowbridge, Billy?"

"Not Trowbridge!" I cried; I couldn't believe it! I'd last seen Trow-bridge in his *pajamas*! Kittredge had accosted him when the round-faced little boy was on his way to brush his teeth. I was very upset to think of Trowbridge dying in Vietnam.

"Yes, I'm afraid so—Trowbridge, too, Billy," Mr. Hadley self-importantly went on. "Alas, yes—young Trowbridge, too."

I saw that Grandpa Harry had disappeared—if not in the way Uncle Bob had recently used the word.

"Not a costume change, let's hope, Bill," Nils Borkman whispered in my ear.

I only then noticed that Mr. Poggio, the grocer, was there—he who'd so enjoyed Grandpa Harry onstage, *as a woman*. In fact, both Mr. and Mrs. Poggio were there, to pay their respects. Mrs. Poggio, I remembered, had *not* enjoyed Grandpa Harry's female impersonations. This sighting caused me to look all around for the disapproving Riptons—Ralph Ripton, the sawyer, and his no-less-disapproving wife. But the Riptons, if they'd come to pay their respects, had left early—as was their habit at the plays put on by the First Sister Players.

I went to see how Uncle Bob was doing; there were a few more empty beer bottles at his feet, and now those feet could no longer locate the bottles and kick them under the couch.

I kicked a few bottles under the couch for him. "You won't be tempted to drive yourself home, will you, Uncle Bob?" I asked him.

"That's why I already put the car keys in your jacket pocket, Billy," my uncle told me.

But when I felt around in my jacket pockets, I found only a squash ball. "Not the car keys, Uncle Bob," I said, showing him the ball.

"Well, I know I put my car keys in *someone's* jacket pocket, Billy," the Racquet Man said.

"Any news from *your* graduating class?" I suddenly asked him; he was drunk enough—I thought I might catch him off-guard. "What news from the Class of '35?" I asked my uncle as casually as I could.

"Nothing from Big Al, Billy—believe me, I would tell you," he said.

Grandpa Harry was making the rounds at his party *as a woman* now; it was at least an improvement that he was acknowledging to everyone that his daughters were dead—not just late for the party, as he'd earlier said. I could see Nils Borkman following his old partner, as if the two of them were on skis and armed, gliding through the snowy woods. Bob dropped another empty beer bottle, and I kicked it under Grandpa Harry's living-room couch. No one noticed the beer bottles, not since Grandpa Harry had reappeared—that is, *not* as Grandpa Harry.

"I'm sorry for your loss, Harry—yours and mine," Uncle Bob said to my grandfather, who was wearing a faded-purple dress I remembered as one of Nana Victoria's favorites. The blue-gray wig was at least "age-appropriate," Richard Abbott would later say—when Richard was able to speak again, which wouldn't be soon. Nils Borkman told me that the falsies must have come from the costume shop at the First Sister Players, or maybe Grandpa Harry had stolen them from the Drama Club at Favorite River Academy.

The withered and arthritic hand that held out a new beer to my uncle Bob did not belong to the caterer with the dyed-red hair. It was Herm Hoyt—he was only a year older than Grandpa Harry, but Coach Hoyt looked a lot more beaten up.

Herm had been sixty-eight when he was coaching Kittredge in '61; he'd looked ready to retire then. Now, at eighty-five, Coach Hoyt had been retired for fifteen years.

"Thanks, Herm," the Racquet Man quietly said, raising the beer to his lips. "Billy here has been asking about our old friend Al."

"How's that duck-under comin' along, Billy?" Coach Hoyt asked.

"I guess you haven't heard from her, Herm," I replied.

"I hope you've been *practicin'*, Billy," the old coach said.

I then told Herm Hoyt a long and involved story about a fellow run-ner I'd met in Central Park. The guy was about my age, I told the coach, and by his cauliflower ears—and a certain stiffness in his shoulders and neck, as he ran—I deduced that he was a wrestler, and when I mentioned wrestling, he thought that I was a wrestler, too.

"Oh, no—I just have a halfway-decent duck-under," I told him. "I'm no wrestler."

But Arthur—the wrestler's name was Arthur—misunderstood me. He thought I meant that I *used to* wrestle, and I was just being modest or self-deprecating.

Arthur had gone on and on (the way wrestlers will) about how I should still be wrestling. "You should be picking up some other moves to go with that duck-under—it's not too late!" he'd told me. Arthur wres-tled at a club on Central Park South, where he said there were a lot of guys "our age" who were still wrestling. Arthur was confident that I could find an appropriate workout partner in my weight-class.

Arthur was unstoppably enthusiastic about my not "quitting" wres-tling, simply because I was in my thirties and no longer competing on a school or college team.

"But I was never on a team!" I tried to tell him.

"Look—I know a lot of guys our age who were never starters," Arthur had told me. "And they're still wrestling!"

Finally, as I told Herm Hoyt, I just became so exasperated with Ar-thur's insistence that I come to wrestling practice at his frigging club, I told him the truth.

"Exactly what did you tell the fella, Billy?" Coach Hoyt asked me.

That I was gay—or, more accurately, bisexual.

"Jeez . . ." Herm started to say.

That a former wrestler, who'd briefly been my lover, had tried to teach me a little wrestling—strictly for my own self-defense. That the former wrestling coach of this same ex-wrestler had also given me some tips.

"You mean that duck-under you mentioned—that's *it?*" Arthur had asked.

"That's it. Just the duck-under," I'd admitted.

"Jeez, Billy . . ." old Coach Hoyt was saying, shaking his head.

"Well, that's the story," I said to Herm. "I *haven't* been practicing the duck-under."

"There's only one wrestlin' club I know on Central Park South, Billy," Herm Hoyt told me. "It's a pretty good one."

"When Arthur understood what my history with the duck-under was, he didn't seem interested in pursuing the matter of my coming to wrestling practice," I explained to Coach Hoyt.

"It might not be the best idea," Herm said. "I don't know the fellas at that club—not anymore."

"They probably don't get many gay guys wrestling there—you know, for self-defense—is that your guess, Herm?" I asked the old coach.

"Has this Arthur fella read your *writin'*, Billy?" Herm Hoyt asked me.

"Have *you?*" I asked Herm, surprised.

"Jeez—sure, I have. Just don't ask me what it's *about*, Billy!" the old wrestling coach said.

"How about Miss Frost?" I suddenly asked him. "Has *she* read my writing?"

"Persistent, isn't he?" Uncle Bob asked Herm.

"She knows you're a writer, Billy—everybody who knows you knows that," the wrestling coach said.

"Don't ask *me* what you write about, either, Billy," Uncle Bob said. He dropped the empty bottle and I kicked it under Grandpa Harry's couch. The woman with the dyed-red hair brought another beer for the Racquet Man. I realized why she'd seemed familiar; all the caterers were from the Favorite River Academy dining service—they were kitchen workers, from the academy dining halls. That woman who kept bringing Bob another beer had been in her forties when I'd last seen her; she came from the *past*, which would always be with me.

"The wrestlin' club is the New York Athletic Club—they have other sports there, for sure, but they weren't bad at wrestlin', Billy. You could probably do some practicin' of your duck-under there," Herm was saying. "Maybe ask that Arthur fella about it, Billy—after all these years, I'll bet you could use some *practicin'*."

"Herm, what if the wrestlers beat the shit out of me?" I asked him. "Wouldn't that kind of defeat the purpose of Miss Frost and you showing me a duck-under in the first place?"

"Bob's asleep, and he's pissed all over himself," the old coach abruptly observed.

"Uncle Bob . . ." I started to say, but Herm Hoyt grabbed the Racquet Man by both shoulders and shook him.

"Bob—stop pissin'!" the wrestling coach shouted.

When Bob's eyes blinked open, he was as caught off-guard as anyone working in the office of Alumni Affairs at Favorite River Academy ever would be.

"España," the Racquet Man said, when he saw me.

"Jeez, Bob—be careful what you say," Herm Hoyt said.

"España," I repeated.

"That's where he is—he says he's never coming back, Billy," Uncle Bob told me.

"That's where *who* is?" I asked my drunken uncle.

Our only conversation, if you could call it that, had been about Kittredge; it was hard to imagine Kittredge speaking Spanish. I knew the Racquet Man didn't mean Big Al—Uncle Bob wasn't telling me that Miss Frost was in Spain, and *she* was never coming back.

"Bob . . ." I started to say, but the Racquet Man had nodded off again. Herm Hoyt and I could see that Bob was still pissing.

"Herm . . ." I started to say.

"Franny Dean, my former wrestlin'-team manager, Billy—*he's* in Spain. Your father is in Spain, Billy, and he's happy there—that's all I know."

"*Where* in Spain, Herm?" I asked the old coach.

"España," Herm Hoyt repeated, shrugging. "Somewhere in Spain, Billy—that's all I can tell ya. Just keep thinkin' about the *happy* part. Your dad is happy, and he's in Spain. Your mom was never happy, Billy."

I knew Herm was right about that. I went looking for Elaine; I wanted to tell her that my father was in Spain. My mother was dead, but my father—whom I'd never known—was alive and happy.

But before I could tell her, Elaine spoke to me first. "We should sleep in your bedroom tonight, Billy—not in mine," she began.

"Okay—" I said.

"If Richard wakes up and decides to *say* something, he shouldn't be alone—we should be there," Elaine went on.

"Okay, but I just found out about something," I told her; she wasn't listening.

"I owe you a blow job, Billy—maybe this is your lucky night," Elaine said. I thought she was drunk, or else I'd misheard her.

"What?" I said.

"I'm sorry for what I said about Rachel. That's what the blow job is for," Elaine explained; she *was* drunk, extending the number of syllables in her words in the overly articulated manner of the Racquet Man.

"You don't *owe* me a blow job, Elaine," I told her.

"You don't want a blow job, Billy?" she asked me; she made "blow job" sound as if it had four or five syllables.

"I didn't say I didn't *want* one," I told her. "España," I said suddenly, because *that's* what I wanted to talk about.

"España?" Elaine said. "Is that a kind of Spanish blow job, Billy?" She was tripping a little, as I led her over to say good night to Grandpa Harry.

"Don't worry, Bill," Nils Borkman suddenly said to me. "I am unloading the rifles! I am keeping a secret of the bullets!"

"España," Elaine repeated. "Is it a *gay* thing, Billy?" she whispered to me.

"No," I told her.

"You'll show me, right?" Elaine asked. I knew that the trick would be keeping her awake until we were back in Bancroft Hall.

"I love you!" I said to Grandpa Harry, hugging him.

"I love *you*, Bill!" Harry told me, hugging me back. (His falsies had to have been modeled on someone with breasts as big as my aunt Muriel's, but I didn't tell my grandfather that.)

"You don't *owe* me anything, Elaine," I was saying, as we left that River Street house.

"Don't say good night to my mom and dad, Billy—don't get anywhere near my dad," Elaine told me. "Not unless you want to hear about more casualties—not unless you have the stomach to listen to more fucking body-counting."

After hearing about Trowbridge, I truly didn't have the stomach for more casualties. I didn't even say good night to Mrs. Hadley, because I could see that Mr. Hadley was loitering around.

"España," I said quietly to myself, as I was helping Elaine up those three flights of stairs in Bancroft Hall; it's a good thing I didn't have to get her as far as *her* bedroom, which was on the frigging fifth floor.

As we were navigating the third-floor dormitory hall, I must have softly said "España" again—not so softly, I guess, because Elaine heard me.

"I'm a little worried about what kind of blow job an España is, exactly. It's not rough stuff, is it, Billy?" Elaine asked me.

There was a boy in his pajamas in the hall—such a little boy, and he had his toothbrush in his hand. From his frightened expression, he obviously didn't know who Elaine and I were; he'd also clearly heard what Elaine had asked about the España blow job.

"We're just fooling around," I told the small boy. "There's not going to be any rough stuff. There's not going to be a blow job!" I said to Elaine and the boy in pajamas. (With his toothbrush, he'd reminded me of Trowbridge, of course.)

"Trowbridge is dead. Did you know Trowbridge? He was killed in Vietnam," I told Elaine.

"I didn't know any Trowbridge," Elaine said; like me, Elaine couldn't stop staring at the young boy in pajamas. "You're crying, Billy—please stop crying," Elaine said. We were leaning on each other when I managed to open the door to silent Richard's apartment. "Don't worry about him crying—his mom just died. He'll be all right," Elaine said to the boy holding his toothbrush. But I had seen Trowbridge standing there, and perhaps I foresaw that there were more casualties coming; maybe I'd imagined all the body-counting in the not-too-distant future.

"Billy, Billy—please stop crying," Elaine was saying. "What did you mean? 'There's not going to be a blow job!' Do you think I'm *bluffing*? You know me, Billy—I've stopped bluffing. I don't *bluff* anymore, Billy," she babbled on.

"My father is alive. He's living in Spain, and he's happy. That's all I know, Elaine," I told her. "My dad, Franny Dean, is living in Spain— España." But that was as far as I got.

Elaine had slipped off her coat as we'd stumbled through Richard and my mother's living room; she'd kicked off her shoes and her skirt, upon entering my bedroom, and she was struggling to unbutton the buttons on her blouse when—on another level of half-consciousness—Elaine saw the bed of my adolescent years and dove for it, or she somehow managed to throw herself on it.

By the time I knelt next to her on the bed, I could see that Elaine had completely passed out; she was limp and unmoving as I took off her blouse and unclasped her rather uncomfortable-looking necklace. I put her to bed in her bra and panties, and went about the usual business of getting into the small bed beside her.

"España," I whispered in the dark.

"You'll show me, right?" Elaine said in her sleep.

I fell asleep thinking about why I had never tried to find my father. A part of me had rationalized this: If he's curious about me, let him find me,

I'd thought. But in truth I had a fabulous father; my stepfather, Richard Abbott, was the best thing that ever happened to me. (My mom had never been happy, but Richard was the best thing that ever happened to her, too; my mother must have been happy with Richard.) Maybe I'd never tried to find Franny Dean because finding him would have made me feel I was betraying Richard.

"What's up with you, Jacques Kittredge?" the Racquet Man had written; of course I fell asleep thinking about that, too.

Chapter 12

A WORLD OF EPILOGUES

Do epidemics herald their own arrivals, or do they generally arrive unannounced? I had two warnings; at the time, they seemed merely coincidental—I didn't heed them.

It was a few weeks after my mother's death before Richard Abbott began to speak again. He continued to teach his classes at the academy— albeit by rote, Richard had even managed to direct a play—but he had nothing personal to say to those of us who loved him.

It was April of that same year ('78) when Elaine told me that Richard had spoken to her mother. I called Mrs. Hadley immediately after I got off the phone with Elaine.

"I know Richard's going to call you, Billy," Martha Hadley told me. "Just don't expect him to be quite his old self."

"How is he?" I asked her.

"I'm trying to say this carefully," Mrs. Hadley said. "I don't want to blame Shakespeare, but there's such a thing as too much graveyard humor—if you ask me."

I didn't know what Martha Hadley meant; I just waited for Richard to call. I think it was May before I finally heard from him, and Richard just started right in—as if we'd never been out of touch.

Given his grief, I would have guessed that Richard hadn't had the time or inclination to read my third novel, but he'd read it. "The same old themes, but better done—the pleas for tolerance never grow tiresome, Bill. Of course, everyone is intolerant of something or someone. Do you know what *you're* intolerant of, Bill?" Richard asked me.

"What would that be, Richard?"

"You're intolerant of intolerance—aren't you, Bill?"

"Isn't that a *good* thing to be intolerant of?" I asked him.

"And you are *proud* of your intolerance, too, Bill!" Richard cried. "You have a most *justifiable* anger at intolerance—at intolerance of sexual differences, especially. God knows, I would never say you're not *entitled* to your anger, Bill."

"God knows," I said cautiously. I couldn't quite see where Richard was going.

"As forgiving as you are of sexual differences—and rightly so, Bill!— you're not *always* so forgiving, are you?" Richard asked.

"Ah, well . . ." I started to say, and then stopped. So *that* was where he was going; I'd heard it before. Richard had told me that I'd not been standing in my mother's shoes in 1942, when I was born; he'd said I couldn't, or shouldn't, judge her. It was my not forgiving her that irked him—it was my intolerance of *her* intolerance that bugged him.

"As Portia says: 'The quality of mercy is not strained.' Act four, scene one—but I know it's not your favorite Shakespeare, Bill," Richard Abbott said.

Yes, we'd fought about *The Merchant of Venice* in the classroom— eighteen years ago. It was one of the few Shakespeare plays we'd read in class that Richard had *not* directed onstage. "It's a comedy—a romantic comedy—but with an unfunny part," Richard had said. He meant Shylock—Shakespeare's incontrovertible prejudice against Jews.

I took Shylock's side. Portia's speech about "mercy" was vapid, Christian hypocrisy; it was Christianity at its most superior-sounding and most saccharine. Whereas Shylock has a point: The hatred of him has taught him to hate. Rightly so!

"I am a Jew," Shylock says—act 3, scene 1. "Hath not a Jew eyes? Hath not a Jew hands, organs, dimensions, senses, affections, passions?" I love that speech! But Richard didn't want to be reminded that I'd *always* been on Shylock's side.

"Your mom is dead, Bill. Have you no feelings for your mother?" Richard asked me.

"No feelings," I repeated. I was remembering her hatred of homosexuals—her rejection of me, not only because I looked like my father but also because I had something of his weird (and unwelcome) sexual orientation.

"How does Shylock put it?" I asked Richard Abbott. (I knew perfectly well how Shylock put it, and Richard had long understood how I'd embraced this.)

"If you prick us, do we not bleed?" Shylock asks. "If you tickle us, do we not laugh? If you poison us, do we not die?"

"Okay, Bill—I know, I know. You're a pound-of-flesh kind of guy," Richard said.

"'And if you wrong us,'" I said, quoting Shylock, "'shall we not revenge? If we are like you in the rest, we will resemble you in that.' And what did they do to Shylock, Richard?" I asked. "They forced him to become a fucking *Christian*!"

"It's a difficult play, Bill—that's why I've not put it onstage," Richard said. "I'm not sure it's suitable for kids in a secondary school."

"How are you doing, Richard?" I asked him, hoping to change the subject.

"I remember that boy who was ready to rewrite Shakespeare—that boy who was so sure the epilogue to *The Tempest* was extraneous," Richard said.

"I remember that boy, too," I told him. "I was wrong about that epilogue."

"If you live long enough, Bill—it's a world of epilogues," Richard Abbott said.

That was the first warning I paid no attention to. Richard was only twelve years older than I was; that's not such a big difference—not when Richard was forty-eight and I was thirty-six. We seemed almost like contemporaries in 1978. I'd been only thirteen when Richard had taken me to get my first library card—that evening when we both met Miss Frost. At twenty-five, Richard Abbott had seemed so debonair to me—and so authoritative.

At thirty-six, I didn't find anyone "authoritative"—not even Larry, not anymore. Grandpa Harry, while he was steadfastly good-hearted, was slipping into strangeness; even to me (a pillar of tolerance, as I saw myself), Harry's eccentricities had been more acceptable onstage. Not even Mrs. Hadley was the authority she once seemed, and while I listened to my best friend, Elaine, who knew me so well, I increasingly took Elaine's advice with a grain of salt. (After all, Elaine wasn't any better—or more reliable—in relationships than I was.) I suppose if I'd heard from Miss Frost—even at the know-it-all age of thirty-six—I might still have found *her* authoritative, but I didn't hear from her.

I did, albeit cautiously, heed Herm Hoyt's advice: The next time I encountered Arthur, that wrestler who was my age and also ran around the reservoir in Central Park, I asked him if I was still welcome to practice my less-than-beginner-level wrestling skills at the New York Athletic Club—that is, now that Arthur understood I was a bisexual man in need of improving my self-defense, and not a real wrestler.

Poor Arthur. He was one of those well-intentioned straight guys who wouldn't have dreamed of being cruel—or even remotely unkind—to gays. Arthur was a liberal, open-minded New Yorker; he not only prided himself on being fair—he was exceedingly fair—but he agonized over what was "right." I could see him suffering over how "wrong" it would be not to invite me to his wrestling club, just because I was—well, as Uncle Bob would say, a little light in the loafers.

My very existence as a bisexual was not welcomed by my gay friends; they either refused to believe that I *really* liked women, or they felt I was somehow dishonest (or hedging my bets) about being gay. To most straight men—even a prince among them, which Arthur truly was—a bisexual man was simply a gay guy. The only part about being bi that even registered with straight men was the *gay* part. That was what Arthur would be up against when he talked about me to his pals at the wrestling club.

This was the end of the freewheeling seventies; while acceptance of sexual differences wasn't necessarily the norm, such acceptance was almost normal in New York—in liberal circles, such acceptance was expected. But I felt responsible for the spot I'd put Arthur in; I had no knowledge of the tight-assed elements in the New York Athletic Club, in those days when the venerable old institution was an all-male bastion.

I have no idea what Arthur had to go through just to get me a guest pass, or an athletic pass, to the NYAC. (Like my final draft classification, or *re*classification, I'm not sure what my stupid pass to the New York Athletic Club was called.)

"Are you crazy, Billy?" Elaine asked me. "Are you trying to get yourself killed? That place is notoriously anti-*everything*. It's anti-*Semitic*, it's anti-*black*."

"It is?" I asked her. "How do you know?"

"It's anti-*women*—I fucking know that!" Elaine had said. "It's an Irish Catholic boys' club, Billy—just the Catholic part ought to have you running for the hills."

"I think you would like Arthur," I told Elaine. "He's a good guy—he really is."

"I suppose he's married," Elaine said with a sigh.

Come to think of it, I had seen a wedding ring on Arthur's left hand. I never fooled around with married men—with married *women*, sometimes, but not with married men. I was bisexual, but I was long over being conflicted. I couldn't stand how conflicted married men were—that is, when they were also interested in gay guys. And according to Larry, all married men were disappointing lovers.

"Why?" I'd asked him.

"They're freaks about gentleness—they must have learned to be gentle from their pushy wives. Those men have no idea how *boring* 'gentle' is," Larry told me.

"I don't think 'gentle' is *always* boring," I said.

"Please pardon me, dear Bill," Larry had said, with that characteristically condescending wave of his hand. "I'd forgotten you were steadfastly a *top*."

I really liked Larry, more and more, as a friend. I had even grown to like how he teased me. We'd both been reading the memoir of a noted actor—"a noted *bi*," Larry called him.

The actor claimed that, all his life, he had "fancied" older women and younger men. "As you might imagine," the noted actor wrote, "when I was younger, there were many older women who were available. Now that I'm older—well, of course, there are many more *available* younger men."

"I don't see my life as that *neat*," I said to Larry. "I don't imagine being bi will ever seem exactly *well rounded*."

"Dear Bill," Larry said—in that way he had, as if he were writing me an important letter. "The man is an *actor*—he *isn't* bi, he's *gay*. No wonder—now that he's older—there are many more younger men around! Those older women were the only women he felt *safe* with!"

"That's not my profile, Larry," I told him.

"But you're still a young man!" Larry had cried. "Just wait, dear Bill—just wait."

• • •

IT BECAME, OF COURSE, a source of both comedy and concern—with
the women I saw and the gay men I knew—that I regularly attended
wrestling practice at the NYAC. My gay friends refused to believe that
I had next to no homoerotic interest in the wrestlers I met at the club,
but my crushes on that kind of wrong person had been a phase for me,
perhaps a part of the coming-out process. (Well, okay—a slowly passing, not-altogether-gone phase.) Straight men didn't often attract me, at
least not very much; that they could sense this, as Arthur did, had made
it increasingly possible for me to have straight men for friends.

Yet Larry insisted that my wrestling practices were a kind of high-
energy, risky cruising; Donna, my dear but easily offended transsexual
friend, dismissed what she called my "duck-under fixation" as the culti-
vation of a death wish. (Soon after this pronouncement, Donna disappeared from New York—to be followed by reports that she'd been sighted
in Toronto.)

As for the wrestlers at the New York Athletic Club, they were
a mixed lot—in every respect, not only in how they treated me. My
women friends, Elaine among them, believed that it was only a matter of
time before I would be beaten to a pulp, but I was not once threatened
(or deliberately hurt) at the NYAC.

The older guys generally ignored me; once someone cheerfully said,
when we were introduced, "Oh, you're the *gay* guy—right?" But he shook
my hand and patted me on the back; later, he always smiled and said
something friendly when we saw each other. We weren't in the same
weight-class. If he was avoiding contact with me—on the mat, I mean—
I wouldn't have known.

There was the occasional mass evacuation of the sauna, when I made
an after-practice appearance there. I spoke to Arthur about it. "Maybe I
should steer clear of the sauna—do you think?"

"That's your call, Billy—that's their problem, not yours," Arthur
said. (I was "Billy" to all the wrestlers.)

I decided, despite Arthur's assurances, to stay out of the sauna. Practices were at seven in the evening; I became almost comfortable going
to them. I was not called—at least not to my face—"the *gay* guy," except
for that one time. I was commonly referred to as "the writer"; most of the
wrestlers hadn't read my sexually explicit novels—those pleas for tolerance of sexual differences, as Richard Abbott would continue to describe

my books—but Arthur had read them. Like many men, he'd told me that his wife was my biggest fan.

I was always hearing that from men about the women in their lives—their wives, their girlfriends, their sisters, even their mothers, were my biggest fans. Women read fiction more than men do, I would guess.

I'd met Arthur's wife. She was very nice; she truly read a lot of fiction, and I liked much of what she liked—as a reader, I mean. Her name was Ellen—one of those perky blondes with a pageboy cut and an absurdly small, thin-lipped mouth. She had the kind of stand-up boobs that belied an otherwise unisex look—boy, was she ever *not* my kind of girl! But she was genuinely sweet to me, and Arthur—bless his heart—was *very* married. There would be no introducing him to Elaine.

In fact, beyond having a beer in the NYAC tap room with Arthur, I did no socializing with the wrestlers I'd met at the club. The wrestling room was then on the fourth floor—at the opposite end of the hall from the boxing room. One of my frequent workout partners in the wrestling room—Jim *Somebody* (I forget his last name)—was also a boxer. All the wrestlers knew I'd had no competitive wrestling experience—that I was there for the self-defense aspect of the sport, period. In support of my self-defense, Jim took me down the hall to the boxing room; he tried to show me how to defend myself from being hit.

It was interesting: I never really learned how to throw a decent punch, but Jim taught me how to cover up—how not to get hit so hard. Occasionally, one of Jim's punches would land a little harder than he'd intended; he always said he was sorry.

In the wrestling room, too, I took some occasional (albeit accidental) punishment—a split lip, a bloody nose, a jammed finger or thumb. Because I was concentrating so hard on various ways to set up (and conceal) my duck-under, I was banging heads a lot; you more or less have to bang heads if you like being in the collar-tie. Arthur inadvertently head-butted me, and I took a few stitches in the area of my right eyebrow.

Well, you should have heard Larry and Elaine—and all the others.

"Macho Man," Larry called me, for a while.

"You're telling me everyone's friendly to you—is that right, Billy?" Elaine asked. "This was just a cordial kind of head-butt, huh?"

But—the teasing from those friends in my writing world notwithstanding—I was learning a little more wrestling. I was getting a *lot* better at the duck-under, too.

"The one-move man," Arthur had called me, in my earliest days in that wrestling room—but, as time went on, I picked up a few other moves. It must have been boring for the real wrestlers to have me as a workout partner, but they didn't complain.

To my surprise, three or four of the old-timers gave me some pointers. (Maybe they appreciated my staying out of the sauna.) There was a fair number of wrestlers in their forties—a few in their fifties, tough old fellas. There were kids right out of college; there were some Olympic hopefuls and former Olympians. There were Russians who'd defected (one Cuban, too); there were many Eastern Europeans, but only two Iranians. There were Greco-Roman guys and freestyle guys, and strictly folkstyle guys—the latter were most in evidence among the kids and the old-timers.

Ed showed me how a cross-leg pull could set up my duck-under; Wolfie taught me an arm-drag series; Sonny showed me the Russian arm-tie and a nasty low-single. I wrote to Coach Hoyt about my progress. Herm and I both knew that I would never become a wrestler—not in my late thirties—but, as for learning to *protect* myself, I was learning. And I liked the 7 P.M. wrestling routine in my life.

"You're becoming a gladiator!" Larry had said; for once, he wasn't teasing me.

Even Elaine withheld her near-constant fears. "Your body is different, Billy—you know that, don't you? I'm not saying you're one of those gym rats who are doing it for cosmetic reasons—I know you have *other* reasons—but you are starting to look a little scary," Elaine said.

I knew I wasn't "scary"—not to anyone. But, as the old decade ended and the eighties began, I was aware of the passing of some ancient, ingrained fears and apprehensions.

Mind you: New York was not a safe city in the eighties; at least it was nowhere near as "safe" as it's become. But I, personally, felt safer—or more secure about who I was—than I'd ever felt before. I'd even begun to think of Miss Frost's fears for me as groundless, or else she'd lived in Vermont too long; maybe she'd been right to fear for my safety in Vermont, but not in New York.

There were times when I didn't really feel like going to wrestling practice at the NYAC, but Arthur and many others had gone out of their way to make me feel welcome there. I didn't want to disappoint them, yet—increasingly—I was thinking: What do you need to defend yourself for? Whom do you need to defend yourself *from*?

There was an effort under way to make me an official member of the New York Athletic Club; I can barely remember the process now, but it was very involved and it took a long time.

"A lifetime membership is the way to go—you don't imagine yourself moving away from New York, do you, Billy?" Arthur had asked; he was sponsoring my membership. It would be a stretch to say I was a famous novelist, but—with a fourth book about to be published—I was at least a well-known one.

Nor did the money matter. Grandpa Harry was excited that I was "keepin' up the wrestlin' "—my guess is that Herm Hoyt had talked to him. Harry said he would happily pay the fee for my lifetime membership.

"Don't put yourself out, Arthur—no more than you already have," I told him. "The club has been good for me, but I wouldn't want you alienating people or losing friends over me."

"You're a shoo-in, Billy," Arthur told me. "It's no big deal being gay."

"I'm bi—" I started to say.

"I mean bi—it's no big deal, Billy," Arthur said. "It's not like it *was*."

"No, I guess it isn't," I said, or so it seemed—as 1980 was soon to become 1981.

How one decade could slide unnoticed into another was a mystery to me, though this period of time was marked by the death of Nils Borkman—and Mrs. Borkman's subsequent suicide.

"They were *both* suicides, Bill," Grandpa Harry had whispered to me over the phone—as if his phone were being tapped.

Nils was eighty-eight—soon to be eighty-nine, had he lived till 1981. It was the regular firearm season for deer—this was shortly before Christmas, 1980—and Nils had blown off the back of his head with a .30-30 carbine while he was transversing the Favorite River Academy athletic fields on his cross-country skis. The students had already gone home for Christmas vacation, and Nils had called his old adversary Chuck Beebe—the game warden who was opposed to Nils and Grandpa Harry making deer-hunting a biathlon event.

"Poachers, Chuck! I have with my own eyes seen them—on the Favorite River athletic fields. I am, as we speak, off to hunt down them!" Nils had urgently shouted into the phone.

"What? *Whoa!*" Chuck had shouted back. "There's poachers in deer season—what are they usin', machine guns or somethin'? Nils?" the game warden had inquired. But Nils had hung up the phone. When Chuck found the body, it appeared that the rifle had been fired while Nils was withdrawing the weapon—from behind himself. Chuck was willing to call the shooting an accident, because he'd long believed that the way Nils and Grandpa Harry hunted deer was dangerous.

Nils had known perfectly well what he was doing. He normally hunted deer with a .30-06. The lighter .30-30 carbine was what Grandpa Harry called a "varmint gun." (Harry hunted deer with it; he said deer were varmints.) The carbine had a shorter barrel; Harry knew that it was easier for Nils to shoot himself in the back of the head with the .30-30.

"But *why* would Nils shoot himself?" I'd asked Grandpa Harry.

"Well, Bill—Nils was Norwegian," Grandpa Harry had begun; it took several minutes for Harry to remember that he'd not told me Nils had been diagnosed with an inoperable cancer.

"Oh."

"Mrs. Borkman will be the next to go, Bill," Grandpa Harry announced dramatically. We'd always joked about Mrs. Borkman being an Ibsen woman, but, sure enough, she shot herself that same day. "Like Hedda—with a handgun, in the temple!" Grandpa Harry had said admiringly—in a not that much later phone call.

I have no doubt that losing his partner and old friend, Nils, precipitated Grandpa Harry's decline. Of course Harry had lost his wife and his only children, too. Thus Richard and I would soon venture down that assisted-living road of committing Grandpa Harry to the Facility, where Harry's "surprise" appearances in drag would quickly wear out his welcome. And—still early in '81, as I recall—Richard and I would move Grandpa Harry back into his River Street home, where Richard and I hired a live-in nurse to look after him. Elmira was the nurse's name; not only did she have fond memories of seeing Harry onstage *as a woman* (when Elmira had been a little girl), but Elmira even participated in choosing Grandpa Harry's dress-of-the-day from his long-hoarded stash of Nana Victoria's clothes.

It was also relatively early in that year ('81) when Mr. Hadley left Mrs. Hadley; as it turned out, he ran off with a brand-new Favorite River Academy graduate. The girl was in her freshman year of college—I can't remember where. She would drop out of college in order to live with Mr.

Hadley, who was sixty-one—Martha Hadley's age, exactly. Mrs. Hadley was my mother's age; she was a whopping ten years older than Richard Abbott, but Elaine must have been right in guessing that her mom had always loved Richard. (Elaine was usually right.)

"What a *melodrama*," Elaine said wearily, when—as early as the summer of '81—Mrs. Hadley and Richard started living together. Old hippie that she was, Martha Hadley refused to get married again, and Richard (I'm sure) was happy just to be in Mrs. Hadley's uncomplaining presence. What did Richard Abbott care about remarrying?

Besides, they both understood that if they *didn't* get married, they would be asked to move out of Bancroft Hall. It may have been the start of the eighties, but it was small-town Vermont, and Favorite River had its share of boarding-school rules. An unmarried couple, living together in a faculty apartment in a prep school—well, this wouldn't quite do. Both Mrs. Hadley and Richard had *had* it with an all-boys' dorm; Elaine and I didn't doubt that. It's entirely possible that Richard Abbott and Martha Hadley decided they would be crazy to get married; by choosing to live together in sin, they got out of living in a dorm!

Mrs. Hadley and Richard had the summer to find a place to live in town, or at least near First Sister—a modest house, something a couple of secondary-school teachers could afford. The place they found was not more than a few doors down River Street from what had once been the First Sister Public Library—now the historical society. The house had gone through a succession of owners in recent years; it needed some repairs, Richard told me somewhat haltingly over the phone.

I sensed his hesitation; if it was money he needed, I would have gladly given him what I could, but I was surprised Richard hadn't asked Grandpa Harry first. Harry loved Richard, and I knew that Grandpa Harry had given his blessing to Richard's living with Martha Hadley.

"The house isn't more than a ten-minute walk from Grandpa Harry's house, Bill," Richard said over the phone. I could tell he was stalling.

"What is it, Richard?" I asked him.

"It's the former Frost home, Bill," Richard said. Given the history of the many recent and unreliable owners, we both knew that no traces of Miss Frost could conceivably have remained. Miss Frost was gone—both Richard Abbott and I knew that. Yet the house being "the former Frost home" was a glimpse into the darkness—the *past* darkness, I thought at the time. I saw no foreshadow of a *future* darkness.

• • •

As FOR MY SECOND warning that a plague was coming, I just plain missed it. There'd been no Christmas card from the Atkins family in 1980; I hadn't noticed. When a card came—it was long after the holiday, but the card still proclaimed "Season's Greetings"—I remember being surprised that Tom hadn't included a review of my fourth novel. (The book wasn't yet published, but I'd sent Atkins a copy of the galleys; I thought that such a faithful fan of my writing deserved a sneak preview. After all, no one else was comparing me favorably to Flaubert!)

But there was nothing enclosed with the "Season's Greetings" card, which arrived sometime in February of '81—at least I think it showed up that late. I noted that the children and the dog looked older. What gave me pause was how much older poor Tom looked; it was almost as if he'd aged several years between Christmases.

My guess was that the photo had been taken on a family ski trip— everyone was dressed for skiing, and Atkins even wore a ski hat. They'd brought the dog *skiing!* I marveled.

The kids looked tanned—the wife, too. Remembering how fair-skinned Tom was, he probably had to be careful about the sun; thus I saw nothing amiss about Tom not being tanned. (Knowing Atkins, he'd probably heeded the earliest alarms about skin cancer and the importance of wearing sunscreen—he'd always been a boy who had heeded every alarm.)

But there was something silvery about Tom's skin color, I thought— not that I could see much of his face, because Atkins's stupid ski hat covered his eyebrows. Yet I could tell—just from that partial view of poor Tom's face—that he'd lost weight. Quite a *lot* of weight, I speculated, but, given the ski clothes, I couldn't really tell. Maybe Atkins had always been a bit hollow-cheeked.

Yet I'd stared at this belated Christmas card for the longest time. There was a look I hadn't seen before in the expression of Tom's wife. How was it possible, in a single expression, to convey a fear of both the unknown and the known?

Mrs. Atkins's expression reminded me of that line in *Madame Bovary*—it's at the end of chapter 6. (The one that goes like a dart to a bull's-eye, or to your heart—"it seemed quite inconceivable that this calm life of hers could really be the happiness of which she used to dream.") Tom's wife didn't look afraid—she seemed *terrified*! But what could possibly have frightened her so?

And where was the smile that the Tom Atkins I knew could rarely suppress for long? Atkins had this goofy, openmouthed smile—with lots of teeth and his tongue showing. But poor Tom had tightly closed his mouth—like a kid who's trying to conceal a wad of chewing gum from a teacher, or like someone who knows his breath is bad.

For some reason, I'd shown the Atkins family photo to Elaine. "You remember Atkins," I said, handing her the late-arriving Christmas card.

"Poor Tom," Elaine automatically said; we both laughed, but Elaine stopped laughing when she had a look at the photograph. "What's the matter with him—what's he got in his *mouth?*" she asked.

"I don't know," I said.

"He's got something in his mouth, Billy—he doesn't want anyone to see it," Elaine told me. "And what's the matter with those children?"

"The *children?*" I asked her. I'd not noticed that anything was wrong with the kids.

"They look like they've been crying," Elaine explained. "*Jesus*—it looks like they cry all the time!"

"Let me see that," I said, taking the photo. The children looked okay to me. "Atkins used to cry a lot," I told Elaine. "He was a real crybaby—maybe the kids got it from Tom."

"Come on, Billy—something's not normal. I mean with all of them," Elaine said.

"The dog looks normal," I said. (I was just fooling around.)

"I'm not talking about the dog, Billy," Elaine said.

IF YOUR PASSAGE THROUGH the Reagan years (1981–89) was unclouded by watching someone you knew die of AIDS, then you don't remember those years (or Ronald Reagan) the way I do. What a decade it was—and we would have that horseback-riding B actor in charge for most of it! (For seven of the eight years he was president, Reagan would not say the *AIDS* word.) Those years have been blurred by the passage of time, and by the conscious and unconscious forgetting of the worst details. Some decades slip by, others drag on; what made the eighties last forever was that my friends and lovers kept dying—into the nineties, and beyond. By '95—in New York, alone—more Americans had died of AIDS than were killed in Vietnam.

It was some months after that February conversation Elaine and I had about the Atkins family photo—I know it was later in '81—when Larry's young lover Russell got sick. (I felt awful that I'd dismissed Russell as a Wall Street guy; I'd called him a poetaster, too.)

I was a snob; I used to turn up my nose at the patrons Larry surrounded himself with. But Larry was a poet—poets don't make any money. Why shouldn't poets, and other artists, have patrons?

PCP was the big killer—a pneumonia (*Pneumocystis carinii*). In young Russell's case, as it often was, this pneumonia was the first presentation of AIDS—a young and otherwise healthy-looking guy with a cough (or shortness of breath) and a fever. It was the X-ray that didn't look great—in the parlance of radiologists and doctors, a "whiteout." Yet there was no suspicion of the disease; there was, at first, the phase of not getting better on antibiotics—finally, there was a biopsy (or lung lavage), which showed the cause to be PCP, that insidious pneumonia. They usually put you on Bactrim; that's what Russell was taking. Russell was the first AIDS patient I watched waste away—and, don't forget, Russell had money *and* he had Larry.

Many writers who knew Larry saw him as spoiled and self-centered—even pompous. I shamefully include my former self in this category of Lawrence Upton observers. But Larry was one of those people who improve in a crisis.

"It should be *me*, Bill," Larry told me when I first paid a visit to Russell. "I've had a life—Russell is just beginning his." Russell was placed in hospice care in his own magnificent Chelsea brownstone; he had his own nurse. All this was new to me then—that Russell had chosen not to go on a breathing machine allowed him to be cared for at home. (Intubating at home is problematic; it's easier to hook a person up to a ventilator in a hospital.) I later saw and remembered that gob of Xylocaine jelly on the tip of the endotracheal tube, but not in Russell's case; he wasn't intubated, not at home.

I remember Larry feeding Russell. I could see the cheesy patches of *Candida* in Russell's mouth, and his white-coated tongue.

Russell had been a beautiful young man; his face would soon be disfigured with Kaposi's sarcoma lesions. A violet-colored lesion dangled from one of Russell's eyebrows where it resembled a fleshy, misplaced earlobe; another purplish lesion drooped from Russell's nose. (The latter was so strikingly prominent that Russell later chose to hide it behind a bandanna.) Larry told me that Russell referred to himself as "the tur-key"—because of the Kaposi's sarcoma lesions.

"Why are they so young, Bill?" Larry kept asking me—when "they," the sheer number of young men who were dying in New York, had made us realize that Russell was just the beginning.

We saw Russell age, in just a few months—his hair thinned, his skin turned leaden, he was often covered with a cool-to-the-touch film of sweat, and his fevers went on forever. The *Candida* went down his throat, into the esophagus; Russell had difficulty swallowing, and his lips were crusted white and fissured. The lymph nodes in his neck bulged. He could scarcely breathe, but Russell refused to go on a ventilator (or to a hospital); in the end, he faked taking the Bactrim—Larry would find the tablets scattered in Russell's bed.

Russell died in Larry's arms; I'm sure Larry wished it had been the other way around. ("He weighed nothing," Larry said.) By then, Larry and I were already visiting friends at St. Vincent's Hospital. As Larry predicted, it would get so crowded at St. Vincent's that you couldn't go to visit a friend, or a former lover, and not encounter someone else you knew. You would glance in a doorway, and there was someone you hadn't known was sick; in more than one instance, Larry claimed, he'd spotted someone he hadn't known was *gay!*

Women found out that their husbands had been seeing men—only when their husbands were dying. Parents learned that their young male children were dying before they knew (or had figured out) that their kids were gay.

Only a few women friends of mine were infected—not many. I was terrified about Elaine; she'd slept with some men I knew were bisexual. But two abortions had taught Elaine to insist on condoms; she was of the opinion that nothing else could keep her from getting pregnant.

We'd had an earlier condom conversation; when the AIDS epidemic started, Elaine had asked me, "You're still a condom guy—right, Billy?" (Since '68! I'd told her.)

"I should be dead," Larry said. He wasn't sick; he looked fine. I wasn't sick, either. We kept our fingers crossed.

It was still in '81, near the end of the year, when there was that bleeding episode in the wrestling room at the New York Athletic Club. I'm not sure if all the wrestlers knew that the AIDS virus was mainly transmitted by blood and semen, because there was a time when hospital workers were afraid they could catch it from a cough or a sneeze, but that day I got a nosebleed in the wrestling room, everyone already knew enough to be scared shitless of blood.

It often happens in wrestling: You don't know you're bleeding until you see your blood on your opponent. I was working out with Sonny; when I saw the blood on Sonny's shoulder, I backed away. "You're bleeding—" I started to say; then I saw Sonny's face. He was staring at my nosebleed. I put my hand to my face and saw the blood—on my hand, on my chest, on the mat. "Oh, it's me," I said, but Sonny had left the wrestling room—running. The locker room, where the training room was, was on another floor.

"Go get the trainer, Billy—tell him we've got blood here," Arthur told me. All the wrestlers had stopped wrestling; no one would touch the blood on the mat. Normally, a nosebleed was no big deal; you just wiped off the mat with a towel. Blood, in a wrestling room, *used to be* of no importance.

Sonny had already sent the trainer to the wrestling room; the trainer arrived with rubber gloves on, and with towels soaked in alcohol. Minutes later, I saw Sonny standing under the shower in the locker room—he was wearing his wrestling gear, even his shoes, in the shower. I emptied out my locker before I took a shower. I wanted to give Sonny time to finish showering before I went anywhere near the shower room. I was betting that Sonny hadn't told the trainer that "the writer" had bled in the wrestling room; Sonny must have told him that "the gay guy" was bleeding. I know that's what *I* would have said to the trainer, at that time.

Arthur saw me only when I was leaving the locker room; I'd showered and dressed, and I had some cautionary cotton balls stuffed up both nostrils—not a drop of blood in sight, but I was carrying a green plastic garbage bag with the entire contents of my locker. I got the garbage bag from a guy in the equipment room; boy, did he look happy I was leaving!

"Are you okay, Billy?" Arthur asked me. Someone would keep asking me that question—for about fourteen or fifteen years.

"I'm going to withdraw my application for lifetime membership, Arthur—if that's okay with you," I said. "The dress code at this place is a nuisance for a writer. I don't wear a coat and tie when I write. Yet I have to put on a coat and tie just to get in the front door here—only to get undressed to wrestle."

"I totally understand, Billy. I just hope you're going to be okay," Arthur said.

"I can't belong to a club with such an uptight dress code. It's all wrong for a writer," I told him.

Some of the other wrestlers were showing up in the locker room after practice—Ed and Wolfie and Jim, my former workout partners, among them. Everyone saw me holding the green plastic garbage bag; I didn't have to tell them it was my last wrestling practice.

I left the club by the back door to the lobby. You look odd carrying a garbage bag on Central Park South. I went out of the New York Athletic Club on West Fifty-eighth Street, where there were a few narrow alleys that served as delivery entrances to the hotels on Central Park South. I knew I would find a Dumpster for my garbage bag, and what amounted to my life as a beginning wrestler in the dawn of the AIDS crisis.

IT WAS SHORTLY AFTER the inglorious nosebleed had ended my wrestling career that Larry and I were having dinner downtown and he told me he'd heard that bottoms were more likely to get sick than tops. I knew tops who had it, but more bottoms got it—this was true. I never knew how Larry managed to have "heard" everything, but he heard right most of the time.

"Blow jobs aren't too terribly risky, Bill—just so you know." Larry was the first person to tell me that. Of course Larry seemed to know (or he assumed) that the number of sex partners in your life was a factor. Ironically, I didn't hear about the *condom* factor from Larry.

Larry had responded to Russell's death by seeking to help every young man he knew who was dying; Larry had an admirably stronger stomach for visiting the AIDS patients we knew at St. Vincent's, and in hospice care, than I did. I could sense myself withdrawing, just as I was aware of people shrinking away from me—not only my fellow wrestlers.

Rachel had retreated immediately. "She may think she can catch the disease from your *writing*, Billy," Elaine told me.

Elaine and I had talked about getting out of New York, but the problem with living in New York for any length of time is that many New Yorkers can't imagine that there's anywhere else they could live.

As more of our friends contracted the virus, Elaine and I would imagine ourselves with one or another of the AIDS-associated, opportunistic illnesses. Elaine developed night sweats. I woke up imagining I could feel the white plaques of *Candida* encroaching on my teeth. (I admitted to Elaine that I often woke up at night and peered into my mouth in a mirror—with a flashlight!) And there was that seborrheic dermatitis; it was flaky and greasy-looking—it cropped up mostly on your eyebrows and scalp, and on the sides of your nose. Herpes could run wild on your lips; the ulcers simply wouldn't heal. There were also those clusters of molluscum; they looked like smallpox—they could completely cover your face.

And there's a certain smell your hair has when it is matted by your sweat and flattened by your pillow. It's not just how translucent-looking and funny-smelling your hair is. It's the salt that dries and hardens on your forehead, from the unremitting fever and the incessant sweating; it's your mucous membranes, too—they get chock-full of yeast. It's a yeasty but, at the same time, fruity smell—the way curd smells, or mildew, or a dog's ears when they're wet.

I wasn't afraid of dying; I was afraid of feeling guilty, forever, because I *wasn't* dying. I couldn't accept that I would or might escape the AIDS virus for as accidental a reason as being told to wear a condom by a doctor who disliked me, or that the random luck of my being a top would or might save me. I was *not* ashamed of my sex life; I was ashamed of myself for not wanting to *be there* for the people who were dying.

"I'm not good at this. You are," I told Larry; I meant more than the hand-holding and the pep talks.

Cryptococcal meningitis was caused by a fungus; it affected your brain, and was diagnosed by a lumbar puncture—it presented with fever and headache and confusion. There was a separate spinal-cord disease, a myelopathy that caused progressive weakness—loss of function in your legs, incontinence. There was little one could do about it—vacuolar myelopathy, it was called.

I was watching Larry empty the bedpan of our friend who had this awful myelopathy; I was truly marveling at Larry—he'd become a saint—when I suddenly realized that I had no difficulty pronouncing the *myelopathy* word, or any of the other AIDS-associated words. (That *Pneumocystis* pneumonia, for example—I could actually say it. Kaposi's sarcoma, those terrible lesions, gave me no pronunciation problem; I could say "cryptococcal meningitis" as if it meant no more to me than the common cold. I didn't even hesitate to pronounce "cytomegalovirus"—a major cause of blindness in AIDS.)

"I should call your mother," I told Elaine. "I seem to be having a pronunciation breakthrough."

"It's just because you're distancing yourself from this disease, Billy," Elaine said. "You're like me—you're imagining yourself as standing on the outside, looking in."

"I should call your mother," I repeated, but I knew Elaine was right.

"Let's hear you say 'penis,' Billy."

"That's not fair, Elaine—that's different."

"Say it," Elaine said.

But I knew how it would sound. It was, is, and will always be *penith* to me; some things never change. I didn't try to say the *penis* word for Elaine. "Cock," I said to her.

I didn't call Mrs. Hadley about my pronunciation breakthrough, either. I *was* trying to distance myself from the disease—even as the epidemic was only beginning. I was already feeling guilty that I didn't have it.

THE 1981 ATKINS CHRISTMAS card came on time that year. No generic "Season's Greetings," more than a month late, but an unapologetic "Merry Christmas" in December.

"Uh-oh," Elaine said, when I showed her the Atkins family photo. "Where's Tom?"

Atkins wasn't in the picture. The names of the family were printed on the Christmas card in small capitals: TOM, SUE, PETER, EMILY & JACQUES ATKINS. (Jacques was the Labrador; Atkins had named the dog after Kittredge!) But Tom had missed the family photograph.

"Maybe he wasn't feeling very photogenic," I said to Elaine.

"His color wasn't so hot last Christmas, was it? And he'd lost all that weight," Elaine said.

"The ski hat was hiding his hair *and* his eyebrows," I added. (There'd been no Tom Atkins review of my fourth novel, I'd noticed. I doubted that Atkins had changed his mind about *Madame Bovary*.)

"Shit, Billy," Elaine said. "What do you make of the message?"

The message, which was written by hand on the back of the Christmas photo, was from the wife. There was not a lot of information in it, and it wasn't very Christmasy.

Tom has mentioned you. He would like to see you.
                                        Sue Atkins

"I think he's dying—that's what I think," I told Elaine.

"I'll go with you, Billy—Tom always liked me," Elaine said.

Elaine was right—poor Tom had always adored her (and Mrs. Hadley)—and, not unlike old times, I felt braver in Elaine's company. If Atkins was dying of AIDS, I was pretty sure his wife would already know everything about that summer twenty years ago, when Tom and I were in Europe together.

That night, I called Sue Atkins. It turned out that Tom had been placed in hospice care at his home in Short Hills, New Jersey. I'd never known what Atkins did, but his wife told me that Tom had been a CEO at a life-insurance company; he'd worked in New York City, five days a week, for more than a decade. I guessed that he'd never felt like seeing me for lunch or dinner, but I was surprised when Sue Atkins said that she'd thought her husband had been seeing me; apparently, there were nights when Tom hadn't made it back to New Jersey in time for dinner.

"It wasn't me he was seeing," I told Mrs. Atkins. I mentioned that Elaine wanted to visit Tom, too—if we weren't "intruding," was how I'd put it.

Before I could explain who Elaine was, Sue Atkins said, "Yes, that would be all right—I've heard all about Elaine." (I didn't ask Mrs. Atkins what she'd heard about me.)

Elaine was teaching that term—grading final papers, I explained on the phone. Perhaps we could come to Short Hills on a Saturday; there wouldn't be all the commuters on the train, I was thinking.

"The children will be home from school, but that will be fine with Tom," Sue said. "Certainly Peter knows who you are. That trip to Europe—" Her voice just stopped. "Peter knows what's going on, and he's devoted to his father," Mrs. Atkins began again. "But Emily—well, she's younger. I'm not sure how much Emily really knows. You can't do much to counter what your kids hear in school from the other kids—not if your kids won't tell you what the other kids are saying."

"I'm sorry for what you're going through," I told Tom's wife.

"I always knew this might happen. Tom was candid about his past," Sue Atkins said. "I just didn't know he'd gone back there. And this terrible disease—" Her voice stopped again.

I was looking at the Christmas card while we spoke on the phone. I'm not good at guessing young girls' ages. I wasn't sure how old Emily was; I just knew she was the younger child. I was estimating that the boy, Peter Atkins, would have been fourteen or fifteen—about the same age poor Tom had been when I'd first met him and thought he was a loser who couldn't even pronounce the *time* word. Atkins had told me he'd called me Bill, instead of Billy, because he noticed that Richard Abbott always called me Bill, and anyone could see how much I loved Richard.

Poor Tom had also confessed to me that he'd overheard Martha Hadley's outburst, when I was seeing Mrs. Hadley in her office and Atkins had been waiting for his turn. "Billy, Billy—you've done nothing *wrong*!" Mrs. Hadley had cried, loud enough for Atkins to have heard her through the closed door. (It was when I'd told Martha Hadley about my crushes on other boys and men, including my slightly fading crush on Richard and my much more devastating crush on Kittredge.)

Poor Tom told me that he'd thought I was having an affair with Mrs. Hadley! "I actually believed you'd just *ejaculated* in her office, or something, and she was trying to assure you that you'd done nothing 'wrong'—that's what I thought she meant by the *wrong* word, Bill," Atkins had confessed to me.

"What an *idiot* you are!" I'd told him; now I felt ashamed.

I asked Sue Atkins how Tom was doing—I meant those opportunistic illnesses I already knew something about, and what drugs Tom was taking. When she said he'd developed a rash from the Bactrim, I knew poor Tom was being treated for the *Pneumocystis* pneumonia. Since Tom was in hospice care at home, he wasn't on a ventilator; his breathing would be harsh and aspirate—I knew that, too.

Sue Atkins also said something about how hard it was for Tom to eat. "He has trouble swallowing," she told me. (Just telling me this made her suppress a cough, or perhaps she'd gagged; she suddenly sounded short of breath.)

"From the *Candida*—he can't eat?" I asked her.

"Yes, it's esophageal candidiasis," Mrs. Atkins said, the terminology sounding oh-so-familiar to her. "And—this is *fairly* recent—there's a Hickman catheter," Sue explained.

"How recent is the Hickman?" I asked Mrs. Atkins.

"Oh, just the last month," she told me. So they were feeding him through the catheter—malnutrition. (With *Candida*, difficulty swallowing usually responded to fluconazole or amphotericin B—unless the yeast had become resistant.)

"If they have you on a Hickman for hyperalimentation feeding, Bill, you're probably starving," Larry had told me.

I kept thinking about the boy, Peter; in the Christmas photo, he reminded me of the Tom Atkins I'd known. I imagined that Peter might be what poor Tom himself had once described as "like us." I was wondering if Atkins had noticed that his son was "like us." That was how Tom had put it, years ago: "Not everyone here understands people like us," he'd said, and I'd wondered if Atkins was making a pass at me. (It had been the first pass that a boy *like me* ever made at me.)

"Bill!" Sue Atkins said sharply, on the phone. I realized I was crying.

"Sorry," I said.

"Don't you dare cry around us when you come here," Mrs. Atkins said. "This family is all cried out."

"Don't let me cry," I told Elaine on that Saturday, not long before Christmas 1981. The holiday shoppers were headed the other way, into New York City. There was almost no one on the train to Short Hills, New Jersey, on that December Saturday.

"How am I supposed to stop you from crying, Billy? I don't have a gun—I can't shoot you," Elaine said.

I was feeling a little jumpy about the *gun* word. Elmira, the nurse Richard Abbott and I had hired to look after Grandpa Harry, ceaselessly complained to Richard about "the gun." It was a Mossberg .30-30 carbine, lever-action—the same type of short-barreled rifle Nils had used to kill himself. (I can't remember, but I think Nils had a Winchester or a Savage, and it wasn't a lever-action; I just know it was also a .30-30 carbine.)

Elmira had complained about Grandpa Harry "excessively cleanin' the damn Mossberg"; apparently, Harry would clean the gun in Nana Victoria's clothes—he got gun oil on a lot of her dresses. It was all the dry-cleaning that upset Elmira. "He's not out shootin'—no more deer-huntin' on skis, not at his age, he's promised me—but he just keeps cleanin' and cleanin' the damn Mossberg!" she told Richard.

Richard had asked Grandpa Harry about it. "There's no point in havin' a gun if you don't keep it clean," Harry had said.

"But perhaps you could wear *your* clothes when you clean it, Harry," Richard had said. "You know—jeans, an old flannel shirt. Something Elmira *doesn't* have to get dry-cleaned."

Harry hadn't responded—that is, not to Richard. But Grandpa Harry told Elmira not to worry: "If I shoot myself, Elmira, I promise I won't leave you with any friggin' dry-cleanin'."

Now, of course, both Elmira and Richard were worried about Grandpa

Harry shooting himself, and I kept thinking about that super-clean .30-30. Yes, I was worried about Grandpa Harry's intentions, too, but—to be honest with you—I was relieved to know the damn Mossberg was ready for action. To be *very* honest with you, I wasn't worrying about Grandpa Harry as much as I was worrying about *me*. If I got the disease, I knew what I was going to do. Vermont boy that I am, I wouldn't have hesitated. I was planning to head home to First Sister—to Grandpa Harry's house on River Street. I knew where he kept that .30-30; I knew where Harry stashed his ammunition. What my grandpa called a "varmint gun" was good enough for me.

In this frame of mind, and determined not to cry, I showed up in Short Hills, New Jersey, to pay a visit to my dying friend Tom Atkins, whom I'd not seen for twenty years—virtually half my life ago.

With half a brain, I might have anticipated that the boy, Peter, would be the one to answer the door. I should have expected to be greeted by a shocking physical resemblance to Tom Atkins—as I first knew him—but I was speechless.

"It's the *son*, Billy—say something!" Elaine whispered in my ear. (Of course I was already struggling to make an effort not to cry.) "Hi—I'm Elaine, this is Billy," Elaine said to the boy with the carrot-colored hair. "You must be Peter. We're old friends of your dad."

"Yes, we've been expecting you—please come in," Peter said politely. (The boy had just turned fifteen; he'd applied to the Lawrenceville School, for what would be his sophomore year, and he was waiting to hear if he got in.)

"We weren't sure what time you were coming, but now is a good time," Peter Atkins was saying, as he led Elaine and me inside. I wanted to hug the boy—he'd used the *time* word twice; he had no trace of a pronunciation problem!—but, under the circumstances, I knew enough not to touch him.

Off to one side of the lavish vestibule was a rather formal-looking dining room—where absolutely no one ate (or had ever eaten), I was thinking—when the boy told us that Charles had just left. "Charles is my dad's nurse," Peter was explaining. "Charles comes to take care of the catheter—you have to keep flushing out the catheter, or it will clot off," Peter told Elaine and me.

"Clot off," I repeated—my first words in the Atkins house. Elaine elbowed me in my ribs.

"My mom is resting, but she'll be right down," the boy was saying. "I don't know where my sister is."

We had stopped alongside a closed door in a downstairs hall. "This used to be my father's study," Peter Atkins said; the boy was hesitating before he opened the door. "But our bedrooms are upstairs—Dad can't climb stairs," Peter continued, not opening the door. "If my sister is in here, with him, she may scream—she's only thirteen, about to be fourteen," the boy told Elaine and me; he had his hand on the doorknob, but he wasn't ready to let us in. "I weigh about a hundred and forty pounds," Peter Atkins said, as matter-of-factly as he could manage. "My dad's lost some weight, since you've seen him," the boy said. "He weighs almost a hundred—maybe ninety-something pounds." Then he opened the door.

"It broke my heart," Elaine told me, later. "How that boy was trying to prepare us." But as I was only beginning to learn about that goddamn disease, there was no way to be prepared for it.

"Oh, there she is—my sister, Emily," Peter Atkins said, when he finally let us enter the room where his dad lay dying.

The dog, Jacques, was a chocolate Labrador with a gray-white muzzle—an old dog, I could tell, not only by his grizzled nose and jaws, but by how slowly and unsteadily the dog came out from under the hospital bed to greet us. One of his hind legs slipped a little on the floor; his tail wagged only slightly, as if it hurt his hips to wag his tail at all.

"Jacques is almost thirteen," Peter told Elaine and me, "but that's pretty old for a dog—and he has arthritis." The dog's cold, wet nose touched my hand and then Elaine's; that was all the old Lab had wanted. There was a subsequent *thump* when the dog lay down under the bed again.

The girl, Emily, was curled up like a second dog at the foot of her father's hospital bed. It was probably of some small comfort to Tom that his daughter was keeping his feet warm. It was an indescribable exertion for Atkins to breathe; I knew that his hands and feet would be cold—the circulation to Tom's extremities was closing down, trying to shunt blood to his brain.

Emily's reaction to Elaine and me was delayed. She sat up and screamed, but belatedly; she'd been reading a book, which flew from her hands. The sound of its fluttering pages was lost to the girl's scream. I saw an oxygen tank in the cluttered room—what had been Atkins's "study," as his son had explained, now converted for a deathwatch.

I also observed that his daughter's scream had little effect on Tom
Atkins—he'd barely moved in the hospital bed. It probably hurt him to
turn his head; yet his bare chest, while the rest of his shrunken body lay
still, was vigorously heaving. The Hickman catheter dangled from the
right side of Tom's chest, where it had been inserted under his clavicle; it
tunneled under the skin a few inches above the nipple, and entered the
subclavian vein below the collarbone.

"These are Dad's old friends, from school, Emily," Peter said irritably
to his little sister. "You knew they were coming."

The girl stalked across the room to her far-flung book; when she'd
retrieved it, she turned and glared. Emily definitely glared at me; she may
have been glaring at her brother and Elaine, too. When the thirteen-
year-old spoke, I felt certain she was speaking only to me, though Elaine
would try in vain to assure me later, on the train, that Tom's daughter
had been addressing both of us. (I don't think so.)

"Are you sick, too?" Emily asked.

"No, I'm not—I'm sorry," I answered her. The girl then marched out
of the room.

"Tell Mom they're here, Emily. Tell Mom!" Peter called after his
angry sister.

"I *will!*" we heard the girl shout.

"Is that you, Bill?" Tom Atkins asked; I saw him try to move his head,
and I stepped closer to the bed. "Bill Abbott—are you here?" Atkins
asked; his voice was weak and terribly labored. His lungs made a thick
gurgling. The oxygen tank must have been for only occasional (and su-
perficial) relief; there probably was a mask, but I didn't see it—the oxygen
was in lieu of a ventilator. Morphine would come next, at the end stage.

"Yes, it's me—Bill—and Elaine is with me, Tom," I told Atkins. I
touched his hand. It was ice-cold and clammy. I could see poor Tom's
face now. That greasy-looking seborrheic dermatitis was in his scalp, on
his eyebrows, and flaking off the sides of his nose.

"Elaine, too!" Atkins gasped. "Elaine and Bill! Are you all right,
Bill?" he asked me.

"Yes, I'm all right," I told him; I'd never felt so ashamed to be "all
right."

There was a tray of medications, and other intimidating-looking
stuff, on the bedside table. (I would remember the heparin solution, for
some reason—it was for flushing out the Hickman catheter.) I saw the

white, cheesy curds of the *Candida* crusting the corners of poor Tom's mouth.

"I did not recognize him, Billy," Elaine would say later, when we were returning to New York. Yet how do you recognize a grown man who weighs only ninety-something pounds?

Tom Atkins and I were thirty-nine, but he resembled a man in his sixties; his hair was not only translucent and thin—what there was of it was completely gray. His eyes were sunken in their sockets, his temples deeply dented, his cheeks caved in; poor Tom's nostrils were pinched tightly together, as if he could already detect the stench of his own ca-daver, and his taut skin, which had once been so ruddy, was an ashen color.

Hippocratic facies was the term for that near-death face—that tightly fitted mask of death, which so many of my friends and lovers who died of AIDS would one day wear. It was skin stretched over a skull; the skin was so improbably hard and tense, you were sure it was going to split.

I was holding one of Tom's cold hands, and Elaine was holding the other one—I could see Elaine trying not to stare at the Hickman cathe-ter in Atkins's bare chest—when we heard the dry cough. For a moment, I imagined that poor Tom had died and his cough had somehow escaped his body. But I saw the son's eyes; Peter knew that cough, and where it came from. The boy turned to the open doorway of the room—where his mother now stood, coughing. It didn't sound like all that serious a cough, but Sue Atkins was having trouble stopping it. Elaine and I had heard that cough before; the earliest stages of *Pneumocystis* pneumonia don't sound too bad. The shortness of breath and the fever were often worse than the cough.

"Yes, I have it," Sue Atkins said; she was controlling the cough, but she couldn't stop it. "In my case, it's just starting," Mrs. Atkins said; she was definitely short of breath.

"I infected her, Bill—that's the story," Tom Atkins said.

Peter, who'd been so poised, was trying to slip sideways past his mother into the hall.

"No—you stay here, Peter. You need to hear what your father has to say to Bill," Sue Atkins told her son; the boy was crying now, but he backed into the room, still looking at the doorway, which his mom was blocking.

"I don't want to stay, I don't want to hear . . ." the boy began; he was shaking his head, as if this were a proven method to make himself stop crying.

"Peter—you have to stay, you have to listen," Tom Atkins said. "Peter is why I wanted to see you, Bill," Tom said to me. "Bill has *some* discernible traces of moral responsibility—doesn't he, Elaine?" Tom suddenly asked her. "I mean Bill's writing—at least his *writing* has discernible traces of moral responsibility, doesn't it? I don't really know Bill anymore," Atkins admitted. (Tom couldn't say more than three or four words without needing to take a breath.)

"Moral responsibility," I repeated.

"Yes, he does—Billy takes moral responsibility. I think so," Elaine said. "I don't mean *only* in your writing, Billy," Elaine added.

"I don't have to stay—I've heard this before," Sue Atkins suddenly said. "You don't have to stay, either, Elaine. We can go try to talk to Emily. She's a challenge to talk to, but she's better with women than she is with men—as a rule. Emily really *hates* men," Mrs. Atkins said.

"Emily screams almost every time she sees a man," Peter explained; he had stopped crying.

"Okay, I'll come with you," Elaine said to Sue Atkins. "I'm not all that crazy about most men, either—I just don't like women at all, usually."

"That's interesting," Mrs. Atkins said.

"I'll come back when it's time to say good-bye," Elaine called to Tom, as she was leaving, but Atkins seemed to ignore the good-bye reference.

"It's amazing how easy time becomes—when there's no more of it, Bill," Tom began.

"Where is Charles—he should be here, shouldn't he?" Peter Atkins asked his dad. "Just look at this room! Why is that old oxygen tank still here? The oxygen doesn't help him anymore," the boy explained to me. "Your lungs need to work in order to have any benefit from oxygen. If you can't breathe in, how are you going to get the oxygen? That's what Charles says."

"Peter, please stop," Tom Atkins said to his son. "I asked Charles for a little privacy—Charles will be back soon."

"You're talking too much, Daddy," the boy said. "You know what happens when you try to talk too much."

"I want to talk to Bill about *you*, Peter," his father said.

"This part is crazy—this part makes no sense," Peter said.

Tom Atkins seemed to be hoarding his remaining breath before he spoke to me: "I want you to keep an eye on my boy when I'm gone, Bill—especially if Peter is 'like us,' but even if he isn't."

"Why me, Tom?" I asked him.

"You don't have any children, do you?" Atkins asked me. "All I'm asking you is to keep one eye on one kid. I don't know what to do about Emily—you might not be the best choice for someone to look after Emily."

"No, no, no," the boy suddenly said. "Emily stays with *me*—she goes where I go."

"You'll have to talk her into it, Peter, and you know how stubborn she is," Atkins said; it was harder and harder for poor Tom to get enough breath. "When I die—when your mom is dead, too—it's *this man here* I want you talking to, Peter. Not your grandfather."

I'd met Tom's parents at our graduation from Favorite River. His father had taken a despairing look at me; he'd refused to shake my hand. That was Peter's grandfather; he hadn't *called* me a fag, but I'd felt him thinking it.

"My father is very . . . unsophisticated," Atkins had told me at the time.

"He should meet my mom," was all I'd said.

Now Tom was asking me to be his son's advice-giver. (Tom Atkins had never been much of a realist.) "Not your grandfather," Atkins said a second time to Peter.

"No, no, no," the boy repeated; he'd started to cry again.

"Tom, I don't know how to be a father—I've had no experience," I said. "And I might get sick, too."

"Yes!" Peter Atkins cried. "What if Bill or Billy, or whatever his name is, gets *sick?*"

"I think I better have a little oxygen, Bill—Peter knows how to do it, don't you, Peter?" Tom asked his son.

"Yes—of course I know how to do it," the boy said; he immediately stopped crying. "*Charles* is the one who should be giving you oxygen, Daddy—and it won't work, anyway!" the fifteen-year-old cried. "You just *think* the oxygen is getting to your lungs; it really isn't." I saw the oxygen mask then—Peter knew where it was—and while the boy attended to the oxygen tank, Tom Atkins smiled proudly at me.

"Peter is a wonderful boy," Atkins said; I saw that Tom couldn't look at his son when he said this, or he would have lost his composure. Atkins was managing to hold himself together by looking at me.

Similarly, when Atkins spoke, I could manage to hold myself together only by looking at his fifteen-year-old son. Besides, as I would say later to Elaine, Peter looked more like Tom Atkins to me than Atkins even remotely looked like himself.

"You weren't this assertive when I knew you, Tom," I said, but I kept my eyes on Peter; the boy was very gently fitting the oxygen mask to his father's unrecognizable face.

"What does 'assertive' mean?" Peter asked me; his father laughed. The laugh made Atkins gasp and cough, but he'd definitely laughed.

"What I mean by 'assertive' is that your dad is someone who takes charge of a situation—he's someone who has confidence in a situation that many people lack confidence in," I said to the boy. (I couldn't believe I was saying this about the Tom Atkins I'd known, but at this moment it was true.)

"Is that any better?" Peter asked his father, who was struggling to breathe the oxygen; Tom was working awfully hard for very little relief, or so it seemed to me, but Atkins managed to nod at his son's question—all the while never taking his eyes off me.

"I don't think the oxygen makes a difference," Peter Atkins said; the boy was examining me more closely than before. I saw Atkins inch his forearm across the bed; he nudged his son with that arm. "So . . ." the boy began, as if this were his idea, as if his dad hadn't already said to him, *When my old friend Bill is here, you be sure to ask him about the summer we spent in Europe together,* or words to that effect. "So . . ." the boy started again. "I understand that you and my dad traveled all over Europe together. So—what was that like?"

I knew I would burst into tears if I so much as glanced at Tom Atkins—who laughed again, and coughed, and gasped—so I just kept looking at Tom's carrot-haired likeness, his darling fifteen-year-old son, and I said, as if I were also following a script, "First of all, I was trying to read this book, but your dad wouldn't let me—not unless I read the whole book out loud to him."

"You read a whole book out loud to him!" Peter exclaimed in disbelief.

"We were both nineteen, but he made me read the entire novel—out loud. And your father *hated* the book—he was actually jealous of one of the characters; he simply didn't want me to spend a single minute *alone* with her," I explained to Peter. The boy was thoroughly delighted now. (I knew what I was doing—I was *auditioning.*)

I guess that the oxygen was working a little—or it was working in Tom's mind—because Atkins had closed his eyes, and he was smiling. It was almost the same goofy smile I remembered, if you could ignore the *Candida*.

"How can you be jealous of a woman in a novel?" Peter Atkins asked me. "This was only make-believe—a made-up story, right?"

"Right," I told Peter, "and she's a miserable woman. She's unhappy all the time, and she eventually poisons herself and dies. Your dad even detested this woman's *feet*!"

"Her *feet*!" the boy exclaimed, laughing more.

"Peter!" we heard his mother calling. "Come here—let your father rest!"

But my audition was doomed from the start.

"It was entirely orchestrated—the whole thing was *rehearsed*. You know that, don't you, Billy?" Elaine would ask me later, when we were on the train.

"I know that *now*," I would tell her. (I didn't know it *then*.)

Peter left the room just as I was getting *started*! I'd had much more to say about that summer Tom Atkins and I spent in Europe, but suddenly young Peter was gone. I thought poor Tom was asleep, but he'd moved the oxygen mask away from his mouth and nose, and—with his eyes still closed—he found my wrist with his cold hand. (At first touch, I'd thought his hand was the old dog's nose.) Tom Atkins wasn't smiling now; he must have known we were alone. I believe Atkins also knew that the oxygen wasn't working; I think he knew that it would never work again. His face was wet with tears.

"*Is* there eternal darkness, Bill?" Atkins asked me. "Is there a monster's face, waiting there?"

"No, no, Tom," I tried to assure him. "It's either *just* darkness—*no* monster, no *anything*—or it's very bright, truly the most amazing light, and there are lots of wonderful things to see."

"No monsters, either way—right, Bill?" poor Tom asked me.

"That's right, Tom—no monsters, either way."

I was aware of someone behind me, in the doorway of the room. It was Peter; he'd come back—I didn't know how long he'd been there, or what he'd overheard.

"Is the monster's face in the darkness in that same book?" the boy asked me. "Is the face also make-believe?"

"Ha!" Atkins cried. "That's a good question, Peter! What do you say to *that*, Bill?" There was a convulsion of coughing then, and more violent gasping; the boy ran to his dad and helped him put the oxygen mask back over his nose and mouth, but the oxygen was ineffective. Atkins's lungs weren't functioning properly—he couldn't draw enough air to help himself.

"Is this a test, Tom?" I asked my old friend. "What do you want from me?"

Peter Atkins just stood there, watching us. He helped his father pull the oxygen mask away from his mouth. "When you're dying, everything is a test, Bill. You'll see," Tom said; with his son's help, Atkins was putting the oxygen mask back in place, but he suddenly stopped the seemingly pointless process.

"It's a made-up story, Peter," I told the boy. "The unhappy woman who poisons herself—even her *feet* are made up. It's make-believe—the monster's face in the darkness, too. It's all *imagined*," I said.

"But *this* isn't 'imagined,' is it?" the boy asked me. "My mom and my dad are dying—that isn't *imagined*, is it?"

"No," I told him. "You can always find me, Peter," I suddenly said to the boy. "I'll be available to you—I promise."

"*There!*" Peter cried—not to me, to his dad. "I got him to say it! Does that make you happy? It doesn't make *me* happy!" the boy cried.

"Peter!" his mom was calling. "Let your father *rest*! Peter?"

"I'm coming!" the boy called; he ran out of the room.

Tom Atkins had closed his eyes again. "Let me know when we're alone, Bill," he gasped; he held the oxygen mask away from his mouth and nose, but I could tell that—as little as the oxygen helped—he wanted it.

"We're alone," I told Atkins.

"I've seen him," Tom whispered hoarsely. "He's not at all who we thought he was—he's more like us than we ever imagined. He's *beautiful*, Bill!"

"*Who's* beautiful—who's more like us than we ever imagined, Tom?" I asked, but I knew that the subject had changed; there'd been only one person Tom and I had always spoken of with fear and secrecy, with love and hatred.

"You know who, Bill—I've seen him," Atkins whispered.

"Kittredge?" I whispered back.

Atkins covered his mouth and nose with the oxygen mask; he was nodding *yes*, but it hurt him to move his head and he was making a torturous endeavor just to breathe.

"Kittredge is *gay*?" I asked Tom Atkins, but this stimulated a prolonged coughing fit, which was followed by a self-contradictory nodding and shaking of his head. With my help, Atkins lifted the oxygen mask away from his mouth and nose—albeit briefly.

"Kittredge looks *exactly* like his mother!" Atkins gasped; then he was back on the mask, making the most horrible sucking sounds. I didn't want to agitate him more than my presence already had. Atkins had closed his eyes again, though his face was frozen in more of a grimace than a smile, when I heard Elaine calling me.

I found Elaine with Mrs. Atkins and the children in the kitchen. "He shouldn't be on the oxygen if no one's watching him—not for long, anyway," Sue Atkins said when she saw me.

"No, Mom—that's not quite what Charles says," Peter corrected her. "We just have to keep checking the tank."

"For God's sake, Peter—please stop criticizing me!" Mrs. Atkins cried; this made her breathless. "That old tank is probably *empty*! Oxygen doesn't really *help* him!" She coughed and coughed.

"Charles shouldn't allow the oxygen tank to be *empty*!" the boy said indignantly. "Daddy doesn't *know* the oxygen doesn't help him—sometimes he *thinks* it helps."

"I hate Charles," the girl, Emily, said.

"Don't hate Charles, Emily—we need Charles," Sue Atkins said, trying to catch her breath.

I looked at Elaine; I felt truly lost. It surprised me that Emily was sitting next to Elaine on a couch facing the kitchen TV, which was off; the girl was curled up beside Elaine, who had her arm around the thirteen-year-old's shoulders.

"Tom believes in your *character*, Bill," Mrs. Atkins said to me (as if my *character* had been under discussion for hours). "Tom hasn't known you for twenty years, yet he believes he can judge your character by the novels you write."

"Which are made up, which are make-believe—right?" Peter asked me.

"Please don't, Peter," Sue Atkins said tiredly, still struggling to suppress that not-so-innocent cough.

"That's right, Peter," I said.

"All this time, I thought Tom was seeing *him*," Sue Atkins said to Elaine, pointing at me. "But Tom must have been seeing that other guy—the one you were *all* so crazy about."

"I don't think so," I said to Mrs. Atkins. "Tom told me he had 'seen' him—not that he '*was* seeing' him. There's a difference."

"Well, what do I know? I'm just the wife," Sue Atkins said.

"Do you mean Kittredge, Billy—is that who she means?" Elaine asked me.

"Yes, that's his name—Kittredge. I think Tom was in love with him—I guess you *all* were," Mrs. Atkins said. She was a little feverish, or maybe it was the drugs she was taking—I couldn't tell. I knew the Bactrim had given poor Tom a rash; I didn't know where. I had only a vague idea of what other side effects were possible with Bactrim. I just knew that Sue Atkins had *Pneumocystis* pneumonia, so she was probably taking Bactrim and she definitely had a fever.

Mrs. Atkins seemed numb, as if she were barely aware that her children, Emily and Peter, were right there with us—in the kitchen.

"Hey—it's just me!" a man's voice called from the vestibule. The girl, Emily, screamed—but she didn't detach herself from Elaine's encompassing arm.

"It's just Charles, Emily," her brother, Peter, said.

"I *know* it's Charles—I hate him," Emily said.

"Stop it, both of you," their mother said.

"Who's Kittredge?" Peter Atkins asked.

"I would like to know who he is, too," Sue Atkins said. "God's gift to men *and* women, I guess."

"What did Tom say about Kittredge, Billy?" Elaine asked me. I'd been hoping to have this conversation on the train, where we would be alone—or not to have it, ever.

"Tom said he had *seen* Kittredge—that's all," I told Elaine. But I knew that *wasn't* all. I didn't know what Atkins had meant—that Kittredge was not at all who we thought he was; that Kittredge was more like us than we ever imagined.

That poor Tom thought Kittredge was *beautiful*—well, *that* I had no trouble imagining. But Atkins had seemed to indicate that Kittredge was and wasn't gay; according to Tom, Kittredge looked *exactly* like his mother! (I wasn't about to tell Elaine *that*!) How could Kittredge look *exactly* like Mrs. Kittredge? I was wondering.

Emily screamed. It must be Charles, the nurse, I thought, but no—it was Jacques, the dog. The old Lab was standing there, in the kitchen.

"It's just Jacques, Emily—he's a *dog,* not a *man,*" Peter said disdainfully to his sister, but the girl wouldn't stop screaming.

"Leave her alone, Peter. Jacques is a *male* dog—maybe that did it," Mrs. Atkins said. But when Emily didn't or couldn't stop screaming, Sue Atkins said to Elaine and me: "Well, it *is* unusual to see Jacques anywhere but at Tom's bedside. Since Tom got sick, that dog won't leave him. We have to drag Jacques outside to *pee!*"

"We have to offer Jacques a treat just to get him to come to the kitchen and *eat,*" Peter Atkins was explaining, while his sister went on screaming.

"Imagine a Lab you have to force to *eat!*" Sue Atkins said; she suddenly looked again at the old dog and started screaming. Now Emily and Mrs. Atkins were both screaming.

"It must be Tom, Billy—something's happened," Elaine said, over the screaming. Either Peter Atkins heard her, or he'd figured it out by himself—he was clearly a smart boy.

"Daddy!" the boy called, but his mother grabbed him and clutched him to her.

"Wait for Charles, Peter—Charles is with him," Mrs. Atkins managed to say, though her shortness of breath had worsened. Jacques (the Labrador) sat there, just breathing.

Elaine and I chose not to "wait for Charles." We left the kitchen and ran along the downstairs hall to the now-open door to Tom's one-time study. (Jacques, who—for a hesitant second—seemed of a mind to follow us, stayed behind on the kitchen floor. The old dog must have known that his master had departed.) Elaine and I entered the transformed room, where we saw Charles bent over the body on the hospital bed, which the nurse had elevated to ease his task. Charles kept his head down; he did not look up at Elaine and me, though it was clear to us both that the nurse knew we were there.

I was horribly reminded of a man I'd seen a few times at the Mineshaft, that S&M club on Washington Street—at Little West Twelfth, in the Meatpacking District. (Larry would tell me the club was closed by the city's Department of Health, but that wouldn't be till '85— four years after AIDS first appeared—which was when Elaine and I were conducting our experiment in living together in San Francisco.)

The Mineshaft had a lot of disquieting action going on: There was a sling, for fist-fucking, suspended from the ceiling; there was a whole wall of glory holes; there was a room with a bathtub, where men were pissed on.

The man Charles closely resembled was a tattooed muscleman with ivory-pale skin; he had a shaved-bald head, with a black patch of whiskers on the point of his chin, and two diamond-stud earrings. He wore a black leather vest and a jockstrap, and a well-shined pair of motorcycle boots, and his job at the Mineshaft was to dispatch people who needed dispatching. He was called Mephistopheles; on his nights "off" from the Mineshaft, he would hang out at a gay black bar called Keller's. I think Keller's was on West Street, on the corner of Barrow, near the Christopher Street pier, but I never went there—no white guys I knew did. (The story I'd heard at the Mineshaft was that Mephistopheles went to Keller's to fuck black guys, or to pick fights with them, and it didn't matter to Mephistopheles which he did; the fucking and the fighting were all the same to him, which was no doubt why he fit right in at an S&M joint like the Mineshaft.)

Yet the male nurse, who was attending so carefully to my dead friend, was not that same Mephistopheles—nor were the ministrations Charles made to poor Tom's remains of a deviant or sexual nature. Charles was fussing over the Hickman catheter dangling from Atkins's unmoving chest.

"Poor Tommy—it's not my job to remove the Hickman," the nurse explained to Elaine and me. "The undertaker will pull it out. You see, there's a cuff—it's like a Velcro collar, around the tube—just inside the point where it enters the skin. Tommy's cells, his skin and body cells, have grown into that Velcro mesh. That's what keeps the catheter in place, so it doesn't fall out or get tugged loose. All the undertaker has to do is give it a very firm jerk, and out it comes," Charles told us; Elaine looked away.

"Maybe we shouldn't have left Tom alone," I told the nurse.

"Lots of people *want* to die alone," the nurse said. "I know Tommy wanted to see you—I know he had something to say. I'll bet he said it, right?" Charles asked me. He looked up at me and smiled. He was a strong, good-looking man with a crew cut and one silver earring—in the upper, cartilaginous part of his left ear. He was clean-shaven, and when he smiled, Charles looked nothing at all like the man I knew as Mephistopheles—a Mineshaft thug-enforcer.

"Yes, I think Tom said what he had to say," I told Charles. "He wanted me to keep an eye on Peter."

"Yes, well—good luck with that. I'm guessing that'll be up to Peter!" Charles said. (I'd not been *entirely* wrong to mistake him for a bouncer at the Mineshaft; Charles had some of the same cavalier qualities.)

"No, no, no!" we could hear young Peter crying all the way from the kitchen. The girl, Emily, had stopped screaming; so had her mom.

Charles was unseasonably dressed for December in New Jersey, the tight black T-shirt showing off his muscles and his tattoos.

"It didn't seem that the oxygen was working," I said to Charles.

"It was working only a little. The problem with PCP is that it's diffuse, it affects *both* lungs, and it affects your ability to get oxygen into your blood vessels—hence into your body," the nurse explained.

"Tom's hands were so cold," Elaine said.

"Tommy didn't want the ventilator," Charles continued; he appeared to be done with the Hickman catheter. The nurse was washing the crusted *Candida* from the area of Atkins's mouth. "I want to clean him up before Sue and the kids see him," Charles said.

"And Mrs. Atkins—her cough," I said. "It's just going to get worse, right?"

"It's a dry cough—sometimes it's *no* cough. People make too much of the cough. It's the shortness of breath that gets worse," the nurse told me. "Tommy just ran out of breath," Charles said.

"Charles—we want to *see* him!" Mrs. Atkins was calling.

"No, no, no," Peter kept crying.

"I *hate* you, Charles!" Emily shouted from the kitchen.

"I know you do, honey!" Charles called back. "Just give me a second—all of you!"

I bent over Atkins and kissed his clammy forehead. "I underestimated him," I said to Elaine.

"Don't cry now, Billy," Elaine told me.

I tensed up suddenly, because I thought Charles was going to hug me or kiss me—or perhaps only push me away from the raised bed—but he was merely trying to give me his business card. "Call me, William Abbott—let me know how Peter can contact you, if he wants to."

"If he wants to," I repeated, taking the nurse's card.

Usually, when anyone addressed me as "William Abbott," I could tell the person was a reader—or that he (or she) at least knew I was "the writer." But beyond my certainty that Charles was gay, I couldn't tell about the *reader* part.

"Charles!" Sue Atkins was calling breathlessly.

Elaine and I, and Charles, were all staring at poor Tom. I can't say that Tom Atkins looked "peaceful," but he was at rest from his terrible exertions to breathe.

"No, no, no," his darling boy was crying—softer now.

Elaine and I saw Charles glance up suddenly at the open doorway. "Oh, it's *you*, Jacques," the nurse said. "It's okay—*you* can come in. Come on."

Elaine and I saw each other flinch. There was no concealing which Jacques we thought had come to say good-bye to Tom Atkins. But in the doorway was *not* the *Zhak* Elaine and I had been expecting. Was it possible that, for twenty years, Elaine and I were anticipating we might see Kittredge again?

In the doorway, the old dog stood—uncertain of his next arthritic step.

"Come on, boy," Charles said, and Jacques limped forward into his former master's former study. Charles lifted one of Tom's cold hands off the side of the bed, and the old Labrador put his cold nose against it.

There were other presences in the doorway—soon to be in the small room with us—and Elaine and I retreated from poor Tom's bedside. Sue Atkins gave me a wan smile. "How nice to have met you, finally," the dying woman said. "Do stay in touch." Like Tom's father, twenty years ago, she didn't shake my hand.

The boy, Peter, didn't once look at me; he ran to his father and hugged the diminished body. The girl, Emily, glanced (albeit quickly) at Elaine; then she looked at Charles and screamed. The old dog just sat there, as he'd sat—expecting nothing—in the kitchen.

All the long way down that hall, through the vestibule (where I only now noticed an undecorated Christmas tree), and out of that *afflicted* house, Elaine kept repeating something I couldn't quite hear. In the driveway was the taxi driver from the train station, whom we'd asked to wait. (To my surprise, we'd been inside the Atkins house only for forty-five minutes or an hour; it had felt, to Elaine and me, as if we'd been there half our lives.)

"I can't hear what you're saying," I said to Elaine, when we were in the taxi.

"What happens to the duck, Billy?" Elaine repeated—loudly enough, this time, so that I could hear her.

Okay, so this is *another* epilogue, I was thinking.

"We are such stuff / As dreams are made on, and our little life / Is rounded with a sleep," Prospero says—act 4, scene 1. At one time, I'd actually imagined that *The Tempest* could and should end there.

How does Prospero begin the epilogue? I was trying to remember. Of course Richard Abbott would know, but even when Elaine and I got back to New York, I knew I didn't want to call Richard. (I wasn't ready to tell Mrs. Hadley about Atkins.)

"First line of the epilogue to *The Tempest*," I said, as casually as I could, to Elaine in that funereal taxi. "You know—the end, spoken by Prospero. How's it begin?"

" 'Now my charms are all o'erthrown,' " Elaine recited. "Is that the bit you mean, Billy?"

"Yes, that's it," I told my dearest friend. That was exactly how I felt—*o'erthrown*.

"Okay, okay," Elaine said, putting her arms around me. "You can cry now, Billy—we both can. Okay, okay."

I was trying not to think of that line in *Madame Bovary*—Atkins had absolutely hated it. You know, that moment after Emma has given herself to the undeserving Rodolphe—when she feels her heart beating, "and the blood flowing in her body like a river of milk." How that image had disgusted Tom Atkins!

Yet, as hard as it was for me to imagine—having seen the ninety-something pounds of Atkins as he lay dying, and his doomed wife, whose blood was no "river of milk" in her diseased body—Tom and Sue Atkins must have felt that way, at least once or twice.

"You're not saying that Tom Atkins told you Kittredge was *gay*—you're not telling me that, are you?" Elaine asked me on the train, as I knew she would.

"No, I'm *not* telling you that—in fact, Tom both nodded and shook his head at the *gay* word. Atkins simply wasn't clear. Tom didn't exactly say what Kittredge is or was, only that he'd 'seen' him, and that Kittredge was 'beautiful.' And there was something else: Tom said Kittredge was not at all who we thought he was, Elaine—I don't know more," I told her.

"Okay. You ask Larry if he's heard anything about Kittredge. I'll check out some of the hospices, if you check out St. Vincent's, Billy," Elaine said.

"Tom never said that Kittredge was *sick*, Elaine."

"If Tom saw him, Kittredge may be sick, Billy. Who knows where Tom went? Apparently, Kittredge went there, too."

"Okay, okay—I'll ask Larry, I'll check out St. Vincent's," I said. I waited a moment, while New Jersey passed by outside the windows of our train. "You're holding out on me, Elaine," I told her. "What makes you think that Kittredge might have the disease? What don't I know about *Mrs.* Kittredge?"

"Kittredge was an experimenter, wasn't he, Billy?" Elaine asked. "That's all I'm going on—he was an experimenter. He would fuck *anyone*, just to see what it was like."

But I knew Elaine so well; I knew when she was lying—a lie of omission, maybe, not the other kind—and I knew I would have to be patient with her, as she had once (for years) been patient with me. Elaine was such a storyteller.

"I don't know what or who Kittredge is, Billy," Elaine told me. (This sounded like the truth.)

"I don't know, either," I said.

Here we were: Tom Atkins had died; yet Elaine and I were even then thinking about Kittredge.

Chapter 13

NOT NATURAL CAUSES

It still staggers me when I remember the impossible expectations Tom Atkins had for our oh-so-youthful romance those many summers ago. Poor Tom was no less guilty of wishful thinking in the desperation of his dying days. Tom hoped I might make a suitable substitute father for his son, Peter—a far-fetched notion, which even that darling fifteen-year-old boy knew would never happen.

I maintained contact with Charles, the Atkins family nurse, for only five or six years—not more. It was Charles who told me Peter Atkins was accepted at Lawrenceville, which—until 1987, a year or two after Peter had graduated—was an all-boys' school. Compared to many New England prep schools—Favorite River Academy included—Lawrenceville was late in becoming coeducational.

Boy, did I ever hope Peter Atkins was *not*—to use poor Tom's words— "like us."

Peter went to Princeton, about five miles northeast of Lawrenceville. When my misadventure of cohabiting with Elaine ended in San Francisco, she and I moved back to New York. Elaine was teaching at Princeton in the academic year of 1987–88, when Peter Atkins was a student there. He showed up in her writing class in the spring of '88, when the fifteen-year-old we'd both met was in his early twenties. Elaine thought Peter was an economics major, but Elaine never paid any attention to what her writing students were majoring in.

"He wasn't much of a writer," she told me, "yet he had no illusions about it."

Peter's stories were all about the suicide—when she was seventeen or eighteen—of his younger sister, Emily.

I'd heard about the suicide from Charles, at the time it happened; she'd always been a "deeply troubled" girl, Charles had written. As for Tom's wife, Sue, she died a long eighteen months after Atkins was gone; she'd had Charles replaced as a nurse almost immediately after Tom's death.

"I can understand why Sue didn't want a gay man looking after her," was all Charles said about it.

I'd asked Elaine if she thought Peter Atkins was gay. "No," she'd said. "Definitely not." Indeed, it was sometime in the late nineties—a couple of years after the worst of the AIDS epidemic—when I was giving a reading in New York, and a ruddy-faced, red-haired young man (with an attractive young woman) approached me at the book signing that followed the event. Peter Atkins must have been in his early thirties then, but I had no trouble recognizing him. He still looked like Tom.

"We got a babysitter for this—that's pretty rare for us," his wife said, smiling at me.

"How are you, Peter?" I asked him.

"I've read all your books," the young man earnestly told me. "Your novels were kind of in loco parentis for me." He said the Latin slowly. "You know, 'in the place of a parent'—kind of," young Atkins said.

We just smiled at each other; there was nothing more to say. He'd said it well, I thought. His father would have been happy how his son turned out—or as happy as poor Tom ever was, about anything. Tom Atkins and I had grown up at a time when we were full of self-hatred for our sexual differences, because we'd had it drummed into our heads that those differences were wrong. In retrospect, I'm ashamed that my expressed hope for Peter Atkins was that he *wouldn't* be like Tom—or like me. Maybe, for Peter's generation, what I should have hoped for him was that he *would* be "like us"—only proud of it. Yet, given what happened to Peter's father and mother—well, it suffices to say that I thought Peter Atkins had been burdened enough.

I SHOULD PEN A brief obituary for the First Sister Players, my hometown's obdurately amateur theatrical society. With Nils Borkman dead, and with the equally violent passing of that little theater's prompter (my mother, Mary Marshall Abbott)—not to mention my late aunt, Muriel Marshall Fremont, who had wowed our town in various strident and big-bosomed roles—the First Sister Players simply slipped away. By the eighties, even in small towns, the old theaters were becoming movie houses; movies were what people wanted to see.

"More folks stayin' home and watchin' television, too, I suppose," Grandpa Harry commented. Harry Marshall himself was "stayin' home"; his days onstage *as a woman* were long gone.

It was Richard who called me, after Elmira found Grandpa Harry's body.

"No more dry-cleanin', Elmira," Harry had said, when he'd earlier seen the nurse hanging Nana Victoria's clean clothes in his closet.

"I musta misheard him," Elmira would later explain to Richard. "I thought he said, '*Not* more dry-cleanin', Elmira'—like he was teasin' me, ya know? But now I'm pretty sure he said, '*No* more dry-cleanin', Elmira'—like he knew *then* what he was gonna do."

As a favor to his nurse, Grandpa Harry had dressed himself as the old lumberman he was—jeans, a flannel shirt, "nothin' fancy," as Elmira would say—and when he'd curled up on his side in the bathtub, the way a child goes to sleep, Harry had somehow managed to shoot himself in the temple with the Mossberg .30-30, so that most of the blood was in the bathtub, and what there was of it that spattered the tile in other parts of the bathroom had presented no insurmountable difficulty for Elmira to clean.

The message on my answering machine, the night before, had been business as usual for Grandpa Harry. "No need to call me back, Bill—I'm turnin' in a bit early. I was just checkin' to be sure you were all right."

That same night—it was November 1984, a little before Thanksgiving—the message on Richard Abbott's answering machine was similar, at least in regard to Grandpa Harry "turnin' in a bit early." Richard had taken Martha Hadley to a movie in town, in what was the former theater for the First Sister Players. But the end of the message Grandpa Harry had left for Richard was a little different from the one Harry left for me. "I miss my girls, Richard," Grandpa Harry had said. (Then he'd curled up in the bathtub and pulled the trigger.) Harold Marshall was ninety, soon to be ninety-one—just a *bit* early to be turning in.

Richard Abbott and Uncle Bob decided to turn that Thanksgiving into what would serve as a remembrance of Grandpa Harry, but Harry's contemporaries—the ones who were still alive—were all in residence at the Facility. (They wouldn't be joining us for Thanksgiving dinner in Grandpa Harry's River Street home.)

Elaine and I drove up from New York together; we'd invited Larry to come with us. Larry was sixty-six; he was without a boyfriend at the moment, and Elaine and I were worried about him. Larry wasn't sick. He didn't have the disease, but he was worn out; Elaine and I had talked about it. Elaine had even said that the AIDS virus was killing Larry—"in another way."

I was happy to have Larry along for the ride. This prevented Elaine from making up any stories about whomever I was seeing at the time, man or woman. Therefore, no one was falsely accused of shitting in the bed.

Richard had invited some foreign students from Favorite River Academy for our Thanksgiving dinner; it was too far for them to go home for such a short school vacation—therefore, we were joined by two Korean girls and a lonely-looking boy from Japan. The rest of us all knew one another—not counting Larry, who'd never been to Vermont before.

Even though Grandpa Harry's River Street house was practically in the middle of town—and a short walk to the Favorite River Academy campus—First Sister itself struck Larry as a "wilderness." God knows what Larry thought of the surrounding woods and fields; the regular firearm season for deer had started, so the sound of shooting was all around. (A "*barbaric* wilderness" was what Larry called Vermont.)

Mrs. Hadley and Richard handled the kitchen chores, with help from Gerry and Helena; the latter was Gerry's new girlfriend—a vivacious, chatty woman who'd just dumped her husband and was coming out, though she was Gerry's age (forty-five) and had two grown children. Helena's "kids" were in their early twenties; they were spending the holiday with her ex-husband.

Larry and Uncle Bob had perplexingly hit it off—possibly because Larry was the exact same age Aunt Muriel would have been if Muriel hadn't been in the head-on collision that also killed my mom. And Larry loved talking to Richard Abbott about Shakespeare. I liked listening to the two of them; in a way, it was like overhearing my adolescence in the Favorite River Academy Drama Club—it was like watching a phase of my childhood pass by.

Since there were now female students at Favorite River, Richard Abbott was explaining to Larry, the casting of the Drama Club plays was very different than it had been when the academy was an all-boys' school. He'd hated having to cast those boys in the female roles, Richard said; Grandpa Harry, who was no "boy," and who'd been outstanding *as a woman,* was an exception (as were Elaine and a handful of other faculty daughters). But now that there were boys *and* girls at his disposal, Richard bemoaned what many theater directors in schools—even in colleges—are often telling me today. More girls *like* theater; there are *always* more girls. There aren't enough boys to cast in all the male parts; you have to look for plays with more female parts for all the girls, because there are almost always more girls than there are female roles to play.

"Shakespeare was very comfortable about switching sexes, Richard," Larry said provocatively. "Why don't you tell your theater kids that in those plays where there are an overabundant number of male parts, you're going to cast all the male roles with *girls,* and that you'll cast the female roles with *boys?* I think Shakespeare would have *loved* that!" (There was little doubt that *Larry* would have loved that. Larry had a gender-lens view of the world, Shakespeare included.)

"That's a very interesting idea, Larry," Richard Abbott said. "But this is *Romeo and Juliet.*" (That would be Richard's next Shakespeare play, I was guessing; I hadn't been paying that close attention to the school-calendar part of the conversation.) "There are only four female roles in the play, and only two of them really matter," Richard continued.

"Yes, yes—I know," Larry said; he was showing off. "There's Lady Montague and Lady Capulet—they're of no importance, as you say. There's really just Juliet and her Nurse, and there must be twenty or more *men!*"

"It's tempting to cast the boys as women, and the other way around," Richard admitted, "but these are just teenagers, Larry. Where do I find a boy with the balls to play Juliet?"

"Ah . . ." Larry said, and stopped. (Even Larry had no answer for that.) I remember thinking how this wasn't, and never would be, my problem. Let it be Richard's problem, I thought; I had other things on my mind.

Grandpa Harry had left his River Street house to me. What was I going to do with a five-bedroom, six-bathroom house in Vermont?

Richard had told me to hang on to it. "You'll get more for it if you sell it later, Bill," he said. (Grandpa Harry had left me a little money, too; I didn't need the additional money I could have gotten by selling that River Street house—at least, not yet.)

Martha Hadley vowed to organize an auction to get rid of the unwanted furniture. Harry had left some money for Uncle Bob, and for Richard Abbott; Grandpa Harry had left the largest sum for Gerry—in lieu of leaving her a share of the house.

It was the house I'd been born in—the house I'd grown up in, until my mom married Richard. Grandpa Harry had said to Richard: "This house should be Bill's. I guess a writer will be okay livin' with the ghosts—Bill can use 'em, can't he?"

I didn't know the ghosts, or if I could use them. That Thanksgiving, what I couldn't quite imagine were the circumstances that would *ever* make me want to live in First Sister, Vermont. But I decided there was no hurry to make a decision about the house; I would hang on to it.

The ghosts sent Elaine from her bedroom to mine—the very first night we slept in that River Street house. I was in my old childhood bedroom when Elaine burst in and crawled into my bed with me. "I don't know who those women think they are," Elaine said, "but I know they're dead, and they're pissed off about it."

"Okay," I told her. I liked sleeping with Elaine, but the next night we moved into one of the bedrooms that had a bigger bed. I saw no ghosts that Thanksgiving holiday—actually, I never saw ghosts in that house.

I'd put Larry in the biggest bedroom; it had been Grandpa Harry's bedroom—the closet was still full of Nana Victoria's clothes. (Mrs. Hadley had promised me she would get rid of them when she and Richard auctioned off the unwanted furniture.) But Larry saw no ghosts; he just had a complaint about the bathtub in that bathroom.

"Uh, Bill—is this the tub where your grandfather—"

"Yes, it is," I quickly told him. "Why?"

Larry had looked for bloodstains, but the bathroom and the tub were spotlessly clean. (Elmira must have scrubbed her ass off in there!) Yet Larry had found something he wanted to show me. There was a chip in the enamel on the floor of the bathtub.

"Was that chip always there?" Larry asked me.

"Yes, always—this bathtub was chipped when I was a small child," I lied.

"So you say, Bill—so you *say*," Larry said suspiciously.

We both knew how the bathtub had been chipped. The bullet from the .30-30 must have passed through Grandpa Harry's head while he had been curled up on his side. The bullet had chipped the enamel on the floor of the bathtub.

"When you're auctioning off the old furniture," I told Richard and Martha privately, "please get rid of that bathtub."

I didn't have to specify *which* bathtub.

"You'll never live in this terrible town, Billy. You're crazy even to imagine you might," Elaine said. It was the night after our Thanksgiving dinner, and perhaps we were lying awake in bed because we'd eaten too much, and we couldn't fall asleep, or maybe we were listening for ghosts.

"When we used to live here, in this terrible town—when we were in those Shakespeare plays—was there ever, in that time at Favorite River, a boy with the balls to play Juliet?" I asked Elaine. I could feel her imagining him, as I was, in the darkness—talk about *listening for ghosts*!

"There was only one boy who had the balls for it, Billy," Elaine answered me, "but he wouldn't have been right for the part."

"Why not?" I asked her. I knew she meant Kittredge; he was pretty enough—he had the balls, all right.

"Juliet is nothing if she's not *sincere*," Elaine said. "Kittredge would have looked the part, of course, but he would have hammed it up, somehow—Kittredge didn't do *sincere*, Billy," Elaine said.

No, he didn't, I thought. Kittredge could have been anyone—he could look the part in any role. But Kittredge was never sincere; he was forever concealed—he was always just playing a part.

AT THAT THANKSGIVING DINNER, there was both awkwardness and comedy. In the latter category, the two Korean girls managed to give the Japanese boy the idea that we were eating a peacock. (I don't know how the girls conveyed the peacock idea to the lonely-looking boy, or why Fumi—the boy—was so stricken at the thought of eating a peacock.)

"No, no—it's a *turkey*," Mrs. Hadley said to Fumi, as if he were having a pronunciation problem.

Since I'd grown up in that River Street house, I found the encyclopedia and showed Fumi what a turkey looked like. "*Not* a peacock," I said. The Korean girls, Su Min and Dong Hee, were whispering in Korean; they were also giggling.

Later, after a lot of wine, it was the vivacious, chatty mother of two—now Gerry's girlfriend—who gave a toast to our extended family for welcoming her to such an "intimate" holiday occasion. It was doubtless the wine, in combination with the *intimate* word, that compelled Helena to deliver an impromptu address on the subject of her vagina— or perhaps she'd meant for her remarks to praise *all* vaginas. "I want to thank you for having me," Helena had begun. Then she got sidetracked. "I used to be someone who *hated* my vagina, but now I love it," she said. She seemed, almost immediately, to think better of her comments, because she quickly said, "Of course, I love Gerry's vagina—that goes without saying, I guess!—but it's because of Gerry that I also love my vagina, and I used to just hate it"; she was standing, a bit unsteadily, with her glass raised. "Thank you for having me," she repeated, sitting down.

I'm guessing that Uncle Bob had probably heard more toasts than anyone else at the dinner table—given all the glad-handing he did for Alumni Affairs, those back-slapping dinner parties with drunken Favorite River alums—but even Uncle Bob was rendered speechless by Helena's toast to at least two vaginas.

I looked at Larry, who I know was bursting with something to say; in an entirely different way from Tom Atkins—who had routinely overreacted to the *vagina* word, or to even the passing thought of a vagina— Larry could be counted on for a vagina reaction. "Don't," I said quietly to him, across the dinner table, because I could always tell when Larry was struggling to restrain himself; his eyes opened very wide and his nostrils flared.

But now it was the Korean girls who'd failed to understand. "A *what?*" Dong Hee had said.

"She hates, now loves, her *what?*" Su Min asked.

It was Fumi's turn to snicker; the Japanese boy had put the peacock-turkey misunderstanding behind him—the lonely-looking young man obviously knew what a vagina was.

"You know, a vagina," Elaine said softly to the Korean girls, but Su Min and Dong Hee had never heard the word—and no one at the dinner table knew the Korean for it.

"My goodness—it's where *babies* come from," Mrs. Hadley tried to explain, but she looked suddenly stricken (perhaps recalling Elaine's abortions).

"It's where everything happens—you know, down there," Elaine said to the Korean girls, but Elaine didn't *do* anything when she said "down there"; she didn't point or gesture, or indicate anything specifically.

"Well, it's not where *everything* happens—I beg to differ," Larry said, smiling; I knew he was just getting started.

"Oh, I'm so sorry—I've had too much to drink, and I forgot there were young people here!" Helena blurted out.

"Don't you worry, dear," Uncle Bob told Gerry's new girlfriend; I could tell Bob liked Helena, who was not at all similar to a long list of Gerry's previous girlfriends. "These kids are from another country, another *culture*; the things we talk about in this country are not necessarily topics for conversation in *Korea,*" the Racquet Man painfully explained.

"Oh, crap!" Gerry cried. "Just try another fucking *word!*" Gerry turned to Su Min and Dong Hee, who were still very much in the dark as far as the *vagina* word was concerned. "It's a twat, a snatch, a quim, a pussy, a muff, a honeypot—it's a *cunt,* for Christ's sake!" Gerry cried, the *cunt* word making Elaine (and even Larry) flinch.

"They get it, Gerry—please," Uncle Bob said.

Indeed, the Korean girls had turned the color of a clean sheet of unlined paper; the Japanese kid had kept up, for the most part, although both "muff" and "honeypot" had surprised him.

"Is there a picture of it somewhere, Bill—if not in the encyclopedia?" Larry asked mischievously.

"Before I forget it, Bill," Richard Abbott interjected—I could tell Richard was tactfully trying to drop the vagina subject—"what about the Mossberg?"

"The *what?*" Fumi asked, in a frightened voice; if the *muff* and *honeypot* vulgarisms for *vagina* had thrown him, the Japanese boy had never heard the *Mossberg* word before.

"What about it?" I asked Richard.

"Shall we auction it off with the furniture, Bill? You don't want to keep that old carbine, do you?"

"I'll hang on to the Mossberg, Richard," I told him. "I'll keep the ammunition, too—if I ever live here, it makes sense to have a varmint gun around."

"You're in town, Billy," Uncle Bob pointed out, about the River Street house. "You're not supposed to shoot in town—not even varmints."

"Grandpa Harry loved that gun," I said.

"He loved his wife's clothes, too, Billy," Elaine said. "Are you going to keep her clothes around?"

"I don't see you becoming a deer hunter, Bill," Richard Abbott said. "Even if you *do* decide to live here." But I wanted that Mossberg .30-30—they could all see that.

"What do you want a gun for, Bill?" Larry asked me.

"I know you're not opposed to *trying* to keep a secret, Billy," Elaine told me. "You're just not any good at keeping secrets."

Elaine had not kept many secrets from me, but if she had a secret, she knew how to keep it; I could never very successfully keep a secret, even when I wanted to keep one.

I could see that Elaine knew why I wanted to hang on to that Mossberg .30-30. Larry knew, too; he was looking at me with a hurt expression—as if he were saying (without actually saying it), "How can you conceive of not letting me *take care of you*—how can you *not* die in my arms, if you're ever dying? How can you even *imagine* sneaking off and shooting yourself, if you get sick?" (That's what Larry's look said, without the words.)

Elaine was giving me the same hurt look as Larry.

"Whatever you want, Bill," Richard Abbott said; Richard looked hurt, too—even Mrs. Hadley seemed disappointed in me.

Only Gerry and Helena had stopped paying attention; they were touching each other under the table. The vagina conversation seemed to have distracted them from what remained of our Thanksgiving dinner. The Korean girls were once more whispering in Korean; the lonely-looking Fumi was writing something down in a notebook not much bigger than the palm of his hand. (Maybe the *Mossberg* word, so he could use it in the next all-male dormitory conversation—such as, "I would really like to get into *her* Mossberg.")

"Don't," Larry said quietly to me, as I'd earlier said across the table to him.

"You should see Herm Hoyt while you're in town, Billy," Uncle Bob was saying—a welcome change of subject, or so I first imagined. "I know the coach would love to have a word with you."

"What about?" I asked Bob, with badly faked indifference, but the Racquet Man was busy; he was pouring himself another beer.

Robert Fremont, my uncle Bob, was sixty-seven. He was retiring next year, but he'd told me that he would continue to volunteer his services to Alumni Affairs, and particularly continue to contribute to the academy's alumni magazine, *The River Bulletin*. Whatever one thought of Uncle Bob's "Cries for Help from the Where-Have-You-Gone? Dept."—well, what can I say?—his enthusiasm for tracking down the school's most elusive alums made him very popular with folks in Alumni Affairs.

"What would Coach Hoyt like to have a word with me about?" I tried asking Uncle Bob again.

"I think you gotta ask him yourself, Billy," the ever-genial Racquet Man said. "You know Herm—he can be a kind of protective fella when it comes to talking about his wrestlers."

"Oh."

Maybe *not* a welcome change of subject, I thought.

IN ANOTHER TOWN, AT a later time, the Facility—"for assisted living, and beyond"—would probably have been named the Pines, or (in Vermont) the Maples. But you have to remember the place was conceived and constructed by Harry Marshall and Nils Borkman; ironically, neither of them would die there.

Someone had just died there, on that Thanksgiving weekend when I went to visit Herm Hoyt. A shrouded body was bound to a gurney, which an elderly, severe-looking nurse was standing guard over in the parking lot. "You're neither the person nor the vehicle I'm waitin' for," she told me.

"I'm sorry," I said.

"It's gonna snow, too," the old nurse said. "Then I'll have to wheel him back inside."

I tried to change the subject from the deceased to the reason for my visit, but—First Sister being the small town it was—the nurse already knew who I was visiting. "The coach is expectin' ya," she said. When she'd told me how to find Herm's room, she added: "You don't look much like a wrestler." When I told her who I was, she said: "Oh, I knew your mother and your aunt—and your grandfather, of course."

"Of course," I said.

"You're the writer," she added, with her eyes focused on the ash-end of her cigarette. I realized that she'd wheeled the body outside because she was a smoker.

I was forty-two that year; I judged the nurse to be at least as old as my aunt Muriel would have been—in the latter half of her sixties. I agreed that I was "the writer," but before I could leave her in the parking lot, the nurse said: "You were a Favorite River boy, weren't ya?"

"Yes, I was—'61," I said. I could see her scrutinizing me now; of course she would have heard everything about me and Miss Frost—everyone of a certain age had heard all about that.

"Then I guess ya knew *this* fella," the old nurse said; she passed her hand over the body bound to the gurney, but she touched nothing. "I'm guessin' he's waitin' in more ways than one!" the nurse said, exhaling an astonishing plume of cigarette smoke. She was wearing a ski parka and an old ski hat, but no gloves—the gloves would have interfered with her cigarette. It was just starting to snow—some scattered flakes were falling, not nearly enough to have accumulated on the body on the gurney.

"He's waitin' for that idiot kid from the funeral home, *and* he's waitin' in whatchamacallit!" the nurse exclaimed.

"Do you mean *purgatory?*" I asked her.

"Yes, I do—what is that, anyway?" she asked me. "*You're* the writer."

"But I don't believe in purgatory, or all the rest of it—" I started to say.

"I'm not askin' ya to believe in it," she said. "I'm askin' ya what it *is!*"

"An intermediate state, after death—" I started to answer her, but she wouldn't let me finish.

"Like Almighty God is decidin' whether to send this fella to the Underworld or the Great Upstairs—isn't that supposed to be what's goin' on there?" the nurse asked me.

"Kind of," I said. I had a limited recollection of what purgatory was *for*—for some kind of expiatory purification, if I remembered correctly. The soul, in that aforementioned intermediate state after death, was expected to *atone* for something—or so I guessed, without ever saying it. "Who is it?" I asked the old nurse; as she had done, I moved my hand safely above the body on the gurney. The nurse narrowed her eyes as she looked at me; it might have been the smoke.

"Dr. Harlow—you remember him, don'tcha? I'm guessin' it won't take the Almighty too long to decide about *him!*" the old nurse said.

I just smiled and left her to wait for the hearse in the parking lot. I didn't believe that Dr. Harlow could ever atone *enough*; I believed he was already in the Underworld, where he belonged. I hoped that the Great Upstairs had no room for Dr. Harlow—he who had been so absolute about my *affliction*.

Herm Hoyt told me that Dr. Harlow had moved to Florida after he'd retired. But when he got sick—he'd had prostate cancer; it had metastasized, as that cancer does, to bone—Dr. Harlow had asked to come back to First Sister. He'd wanted to spend his last days in the Facility. "I can't figure out why, Billy," Coach Hoyt said. "Nobody here ever liked him." (Dr. Harlow had died at age seventy-nine; I hadn't seen the bald-headed owl-fucker since he'd been a man in his fifties.)

But Herm Hoyt hadn't asked to see me because he'd wanted to tell me about Dr. Harlow.

"I'm guessing you've heard from Miss Frost," I said to her old wrestling coach. "Is she all right?"

"Funny—that's what she wanted to know about *you*, Billy," Herm said.

"You can tell her I'm all right," I said quickly.

"I never asked her to tell me the sexual details—in fact, I would just as soon know nothin' about that stuff, Billy," the coach continued. "But she said there's somethin' you should know—so you won't worry about her."

"You should tell Miss Frost I'm a top," I told him, "and I've been wearing condoms since '68. Maybe she won't worry too much about me, if she knows that," I added.

"Jeez—I'm too old for more sexual details, Billy. Just let me finish what I started to say!" Herm said. He was ninety-one, not quite a year older than Grandpa Harry, but Herm had Parkinson's, and Uncle Bob had told me that the coach was having difficulty with one of his medications; it was something Herm was supposed to take for his heart, or so Bob had thought. (The Parkinson's was why Coach Hoyt had moved into the Facility in the first place.)

"I'm not even pretendin' that I understand this, Billy, but here's what Al wanted you to know—forgive me, what *she* wanted you to know. She doesn't actually have sex," Herm Hoyt told me. "She means *not with anybody*, Billy—she just doesn't ever *do* it. She's gone to a world of trouble to make herself a woman, but she doesn't ever have sex—not with men *or* women, I'm tellin' you, not *ever*. There's somethin' *Greek* about what she does—she said you knew all about it, Billy."

"Intercrural," I said to the old wrestling coach.

"That's it—that's what she called it!" Herm cried. "It's nothin' but rubbin' your thing between the other fella's thighs—it's just *rubbin'*, isn't it?" the wrestling coach asked me.

"I'm pretty sure you can't get AIDS that way," I told him.

"But she was *always* this way, Billy—that's what she wants you to know," Herm said. "She became a woman, but she could never pull the trigger."

"Pull the trigger," I repeated. For twenty-three years, I had thought of Miss Frost as *protecting* me; I'd not once imagined that—for whatever reasons, even unwillingly, or unconsciously—she was also protecting *herself*.

"No penetratin', no bein' penetrated—just *rubbin'*," Coach Hoyt repeated. "Al said—*she* said; I'm sorry, Billy—'That's as far as I can go, Herm. That's all I can do, and all I ever will do. I just like to look the part, Herm, but I can't ever pull the trigger.' That's what she told me to tell you, Billy."

"So she's *safe*," I said. "She really *is* all right, and she's going to stay all right."

"She's sixty-seven, Billy. What do you mean, 'she's *safe*'—what do you mean, 'she's gonna *stay* all right'? Nobody *stays* all right, Billy! Gettin' old isn't *safe*!" Coach Hoyt exclaimed. "I'm just tellin' you she doesn't have AIDS. She didn't want you worryin' about her havin' *AIDS*, Billy."

"Oh."

"Al Frost—sorry, *Miss* Frost to you—never did anything *safe*, Billy. Shit," the old coach said, "she may look like a woman—I know she's got the moves down pat—but she still *thinks*, if you can call it that, like a fuckin' wrestler. It's just not safe to look and act like a woman, when you still believe you could be *wrestlin'*, Billy—that's not safe at all."

Fucking *wrestlers*! I thought. They were all like Herm: Just when you imagined they were *finally* talking about other things, they kept coming back to the frigging *wrestling*; they were *all* like that! It didn't make me miss the New York Athletic Club, I can tell you. But Miss Frost *wasn't* like other wrestlers; she'd put the wrestling behind her—at least that had been my impression.

"What are you saying, Herm?" I asked the old coach. "Is Miss Frost going to pick up some guy and try to *wrestle* him? Is she going to pick a fight?"

"Some guys aren't gonna be satisfied with the *rubbin'* part, are they?" Herm asked me. "She won't pick a fight—she doesn't *pick* fights, Billy— but I know Al. She's not gonna back down from a fight—not if some dickhead who wanted more than a *rubbin'* picks a fight with her."

I didn't want to think about it. I was still trying to adjust to the *intercrural* part; I was frankly relieved that Miss Frost didn't—that she truly *couldn't*— have AIDS. At the time, that was more than enough to think about.

Yes, it crossed my mind to wonder if Miss Frost was happy. Was she disappointed in herself that she could never pull the trigger? "I just like to look the part," Miss Frost had told her old coach. Didn't that sound theatrical, perhaps to put Herm at ease? Didn't that sound like she was *satisfied* with intercrural sex? That was more than enough to think about, too.

"How's that duck-under, Billy?" Coach Hoyt asked me.

"Oh, I've been practicing," I told him—kind of a white lie, wasn't it? Herm Hoyt looked frail; he was trembling. Maybe it was the Parkinson's, or one of the medications he was taking—the one for his heart, if Uncle Bob was right.

We hugged each other good-bye; it was the last time I would see him. Herm Hoyt would die of a heart attack at the Facility; Uncle Bob would be the one to break the news to me. "The coach is gone, Billy—you're on your own with the duck-unders." (It would be just a few years down the road; Herm Hoyt would be ninety-five, if I remember correctly.)

When I left the Facility, the old nurse was still standing outside smoking, and Dr. Harlow's shrouded body was still lying there, bound to the gurney. "Still waitin'," she said, when she saw me. The snow was now starting to accumulate on the body. "I've decided *not* to wheel him back inside," the nurse informed me. "He can't feel the snow fallin' on him."

"I'll tell you something about him," I said to the old nurse. "He's exactly the same now as he always was—dead certain."

She took a long drag on her cigarette and blew the smoke over Dr. Harlow's body. "I'm not quarrelin' with *you* over language," she told me. "*You're* the writer."

ONE SNOWY DECEMBER NIGHT after that Thanksgiving, I stood on Seventh Avenue in the West Village, looking uptown. I was outside that last stop of a hospital, St. Vincent's, and I was trying to force myself to go inside. Where Seventh Avenue ran into Central Park—exactly at that distant intersection—was the coat-and-tie, all-male bastion of the New York Athletic Club, but the club was too far north from where I stood for me to see it.

My feet wouldn't move. I couldn't have crawled as far as West Twelfth Street, or to West Eleventh; if a speeding taxi had collided with another taxi at the nearby intersection of Greenwich Avenue and Seventh, I couldn't have saved myself from the flying debris.

The falling snow made me miss Vermont, but I was absolutely paralyzed at the thought of moving "home"—so to speak—and Elaine had

suggested we try living together, but not in New York. I was further paralyzed by the idea of trying to live *anywhere* with Elaine; I both wanted to
try it and was afraid to do it. (I unfortunately suspected that Elaine was
motivated to live with me because she mistakenly believed this would
"save" me from having sex with men—and I would therefore be "safe"
from ever getting AIDS—but I knew that no one person could rescue me
from wanting to have sex with men *and* women.)

And if the abovementioned thoughts weren't paralyzing enough, I
was also rooted like a tree to that Seventh Avenue sidewalk because
I was utterly ashamed of myself. I was—once again—poised to cruise
those mournful corridors of St. Vincent's, *not* because I'd come to visit
and comfort a dying friend or a former lover, but because I was, absurdly,
looking for Kittredge.

It was almost Christmas, 1984, and Elaine and I were still searching that sacred hospital—and various hospices—for a cruel boy who had
abused us when we were all oh-so-young.

Elaine and I had been looking for Kittredge for three years. "Let him
go," Larry had told us both. "If you find him, he'll only disappoint you—
or hurt you again. You're both in your forties. Aren't you a little old to be
exorcising a demon from your unhappy lives as *teenagers?*" (There was no
way Lawrence Upton could say the *teenagers* word nicely.)

These factors must have contributed to my paralysis on Seventh
Avenue in the West Village this snowy December night, but the fact
that Elaine and I were behaving as if we were teenagers—that is, as far
as Kittredge was concerned—doubtless contributed to my tears. (As a
teenager, I had cried a lot.) Thus I was standing outside St. Vincent's
crying, when the older woman in the fur coat came up to me. She was an
expensive-looking little woman in her sixties, but she was notably pretty;
I might have recognized her if she'd still been attired in the sleeveless
dress and straw hat she was wearing on the occasion of my first meeting
her, when she'd declined to shake my hand. When Delacorte had introduced me to his mom at our graduation from Favorite River, he'd told
her: "This is the guy who was *going to be* Lear's Fool."

No doubt Delacorte had also told his mother the story of my having
had sex with the transsexual town librarian, which had prompted Mrs.
Delacorte to say—as she said again to me that wintry night on Seventh
Avenue—"I'm so sorry for your *troubles.*"

I couldn't speak. I knew that I knew her, but it had been twenty-three years; I didn't remember *how* I knew her, or when and where. But now she was not opposed to touching me; she grasped both my hands and said, "I know it's hard to go in there, but it means so much to the one you're visiting. I'll go with you, I'll help you do this—if you help me. It's even hard for me, you know. It's my *son* who's dying," Mrs. Delacorte told me, "and I wish I could *be* him. I want *him* to be the one who's going to go on living. I don't want to go on living *without* him!" she cried.

"Mrs. *Delacorte?*" I guessed—only because I saw something in her tormented face that reminded me of Delacorte's near-death expressions as a wrestler.

"Oh, it's *you!*" she cried. "You're that *writer* now—Carlton talks about you. You're Carlton's friend from school. You've come to see *Carlton*, haven't you? Oh, he'll be so glad to see you—you *must* come inside!"

Thus I was dragged to Delacorte's deathbed in that hospital where so many ill and wasting-away young men were lying in their beds, dying.

"Oh, *Carlton*—look who's here, look who's come to see you!" Mrs. Delacorte announced in that doorway, which was like so many hopeless doorways in St. Vincent's. I hadn't even known Delacorte's first name; at Favorite River, no one had ever called him *Carlton*. He was just plain Delacorte there. (Once Kittredge had called him Two Cups, because of the paper cups that so often accompanied him—due to the insane weight-cutting, and the constant rinsing and spitting, which Delacorte had been briefly famous for.)

Of course, I'd seen Delacorte when he was cutting weight for wrestling—when he looked like he was starving—but he was *really* starving now. (It suffices to say that I knew what the Hickman catheter in Delacorte's skeletal birdcage of a chest was for.) They'd had him on a breathing machine, Mrs. Delacorte had told me when we were en route to his room, but he was off it for now. They'd been experimenting with sublingual morphine, versus morphine elixir, Mrs. Delacorte had also explained; Delacorte was on morphine, either way.

"At this point, the suction is very important—to help clear secretions," Mrs. Delacorte had said.

"At this point, yes," I'd lamely repeated. I was numb; I felt frozen on my feet, as if I were still standing paralyzed on Seventh Avenue in the falling snow.

"This is the guy who was *going to be* Lear's Fool," Delacorte was struggling to say to his mother.

"Yes, yes—I know, dear, I know," the little woman was telling him.

"Did you bring more cups?" he asked her. I saw he was holding two paper cups; they were absolutely empty cups, his mother would later tell me. She was always bringing more cups, but there was no need for rinsing and spitting now; in fact, when they were trying the morphine under his tongue, Delacorte wasn't supposed to rinse or spit—or so Mrs. Delacorte thought. He just wanted to *hold* the paper cups for some foolish reason, she said.

Delacorte also had cryptococcal meningitis; his brain was affected—he had headaches, his mom told me, and he was often delirious. "This guy was Ariel in *The Tempest*," Delacorte said to his mother, upon my first visit to his room—and on the occasion of every later visit. "He was Sebastian in *Twelfth Night*," Delacorte told his mom repeatedly. "It was the *shadow* word that prevented him from being Lear's Fool, which was why I got the part," Delacorte raved.

Later, when I visited him with Elaine, Delacorte even reiterated my onstage history to her. "He didn't come to see me die, when I was Lear's Fool—of course I understand," Delacorte said in a most heartfelt way to Elaine. "I do appreciate that he's come to see me die now—you've both come now, and I truly appreciate it!" he told us.

Delacorte not once called me by name, and I truly can't remember if he ever did; I don't recall him once addressing me as either Bill or Billy when we were Favorite River students. But what does that matter? I didn't even know what his first name *was*! Since I'd not seen him onstage as Lear's Fool, I have a more permanent picture of Delacorte from *Twelfth Night*; he played Sir Andrew Aguecheek—declaring to Sir Toby Belch (Uncle Bob), "O, had I but followed the arts!"

Delacorte died after several days of near-total silence, with the two clean paper cups held shakily in his hands. Elaine was there that day, with Mrs. Delacorte and me, and—coincidentally—so was Larry. He'd spotted Elaine and me from the doorway of Delacorte's room, and had poked his head inside. "Not the one you were looking for, or is it?" Larry had asked.

Elaine and I both shook our heads. A very tired Mrs. Delacorte was dozing while her son slipped away. There was no point in introducing Delacorte to Larry; Delacorte, by his silence, seemed to have already slipped away, or else he was headed in that direction—nor did Elaine and I disturb Mrs. Delacorte to introduce her to Larry. (The little woman hadn't slept a wink for God knows how long.)

Naturally, Larry was the AIDS authority in the room. "Your friend hasn't got long," he whispered to Elaine and me; then he left us there. Elaine took Mrs. Delacorte to the women's room, because the exhausted mother was so worn out she looked as if she might fall or become lost if she went by herself.

I was alone with Delacorte only a moment. I'd grown so accustomed to his silence, I first thought that someone else had spoken. "Have you seen him?" came the faintest whisper. "Leave it to him—he was never the one to be satisfied with just *fitting in*!" Delacorte breathlessly cried.

"Who?" I whispered in the dying man's ear, but I knew who. Who *else* would Delacorte have had on his demented mind at that instant, or almost the instant, of his death? Delacorte died minutes later, with his mother's small hands on his wasted face. Mrs. Delacorte asked Elaine and me if she could have a moment alone with her son's body; of course we complied.

Bullshit or not, it was Larry who later told us that we *shouldn't* have left Mrs. Delacorte alone in the room with her son's body. "A single mom, right—an only child, I'm guessing?" Larry said. "And when there's a Hickman catheter, Bill, you don't want to leave *any* loved one alone with the body."

"I didn't *know*, Larry—I've never *heard* of such a thing!" I told him.

"Of course you haven't heard of such a thing, Bill—you're not *involved*! How would you have *heard*? You're exactly like him, Elaine," Larry told her. "The two of you are keeping *such* a distance from this disease—you're barely *bystanders*!"

"Don't pull rank on us, Larry," Elaine said.

"Larry is *always* pulling rank, one way or another," I said.

"You know, you're not just bisexual, Bill. You're bi-*everything*!" Larry told me.

"What's that supposed to mean?" I asked him.

"You're a solo pilot, aren't you, Bill?" Larry asked me. "You're cruising solo—no copilot has any clout with you." (I still have no idea what Larry meant.)

"Don't pull rank on us, Mr. Florence Fucking Nightingale," Elaine said to Larry.

Elaine and I had been standing in the corridor outside Delacorte's room, when one of the nurses passed by and paused to speak to us. "Is Carlton—" the nurse started to say.

"Yes, he's gone—his mother is with him," Elaine said.

"Oh, dear," the nurse said, stepping quickly into Delacorte's room, but she got there too late. Mrs. Delacorte had done what she wanted to do—what she'd probably *planned* to do, once she knew her son was going to die. She must have had the needle and a syringe in her purse. She'd stuck the needle into the end of the Hickman catheter; she'd drawn some blood out of the Hickman, but she emptied that first syringe into the wastebasket. The first syringe was mostly full of heparin. Mrs. Delacorte had done her homework; she knew that the second syringe would be almost entirely Carlton's blood, teeming with the virus. Then she'd injected herself, deep into her gluteus, with about five milliliters of her son's blood. (Mrs. Delacorte would die of AIDS in 1989; she died in hospice care in her apartment, in New York.)

At Elaine's insistence, I took Mrs. Delacorte uptown in a taxi—after she'd given herself a lethal dose of her beloved Carlton's blood. She had a tenth-floor apartment in one of those innocuously perfect buildings with an awning and a doorman on Park Avenue and East Seventy- or Eighty-something.

"I don't know about you, but *I'm* going to have a drink," she told me. "Please come in." I did.

It was hard to fathom why Delacorte had died at St. Vincent's, when Mrs. Delacorte could clearly have provided more comfortable hospice care for him in her own Park Avenue apartment. "Carlton always objected to feeling privileged," Mrs. Delacorte explained. "He wanted to die like Everyman—that's what he said. He wouldn't let me provide him with hospice care here, even though they could probably have used the extra room at St. Vincent's—as I told him, many times," she said.

They no doubt *did* need the extra room at St. Vincent's, or they soon would. (Some people waited to die in the corridors there.)

"Would you like to see Carlton's room?" Mrs. Delacorte asked me, when we both had a drink in hand, and I don't drink—nothing but beer. I had a whiskey with Mrs. Delacorte; maybe it was bourbon. I would have done anything that little woman wanted. I even went with her to Delacorte's childhood room.

I found myself in a museum of what had been Carlton Delacorte's privileged life in New York, before he'd been sent "away" to Favorite River Academy; it was a fairly common story that Delacorte's leaving home had coincided with his parents getting a divorce, about which Mrs. Delacorte was candid with me.

More surprising, Mrs. Delacorte was no less candid about the prevailing cause of her separation and divorce from young Carlton's father; her husband had been a raving homo-hater. The man had called Carlton a fairy and a little fag; he'd berated Mrs. Delacorte for allowing the effeminate boy to dress up in his mother's clothes and paint his lips with her lipstick.

"Of course I *knew*—probably long before Carlton did," Mrs. Delacorte told me. She seemed to be favoring her right buttock; such a deep intramuscular injection had to hurt. "Mothers *know*," she said, unconsciously limping a little. "You can't *force* children to become something they're not. You can't simply tell a boy not to play with dolls."

"No, you can't," I said; I was looking at all the photographs in the room—pictures of the unguarded Delacorte, before I knew him. He'd been just a little boy once—one who'd like nothing better than to dress and make himself up as a little girl.

"Oh, look at this—just look," the little woman suddenly said; the ice cubes were clicking together in her near-empty glass as she reached and untacked a photo from a bulletin board of photographs in her departed son's bedroom. "Look at how *happy* he was!" Mrs. Delacorte cried, handing me the photo.

I'm guessing that Delacorte was eleven or twelve in the picture; I had no difficulty recognizing his impish little face. Certainly, the lipstick had accentuated his grin. The cheap mauve wig—with a pink streak—was ridiculous; it was one of those wigs you can find in a Halloween-type costume shop. And of course Mrs. Delacorte's dress was too big for the boy, but the overall effect was hilarious and endearing—well, not if you were Mr. Delacorte, I guess. There was a taller, slightly older-looking girl in the photograph with Delacorte—a very pretty girl, but with short hair (as closely cut as a boy's) and an arrestingly confident but tight-lipped smile.

"This day didn't end well. Carlton's father came home and was furious to see Carlton like this," Mrs. Delacorte was saying as I looked more closely at the photo. "The boys had been having such a wonderful time, and that tyrant of a man ruined it!"

"The boys," I repeated. The very pretty girl in the photograph was Jacques Kittredge.

"Oh, you know him—I know you do!" Mrs. Delacorte said, pointing at the oh-so-perfectly cross-dressed Kittredge. He'd applied his lipstick far more expertly than Delacorte had applied his, and one of Mrs. Delacorte's beautiful but old-fashioned dresses was an exquisite fit. "The *Kittredge* boy," the little woman said. "He went to Favorite River—he was a wrestler, too. Carlton was always in awe of him, I think, but he was a devil—that boy. He could be charming, but he was a devil."

"How was Kittredge a devil?" I asked Mrs. Delacorte.

"I know he stole my clothes," she said. "Oh, I gave him some old things I didn't want—he was always asking me if he could have my clothes! 'Oh, *please*, Mrs. Delacorte,' he would say, 'my mother's clothes are *huge*, and she doesn't let me try them on—she says I always mess them up!' He just went on, and on, like that. And then my clothes started disappearing—I mean things I know perfectly well I would *never* have given him."

"Oh."

"I don't know about you," Mrs. Delacorte said, "but *I'm* going to have another drink." She left me to fix herself a second whiskey; I looked at all the other photos on the bulletin board in Delacorte's childhood bedroom. There were three or four photographs with Kittredge in the picture—always *as a girl*. When Mrs. Delacorte came back to her dead son's room, I was still holding the photo she'd handed me.

"Please take it," she told me. "I don't like remembering how that day ended."

"Okay," I said. I still have that photograph, though I don't like remembering any part of the day Carlton Delacorte died.

DID I TELL ELAINE about Kittredge and Mrs. Delacorte's clothes? Did I show Elaine that photo of Kittredge *as a girl*? No, of course not—Elaine was holding out on *me*, wasn't she?

Some guy Elaine knew got a Guggenheim; he was a fellow writer, and he told Elaine that his seedy eighth-floor apartment on Post Street was the perfect place for two writers.

"Where's Post Street?" I asked Elaine.

"Near Union Square, he said—it's in San Francisco, Billy," Elaine told me.

I didn't know San Francisco at all; I only knew there were a lot of gays there. Of course I knew there were gay men dying in big numbers in San Francisco, but I didn't have any close friends or former lovers there, and Larry wouldn't be there to bully me about getting more *involved*. There was another incentive: Elaine and I couldn't (or wouldn't) keep looking for Kittredge—not in San Francisco, or so we'd thought.

"Where's your friend going on his Guggenheim?" I asked Elaine.

"Somewhere in Europe," Elaine said.

"Maybe we should try living together in Europe," I suggested.

"The apartment in San Francisco is available now, Billy," Elaine told me. "And, for a place that will accommodate two writers, it's so *cheap*."

When Elaine and I got a look at our view from the eighth floor of that rat's-ass apartment—those uninspiring rooftops on Geary Street, and that bloodred vertical sign for the Hotel Adagio (the neon for HOTEL was burned out before we arrived in San Francisco)—we could understand why that two-writer apartment was so *cheap*. It should have been *free*!

But if Tom and Sue Atkins dying of AIDS struck Elaine and me as too much, we couldn't stand what Mrs. Delacorte had done to herself, nor have I *ever* heard that such a drawn-out death was a common suicide plan of the loved ones of AIDS victims, particularly (as Larry had so knowingly told Elaine and me) among single moms who were losing their only children. But, as Larry also said, how would I have heard about anything like that? (It was true, as he'd said, that I wasn't *involved*.)

"You're going to try living together in San Francisco," Larry said to Elaine and me, as if we were runaway children. "Oh, my—a little late to be *lovebirds*, isn't it?" (I thought Elaine was going to hit him.) "And, pray tell, what made you choose San Francisco? Have you heard there are no gay men dying there? Maybe we *all* should move to San Francisco!"

"Fuck you, Larry," Elaine said.

"Dear Bill," Larry said, ignoring her, "you can't run away from a plague—not if it's *your* plague. And don't tell me that AIDS is too Grand Guignol for your taste! Just look at what you *write*, Bill—*overkill* is your middle name!"

"You've taught me a lot," was all I could tell him. "I didn't stop loving you, Larry, just because I stopped being your lover. I still love you."

"More overkill, Bill," was all Larry said; he couldn't (or wouldn't) even look at Elaine, and I knew how fond he was of her—*and* of her writing.

"I was never as intimate with anyone as I was with that awful woman," Elaine had told me about Mrs. Kittredge. "I will never be as close to anyone again."

"*How* intimate?" I'd asked her; she'd not answered me.

"It's his mother who *marked* me!" Elaine had cried, about that afore-mentioned *awful woman*. "It's *her* I'll never forget!"

"Marked you *how?*" I'd asked her, but she'd begun to cry, and we had done our *adagio* thing; we'd just held each other, saying nothing—doing our *slowly, softly, gently* routine. That was how we'd lived together in San Francisco, for what amounted to almost all of 1985.

A lot of people left where they were living in the middle of the AIDS crisis; many of us moved somewhere else, hoping it would be better—but it wasn't. There was no harm in trying; at least living together didn't harm Elaine and me—it just didn't work out for us to be lovers. "If that part were ever going to work," Martha Hadley would tell us, but only after we'd ended the experiment, "I think it would have clicked when you were kids—not in your forties."

Mrs. Hadley had a point, as always, but Elaine and I didn't entirely have a bad year together. I kept the photograph of Kittredge and Delacorte in dresses and lipstick as a bookmark in whatever book I was reading, and I left the particular book lying around in the usual places—on the night table on my side of the bed; on the kitchen countertop, next to the coffeemaker; in the small, crowded bathroom, where it would be in Elaine's way. Well, Elaine's eyesight was awful.

It took almost a year for Elaine to *see* that photo; she came out of the bathroom, naked—she was holding the picture in one hand, and the book I'd been reading in the other. She had her glasses on, and she threw the book at me!

"Why didn't you just *show* it to me, Billy? I knew it was Delacorte, months ago," Elaine told me. "As for the other kid, I just thought he was a *girl!*"

"Quid pro quo," I said to my dearest friend. "You've got something to tell me, too—don't you?"

It's easy to see, with hindsight, how it might have gone better for us in San Francisco if we'd just told each other what we knew about Kittredge when we'd first heard about it, but you live your life at the time you live it—you don't have much of an overview when what's happening to you is still happening.

The photograph of Kittredge *as a girl* did not make him look—as his mother had allegedly described him to Elaine—like a "sickly little boy"; he (or that pretty girl in the picture) didn't look like a child who had "no confidence," as Mrs. Kittredge had supposedly told Elaine. Kittredge didn't look like a kid who was "picked on by the other children, especially by the boys," or so (I'd been told) that awful woman had said.

"Mrs. Kittredge *said* that to you, right?" I asked Elaine.

"Not exactly," Elaine mumbled.

It had been even harder for me to believe that Kittredge "was once intimidated by girls," not to mention that Mrs. Kittredge had seduced her son so that he would gain confidence—not that I'd ever completely believed this had happened, as I reminded Elaine.

"It happened, Billy," Elaine said softly. "I just didn't like the reason—I changed the *reason* it happened."

I told Elaine about Kittredge stealing Mrs. Delacorte's clothes; I told her what Delacorte had breathlessly cried, just before he died. Delacorte had clearly meant Kittredge—"he was never the one to be satisfied with just *fitting in!*"

"I didn't want you to like him or forgive him, Billy," Elaine told me. "I hated him for the way he just handed me over to his mother; I didn't want you to pity him, or have sympathy for him. I wanted you to hate him, too."

"I *do* hate him, Elaine," I told her.

"Yes, but that's not all you feel for him—I know," she told me.

Mrs. Kittredge *had* seduced her son, but no real or imagined lack of confidence on the young Kittredge's part was ever the reason. Kittredge had always been very confident—even (indeed, most of all) about wanting to be a *girl*. His vain and misguided mother had seduced him for the most familiar and stupefying reasoning that many gay or bi young men commonly encounter—if not *usually* from their own mothers. Mrs. Kittredge believed that all her little boy needed was a positive sexual experience with a woman—that would surely bring him to his senses!

How many of us gay or bi men have heard this bullshit before? Someone who ardently believes that all we need is to get laid—that is, the "right" way—and we'll never so much as *imagine* having sex with another man!

"You should have told me," I said to Elaine.

"You should have shown me the photograph, Billy."

"Yes, I should have—we both 'should have.'"

Tom Atkins and Carlton Delacorte had seen Kittredge, but how recently had they seen him—and where? What was clear to Elaine and me was that Atkins and Delacorte had seen Kittredge *as a woman*.

"A pretty one, too, I'll bet," Elaine said to me. Atkins had used the *beautiful* word.

It had been hard enough for Elaine and me, just living together in San Francisco. With Kittredge back on our minds—not to mention the *as a woman* part—staying together in San Francisco seemed no longer tenable.

"Just don't call Larry—not yet," Elaine said.

But I *did* call Larry; for one thing, I wanted to hear his voice. And Larry knew everything and everyone; if there was an apartment to rent in New York, Larry would know where it was and who owned it. "I'll find you a place to stay in New York," I told Elaine. "If I can't find two places in New York, I'll try living in Vermont—you know, I'll just *try* it."

"Your house has no furniture in it, Billy," Elaine pointed out.

"Ah, well . . ."

That was when I called Larry.

"I just have a cold—it's nothing, Bill," Larry said, but I could hear his cough, and that he was struggling to suppress it. There was no pain with that dry PCP cough; it wasn't a cough like the one you get with pleurisy, and there was no phlegm. It was the shortness of breath that was worrisome about *Pneumocystis* pneumonia, and the fever.

"What's your T-cell count?" I asked him. "When were you going to tell me? Don't bullshit me, Larry!"

"Please come home, Bill—you *and* Elaine. Please, *both* of you, come home," Larry said. (Just that—not a long speech—and he was out of breath.)

Where Larry lived, and where he would die, was on a pretty, tree-lined part of West Tenth Street—just a block north of Christopher Street, and an easy walk to Hudson Street or Sheridan Square. It was a narrow, three-story town house, generally not affordable to a poet—or to most other writers, Elaine and me included. But an iron-jawed heiress and grande dame among Larry's poetry patrons—the *patroness*, as I thought of her—had left the house to Larry, who would leave it to Elaine and me. (Not that Elaine and I could afford to keep it—we would eventually be forced to sell that lovely house.)

When Elaine and I moved in—to help the live-in nurse look after Larry—it was not the same as living "together"; we were done with that experiment. Larry's house had five bedrooms; Elaine and I had our own bedrooms and our own bathrooms. We took turns doing the night shift with Larry, so the sleep-in nurse could actually sleep; the nurse, whose name was Eddie, was a calm young man who tended to Larry all day—in theory, so that Elaine and I could write. But Elaine and I didn't write very much, or very well, in those many months when Larry was wasting away.

Larry was a good patient, perhaps because he'd been an excellent nurse to so many patients before he got sick. Thus my mentor, and my old friend and former lover, became (when he was dying) the same man I'd admired when I first met him—in Vienna, more than twenty years before. Larry would be spared the worst progression of the esophageal candidiasis; he had no Hickman catheter. He wouldn't hear of a ventilator. He did suffer from the spinal-cord disease vacuolar myelopathy; Larry grew progressively weak, he couldn't walk or even stand, and he was incontinent—about which he was, but only at first, vain and embarrassed. (Truly not for long.) "It's my *penis*, again, Bill," Larry would soon say with a smile, whenever there was an incontinence issue.

"Ask Billy to say the plural, Larry," Elaine would chime in.

"Oh, I know—have you ever heard anything quite like it?" Larry would exclaim. "Please say it, Bill—give us the *plural*!"

For Larry, I would do it—well, for Elaine, too. They just loved to hear that frigging plural. "Penith-zizzes," I said—always quietly, at first.

"What? I can't hear you," Larry would say.

"Louder, Billy," Elaine said.

"Penith-zizzes!" I would shout, and then Larry and Elaine would join in—all of us crying out, as loudly as we could. *"Penith-zizzes!"*

One night, our exclamations woke poor Eddie, who was trying to sleep. "What's wrong?" the young nurse asked. (There he was, in his pajamas.)

"We're saying 'penises' in another language," Larry explained. "Bill is teaching us." But it was Larry who taught me.

As I said once to Elaine: "I'll tell you who my teachers were—the ones who meant the most to me. Larry, of course, but also Richard Abbott, and—maybe the most important of all, or at the most important *time*—your mother."

Lawrence Upton died in December of '86; he was sixty-eight. (It's hard to believe, but Larry was almost the same age I am *now*!) He lived for a year in hospice care, in that house on West Tenth Street. He died on Elaine's shift, but she came and woke me up; that was the deal Elaine and I had made with each other, because we'd both wanted to be there when Larry died. As Larry had said about Russell, the night Russell died in Larry's arms: "He weighed nothing."

The night Larry died, both Elaine and I lay beside him and cradled him in our arms. The morphine was playing tricks on Larry; who knows how consciously (or not) Larry said what he said to Elaine and me? "It's my *penis* again," Larry told us. "And again, and again, and again—it's *always* my penis, isn't it?"

Elaine sang him a song, and he died when she was still singing.

"That's a beautiful song," I told her. "Who wrote it? What's it called?"

"Felix Mendelssohn wrote it," Elaine said. "Never mind what it's called. If you ever die on me, Billy, you'll hear it again. I'll tell you then what it's called."

THERE WERE A COUPLE of years when Elaine and I rattled around in that too-grand town house Larry had left us. Elaine had a vapid, nondescript boyfriend, whom I disliked for the sole reason that he wasn't substantial enough for her. His name was Raymond, and he burned his toast almost every morning, setting off the frigging smoke detector.

I was on Elaine's shit list for much of that time, because I was seeing a transsexual who kept urging Elaine to wear sexier-looking clothes; Elaine wasn't inclined to "sexier-looking."

"Elwood has bigger boobs than I have—*everybody* has," Elaine said to me. Elaine purposely called my transsexual friend Elwood, or Woody. My transsexual friend called herself El. Soon everyone would be using the *transgender* word; my friends told me I should use it, too—not to mention those terribly correct young people giving me the hairy eyeball because I continued to say "transsexual" when I was supposed to say "transgender."

I just love it when certain people feel free to tell *writers* what the correct words are. When I hear the same people use *impact* as a verb, I want to throw up!

It suffices to say that the late eighties were a time of transition for Elaine and me, though some people apparently had nothing better to do than update the frigging gender language. It was a trying two years, and the financial effort to own and maintain that house on West Tenth Street—including the killer taxes—put a strain on our relationship.

One evening, Elaine told me the story that she was sure she'd spotted Charles, poor Tom's nurse, in a room at St. Vincent's. (I'd stopped hearing from Charles.) Elaine had peered into a doorway—she was looking for someone else—and there was this shriveled former bodybuilder, his wrinkled and ruined tattoos hanging illegibly from the stretched and sagging skin of his once-powerful arms.

"Charles?" Elaine had said from the doorway, but the man had roared like an animal at her; Elaine had been too frightened to go inside the room.

I was pretty sure I knew who it was—not Charles—but I went to St. Vincent's to see for myself. It was the winter of '88; I'd not been inside that last-stop hospital since Delacorte had died and Mrs. Delacorte had injected herself with his blood. I went one more time—just to be certain that the roaring animal Elaine had seen wasn't Charles.

It was that terrifying bouncer from the Mineshaft, of course—the one they called Mephistopheles. He roared at me, too. I never set foot in St. Vincent's again. (Hello, Charles—if you're out there. If you're not, I'm sorry.)

That same winter, one night when I was out with El, I was told another story. "I just heard about this girl—you know, she was like me but a little older," El said.

"Uh-huh," I said.

"I think you knew her—she went to Toronto," El said.

"Oh, you must mean Donna," I said.

"Yeah, that's her," El said.

"What about her?" I asked.

"She's not doing too well—that's what I heard," El told me.

"Oh."

"I didn't say she was *sick*," El said. "I just heard she's not doing too well, whatever that means. I guess she was someone *special* to you, huh? I heard that, too."

I didn't do anything with this information, if you could call it that. But that night was when I got the call from Uncle Bob about Herm Hoyt dying at age ninety-five. "The coach is gone, Billy—you're on your own with the duck-unders," Bob said.

No doubt, that must have distracted me from following up on El's story about Donna. The next morning, Elaine and I had to open all the windows in the kitchen to get rid of the smoke from Raymond burning his frigging toast, and I said to Elaine: "I'm going to Vermont. I have a house there, and I'm going to try living in it."

"Sure, Billy—I understand," Elaine said. "This is too much house for us, anyway—we should sell it."

That clown Raymond just sat there, eating his burned toast. (As Elaine would say later, Raymond was probably wondering where he was going to live next; he must have known it wouldn't be with Elaine.)

I said good-bye to El—either that same day or the next one. She wasn't very understanding about it.

I called Richard Abbott and got Mrs. Hadley on the phone. "Tell Richard I'm going to try it," I told her.

"I've got my fingers crossed for you, Billy—Richard and I would *love* it if you were living here," Martha Hadley said.

That was why I was living in Grandpa Harry's River Street house, now mine, on the morning Uncle Bob called me from the office of Alumni Affairs at the academy.

"It's about Big Al, Billy," Bob said. "This isn't an obituary I would ever run, unedited, in *The River Bulletin*, but I gotta run the unedited version by you."

It was February 1990 in First Sister—colder than a witch's tit, as we say in Vermont.

Miss Frost was the same age as the Racquet Man; she'd died from injuries she suffered in a fight in a bar—she was seventy-three. The injuries were mostly head injuries, Uncle Bob told me. Big Al had found herself in a barroom brawl with a bunch of airmen from Pease Air Force Base in Newington, New Hampshire. The bar had been in Dover, or maybe in Portsmouth—Bob didn't have all the details.

"What's 'a bunch,' Bob—how many airmen were there?" I asked him.

"Uh, well, there was one airman first-class, and one airman basic, and a couple more who were only identified by the *airmen* word—that's all I can tell you, Billy," Uncle Bob said.

"*Young* guys, right? *Four* of them? Were there four of them, Bob?" I asked him.

"Yes, four. I assume they were young, Billy—if they were enlisted men and still in service. But I'm just guessing about their ages," Uncle Bob told me.

Miss Frost had probably received her head injuries after the four of them finally managed to get her down; I imagine it took two or three of them to hold her down, while the fourth man had kicked her in the head.

All four men had been hospitalized, Bob told me; the injuries to two of the four were listed as "serious." But none of the airmen had been charged; at that time, Pease was still a SAC base. According to Uncle Bob, the Strategic Air Command "disciplined" its own, but Bob admitted that he didn't truly understand how the "legal stuff" (when it came to the military) really worked. The four airmen were never identified by name, nor was there any information as to *why* four young men had a fight with a seventy-three-year-old woman, who—in their eyes—may or may not have been acceptable *as a woman.*

My guess, and Bob's, was that Miss Frost might have had a past relationship—or just a previous meeting—with one or more of the airmen. Maybe, as Herm Hoyt had speculated to me, one of the fellas had objected to the *intercrural* sex; he might have found it insufficient. Perhaps, given how young the airmen were, they knew of Miss Frost only "by reputation"; it might have been enough provocation to them that she was, in their minds, not a *real* woman—it might have been only that. (Or they were frigging homophobes—it might have been *only that,* too.)

Whatever led to the altercation, it was apparent—as Coach Hoyt had predicted—that Big Al would never back down from a fight.

"I'm sorry, Billy," Uncle Bob said.

Later, Bob and I agreed we were glad that Herm Hoyt hadn't lived to hear about it. I called Elaine in New York that night. She had her own small place in Chelsea, just a little northwest of the West Village and due north of the Meatpacking District. I told Elaine about Miss Frost, and I asked her to sing me that Mendelssohn song—the one she'd said she was saving for me, the same one she'd sung for Larry.

"I promise I won't die on your shift, Elaine. You'll never have to sing that song for me. Besides, I need to hear it now," I told her.

As for the Mendelssohn song, Elaine explained it was a small part of *Elijah*—Mendelssohn's longest work. It comes near the end of that oratorio, after God arrives (in the voice of a small child), and the angels sing blessings to Elijah, who sings his last aria—"For the Mountains Shall Depart." That's what Elaine sang to me; her alto voice was big and strong, even over the phone, and I said good-bye to Miss Frost, listening to the same music I'd heard when I was saying good-bye to Larry. Miss Frost had been lost to me for almost thirty years, but that night I knew she was gone for good, and all that Uncle Bob would say about her in *The River Bulletin* wasn't nearly enough.

> Sad tidings for the Class of '35! Al Frost: born, First Sister,
> Vermont, 1917; wrestling team captain, 1935 (undefeated);
> died, Dover or Portsmouth, New Hampshire, 1990.

"That's *it?*" I remember asking Uncle Bob.

"Shit, Billy—what else can we say in an alumni magazine?" the Racquet Man said.

When Richard and Martha were auctioning off the old furniture from Grandpa Harry's River Street house, they told me they'd found thirteen beer bottles under the living-room couch—all Uncle Bob's. (If I had to bet, all from that one party to commemorate Aunt Muriel and my mother.)

"Way to go, Bob!" I'd said to Mrs. Hadley and Richard.

I knew the Racquet Man was right. What *can* you say in a frigging alumni magazine about a transsexual wrestler who was killed in a bar fight? Not much.

I T   WAS   A   COUPLE of years later—I was slowly adjusting to living in Vermont—when I got a late-night phone call from El. It took me a second or two to recognize her voice; I think she was drunk.

"You know that friend of yours—the girl like me, but she's older?" El asked.

"You mean Donna," I said, after a pause.

"Yeah, Donna," El said. "Well, she *is* sick now—that's what I heard."

"Thank you for telling me," I was saying, when El hung up the phone. It was too late to call anybody in Toronto; I just slept on the news. I'm guessing this would have been 1992 or '93; it may even have been early in 1994. (After I moved to Vermont, I didn't pay such close attention to time.)

I had a few friends in Toronto; I asked around. I was told about an excellent hospice there—everyone I knew said it was quite a wonderful place, under the circumstances. Casey House, it was called; just recently, someone told me it still exists.

The director of nursing at Casey House, at that time, was a great guy; his first name was John, if I remember correctly, and I think he had an

Irish last name. Since I'd moved back to First Sister, I was discovering that I wasn't very good at remembering names. Besides, whenever this was, exactly—when I heard about Donna being sick—I was already fifty, or in my fifties. (It wasn't just *names* I had trouble remembering!)

John told me that Donna had been admitted to hospice care several months before. But Donna was "Don" to the nurses and other caregivers at Casey House, John had explained to me.

"Estrogen has side effects—in particular, it can affect the liver," John told me. Furthermore, estrogens can cause a kind of hepatitis; the bile stagnates and builds. "The itching that occurs with this condition was driving Don nuts," was how John put it. It was Donna herself who'd told everyone to call her Don; upon stopping the estrogens, her beard came back.

It seemed exceptionally unfair to me that Donna, who had worked so hard to feminize herself, was not only dying of AIDS; she was being forced to return to her former male self.

Donna also had cytomegalovirus. "In this case, the blindness may be a blessing," John told me. He meant that Donna was spared *seeing* her beard, but of course she could feel it—even though one of the nurses shaved her face every day.

"I just want to prepare you," John said to me. "Watch yourself. Don't call him 'Donna.' Just try not to let that name slip." In our phone conversations, I'd noticed that the director of nursing was careful to use the *he* and *him* words while discussing "Don." John not once said *she* or *her* or *Donna.*

Thus prepared, I found my way to Huntley Street in downtown Toronto—a small residential-looking street, or so it seemed to me (between Church Street and Sherbourne Street, if you know the city). Casey House itself was like a very large family's home; it had as pleasant and welcoming an atmosphere as was possible, but there's only so much you can do about bedsores and muscular wasting—or the lingering smell, no matter how hard you try to mask it, of fulminant diarrhea. Donna's room had an almost-nice lavender smell. (A bathroom deodorizer, a perfumed disinfectant—not one I would choose.) I must have held my breath.

"Is that you, Billy?" Donna asked; white splotches clouded her eyes, but she could hear okay. I'll bet she'd heard me hold my breath. Of course they'd told her I was coming, and a nurse had very recently shaved her; I was unused to the masculine smell of the shaving cream, or maybe it was an after-shave gel. Yet, when I kissed her, I could feel the beard on Donna's cheek—as I'd not once felt it when we were making love—and I could see the shadow of a beard on her clean-shaven face. She was taking Coumadin; I saw the pills on the bedside table.

I was impressed by what a good job the nurses were doing at Casey House; they were experts at accomplishing all they could to make Donna comfortable, including (of course) the pain control. John had explained to me the subtleties of sublingual morphine versus morphine elixir versus fentanyl patch, but I hadn't really been listening. John also told me that Don was using a special cream that seemed to help control his itching, although the cream was exposing Don to "a lot of steroids."

Suffice it to say, I saw that Donna was in good and caring hands at Casey House—even though she was blind, and she was dying *as a man*. While I was visiting with Donna, two of her Toronto friends also came to see her—two *very* passable transsexuals, each of them clearly dedicated to living her life *as a woman*. When Donna introduced us, I very much had the feeling that she'd forewarned them I would be there; in fact, Donna might have asked her friends to stop by when I was with her. Maybe Donna wanted me to see that she'd found "her people," and that she'd been happy in Toronto.

The two transsexuals were very friendly to me—one of them flirted with me, but it was all for show. "Oh, you're the *writer*—we know all about you!" the more outgoing but *not* flirtatious one said.

"Oh, yeah—the *bi* guy, right?" the one who was coming on to me said. (She definitely wasn't serious about it. The flirting was entirely for Donna's amusement; Donna had always loved flirting.)

"Watch out for her, Billy," Donna told me, and all three of them laughed. Given Atkins, given Delacorte, given Larry—not to mention those airmen who killed Miss Frost—it wasn't a terribly painful visit. At one point, Donna even said to her flirtatious friend, "You know, Lorna— Billy never complained that I had *too big* a cock. You *liked* my cock, didn't you, Billy?" Donna asked me.

"I certainly did," I told her, being careful *not* to say, "I certainly did, *Donna*."

"Yeah, but you told me Billy was a *top*," Lorna said to Donna; the other transsexual, whose name was Lilly, laughed. "Try being a *bottom* and see what *too big* a cock does to you!"

"You see, Billy?" Donna said. "I told you to watch out for Lorna. She's already found a way to let you know she's a bottom, and that she likes *little* cocks."

The three friends all laughed at that—I had to laugh, too. I only noticed, when I was saying good-bye to Donna, that her friends and I had not once called her by name—not Donna *or* Don. The two transsexuals waited for me when I was saying good-bye to John; I would have hated his job.

I walked with Lorna and Lilly to the Sherbourne subway station; they were taking the subway home, they said. By the way they said the *home* word, and the way they were holding hands, I got the feeling that they lived together. When I asked them where I could catch a taxi to take me back to my hotel, Lilly said, "I'm glad you mentioned what hotel you're staying in—I'll be sure to tell Donna that you and Lorna got in a *lot* of trouble."

Lorna laughed. "I'll probably tell Donna that you and Lilly got in trouble, too," Lorna told me. "Donna loves it when I say, 'Lilly never knew a cock she didn't like, big *or* little'—that cracks her up."

Lilly laughed, and I did, too, but the flirting was finished. It had all been for Donna. I kissed Donna's two friends good-bye at the Sherbourne subway station, their cheeks perfectly soft and smooth, with no hint of a beard—absolutely nothing you could feel against your face, and not the slightest shadow on their pretty faces. I still have dreams about those two.

I was thinking, as I kissed them good-bye, of what Elaine told me Mrs. Kittredge had said, when Elaine was traveling in Europe with Kittredge's mother. (This was what Mrs. Kittredge *really* said—not the story Elaine first told me.)

"I don't know what your son wants," Elaine had told Kittredge's mother. "I just know he always wants *something*."

"I'll tell you what he wants—even more than he wants to fuck us," Mrs. Kittredge said. "He wants to *be* one of us, Elaine. He doesn't want to be a boy or a man; it doesn't matter to him that he's finally so *good* at being a boy or a man. He never *wanted* to be a boy or a man in the first place!"

But if Kittredge was a woman now—if he was like Donna had been, or like Donna's two very "passable" friends—and if Kittredge had AIDS and was dying somewhere, what if they'd had to stop giving Kittredge the estrogens? Kittredge had a *very* heavy beard; I could still feel, after more than thirty years, how heavy his beard was. I had so often, and for so long, imagined Kittredge's beard scratching against my face.

Do you remember what he said to me, about transsexuals? "I regret I've never tried one," Kittredge had whispered in my ear, "but I have the impression that if you pick up one, the others will come along." (He'd been talking about the transvestites he'd seen in Paris.) "I think, if I were going to try it, I would try it in Paris," Kittredge had said to me. "But *you*, Nymph—you've already *done* it!" Kittredge had cried.

Elaine and I had seen Kittredge's single room at Favorite River Academy, most memorably (to me) the photograph of Kittredge and his mother that was taken after a wrestling match. What Elaine and I had noticed, simultaneously, was that an unseen hand had cut off Mrs. Kittredge's face and glued it to Kittredge's body. There was Kittredge's mother in Kittredge's wrestling tights and singlet. And there was Kittredge's handsome face glued to his mother's beautiful and exquisitely tailored body.

The truth was, Kittredge's face had *worked* on a woman's body, with a woman's clothes. Elaine had convinced me that Kittredge must have been the one who switched the faces in the photograph; Mrs. Kittredge couldn't have done it. "That woman has no imagination and no sense of humor," Elaine had said, in her authoritarian way.

I was back home from Toronto, having said good-bye to Donna. Lavender would never smell the same to me again, and you can imagine what an anticlimax it would be when Uncle Bob called me in my River Street house with the latest news of a classmate's death.

"You've lost another classmate, Billy—not your favorite person, if memory serves," the Racquet Man said. As vague as I am concerning when I heard the news about Donna, I can tell you *exactly* when it was that Uncle Bob called me with the news about Kittredge.

I'd just celebrated my fifty-third birthday. It was March 1995; there was still a lot of snow on the ground in First Sister, with nothing but mud season to look forward to.

Elaine and I had been talking about taking a trip to Mexico; she'd been looking at houses to rent in Playa del Carmen. I would have happily gone to Mexico with her, but she was having a boyfriend problem: Her boyfriend was a tight-assed turd who didn't want Elaine to go anywhere with me.

"Didn't you tell him we don't do it?" I asked her.

"Yes, but I also told him that we *used to* do it—or that we tried to," Elaine said, revising herself.

"Why did you tell him that?" I asked her.

"I'm trying out a new honesty policy," Elaine answered. "I'm not making up so many stories, or I'm trying not to."

"How is this policy working out with your *fiction* writing?" I asked her.

"I don't think I can go to Mexico with you, Billy—not right now," was all she'd said.

I'd had a recent boyfriend problem of my own, but when I dumped the boyfriend, I had rather soon developed a girlfriend problem. She was a first-year faculty member at Favorite River, a young English teacher. Mrs. Hadley and Richard had introduced us; they'd invited me to dinner, and there was Amanda. When I first saw her, I thought she was one of Richard's students—she looked that young to me. But she was an anxious young woman in her late twenties.

"I'm almost thirty," Amanda was always saying, as if she was anxious that she was too young-looking; therefore, saying she would soon be thirty made her seem older.

When we started sleeping together, Amanda was anxious about where we did it. She had a faculty apartment in one of the girls' dorms at Favorite River; when I spent the night with her there, the girls in the dormitory knew about it. But, most nights, Amanda had dorm duty—she couldn't stay with me in my house on River Street. The way it was working out, I wasn't sleeping with Amanda nearly enough—that was the developing problem. And then, of course, there was the *bi* issue: She'd read all my novels, she said she *loved* my writing, but that I was a bi guy made her anxious, too.

"I just can't believe you're fifty-*three!*" Amanda kept saying, which confused me. I couldn't tell if she meant I seemed so much younger than I was, or that she was appalled at herself for dating an *old* bi guy in his fifties.

Martha Hadley, who was seventy-five, had retired, but she still met with individual students who had "special needs"—pronunciation problems included. Mrs. Hadley had told me that Amanda suffered from pronunciation problems. "That wasn't why you introduced us, was it?" I asked Martha.

"It wasn't *my* idea, Billy," Mrs. Hadley said. "It was Richard's idea to introduce you to Amanda, because she is such a fan of your *writing*. I never thought it was a good idea—she's way too young for you, and she's anxious about everything. I can only imagine that, because you are *bi*—well, that's got to keep Amanda awake at night. She can't *pronounce* the word *bisexual!*"

"Oh."

That's what was going on in my life when Uncle Bob called me about Kittredge. That's why I said, half seriously, I had "nothing but mud season to look forward to"—nothing except my writing. (Moving to Vermont had been good for my writing.)

The account of Kittredge's death had been submitted to the Office of Alumni Affairs by Mrs. Kittredge.

"Do you mean he had a wife, or do you mean his mother?" I asked Uncle Bob.

"Kittredge had a wife, Billy, but we heard from the mother."

"Jesus—how old would *Mrs.* Kittredge be?" I asked Bob.

"She's only seventy-two," my uncle answered; Uncle Bob was seventy-eight, and he sounded a little insulted by my question. Elaine had told me that Mrs. Kittredge had only been eighteen when Kittredge was born.

According to Bob—that is, according to Mrs. Kittredge—my former heartthrob and tormentor had died in Zurich, Switzerland, "of natural causes."

"Bullshit, Bob," I said. "Kittredge was only a year older than I am—he was fifty-four. What 'natural causes' can kill you when you're fifty-fucking-four?"

"My thoughts exactly, Billy—but that's what his mom said," the Racquet Man replied.

"From what I've heard, I'll bet Kittredge died of AIDS," I said.

"What mother of Mrs. Kittredge's generation would be likely to tell her son's old school *that?*" Uncle Bob asked me. (Indeed, Sue Atkins had reported only that Tom Atkins had died "after a long illness.")

"You said Kittredge had a *wife*," I replied to my uncle.

"He is survived by his wife and his son—an only child—and by his mother, of course," the Racquet Man told me. "The boy is named after his father—another Jacques. The wife has a German-sounding name. You studied German, didn't you, Billy? What kind of name is Irmgard?" Uncle Bob asked.

"Definitely German-sounding," I said.

If Kittredge had wasted away in Zurich—even if he'd died in Switzerland "of natural causes"—possibly his wife was Swiss, but *Irmgard* was a German name. Boy, was that ever a tough Christian name to carry around! It was terribly old-fashioned; one immediately felt the stiffness of the person wearing that heavy name. I thought it was a suitable name for an elderly schoolmistress, a strict disciplinarian.

I was guessing that the only child, the son named Jacques, would have been born sometime in the early seventies; that would have been right on schedule for the kind of career-oriented young man I imagined Kittredge was, in those early years—given the MFA from Yale, given his first few steps along a no doubt bright and shining career path in the world of *drama*. Only at the appropriate time would Kittredge have paused, and found a wife. And *then* what? How had things unraveled after that?

"That fucker—God *damn* him!" Elaine cried, when I told her Kittredge had died. She was furious—it was as if Kittredge had *escaped*, somehow. She couldn't speak about the "of natural causes" bullshit, not to mention the wife. "He can't get away with this!" Elaine cried.

"Elaine—he *died*. He didn't get away with anything," I said, but Elaine cried and cried.

Unfortunately, it was one of the few nights when Amanda didn't have dorm duty; she was staying with me in the River Street house, and so I had to tell her about Kittredge, and Elaine, and all the rest.

No doubt, this history was more bi—and gay, and "transgender" (as Amanda would say)—in nature than anything Amanda had been forced to imagine, although she kept saying how much she *loved* my writing, where she'd no doubt encountered a world of sexual "differences" (as Richard would say).

I blame myself for not saying anything to Amanda about the frigging ghosts in that River Street house; only other people saw them—they never bothered *me*! But Amanda got up to go to the bathroom—it was the middle of the night—and her screaming woke me. It was a brand-new bathtub in that bathroom—it was *not* the same tub Grandpa Harry had pulled the trigger in, just the same bathroom—but, when Amanda finally calmed down enough to tell me what happened (when she was sitting on the toilet), it had no doubt been Harry she'd seen in that brand-new bathtub.

"He was curled up like a little boy in the bathtub—he *smiled* at me when I was peeing!" Amanda, who was still sobbing, explained.

"I'm really sorry," I said.

"But he was no little boy!" Amanda moaned.

"No, he wasn't—that was my grandfather," I tried to tell her calmly. Oh, that Harry—he certainly loved a new audience, even as a ghost! (Even *as a man!*)

"At first, I didn't see the rifle—but he *wanted* me to see it, Billy. He showed me the gun, and then he shot himself in the head—his head went all over the place!" Amanda wailed.

Naturally, I had some explaining to do; I had to tell her everything about Grandpa Harry. We were up all night. Amanda would not go to the bathroom by herself in the morning—she wouldn't even be alone in one of the other bathrooms, which I'd suggested. I understood; I was very understanding. I've never seen a frigging ghost—I'm sure they're frightening.

I guess the last straw, as I would later explain to Mrs. Hadley and Richard, was that Amanda was so rattled in the morning—after all, the anxious young woman hadn't had a good night's sleep—she opened the door to my bedroom closet, thinking she was opening the door to the up-stairs hall. And there was Grandpa Harry's .30-30 Mossberg; I keep that old carbine in my closet, where it just leans against a wall.

Amanda screamed and screamed—Christ, she wouldn't stop scream-ing. "You kept the actual gun—you keep it in your bedroom closet! Who would ever keep the very same gun his grandfather used to blow himself all over the bathroom, Billy?" Amanda yelled at me.

"Amanda has a point about the gun, Bill," Richard would say to me, when I told him that Amanda and I were no longer seeing each other.

"*Nobody* wants you to have that gun, Billy," Martha Hadley said.

"If you get rid of the gun, maybe the ghosts will leave, Billy," Elaine told me.

But those ghosts have never appeared to me; I think you have to be receptive to see ghosts like that, and I guess I'm not "receptive" in that way. I have my own ghosts—my own "terrifying angels," as I (more than once) have thought of them—but *my* ghosts don't live in that River Street house in First Sister, Vermont.

I would go to Mexico, alone, that mud season of 1995. I rented a house Elaine told me about in Playa del Carmen. I drank a lot of *cerveza*, and I picked up a handsome, swashbuckling-looking guy with a pencil-thin mustache and dark sideburns; honestly, he looked like one of the actors who played Zorro—one of the old black-and-white versions. We had fun, we drank a lot more *cerveza*, and when I came back to Vermont, it was almost looking like spring.

Not much would happen to me—not for fifteen years—except that I became a teacher. The private schools—you're supposed to call them "independent" schools, but I still let the *private* word slip out—aren't so strict about the retirement age. Richard Abbott wouldn't retire from Favorite River Academy until he was in his early seventies, and even after he retired, Richard went to all the productions of the school's Drama Club.

Richard wasn't very happy about his various replacements—well, nobody was happy about that lackluster bunch of buffoons. There wasn't anyone in the English Department who had Richard's feelings for Shakespeare, and there was no one who knew shit about theater. Martha Hadley and Richard were all over me to get *involved* at the academy.

"The kids read your novels, Billy," Richard kept telling me.

"Especially—you know—the kids who are sexually *different*, Billy," Mrs. Hadley said; she was still working with individual "cases" (as she called them) in her eighties.

It was from Elaine that I first heard there were groups for lesbian, gay, bi, and transgender kids on college campuses. It was Richard Abbott—in his late seventies—who told me there was even such a group of kids at Favorite River Academy. It was hard for a bi guy of my generation to imagine such organized and recognized groups. (They were becoming so common, these groups were known by their initials. When I first heard about this, I couldn't believe it.)

When Elaine was teaching at NYU, she invited me to come give a reading from a new novel to the LGBT group on campus. (I was so out of it; it took me days of reciting those initials before I could keep them in the correct order.)

It would have been the fall term of 2007 at Favorite River Academy when Mrs. Hadley told me there was someone special she and Richard wanted me to meet. I immediately thought it was a new teacher at the academy—someone in the English Department, either a pretty woman or a cute guy, I guessed, or possibly this "special" person had just been hired to breathe a hope of new life into the failing, all-but-expired Drama Club at Favorite River.

I was remembering Amanda—*that's* where I thought this matchmaking enterprise of Martha Hadley's (and Richard's) was headed. But, no—not at my age. I was sixty-five in the fall of 2007. Mrs. Hadley and Richard weren't trying to fix me up. Martha Hadley was a spry eighty-seven, but one slip on the ice or in the snow—one bad fall, a broken hip—and she would be checking into the Facility. (Mrs. Hadley would soon be checking in there, anyway.) And Richard Abbott was no longer leading-man material; at seventy-seven, Richard had come partway out of retirement to teach a Shakespeare course at Favorite River, but he didn't have the stamina to put Shakespeare onstage anymore. Richard was just reading the plays with some first-year kids at the academy; all of them were starting freshmen at the school. (Kids in the Class of *2011*! I couldn't imagine being that young again!)

"We want to introduce you to a new *student*, Bill," Richard said; he was rather indignant at the very idea of him (or Martha) finding me a likely date.

"A new freshman, Billy—someone special," Mrs. Hadley said.

"Someone with pronunciation problems, you mean?" I asked Martha Hadley.

"We're not trying to fix you up with a teacher, Bill. We think you should *be* a teacher," Richard said.

"We want you to meet one of the new LGBT kids, Billy," Mrs. Hadley told me.

"Sure—why not?" I said. "I don't know about being a teacher, but I'll meet the kid. Boy or girl?" I remember asking Martha Hadley and Richard. They just looked at each other.

"Ah, well—" Richard started to say, but Mrs. Hadley interrupted him.

Martha Hadley took my hands in hers, and squeezed them. "Boy or girl, Billy," she said. "Well, that's the question. That's why we want you to meet him, or her—that's the question."

"Oh," I said. That was how and why I became a teacher.

THE RACQUET MAN WAS ninety when he checked into the Facility; this followed two hip-replacement surgeries, and a fall downstairs when he was supposed to be healing from the second surgery. "I'm starting to feel like an old fella, Billy," Bob told me when I went to visit him in the Facility in the autumn of 2007—the same September Mrs. Hadley and Richard introduced me to the LGBT kid, the one who would change my life.

Uncle Bob was recovering from pneumonia—the result of being bed-ridden for a period of time after he fell. From the AIDS epidemic, I still had a vivid memory of *that* pneumonia—the one so many people never recovered from. I was happy to see Bob up and about, but he'd decided he was staying at the Facility.

"I gotta let these folks look after me, Billy," the Racquet Man said. I understood how he felt; Muriel had been gone for almost thirty years, and Gerry, who was sixty-eight, had just started living with a new girl-friend in California.

"Vagina Lady," which had been Elaine's name for Helena, was long gone. No one had met Gerry's new girlfriend, but Gerry had written me about her. She was "only" my age, Gerry told me—as if the girl were under the age of consent.

"The next thing you know, Billy," Uncle Bob told me, "they'll start legalizing same-sex marriage all over the place, and Gerry will be *marry-ing* her next new girlfriend. If I stay put in the Facility, Gerry will have to get married in *Vermont!*" the Racquet Man exclaimed, as if the very idea of *that* ever happening was beyond credibility.

Thus assured that my ninety-year-old uncle Bob was safe at the Fa-cility, I made my way to Noah Adams Hall, which was the building for English and foreign-language studies at Favorite River; I was meeting the "special" new student in Richard's ground-floor office, which was adja-cent to Richard's classroom. Mrs. Hadley was also meeting us there.

To my horror, Richard's office hadn't changed; it was awful. There was a fake-leather couch that smelled worse than any dog bed you've ever smelled; there were three or four straight-backed wooden chairs, of the kind with those arms that have a flat mini-desk for writing. There was Richard's desk, which was always a mountain of upheaval; a pile of opened books and loose papers obscured the writing surface. Richard's desk chair was on casters, so that Richard could slide all around his of-fice in a seated position—which, to the students' general amusement, Richard did.

What *had* changed at Favorite River, since my days at the formerly all-boys' school, was not only the girls—it was the dress code. If there was one in 2007, I couldn't tell you what it was; coats and ties were no longer re-quired. There was some vague rule against "torn" jeans—this meant jeans that were tattered or slashed. There was a rule that you couldn't come to the dining hall in your pajamas, and another one, which was always being protested, that concerned the girls' bare midriffs—how *much* midriff could be bare was the issue. Oh, and so-called plumbers' cracks were deemed offensive—this was most offensive, I was told, when the "cracks" belonged to the boys. Both the girls' bare midriffs and the boys' plumbers' cracks were hotly debated rules, which were constantly under revision in infinitesimal ways. They were sexually discriminatory rules, the students said; girls' midriffs and boys' cracks were being singled out as "bad."

Here I'd been expecting Martha and Richard's "special" student to be some cutting-edge hermaphrodite—a kind of alluring-to-everyone mélange of reproductive organs, a he or a she as sexually beguiling as the mythological combination of a nymph and a satyr in a Fellini film—but there in Richard's office, slouched on that dog bed of a couch, was a sloppily dressed, slightly overweight boy with a brightly inflamed pimple on his neck and only the spottiest evidence of a prepubescent beard. That zit was almost as angry-looking as the boy himself. When he saw me, his eyes narrowed—either in resentment or due to the effort he was making to scrutinize me more closely.

"Hi, I'm Bill Abbott," I said to the boy.

"This is George—" Mrs. Hadley started to say.

"*Georgia,*" the boy quickly corrected her. "I'm Georgia Montgomery—the kids call me Gee."

"Gee," I repeated.

"Gee will do for now," the boy said, "but I'm *going to be* Georgia. This *isn't* my body," he said angrily. "I'm not what you see. I'm becoming someone else."

"Okay," I said.

"I came to this school because *you* went here," the boy told me.

"Gee was in school in California," Richard started to explain.

"I thought there might be other transgender kids here," Gee told me, "but there aren't—nobody who's out, anyway."

"His parents—" Mrs. Hadley tried to tell me.

"*Her* parents," Gee corrected Martha.

"Gee's parents are very *liberal,*" Martha said to me. "They *support* you, don't they?" Mrs. Hadley asked the boy—or the girl-in-progress, if that's who he or she was.

"My parents *are* liberal, and they *do* support me," Gee said, "but my parents are also afraid of me—they say 'yes' to everything, like my coming all the way to Vermont."

"I see," I said.

"I've read all your books," Gee told me. "You're pretty angry, aren't you? You're pretty pessimistic, anyway. You don't see all the sexual intolerance ending anytime soon, do you?" the boy asked me.

"I write *fiction*," I cautioned him. "I'm not necessarily as pessimistic about real life as I am when I make up a story."

"You seem pretty angry," the boy insisted.

"We should leave these two alone, Richard," Mrs. Hadley said.

"Yes, yes—you're on your own, Bill," Richard said, patting me on the back. "Ask Bill to tell you about a transsexual he knew, Gee," Richard said to the girl-in-progress, as he was leaving.

"*Transgender*," Gee corrected Richard.

"Not to me," I told the kid. "I know the language changes; I know I'm an old man, and out of date. But the person I knew was a transsexual to me. At that time, that's who she was. I say 'transsexual.' If you want to hear the story, you'll just have to get used to that. Don't correct *my* language," I told the kid. He just sat there on that smelly couch, staring at me. "I'm a liberal, too," I told him, "but I don't say 'yes' to everything."

"We're reading *The Tempest* in Richard's class," Gee said—apropos of nothing, or so I thought. "It's too bad we can't put it onstage," the boy added, "but Richard has assigned us parts to read in class. I'm Caliban— I'm the monster, naturally."

"I was Ariel once," I told him. "I saw my grandfather do Caliban onstage; he played Caliban *as a woman*," I said to the girl-in-progress.

"Really?" the kid asked me; he smiled for the first time, and I could suddenly see it. He had a pretty girl's smile; it was hidden in the boy's unformed face, and further concealed by his sloppy boy's body, but I could see the *her* in him. "Tell me about the transgender you knew," the kid told me.

"*Transsexual*," I said.

"Okay—please tell me about her," Gee asked me.

"It's a long story, Gee—I was in love with her," I told him—I told *her*, I should say.

"Okay," she repeated.

Later that day, we went together to the dining hall. The kid was only fourteen, and she was famished. "You see that jock over there?" Gee asked me; I couldn't see which jock Gee meant, because there was a whole table of them—football players, from the look of them. I just nodded.

"He calls me Tampon, or sometimes just George—not Gee. Needless to say, never Georgia," the kid said, smiling.

"Tampon is pretty terrible," I told the girl.

"Actually, I prefer it to George," Gee told me. "You know, Mr. A., *you* could probably direct *The Tempest,* couldn't you—if you wanted to? That way, we could put Shakespeare onstage."

No one had ever called me Mr. A.; I must have liked it. I'd already decided that if Gee wanted to be a girl this badly, she had to be one. I wanted to direct *The Tempest,* too.

"Hey, Tampon!" someone called.

"Let's have a word with the football players," I told Gee. We went over to their table; they instantly stopped eating. They saw the tragic-looking mess of a boy—the transgender wannabe, as they probably thought of him—and they saw me, a sixty-five-year-old man, whom they might have mistaken for a faculty member (I soon would be). After all, I looked way too old to be Gee's father.

"This is Gee—that's her name. Remember it," I said to them. They didn't respond. "Which of you called Gee 'Tampon'?" I asked them; there was no response to my question, either. (Fucking bullies; most of them are cowards.)

"If someone mistakes you for a tampon, Gee—whose fault is it, if you don't speak up about it?" I asked the girl, who still looked like a boy.

"That would be my fault," Gee said.

"What's her name?" I asked the football players.

All but one of them called out, "Gee!" The one who hadn't spoken, the biggest one, was eating again; he was looking at his food, not at me, when I spoke to him.

"What's her name?" I asked again; he pointed to his mouth, which was full.

"I'll wait," I told him.

"He's *not* on the faculty," the big football player said to his team-mates, when he'd swallowed his food. "He's just a writer who lives in town. He's some old gay guy who lives here, and he went to school here. He can't tell us what to do—he's not on the faculty."

"What's her name?" I asked him.

"Douche Bag?" the football player asked me; he was smiling now—so were the other football players.

"You see why I'm 'pretty angry,' as you say, Gee?" I asked the fourteen-year-old. "Is this the guy who calls you Tampon?"

"Yes—that's him," Gee said.

The football player, the one who knew who I was, had stood up from the table; he was a very big kid, maybe four inches taller than I am, and easily twenty or thirty pounds heavier.

"Get lost, you old fag," the big kid said to me. I thought it would be better if I could get him to say the *fag* word to Gee. I knew I would have the fucker then; the dress code may have relaxed at Favorite River, but there were other rules in place—rules that didn't exist when I'd been a student. You couldn't get thrown out of Favorite River for saying *tampon* or *douche bag*, but the *fag* word was in the category of hate. (Like the *nigger* word and the *kike* word, the *fag* word could get you in trouble.)

"Fucking *football* players," I heard Gee say; it was something Herm Hoyt used to say. (Wrestlers are rather contemptuous about how tough football players *think* they are.) That young transgender-in-progress must have been reading my mind!

"What did you say, you little fag?" the big kid said. He took a cheap shot at Gee—he smacked the heel of his hand into the fourteen-year-old's face. It must have hurt her, but I saw that Gee wasn't going to back down; her nose was starting to bleed when I stepped between them.

"That's enough," I said to the big kid, but he bumped me with his chest. I saw the right hook coming, and took the punch on my left forearm—the way Jim *Somebody* had shown me, down that fourth-floor hall in the boxing room at the NYAC. The football player was a little surprised when I reached up and caught the back of his neck in a collar-tie. He pushed back against me, hard; he was a heavy kid, and he leaned all his weight on me—just what you want your opponent to do, if you have a halfway-decent duck-under.

The dining-hall floor was a lot harder than a wrestling mat, and the big kid landed awkwardly, with all his weight (and most of mine) on one shoulder. I was pretty sure he'd separated that shoulder, or he had broken his collarbone—or both. At the time, he was just lying on the floor, try-ing not to move that shoulder or his upper arm.

"Fucking *football* players," Gee repeated, this time to the whole table of them. They could see her nose was bleeding more.

"For the fourth time, what's her name?" I asked the big kid lying on the floor.

"Gee," the douche-bag, tampon guy said. It turned out that he was a PG—a nineteen-year-old postgraduate who'd been admitted to Favorite River to play football. Either the separated shoulder or the broken collarbone would cause him to miss the rest of the football season. The academy didn't expel him for the *fag* word, but he was put on probation. (Both Gee and I had hoped that her nose was broken, but it wasn't.) The PG would be thrown out of school the following spring for using the *dyke* word, in reference to a girl who wouldn't sleep with him.

When I agreed to teach part-time at Favorite River, I said I would do so only on the condition that the academy make an effort to educate new students, especially the older PGs, on the subject of the liberal culture at Favorite River—I meant, of course, in regard to our acceptance of sexual diversity.

But there in the dining hall, on that September day in 2007, I didn't have anything more of an *educative* nature to say to the football players.

My new protégée, Gee, however, had more to say to those jocks, who were still sitting at their table. "I'm going to become a girl," she told them bravely. "One day, I'll be Georgia. But, for now, I'm just Gee, and you can see me as Caliban in Shakespeare's *The Tempest*."

"Perhaps it will be a winter-term play," I cautioned the football players, not that I expected any of them to come see it. I just thought that I might need that long to get the kids ready; all the students in Richard's Shakespeare class were freshmen. I would open auditions to the entire school, but I feared that the kids who would be most interested in the play were (like Gee) only freshmen.

"There's one more thing," my protégée said to the football players. Her nose was streaming blood, but I could tell Gee was happy about that. "Mr. A. is *not* an old *gay* guy—he's an old *bi* guy. You got that?"

I was impressed that the football players nodded. Well, okay, not the big one on the dining-hall floor; he was just lying there, not moving. I only regret that Miss Frost and Coach Hoyt didn't see me hit that duck-under. If I do say so myself, it was a pretty good duck-under—my one move.

Chapter 14

TEACHER

All that had happened three years ago, when Gee was just a freshman. You should have seen Gee at the start of her senior year, in the fall term of 2010—at seventeen, that girl was a knockout. Gee would turn eighteen her senior year; she would graduate, on schedule, with the Class of 2011. All I'm saying is, you should have seen her when she was a senior. Mrs. Hadley and Richard were right: Gee was special.

That fall term of 2010, we were in rehearsals for what Richard called "the fall Shakespeare." We would be performing *Romeo and Juliet* in that most edgy time—the brief bit of school that remains between the Thanksgiving break and Christmas vacation.

As a teacher, I can tell you that's a terrible time: The kids are woefully distracted, they have exams, they have papers due—and, to make it worse, the fall sports have been replaced by the winter ones. There is much that's new, but a lot that's old; everyone has a cough, and tempers are short.

The Drama Club at Favorite River had last put on *Romeo and Juliet* in the winter of '85, which was twenty-five years ago. I still remembered what Larry had said to Richard about casting a boy as Juliet. (Larry thought Shakespeare would have *loved* the idea!) But Richard had asked, "Where do I find a boy with the balls to play Juliet?" Not even Lawrence Upton could find an answer for that.

Now I knew a boy with the balls to play Juliet. I had Gee, and—*as a girl*—Gee was just about perfect. At seventeen, Gee still actually had balls, too. She'd begun the extensive psychological examinations—the counseling and psychotherapy—necessary for young people who are serious about gender reassignment. I don't believe that her beard had yet been removed by the process of electrolysis; Gee may not have been old enough for electrolysis, but I don't really know. I *do* know that, with her parents' and her doctor's approval, Gee was receiving injections of female hormones; if she stayed committed to her sex change, she would have to continue to take those hormones for the rest of her life. (I had no doubt that Gee, soon to be *Georgia*, Montgomery would stay committed.)

What was it Elaine once said, about the possibility of *Kittredge* playing Juliet? It wouldn't have worked, we agreed. "Juliet is nothing if she's not *sincere*," Elaine had said.

Boy, did I ever have a Juliet who was *sincere*! Gee had always had balls, but now she had breasts—small but very pretty ones—and her hair had acquired a new luster. My, how her eyelashes had grown! Gee's skin had become softer, and the acne was altogether gone; her hips had spread, though she'd actually lost weight since her freshman year—her hips were already womanly, if not yet curvaceous.

What's more important, the whole community at Favorite River Academy knew who (and what) Gee Montgomery was. Sure, there were still a few jocks who hadn't entirely accepted how sexually *diverse* a school we were trying to be. There will always be a few troglodytes.

Larry would have been proud of me, I thought. In a word, it might have surprised Larry to see how *involved* I was. Political activism didn't come naturally to me, but I was at least a *little* active politically. I'd traveled to some college campuses in our state. I'd spoken to the LGBT groups at Middlebury College and the University of Vermont. I'd supported the same-sex marriage bill, which the Vermont State Senate passed into law—over the veto of our Republican governor, a troglodyte.

Larry would have laughed to see me supporting gay marriage, because Larry knew what I thought of *any* marriage. "Old Mr. Monogamy," Larry would have teased me. But gay marriage is what the gay and bi kids want, and I support those kids.

"I see a future hero in you!" Grandpa Harry had told me. I wouldn't go that far, but I hope Miss Frost might have approved of me. In my own way, I was *protecting* someone—I'd protected Gee. I was a worthwhile person in Gee's life. Maybe Miss Frost would have liked me for that.

This was my life at age sixty-eight. I was a part-time English teacher at my old school, Favorite River Academy; I also directed the Drama Club there. I was a writer, and an occasional political activist—on the side of LGBT groups, everywhere. Oh, forgive me; the language, I know, keeps changing.

A very young teacher at Favorite River told me it was no longer appropriate (or inclusive enough) to say LGBT—it was supposed to be LGBTQ.

"What is the fucking Q for?" I asked the teacher. "*Quarrelsome*, perhaps?"

"No, Bill," the teacher said. "*Questioning*."

"Oh."

"I remember you at the *questioning* phase, Billy," Martha Hadley told me. Ah, well—yes, I remember me at that phase, too. I'm okay about saying LGBTQ; at my age, I just have trouble remembering the frigging Q!

Mrs. Hadley lives in the Facility now. She's ninety, and Richard visits her every day. I visit Martha twice a week—at the same time I visit Uncle Bob. At ninety-three, the Racquet Man is doing surprisingly well—that is, physically. Bob's memory isn't all it was, but that's a good fella's failing. Sometimes, Bob even forgets that Gerry and her California girlfriend—the one who's as old as I am—were married in Vermont this year.

It was a June 2010 wedding; we had it at my house on River Street. Both Mrs. Hadley and Uncle Bob were there—Martha in a wheelchair. The Racquet Man was pushing Mrs. Hadley around.

"Are you sure you don't want me to take over pushing the wheelchair, Bob?" Richard and I and Elaine kept asking.

"What makes you think I'm *pushing* it?" the Racquet Man asked us. "I'm just *leaning* on it!"

Anyway, when Uncle Bob asks me when Gerry's wedding is, I have to keep reminding him that she's already married.

It was, in part, Bob's forgetfulness that almost caused me to miss one small highlight of my life—a small but truly important highlight, I think.

"What are you going to do about Señor Bovary, Billy?" Uncle Bob asked me, when I was driving him back to the Facility from Gerry's wedding.

"Señor who?" I asked the Racquet Man.

"Shit, Billy—I'm sorry," Uncle Bob said. "I can't remember my Alumni Affairs anymore—as soon as I hear something, I seem to forget it!"

But it wasn't exactly in the category of an announcement for publication in *The River Bulletin;* it was just a query that came to Bob, in care of the "Cries for Help from the Where-Have-You-Gone? Dept."

Please pass this message along to young William,

the carefully typed letter began.

> His father, William Francis Dean, would like to know how his son is—even if the old prima donna himself won't write his son and just <u>ask</u> him. There was an AIDS epidemic, you know; since he's still writing books, we assume that young William survived it. But how's his health? As we say over here—if you would be so kind as to ask young William— <u>Cómo está</u>? And please tell young William, if he wants to see us before we die, he ought to pay us a <u>visit</u>!

The carefully typed letter was from my father's longtime lover—the toilet-seat skipper, the reader, the guy who reconnected with my dad on the subway and *didn't* get off at the next station.

He had typed, not signed, his name:

Señor Bovary

I WENT ONE SUMMER recently, with a somewhat cynical Dutch friend, to the gay-pride parade in Amsterdam; that city is a hopeful experiment, I have long believed, and I loved the parade. There were surging tides of men dancing in the streets—guys in purple and pink leather, boys in Speedos with leopard spots, men in jockstraps, kissing, one woman sleekly covered with wet-looking green feathers and sporting an all-black strap-on cock. I said to my friend that there were many cities where they preached tolerance, but Amsterdam truly practiced it—even *flaunted* it. As I spoke, a long barge glided by on one of the canals; an all-girls' rock band was playing onboard, and there were women wearing transparent leotards and waving to us onshore. The women were waving dildoes.

But my cynical Dutch friend gave me a tired (and barely tolerant) look; he seemed as indifferent to the gay goings-on as the mostly foreign-born prostitutes in the windows and doorways of de Wallen, Amsterdam's red-light district.

"Amsterdam is so *over*," my Dutch friend said. "The new scene for gays in Europe is Madrid."

"Madrid," I repeated, the way I do. I was an old bi guy in his sixties, living in Vermont. What did I know about the new scene for gays in Europe? (What did I know about any frigging *scene*?)

It was on Señor Bovary's recommendation that I stayed at the Santo Mauro in Madrid; it was a pretty, quiet hotel on the Zurbano—a narrow, tree-lined street (a residential but boring-looking neighborhood) "within walking distance of Chueca." Well, it was a *long* walk to Chueca, "the gay district of Madrid"—as Señor Bovary described Chueca in his email to me. Bovary's typed letter, which was mailed to Uncle Bob at Favorite River's Office of Alumni Affairs, had not included a return address—just an email address and Señor Bovary's cell-phone number.

The initial contact, by letter, and my follow-up email communication with my father's enduring partner, suggested a curious combination of the old-fashioned and the contemporary.

"I believe that the Bovary character is your dad's age, Billy," Uncle Bob had forewarned me. I knew, from the 1940 *Owl*, that William Francis Dean had been born in 1924, which meant that my father and Señor Bovary were eighty-six. (I also knew from the same '40 *Owl* that Franny Dean had wanted to be a "performer," but performing *what*?)

From the emails of "the Bovary character," as the Racquet Man had called my dad's lover, I understood that my father had not been informed of my coming to Madrid; this was entirely Señor Bovary's idea, and I was following his instructions. "Have a walk around Chueca on the day you arrive. Go to bed early that first night. I'll meet you for dinner on your second night. We'll take a stroll; we'll end up in Chueca, and I'll bring you to the club. If your father knew you were coming, it would just make him self-conscious," Señor Bovary's email said.

What club? I wondered.

"Franny wasn't a bad guy, Billy," Uncle Bob had told me, when I was still a student at Favorite River. "He was just a little light in his loafers, if you know what I mean." Probably the place Bovary was taking me in Chueca was *that* sort of club. But what *kind* of gay club was it? (Even an old bi guy in Vermont knows there's more than one kind of gay club.)

In the late afternoon in Chueca, most of the shops were still closed for siesta in the ninety-degree heat; it was a dry heat, however—very agreeable to a visitor coming to Madrid from the blackfly season in Vermont. I had the feeling that the Calle de Hortaleza was a busy street of commercialized gay sex; it had a sex-tourism atmosphere, even at the siesta time of day. There were some lone older men around, and only occasional groups of young gay guys; there would have been more of both types on a weekend, but this was a workday afternoon. There was not much of a lesbian presence—not that I could see, but this was my first look at Chueca.

There was a nightclub called A Noite on Hortaleza, near the corner of the Calle de Augusto Figueroa, but you don't notice nightclubs during the day. It was the out-of-place Portuguese name of the club that caught my eye—*a noite* means "the night" in Portuguese—and those tattered billboards advertising shows, including one with drag queens.

The streets between the Gran Vía and the metro station in the Plaza de Chueca were crowded with bars and sex shops and gay clothing stores. Taglia, the wig shop on the Calle de Hortaleza, was opposite a bodybuilders' gym. I saw that Tintin T-shirts were popular, and—on the corner of the Calle de Hernán Cortés—there were male mannequins in thongs in the storefront window. (There's one thing I'm glad to be too old for: thongs.)

Fighting jet lag, I was just trying to get through the day and to stay up late enough to have an early dinner at my hotel before I went to bed. I was too tired to appreciate the muscle-bound waiters in T-shirts at the Mama Inés Café on Hortaleza; there were mostly men in couples, and a woman who was alone. She was wearing flip-flops and a halter top; she had an angular face and looked very sad, resting her mouth on one hand. I almost tried to pick her up. I remember wondering if, in Spain, the women were very thin until they suddenly became fat. I was noticing a certain type of man—skinny in a tank top, but with a small and helpless-looking potbelly.

I had a *café con leche* as late as 5 P.M.—very unlike me, too late in the day for me to drink coffee, but I was trying to stay awake. I later found a bookstore on the Calle de Gravina—Libros, I believe it was called. (I'm not kidding, a bookstore called "Books.") The English novel, in English, was well represented there, but there was nothing contemporary—not even from the twentieth century. I browsed the fiction section for a while. Diagonally across the street, on the corner of San Gregorio, was what looked like a popular bar—the Ángel Sierra. The siesta must have been over by the time I left the bookstore, because that bar was beginning to get crowded.

I passed a coffeehouse, also on the Calle de Gravino, with some older, stylishly dressed lesbians sitting at a window table—to my limited knowledge, the only lesbians I spotted in Chueca, and almost the only women I saw anywhere in that district. But it was still early in the evening, and I knew that everything in Spain happens late. (I'd been in Barcelona before, on translation trips. My Spanish-language publisher is based there.)

As I was leaving Chueca—for that long walk back to the Santo Mauro—I stopped in at a bear bar on the Calle de las Infantas. The bar called Hot was packed with men standing chest to chest and back to back. They were older men, and you know what bears are like— ordinary-looking men, chubby guys with beards, many beer drinkers among them. It was Spain, so of course there was a lot of smoking; I didn't stay long, but Hot had a friendly atmosphere. The shirtless bartenders were the youngest guys in the place—they were hot, all right.

THE DAPPER LITTLE MAN who met me at a restaurant in the Plaza Mayor the following night did not immediately summon to mind a young soldier with his pants down at his ankles, reading *Madame Bovary* in a storm at sea, while—on his bare bum—he skipped over a row of toilet seats to meet my young father.

Señor Bovary's hair was neatly trimmed and all white, as were the short bristles of his no-nonsense mustache. He wore a pressed, short-sleeved white shirt with two breast pockets—one for his reading glasses, the other armed with pens. His khaki trousers were sharply creased; perhaps the only contemporary components of the fastidious man's old-fashioned image were his sandals. They were the kind of sandals that young outdoorsmen wear when they wade in raging rivers and run through fast-flowing streams—those sandals that have the built-up and serious-looking treads of running shoes.

"Bovary," he said; he extended his hand, palm down, so that I didn't know if he expected me to shake it or kiss it. (I shook it.)

"I'm so glad you contacted me," I told him.

"I don't know what your father has been waiting for, now that your mother—*una mujer difícil*, 'a difficult woman'—has been dead for thirty-two years. It *is* thirty-two, isn't it?" the little man asked.

"Yes," I said.

"Let me know what your HIV status is; I'll tell your father," Bovary said. "He's dying to hear, but I know him—he'll never ask you himself. He'll just worry about it after you've gone back home. He's an impossible procrastinator!" Bovary exclaimed affectionately, giving me a small, twinkling smile.

I told him: I keep testing negative; I don't have HIV disease.

"No toxic cocktail for you—that's the ticket!" Señor Bovary exclaimed. "We don't have the virus, either—if you're interested. I admit to having had sex only with your father, and—save that truly *disastrous* dalliance with your mom—your dad has had sex only with me. How *boring* is that?" the little man asked me, smiling more. "I've read your *writing*—so, of course, has your father. On the evidence of what you've written about—well, one can't blame your dad for worrying about *you!* If half of what you write about has *happened* to you, you must have had sex with *everyone!*"

"With men and women, yes—with *everyone*, no," I said, smiling back at him.

"I'm only asking because he *won't* ask. Honestly, you'll meet your father, and you'll feel you've had *interviews* that are more in-depth than anything he'll ask you or even *say* to you," Señor Bovary warned me. "It isn't that he doesn't *care*—I'm not exaggerating when I say he's *always* worrying about you—but your father is a man who believes your privacy is not to be invaded. Your dad is a *very* private man. I've only ever seen him be public about one thing."

"And that is?" I asked.

"I'm not going to spoil the show. We should be going, anyway," Señor Bovary said, looking at his watch.

"*What* show?" I asked him.

"Look, I'm not the performer—I just manage the money," Bovary said. "You're the *writer* in the family, but your father *does* know how to tell a story—even if it's always the same story."

I followed him, at a fairly fast pace, from the Plaza Mayor to the Puerta del Sol. Bovary must have had those special sandals because he was a walker; I'll bet he walked everywhere in Madrid. He was a trim, fit man; he'd had very little to eat for dinner, and nothing to drink but mineral water.

It was probably nine or ten o'clock at night, but there were a lot of

people in the streets. As we walked up Montero, we passed some prostitutes—"working girls," Bovary called them.

I heard one of them say the *guapo* word.

"She says you're handsome," Señor Bovary translated.

"Perhaps she means *you*," I told him; he was *very* handsome, I
thought.

"She doesn't mean me—she *knows* me," was all Bovary said. He was
all business—Mr. Money Manager, I was thinking.

Then we crossed the Gran Vía into Chueca, by that towering building—the Telefónica. "We're still a little early," Señor Bovary was saying,
as he looked again at his watch. He seemed to consider (then he recon-
sidered) taking a detour. "There's a bear bar on this street," he said, pausing at the intersection of Hortaleza and the Calle de las Infantas.

"Yes, Hot—I had a beer there last night," I told him.

"Bears are all right, if you like *bellies*," Bovary said.

"I have nothing against bears—I just like beer," I said. "It's all I
drink."

"I just drink *agua con gas*," Señor Bovary said, giving me his small,
twinkling smile.

"Mineral water, with bubbles—right?" I asked him.

"I guess we both like *bubbles*," was all Bovary said; he had continued
walking along Hortaleza. I wasn't paying very close attention to the street,
but I recognized that nightclub with the Portuguese name—A Noite.

When Señor Bovary led me inside, I asked, "Oh, is *this* the club?"

"Mercifully, *no*," the little man replied. "We're just killing time. If
the show were starting *here*, I wouldn't have brought you, but the show
starts very late here. It's safe just to have a drink."

There were some skinny gay boys hanging around the bar. "If you
were alone, they'd be all over you," Bovary told me. It was a black marble
bar, or maybe it was polished granite. I had a beer and Señor Bovary had
an *agua con gas* while we waited.

There was a blue-tinted ballroom and a proscenium stage at A Noite;
they were playing Sinatra songs backstage. When I quietly used the *retro*
word for the nightclub, all Bovary said was, "To be kind." He kept checking his watch.

When we went out on Hortaleza again, it was almost 11 P.M.; I had
never seen as many people on the street. When Bovary brought me to
the club, I realized I'd walked past it and not noticed it—at least twice. It

was a very small club with a long line out front—on Hortaleza, between the Calle de las Infantas and San Marcos. The name of the club I saw only now—for the first time. The club was called SEÑOR BOVARY.

"Oh," I said, as Bovary led me around the line to the stage door.

"We'll see Franny's show, *then* you'll meet him," the little man was saying. "If I'm lucky, he won't see you with me till the end of his routine—or *near* the end, anyway."

The same types I'd seen at A Noite, those skinny gay boys, were crowding the bar, but they made room for Señor Bovary and me. Onstage was a transsexual dancer, very passable—nothing *retro* about her.

"Shameless catering to straight guys," Bovary whispered in my ear. "Oh, and guys like *you*, I suppose—is she your type?"

"Yes, definitely," I told him. (I thought the lime-green strobe pulsing on the dancer was a little tacky.)

It wasn't exactly a strip show; the dancer had certainly had her boobs done, and she was very proud of them, but she never took off the thong. The crowd gave her a big hand when she exited the stage, passing through the audience—even passing by the bar, still in her thong but carrying the rest of her clothes. Bovary said something to her in Spanish, and she smiled.

"I told her you were a very important guest, and that she was *definitely* your type," the little man said mischievously to me. When I started to say something, he put an index finger to his lips and whispered: "I'll be your translator."

I first thought he was making a joke—about translating for me, if I were later to find myself with the transsexual dancer—but Bovary meant that he would translate for my father. "Franny! Franny! Franny!" voices in the crowd kept calling.

From the instant Franny Dean came onstage, there were ooohs and ahhhs; it wasn't just the glitter and drop-dead décolletage of the dress, but with that plunging neckline and the poised way my father carried it off, I could see why Grandpa Harry had a soft spot for William Francis Dean. The wig was a jet-black mane with silver sparkles; it matched the dress. The falsies were modest—small, like the rest of him—and the pearl necklace wasn't ostentatious, yet it picked up the powder-blue light onstage. That same powder-blue light had turned all the white onstage and in the audience a pearl-gray color—even Señor Bovary's white shirt, where we sat at the bar.

"I have a little story to tell you," my dad told the crowd, in Spanish. "It won't take very long," he said with a smile; his old, thin fingers toyed with his pearls. "Maybe you've heard this before?" he asked—as Bovary whispered, in English, in my ear.

"*Sí!*" shouted the crowd, in chorus.

"Sorry," my father replied, "but it's the only story I know. It's the story of my life, and the one love in it."

I already knew the story. It was, in part, what he'd told me when I was recovering from scarlet fever—only in more detail than a child could possibly have remembered.

"Imagine meeting the love of your life on a *toilet!*" Franny Dean cried. "We were in a latrine, awash with seawater; we were on a ship, awash with *vomit!*"

"*Vómito!*" the crowd repeated, in a unified cry.

I was amazed how many of them had heard the story; they knew it by heart. There were many older people in the audience, both men and women; there were young people, too—mostly boys.

"There's no sound quite like the sound of a human derrière, passing a succession of toilet seats—that *slapping* sound, as the love of your life approaches, coming nearer and nearer," my father said; he paused and took a deep breath while many of the young boys in the audience dropped their pants down to their ankles (their underpants, too) and slapped one another on their bare asses.

My father exhaled onstage and said, with a condemning sigh, "No, not like that—it was a *different* slapping sound, more *refined.*" In his glittering black dress with the plunging neckline, my dad paused again—while those chastised boys pulled up their pants, and the audience settled down.

"Imagine *reading* in a storm at sea. How much of a reader would you need to be?" my father asked. "I've been a reader all my life. I knew that if I *ever* met the love of my life, he would have to be a reader, too. But, oh—to first make *contact* with him *that* way! Cheek to cheek, so to speak," my dad said, jutting out one skinny hip and slapping himself on the buttocks.

"Cheek to cheek!" the crowd cried—or however you say that in Spanish. (I can't remember.) He'd met Bovary on a toilet, butt to butt; how perfect was that?

There wasn't much more to the show. When my father's story, about the love of his life, was finished, I noticed that many of the older people in the audience quickly slipped away—as did nearly all the women. The women who stayed, I realized only later—as I was leaving—were the transsexuals and the transvestites. (The young boys stayed, and by the time I left the club, there were many more of them—in addition to some older men, who were mostly alone, no doubt on the prowl.)

Señor Bovary led me backstage to meet my father. "Don't be disappointed," he kept whispering in my ear, as if he were still translating and we were still sitting at the bar.

My father, standing in his dressing room, was already stripped to the waist—wig off—by the time Bovary and I got backstage. William Francis Dean had a snow-white crew cut and the starved-down, muscular body of a lightweight wrestler or a jockey. The little falsies, and a bra no bigger than Elaine's—the one I used to wear when I was sleeping—were on my dad's dressing-room table, all heaped together with the pearl necklace. The dress, which unzipped from the back, had been undone only as far as my father's slender waist, and he'd slipped the top half off his shoulders.

"Shall I unzip you the rest of the way, Franny?" Señor Bovary asked the performer. My father turned his back to Bovary, allowing his lover to unzip him. Franny Dean stepped out of the dress, revealing only a tight black girdle; he'd already unfastened his black stockings from the girdle—the stockings were rolled at his narrow ankles. When my dad sat at his dressing-room table, he pulled the rolled-down stockings off his small feet and threw them at Señor Bovary. (All this before he began to remove his makeup, starting with the eyeliner; he'd already removed the fake eyelashes.)

"It's a good thing I didn't see you *whispering* to young William at the bar until I was almost done with the Boston part of the story," my father said peevishly to Bovary.

"It's a good thing *someone* invited young William to come see you before you're dead, Franny," Señor Bovary told him.

"Mr. Bovary *exaggerates*, William," my dad told me. "As you can see for yourself, I'm *not* dying."

"I'll leave you two alone," Mr. Bovary told us in a wounded tone.

"Don't you dare," my dad said to the love of his life.

"I dare not," Bovary replied, with droll resignation. He gave me a long-suffering look, of the you-see-what-I-put-up-with kind.

"What's the point of having a love of your life, if he's not *always* with you?" my father asked me.

I didn't know what to say; I was quite at a loss for words.

"Be nice, Franny," Señor Bovary told him.

"Here's what women do, William—small-town girls, anyway," my father said. "They find something they love about you—even if there's just one thing they find endearing. For example, your mother liked to dress me up—and I liked it, too."

"Maybe *later*, Franny—maybe say this to young William *after* you've had a chance to get to know each other," Mr. Bovary suggested.

"It's too late for young William and me to get to know each other. We were denied that opportunity. Now we already are who we are, aren't we, William?" my dad asked me. Once again, I didn't know what to say.

"Please *try* to be nicer, Franny," Bovary told him.

"Here's what women do, as I was saying," my father continued. "Those things they *don't* love about you—those things they don't even *like*—well, guess what women do about *those* things? They imagine they can *change* those things—*that's* what women do! They imagine they can change you," my father said.

"You knew *one* girl, Franny, *una mujer difícil*—" Mr. Bovary started to say.

"Now who's not being *nice?*" my dad interrupted him.

"I've known some *men* who tried to change me," I told my father.

"I can't compete with everyone *you've* known, William—I couldn't possibly claim to have had *your* experience," my dad said. I was surprised he was a prig.

"I used to wonder where I came from," I told him. "Those things in myself that I didn't understand—those things I was *questioning*, especially. You know what I mean. How much of me came from my mother? There was little that came from her that I could see. And how much of me came from *you*? There was a time when I thought about that, quite a lot," I told him.

"We heard about you beating up some boy," my father said.

"Say this *later*, Franny," Mr. Bovary pleaded with him.

"You beat up a kid at school—rather recently, wasn't it?" my dad asked me. "Bob told me about it. The Racquet Man was quite proud of you for it, but I found it upsetting. You didn't get *violence* from me—you didn't get *aggression*. I wonder if all that anger doesn't come from those *Winthrop women*," he told me.

"He was a *big* kid," I said. "He was nineteen, a football player—a fucking bully."

But my father and Señor Bovary looked as though they were ashamed of me. I was on the verge of explaining Gee to them—how she'd been only fourteen, a boy becoming a girl, and the nineteen-year-old thug had hit her in the face, bloodying her nose—but I suddenly thought that I didn't owe these disapproving old queens an explanation. I didn't give a shit about that football player.

"He called me a *fag*," I told them. I guessed that would make them sniffy.

"Oh, did you hear that?" my dad asked the love of his life. "Not the *fag* word! Can you imagine being called a fag and *not* beating the shit out of someone?" my father asked his lover.

"Nicer—try being nicer, Franny," Bovary said, but I saw that he was smiling. They were a cute couple, but prissy—made for each other, as they say.

My dad stood up and hooked his thumbs into the tight waistband of his girdle. "If you gentlemen would be so kind as to give me a little *privacy*," he said. "This ridiculous undergarment is killing me."

I went back to the bar with Bovary, but there would be no hope of further conversation there; the skinny gay boys had multiplied, in part because there were more older men by themselves at the bar. There was an all-boys' band playing in a pink strobe light, and men and boys were dancing together out on the dance floor; some of the T-girls were dancing, too, either with a boy or with one another.

When my father joined us at the bar, he was the picture of masculine conformity; in addition to those athletic-looking sandals (like Bovary's), my dad was wearing a tan-colored sports jacket with a dark-brown handkerchief in the breast pocket of the jacket. The murmur of "Franny!" passed through the crowd as we were leaving the club.

We were walking on Hortaleza, just past the Plaza de Chueca, when a gang of young men recognized my father; even *as a man*, Franny must have been famous in that district. "*Vómito!*" one of the young men cheerfully greeted him.

"*Vómito!*" my dad happily said back to him; I could see he was pleased that they knew who he was, even *not* as a woman.

I was struck that, well after midnight, there were throngs of people in the streets of Chueca. But Bovary told me there was a good chance of a smoking ban making Chueca even noisier and more crowded at night. "All the men will be standing outside the clubs and bars, on these narrow streets—all of them drinking and smoking, and shouting to be heard," Señor Bovary said.

"Think of all the *bears*!" my father said, wrinkling his nose.

"William has nothing against bears, Franny," Bovary gently said. I saw that they were holding hands, partners in propriety.

They walked me all the way back to the Santo Mauro, my hotel on the Zurbano.

"I think you should admit to your son, Franny, that you're a *little* proud of him for beating up that bully," Bovary said to my father in the courtyard of the Santo Mauro.

"It *is* appealing to know I have a son who can beat the shit out of somebody," my father said.

"I didn't beat the shit out of him. It was one move—he just fell awkwardly, on a hard surface," I tried to explain.

"That's not what the Racquet Man said," my dad told me. "Bob made me believe you wiped the floor with the fucker."

"Good old Bob," I said.

I offered to call them a taxi; I didn't know that they lived in the neighborhood. "We're right around the corner from the Santo Mauro," Señor Bovary explained. This time, when he offered me his hand, palm down, I took his hand and kissed it.

"Thank you for making this happen," I said to Bovary. My father stepped forward and gave me a sudden hug; he also gave me a quick, dry kiss on both my cheeks—he was so *very* European.

"Maybe, when I come back to Spain—for my next Spanish translation—maybe I can come see you again, or you can come to Barcelona," I said to my father. But, somehow, this seemed to make my dad uncomfortable.

"Maybe," was all my father said.

"Perhaps nearer that time would be a good time to talk about it," Mr. Bovary suggested.

"My *manager*," my dad said, smiling at me but pointing to Señor Bovary.

"*And* the love of your life!" Bovary cried happily. "Don't you ever forget it, Franny!"

"How could I?" my father said to us. "I keep telling the story, don't I?"

I sensed that this was good-bye; it seemed unlikely that I would see them again. (As my father had said: "We already are who we are, aren't we?")

But the *good-bye* word felt too final; I couldn't say it.

"*Adiós*, young William," Señor Bovary said.

"*Adiós*," I said to him. They were walking away—holding hands, of course—when I called after my father. "*Adiós*, Dad!"

"Did he call me 'Dad'—is that what he said?" my father asked Mr. Bovary.

"He did—he distinctly did," Bovary told him.

"*Adiós*, my son!" my father said.

"*Adiós!*" I kept calling to my dad and the love of his life, until I could no longer see them.

AT FAVORITE RIVER ACADEMY, the black-box theater in the Webster Center for the Performing Arts was not the main stage in that relatively new but brainless building—well intentioned, to be kind, but stupidly built.

Times have changed: Students today don't study Shakespeare the way I did. Nowadays, I could not fill the seats for a main-stage performance of any Shakespeare play, not even *Romeo and Juliet*—not even with a former boy playing Juliet! The black box was a better teaching tool for my actors, anyway, and it was great for smaller audiences. The students were much more relaxed in our black-box productions, but we all complained about the mice. It may have been a relatively new building, but—due to either faulty design or misguided contracting—the crawl space under the Webster Center was poorly insulated and had not been mouse-proofed.

When it starts to get cold, any stupidly built building in Vermont will have mice. The kids working with me in our black-box production of *Romeo and Juliet* called them "stage mice"; I can't tell you why, except that the mice had occasionally been spotted onstage.

It was cold that November. The Thanksgiving break was only a week away, and we already had snow on the ground—it was even cold, for that time of year, for *Vermont*. (No wonder the mice had moved indoors.)

I'd just persuaded Richard Abbott to move into the River Street house with me; at eighty, Richard hardly needed to spend another winter in Vermont in a house by himself—he was on his own now that Martha was in the Facility. I gave Richard what had been my bedroom as a child, and that bathroom I'd once shared with Grandpa Harry.

Richard didn't complain about the ghosts. Maybe he would have, if he'd ever encountered Nana Victoria's ghost, or Aunt Muriel's—or even my mother's—but the only ghost Richard ever saw was Grandpa Harry's. Naturally, Harry's ghost showed up a few times in that bathroom he'd once shared with me—thankfully, *not* in that bathtub.

"Harry appears to be confused, as if he's lost his toothbrush," was all Richard ever said about Grandpa Harry's ghost.

The bathtub Harry had blown his brains out in was gone. If Grandpa Harry was actually going to *repeat* blowing his brains out in a bathroom, it would be the master bathroom—the one I now used—and that inviting new bathtub (the way Harry had *repeated* himself for Amanda).

But, as I've told you, I never saw the ghosts in that River Street house. There was the one morning when I woke up and found my clothes—neatly arranged, in the order I would put them on—at the foot of my bed. These were clean clothes, my jeans on the bottom of the pile; the shirt was perfectly folded, with my socks and underwear on top. It was precisely the way my mother used to prepare my clothes for me when I was a little boy. She must have done this every night, after I'd fallen asleep. (She'd stopped doing this around the time when I became a teenager or shortly before.) I had completely forgotten how she'd once loved me. My guess is that her ghost wanted to remind me.

It happened only that one morning, but it was enough to make me remember when I had loved her—without reservation. Now, after those many years when I had lost her affection and believed I no longer loved her, I was able to mourn her—the way we are supposed to mourn our parents when they're gone.

WHEN I FIRST MOVED into the River Street house, I found Uncle Bob standing beside a box of books in the downstairs hall. Aunt Muriel had wanted me to have these "monuments of world literature," Bob had struggled to explain, but Muriel's ghost hadn't delivered the books—Uncle Bob had brought the box. He'd belatedly discovered that Muriel had intended to give me the books, but that fatal car crash must have interrupted her plans. Uncle Bob hadn't noticed that the books were for me; there was a note inside the box, but some years had passed before Bob read it.

"*These books are by your forebears, Billy,*" Aunt Muriel had written, in her unmistakably assertive longhand. "*You're the writer in the family—you should have them.*"

"I'm afraid I don't know *when* she was intending to give them to you, Billy," Bob sheepishly said.

The *forebears* word is worth noting. At first, I was flattered by the company of the esteemed writers Muriel had selected for me; it was a highly literary collection of works. There were two plays by García Lorca—*Blood Wedding* and *The House of Bernarda Alba*. (I hadn't known that Muriel knew I loved Lorca—his poems, too.) There were three plays by Tennessee Williams; maybe Nils Borkman had given these plays to Muriel, I'd first thought. There was a book of poems by W. H. Auden, and poems by Walt Whitman and Lord Byron. There were those unsurpassed novels by Herman Melville and E. M. Forster—I mean *Moby-Dick* and *Howards End*. There was *Swann's Way* by Marcel Proust. Yet I still didn't understand why my aunt Muriel had gathered these particular writers together and called them my "forebears"—not until I unearthed, from the bottom of the box, two little books that lay touching each other: Arthur Rimbaud's *A Season in Hell* and James Baldwin's *Giovanni's Room*.

"Oh," I said to Uncle Bob. My *gay* forebears, Aunt Muriel must have thought—my not-so-straight brethren, I could only guess.

"I think your aunt meant this in a *positive* way, Billy," Uncle Bob said.

"You think so?" I asked the Racquet Man. We both stood there in the downstairs hall, trying to imagine Muriel putting these books in a box for me in a *positive* way.

I never told Gerry about her mother's gift to me—fearing that Muriel might have left nothing, or worse, for Gerry. I didn't ask Elaine if *she* thought Muriel had intended these books for me in a *positive* way. (Elaine's opinion of Muriel was that my aunt had been *born* a menacing ghost.)

It was the phone call from Elaine—late one night, in my River Street house—that reminded me of Esmeralda, gone from my life (but not from my mind) these many years. Elaine was crying into the phone; yet another bad boyfriend had dumped her, but this one had made cruel comments about my dear friend's vagina. (I'd never told Elaine my unfortunate, not-a-ballroom appraisal of Esmeralda's vagina—boy, was this ever not the night to tell Elaine *that* story!)

"You're always telling me how you love my little breasts, Billy," Elaine was saying, between sobs, "but you've never said anything about my vagina."

"I *love* your vagina!" I assured her.

"You're not just saying that, are you, Billy?"

"No! I think your vagina is *perfect!*" I told her.

"Why?" Elaine asked; she'd stopped crying.

I was determined not to make the Esmeralda mistake with my dearest friend. "Ah, well—" I began, and then paused. "I'll be absolutely honest with you, Elaine. Some vaginas feel as big as ballrooms, whereas *your* vagina feels just right. It's the perfect size—perfect for *me*, anyway," I said, as casually as I could.

"Not a ballroom—is that what you're saying, Billy?"

How did I end up here again? I was thinking. "Not a ballroom, in a *positive* way!" I cried.

Elaine's nearsightedness was a thing of the past; she'd had that Lasik surgery—it was as if she were seeing for the first time. Before the surgery, when she'd had sex, she always took her glasses off—she'd never had a really good look at a penis. Now she could actually see penises; she didn't like the looks of some of them—"of *most* of them," Elaine had said. She'd told me that, the next time we were together, she wanted to take a good look at *my* penis. I thought it was a little tragic that Elaine didn't know another guy well enough to feel comfortable about staring at his penis, but what are friends for?

"So my vagina is 'not a ballroom' in a *positive* way?" Elaine now said on the phone. "Well, that sounds okay. I can't wait to get a good look at your penis, Billy—I know you'll take my staring at your penis in a *positive* way."

"I can't wait, too," I told her.

"Just remember who's the *perfect* size for you, Billy," Elaine said.

"I love you, Elaine," I told her.

"I love you, too, Billy," Elaine said.

Thus was my not-a-ballroom faux pas put to rest—thus that ghost departed. Thus did my worst memory of Esmeralda (*that* terrifying angel) take flight.

IT WAS THE THIRD week of November 2010—for as long as I live, I won't forget this. I had my hands full with *Romeo and Juliet*; I had a terrific cast of kids, and (as you know) a Juliet with all the balls a director could ever ask for.

The stage mice chiefly bothered the few females in that cast—namely, my Lady Montague and my Lady Capulet, and my Nurse. As for my Juliet, Gee didn't shriek when the stage mice were scurrying around; Gee tried to stomp on the disruptive little rodents. Gee and my bloodthirsty Tybalt had killed some stage mice by stomping on them, but my Mercutio and my Romeo were the experts in my cast at setting the mousetraps. I was constantly reminding them that they had to disarm the mousetraps when our *Romeo and Juliet* was in performance. I didn't want that grisly snapping sound—or the occasional death squeal of a stage mouse—to interrupt the show.

My Romeo was a cow-eyed boy of strictly conventional handsomeness, but he had exceptionally good diction. He could say that act 1, scene 1 line (of utmost importance) so that the audience could really hear it. "Here's much to do with hate, but more with love"—that one.

It was also important to Gee that—as she told me—my Romeo was not her type. "But I'm okay about kissing him," she'd added.

Fortunately, my Romeo was okay about kissing Gee—despite everyone in our school knowing that Gee had balls (and a penis). It would have taken a brave boy at Favorite River to have ventured to *date* Gee; it hadn't happened. Gee had always lived in a girls' dorm; even with balls and a penis, Gee would never bother the girls, and the girls knew it. The girls had not once bothered Gee, either.

Putting Gee in a boys' dorm might have been asking for trouble; Gee liked boys, but because Gee was a boy who was trying to become a girl, some of the boys *definitely* would have bothered her.

No one had imagined—least of all, me—that Gee would turn out to be such a pretty young woman. No doubt, there were boys at Favorite River Academy who had a serious crush on her—straight boys, because Gee was completely passable, and those gay boys who were turned on by Gee *because* she had balls and a penis.

Richard Abbott and I took turns driving Gee out to see Martha at the Facility. At ninety, Mrs. Hadley was a kind of wise grandmother to Gee; Martha told Gee not to date any boys at Favorite River.

"Save the dating for when you get to college," Mrs. Hadley had advised her.

"That's what I'm doing—I'm waiting on the dating," Gee Montgomery had told me. "All the guys at Favorite River are too immature for me, anyway," she said.

There was one boy who seemed *very* mature to me—at least physically. He was, like Gee, a senior, but he was also a wrestler, which was why I had cast him as the fiery-tempered Tybalt—a kinsman to the Capulets, and the hothead who is most responsible for what happens in the play. Oh, I know, it is the long-standing discord between the Montagues and the Capulets that brings about the deaths of Romeo and Juliet, but Tybalt is the catalyst. (I hope Herm Hoyt and Miss Frost would have forgiven me for casting a wrestler as my catalyst.)

My Tybalt was the most mature-looking boy at Favorite River—a four-year varsity wrestler from Germany. Manfred was a light-heavyweight; his English was correct, and very carefully enunciated, but he'd retained a slight accent. I'd told Manfred to let us hear the accent in *Romeo and Juliet*. How wicked of me—to have my Tybalt be a wrestler with a German accent. But, to tell you the truth, I was a little worried about how big a crush Manfred might have had on Gee. (And I know Gee liked him.) If there was a boy at Favorite River who was conceivably courageous enough to date Gee Montgomery—that is, even to *ask* her for a date—that boy, who very much looked like a man, was my hot-blooded Tybalt.

By that Wednesday, we were off-script in *Romeo and Juliet*—we were in the fine-tuning phase. Our rehearsal was later in the evening than usual; we had an 8 P.M. start—due to Manfred being at a pre-season wrestling match somewhere in Massachusetts.

I'd gone to the theater close to our usual rehearsal time, about 6:45 or 7:00 on that Wednesday, and—as I expected—most of my cast would show up early as well. Come 8:00, we would *all* be waiting for Manfred— my most combative Tybalt.

I was having a political conversation with my Benvolio, one of my gay boys. He was very active in the campus LGBTQ group, and we were talking about the election of the new governor of Vermont, a Democrat—"our gay-rights governor," my Benvolio was in the midst of saying.

Suddenly, he interrupted himself and said: "I forgot to tell you, Mr. A. There's a guy looking for you. He was in the dining hall, asking about you."

I'd actually been in the dining hall for a quick bite to eat earlier that same evening, and someone else had told me there was a guy asking where he might find me. A young woman in the English Department had told me—a kind of Amanda-type, but *not*. (Amanda had moved on, to my relief.)

"How old a guy?" I'd asked this young faculty person. "What did he look like?"

"My age, or only a little older—good-looking," she'd told me. I was guessing that this young English teacher was in her early thirties—maybe mid-thirties.

"How old a man, would you guess?" I asked my young Benvolio. "What did he look like?"

"*Late* thirties, maybe," my Benvolio answered. "*Very* handsome—*hot, if you ask me*," the gay boy said, smiling. (He was an excellent Benvolio to my cow-eyed Romeo, I was thinking.)

My cast was showing up in the black box—some arriving alone, some in twos or threes. If Manfred got back from his wrestling match ahead of schedule, we could start our rehearsal; most of the kids still had homework to do—they would have a late night.

Here came my clergymen, my Friar Lawrence and my Friar John, and my officious-sounding Apothecary. Here came my chatterboxes—two junior girls, my Lady Montague and my Lady Capulet. And there was my Mercutio—only a sophomore, but a long-legged and talented one. He had the requisite charm and derring-do for the likable but doomed Mercutio.

Straggling into the black box, not quite last, were various Attendants, Maskers, Torchbearers, my Boy with a drum (a tiny freshman, who could have played a dwarf), several Servingmen (including Tybalt's page), sundry Gentlemen and Gentlewomen—and my Paris, my Prince Escalus, and the others. My Nurse came at the end, shoving my Balthasar and my Petruchio ahead of her. Juliet's Nurse was a stalwart girl—a field-hockey player, and one of the most outspoken lesbians in the LGBTQ group. My Nurse did not countenance most male behavior—including gay and bi male behavior. I was very fond of her. If there were ever any trouble—a food fight in the dining hall, or a disaffected student with a weapon—I knew I could count on Juliet's Nurse to watch my back. She had a grudging respect for Gee, but I knew they weren't friends.

And where was Gee? I began to wonder. My Juliet was usually the first to arrive at the theater.

"There's a guy looking for you, Mr. A.—some creep who thinks very highly of himself," Juliet's Nurse told me. "I think he's hitting on Gee, or maybe he's just walking with her and talking to her. They're on their way here, anyway," my Nurse said.

But I did not, at first, see the stranger; when I spotted Gee, she was alone. I'd been discussing Mercutio's death scene with my long-legged Mercutio. I was agreeing with him that there is, as my talented sophomore put it, some black humor involved, when Mercutio first describes the seriousness of his stab wound to Romeo—"'tis not so deep as a well, nor so wide as a church door, but 'tis enough. 'Twill serve. Ask for me tomorrow, and you shall find me a grave man." Yet I cautioned my Mercutio not to make it the least bit *funny* when he curses the Capulets and the Montagues: "A plague o' both your houses!"

"Sorry I'm a little late, Mr. A.—I got delayed," Gee said; she looked flushed, even red-cheeked, but it was cold outside. There was no one with her.

"I heard some guy was bothering you," I told her.

"He wasn't bothering *me*—he's got a thing about *you*," my Juliet told me.

"He looked like he was hitting on you," my sturdy Nurse said to her.

"No one's hitting on me till I get to college," Gee told her.

"Did the man say what he wanted?" I asked Gee; she shook her head.

"I think it's personal, Mr. A.—the guy is upset about something," Gee said.

We were all standing in the stage area, which was brightly lit; my stage manager had already dimmed the houselights. In our black box, we can position the audience where we want them; we can move the seats around. Sometimes, the audience completely encircles the stage or sits facing one another with the stage between them. For *Romeo and Juliet*, I had all the seats form a shallow horseshoe around the stage. With the houselights dimmed, but not dark, I could watch the rehearsals from any seat in the audience and still see well enough to read my notes—or write new notes.

It was my gay Benvolio who whispered in my ear, while all of us were still waiting for Manfred (my trouble-making Tybalt) to get back to campus from his wrestling match. "Mr. A.—I see him," my Benvolio whispered. "That guy who's looking for you—he's in the audience." With the houselights dimmed, I could not make out the man's face; he was sitting in the middle of the horseshoe-shaped seats, about four or five rows back—just out of reach of the spotlights illuminating our stage.

"Should we call Security, Mr. A.?" Gee asked me.

"No, no—I'll just see what he wants," I told her. "If I appear to be stuck in an unwelcome conversation, just come interrupt us—pretend you have to ask me something about the play. Make up anything that comes to mind," I said.

"You want me to come with you?" my bold Nurse, the field-hockey player, asked me.

"No, no," I told the fearless girl, who was spoiling for a fight. "Just be sure I know when Manfred gets here."

We were at that point in our rehearsals where I like to have the kids run their lines consecutively; I didn't want to be rehearsing either piece-meal or out of sequence. My ever-ready Tybalt is an inciting presence in act 1, scene 1. (*Enter Tybalt, drawing his sword*, as the stage directions say.) The only rehearsing I wanted to do without Manfred was that small set piece the Chorus says, the prologue to the play.

"Listen up, Chorus," I said. "Run through the prologue a couple of times. Take note that the most important line ends not with a comma, but a semicolon; pay attention to that semicolon. 'A pair of star-crossed lovers take their life'; please *pause* after the semicolon."

"We're here, if you need us, Mr. A.," I heard Gee say—as I went up an aisle to the fourth or fifth row of seats, into the dimly lit audience.

"Hey, *Teacher*," I heard the man say, maybe a split second before I could clearly see him. He might as well have said, "Hey, *Nymph*"—that's how familiar his voice was to me, almost fifty years after I'd last heard it. His handsome face, his wrestler's build, his slyly confident smile—they were all familiar to me.

But you're supposed to be *dead*! I was thinking—the "of natural causes" was the only doubtful part. Yet *this* Kittredge, of course, couldn't have been *my* Kittredge. This Kittredge was only slightly more than half my age; if he'd been born in the early seventies, when I'd imag-ined Kittredge's son had been born, he would have been in his late thir-ties—thirty-seven or thirty-eight, I would have guessed, upon meeting Kittredge's only child.

"It's truly striking how much you look like your father," I said to young Kittredge, holding out my hand; he declined to shake it. "Well, of course, I mean if I had seen your father at your age—you look as I *imagine* he must have looked in his late thirties."

"My father didn't look at all like me when he was my age," the young man said. "He was already in his early thirties when I was born; by the time I was old enough to remember what he looked like, he already looked like a woman. He hadn't had the surgical reassignment yet, but he was very passable as a woman. I didn't *have* a father. I had two moth-ers—one of them was hysterical most of the time, and the other one had a penis. After the surgery, as I understand it, he had some kind of vagina. He died of AIDS—I'm surprised you *haven't*. I've read all your novels," young Kittredge added, as if everything in my writing had indicated to him that I easily could have died of AIDS—or that I *should* have.

"I'm sorry," was all I could say to him; as Gee had said, he was upset. As I could see for myself, he was angry. I tried to make small talk. I asked him what his dad had done for a living, and how Kittredge had met Irmgard, the wife—this angry young man's mother.

They'd met skiing—Davos, or maybe Klosters. Kittredge's wife was Swiss, but she'd had a German grandmother; that's where the *Irmgard* came from. Kittredge and Irmgard had homes in the ski town and in Zurich, where they'd both worked at the Schauspielhaus. (It was quite a famous theater.) I imagined that Kittredge had liked living in Europe; no doubt, he was used to Europe, because of his mother. And maybe a sex-change surgery was more easily arranged in Europe—I had no idea, really.

Mrs. Kittredge—the mom, I mean, *not* the wife—had killed herself soon after Kittredge's death. (There was no doubt she'd been his real mother.) "Pills," was all the grandson would say about it; he clearly wasn't interested in talking to me about anything except the fact that his father became a woman. I began to get the feeling that young Kittredge believed I had something to do with what he saw as a despicable alteration.

"How was his German?" I asked Kittredge's son, but that was of no concern to the angry young man.

"His German was passable—not *as* passable as he was as a woman. He didn't make any effort to improve his German," Kittredge's son told me. "My father never worked as hard at *anything* as he worked at becoming a woman."

"Oh."

"When he was dying, he told me that something happened here—when you knew him," Kittredge's son said to me. "Something *started* here. He admired you—he said you had balls. You did something 'inspiring,' or so he told me. There was a transsexual involved—someone older, I think. Maybe you both knew her. Maybe my father admired her, too—maybe *she* inspired him."

"I saw a photo of your father when he was younger—before he came here," I told young Kittredge. "He was dressed and made up as a very pretty girl. I think something *started*, as you say, before he met me—and all the rest of it. I could show you that photo, if you—"

"I've seen those photographs—I don't need to see another one!" Kittredge's son said angrily. "What about the transsexual? How did you two *inspire* my father?"

"I'm surprised to hear he 'admired' me—I can't imagine that I did anything he would have found 'inspiring.' I never thought he even *liked* me. In fact, your father was always rather cruel to me," I told Kittredge's son.

"What about the transsexual?" young Kittredge asked me again.

"I knew the transsexual—your father met her only once. I was *in love with* the transsexual. What happened with the transsexual happened to *me!*" I cried. "I don't know what happened to your father."

"*Something* happened here—that's all I know," the son said bitterly. "My father read all your books, obsessively. What was he looking for in your novels? I've read them—I never found my father there, not that I would necessarily have recognized him in your pages."

I thought of *my* father, then, and I said—as gently as I could manage—to Kittredge's angry son, "We already are who we are, aren't we? I can't make your father comprehensible to you, but surely you can have some *sympathy* for him, can't you?" (I'd never imagined myself asking anyone to have *sympathy* for Kittredge!)

I had once believed that if Kittredge was gay, he sure looked like a top to me. Now I wasn't so sure. When Kittredge had met Miss Frost, I'd seen him change from dominant to submissive—in about ten seconds.

Just then Gee was there, in the row of seats beside us. My cast for *Romeo and Juliet* had surely heard the raised voices; they must have been worried about me. No doubt, they could hear how angry young Kittredge was. To me, he seemed just a callow, disappointing reflection of his father.

"Hi, Gee," I said. "Is Manfred here? Are we ready?"

"No—we still don't have our Tybalt," Gee told me. "But I have a question. It's about act one, scene five—it's the very first thing I say, when the Nurse tells me Romeo is a Montague. You know, when I learn I'm in love with the son of my enemy—it's that couplet."

"What about it?" I asked her; she was stalling for us both, I could see. We wanted Manfred to arrive. Where was my easily outraged Tybalt when I needed him?

"I don't think I should sound sorry for myself," Gee continued. "I don't think of Juliet as self-pitying."

"No, she's not," I said. "Juliet may sound fatalistic—at times—but she shouldn't sound self-pitying."

"Okay—let me say it," Gee said. "I think I've got it—I'm just saying it as it *is*, but I'm not complaining about it."

"This is my Juliet," I told young Kittredge. "My best girl, Gee. Okay," I said to Gee, "let's hear it."

" 'My only love sprung from my only hate! / Too early seen unknown, and known too late!' " my Juliet said.

"That couldn't be better, Gee," I told her, but young Kittredge was just staring at her; I couldn't tell if he admired her or suspected her.

"What kind of name is *Gee?*" Kittredge's son asked her. I could see that my best girl's confidence was a little shaken; here was a handsome, rather worldly-looking man—someone *not* from our Favorite River community, where Gee had earned our respect and had developed much confidence in herself *as a woman*. I could see that Gee was doubting herself. I knew what she was thinking—in young Kittredge's presence, and under his intimidating scrutiny. Do I look *passable?* Gee was wondering.

"Gee is just a made-up name," the young girl evasively told him.

"What's your *real* name?" Kittredge's son asked her.

"I was George Montgomery, at birth. I'm going to be *Georgia* Montgomery later," Gee told him. "Right now, I'm just Gee. I'm a boy who's becoming a girl—I'm *in transition*," my Juliet said to young Kittredge.

"That couldn't be better, Gee," I told her again. "I think you said that perfectly."

One glance at Kittredge's son told me: He'd had no idea that Gee was a work-in-progress; he hadn't known she was a transgender kid, on her brave way to becoming a woman. One glance at Gee told me that she knew she'd been *passable*; I think that gave my Juliet a ton of confidence. I realize now that if Kittredge's son had said anything disrespectful to Gee, I would have tried to kill him.

At that moment, Manfred arrived. "The wrestler is here!" someone shouted—my Mercutio, maybe, or it might have been my gay Benvolio.

"We have our Tybalt!" my strong Nurse called to Gee and me.

"Ah, at last," I said. "We're ready."

Gee was running toward the stage—as if her next life depended on starting this delayed rehearsal. "Good luck—break a leg," young Kittredge called after her. Just like his father—you couldn't read his tone of voice. Was he being sincere or sarcastic?

I could see that my most assertive Nurse had pulled Manfred aside. No doubt, she was filling the hot-tempered Tybalt in—she wanted "the wrestler" to know there was a potential problem, a creep (as she'd called young Kittredge) in the audience. I was ushering Kittredge's son to an aisle between the horseshoe-shaped seats, just accompanying the young man to the nearest exit, when Manfred presented himself in the aisle—as ready for a fight as Tybalt ever was.

When Manfred wanted to speak privately to me, he always spoke in German; he knew I'd lived in Vienna and could still speak a little German, albeit badly. Manfred politely asked if there was anything he could do to help me—in German.

Fucking *wrestlers*! I saw that my Tybalt had lost half his mustache; they'd had to shave one side of his lip before they gave him the stitches! (Manfred would have to shave the other half of his lip before we were in performance; I don't know about you, but I've never seen a Tybalt with only half a mustache.)

"Your German is pretty good," young Kittredge, sounding surprised, said to Manfred.

"It ought to be—I'm German," Manfred told him aggressively, in English.

"This is my Tybalt. He's also a wrestler, like your father," I said to Kittredge's son. They shook hands a little tentatively. "I'll be right there, Manfred—you can wait onstage for me. Nice lip," I told him, as he was going down the aisle to the stage.

Young Kittredge reluctantly shook my hand at the exit door. He was still agitated; he'd had more to say, but—in at least one way—he was *not* like his father. Whatever one thinks of Kittredge, I can tell you this: He was a cruel fucker, but he was a fighter. The son, whether he had wrestled or not, needed just one look at Manfred; Kittredge's son was no fighter.

"Look, here it is—I just have to say this," young Kittredge said; he almost couldn't look at me. "I don't know you, I admit—I don't have a clue who my father really was, either. But I've read all your books, and I know what you do—I mean, in your *writing*. You make all these sexual extremes seem normal—that's what you do. Like Gee, that *girl*, or whatever she is—or what she's *becoming*. You create these characters who are so sexually 'different,' as *you* might call them—or 'fucked up,' which is what *I* would call them—and then you expect us to *sympathize* with them, or feel sorry for them, or something."

"Yes, that's more or less what I do," I told him.

"But so much of what you describe is not *natural*!" Kittredge's son cried. "I mean, I know what you *are*—not only from your writing. I've read what you say about yourself, in interviews. What you are isn't *natural*—you aren't *normal*!"

He'd held his voice down when he was talking about Gee—I'll give him credit for that—but now Kittredge's son had raised his voice again. I knew that my stage manager—not to mention the entire cast for *Romeo and Juliet*—could hear every word. It was suddenly so quiet in our little black-box theater; I swear you could have heard a stage mouse fart.

"You're *bisexual*, aren't you?" Kittredge's son then asked me. "Do you think *that's* normal, or natural—or *sympathetic*? You're a *switch-hitter*!" he said, opening the exit door; thank goodness, everyone could see he was finally leaving.

"My dear boy," I said sharply to young Kittredge, in what has become my lifelong imitation of the way Miss Frost so pointedly and thrillingly spoke to me.

"My dear boy, please don't put a *label* on me—don't make me a *category* before you get to know me!" Miss Frost had said to me; I've never forgotten it. Is it any wonder that this was what I said to young Kittredge, the cocksure son of my old nemesis and forbidden love?

Acknowledgments

Jamey Bradbury
Rob Buyea
David Calicchio
Dean Cooke
Emily Copeland
Peter Delacorte
David Ebershoff
Amy Edelman
Marie-Anne Esquivié
Paul Fedorko
Vicente Molina Foix
Rodrigo Fresán
Ruth Geiger
Ron Hansen
Sheila Heffernon
Alan Hergott
Everett Irving
Janet Turnbull Irving
Josée Kamoun
Jonathan Karp
Katie Kelley
Rick Kelley
Kate Medina
Jan Morris
Anna von Planta
David Rowland
Marty Schwartz
Nick Spengler
Helga Stephenson
Abraham Verghese
Edmund White

About John Irving

The World According to Garp, which won the National Book Award in 1980, was John Irving's fourth novel and his first international bestseller; it also became a George Roy Hill film. Tony Richardson wrote and directed the adaptation for the screen of *The Hotel New Hampshire* (1984). Irving's novels are now translated into thirty-five languages, and he has had nine international bestsellers. Worldwide, the Irving novel most often called "an American classic" is *A Prayer for Owen Meany* (1989), the portrayal of an enduring friendship at that time when the Vietnam War had its most divisive effect on the United States.

In 1992, John Irving was inducted into the National Wrestling Hall of Fame in Stillwater, Oklahoma. (He competed as a wrestler for twenty years, until he was thirty-four, and coached the sport until he was forty-seven.) In 2000, Irving won the Oscar for Best Adapted Screenplay for *The Cider House Rules,* a Lasse Hallström film that earned seven Academy Award nominations. Tod Williams wrote and directed *The Door in the Floor,* the 2004 film adapted from Irving's ninth novel, *A Widow for One Year.*

In One Person is John Irving's thirteenth novel.